WALLFLOWER

Iasmin Omar Ata

Viking

VIKING
An imprint of Penguin Random House LLC
1745 Broadway, New York, NY 10019
penguinrandomhouse.com

Copyright © 2026 by Iasmin Omar Ata

Penguin Random House values and supports copyright. Copyright fuels creativity, encourages diverse voices, promotes free speech, and creates a vibrant culture. Thank you for buying an authorized edition of this book and for complying with copyright laws by not reproducing, scanning, or distributing any part of it in any form without permission. You are supporting writers and allowing Penguin Random House to continue to publish books for every reader. Please note that no part of this book may be used or reproduced in any manner for the purpose of training artificial intelligence technologies or systems.

Viking & colophon are registered trademarks of Penguin Random House LLC.

Edited by Meriam Metoui   Design by Kate Renner

The art for this book was created using Clip Studio on iPad with a variety of brushes.
No AI was used in the creation of art for this book.

Library of Congress Cataloging-in-Publication Data is available.

Manufactured in China
TOPL

ISBN 9780593117149 (hardcover)
1 3 5 7 9 10 8 6 4 2

ISBN 9780593117156 (paperback)
1 3 5 7 9 10 8 6 4 2

The authorized representative in the EU for product safety and compliance is Penguin Random House Ireland, Morrison Chambers, 32 Nassau Street, Dublin D02 YH68, Ireland.
https://eu-contact.penguin.ie.

*To my father, Omar, and auntie Layla;
for the home-cooked meals,
the great advice,
and the unconditional love*

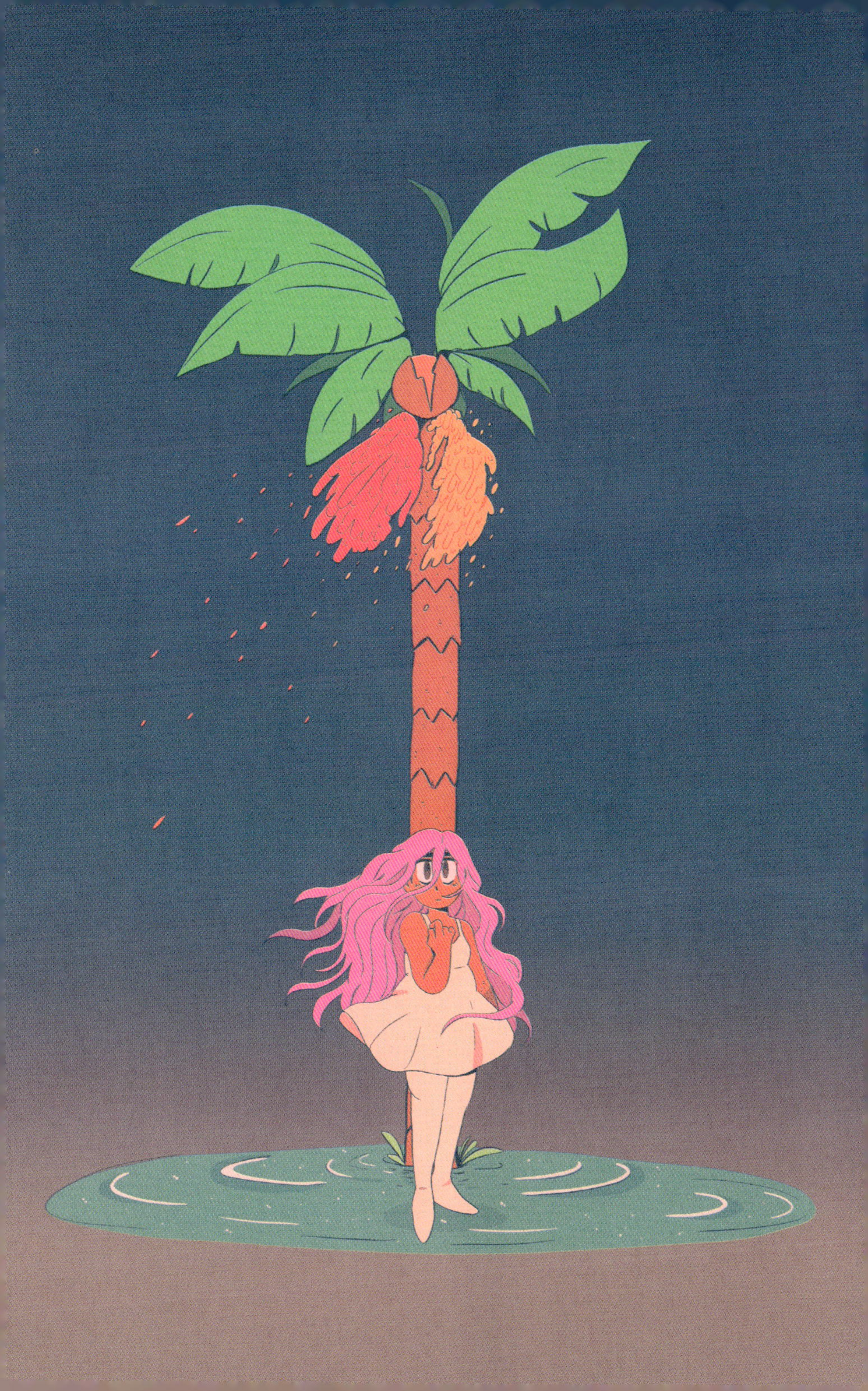

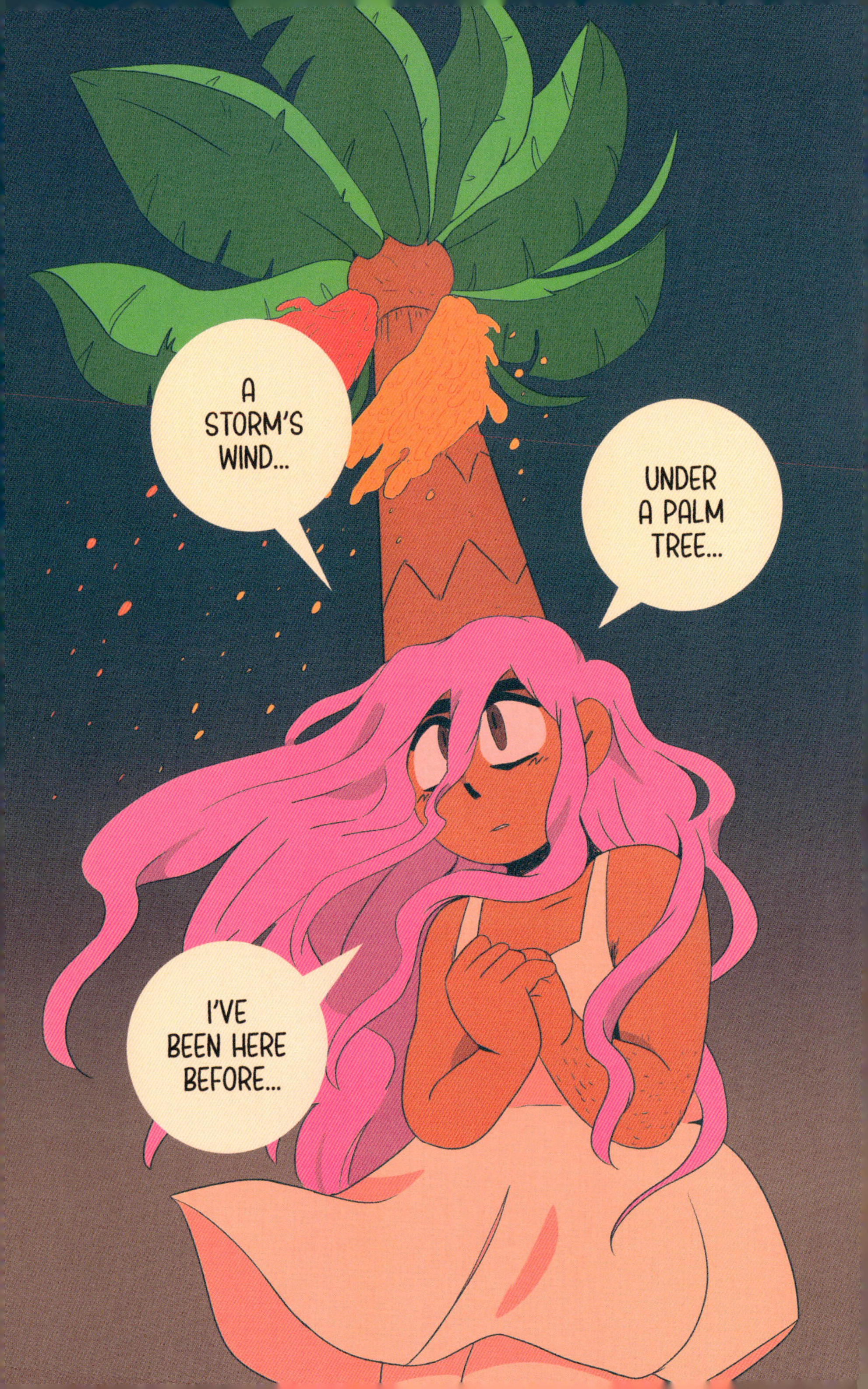
A STORM'S WIND...
UNDER A PALM TREE...
I'VE BEEN HERE BEFORE...

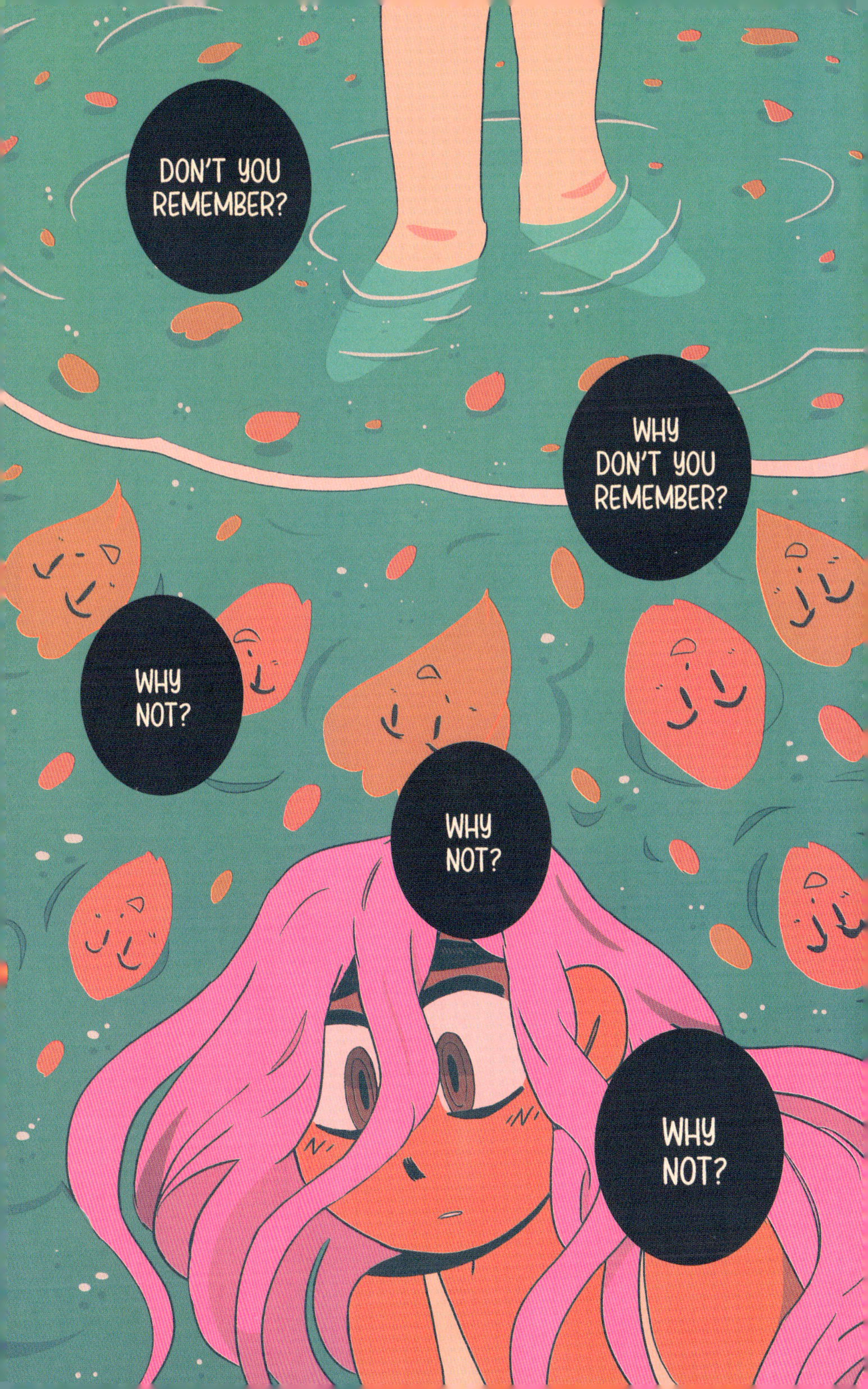
DON'T YOU REMEMBER?
WHY DON'T YOU REMEMBER?
WHY NOT?
WHY NOT?
WHY NOT?

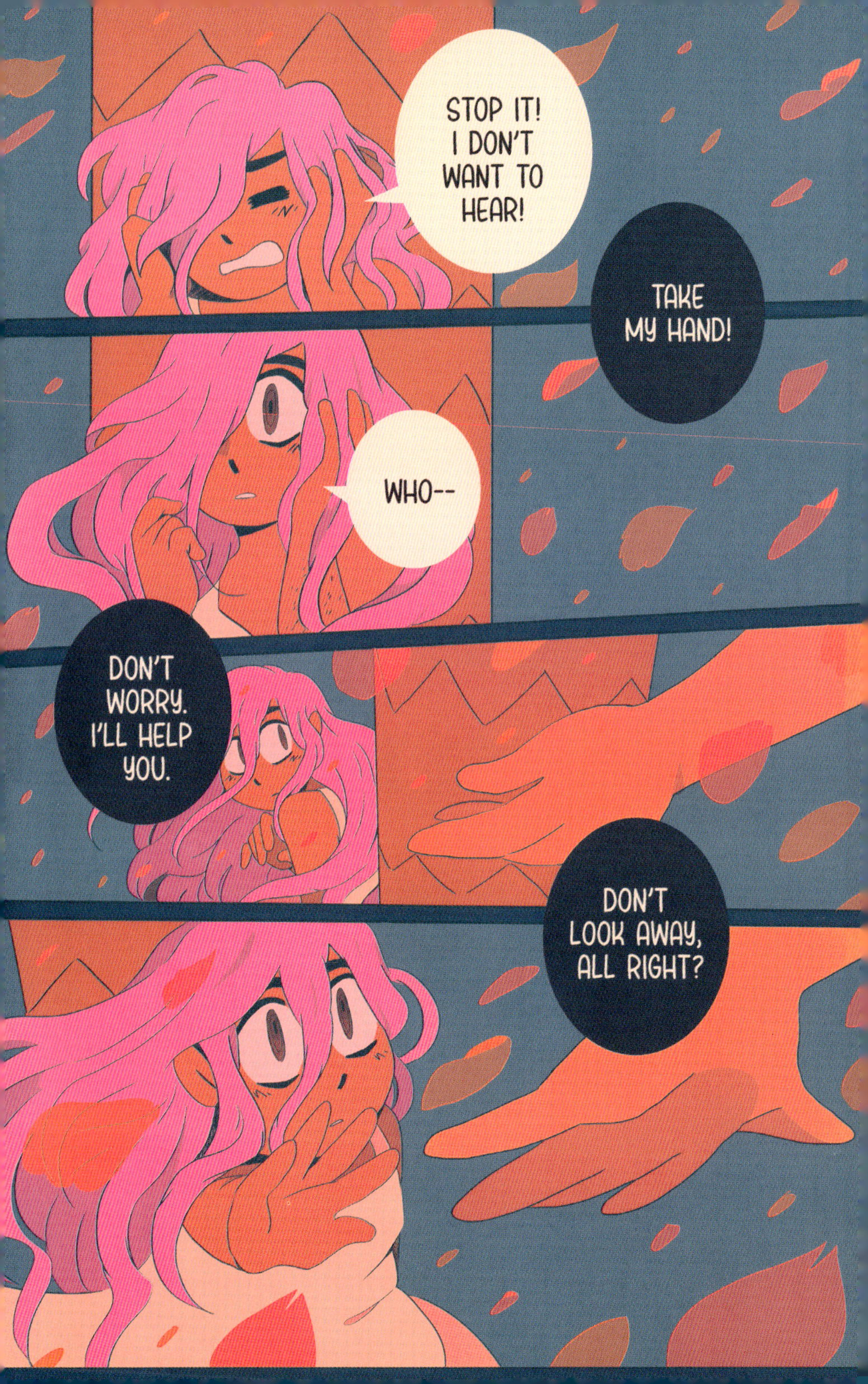
STOP IT! I DON'T WANT TO HEAR!
TAKE MY HAND!
WHO--
DON'T WORRY. I'LL HELP YOU.
DON'T LOOK AWAY, ALL RIGHT?

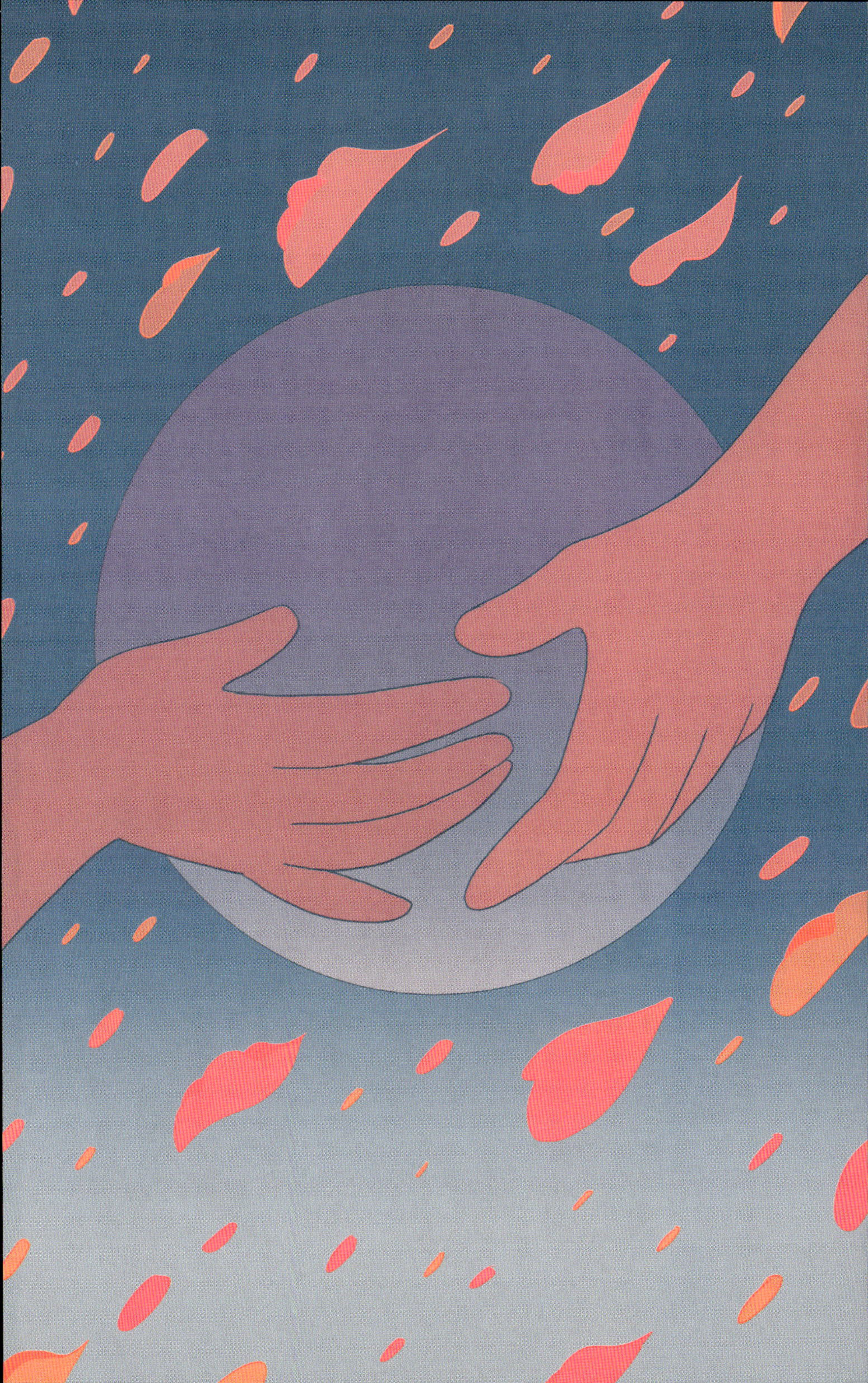

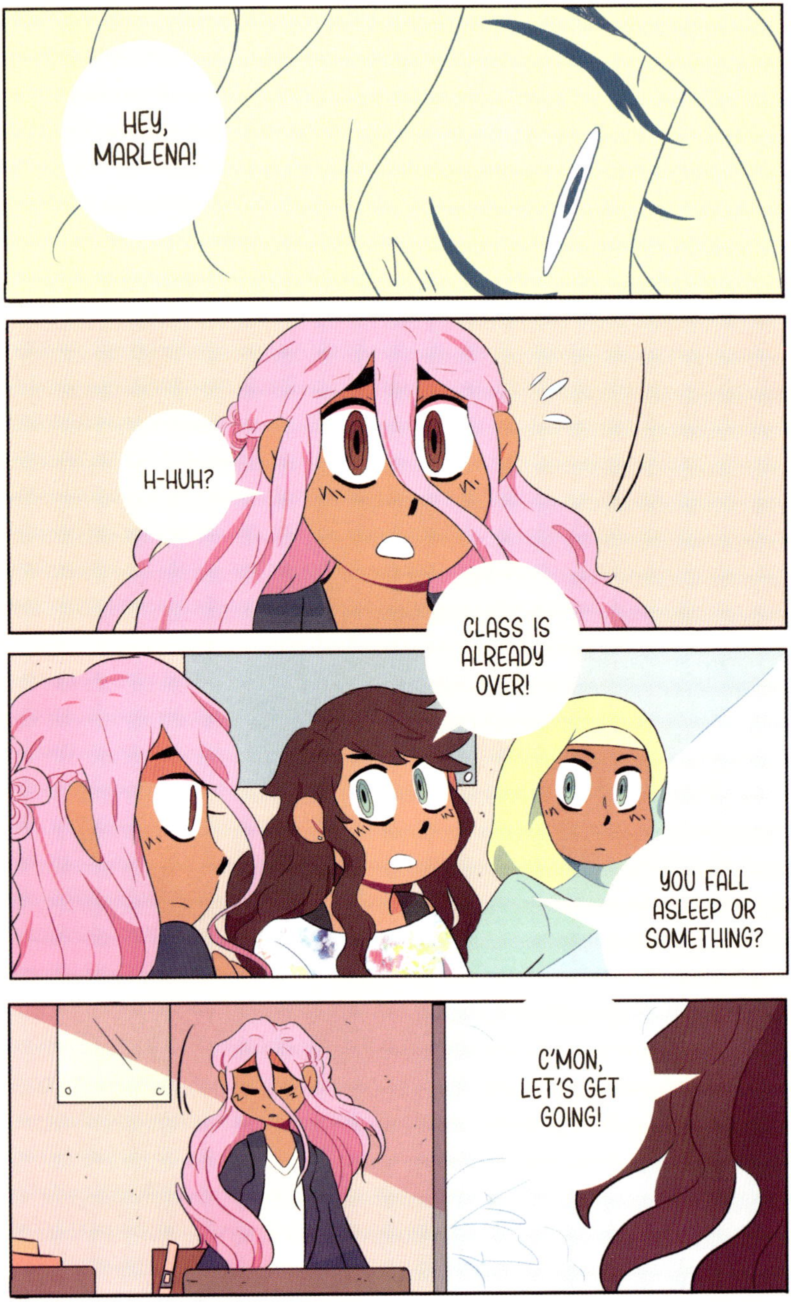
HEY, MARLENA!
H-HUH?
CLASS IS ALREADY OVER!
YOU FALL ASLEEP OR SOMETHING?
C'MON, LET'S GET GOING!

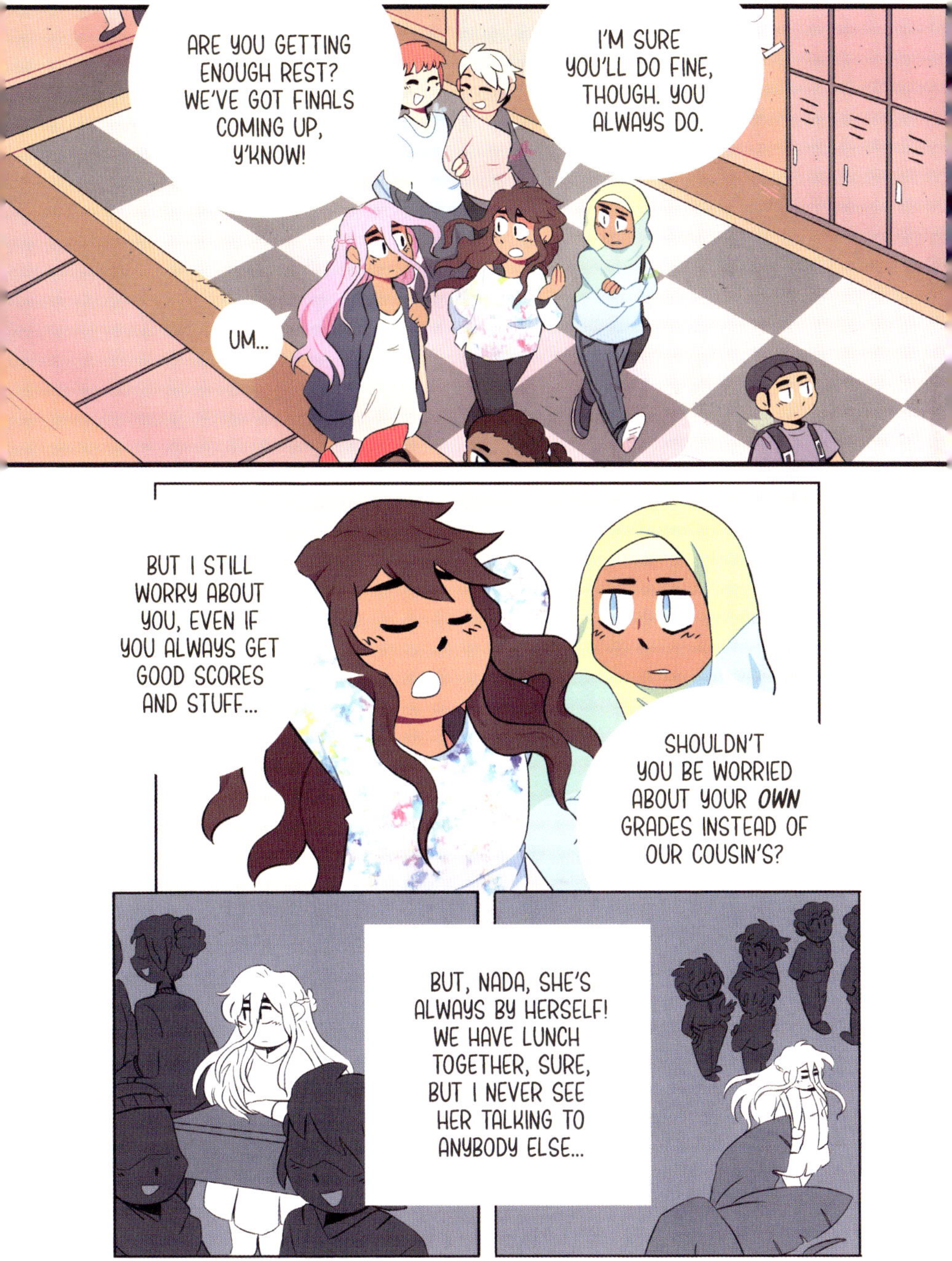
ARE YOU GETTING ENOUGH REST? WE'VE GOT FINALS COMING UP, Y'KNOW!
I'M SURE YOU'LL DO FINE, THOUGH. YOU ALWAYS DO.
UM...
BUT I STILL WORRY ABOUT YOU, EVEN IF YOU ALWAYS GET GOOD SCORES AND STUFF...
SHOULDN'T YOU BE WORRIED ABOUT YOUR *OWN* GRADES INSTEAD OF OUR COUSIN'S?
BUT, NADA, SHE'S ALWAYS BY HERSELF! WE HAVE LUNCH TOGETHER, SURE, BUT I NEVER SEE HER TALKING TO ANYBODY ELSE...

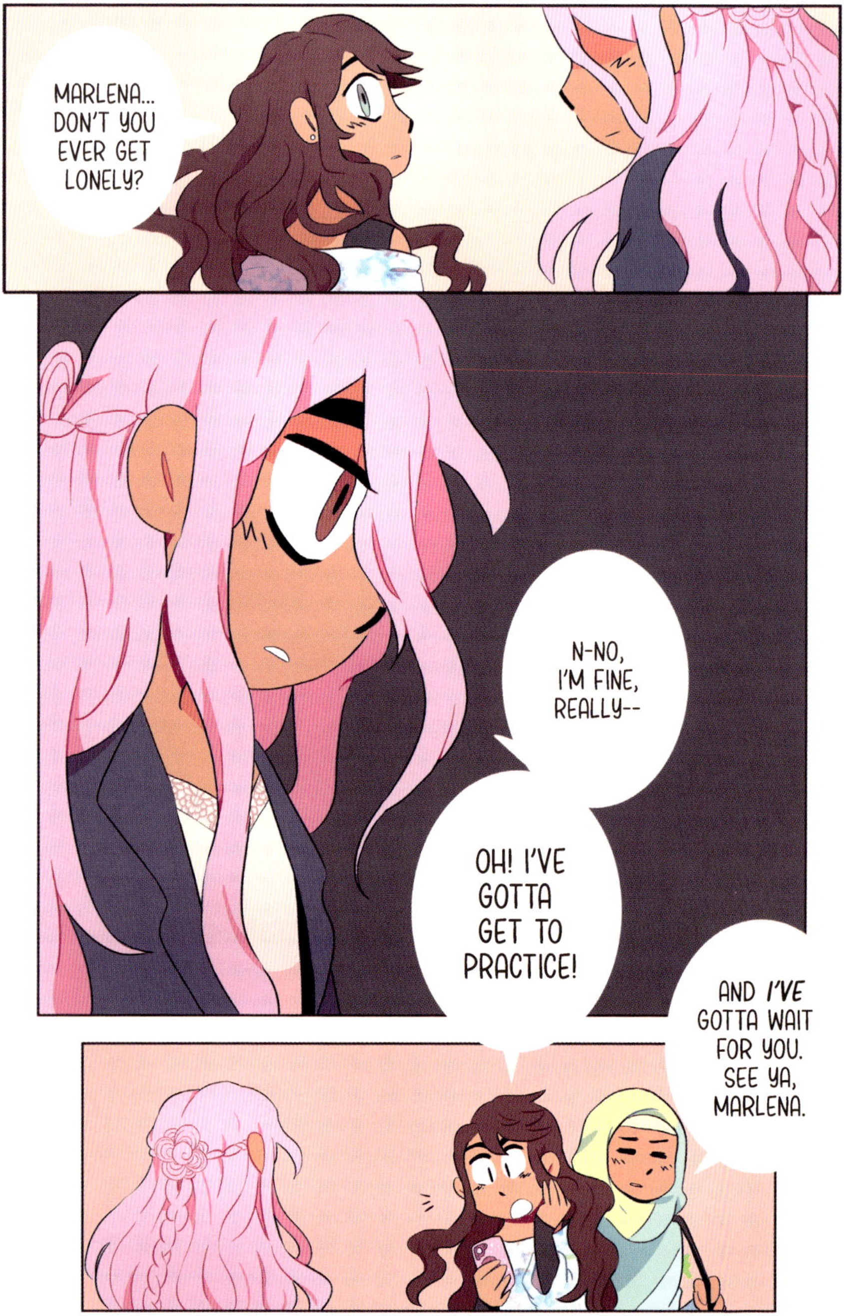
MARLENA... DON'T YOU EVER GET LONELY?
N-NO, I'M FINE, REALLY--
OH! I'VE GOTTA GET TO PRACTICE!
AND *I'VE* GOTTA WAIT FOR YOU. SEE YA, MARLENA.

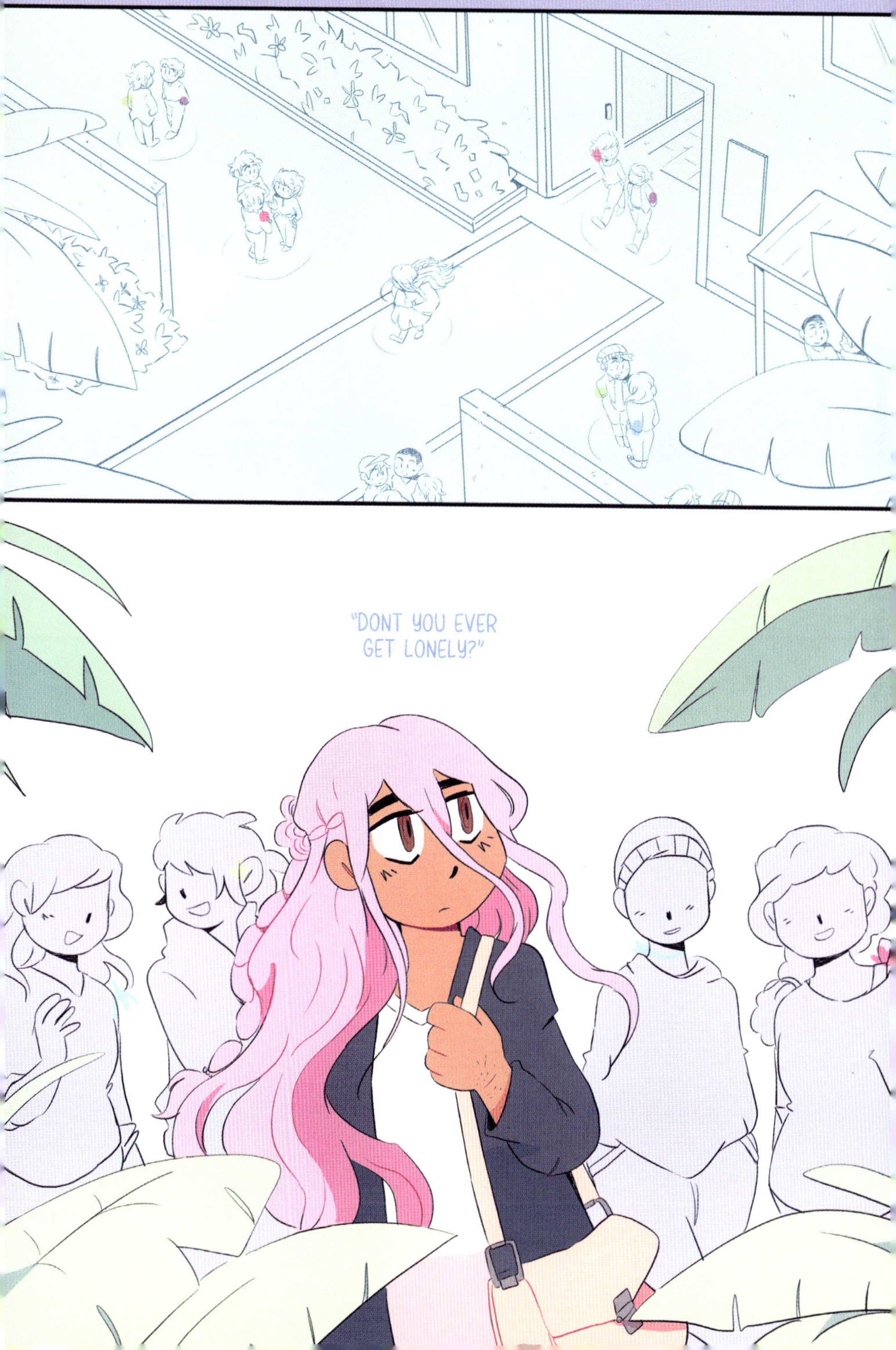
"DONT YOU EVER
GET LONELY?"

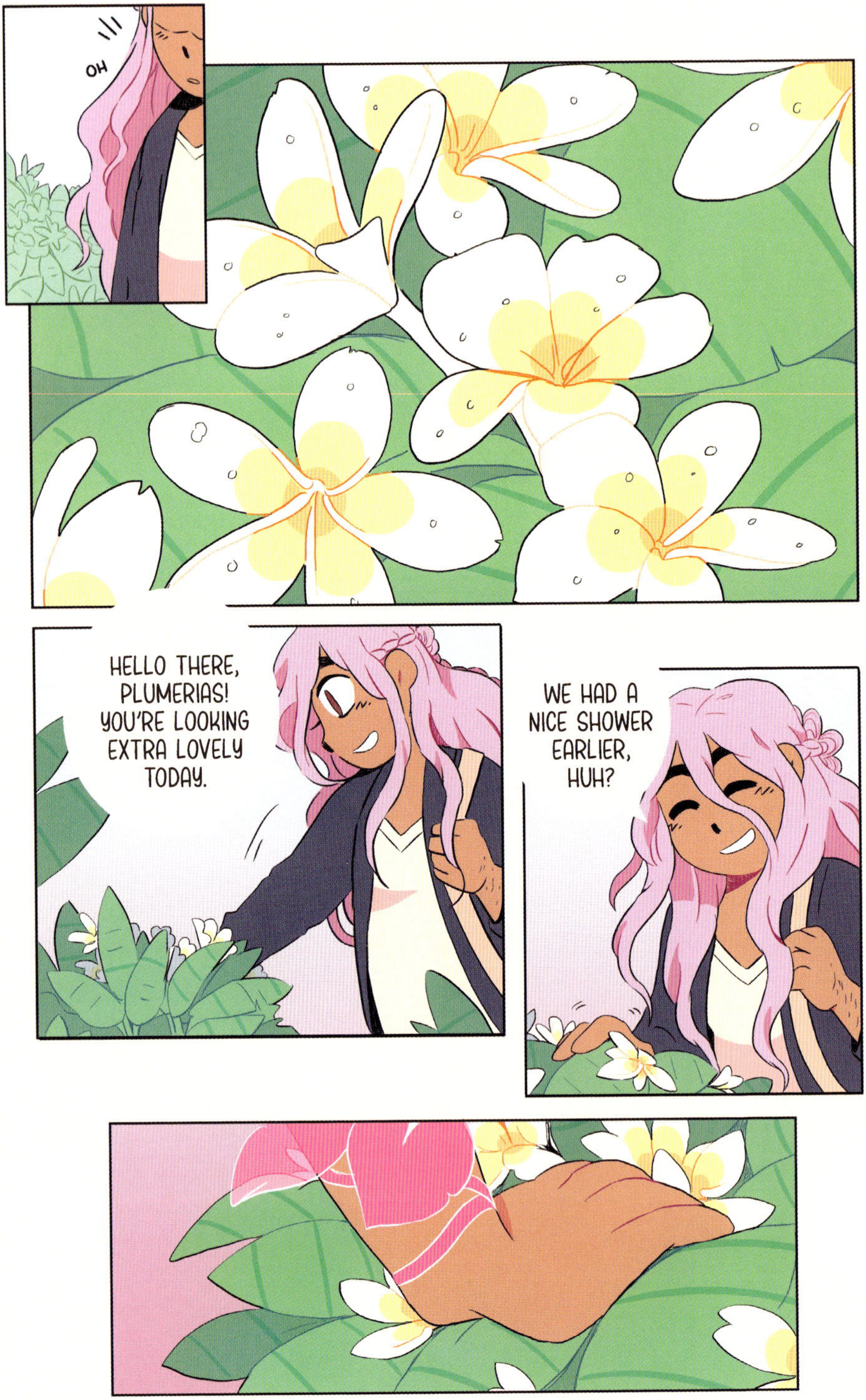
OH
HELLO THERE, PLUMERIAS! YOU'RE LOOKING EXTRA LOVELY TODAY.
WE HAD A NICE SHOWER EARLIER, HUH?

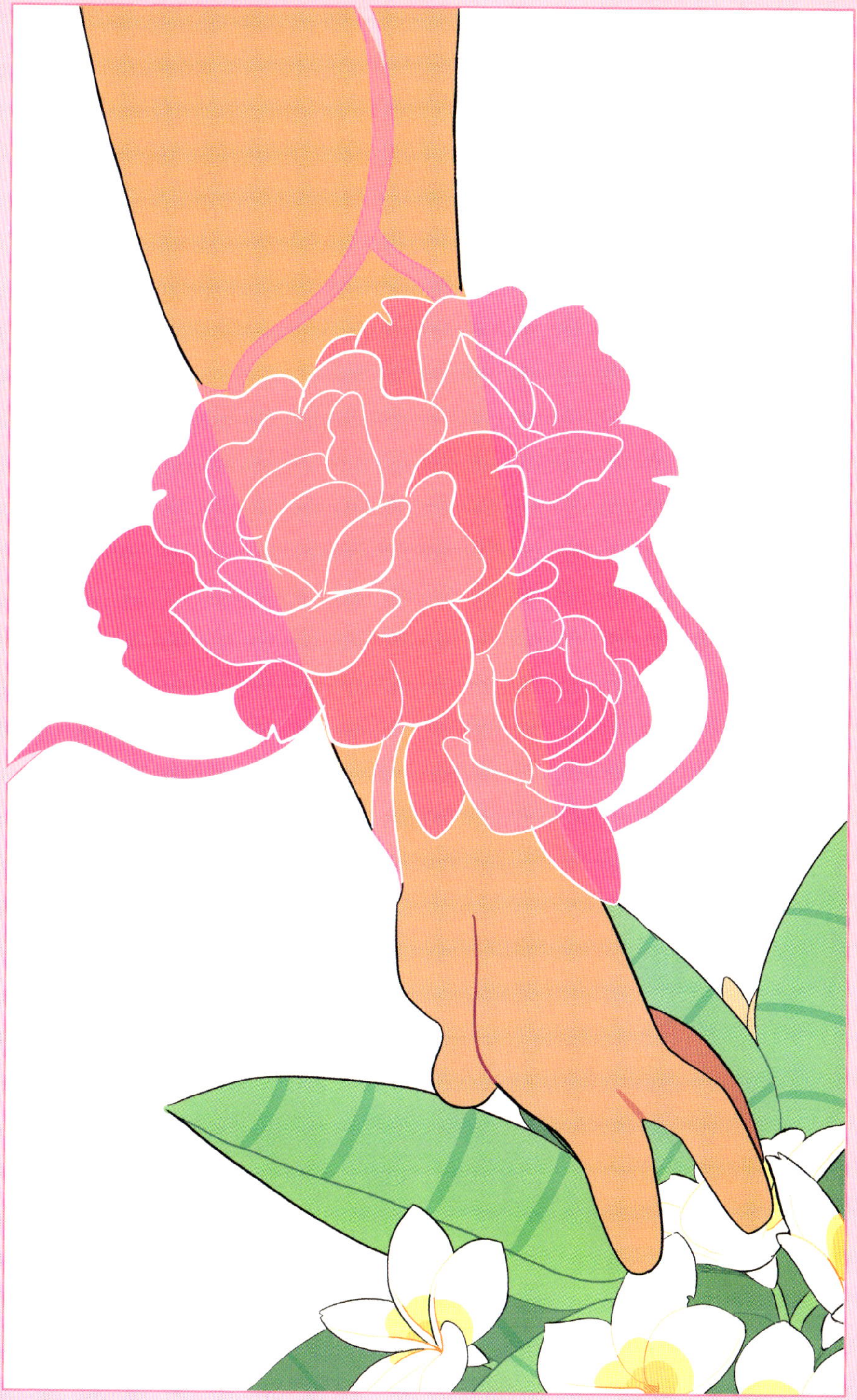

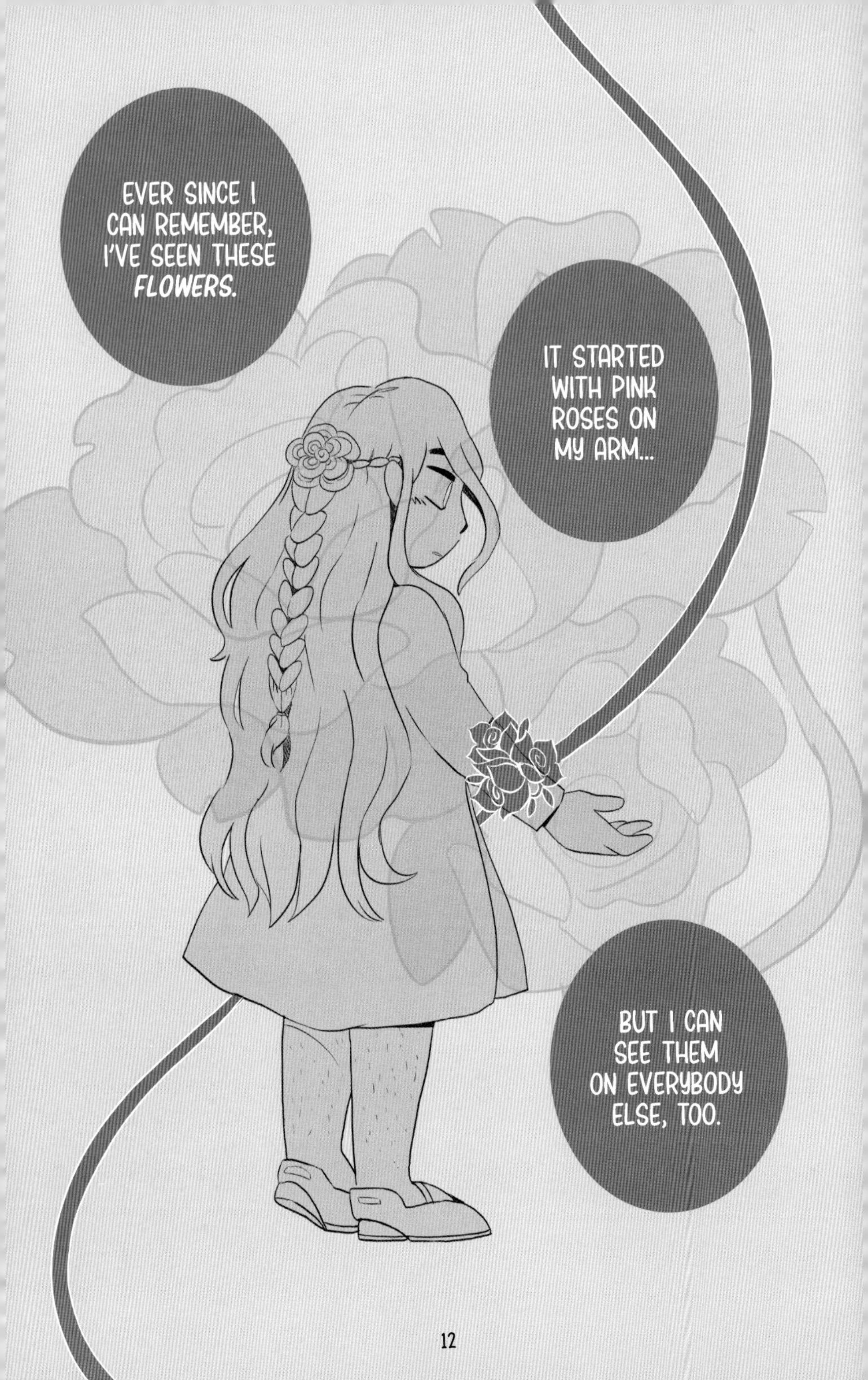
EVER SINCE I CAN REMEMBER, I'VE SEEN THESE *FLOWERS.*
IT STARTED WITH PINK ROSES ON MY ARM...
BUT I CAN SEE THEM ON EVERYBODY ELSE, TOO.

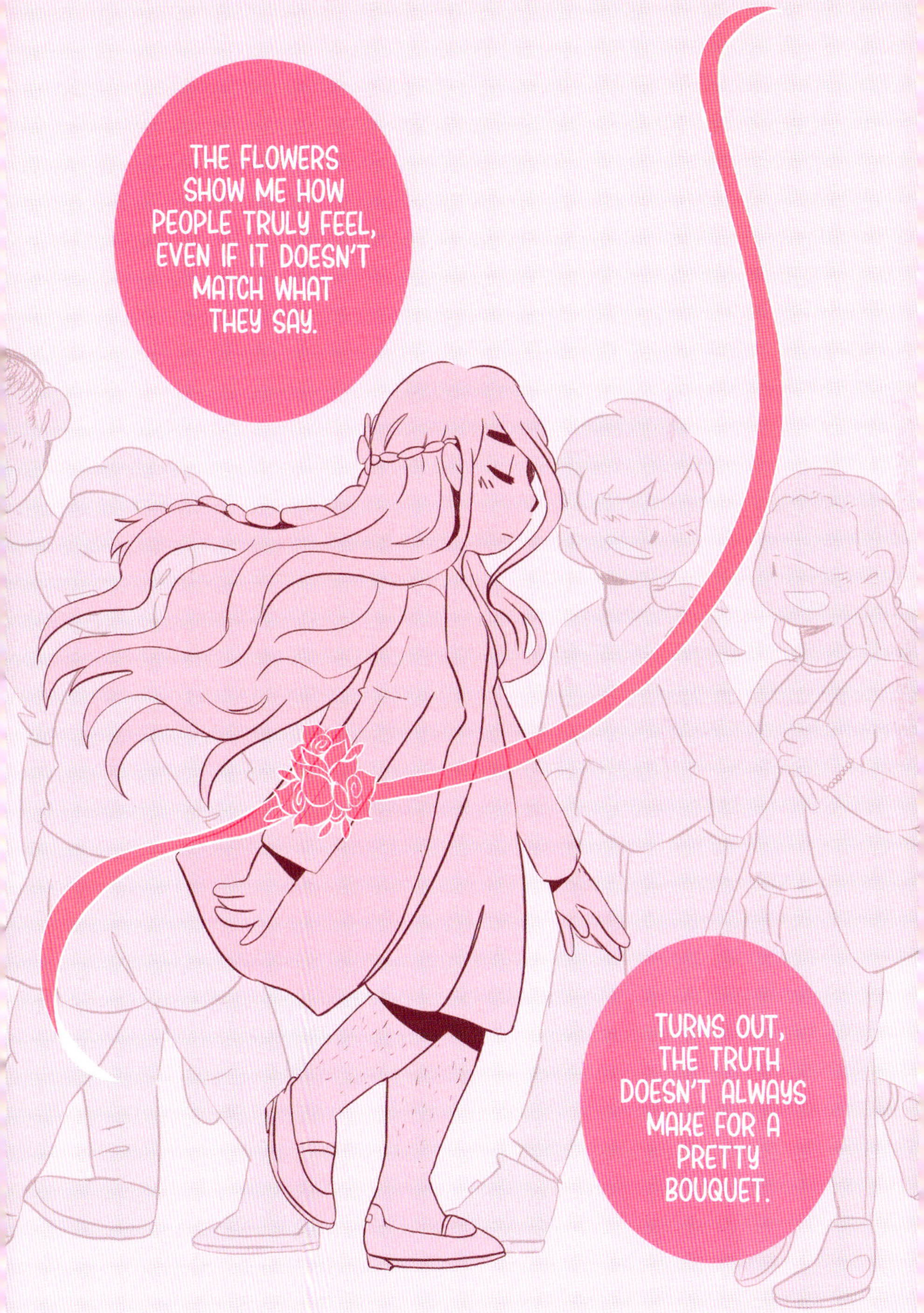
THE FLOWERS SHOW ME HOW PEOPLE TRULY FEEL, EVEN IF IT DOESN'T MATCH WHAT THEY SAY.
TURNS OUT, THE TRUTH DOESN'T ALWAYS MAKE FOR A PRETTY BOUQUET.

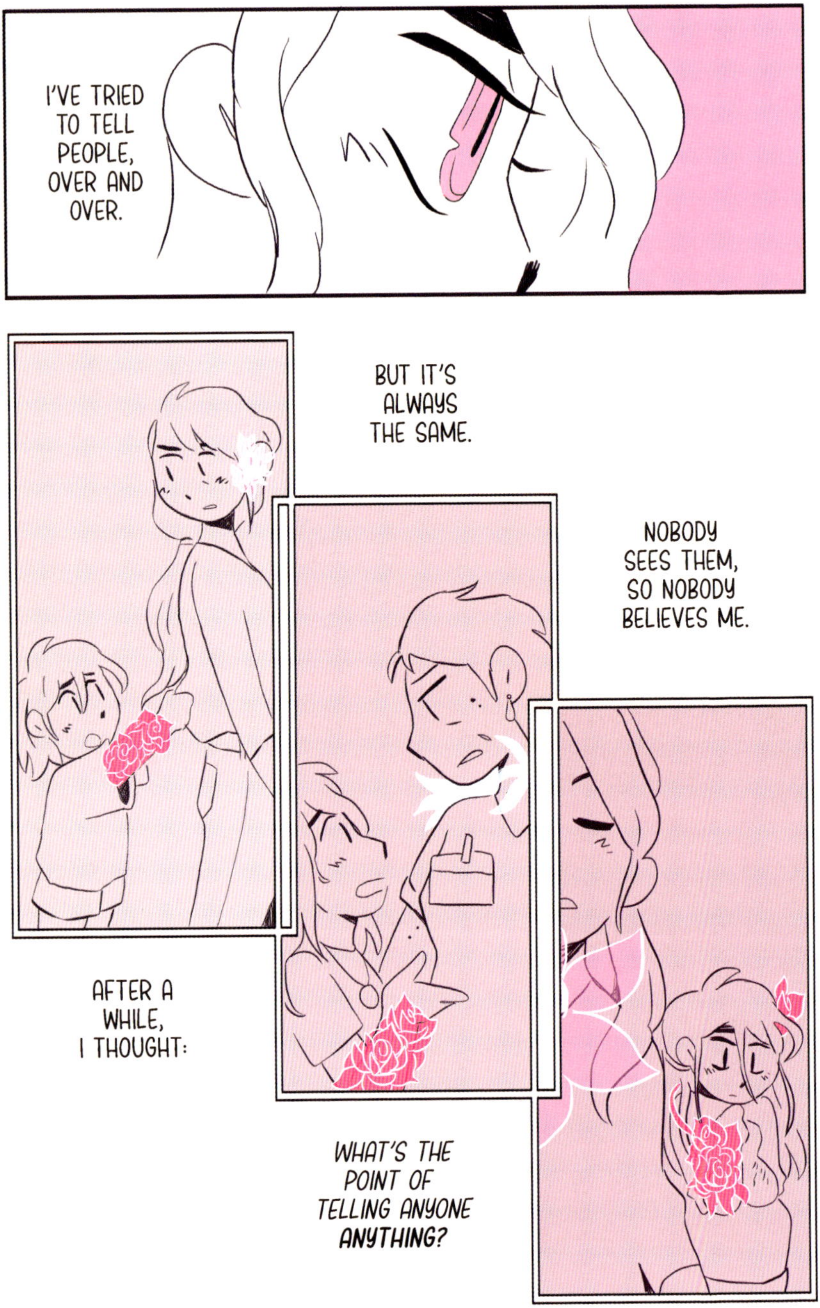
I'VE TRIED TO TELL PEOPLE, OVER AND OVER.
BUT IT'S ALWAYS THE SAME.
NOBODY SEES THEM, SO NOBODY BELIEVES ME.
AFTER A WHILE, I THOUGHT:
WHAT'S THE POINT OF TELLING ANYONE ***ANYTHING?***

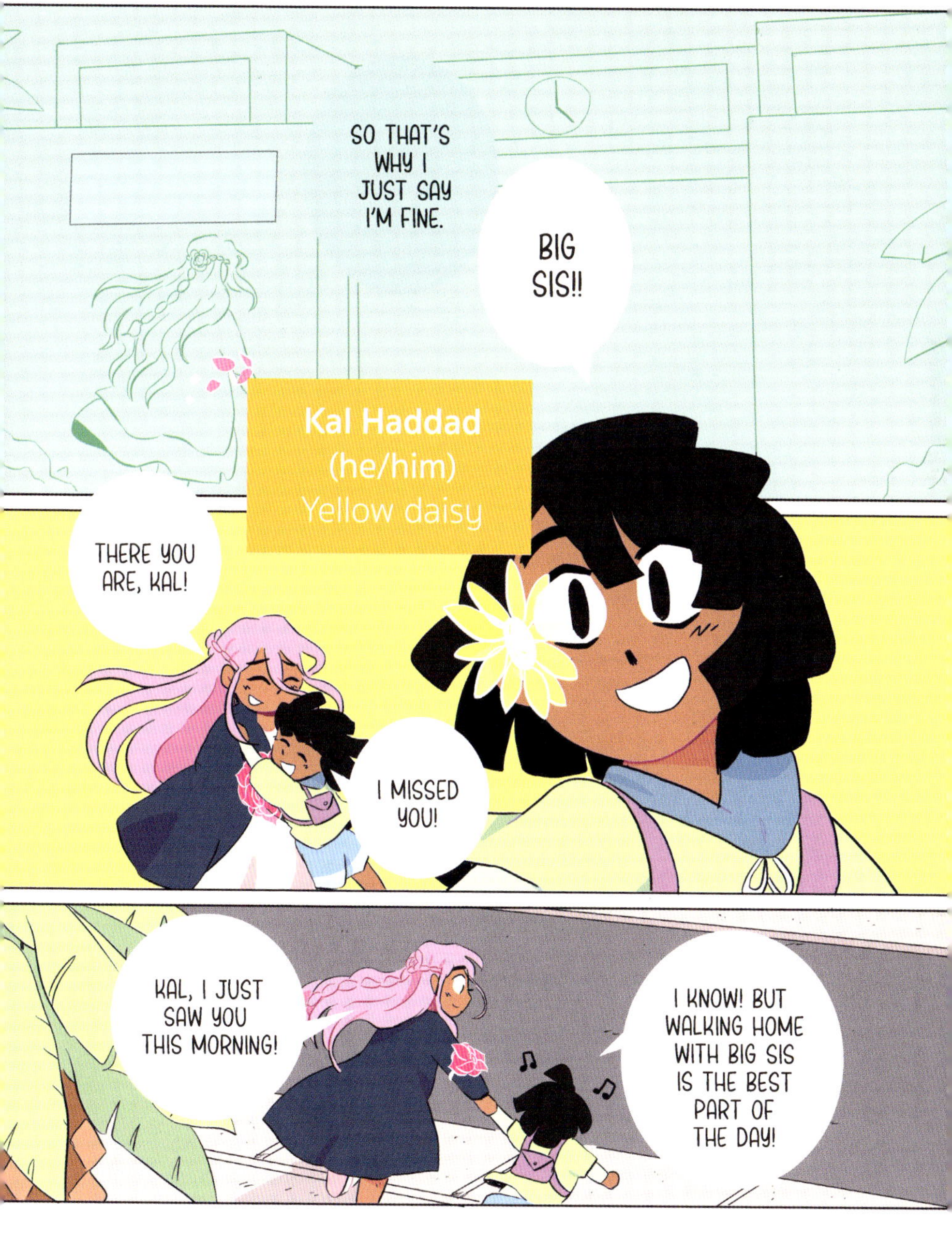
SO THAT'S WHY I JUST SAY I'M FINE.
BIG SIS!!
Kal Haddad (he/him) Yellow daisy
THERE YOU ARE, KAL!
I MISSED YOU!
KAL, I JUST SAW YOU THIS MORNING!
I KNOW! BUT WALKING HOME WITH BIG SIS IS THE BEST PART OF THE DAY!

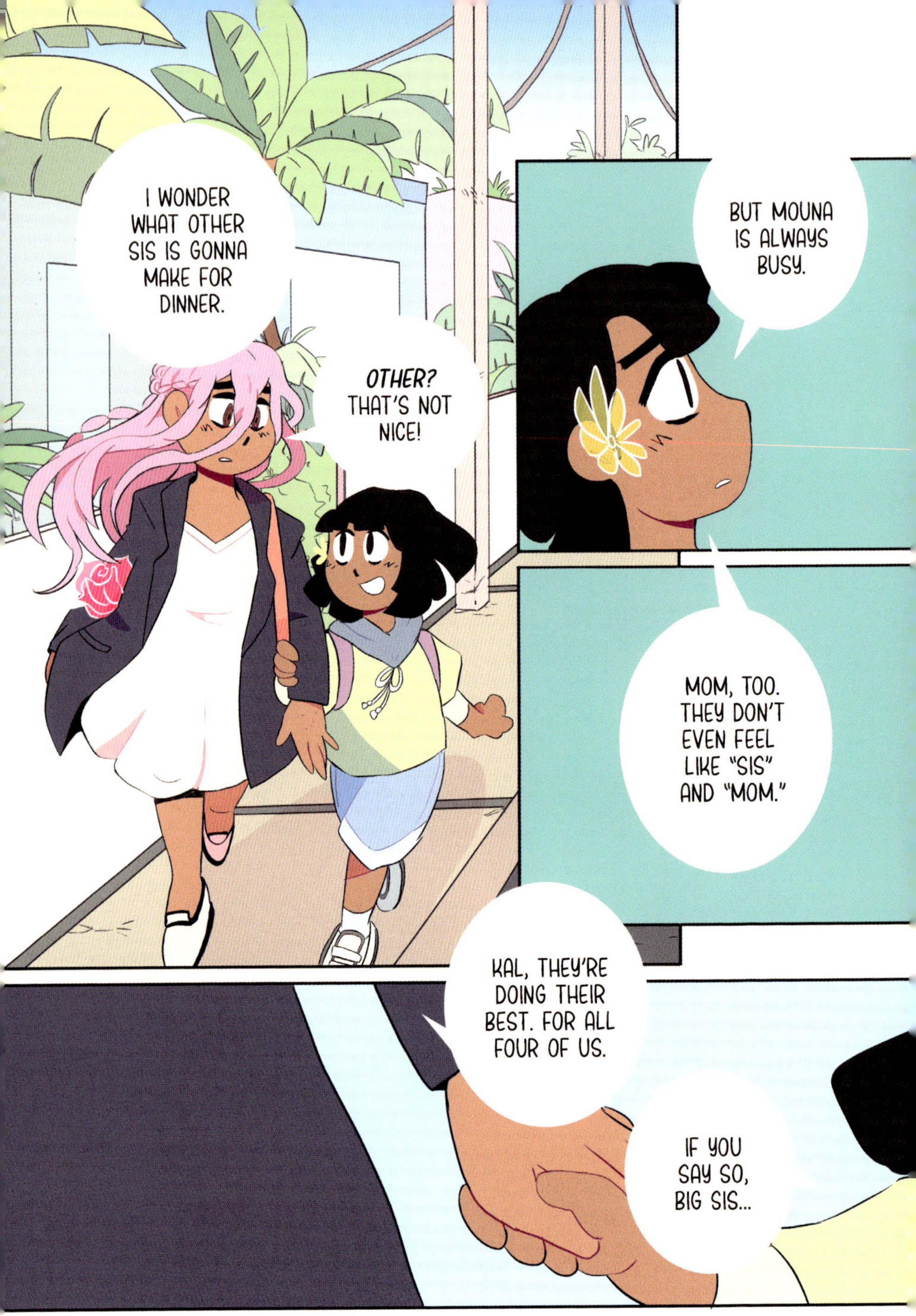
I WONDER WHAT OTHER SIS IS GONNA MAKE FOR DINNER.
OTHER? THAT'S NOT NICE!
BUT MOUNA IS ALWAYS BUSY.
MOM, TOO. THEY DON'T EVEN FEEL LIKE "SIS" AND "MOM."
KAL, THEY'RE DOING THEIR BEST. FOR ALL FOUR OF US.
IF YOU SAY SO, BIG SIS...

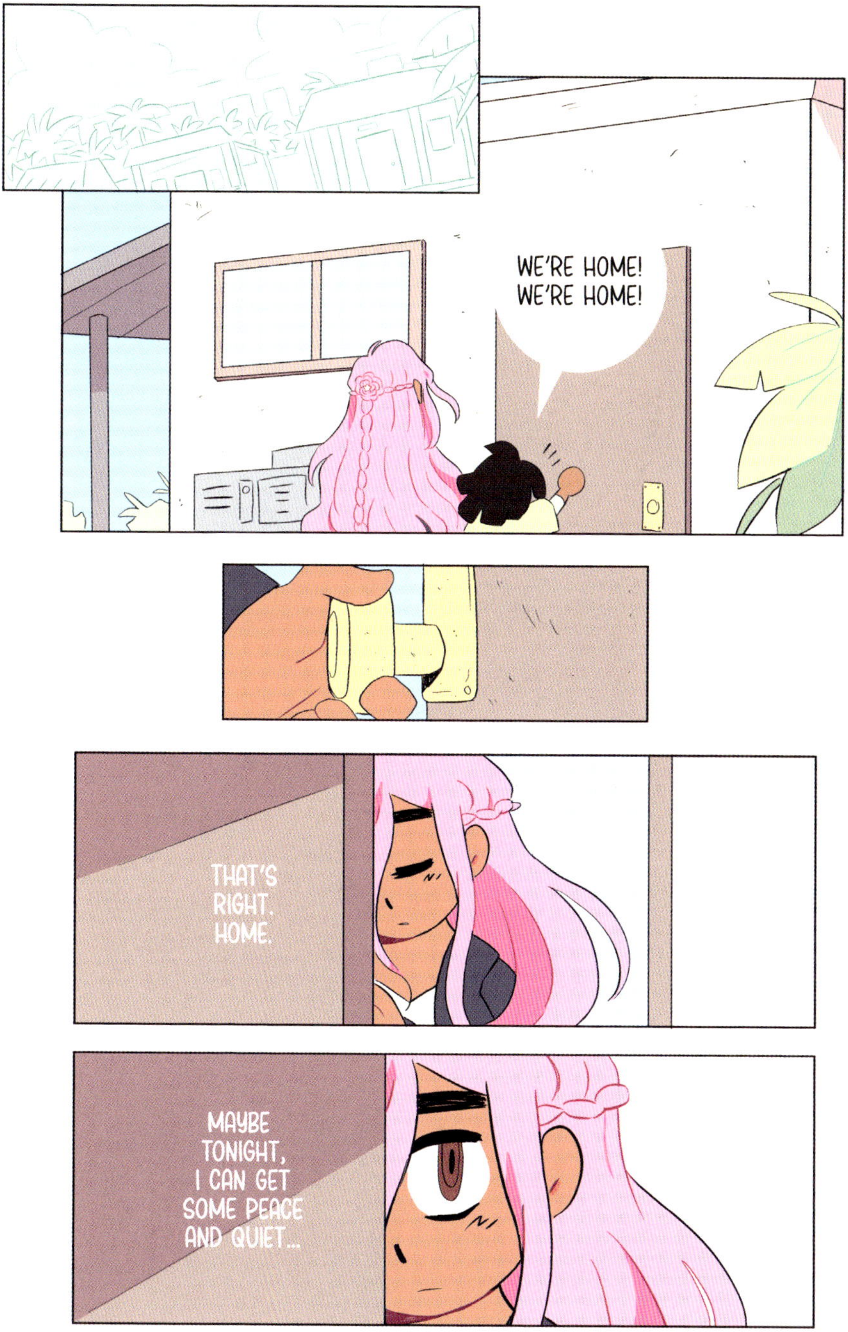
WE'RE HOME! WE'RE HOME!
THAT'S RIGHT. HOME.
MAYBE TONIGHT, I CAN GET SOME PEACE AND QUIET...

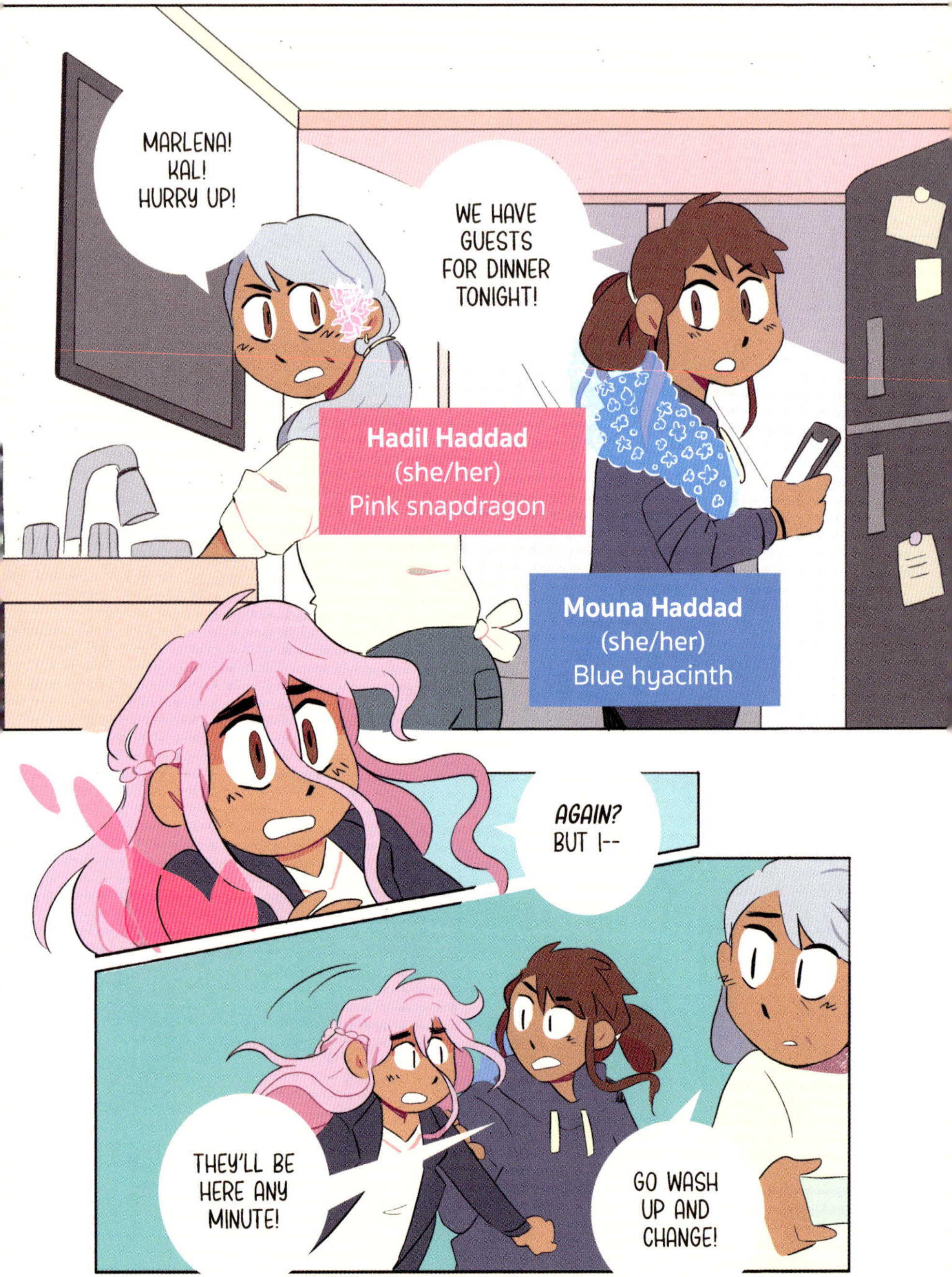
MARLENA! KAL! HURRY UP!
WE HAVE GUESTS FOR DINNER TONIGHT!
Hadil Haddad (she/her) Pink snapdragon
Mouna Haddad (she/her) Blue hyacinth
AGAIN? BUT I--
THEY'LL BE HERE ANY MINUTE!
GO WASH UP AND CHANGE!

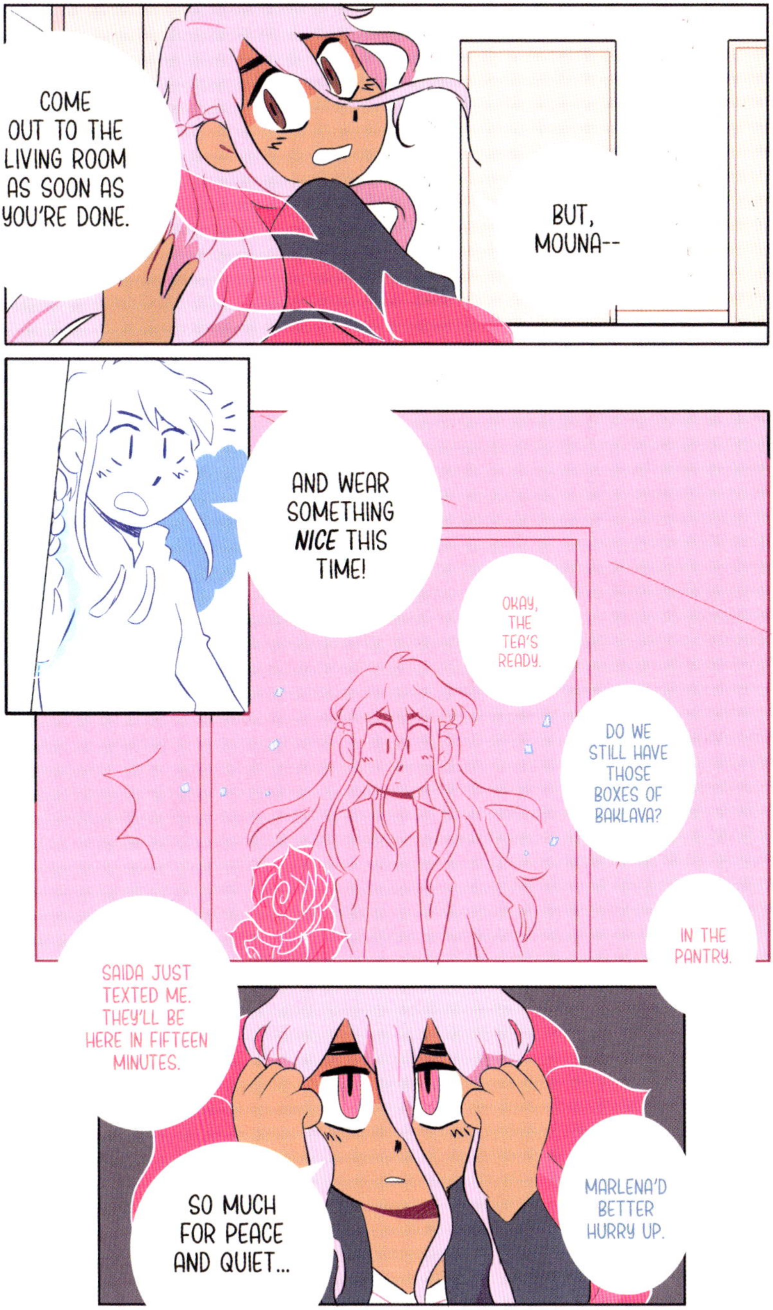
COME OUT TO THE LIVING ROOM AS SOON AS YOU'RE DONE.
BUT, MOUNA--
AND WEAR SOMETHING *NICE* THIS TIME!
OKAY, THE TEA'S READY.
DO WE STILL HAVE THOSE BOXES OF BAKLAVA?
IN THE PANTRY.
SAIDA JUST TEXTED ME. THEY'LL BE HERE IN FIFTEEN MINUTES.
MARLENA'D BETTER HURRY UP.
SO MUCH FOR PEACE AND QUIET...

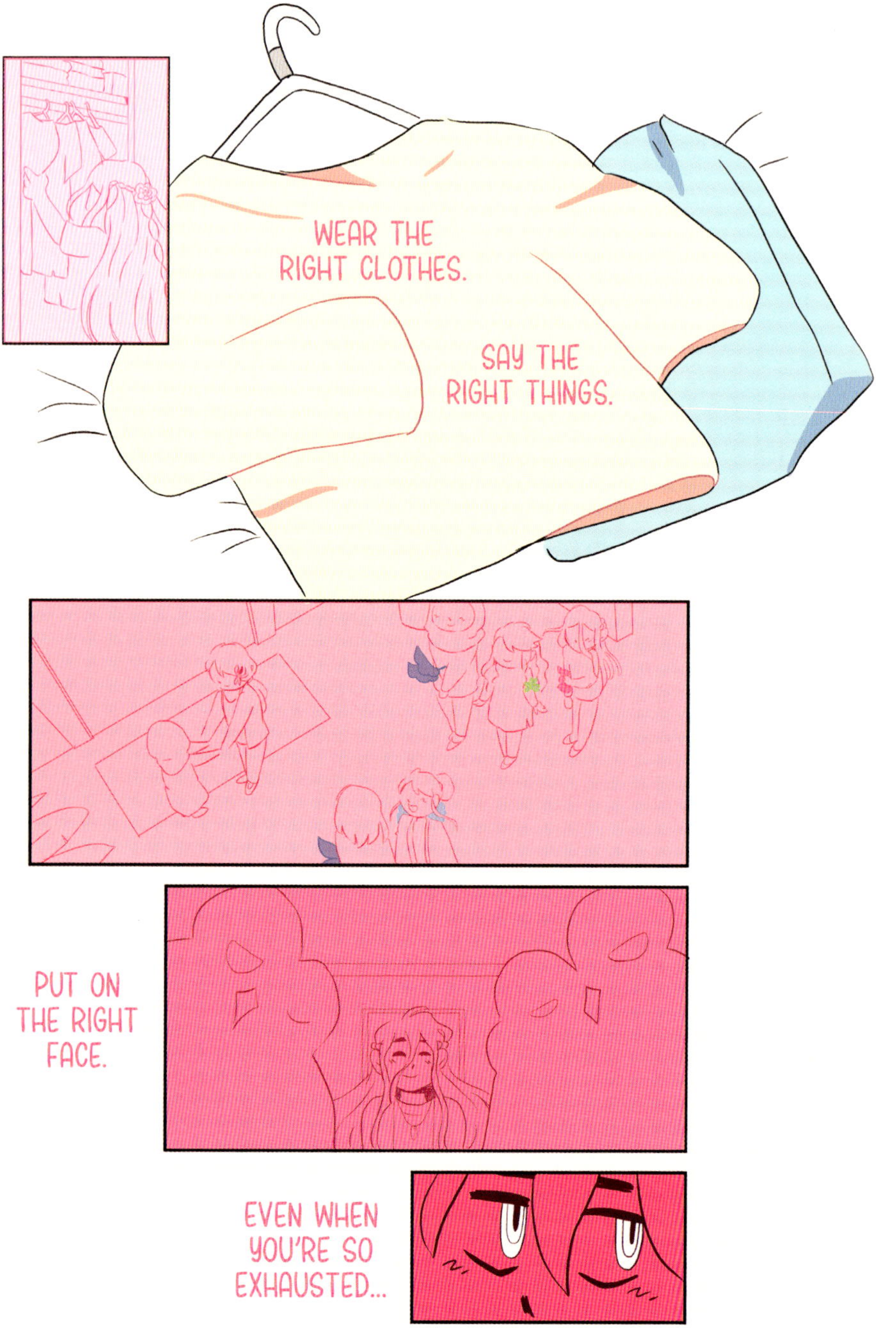
WEAR THE RIGHT CLOTHES.
SAY THE RIGHT THINGS.
PUT ON THE RIGHT FACE.
EVEN WHEN YOU'RE SO EXHAUSTED...

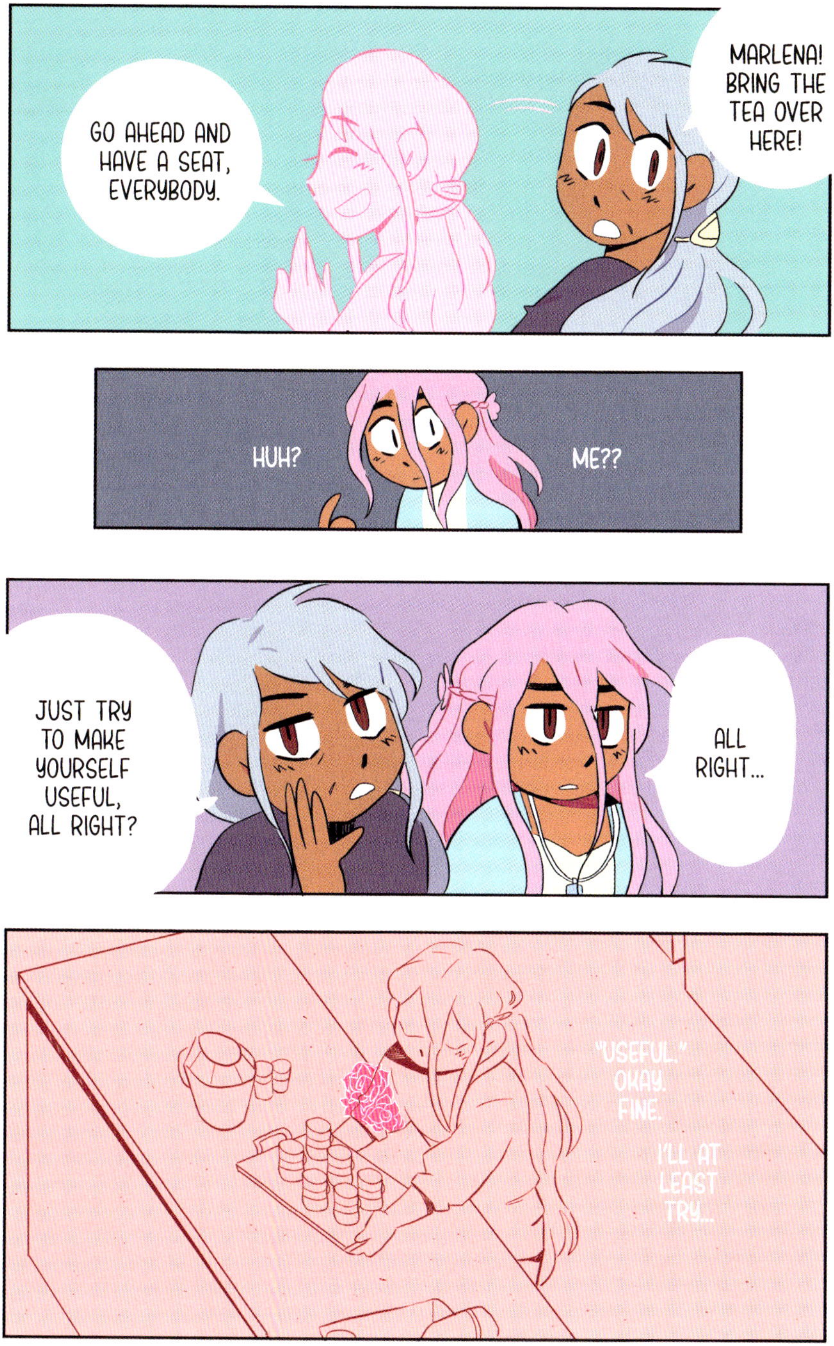
GO AHEAD AND HAVE A SEAT, EVERYBODY.
MARLENA! BRING THE TEA OVER HERE!
HUH?
ME??
JUST TRY TO MAKE YOURSELF USEFUL, ALL RIGHT?
ALL RIGHT...
"USEFUL." OKAY. FINE.
I'LL AT LEAST TRY...

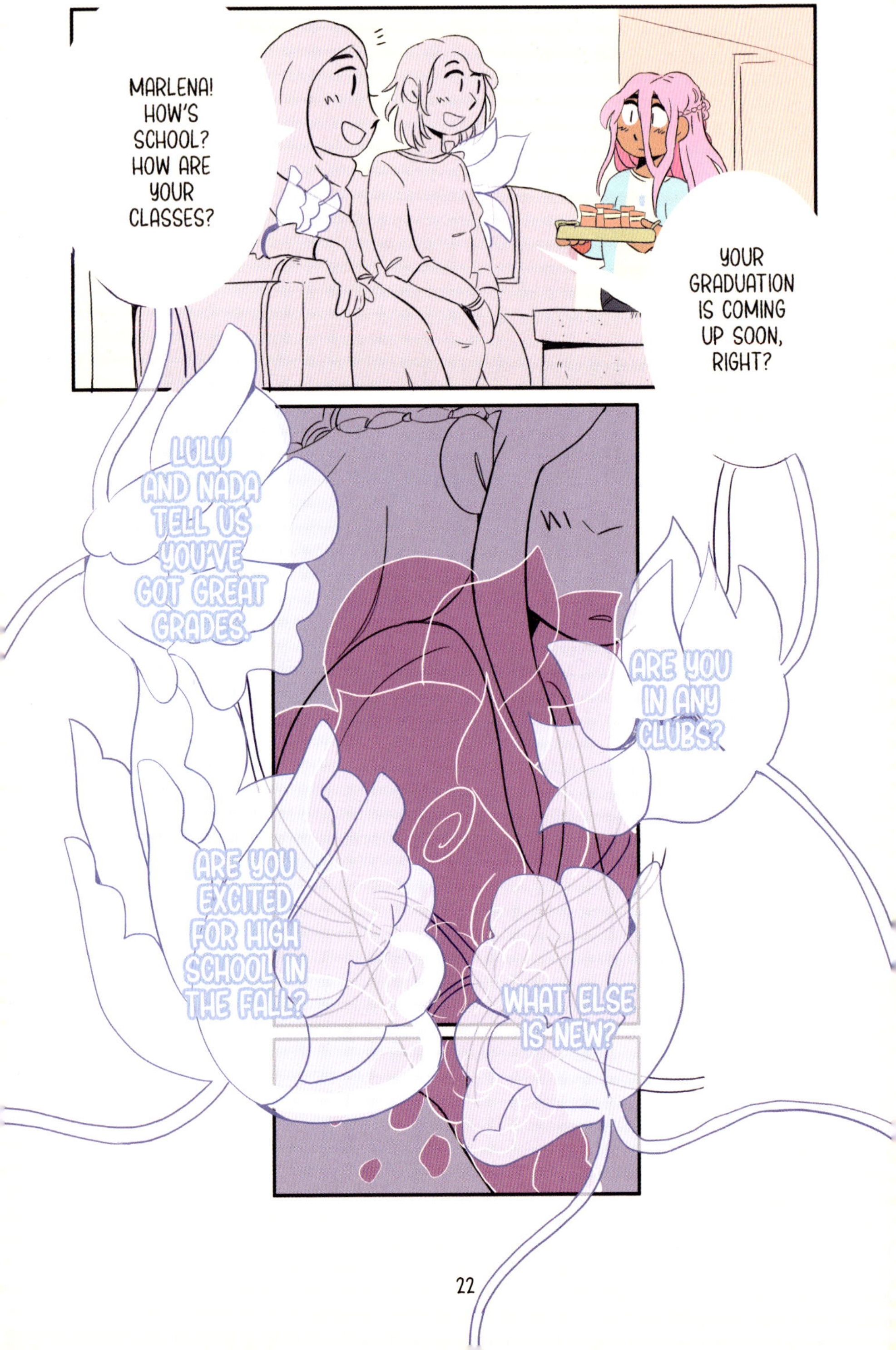
MARLENA! HOW'S SCHOOL? HOW ARE YOUR CLASSES?
YOUR GRADUATION IS COMING UP SOON, RIGHT?
LULU AND NADA TELL US YOU'VE GOT GREAT GRADES.
ARE YOU IN ANY CLUBS?
ARE YOU EXCITED FOR HIGH SCHOOL IN THE FALL?
WHAT ELSE IS NEW?

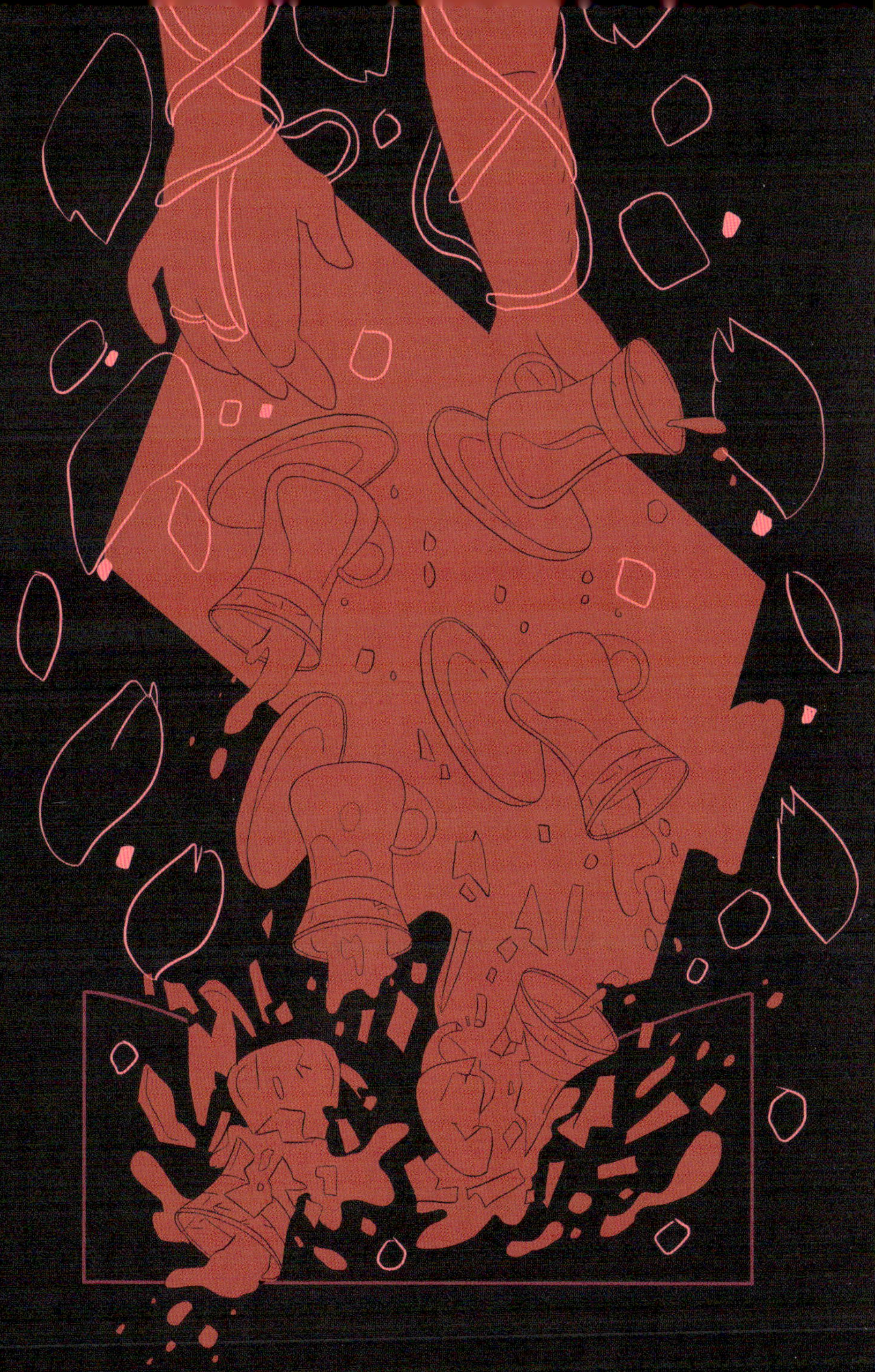

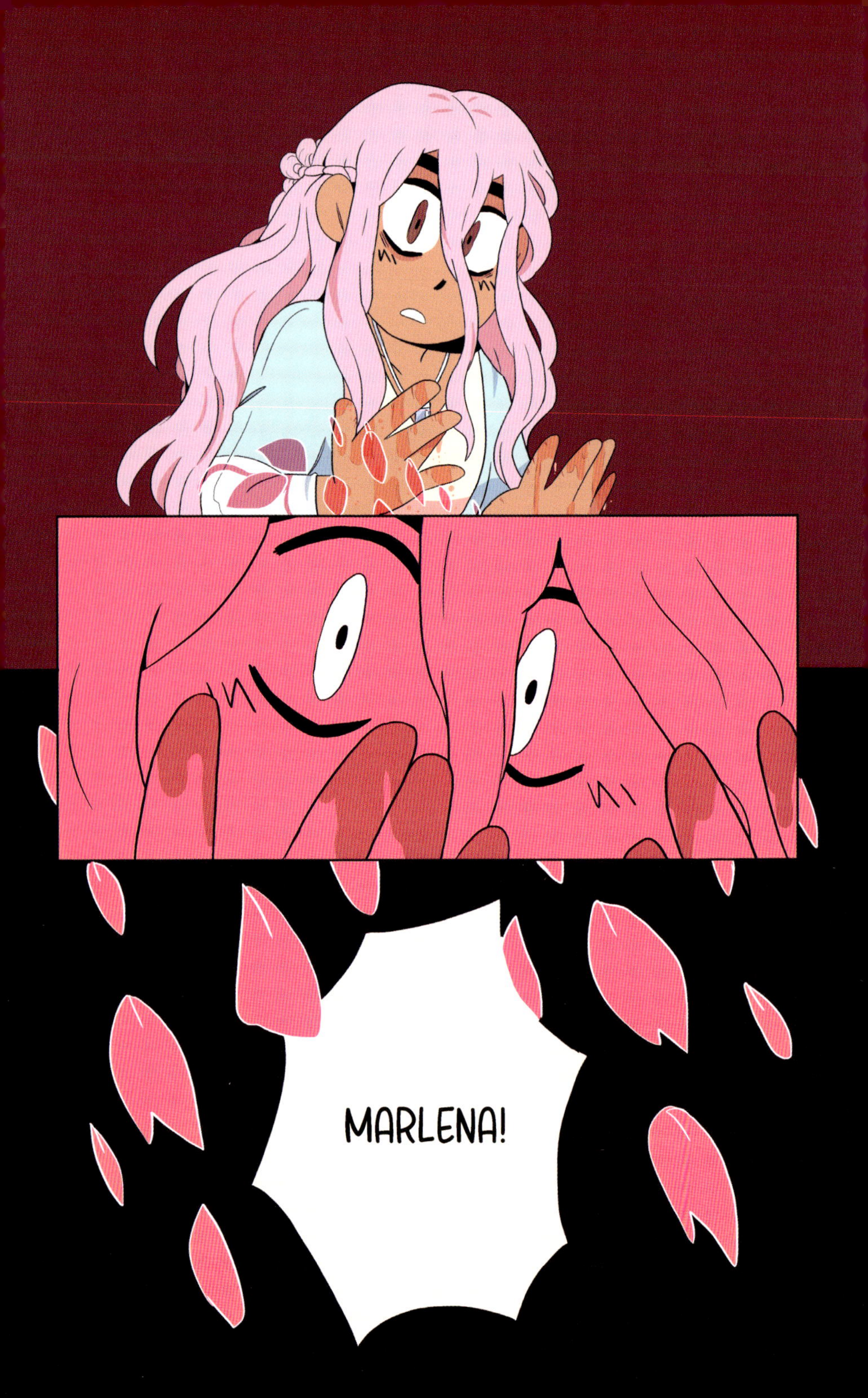
MARLENA!

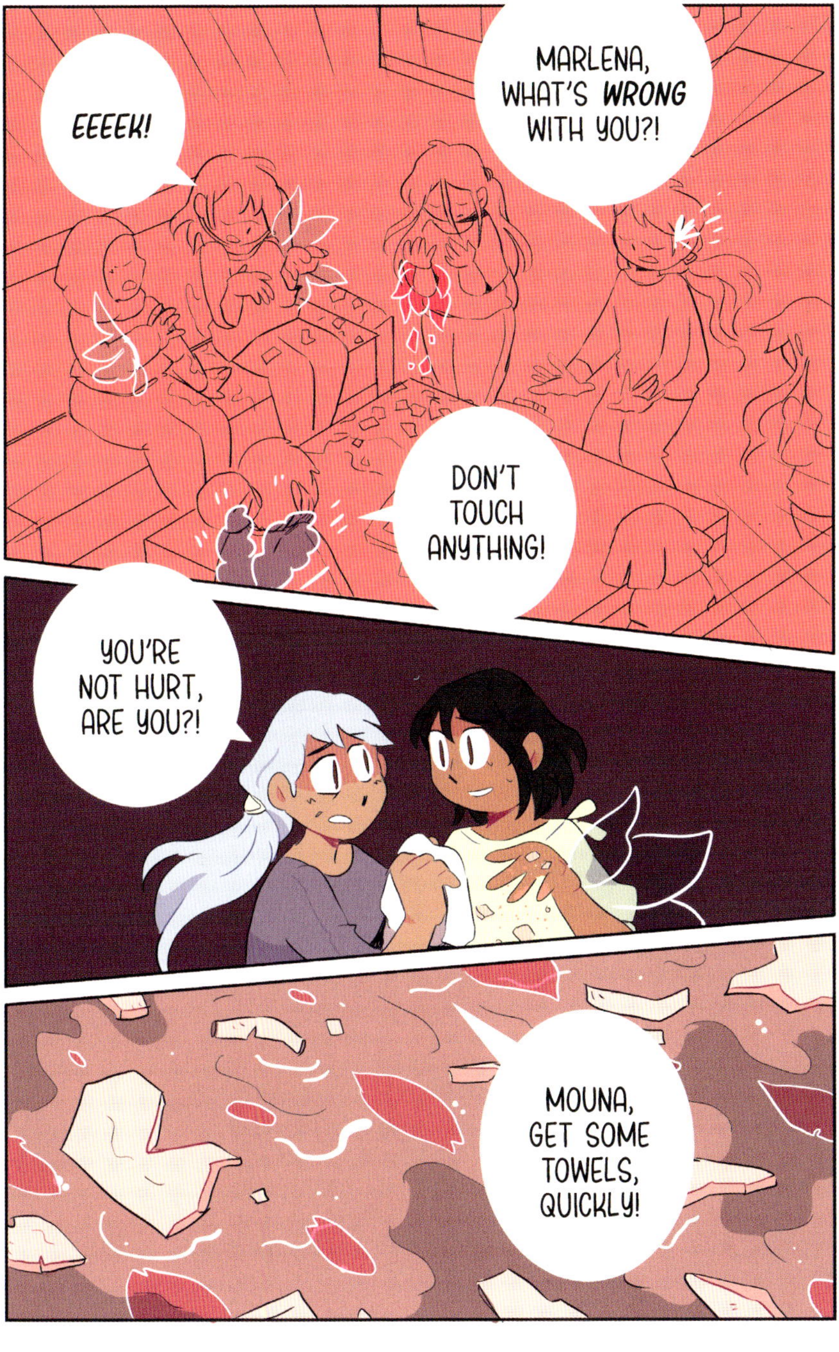
EEEEK!
MARLENA, WHAT'S **WRONG** WITH YOU?!
DON'T TOUCH ANYTHING!
YOU'RE NOT HURT, ARE YOU?!
MOUNA, GET SOME TOWELS, QUICKLY!

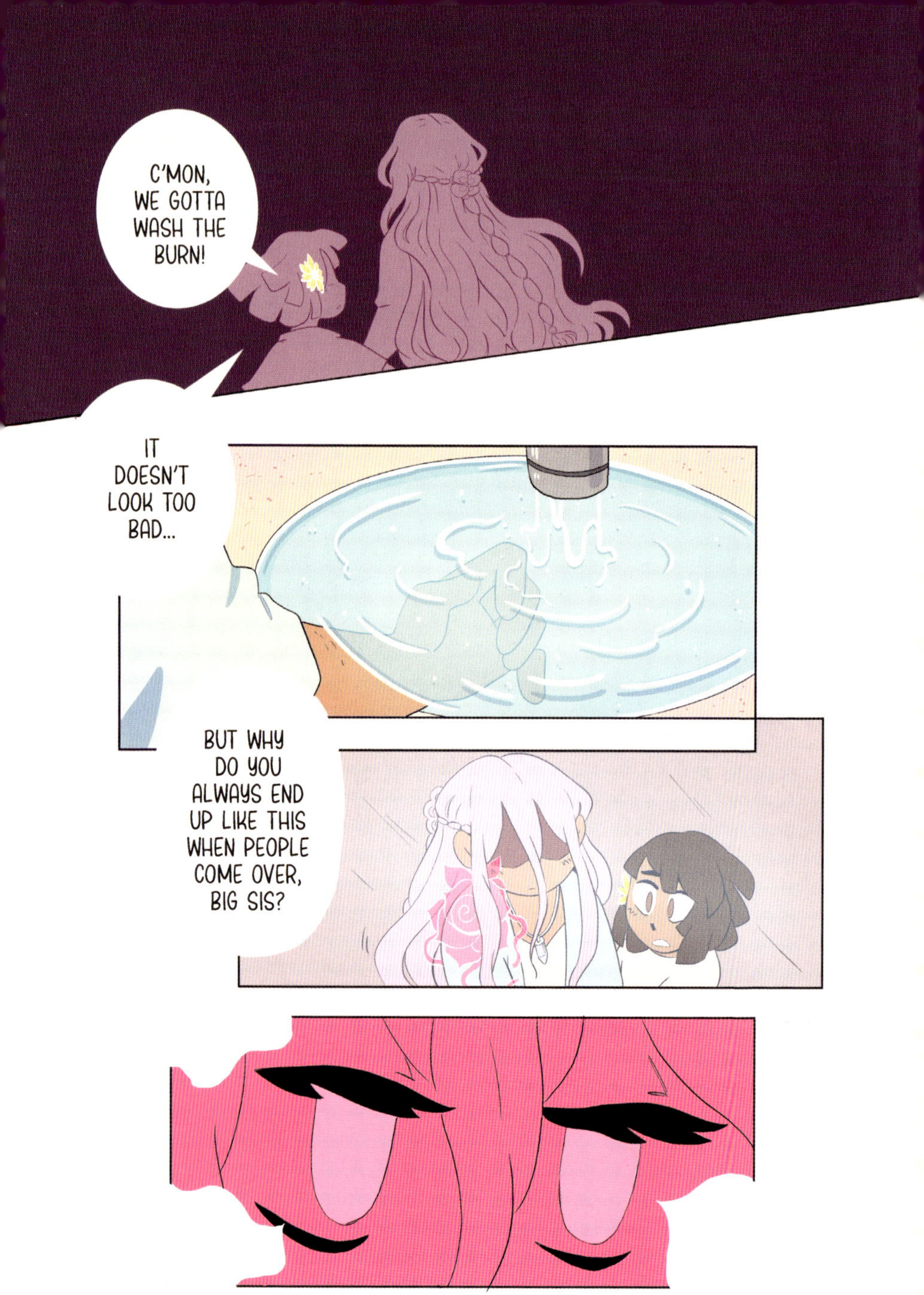
C'MON, WE GOTTA WASH THE BURN!
IT DOESN'T LOOK TOO BAD...
BUT WHY DO YOU ALWAYS END UP LIKE THIS WHEN PEOPLE COME OVER, BIG SIS?

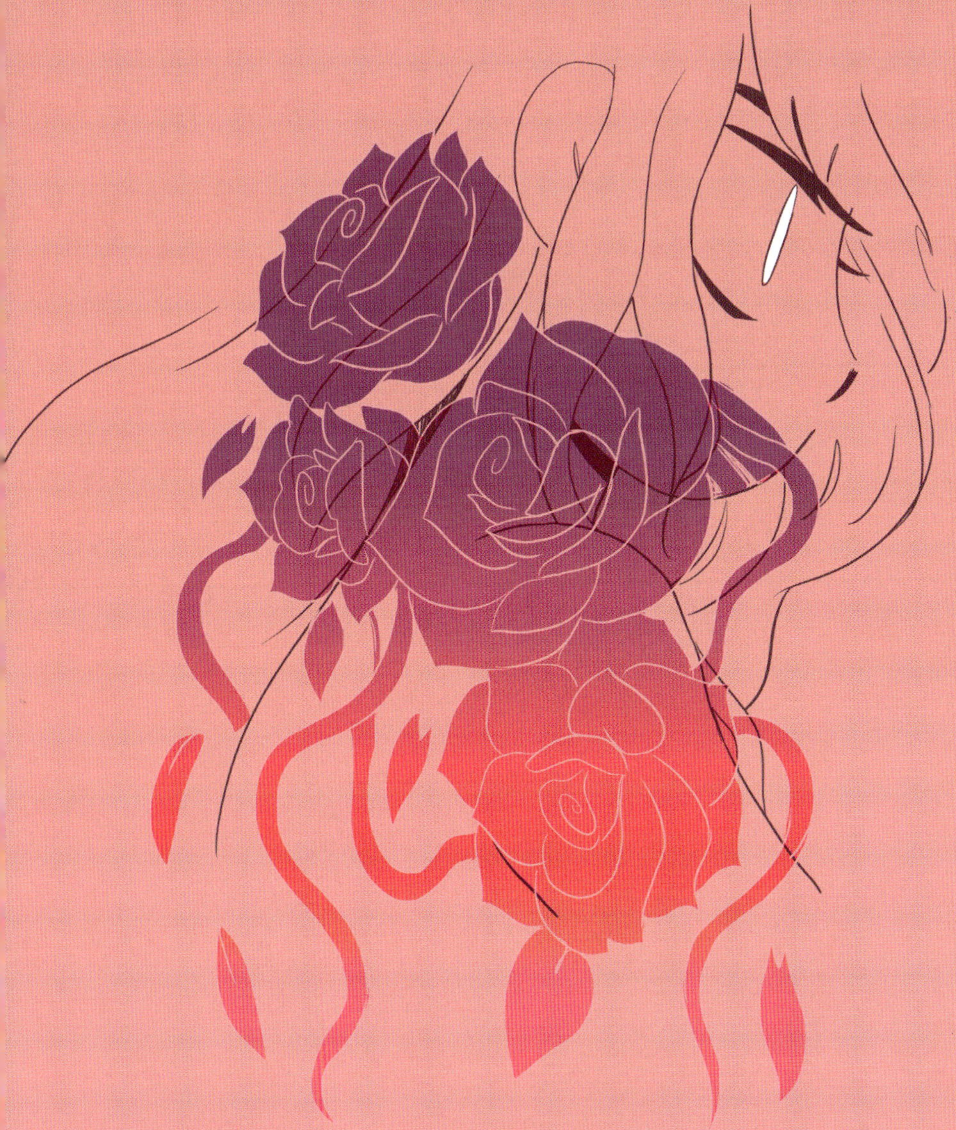

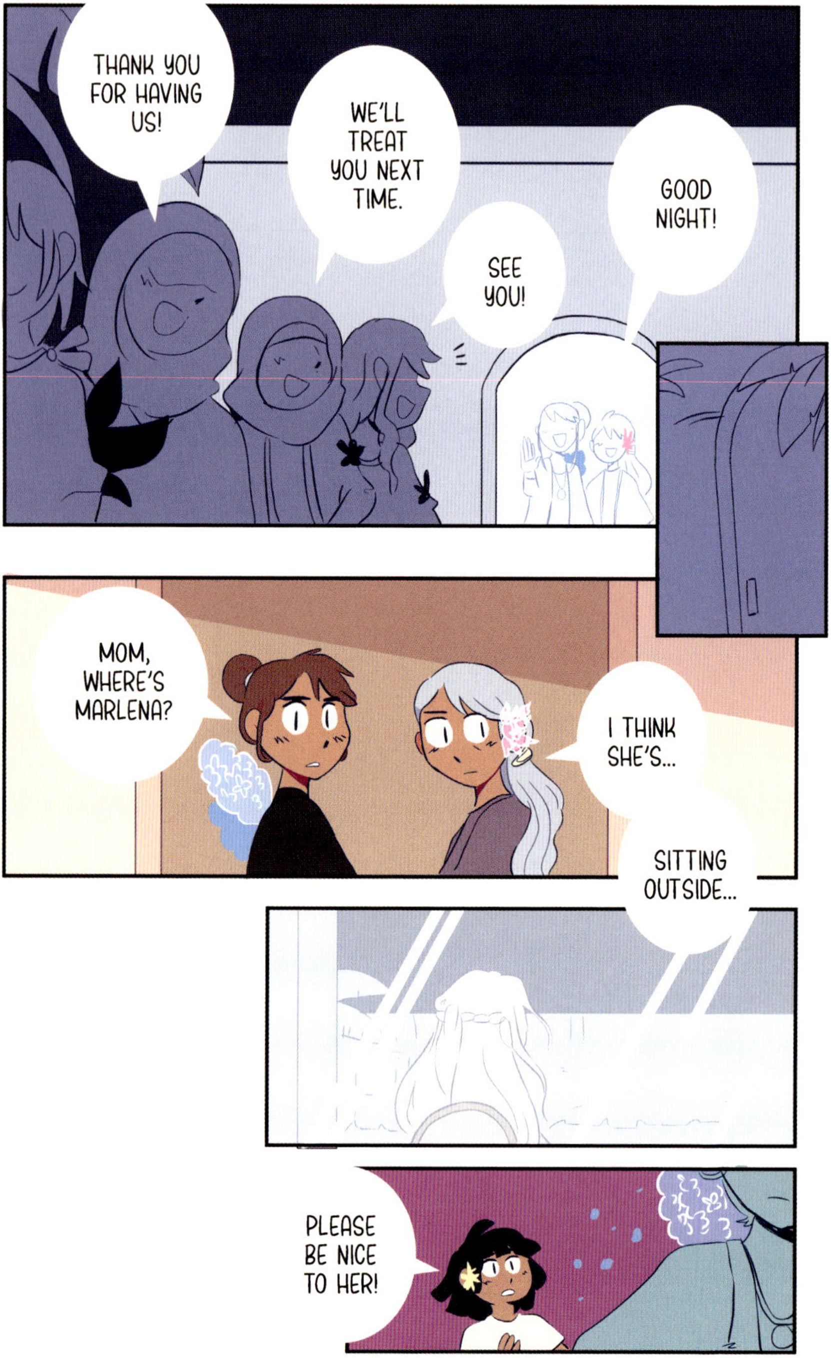
THANK YOU FOR HAVING US!
WE'LL TREAT YOU NEXT TIME.
SEE YOU!
GOOD NIGHT!
MOM, WHERE'S MARLENA?
I THINK SHE'S...
SITTING OUTSIDE...
PLEASE BE NICE TO HER!

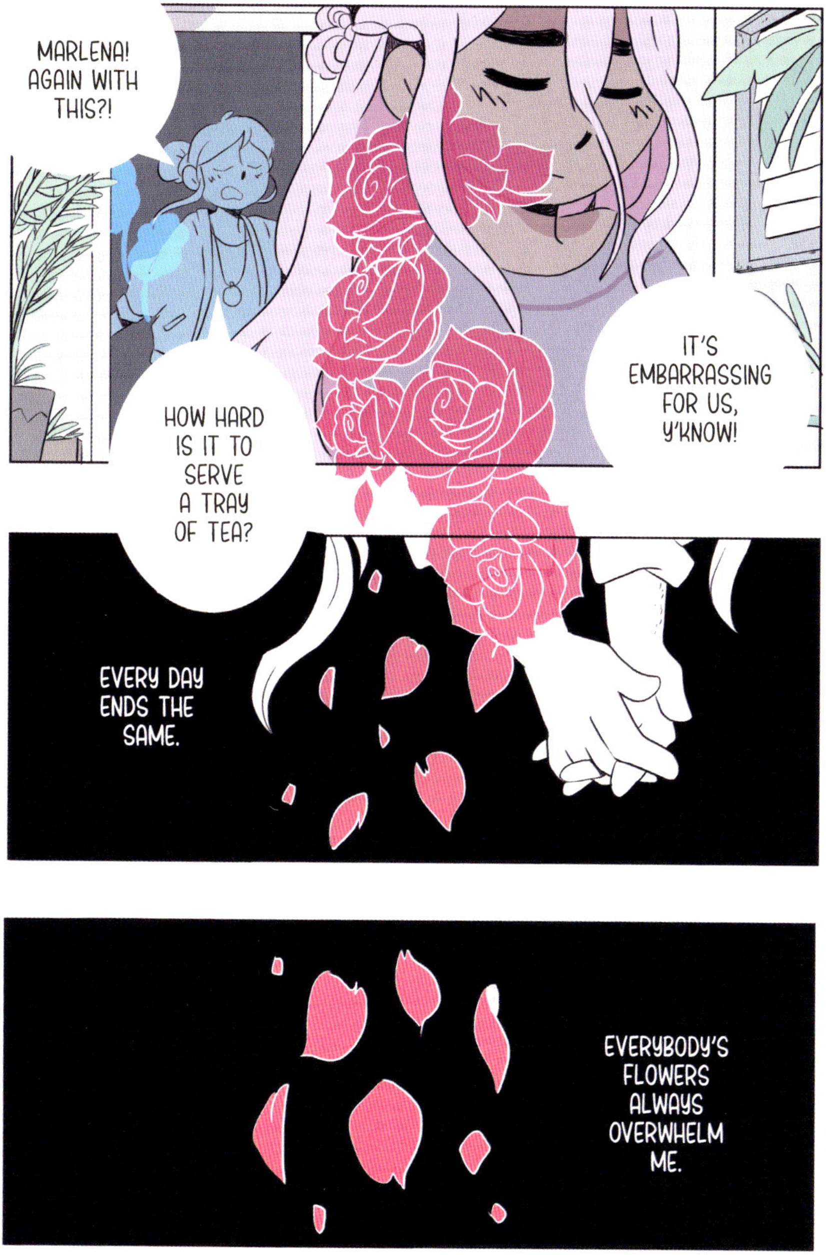
MARLENA! AGAIN WITH THIS?!
HOW HARD IS IT TO SERVE A TRAY OF TEA?
IT'S EMBARRASSING FOR US, Y'KNOW!
EVERY DAY ENDS THE SAME.
EVERYBODY'S FLOWERS ALWAYS OVERWHELM ME.

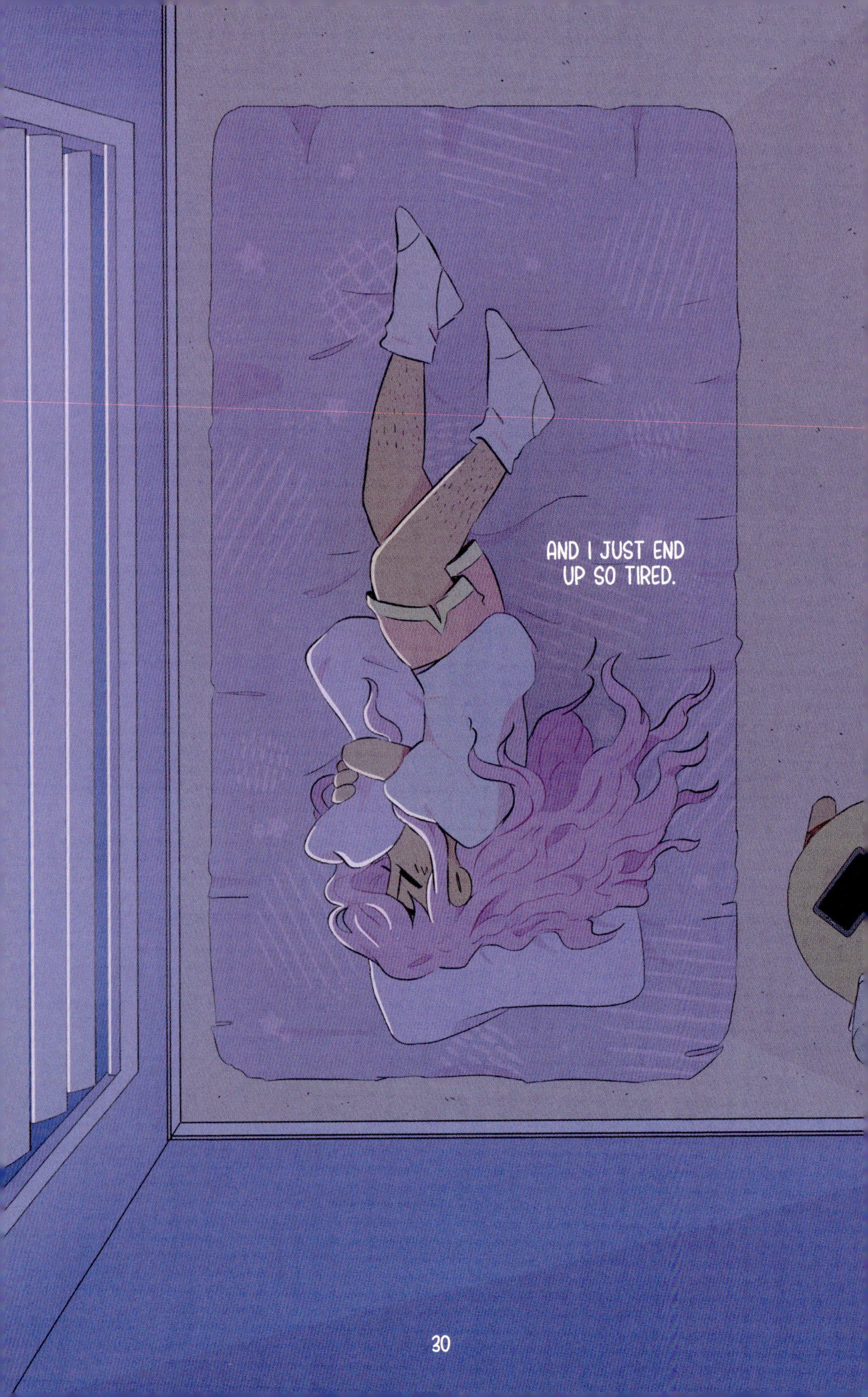
AND I JUST END UP SO TIRED.

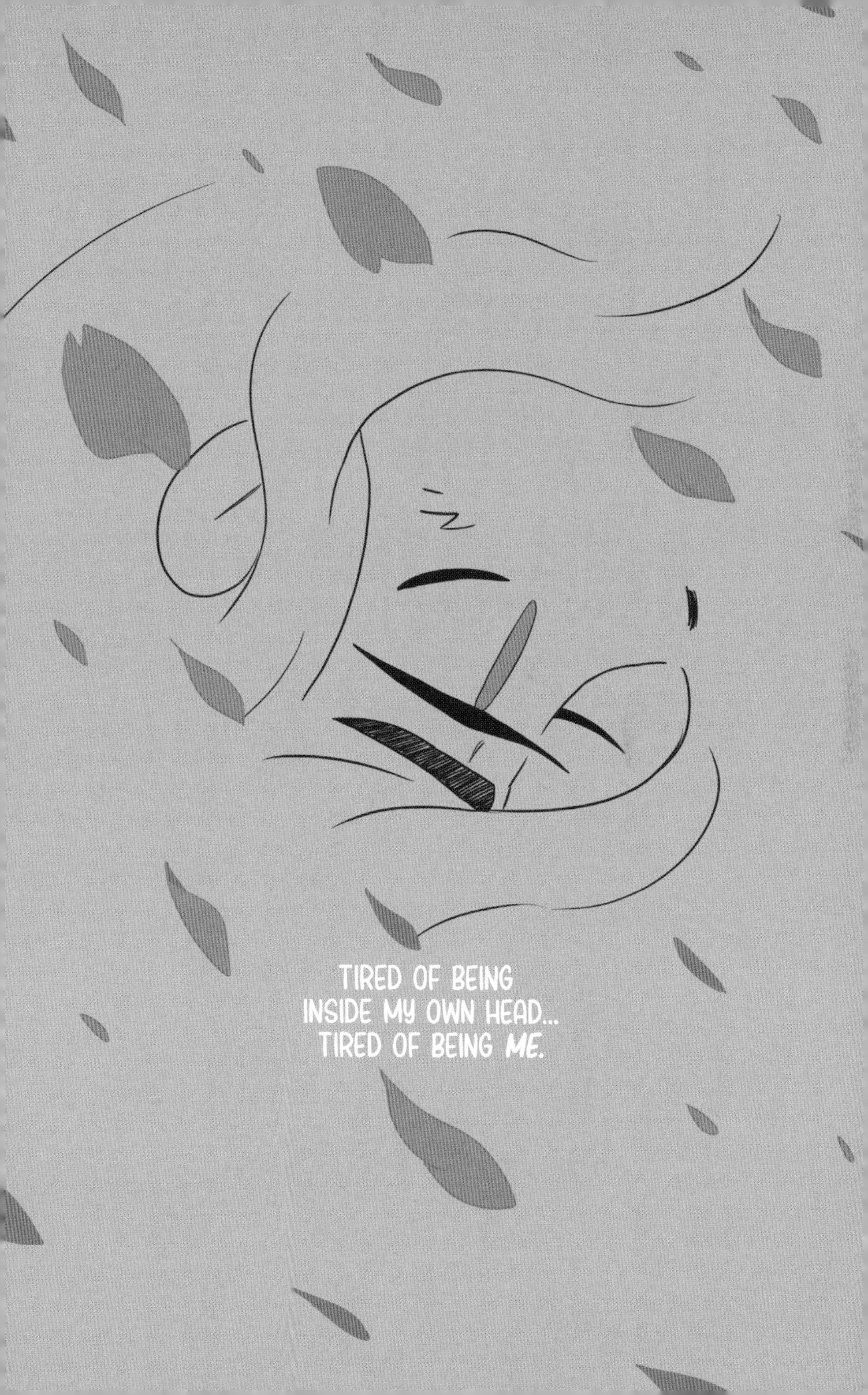
TIRED OF BEING
INSIDE MY OWN HEAD...
TIRED OF BEING *ME.*

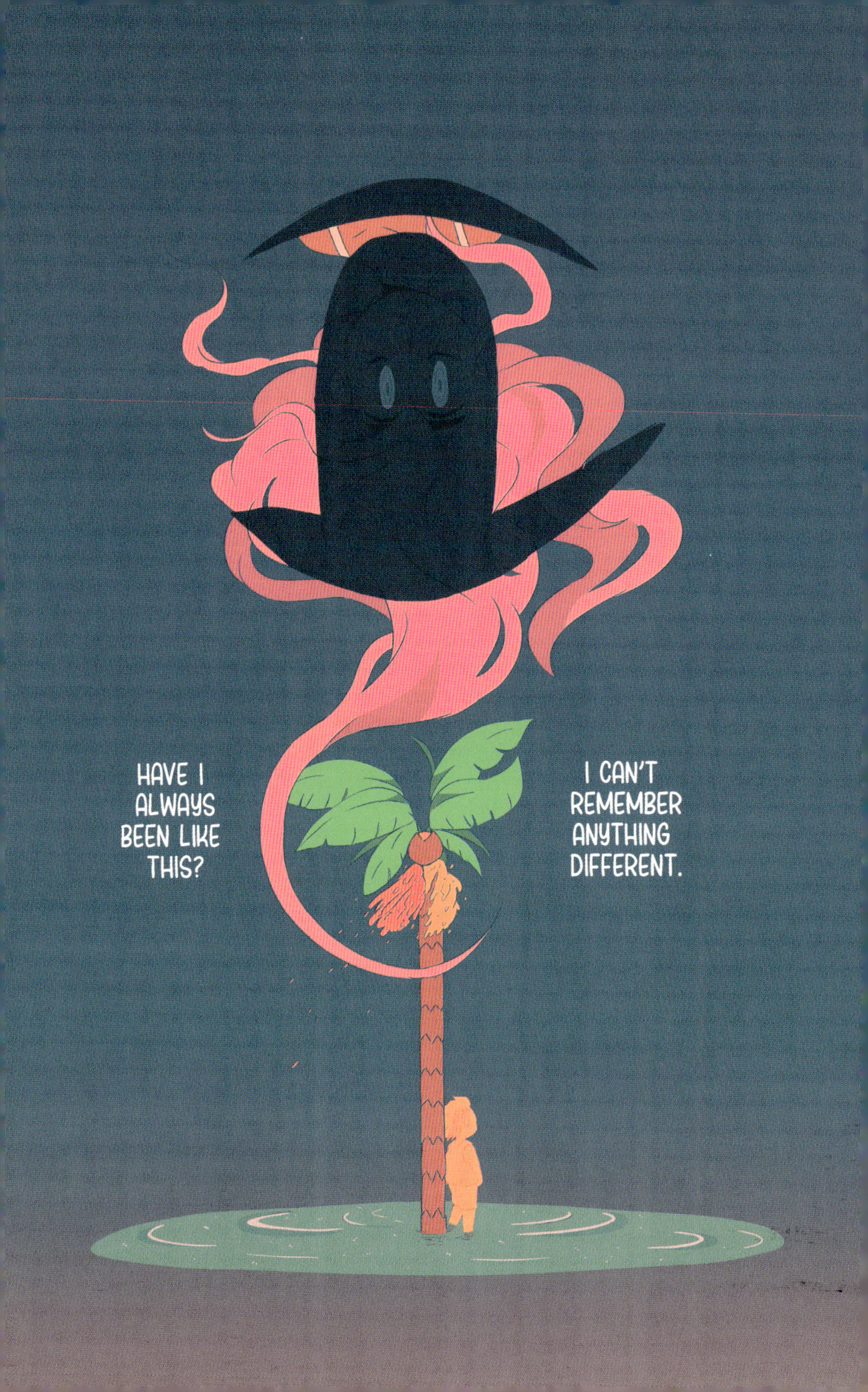
HAVE I ALWAYS BEEN LIKE THIS?
I CAN'T REMEMBER ANYTHING DIFFERENT.

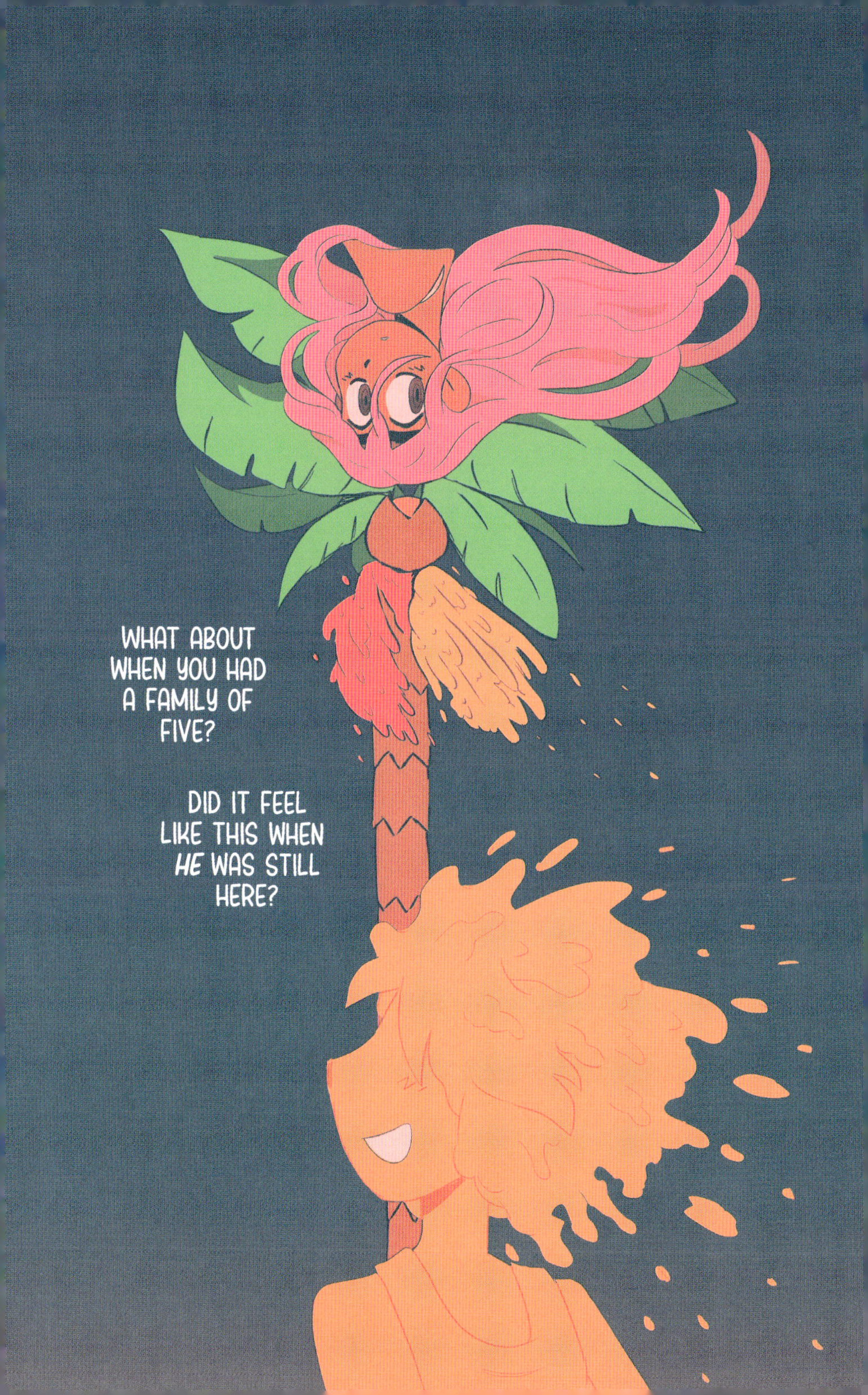
WHAT ABOUT WHEN YOU HAD A FAMILY OF FIVE?
DID IT FEEL LIKE THIS WHEN *HE* WAS STILL HERE?

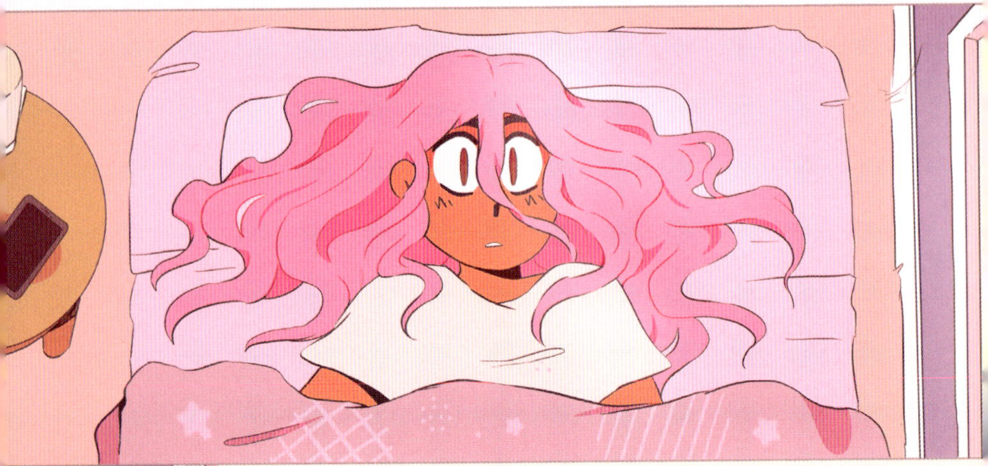

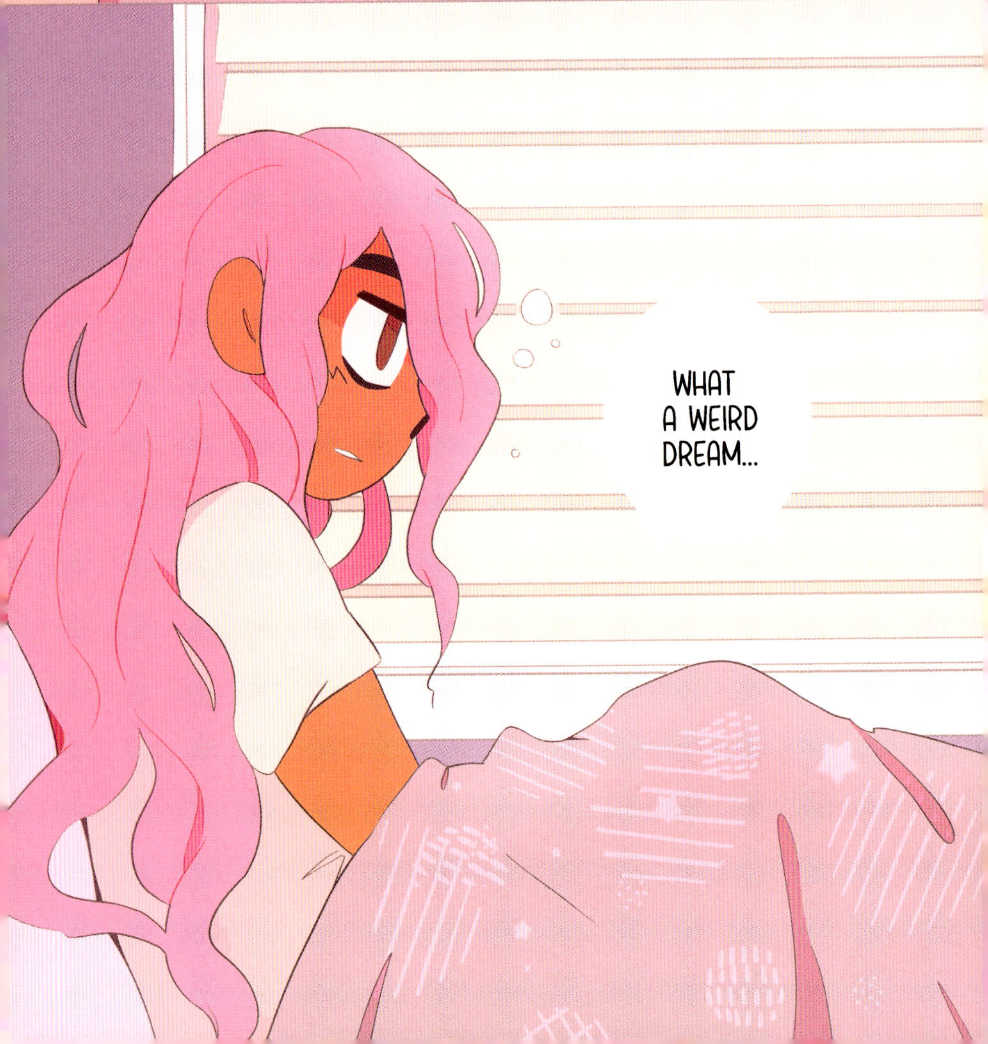
WHAT A WEIRD DREAM...

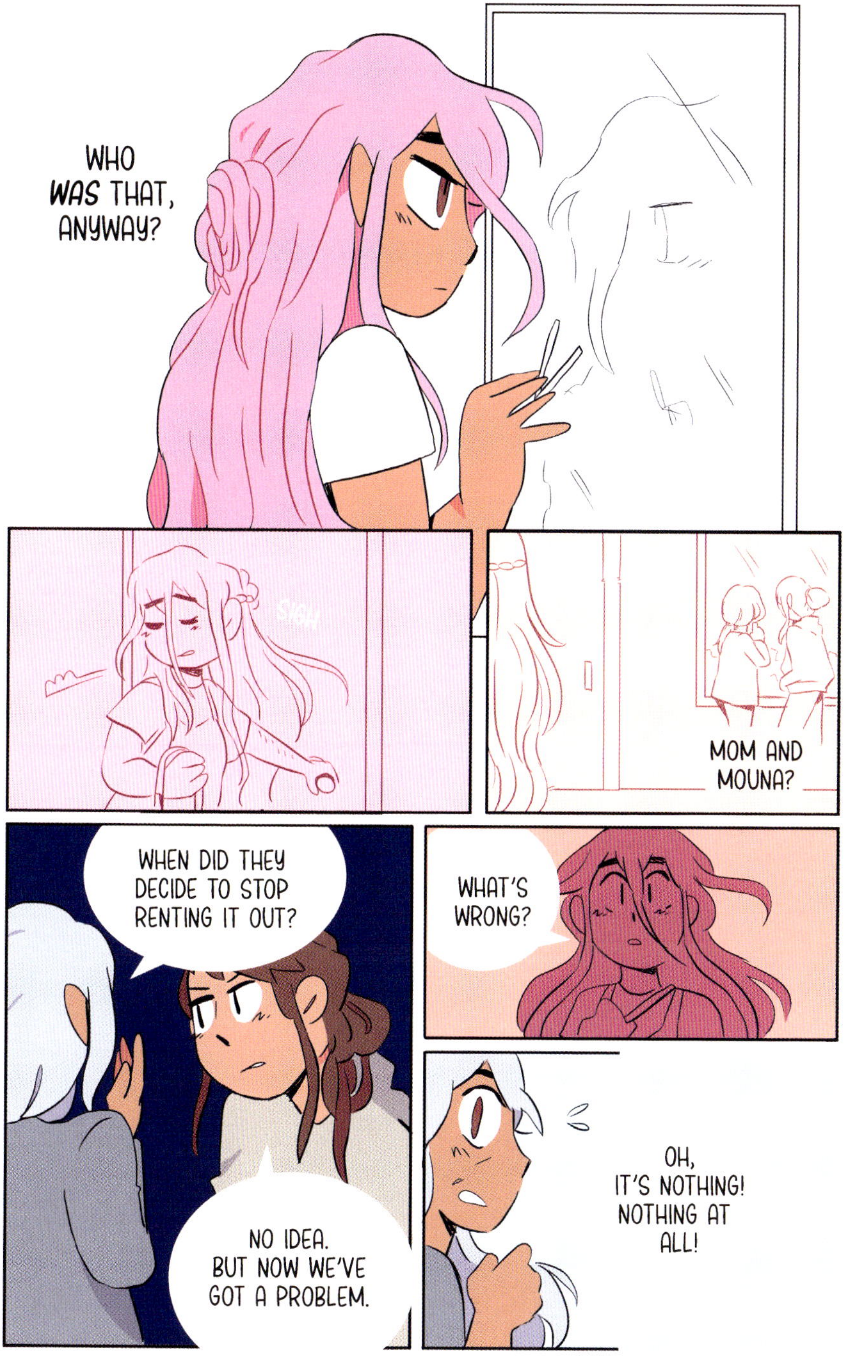
WHO WAS THAT, ANYWAY?
SHOW
MOM AND MOUNA?
WHEN DID THEY DECIDE TO STOP RENTING IT OUT?
NO IDEA. BUT NOW WE'VE GOT A PROBLEM.
WHAT'S WRONG?
OH, IT'S NOTHING! NOTHING AT ALL!

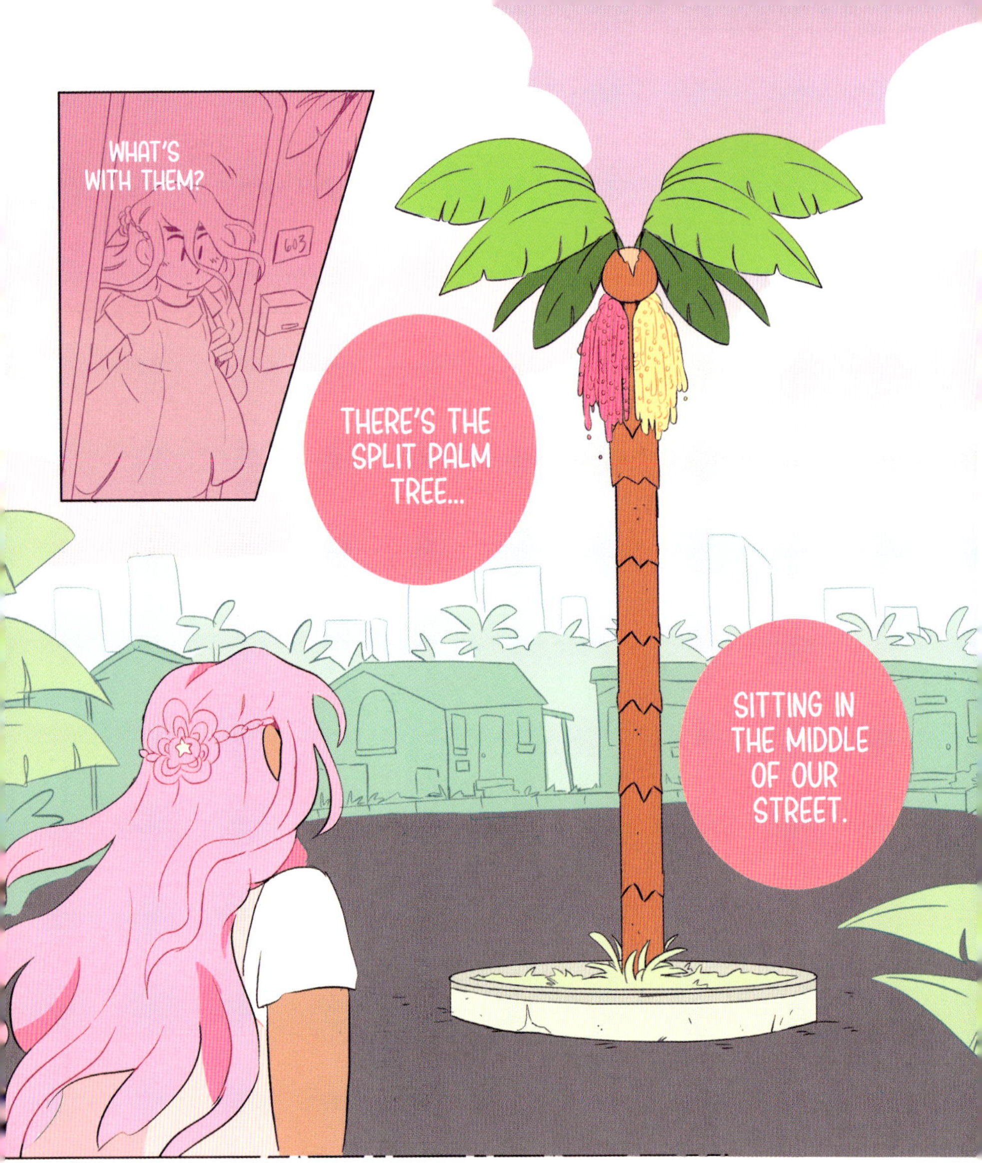
WHAT'S WITH THEM?
603
THERE'S THE SPLIT PALM TREE...
SITTING IN THE MIDDLE OF OUR STREET.

EVER SINCE I CAN REMEMBER,
IT'S BEEN STRANGELY SPLIT IN HALF LIKE THAT.
BUT I DON'T KNOW HOW IT GOT THAT WAY.

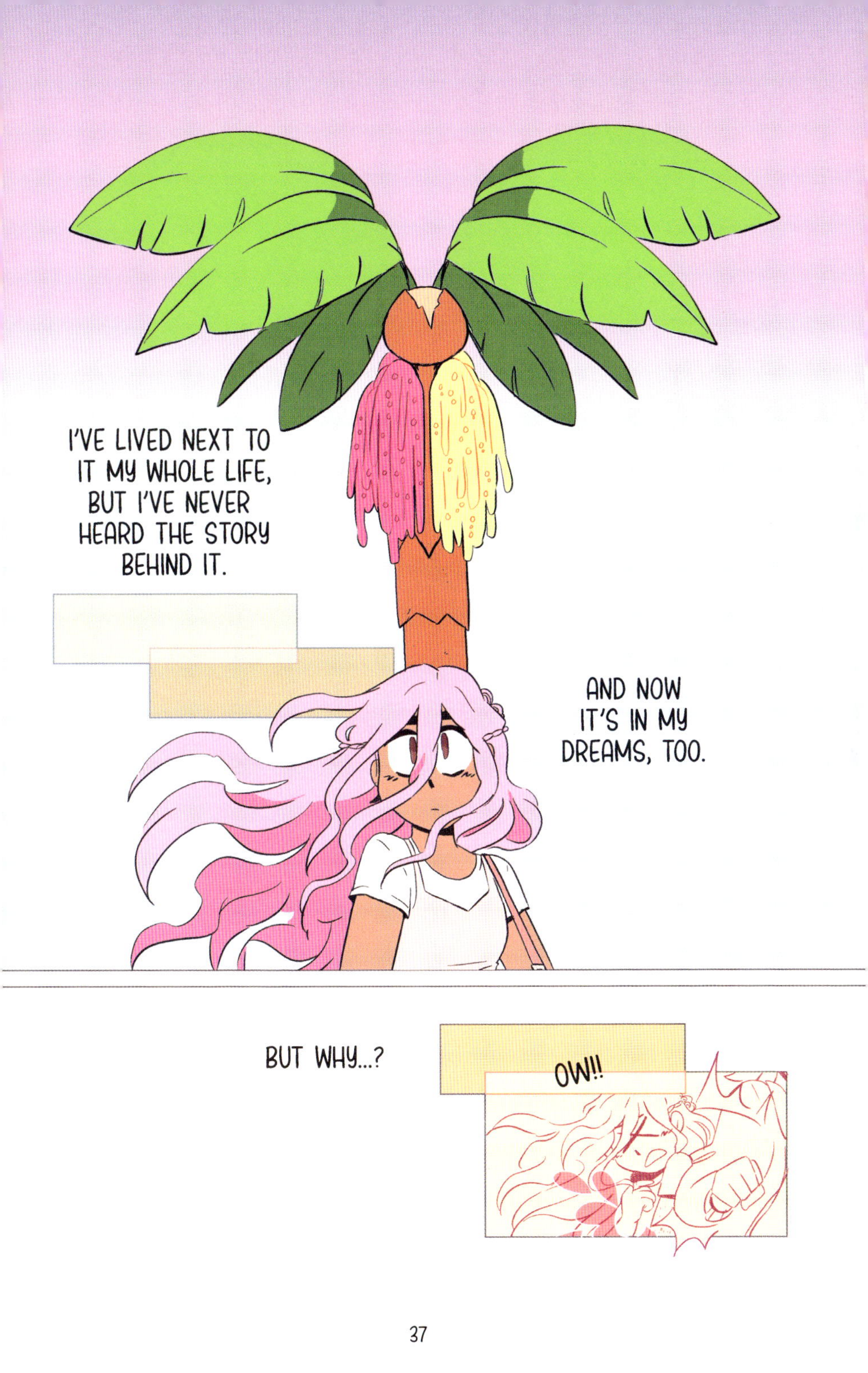

I'VE LIVED NEXT TO IT MY WHOLE LIFE, BUT I'VE NEVER HEARD THE STORY BEHIND IT.
AND NOW IT'S IN MY DREAMS, TOO.
BUT WHY...?
OW!!

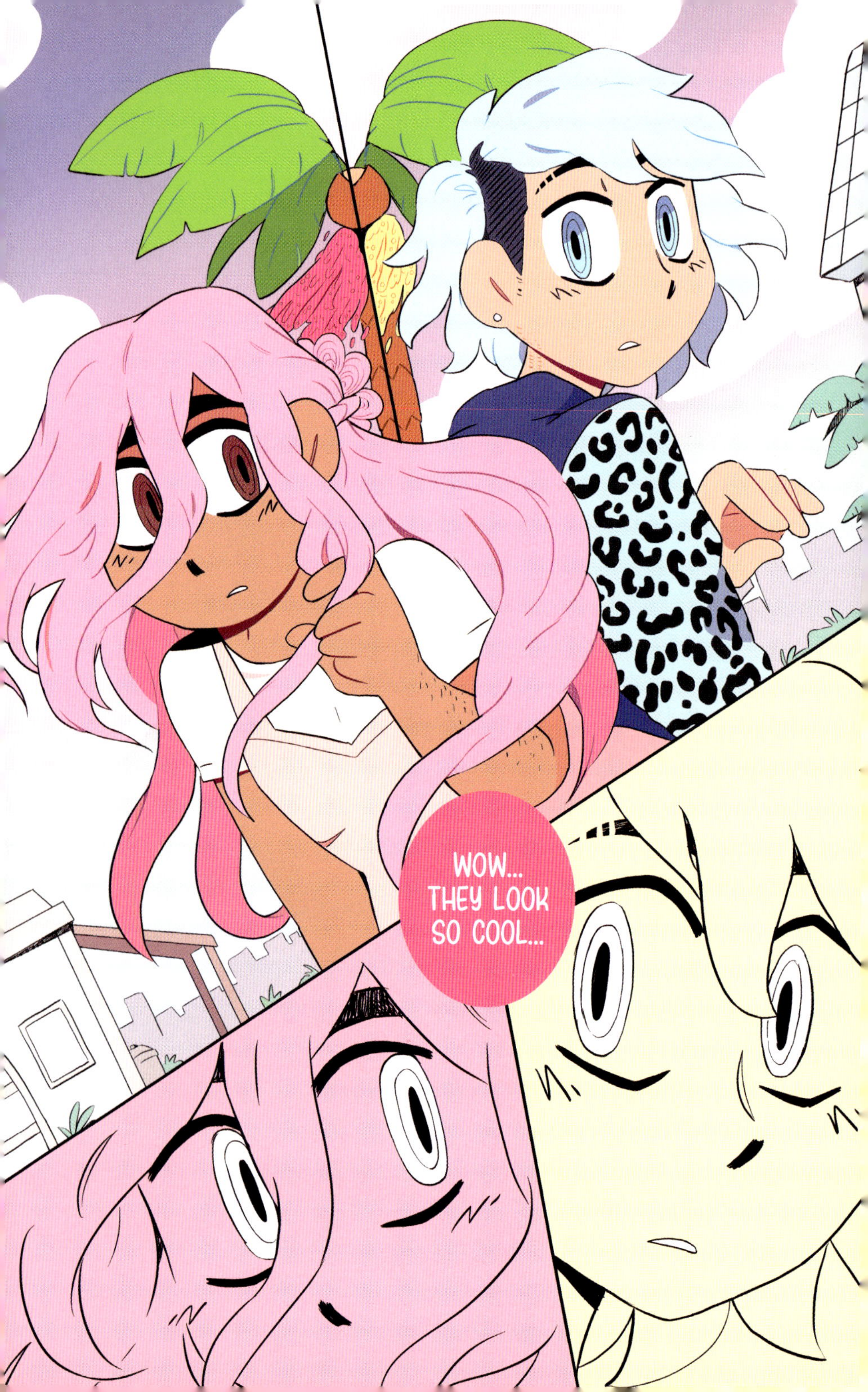
WOW... THEY LOOK SO COOL...

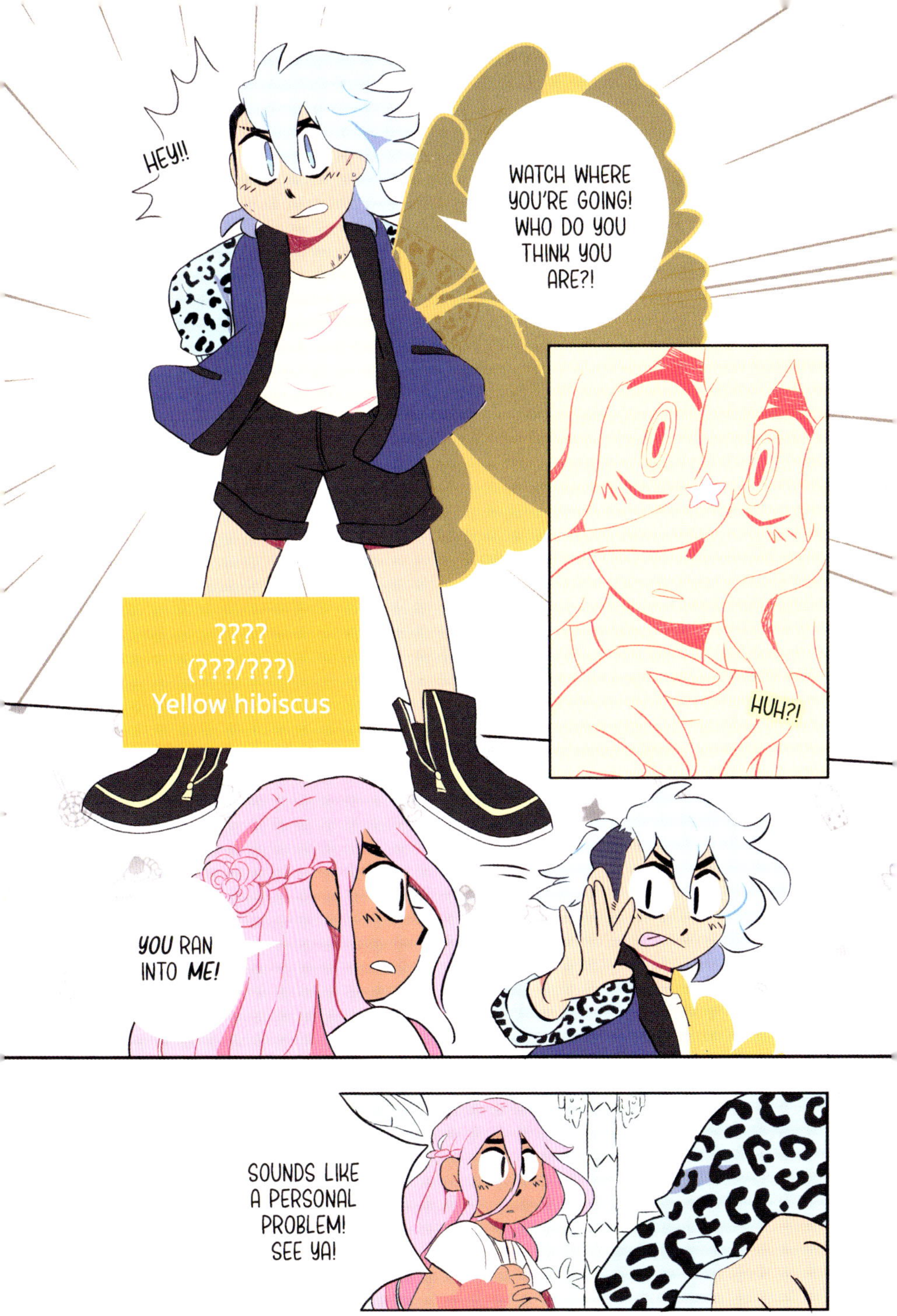
HEY!!
WATCH WHERE YOU'RE GOING! WHO DO YOU THINK YOU ARE?!
????
(???/???)
Yellow hibiscus
HUH?!
YOU RAN INTO ME!
SOUNDS LIKE A PERSONAL PROBLEM! SEE YA!

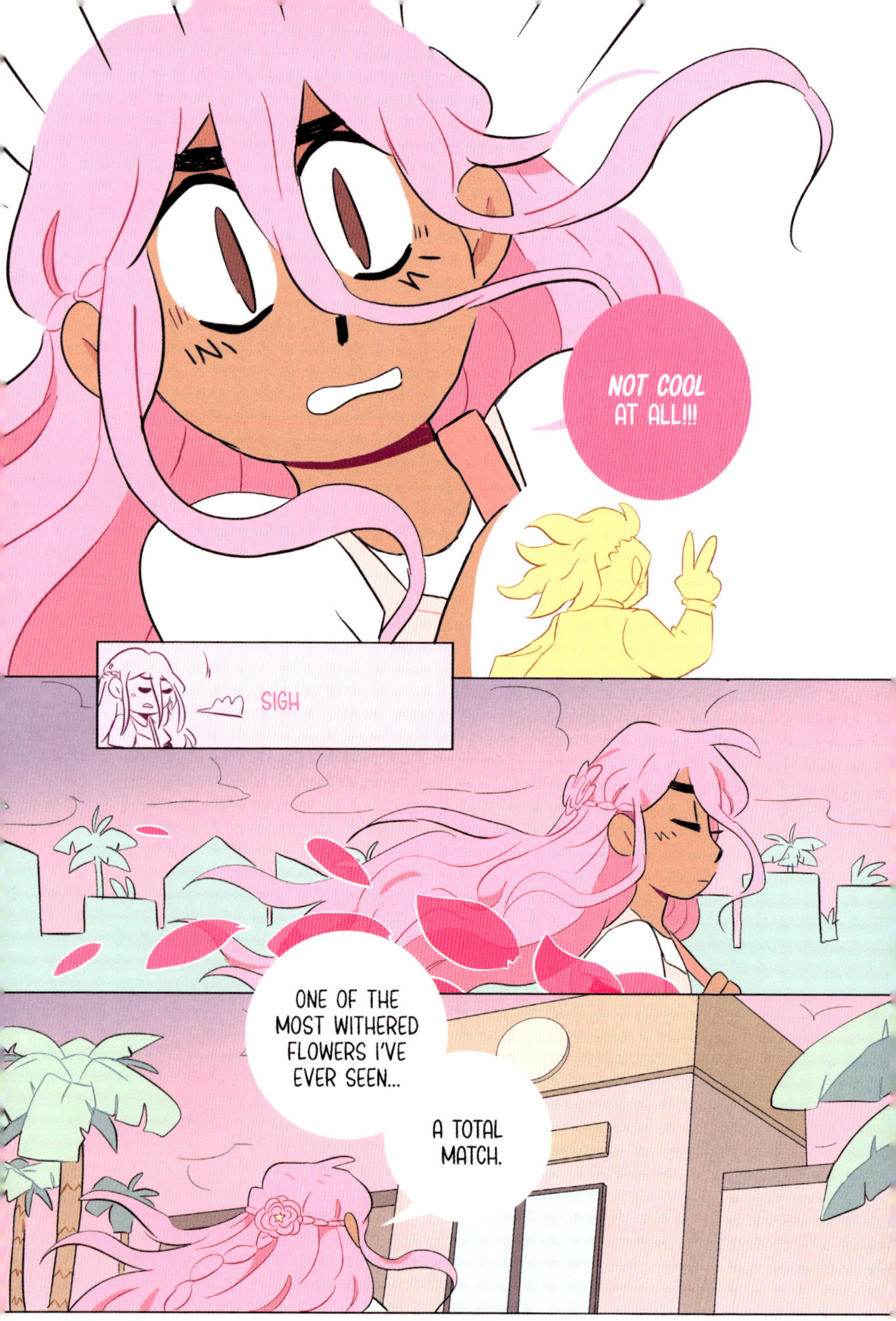
NOT COOL AT ALL!!!
SIGH
ONE OF THE MOST WITHERED FLOWERS I'VE EVER SEEN...
A TOTAL MATCH.

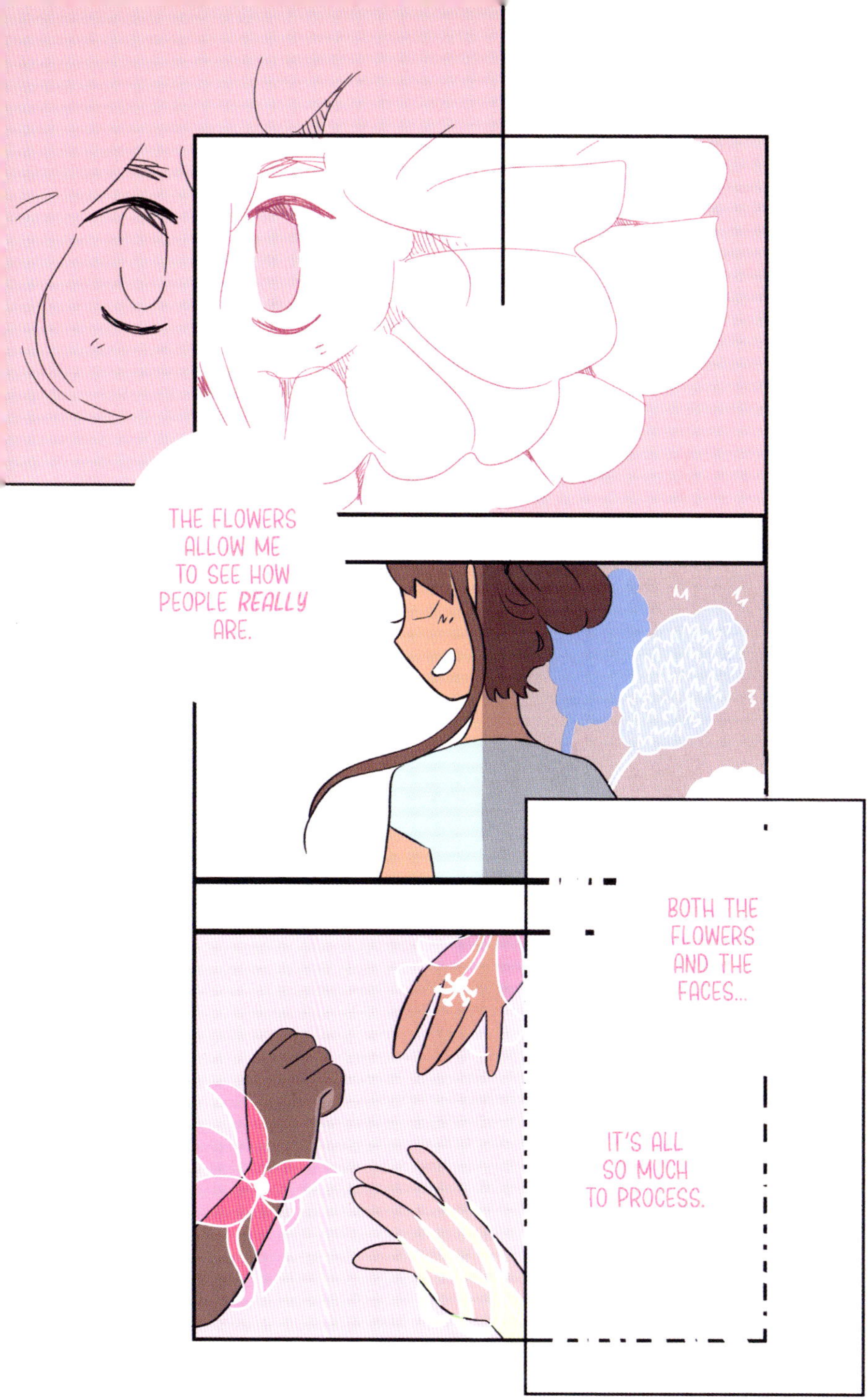
THE FLOWERS ALLOW ME TO SEE HOW PEOPLE *REALLY* ARE.
BOTH THE FLOWERS AND THE FACES...
IT'S ALL SO MUCH TO PROCESS.

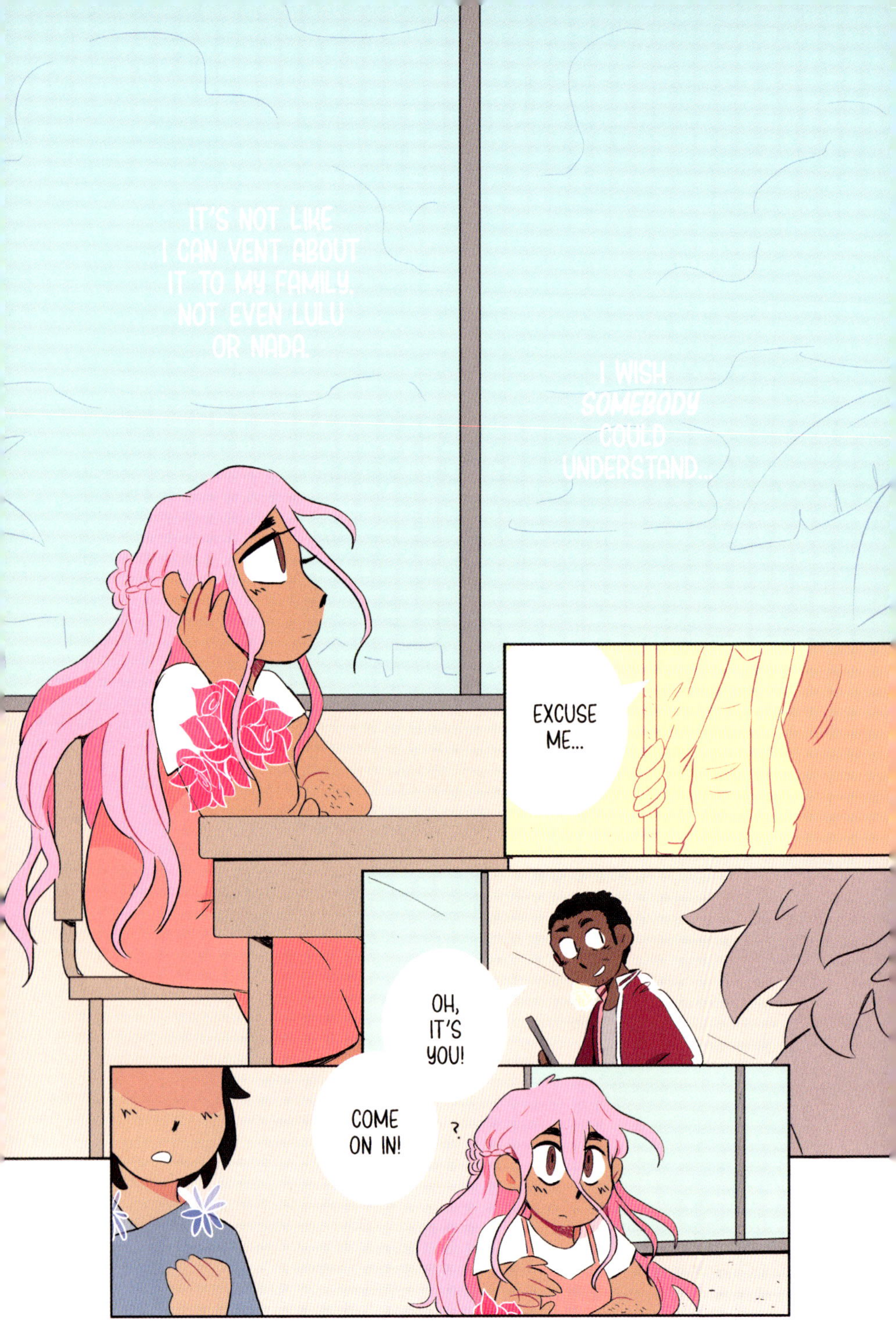

IT'S NOT LIKE I CAN VENT ABOUT IT TO MY FAMILY, NOT EVEN LULU OR NADA.
I WISH *SOMEBODY* COULD UNDERSTAND...
EXCUSE ME...
OH, IT'S YOU!
COME ON IN!
?

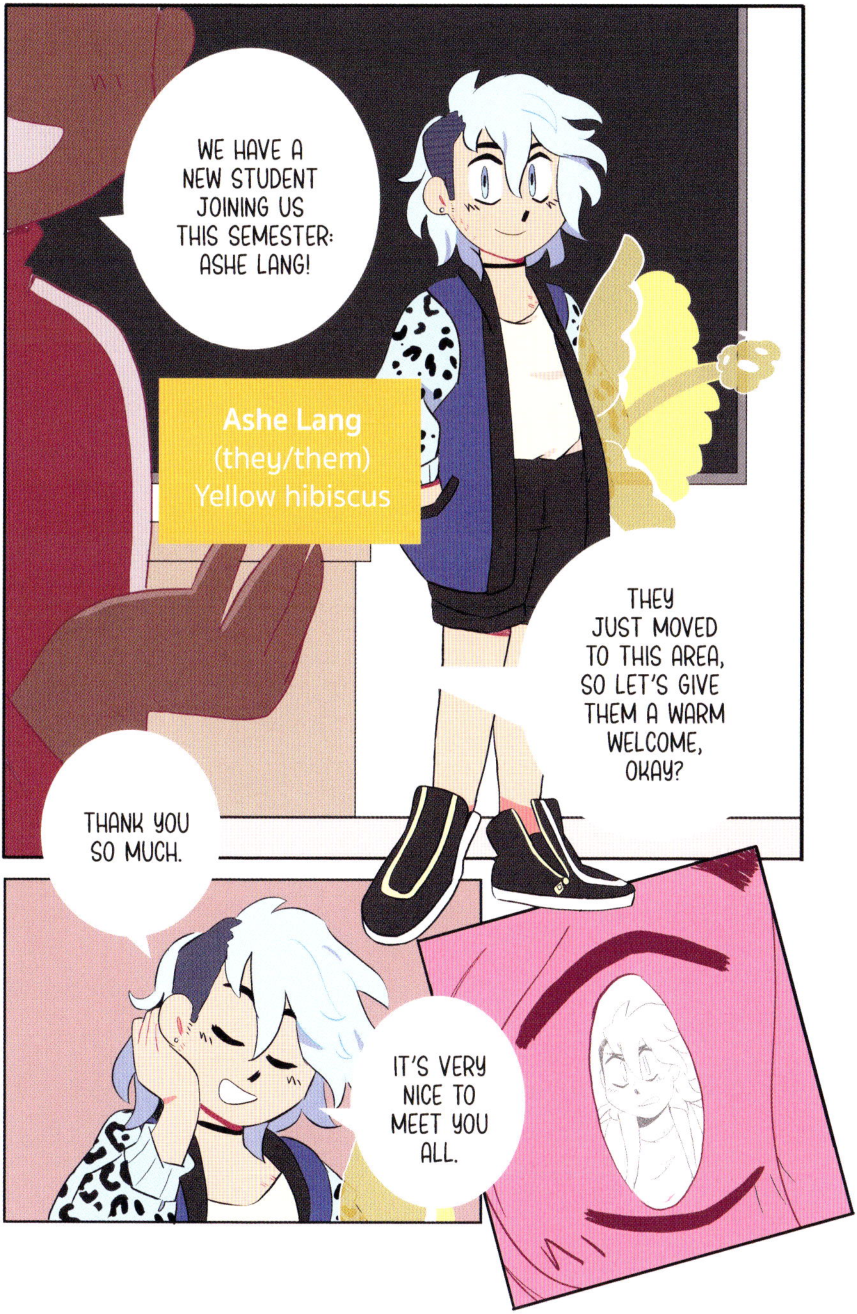
WE HAVE A NEW STUDENT JOINING US THIS SEMESTER: ASHE LANG!
Ashe Lang
(they/them)
Yellow hibiscus
THEY JUST MOVED TO THIS AREA, SO LET'S GIVE THEM A WARM WELCOME, OKAY?
THANK YOU SO MUCH.
IT'S VERY NICE TO MEET YOU ALL.

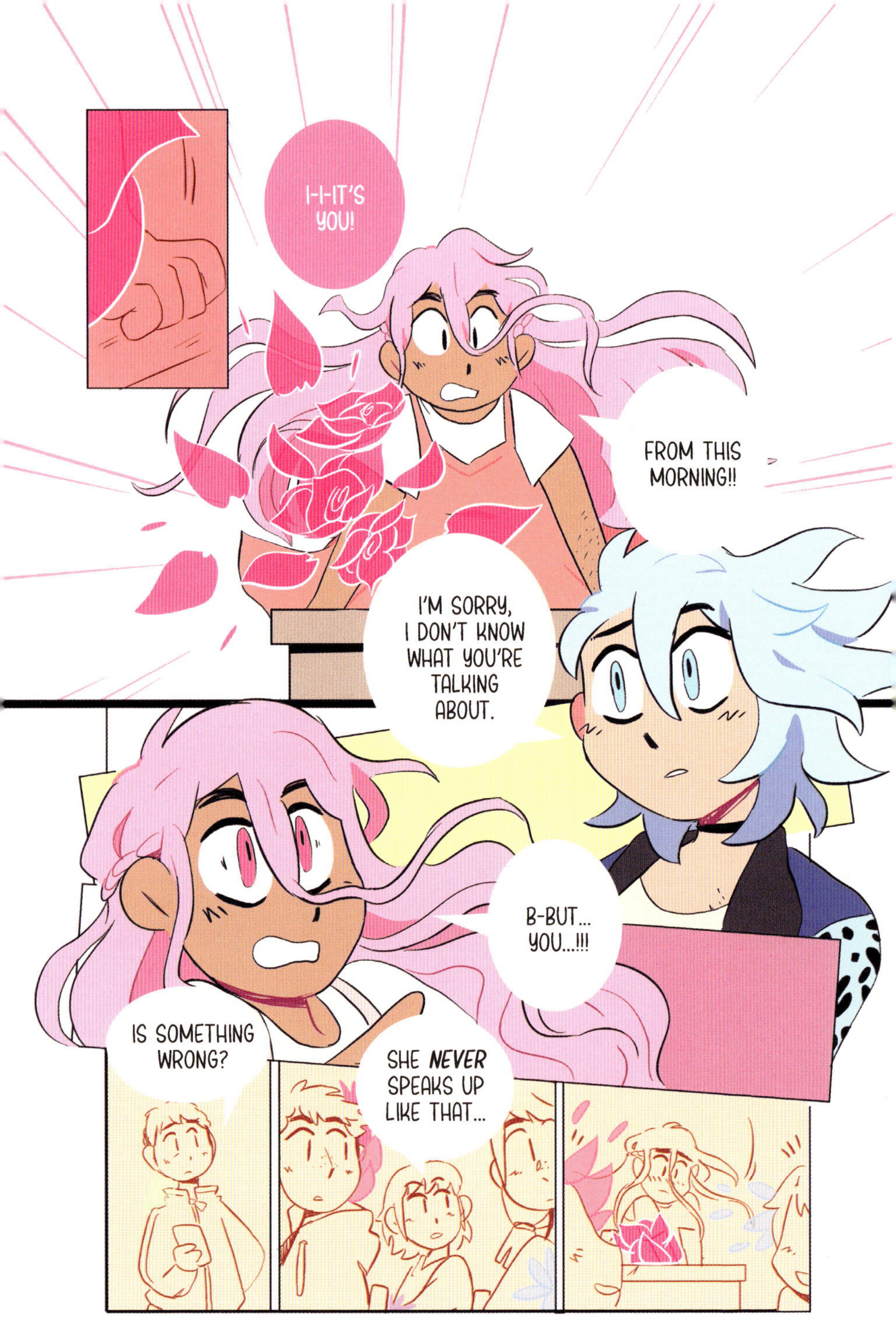
I-I-IT'S YOU!
FROM THIS MORNING!!
I'M SORRY, I DON'T KNOW WHAT YOU'RE TALKING ABOUT.
B-BUT... YOU...!!!
IS SOMETHING WRONG?
SHE *NEVER* SPEAKS UP LIKE THAT...

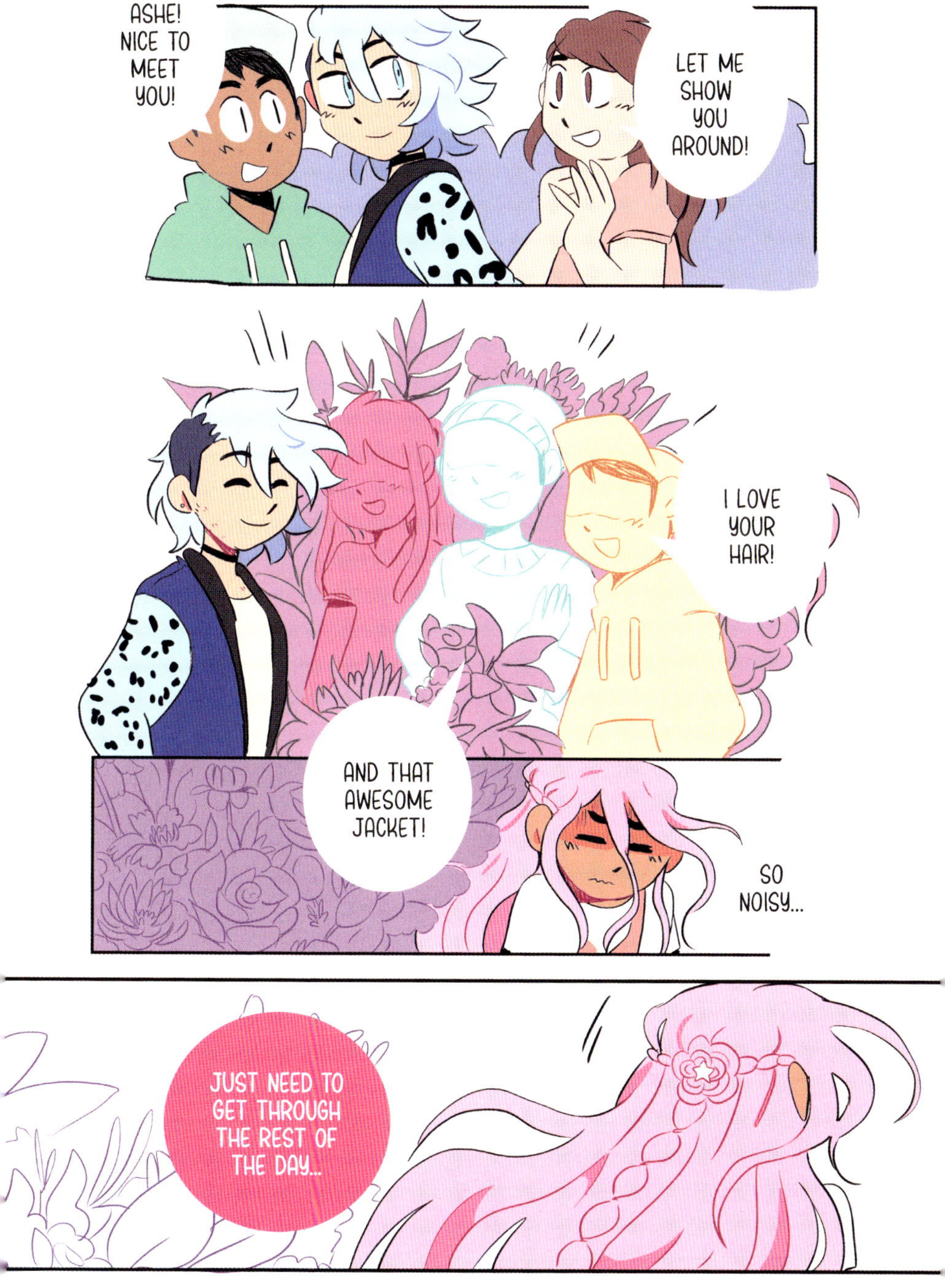
ASHE! NICE TO MEET YOU!
LET ME SHOW YOU AROUND!
I LOVE YOUR HAIR!
AND THAT AWESOME JACKET!
SO NOISY...
JUST NEED TO GET THROUGH THE REST OF THE DAY...

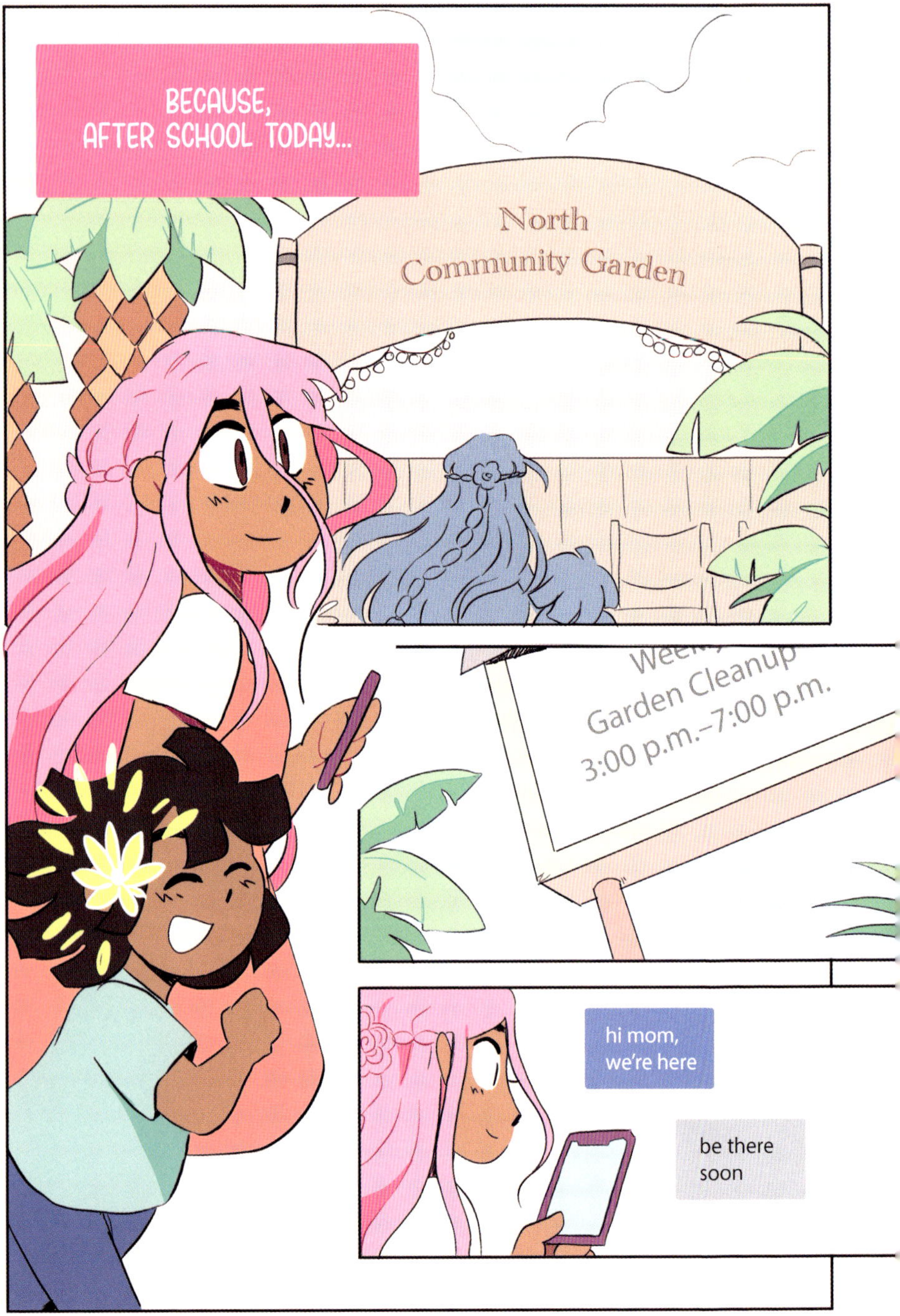
BECAUSE,
AFTER SCHOOL TODAY...
North
Community Garden
Garden Cleanup
3:00 p.m.–7:00 p.m.
hi mom,
we're here
be there
soon

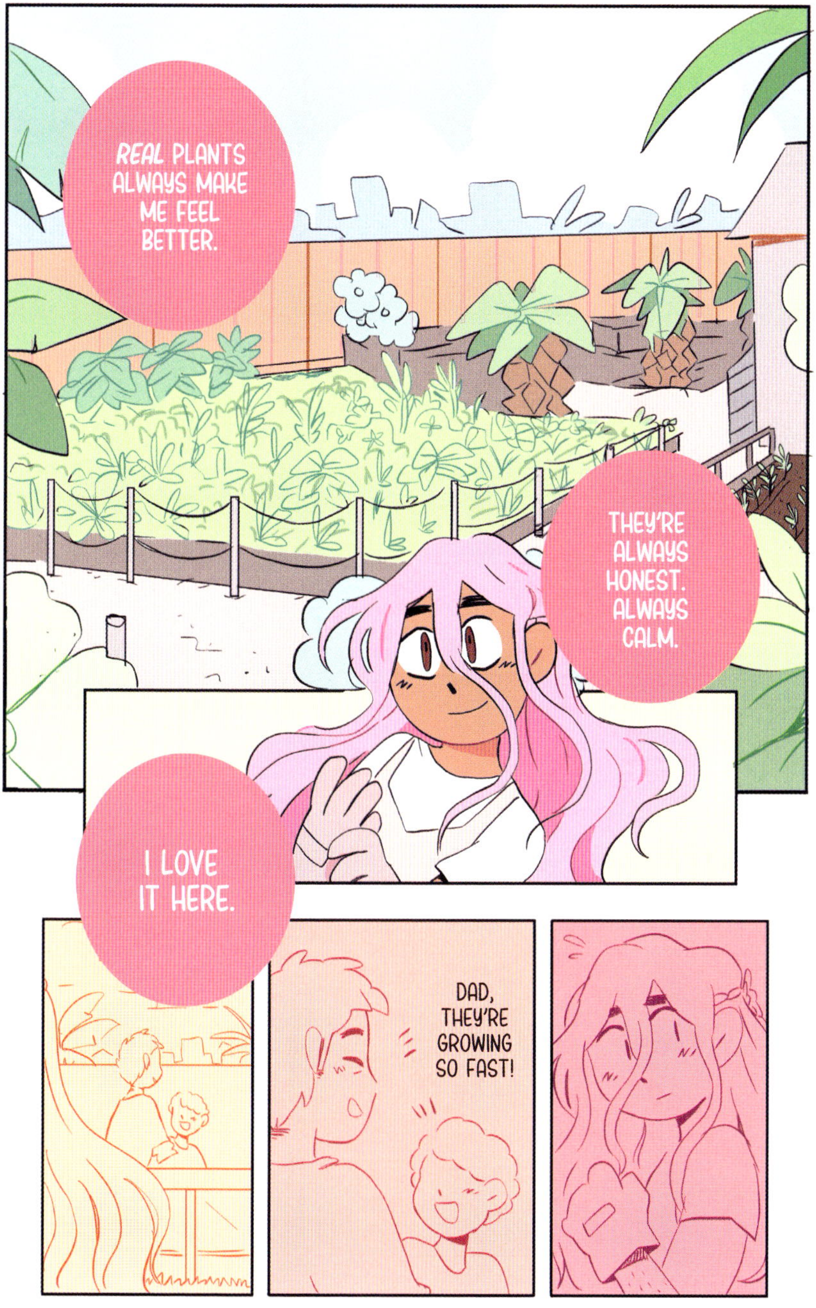
REAL PLANTS ALWAYS MAKE ME FEEL BETTER.
THEY'RE ALWAYS HONEST. ALWAYS CALM.
I LOVE IT HERE.
DAD, THEY'RE GROWING SO FAST!

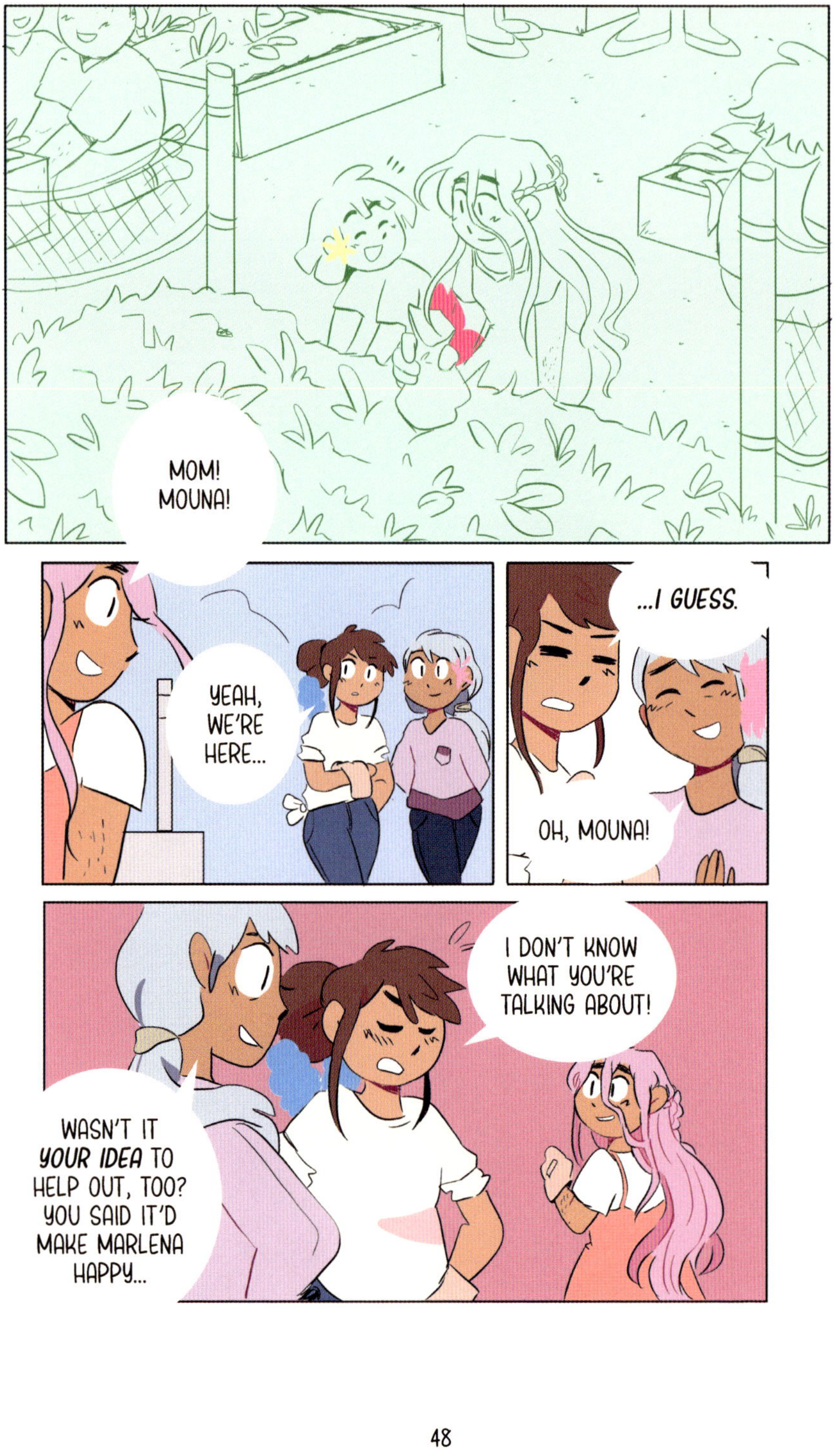
MOM!
MOUNA!
YEAH, WE'RE HERE...
...I GUESS.
OH, MOUNA!
I DON'T KNOW WHAT YOU'RE TALKING ABOUT!
WASN'T IT *YOUR IDEA* TO HELP OUT, TOO? YOU SAID IT'D MAKE MARLENA HAPPY...

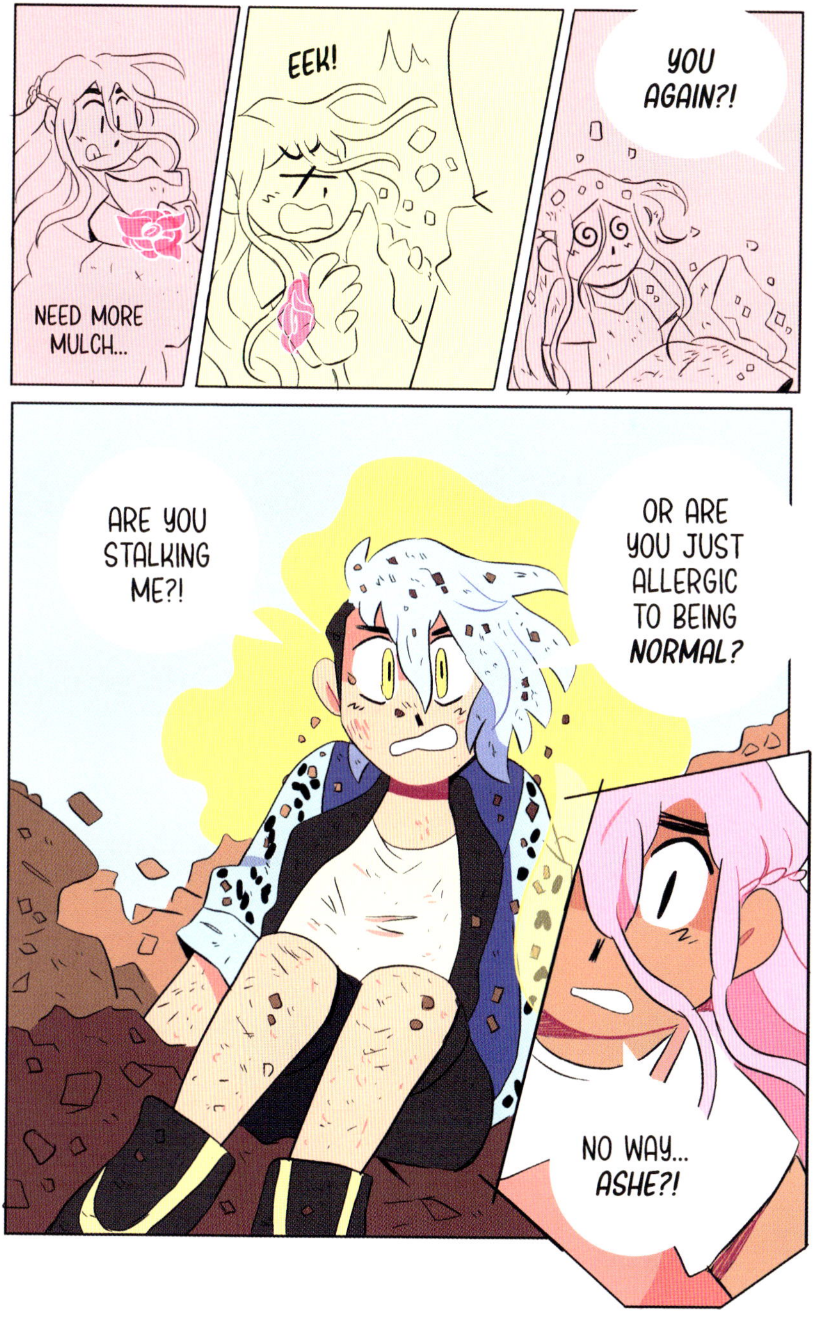
NEED MORE MULCH...
EEK!
YOU AGAIN?!
ARE YOU STALKING ME?!
OR ARE YOU JUST ALLERGIC TO BEING NORMAL?
NO WAY... ASHE?!

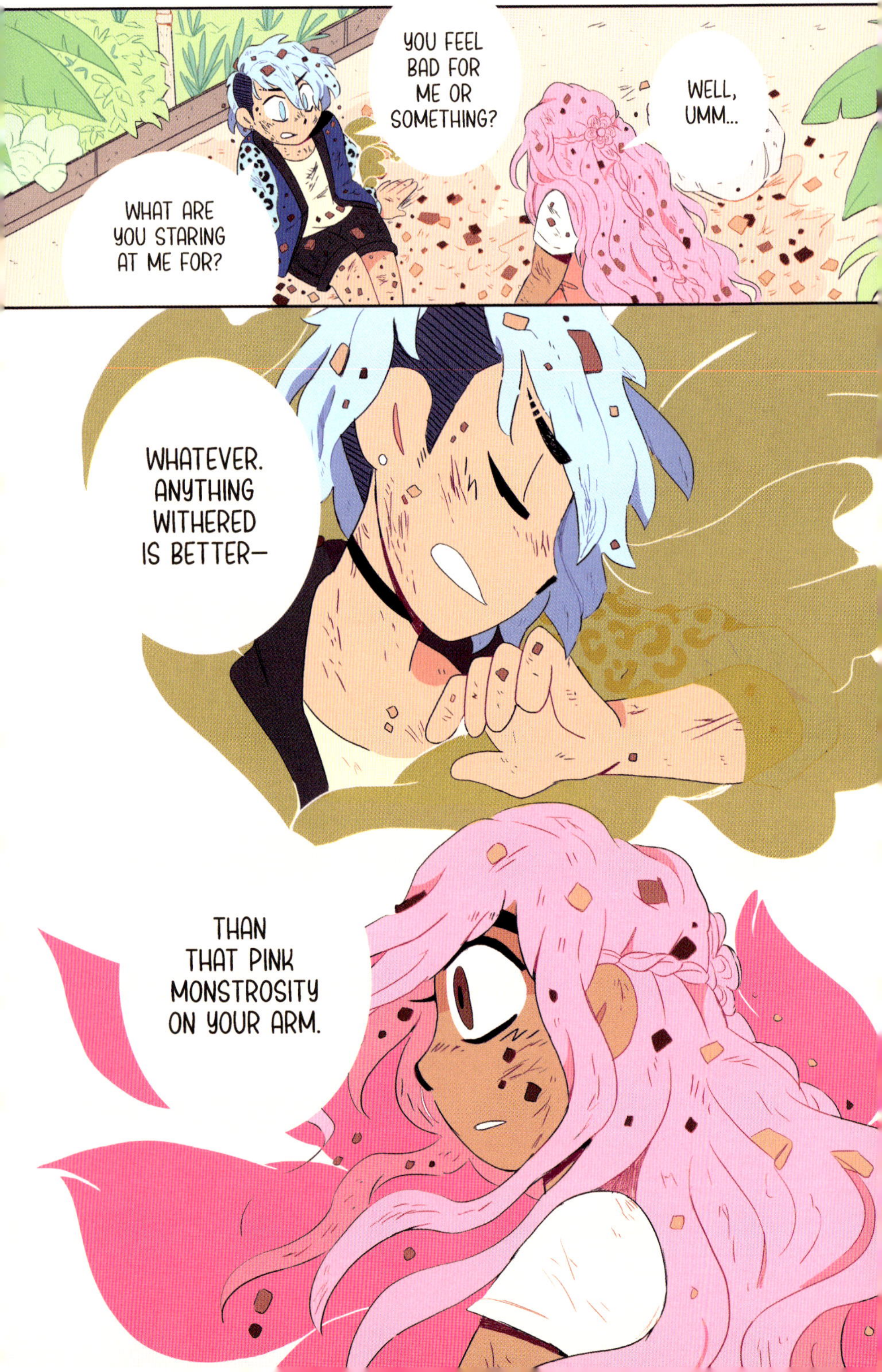
WHAT ARE YOU STARING AT ME FOR?
YOU FEEL BAD FOR ME OR SOMETHING?
WELL, UMM...
WHATEVER. ANYTHING WITHERED IS BETTER—
THAN THAT PINK MONSTROSITY ON YOUR ARM.

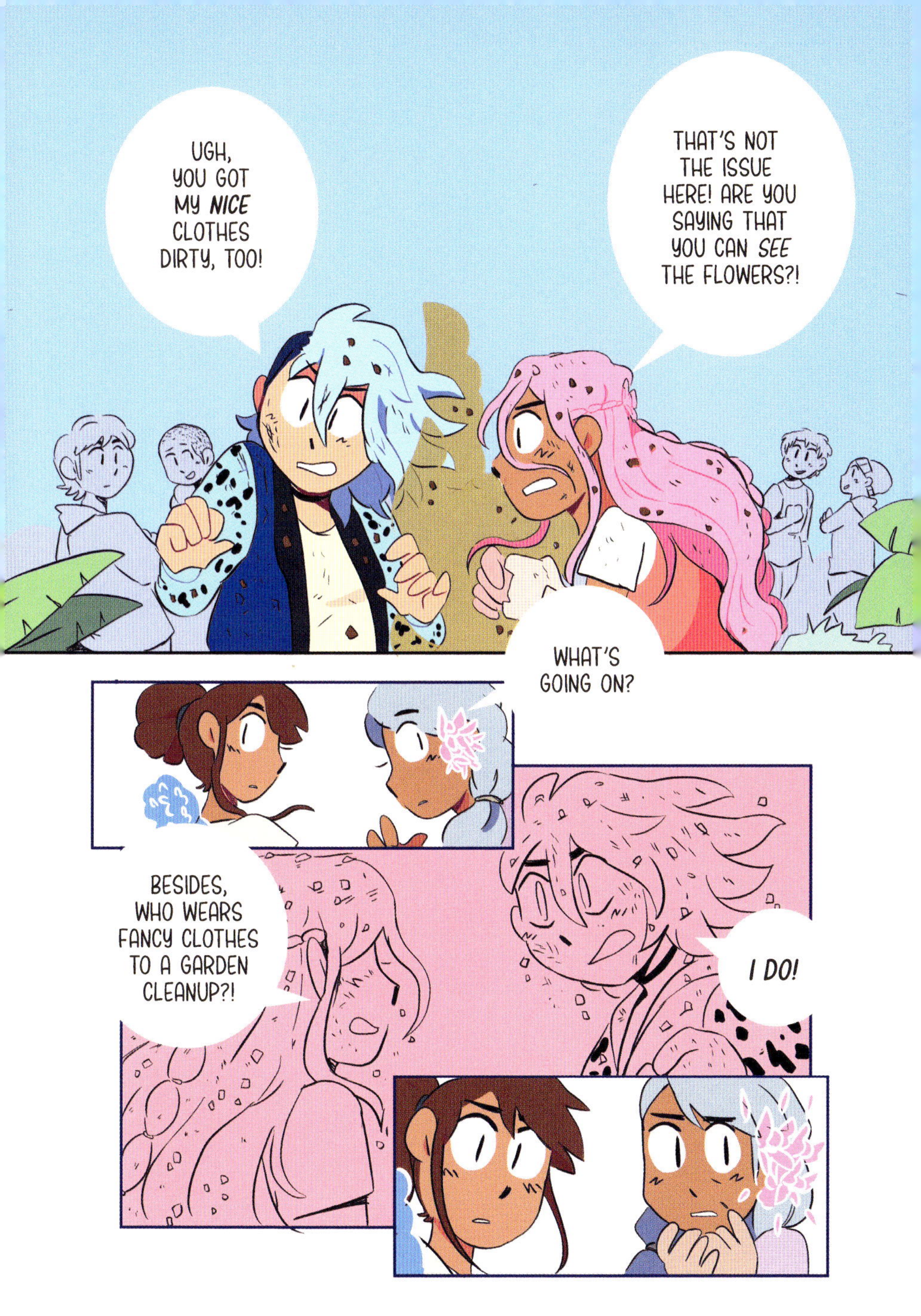
UGH, YOU GOT MY *NICE* CLOTHES DIRTY, TOO!
THAT'S NOT THE ISSUE HERE! ARE YOU SAYING THAT YOU CAN *SEE* THE FLOWERS?!
WHAT'S GOING ON?
BESIDES, WHO WEARS FANCY CLOTHES TO A GARDEN CLEANUP?!
I DO!

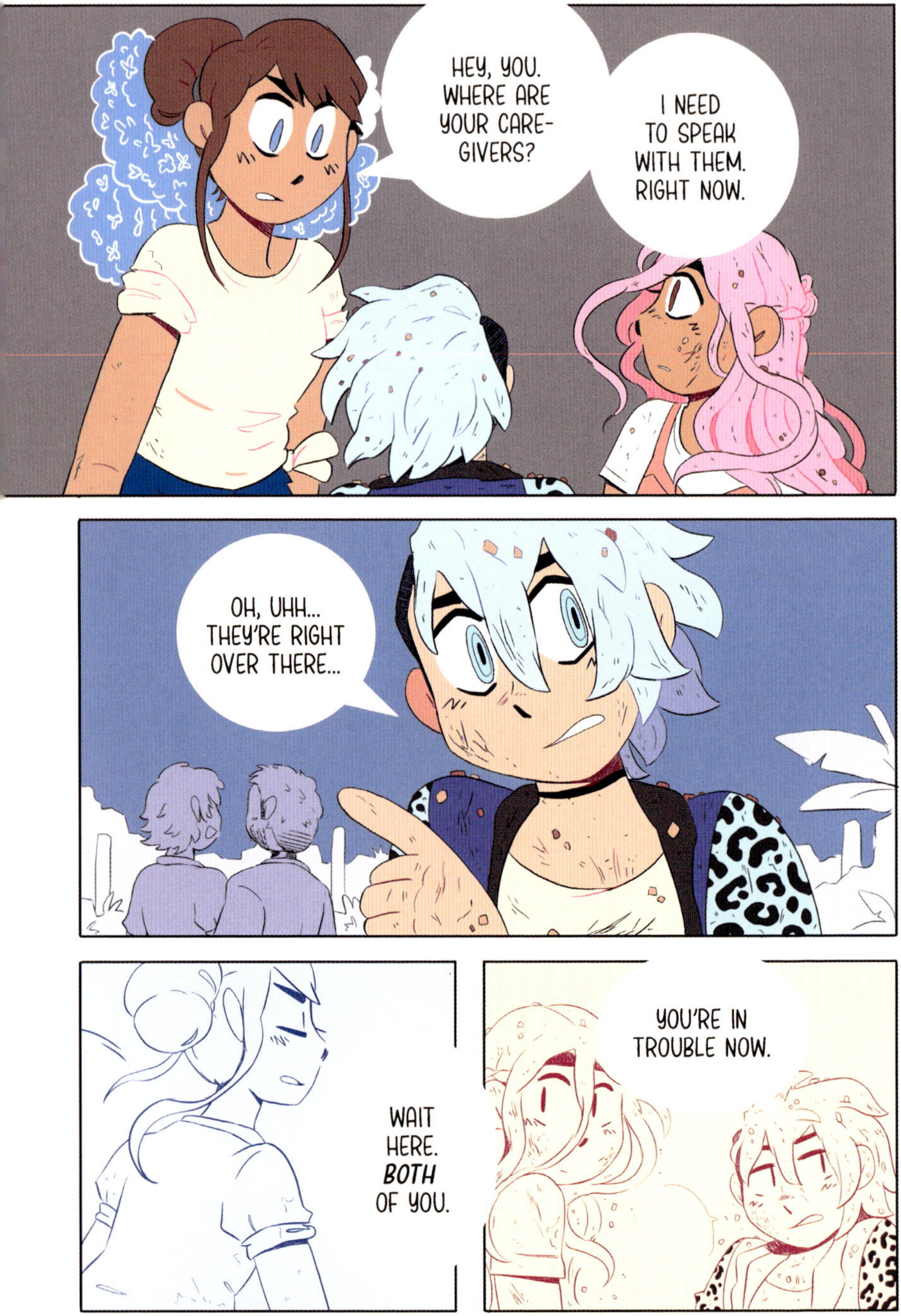
HEY, YOU. WHERE ARE YOUR CARE-GIVERS?
I NEED TO SPEAK WITH THEM. RIGHT NOW.
OH, UHH... THEY'RE RIGHT OVER THERE...
WAIT HERE. ***BOTH*** OF YOU.
YOU'RE IN TROUBLE NOW.

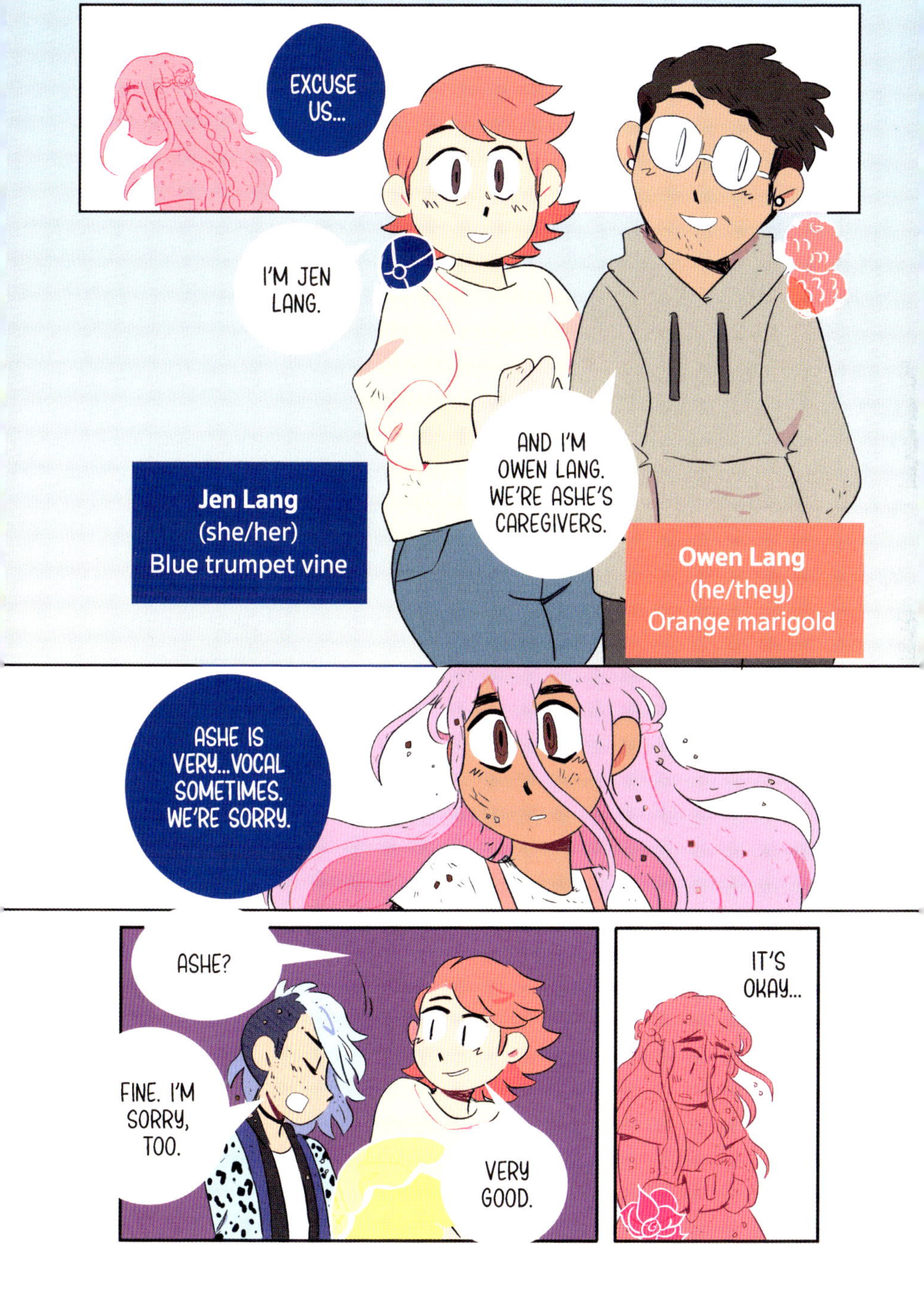

EXCUSE US...
I'M JEN LANG.
AND I'M OWEN LANG. WE'RE ASHE'S CAREGIVERS.
Jen Lang
(she/her)
Blue trumpet vine
Owen Lang
(he/they)
Orange marigold
ASHE IS VERY...VOCAL SOMETIMES. WE'RE SORRY.
ASHE?
FINE. I'M SORRY, TOO.
VERY GOOD.
IT'S OKAY...

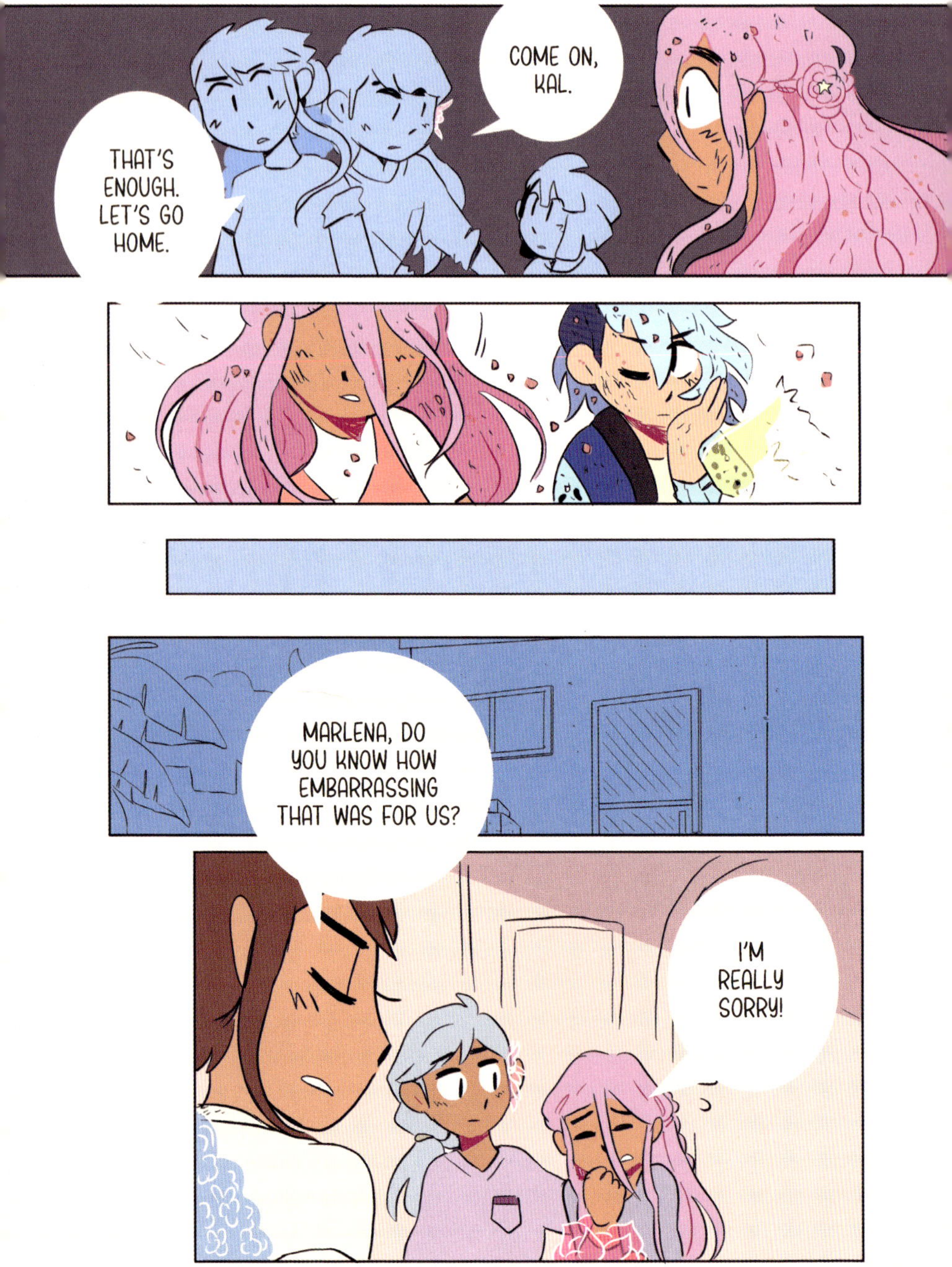
COME ON, KAL.
THAT'S ENOUGH. LET'S GO HOME.
MARLENA, DO YOU KNOW HOW EMBARRASSING THAT WAS FOR US?
I'M REALLY SORRY!

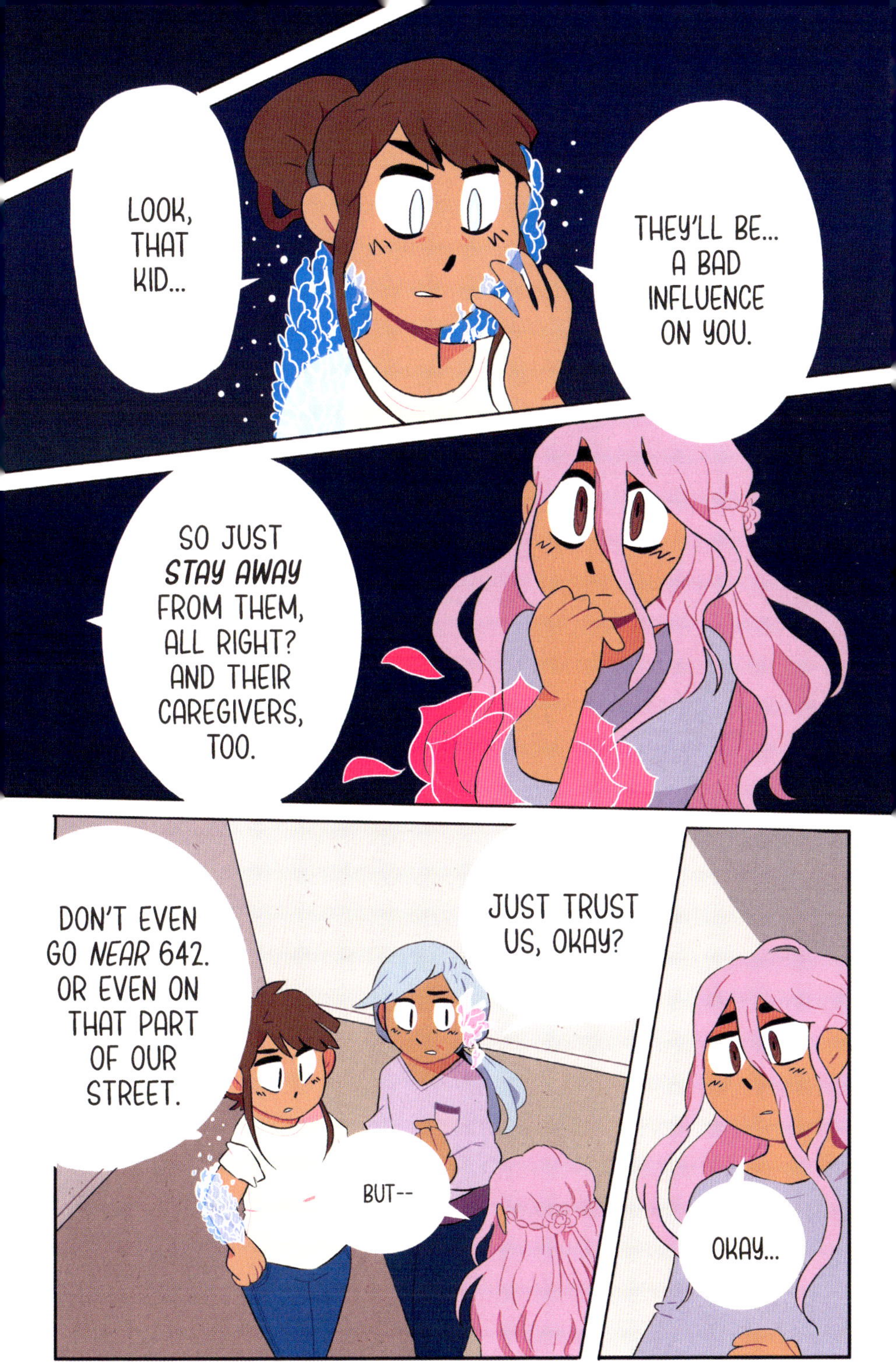
LOOK, THAT KID...
THEY'LL BE... A BAD INFLUENCE ON YOU.
SO JUST *STAY AWAY* FROM THEM, ALL RIGHT? AND THEIR CAREGIVERS, TOO.
DON'T EVEN GO *NEAR* 642. OR EVEN ON THAT PART OF OUR STREET.
JUST TRUST US, OKAY?
BUT--
OKAY...

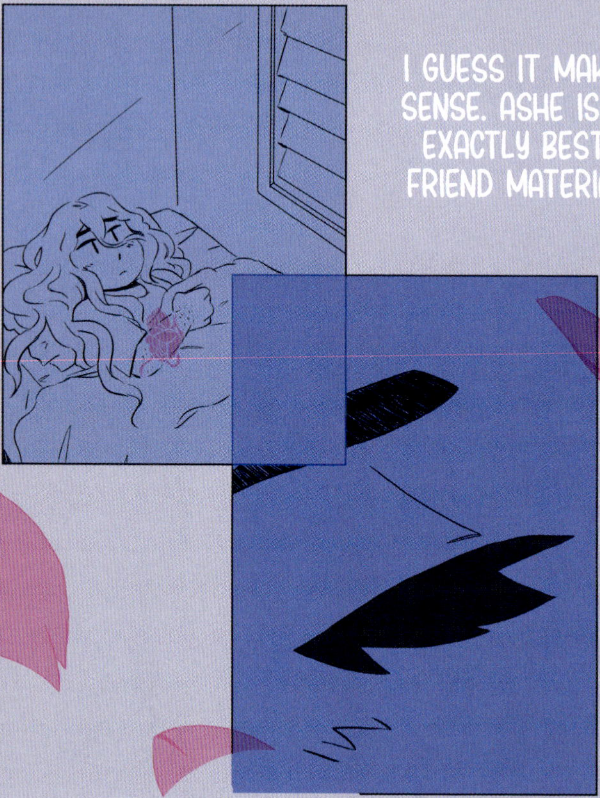

I GUESS IT MAKES SENSE. ASHE ISN'T EXACTLY BEST-FRIEND MATERIAL.

BUT JEN AND OWEN SEEMED NICE ENOUGH.

MOM AND MOUNA ACTED KINDA STRANGE... WHAT ARE THEY NOT TELLING ME?

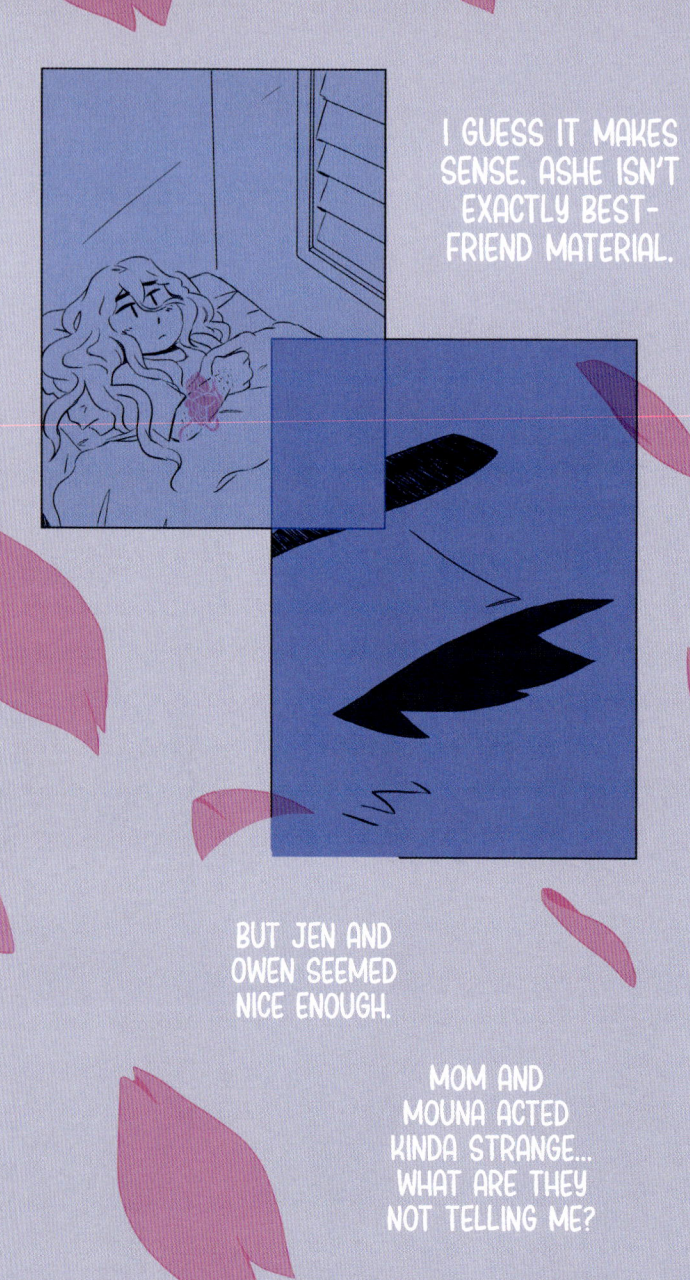

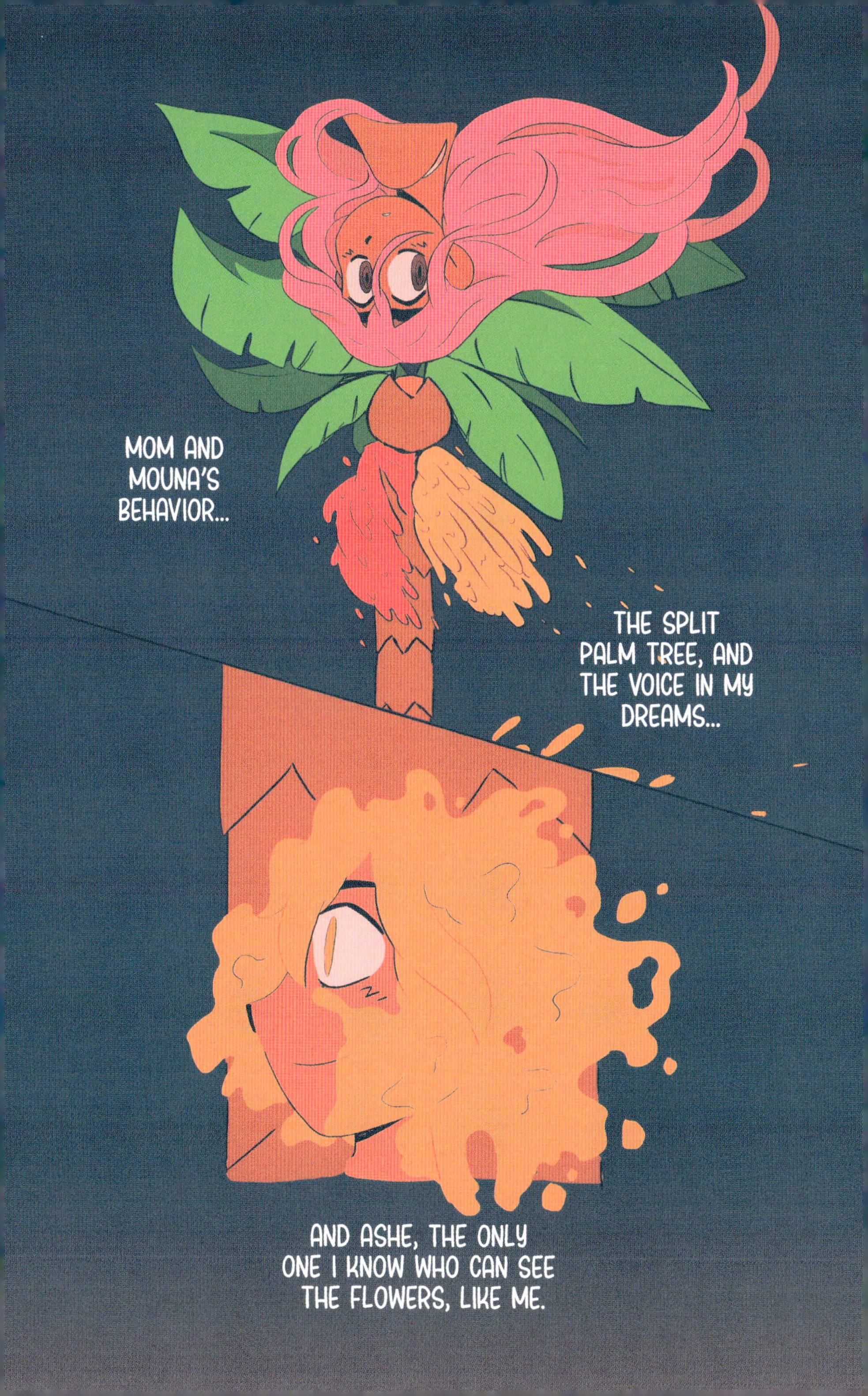
MOM AND MOUNA'S BEHAVIOR...
THE SPLIT PALM TREE, AND THE VOICE IN MY DREAMS...
AND ASHE, THE ONLY ONE I KNOW WHO CAN SEE THE FLOWERS, LIKE ME.

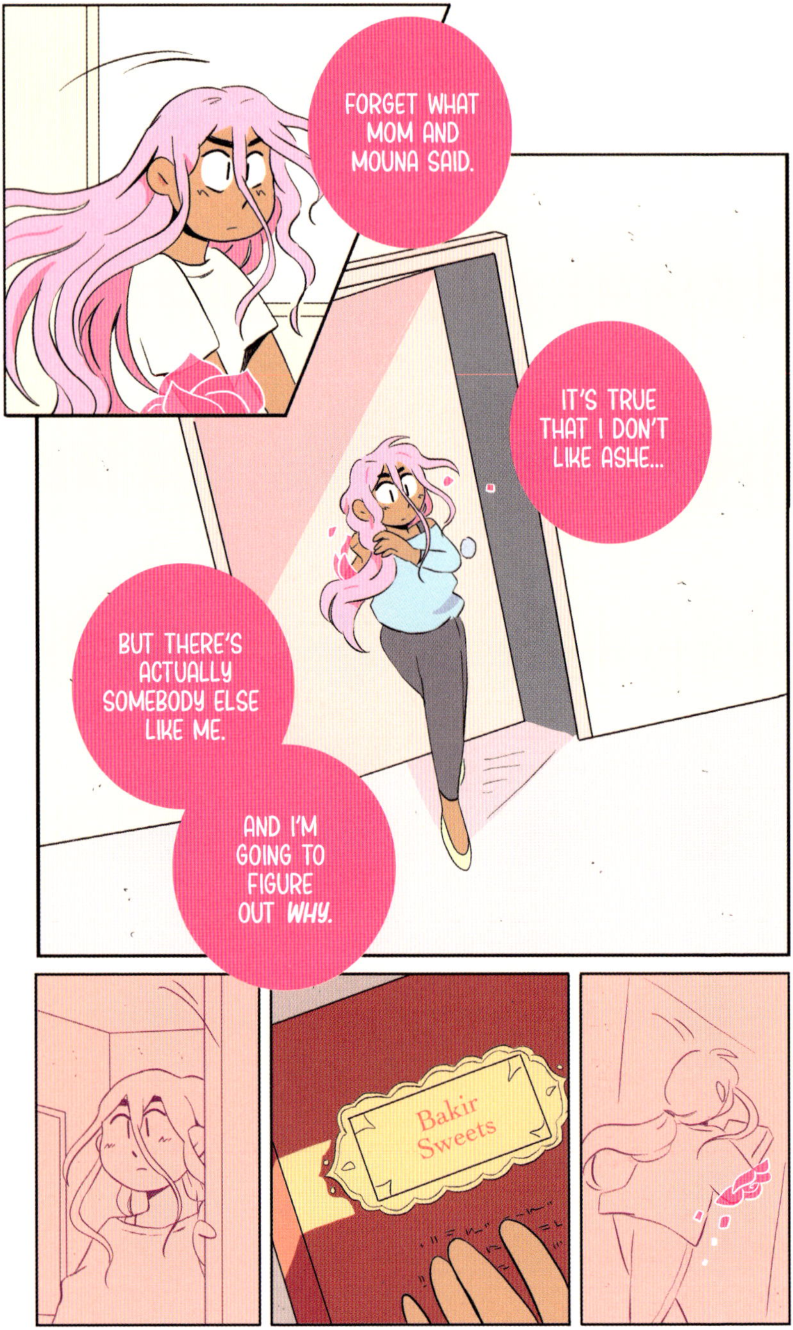
FORGET WHAT MOM AND MOUNA SAID.
IT'S TRUE THAT I DON'T LIKE ASHE...
BUT THERE'S ACTUALLY SOMEBODY ELSE LIKE ME.
AND I'M GOING TO FIGURE OUT *WHY*.
Bakir Sweets

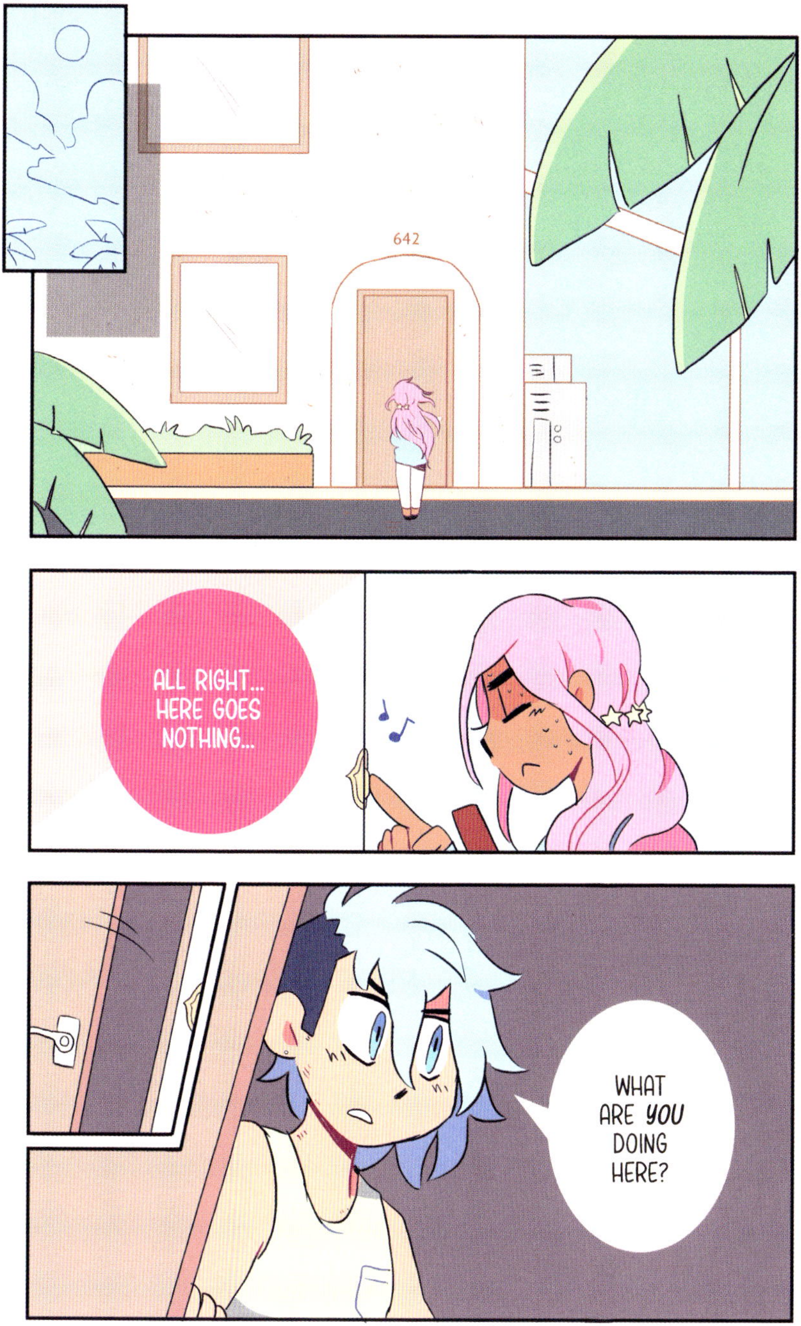
642
ALL RIGHT... HERE GOES NOTHING...
WHAT ARE *YOU* DOING HERE?

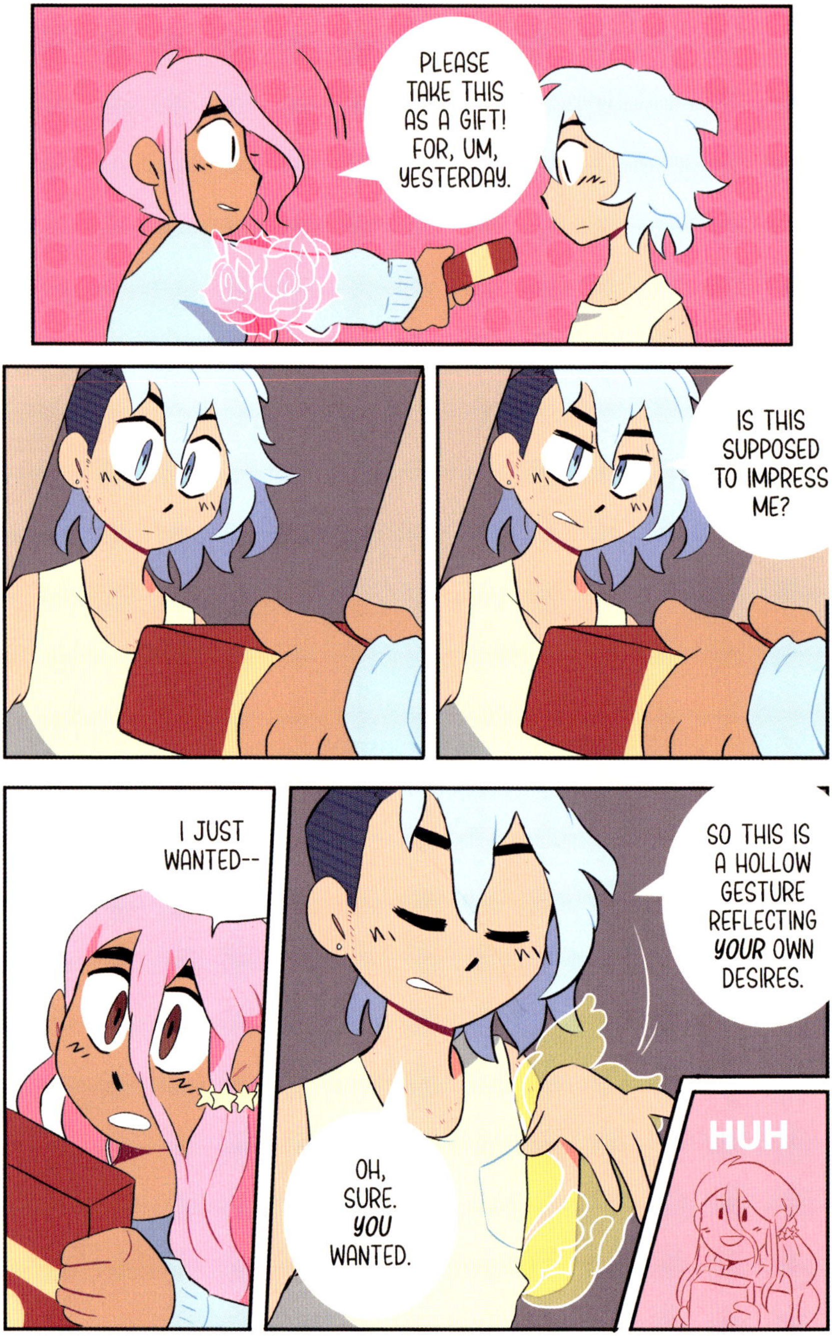

PLEASE TAKE THIS AS A GIFT! FOR, UM, YESTERDAY.
IS THIS SUPPOSED TO IMPRESS ME?
I JUST WANTED--
SO THIS IS A HOLLOW GESTURE REFLECTING *YOUR* OWN DESIRES.
OH, SURE. *YOU* WANTED.
HUH

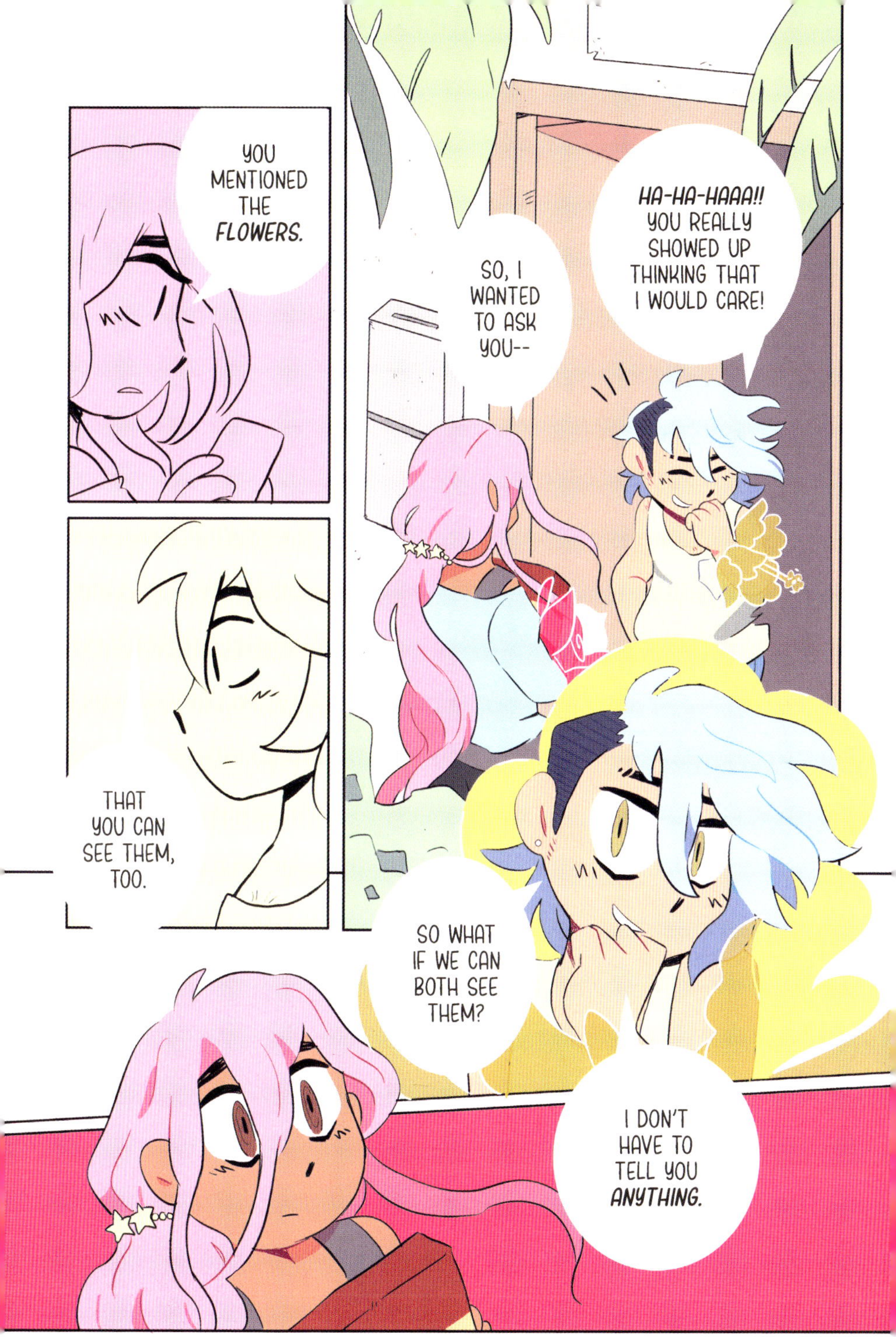
YOU MENTIONED THE *FLOWERS.*
THAT YOU CAN SEE THEM, TOO.
SO, I WANTED TO ASK YOU--
HA-HA-HAAA!! YOU REALLY SHOWED UP THINKING THAT I WOULD CARE!
SO WHAT IF WE CAN BOTH SEE THEM?
I DON'T HAVE TO TELL YOU *ANYTHING.*

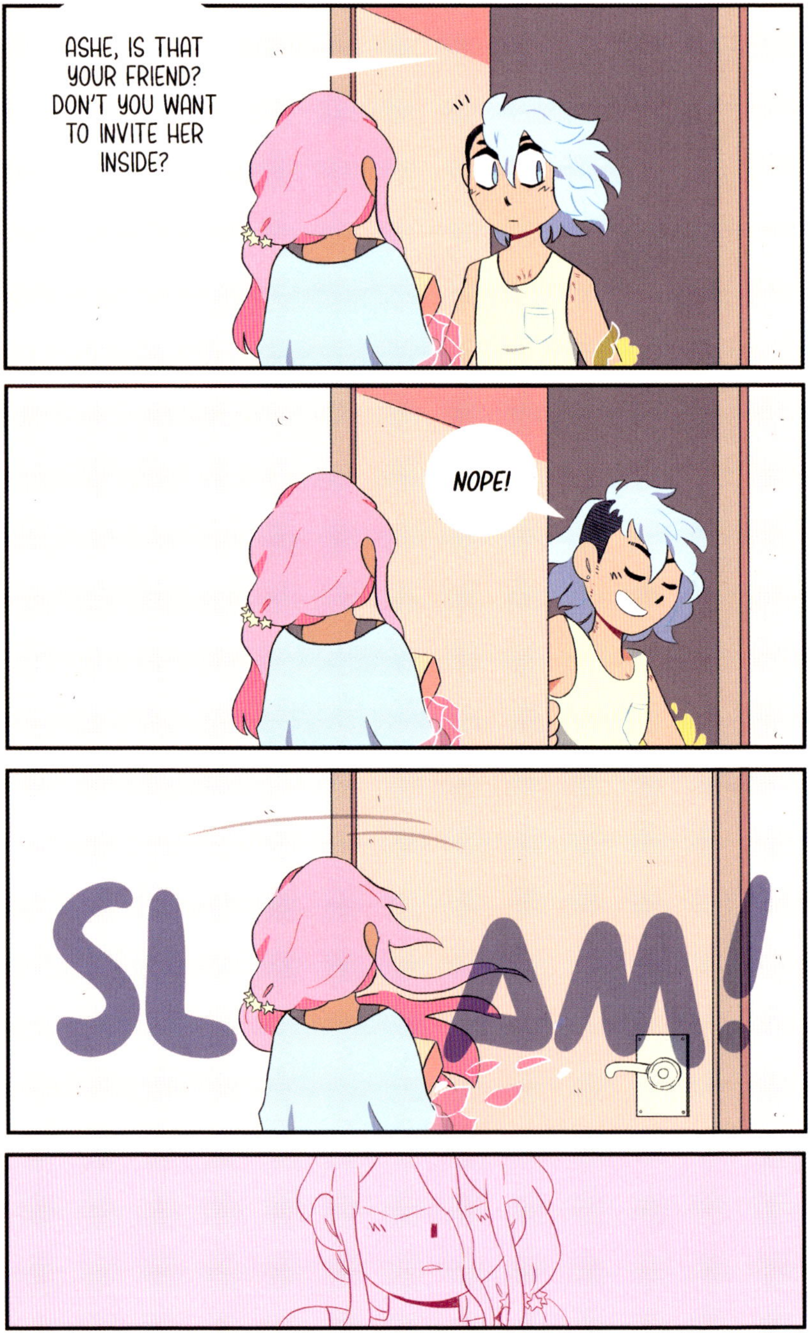
ASHE, IS THAT YOUR FRIEND? DON'T YOU WANT TO INVITE HER INSIDE?
NOPE!
SLAM!

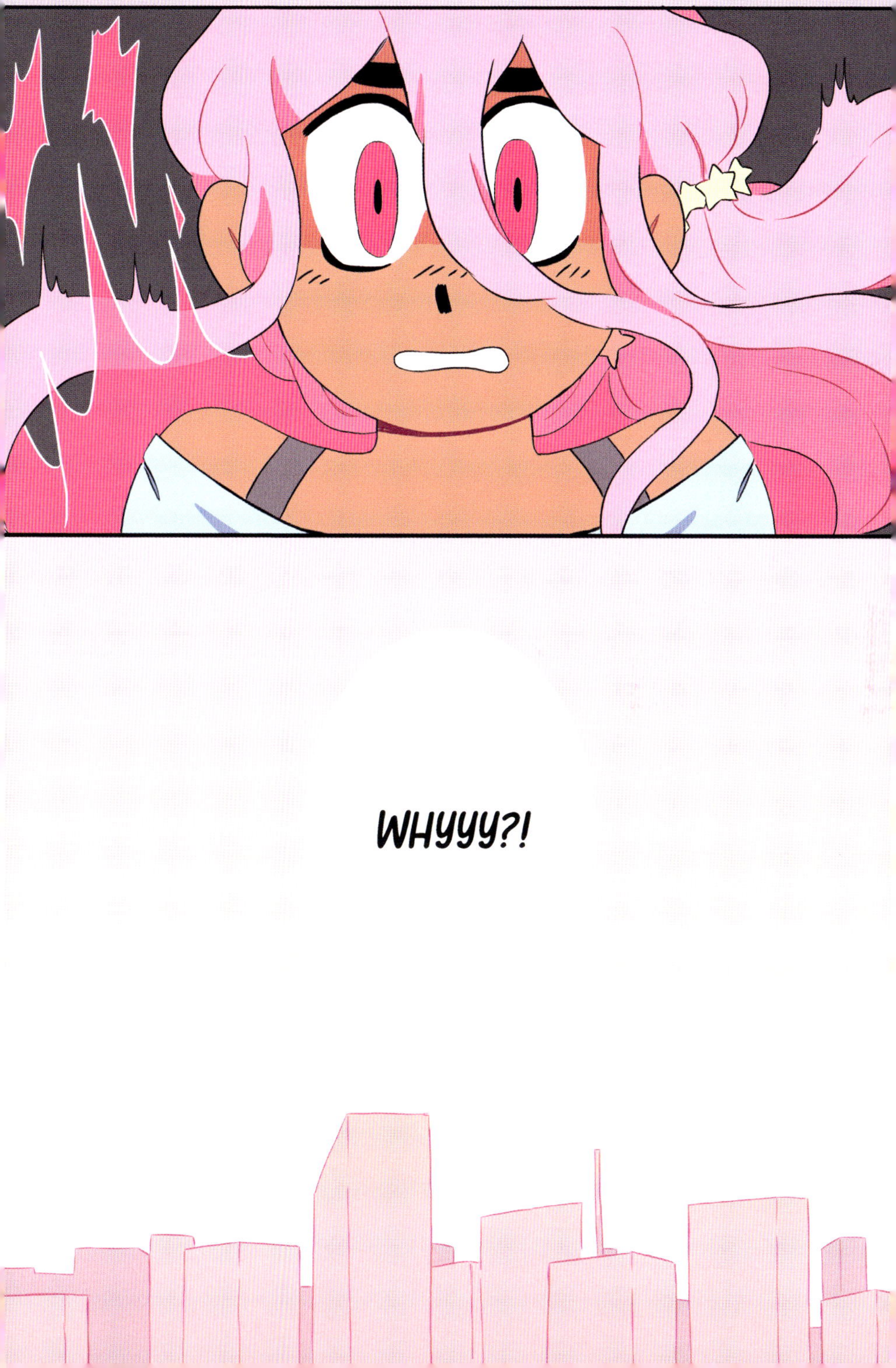
WHYYY?!

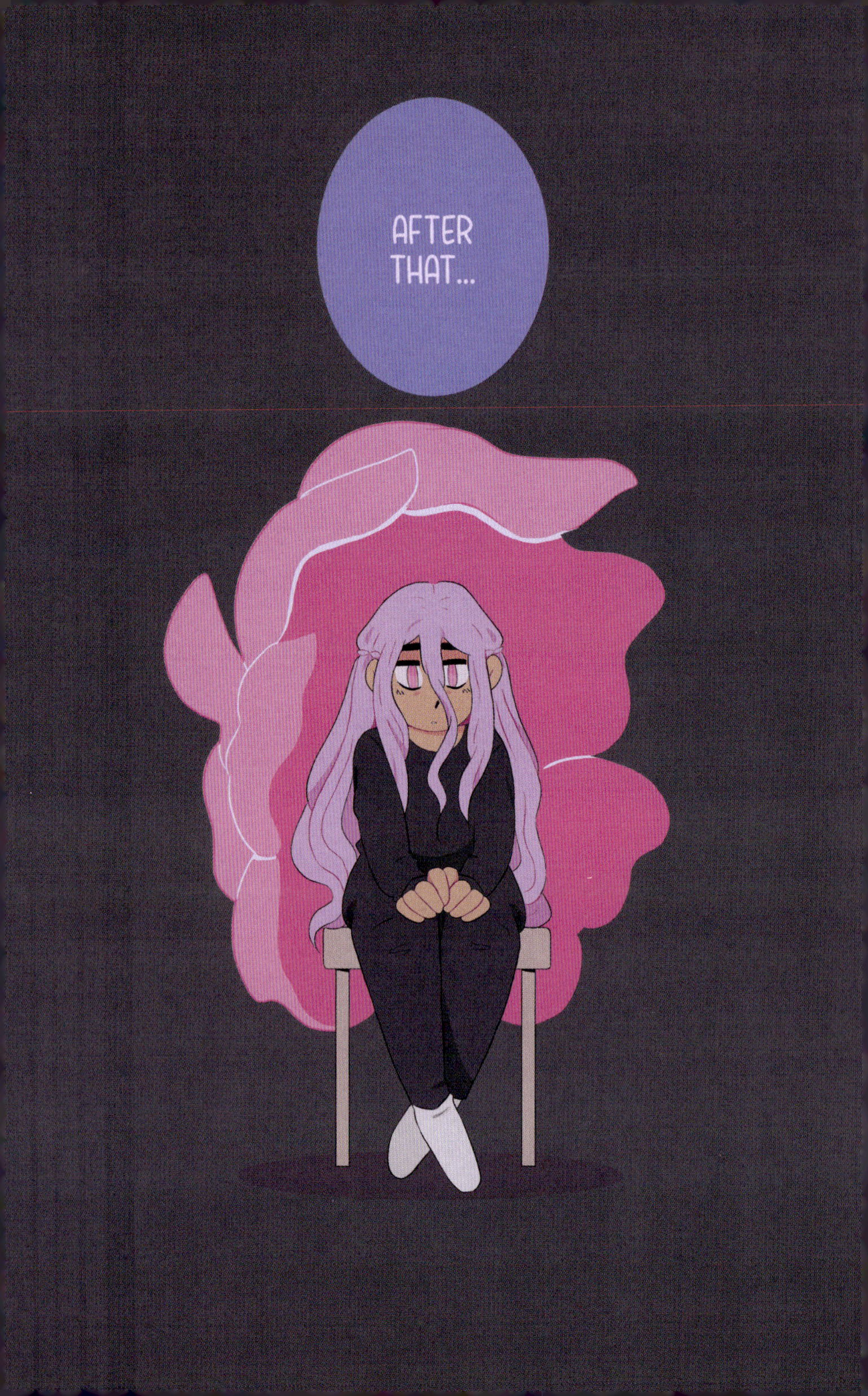
AFTER THAT...

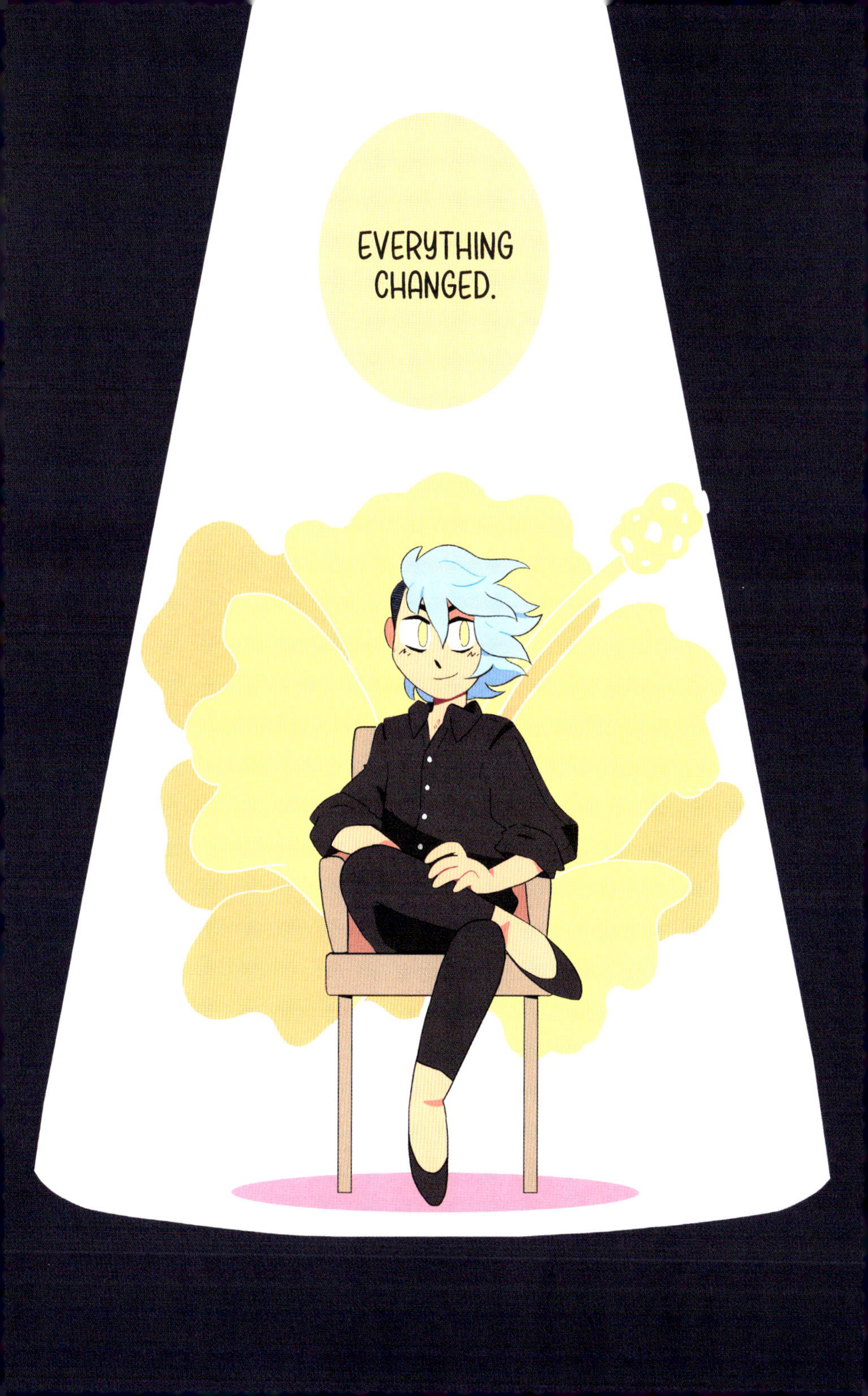
EVERYTHING CHANGED.

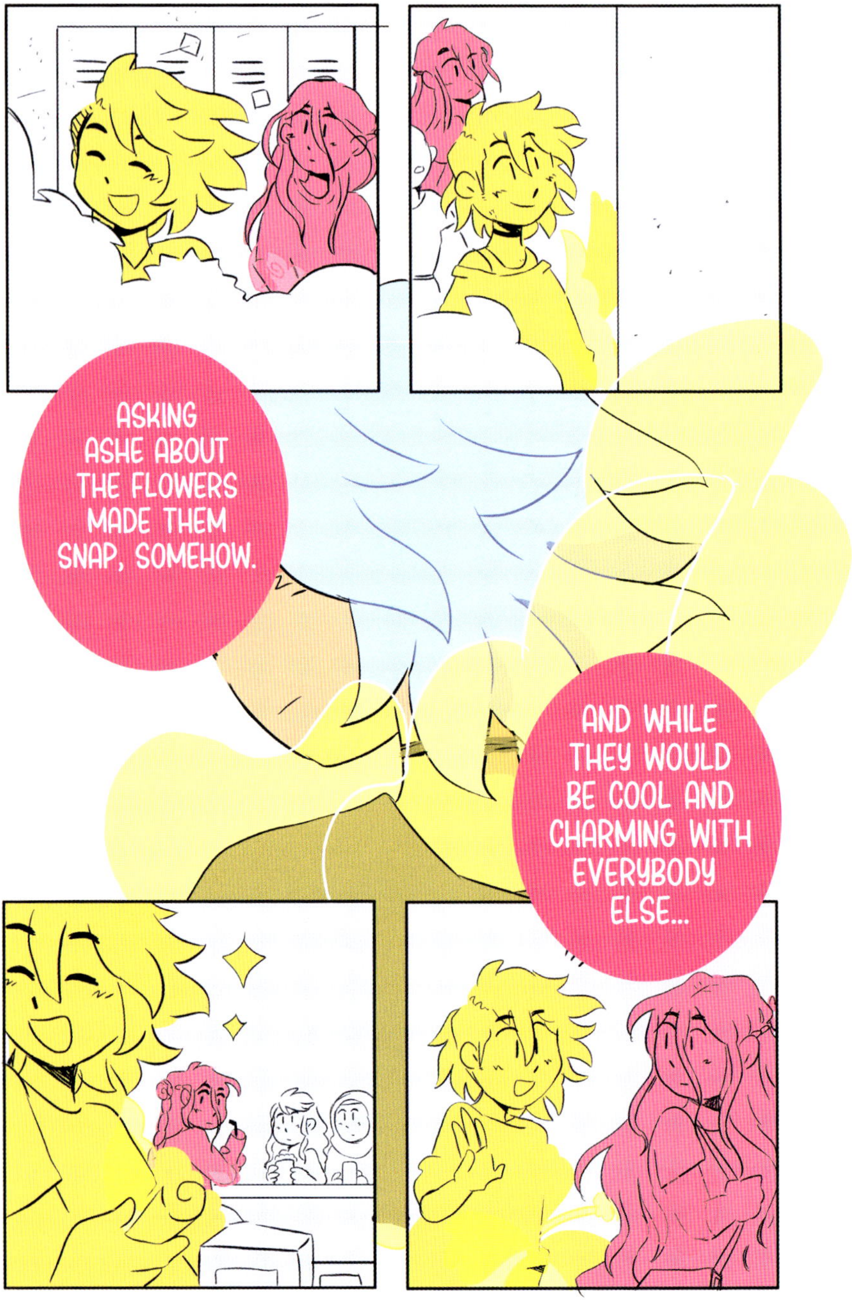
ASKING ASHE ABOUT THE FLOWERS MADE THEM SNAP, SOMEHOW.
AND WHILE THEY WOULD BE COOL AND CHARMING WITH EVERYBODY ELSE...

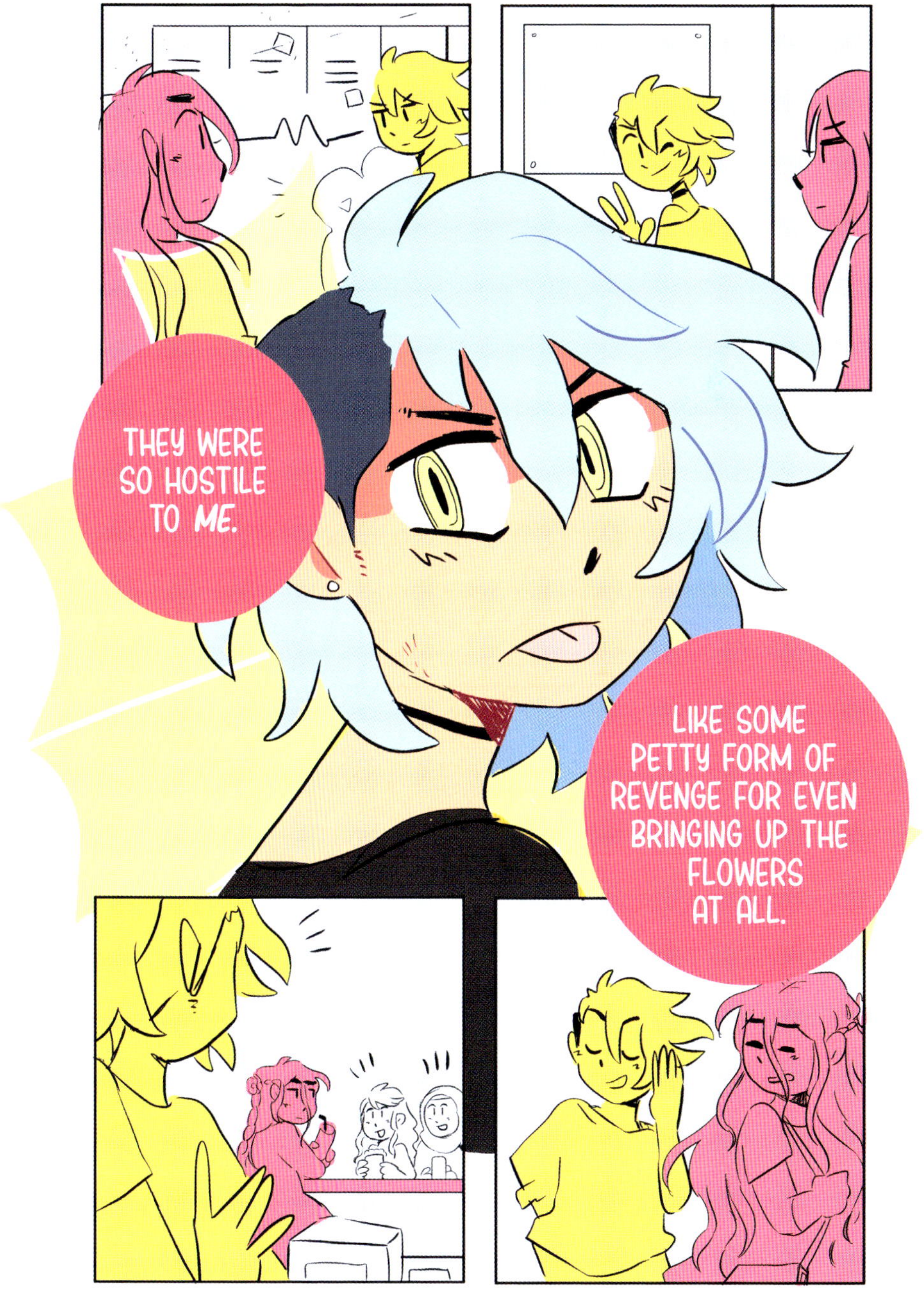
THEY WERE SO HOSTILE TO *ME*.
LIKE SOME PETTY FORM OF REVENGE FOR EVEN BRINGING UP THE FLOWERS AT ALL.

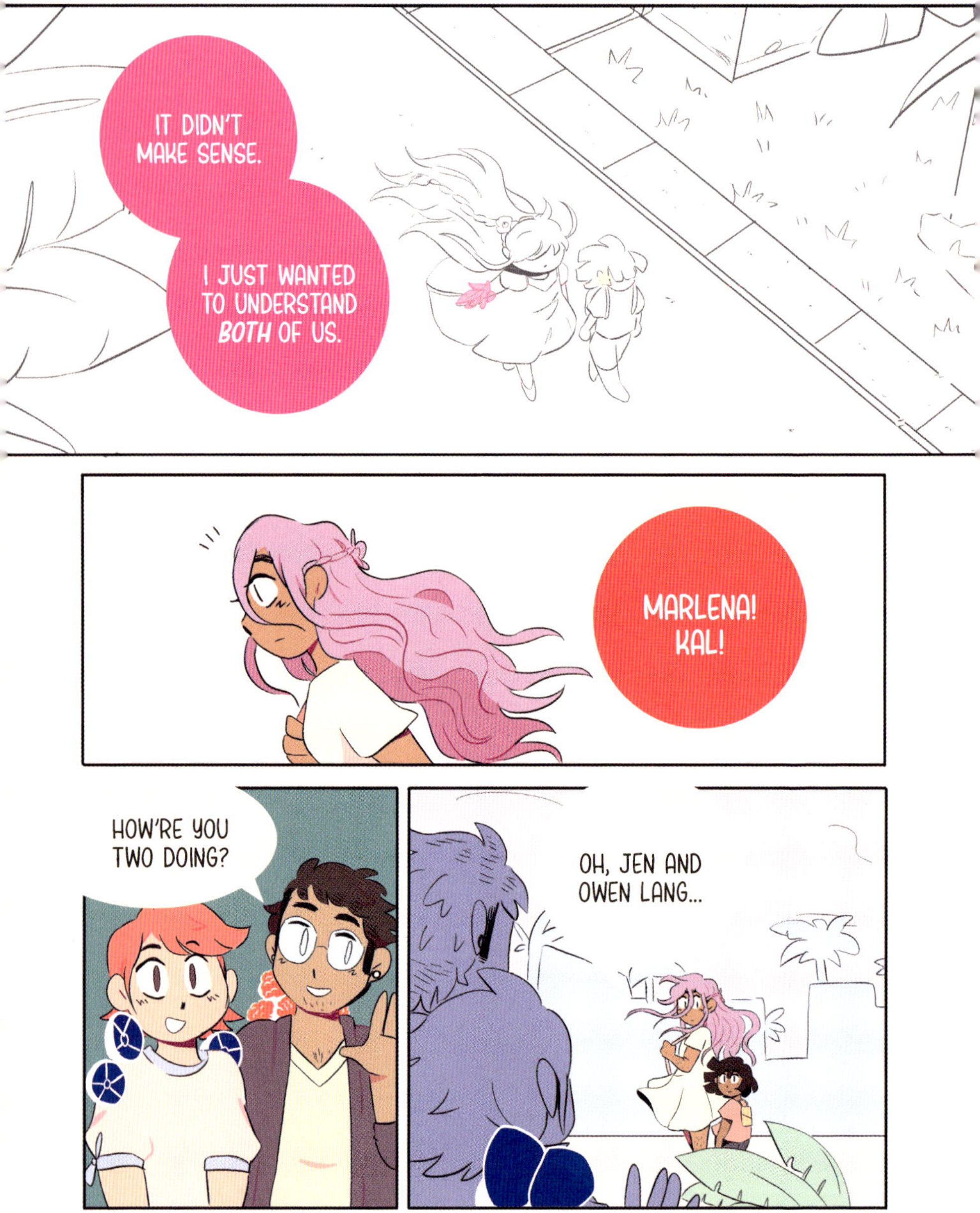
IT DIDN'T MAKE SENSE.
I JUST WANTED TO UNDERSTAND *BOTH* OF US.
MARLENA! KAL!
HOW'RE YOU TWO DOING?
OH, JEN AND OWEN LANG...

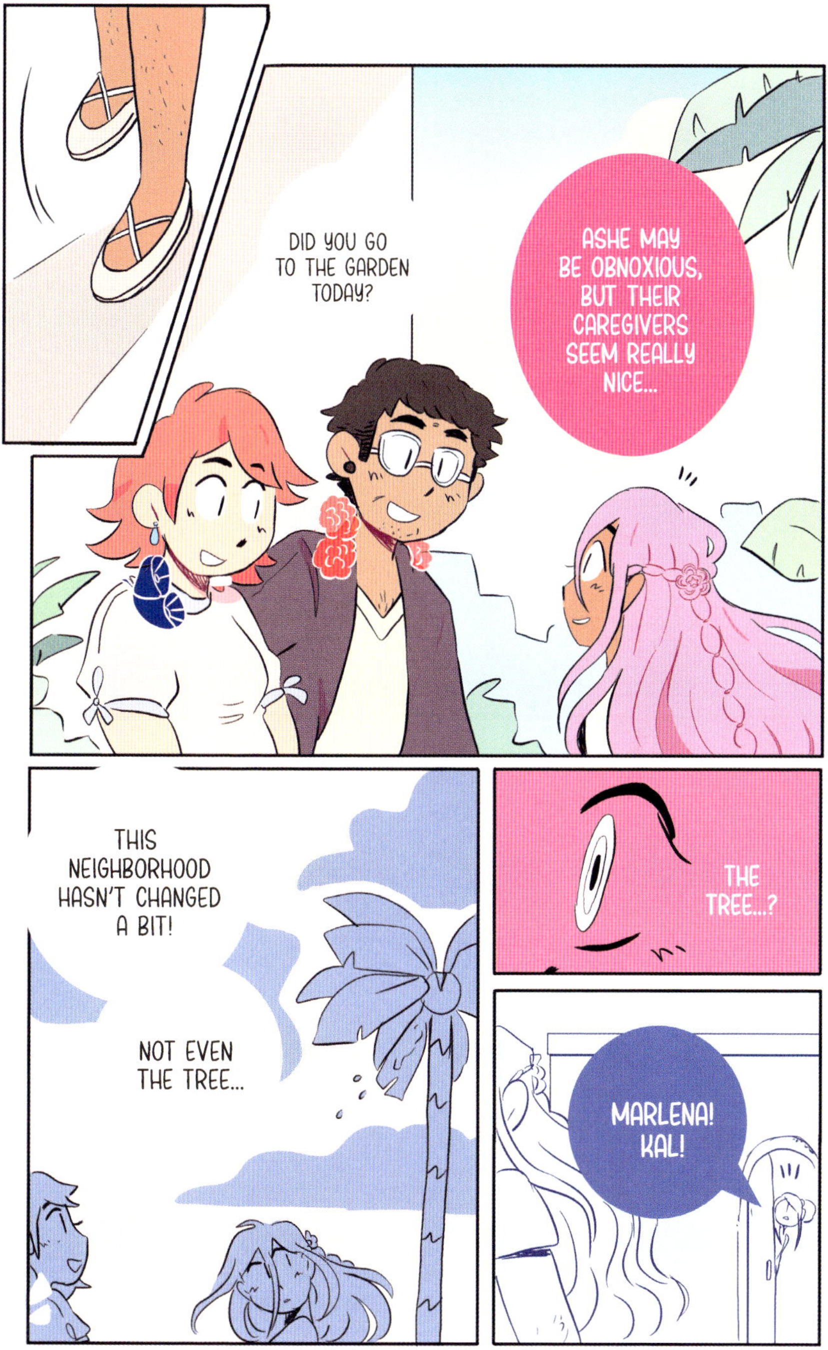
DID YOU GO TO THE GARDEN TODAY?
ASHE MAY BE OBNOXIOUS, BUT THEIR CAREGIVERS SEEM REALLY NICE...
THIS NEIGHBORHOOD HASN'T CHANGED A BIT!
NOT EVEN THE TREE...
THE TREE...?
MARLENA! KAL!

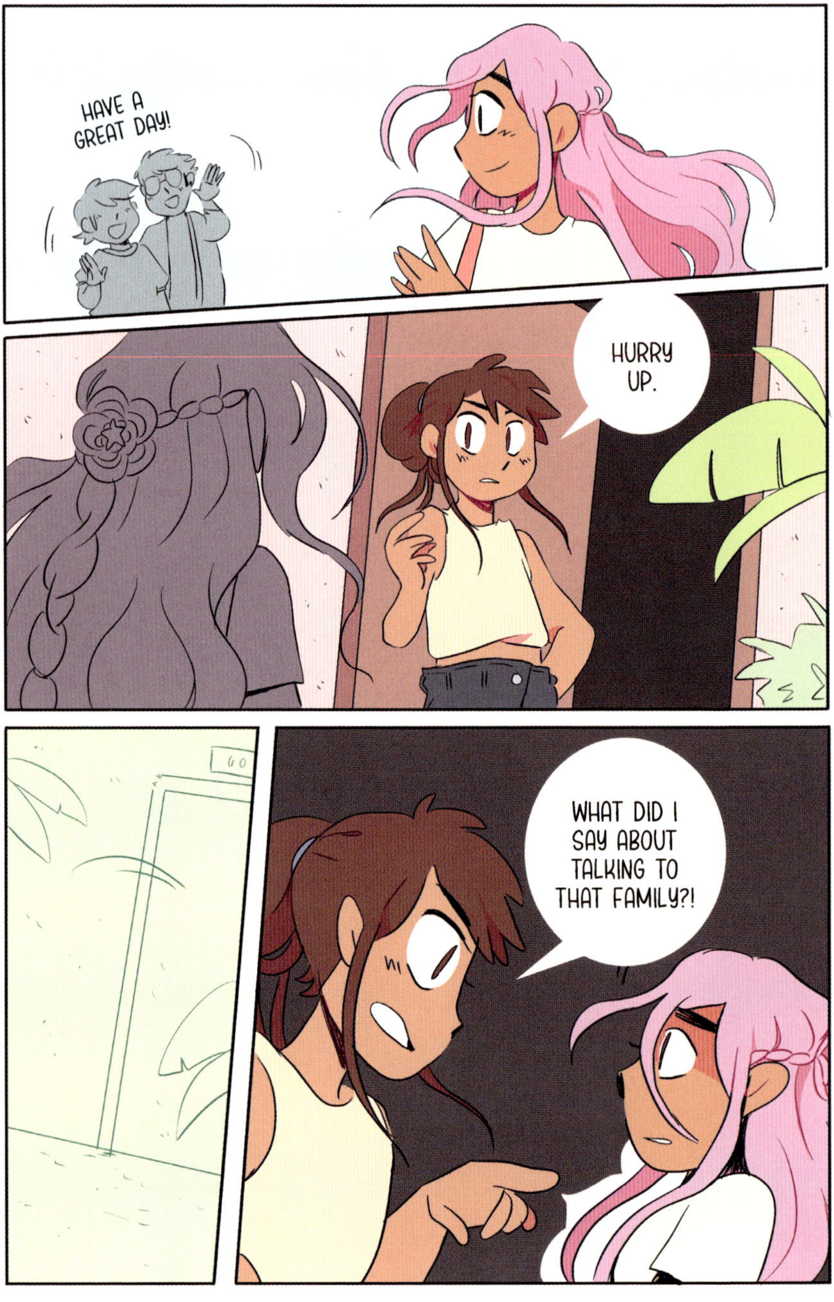
HAVE A GREAT DAY!
HURRY UP.
WHAT DID I SAY ABOUT TALKING TO THAT FAMILY?!

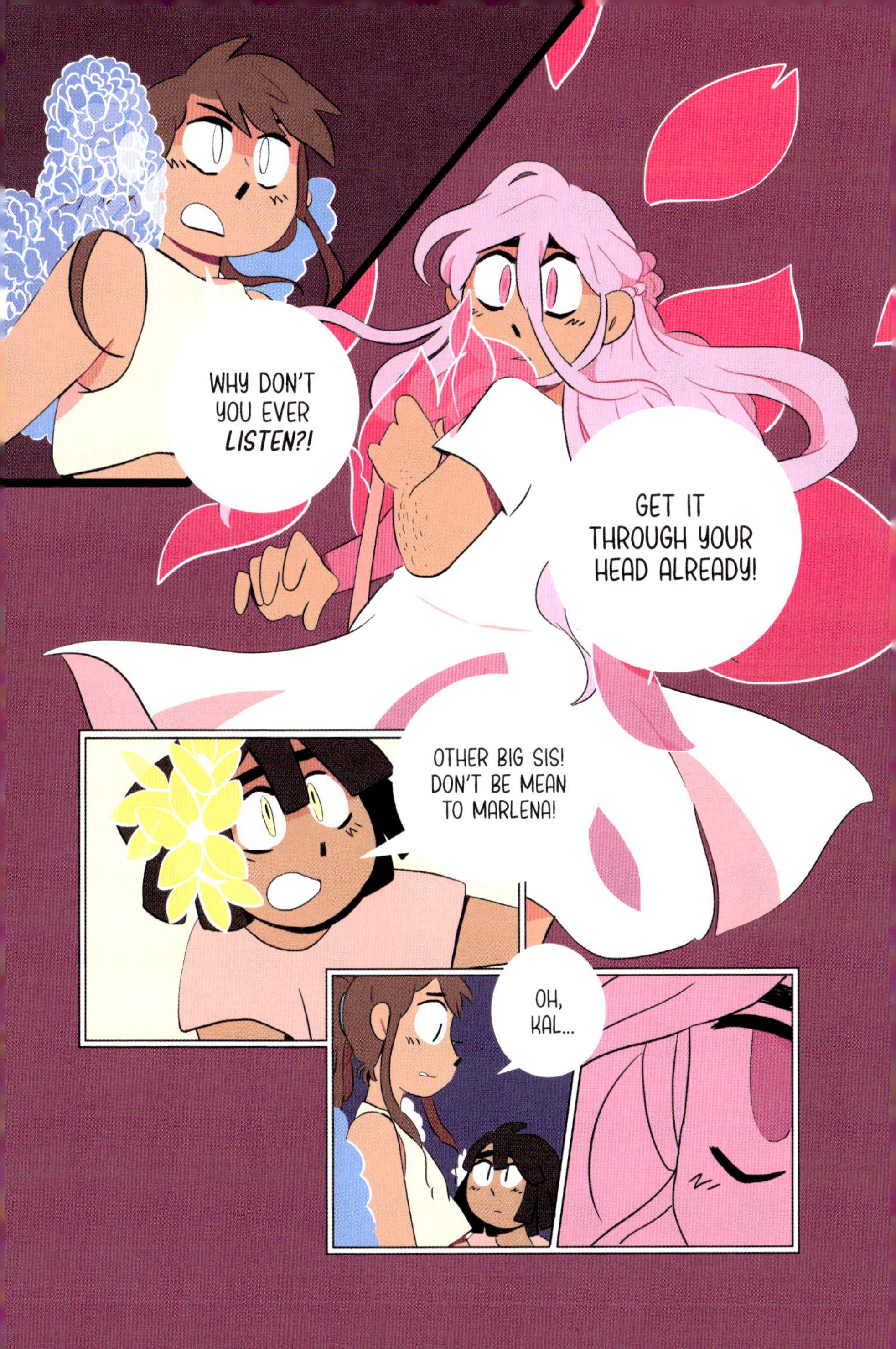
WHY DON'T YOU EVER *LISTEN?!*
GET IT THROUGH YOUR HEAD ALREADY!
OTHER BIG SIS! DON'T BE MEAN TO MARLENA!
OH, KAL...

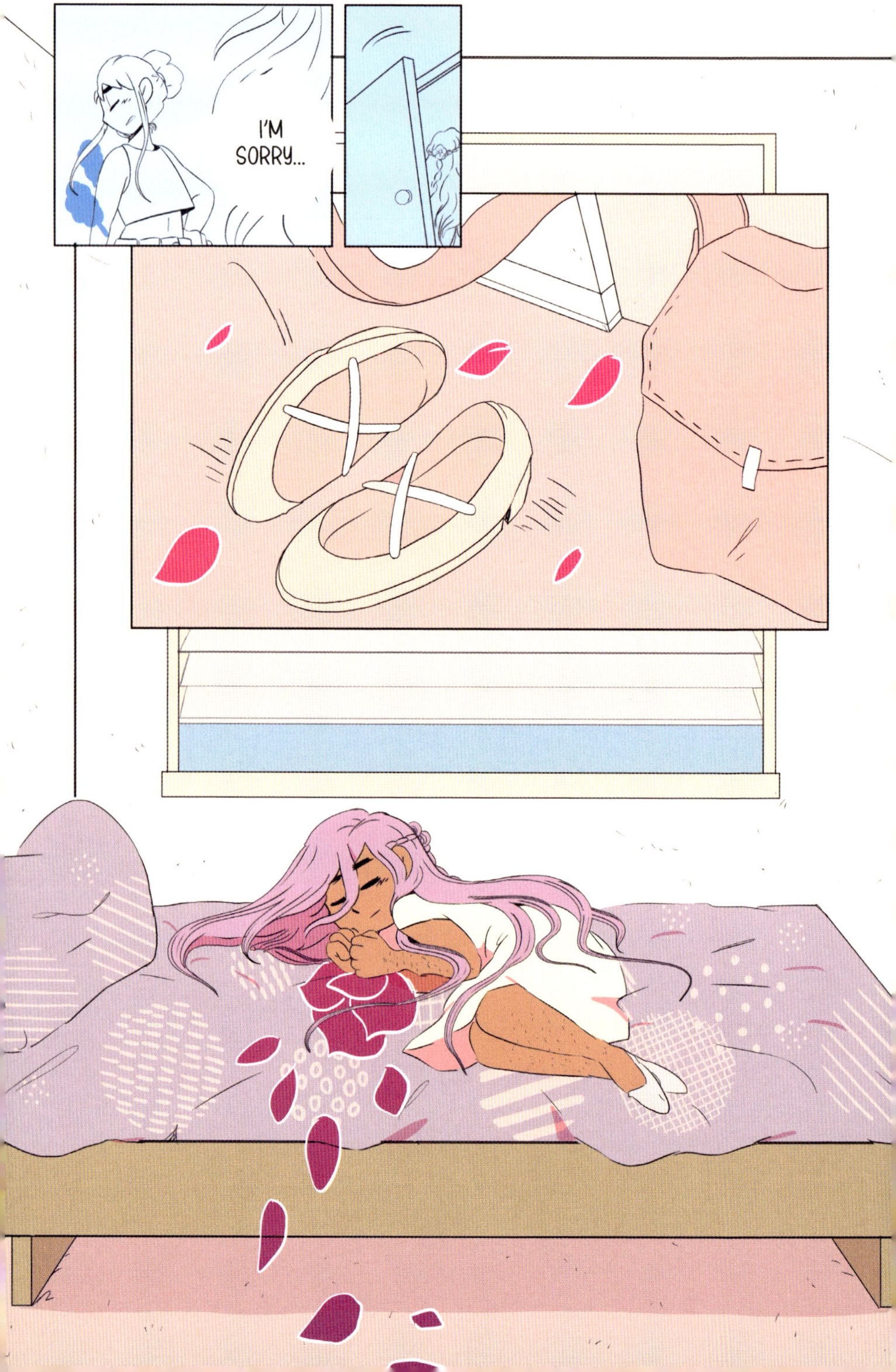
I'M SORRY...

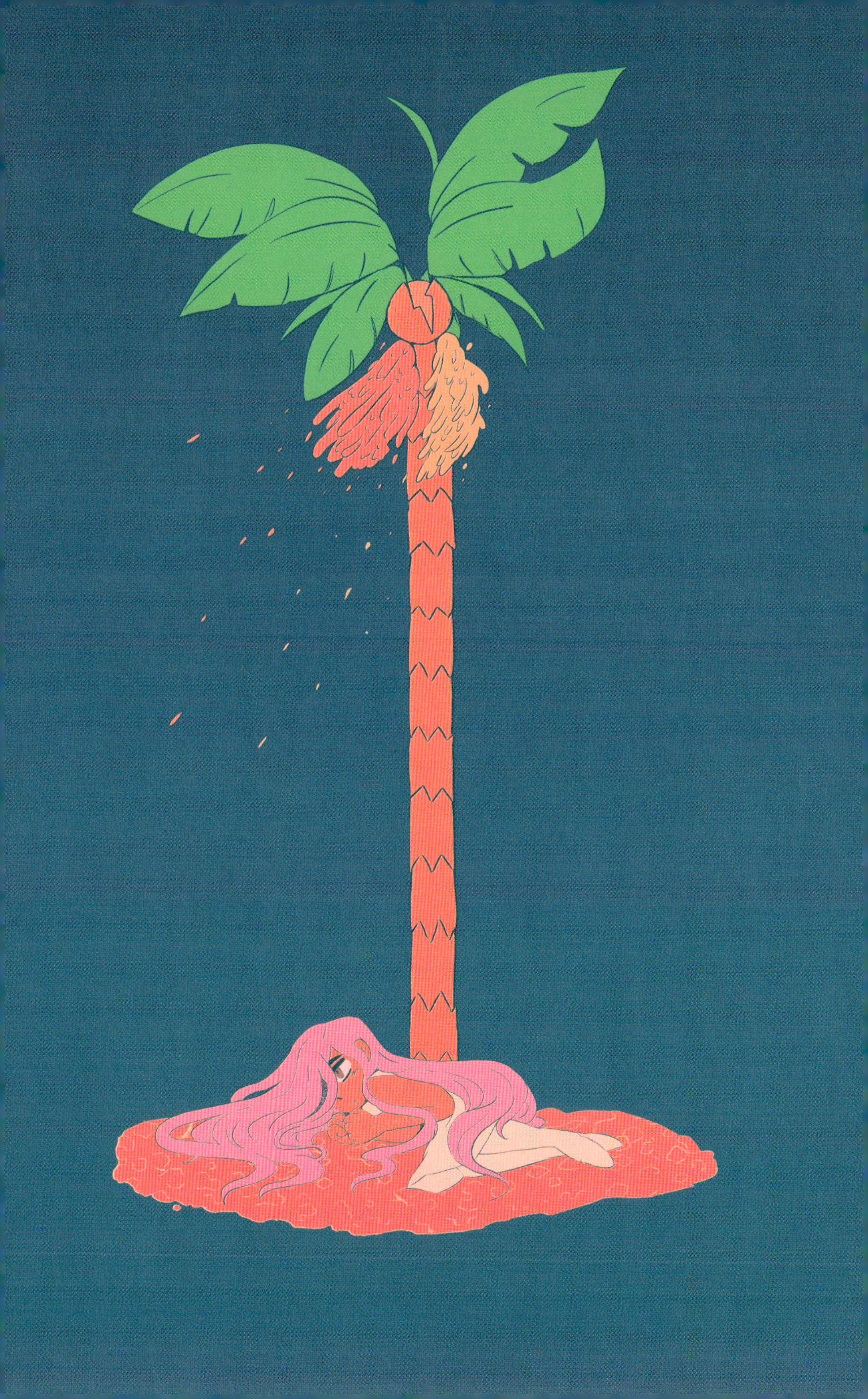

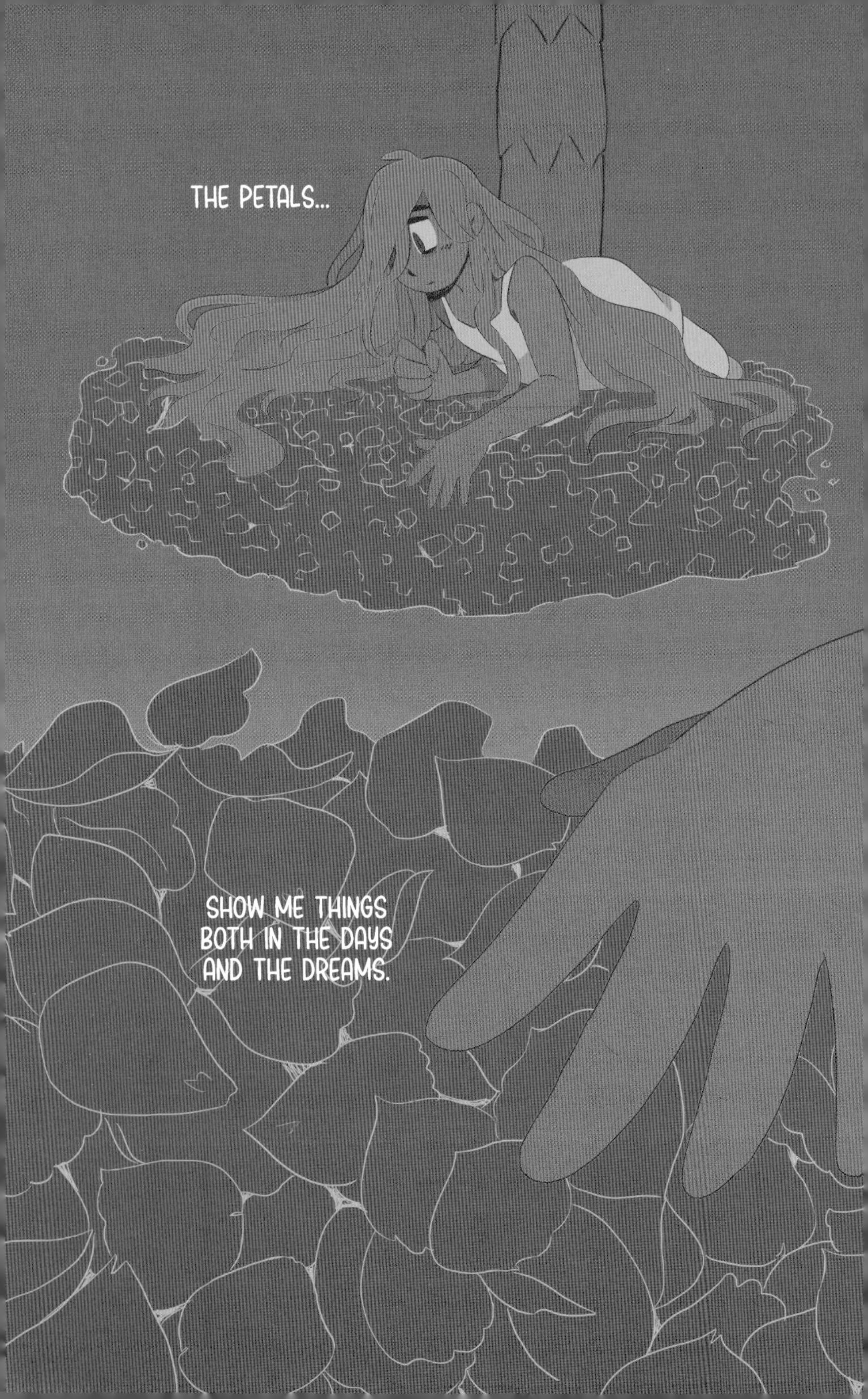
THE PETALS...
SHOW ME THINGS BOTH IN THE DAYS AND THE DREAMS.

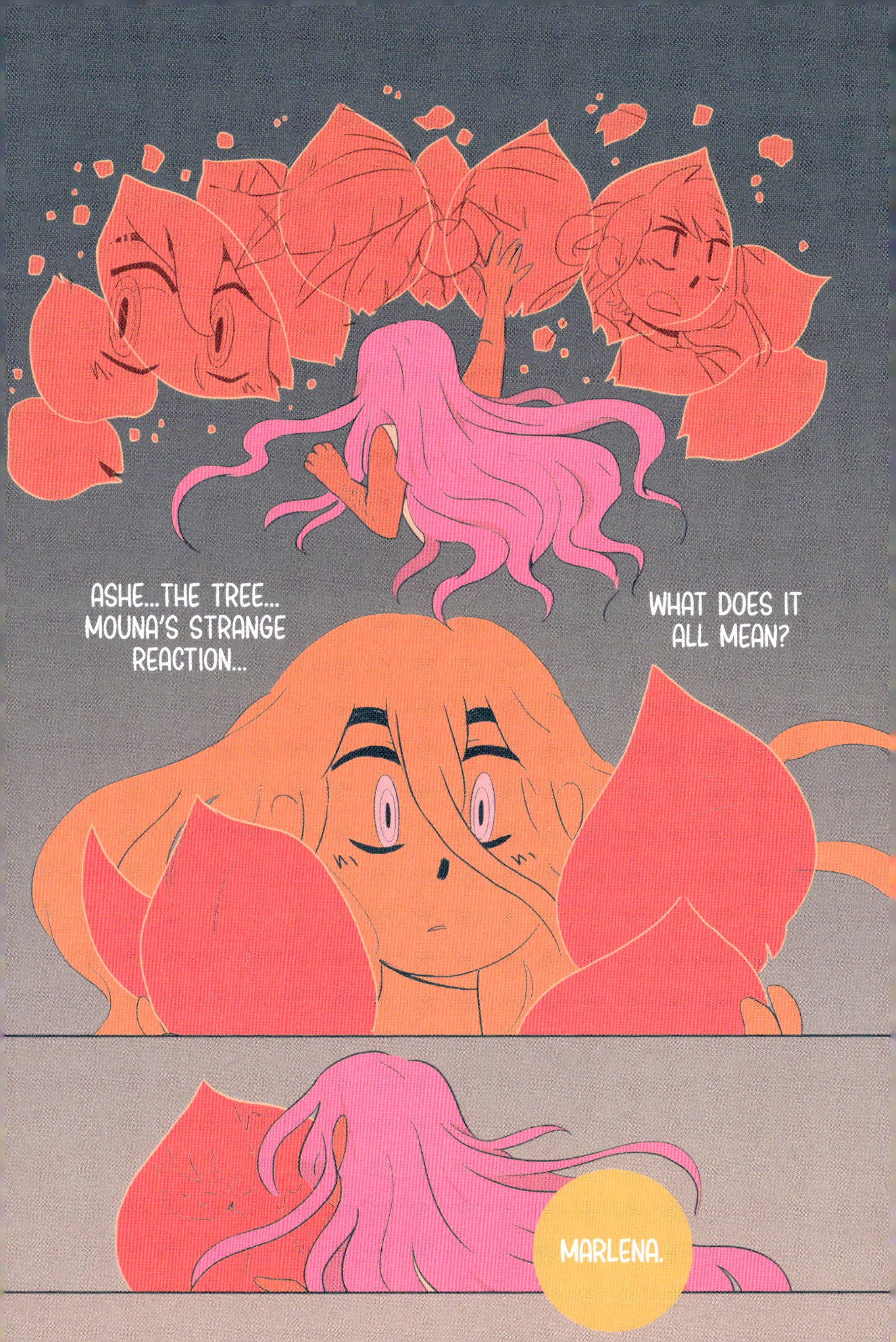
ASHE...THE TREE... MOUNA'S STRANGE REACTION...
WHAT DOES IT ALL MEAN?
MARLENA.

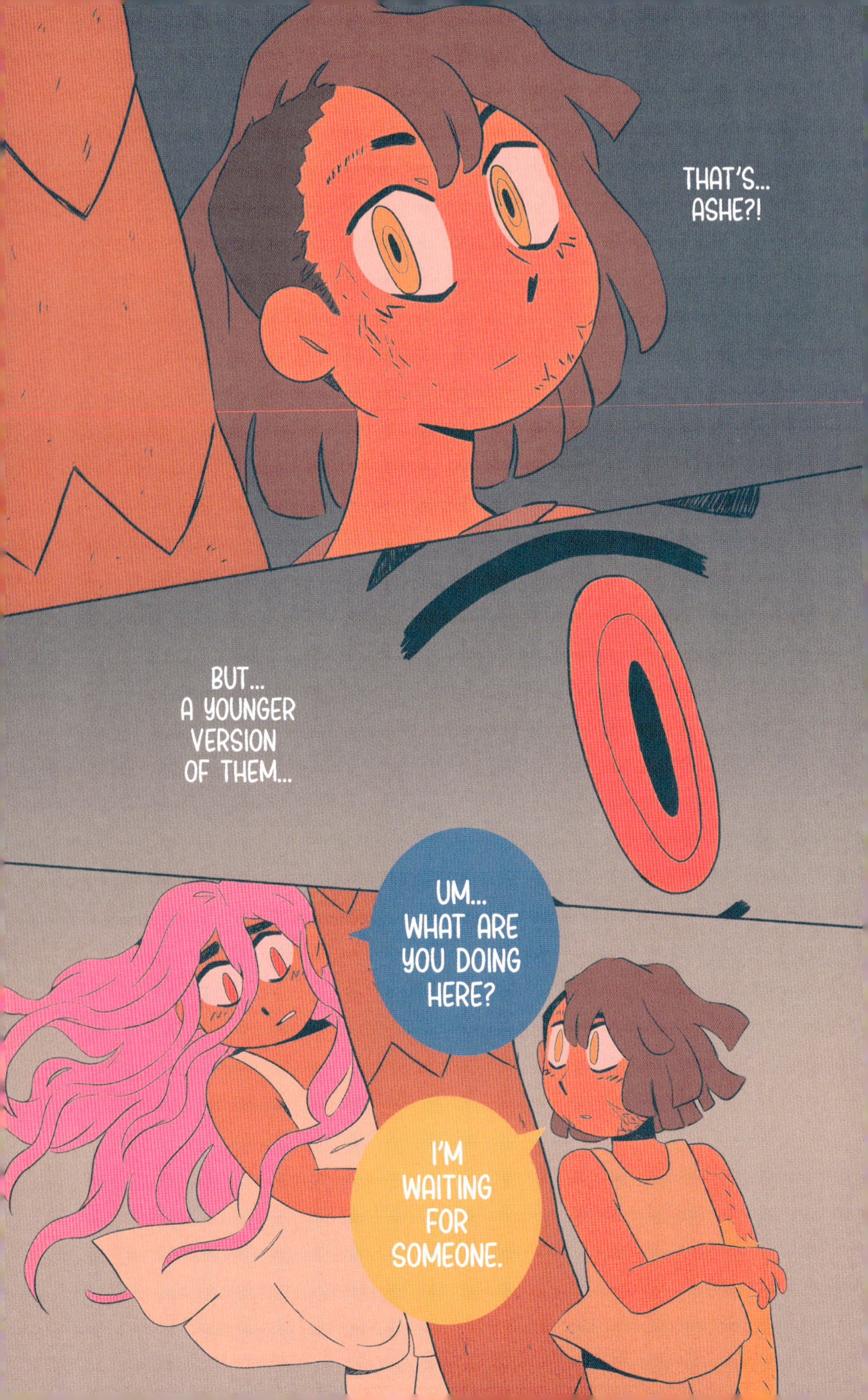
THAT'S... ASHE?!
BUT... A YOUNGER VERSION OF THEM...
UM... WHAT ARE YOU DOING HERE?
I'M WAITING FOR SOMEONE.

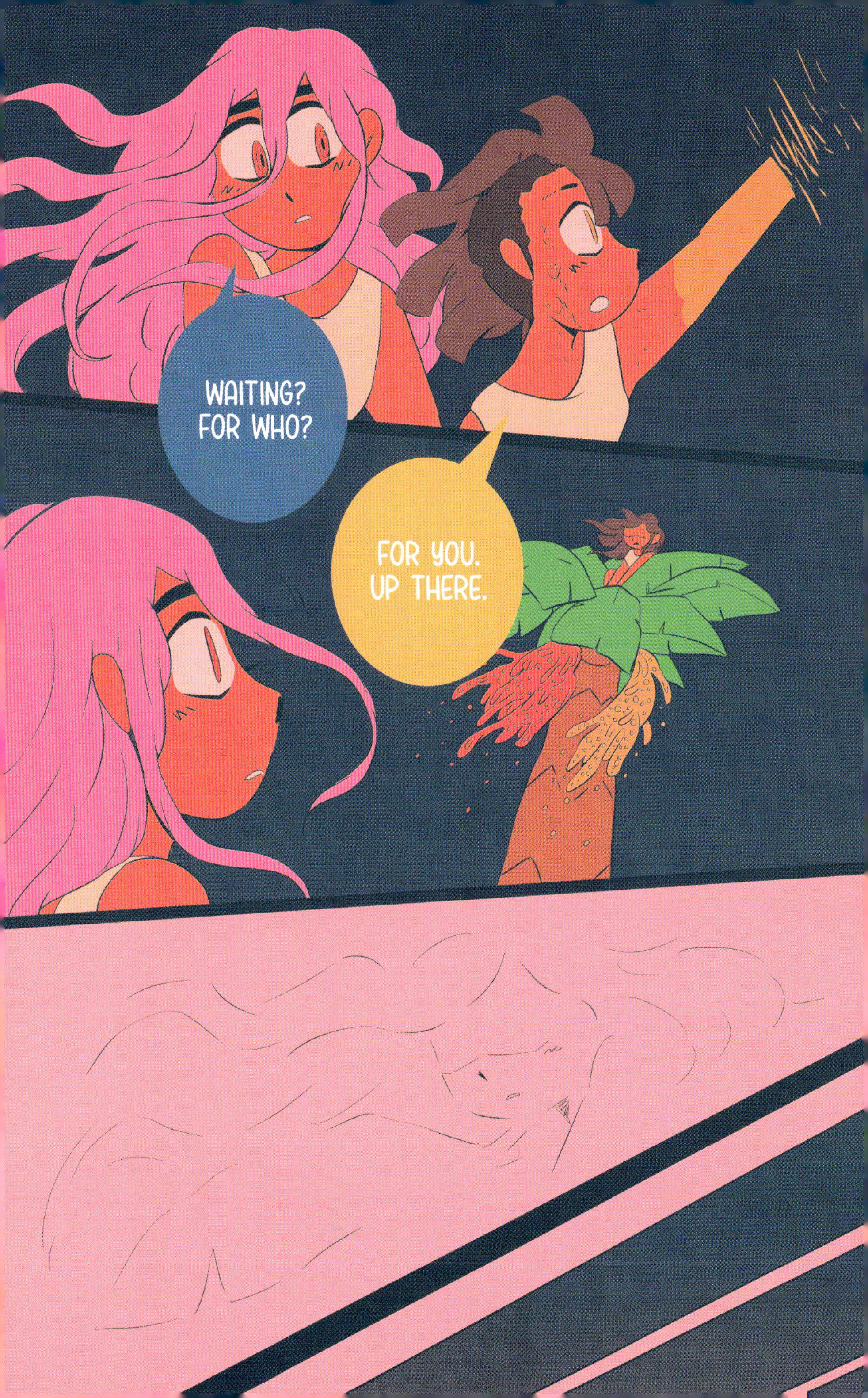
WAITING? FOR WHO?
FOR YOU. UP THERE.

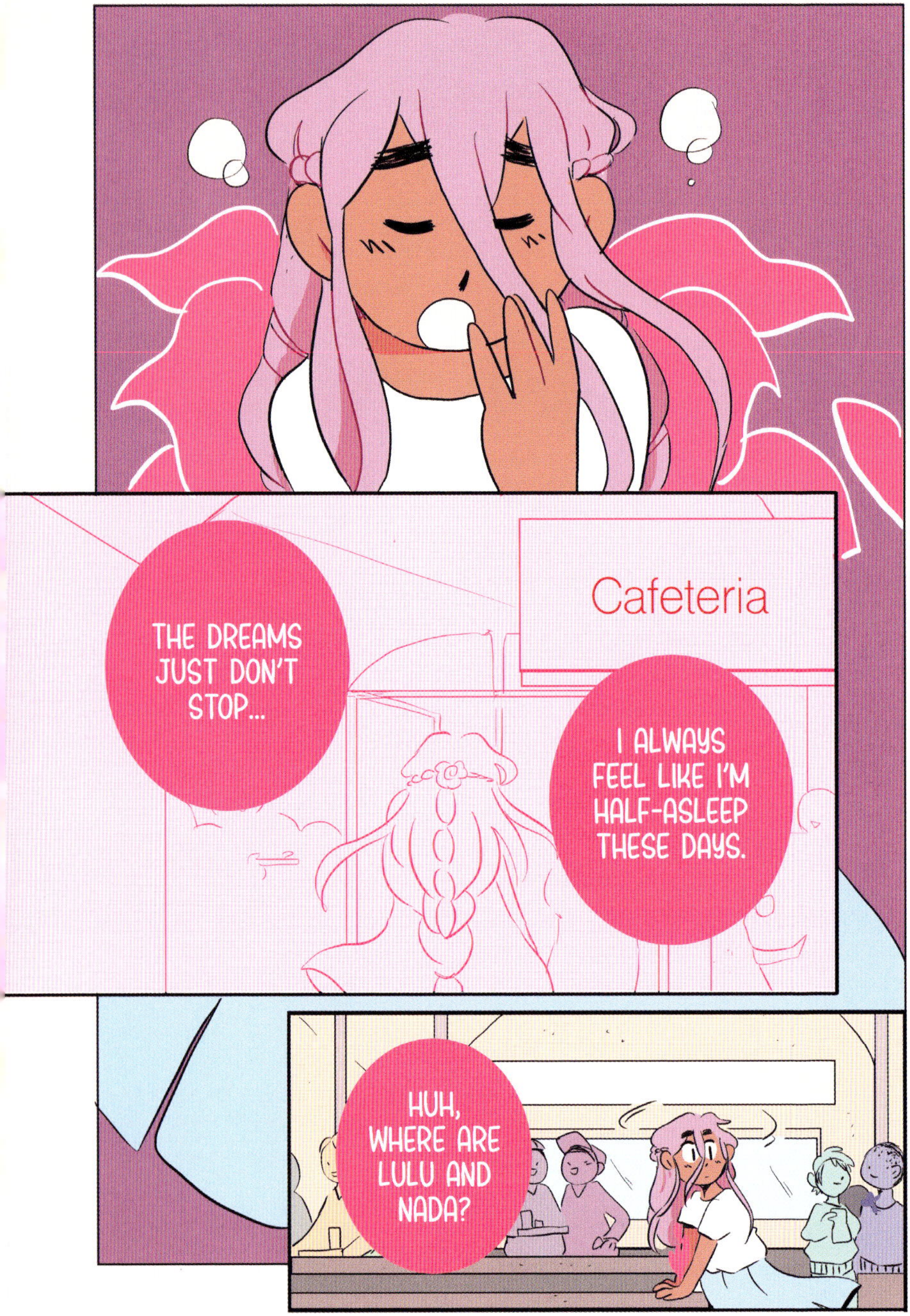
THE DREAMS JUST DON'T STOP...
Cafeteria
I ALWAYS FEEL LIKE I'M HALF-ASLEEP THESE DAYS.
HUH, WHERE ARE LULU AND NADA?

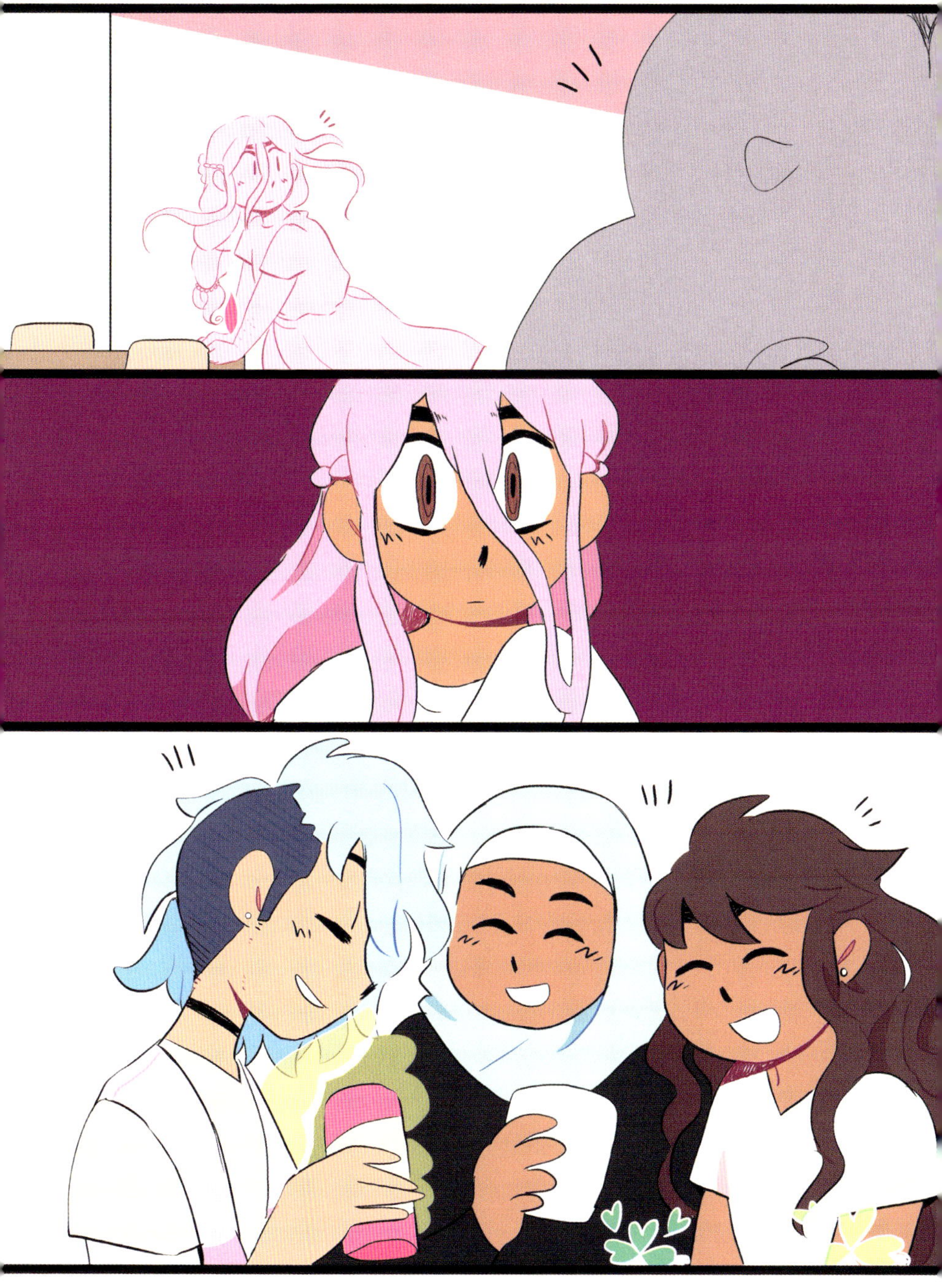

IF ONLY I COULD BE MORE LIKE THEM...

THINGS WOULD BE DIFFERENT.

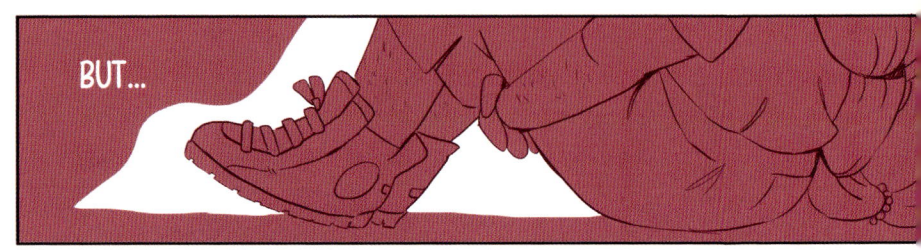

BUT...

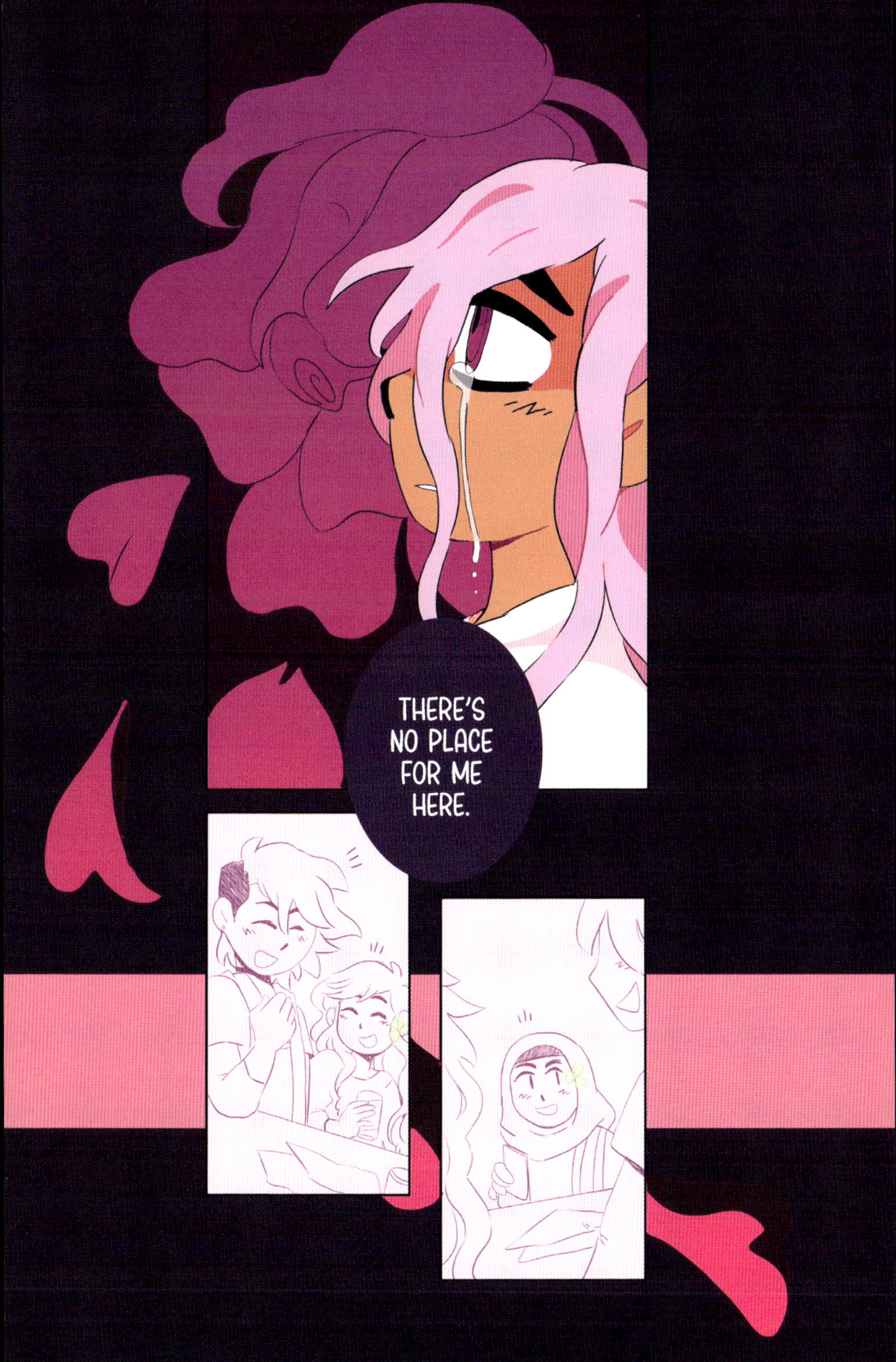
THERE'S NO PLACE FOR ME HERE.

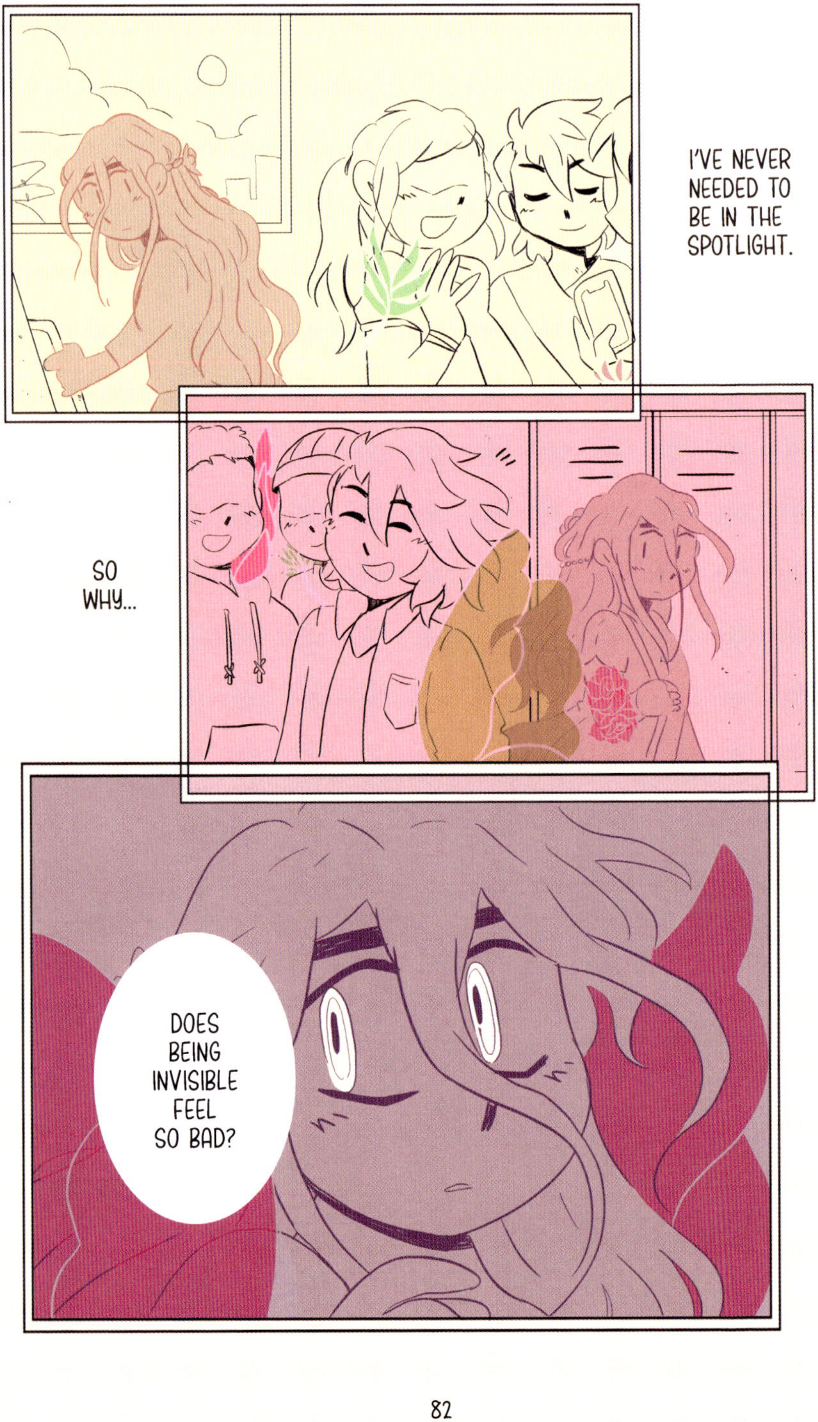
I'VE NEVER NEEDED TO BE IN THE SPOTLIGHT.
SO WHY...
DOES BEING INVISIBLE FEEL SO BAD?

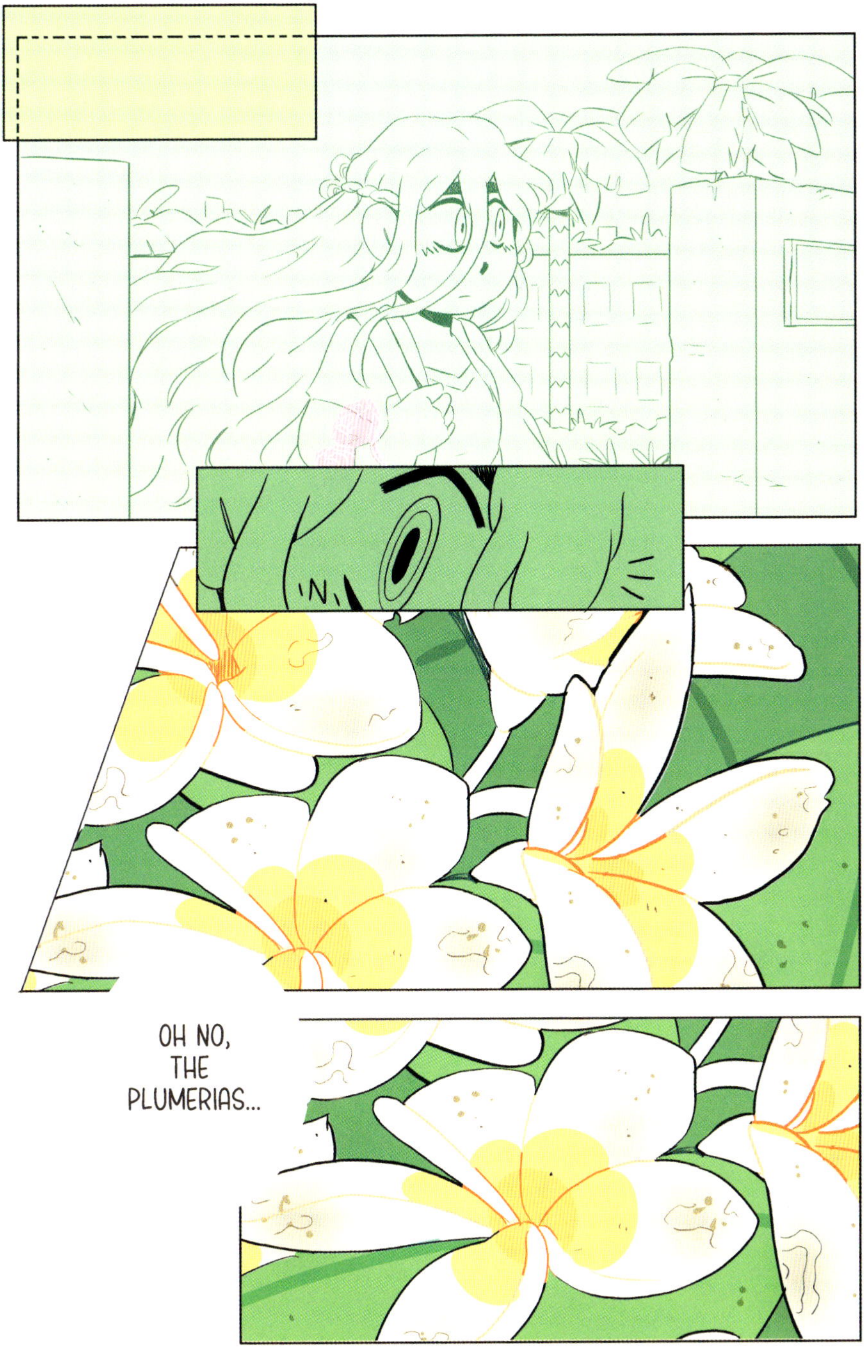
OH NO,
THE
PLUMERIAS...

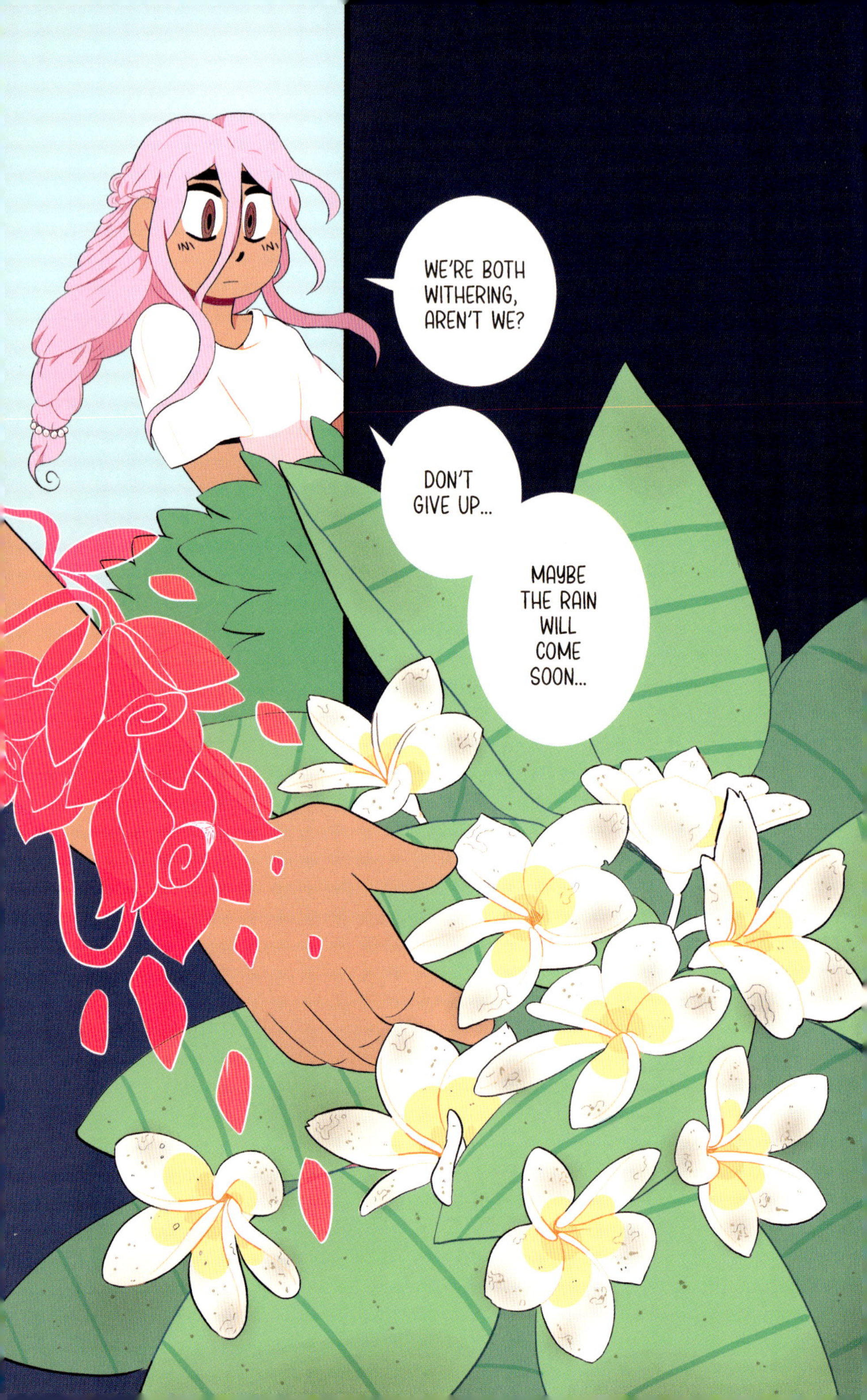
WE'RE BOTH WITHERING, AREN'T WE?
DON'T GIVE UP...
MAYBE THE RAIN WILL COME SOON...

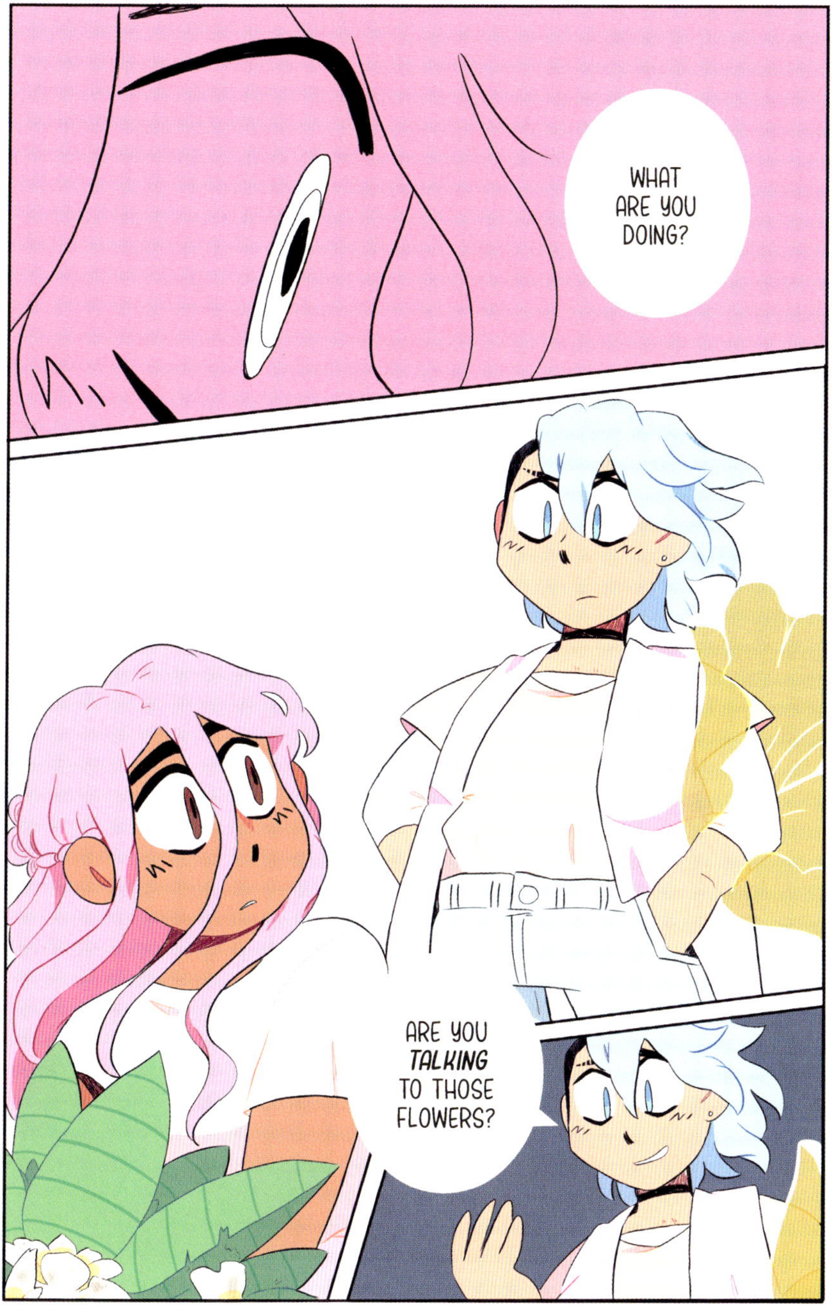
WHAT ARE YOU DOING?
ARE YOU TALKING TO THOSE FLOWERS?

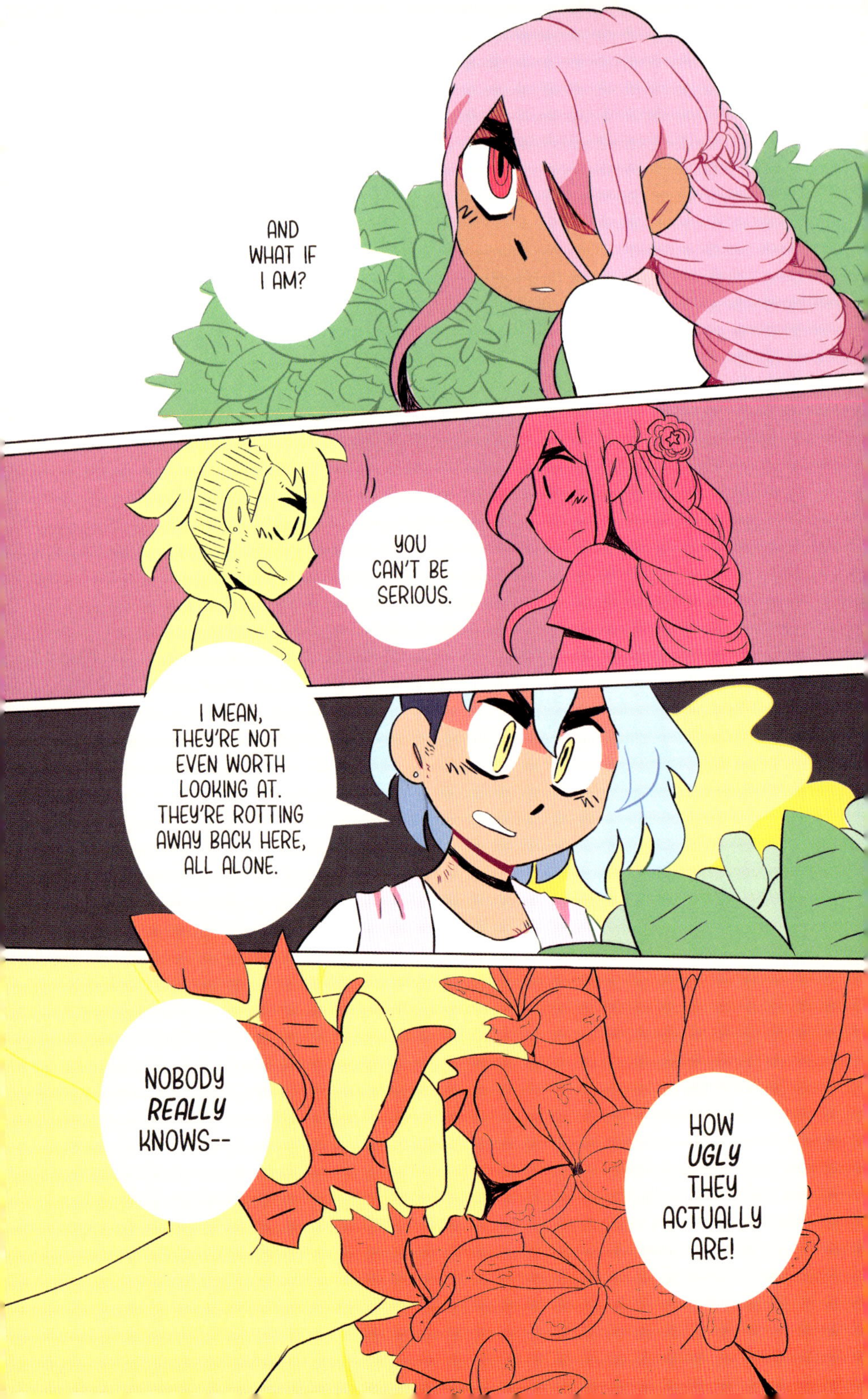
AND WHAT IF I AM?
YOU CAN'T BE SERIOUS.
I MEAN, THEY'RE NOT EVEN WORTH LOOKING AT. THEY'RE ROTTING AWAY BACK HERE, ALL ALONE.
NOBODY *REALLY* KNOWS--
HOW *UGLY* THEY ACTUALLY ARE!

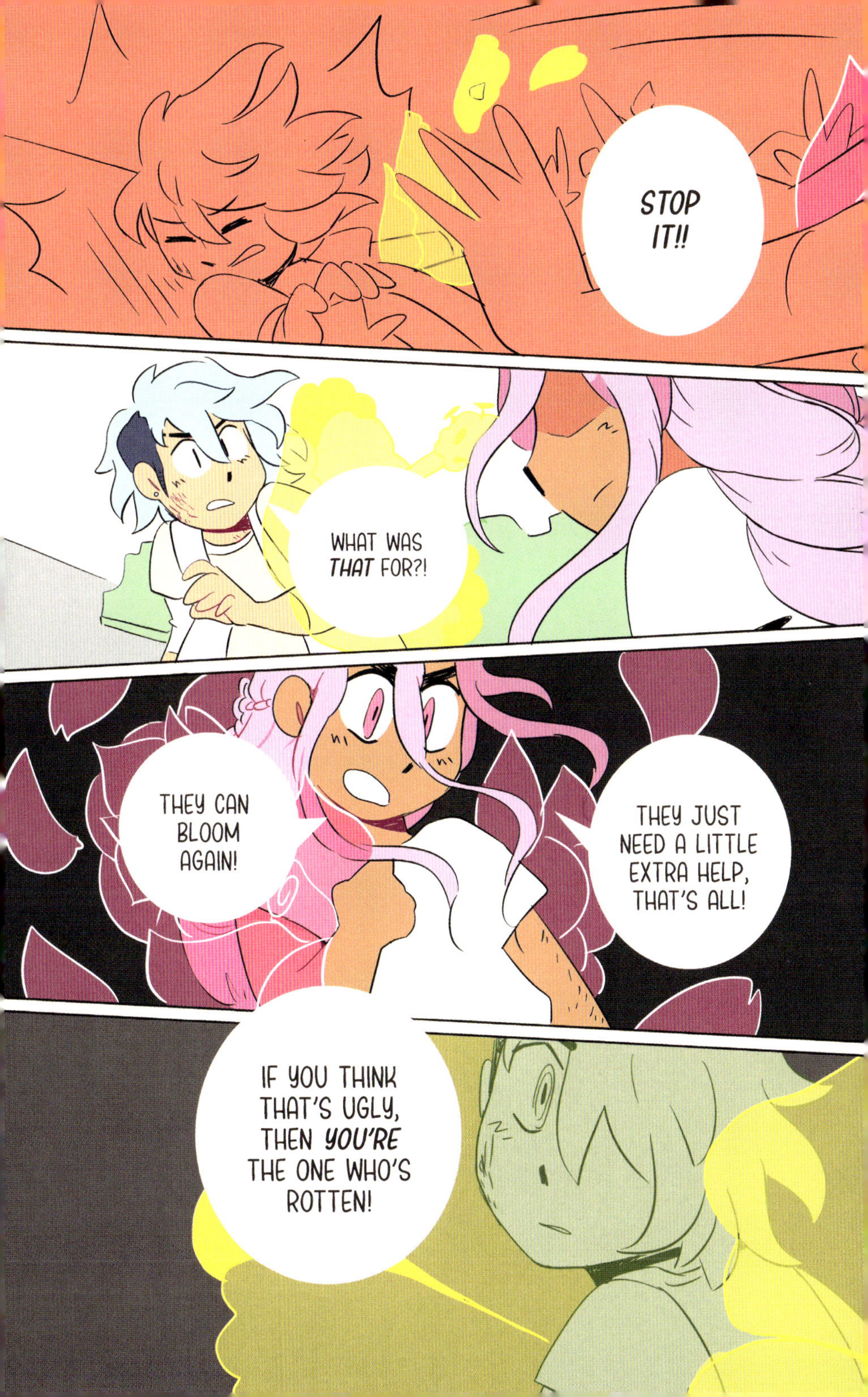
STOP IT!!
WHAT WAS *THAT* FOR?!
THEY CAN BLOOM AGAIN!
THEY JUST NEED A LITTLE EXTRA HELP, THAT'S ALL!
IF YOU THINK THAT'S UGLY, THEN *YOU'RE* THE ONE WHO'S ROTTEN!

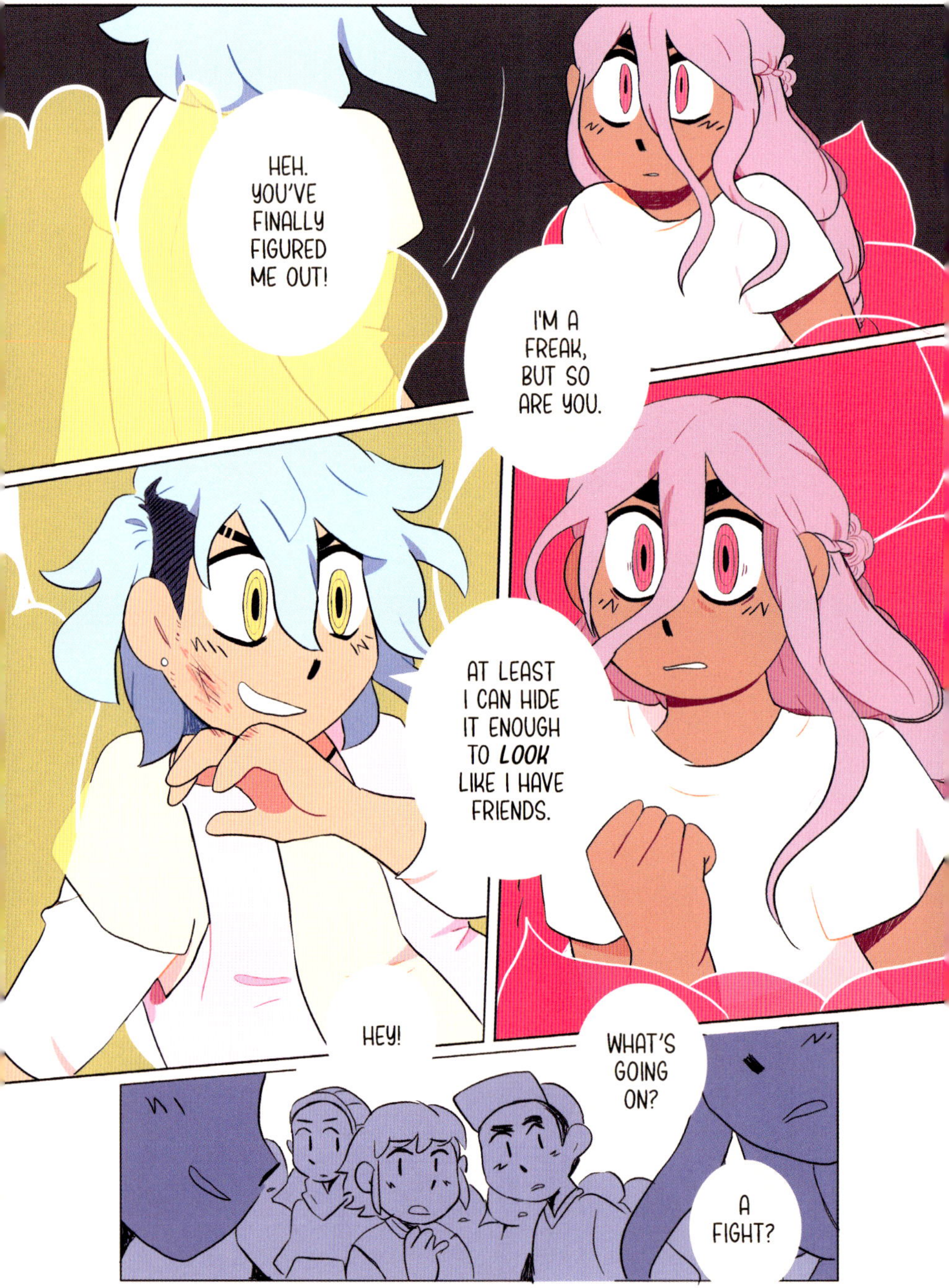
HEH. YOU'VE FINALLY FIGURED ME OUT!
I'M A FREAK, BUT SO ARE YOU.
AT LEAST I CAN HIDE IT ENOUGH TO *LOOK* LIKE I HAVE FRIENDS.
HEY!
WHAT'S GOING ON?
A FIGHT?

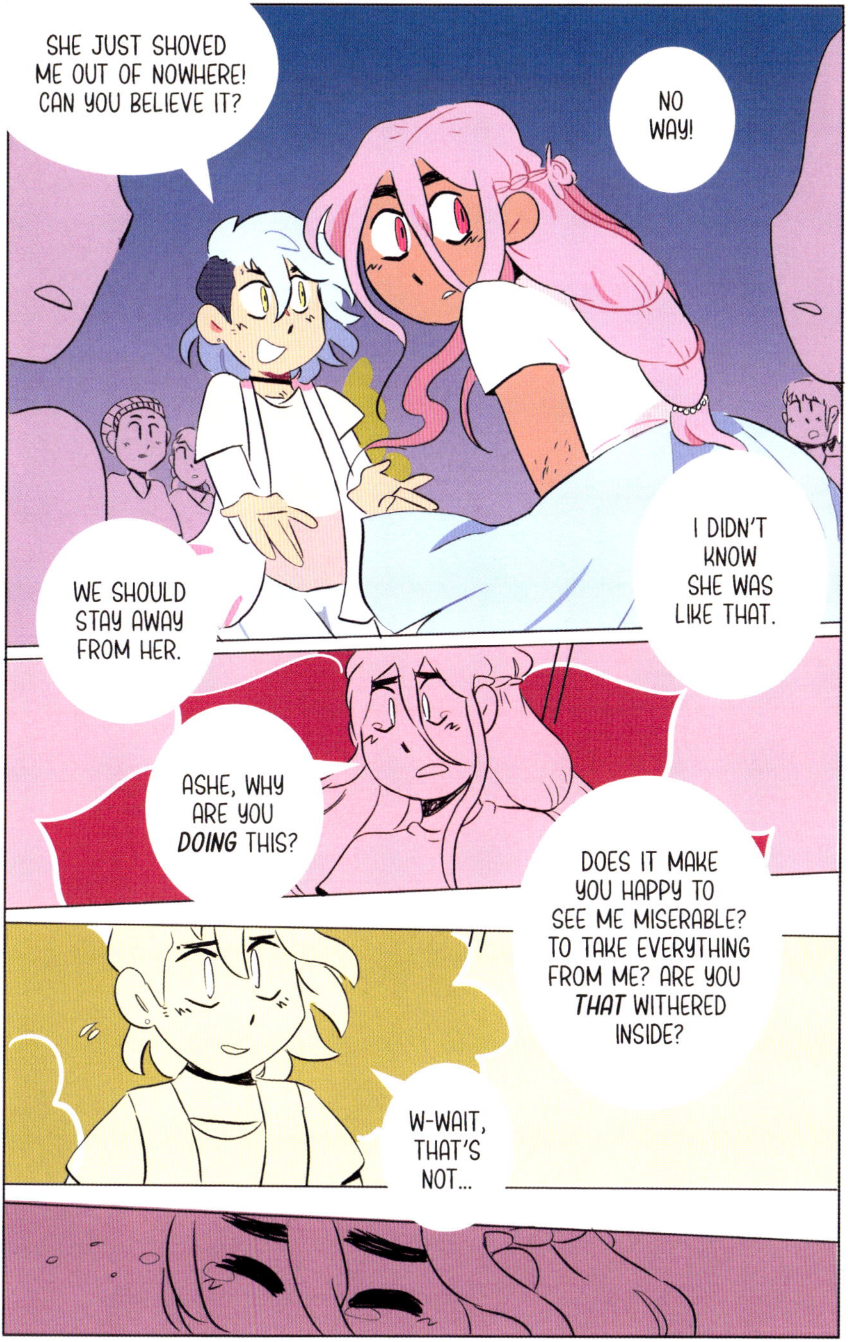
SHE JUST SHOVED ME OUT OF NOWHERE! CAN YOU BELIEVE IT?
NO WAY!
WE SHOULD STAY AWAY FROM HER.
I DIDN'T KNOW SHE WAS LIKE THAT.
ASHE, WHY ARE YOU *DOING* THIS?
DOES IT MAKE YOU HAPPY TO SEE ME MISERABLE? TO TAKE EVERYTHING FROM ME? ARE YOU *THAT* WITHERED INSIDE?
W-WAIT, THAT'S NOT...

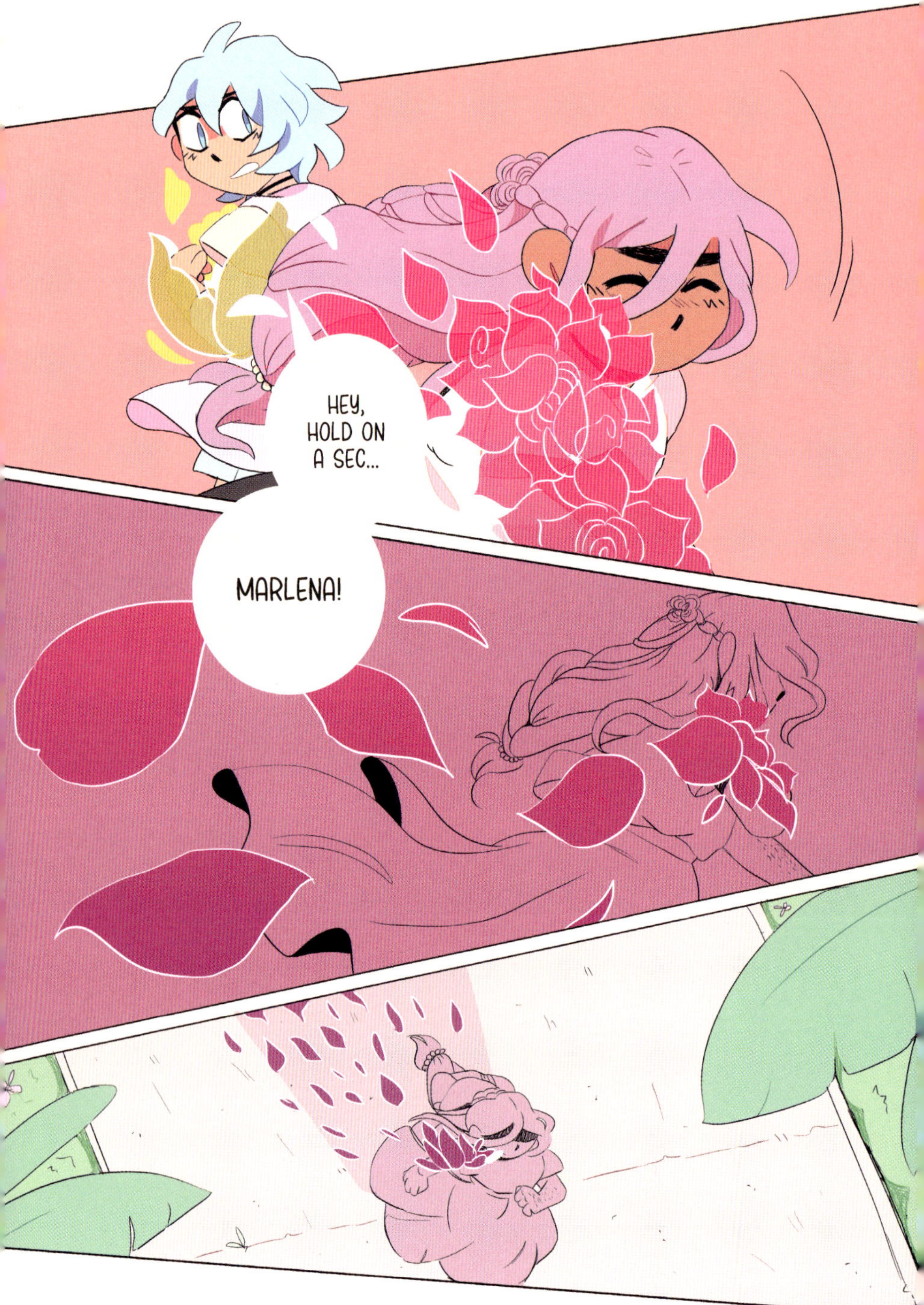
HEY, HOLD ON A SEC...
MARLENA!

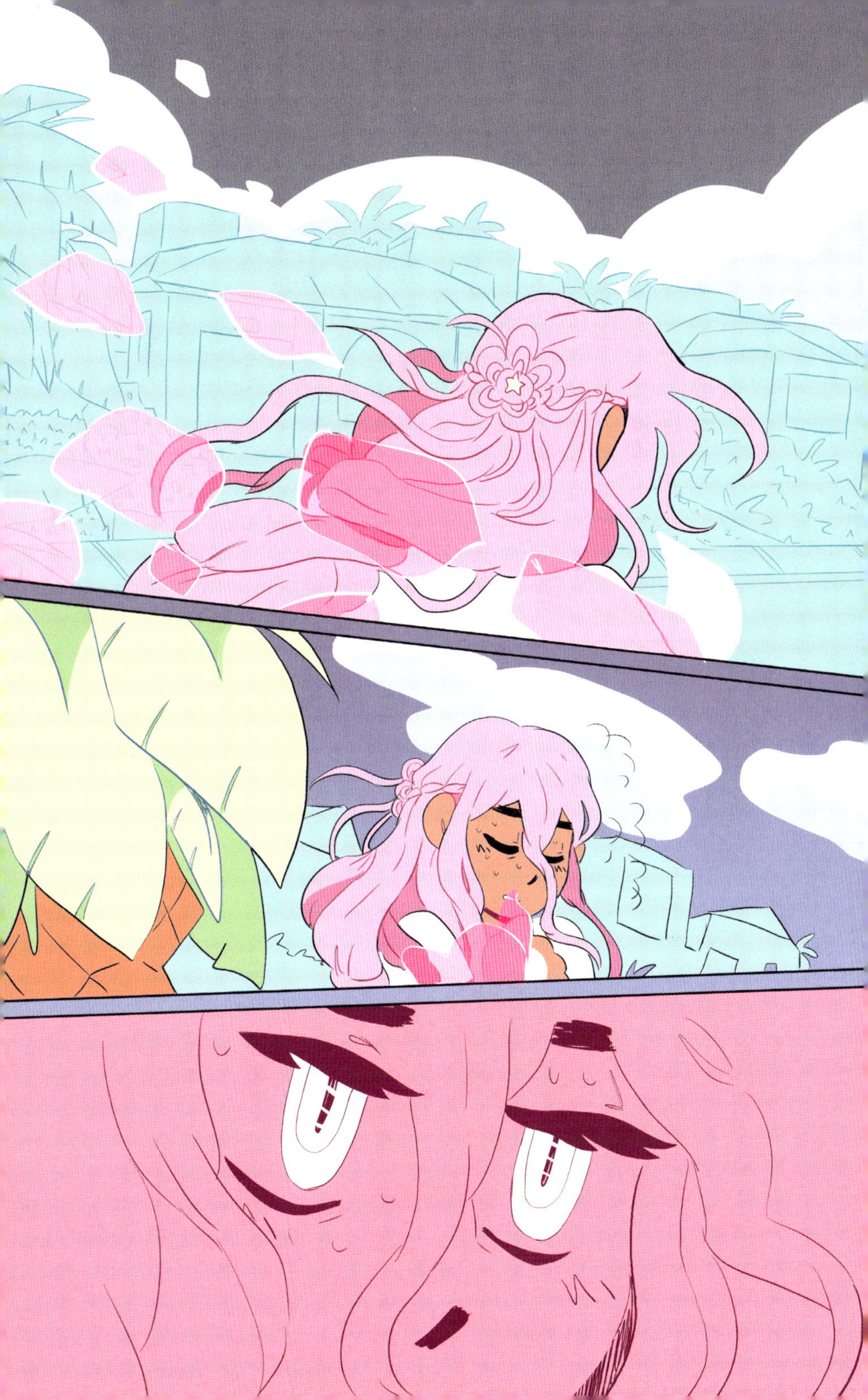

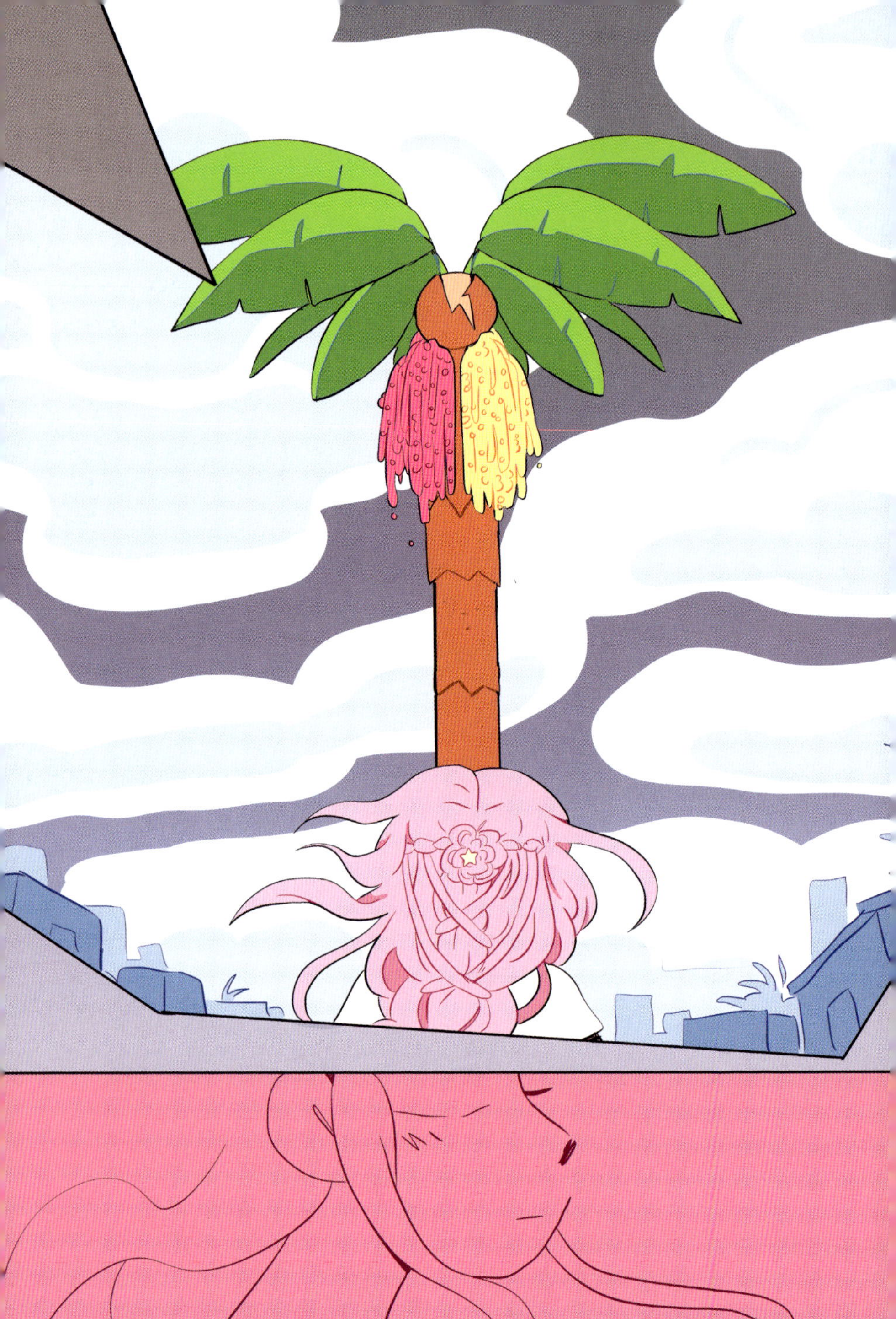

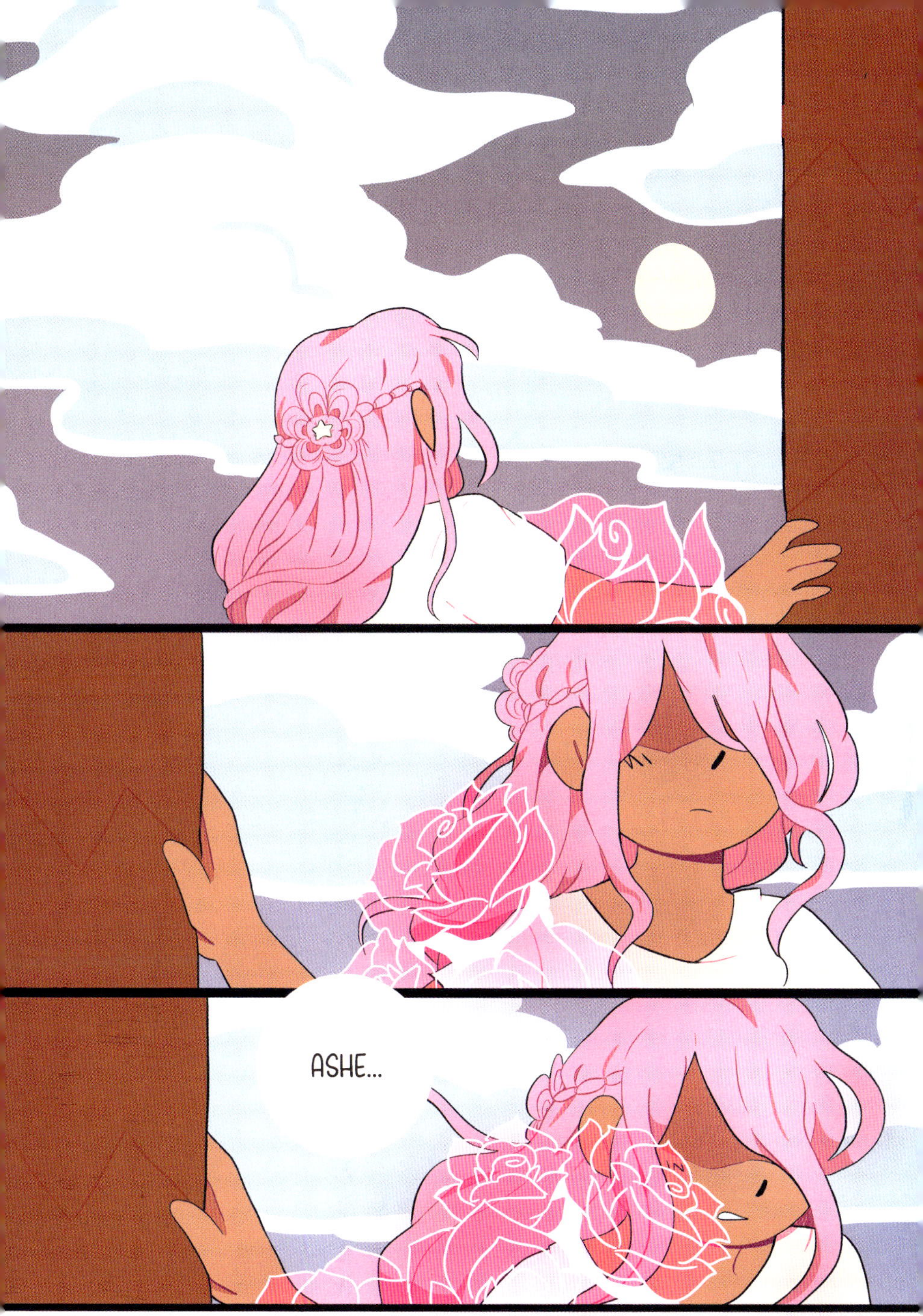
ASHE...

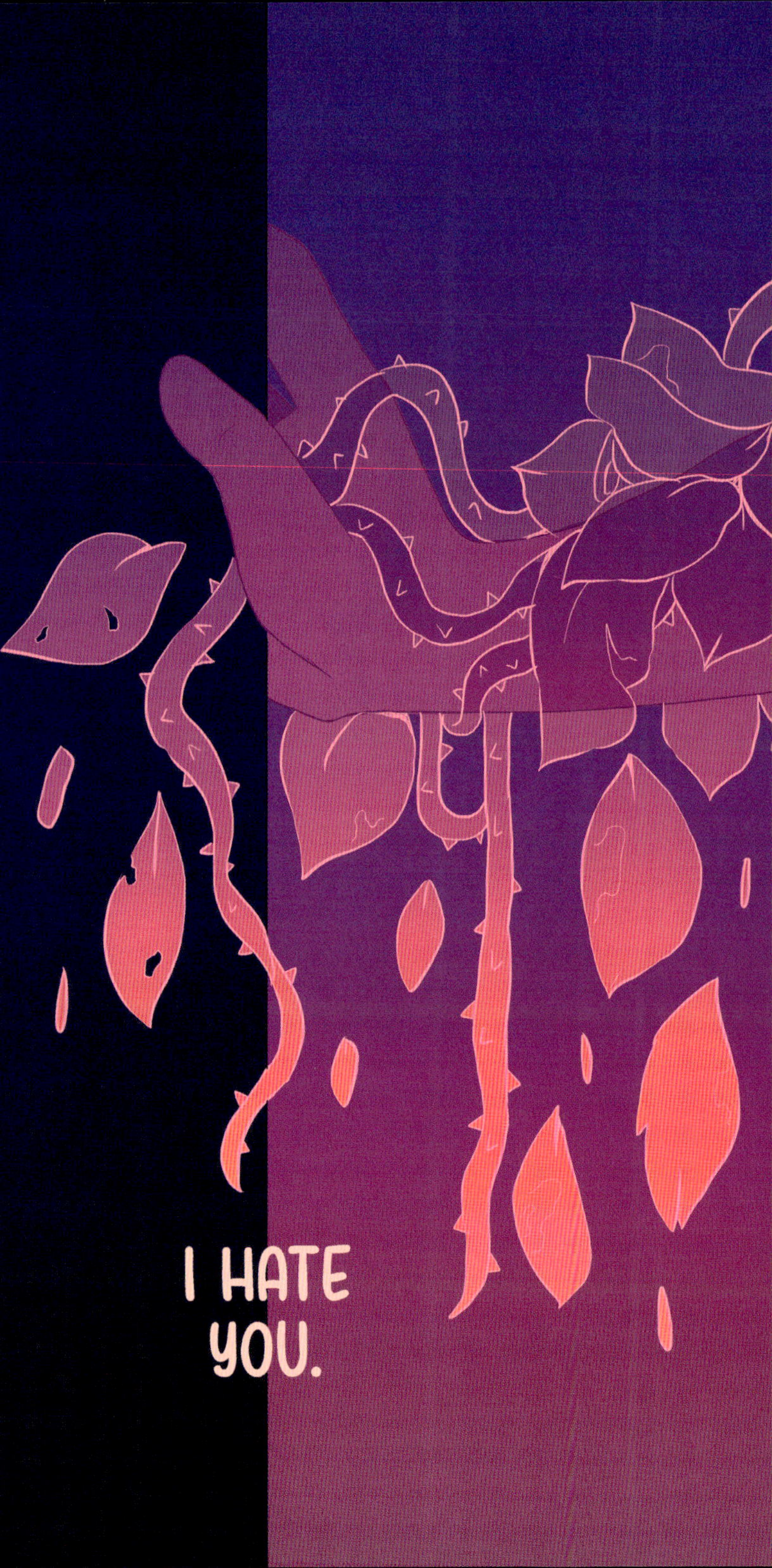
I HATE YOU.

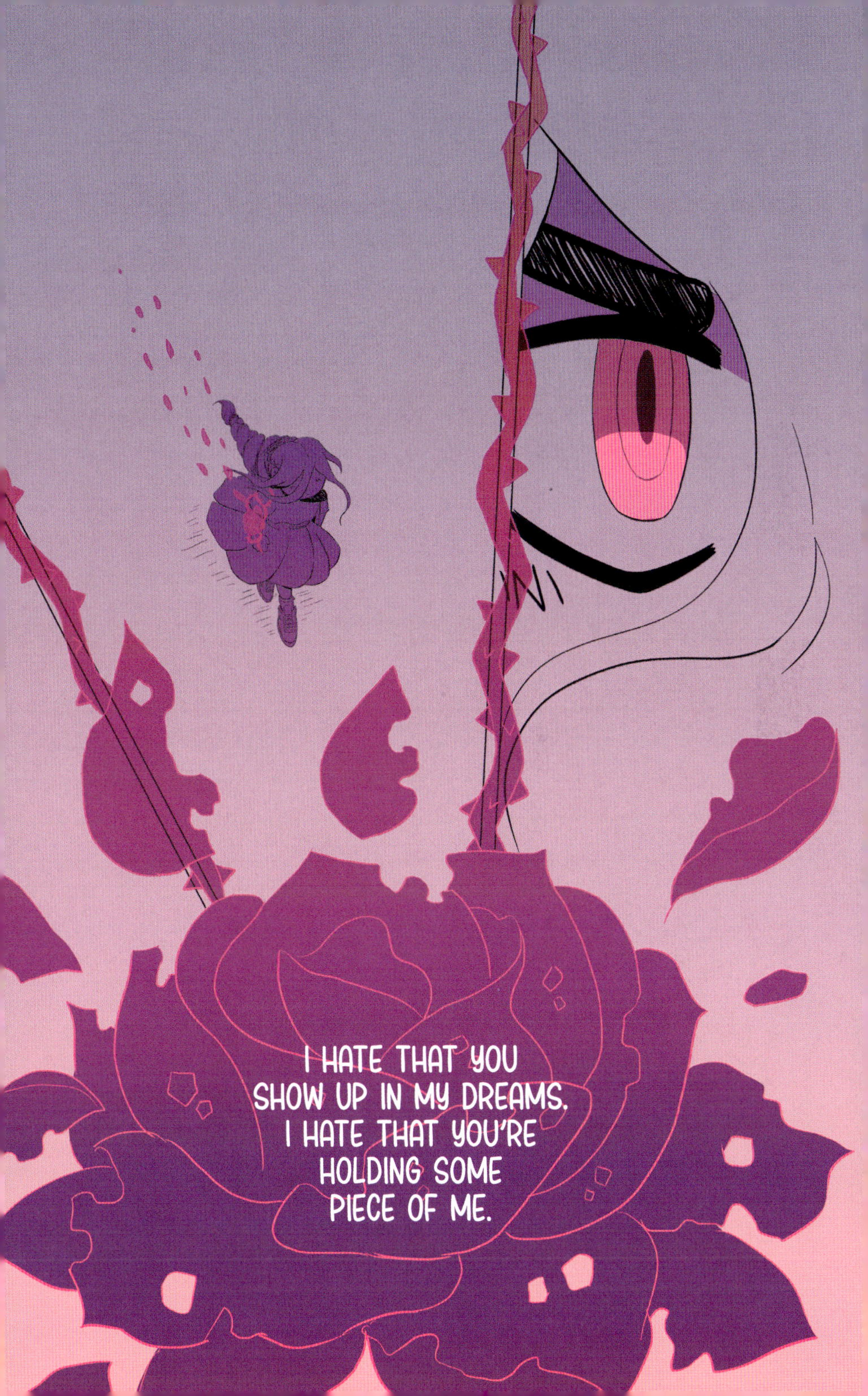
I HATE THAT YOU SHOW UP IN MY DREAMS. I HATE THAT YOU'RE HOLDING SOME PIECE OF ME.

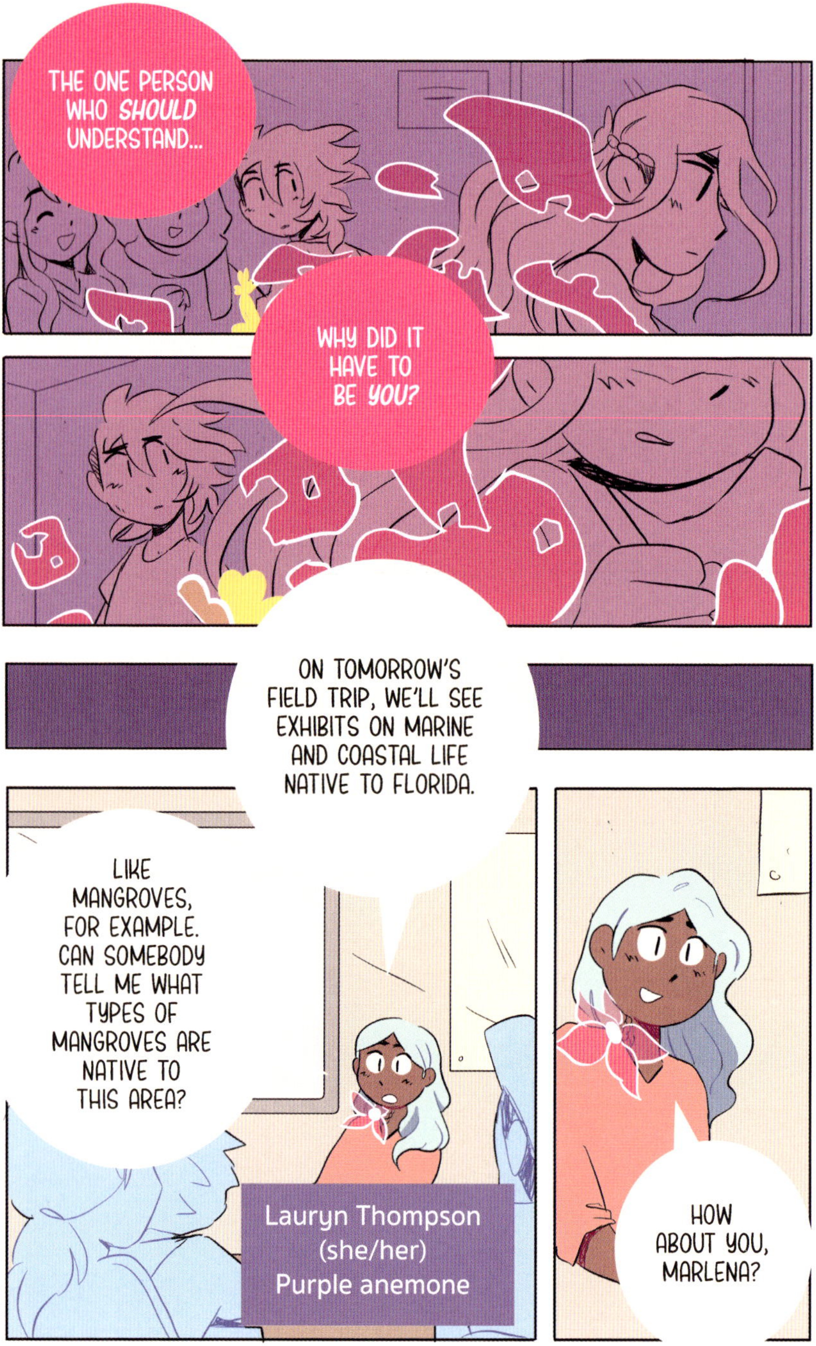
THE ONE PERSON WHO *SHOULD* UNDERSTAND...
WHY DID IT HAVE TO BE *YOU?*
ON TOMORROW'S FIELD TRIP, WE'LL SEE EXHIBITS ON MARINE AND COASTAL LIFE NATIVE TO FLORIDA.
LIKE MANGROVES, FOR EXAMPLE. CAN SOMEBODY TELL ME WHAT TYPES OF MANGROVES ARE NATIVE TO THIS AREA?
Lauryn Thompson (she/her) Purple anemone
HOW ABOUT YOU, MARLENA?

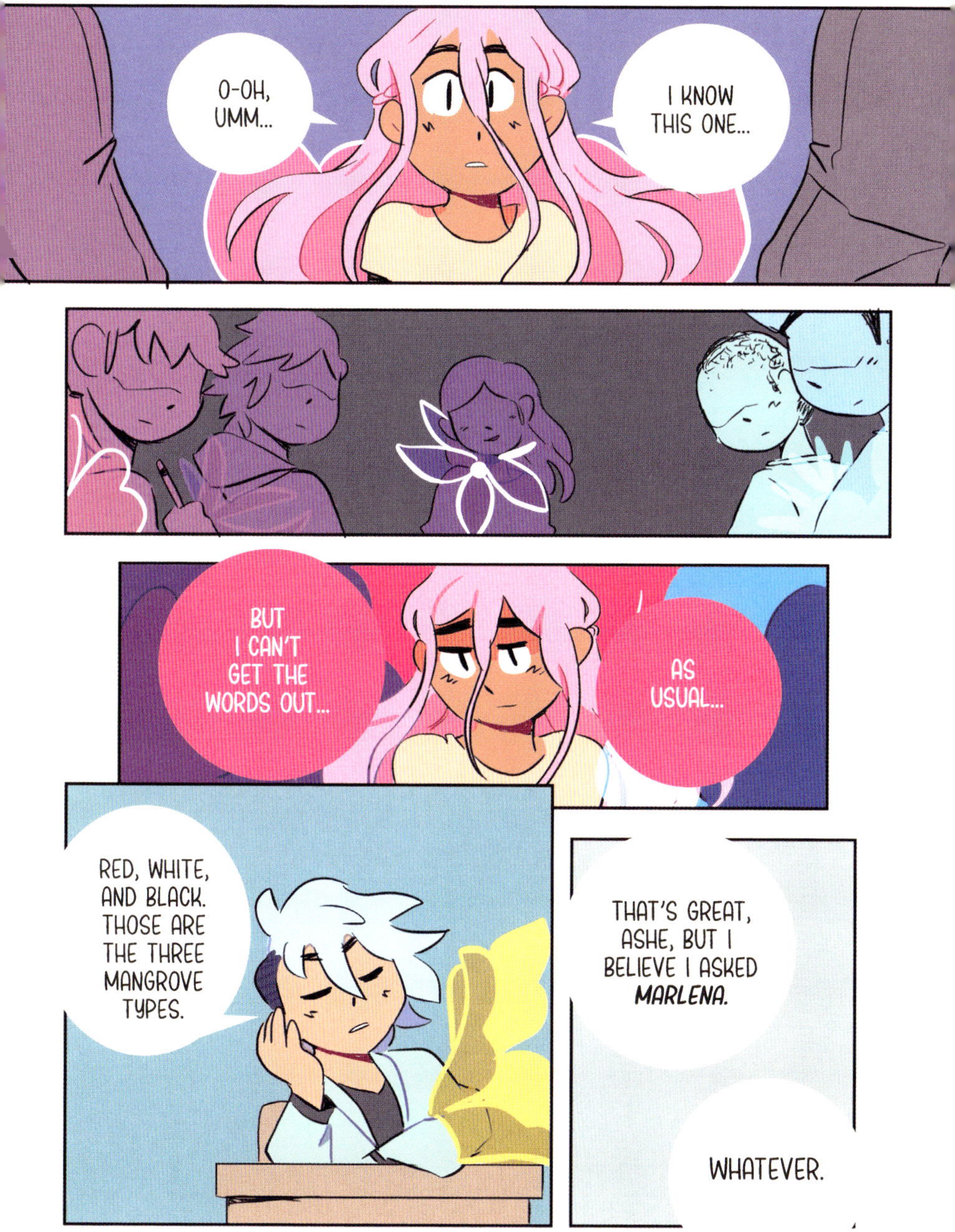
O-OH, UMM...
I KNOW THIS ONE...
BUT I CAN'T GET THE WORDS OUT...
AS USUAL...
RED, WHITE, AND BLACK. THOSE ARE THE THREE MANGROVE TYPES.
THAT'S GREAT, ASHE, BUT I BELIEVE I ASKED **MARLENA.**
WHATEVER.

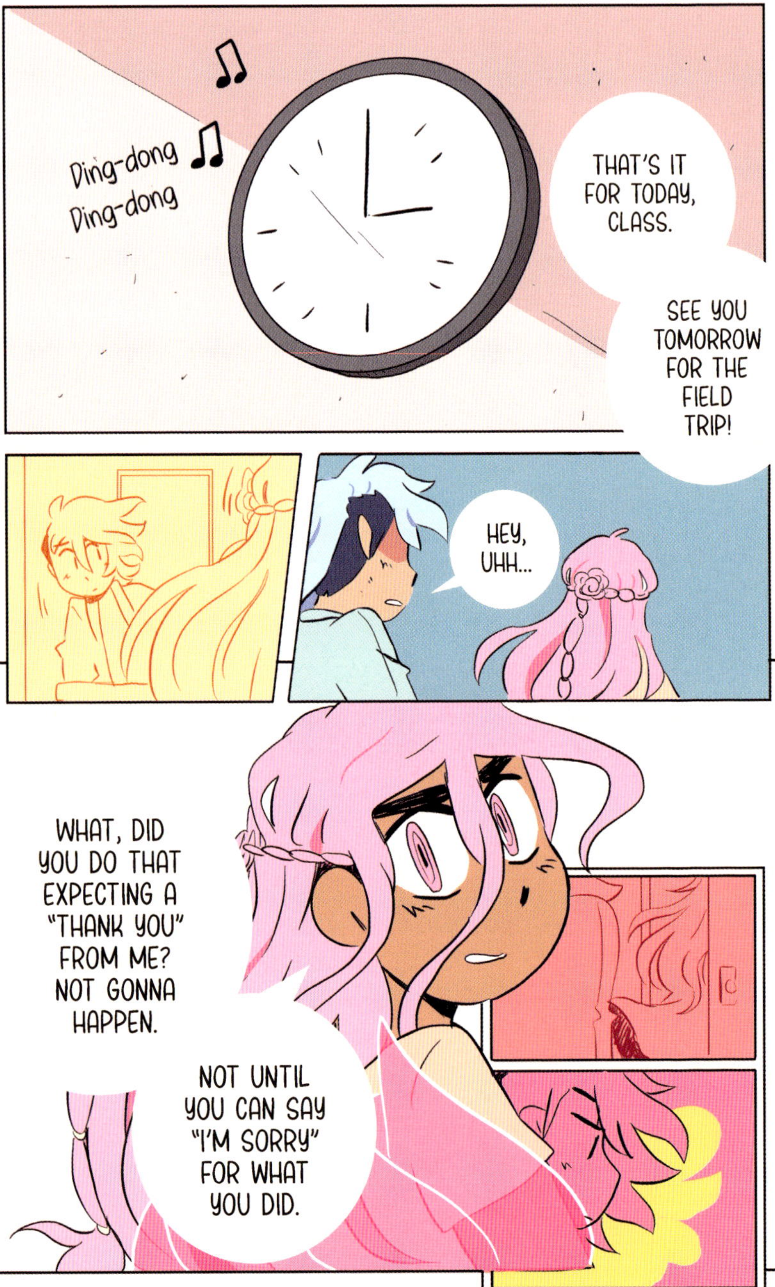
Ding-dong
Ding-dong
THAT'S IT FOR TODAY, CLASS.
SEE YOU TOMORROW FOR THE FIELD TRIP!
HEY, UHH...
WHAT, DID YOU DO THAT EXPECTING A "THANK YOU" FROM ME? NOT GONNA HAPPEN.
NOT UNTIL YOU CAN SAY "I'M SORRY" FOR WHAT YOU DID.

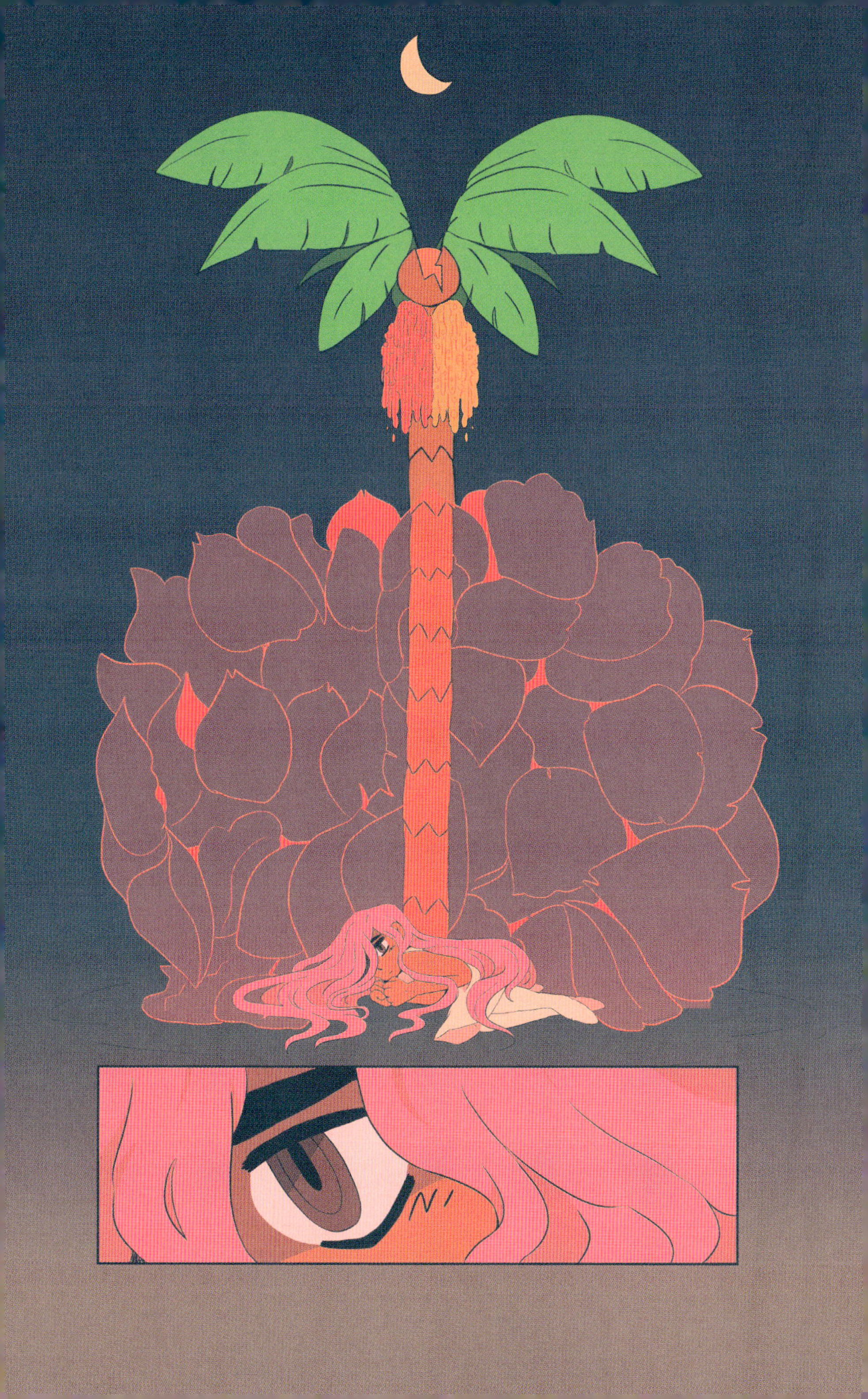

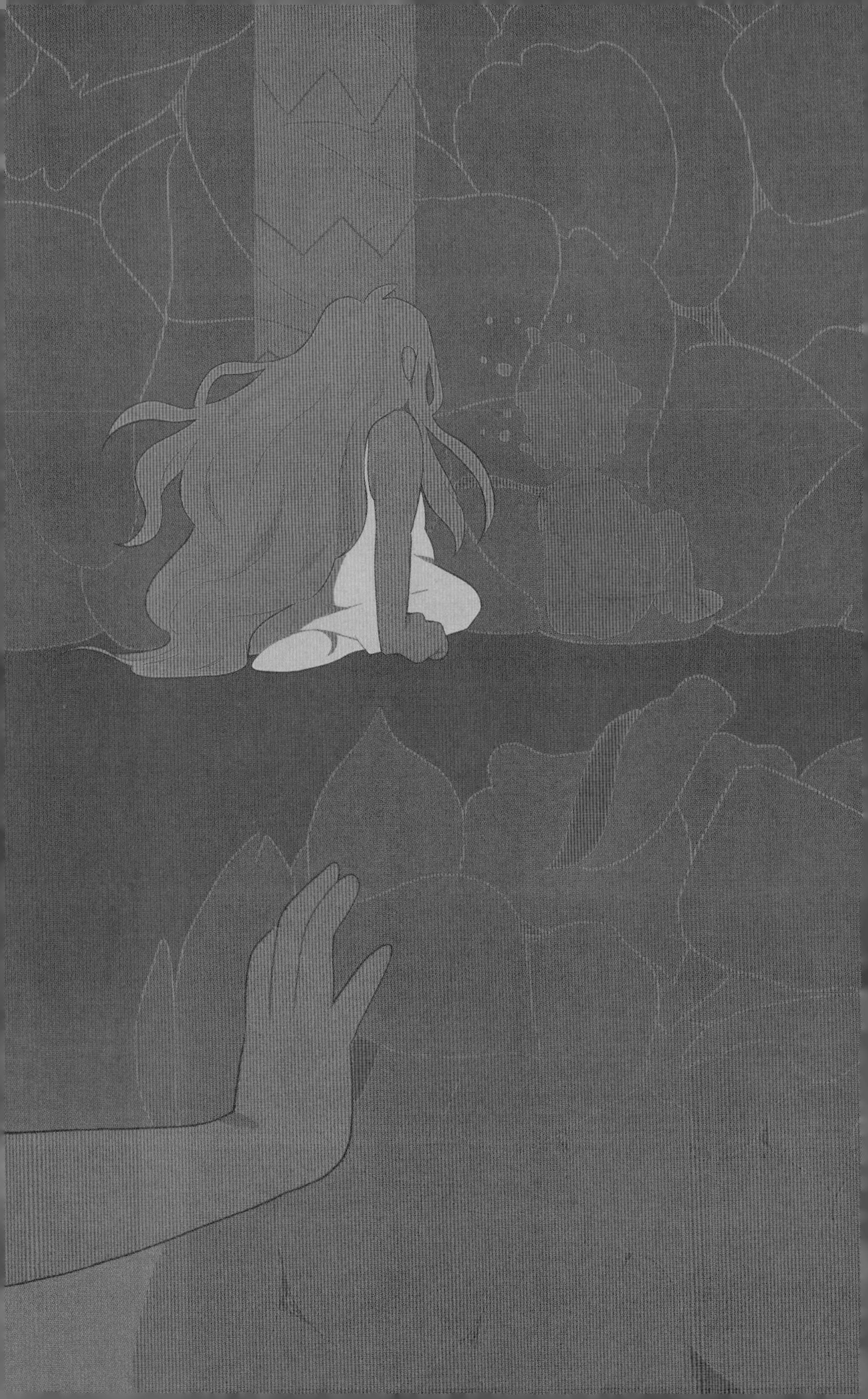

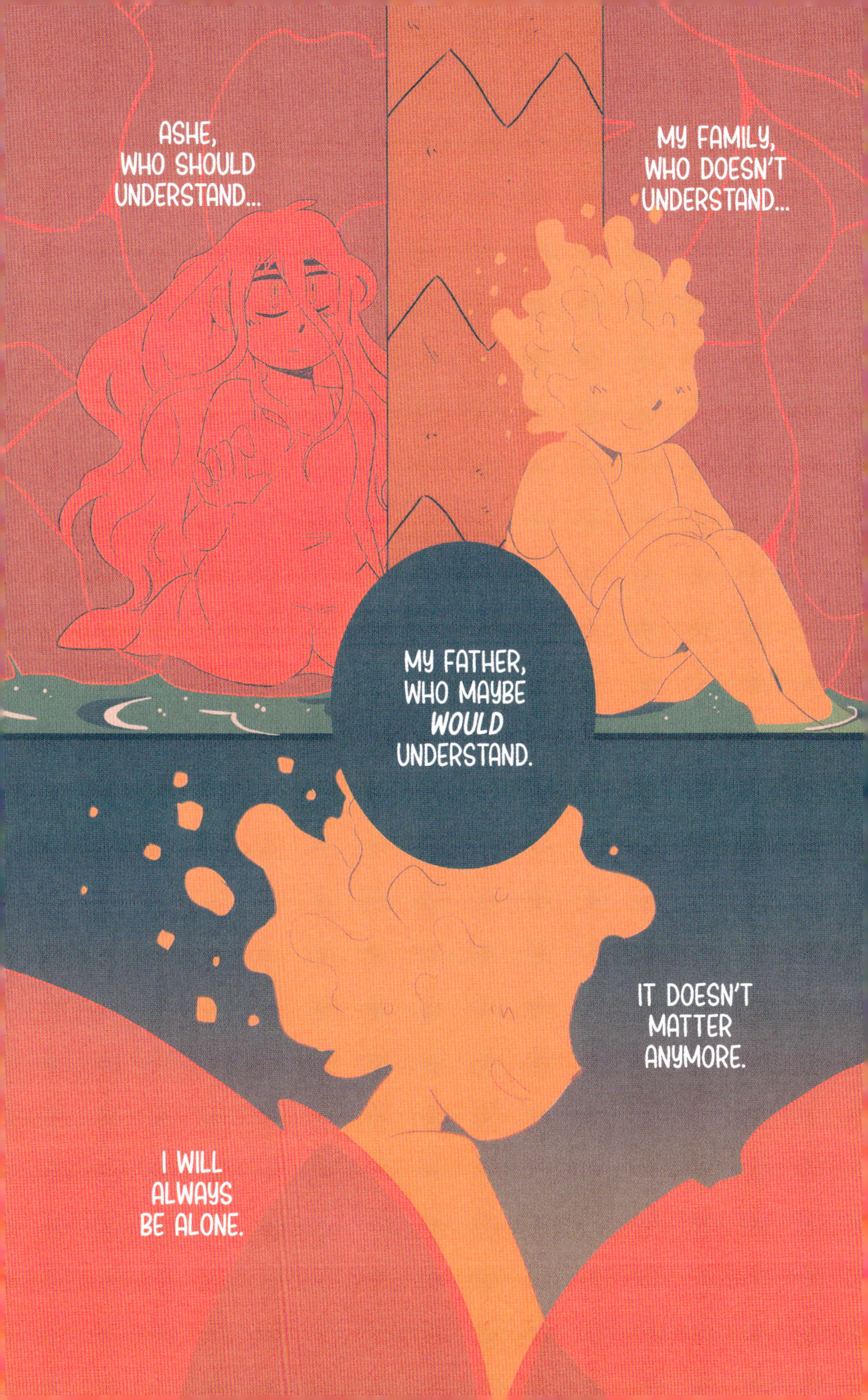
ASHE, WHO SHOULD UNDERSTAND...
MY FAMILY, WHO DOESN'T UNDERSTAND...
MY FATHER, WHO MAYBE *WOULD* UNDERSTAND.
IT DOESN'T MATTER ANYMORE.
I WILL ALWAYS BE ALONE.

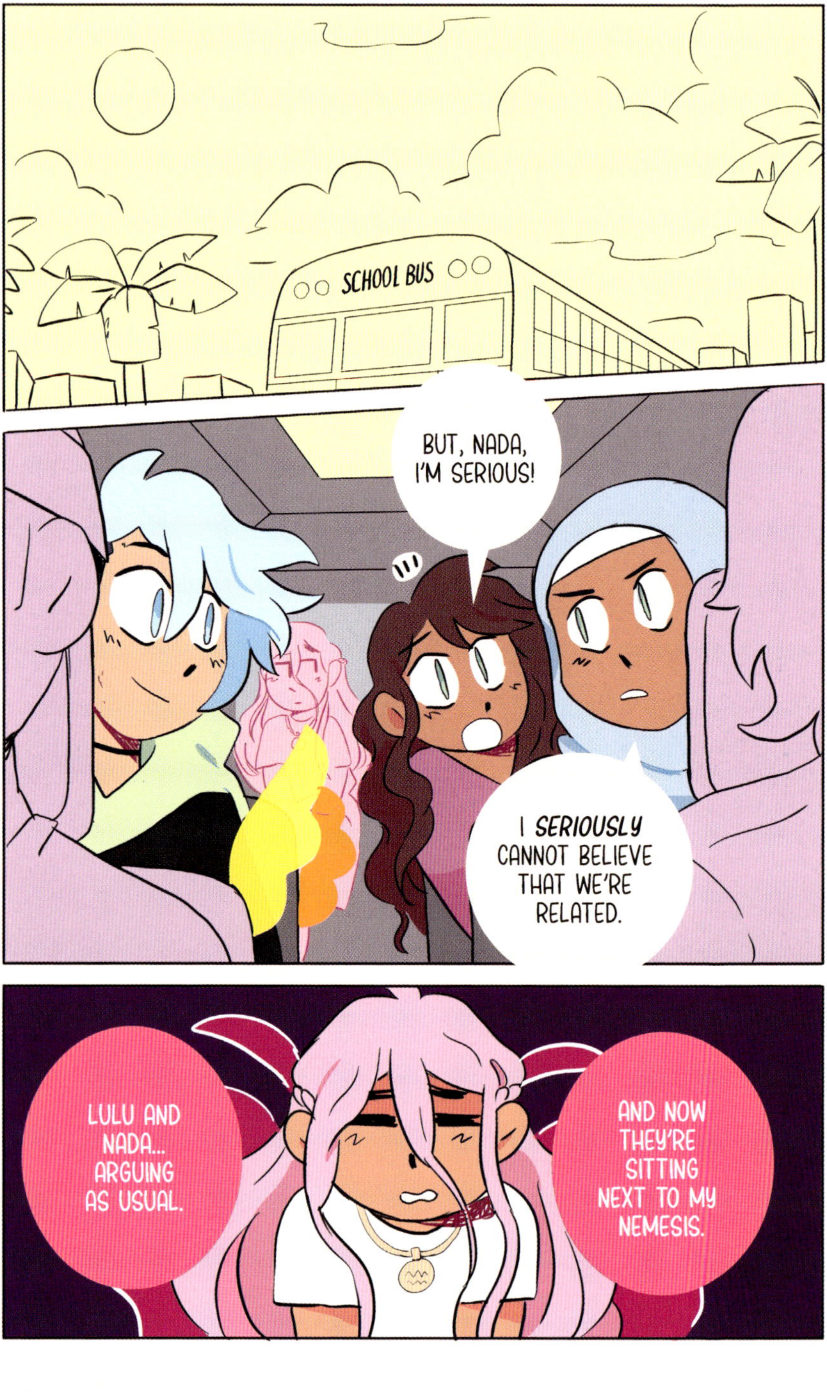
SCHOOL BUS
BUT, NADA, I'M SERIOUS!
I *SERIOUSLY* CANNOT BELIEVE THAT WE'RE RELATED.
LULU AND NADA... ARGUING AS USUAL.
AND NOW THEY'RE SITTING NEXT TO MY NEMESIS.

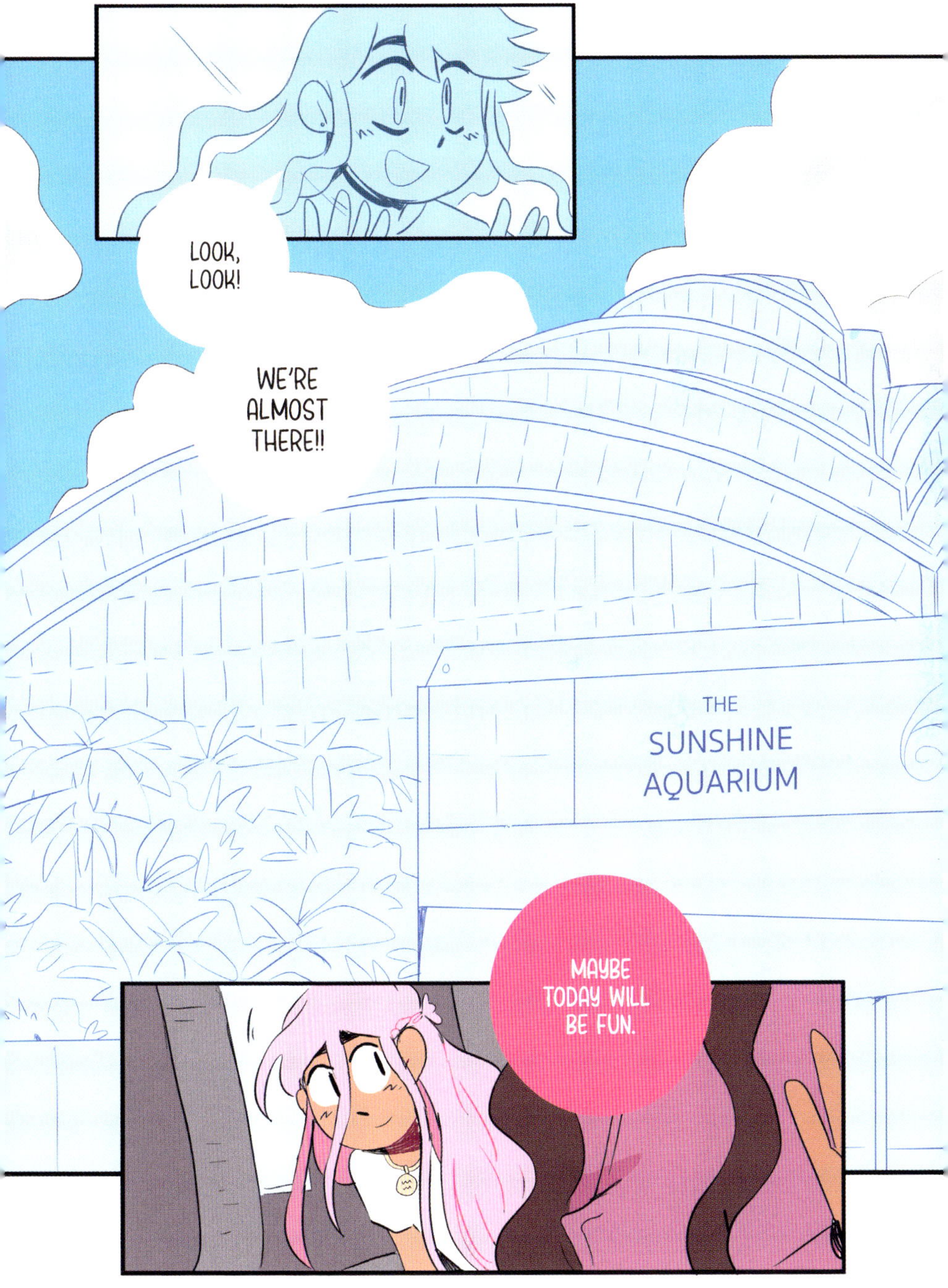
LOOK, LOOK!
WE'RE ALMOST THERE!!
THE SUNSHINE AQUARIUM
MAYBE TODAY WILL BE FUN.

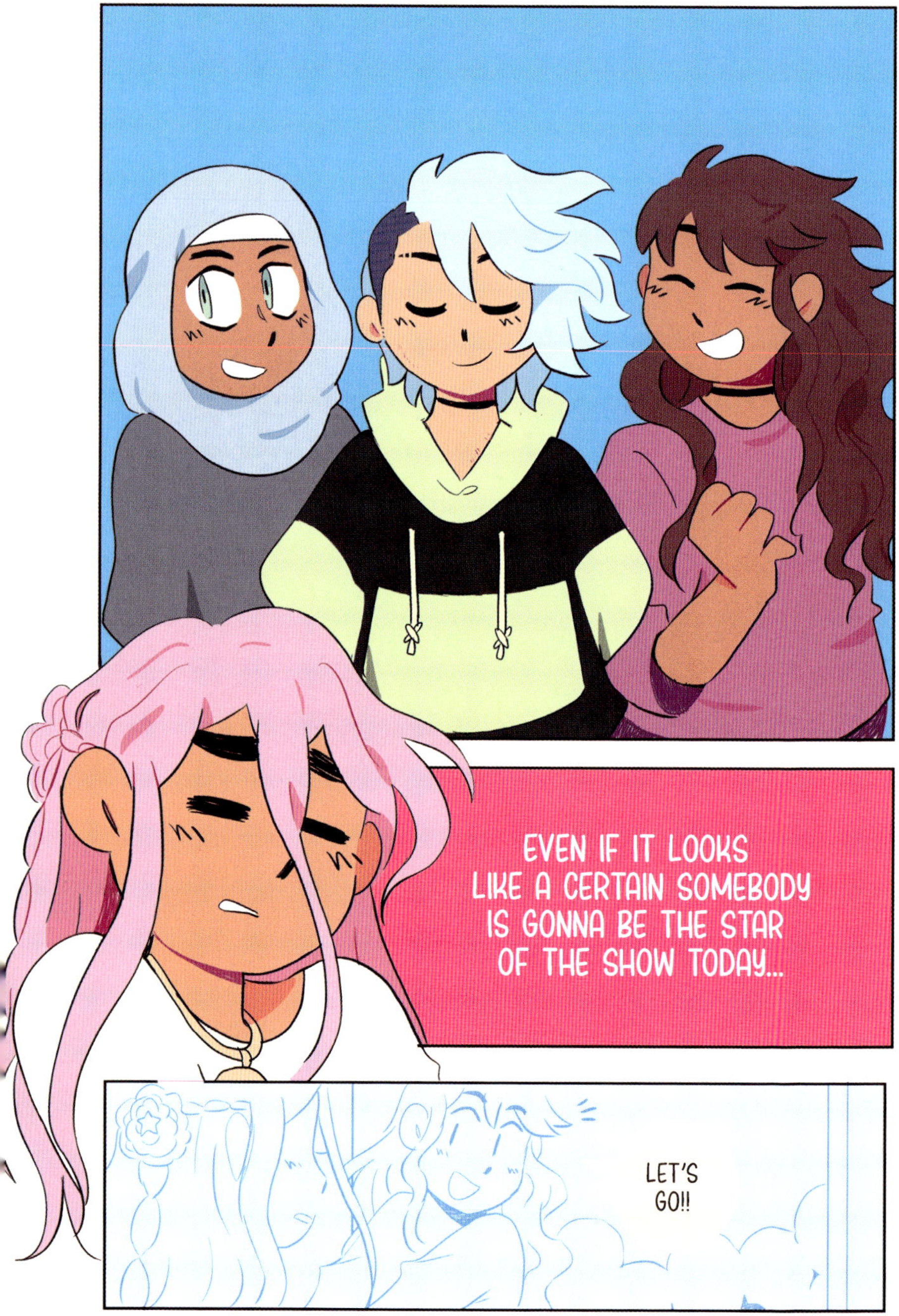
EVEN IF IT LOOKS LIKE A CERTAIN SOMEBODY IS GONNA BE THE STAR OF THE SHOW TODAY...
LET'S GO!!

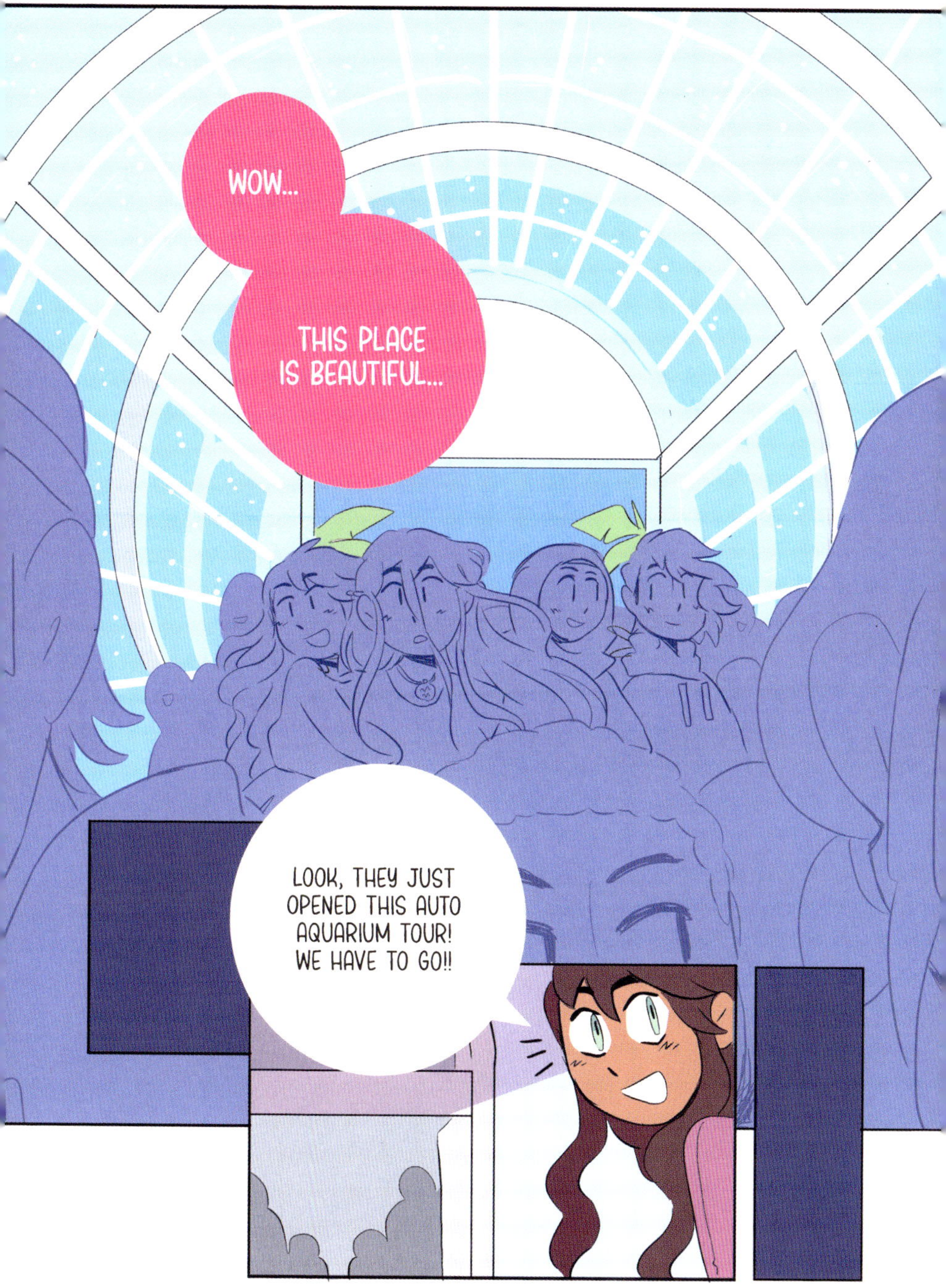
WOW...
THIS PLACE IS BEAUTIFUL...
LOOK, THEY JUST OPENED THIS AUTO AQUARIUM TOUR! WE HAVE TO GO!!

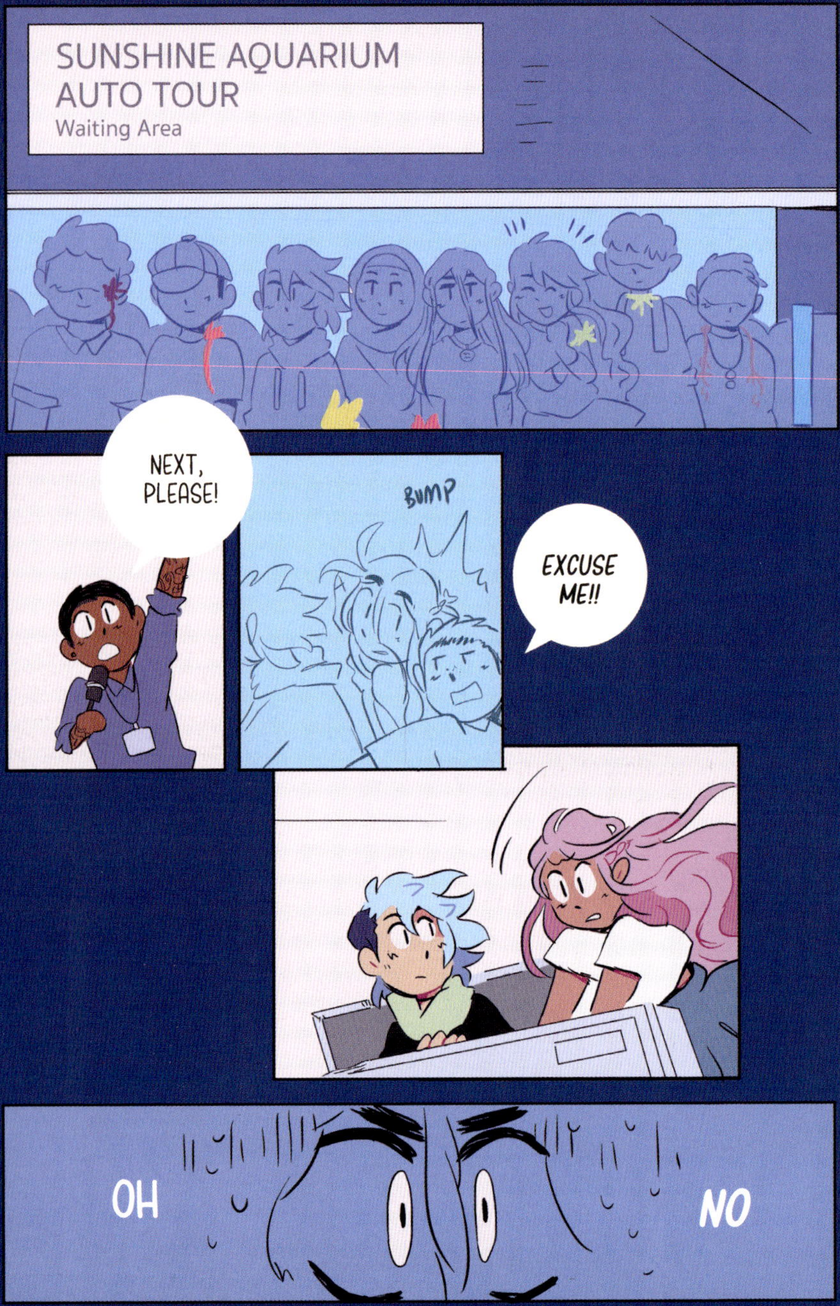
SUNSHINE AQUARIUM
AUTO TOUR
Waiting Area
NEXT, PLEASE!
BUMP
EXCUSE ME!!
OH
NO

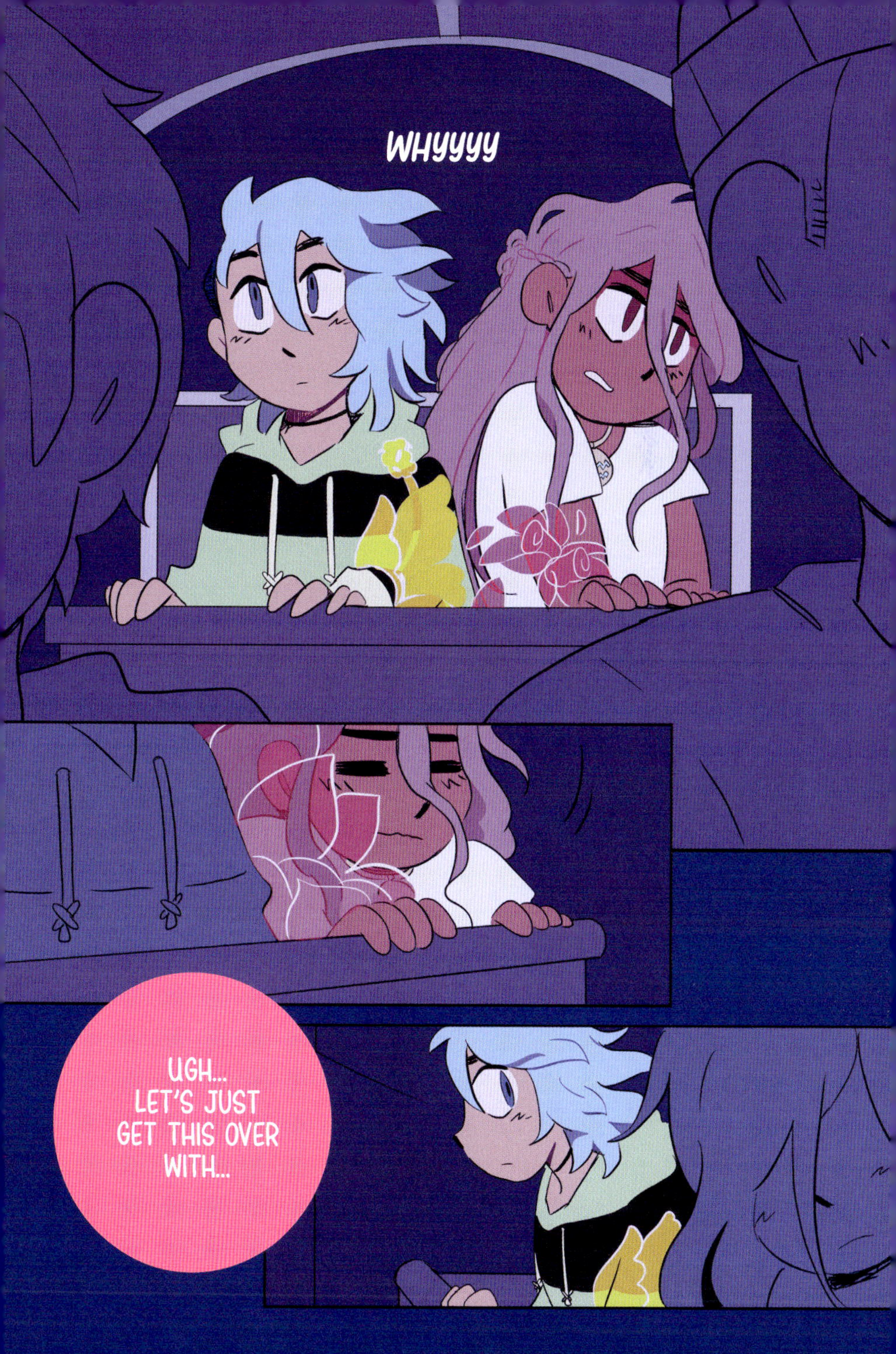
WHYYYY
UGH... LET'S JUST GET THIS OVER WITH...

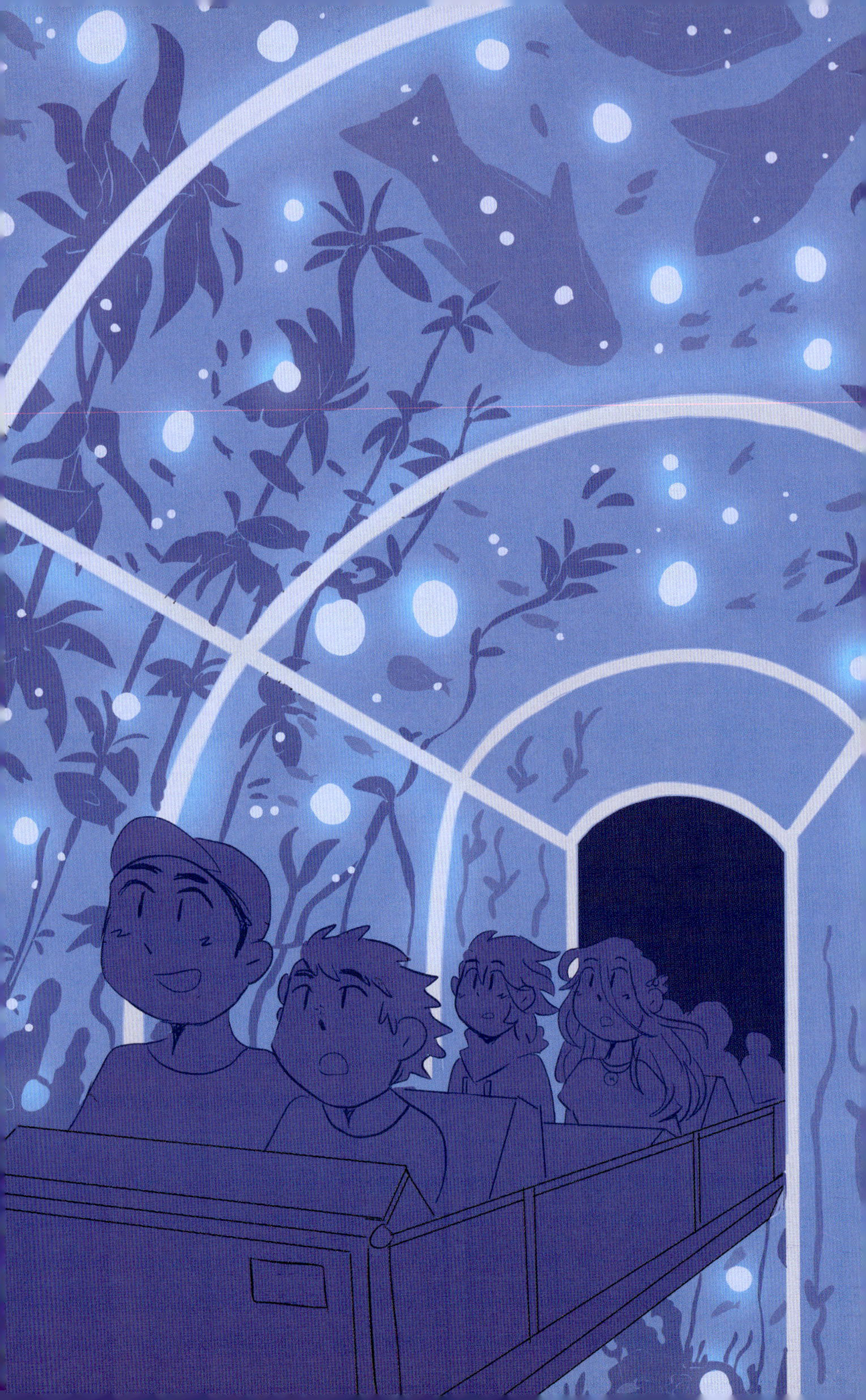

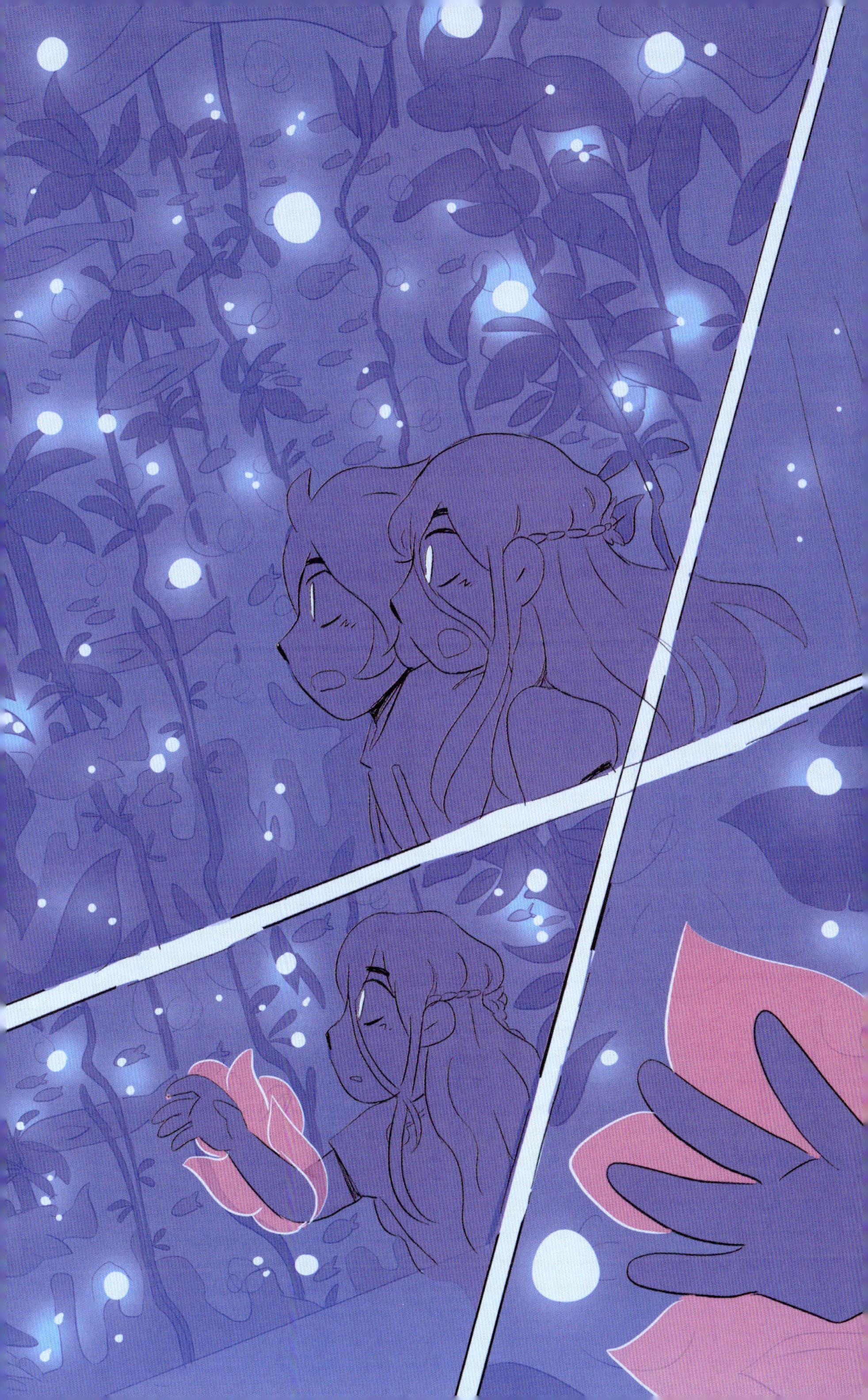

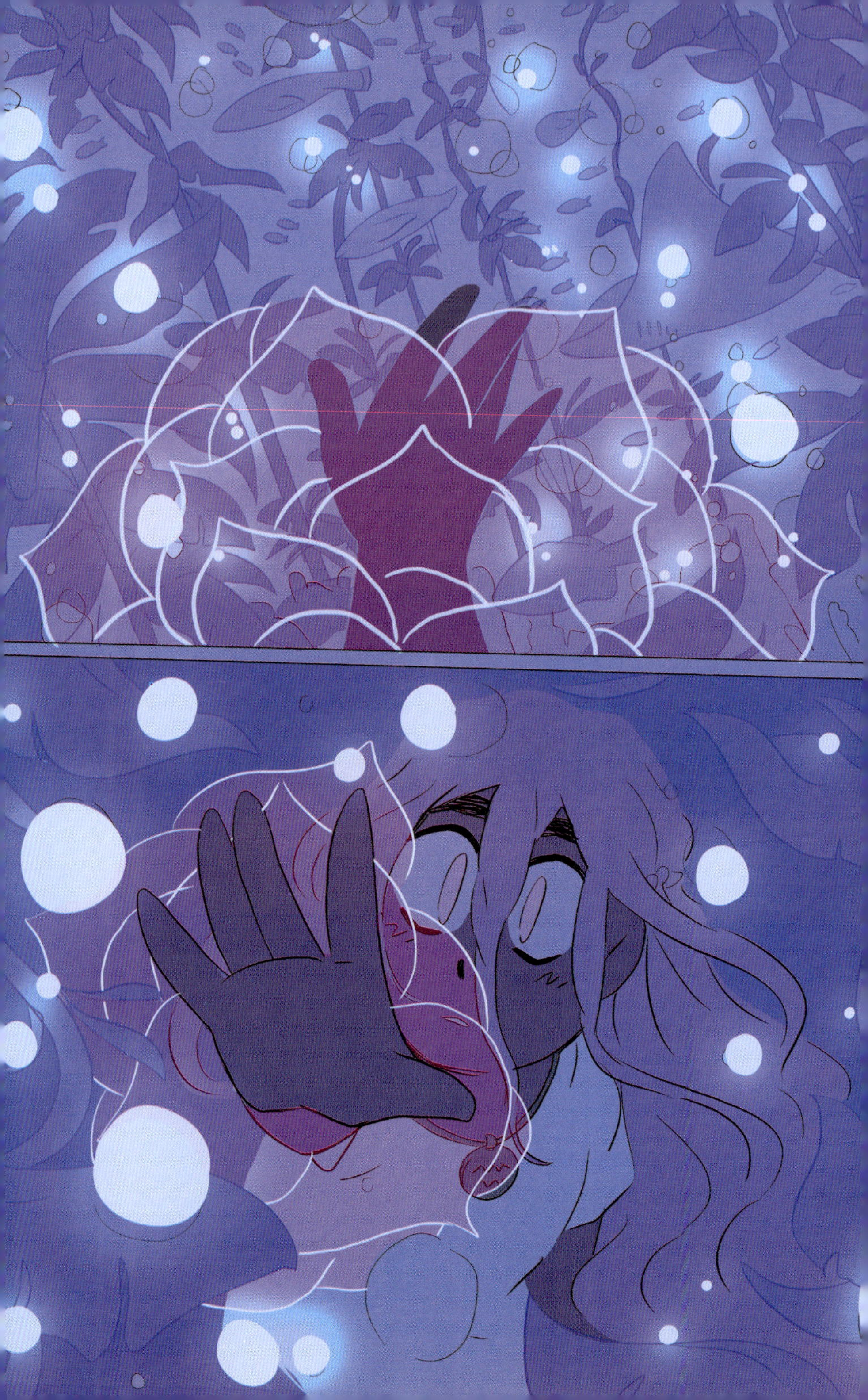

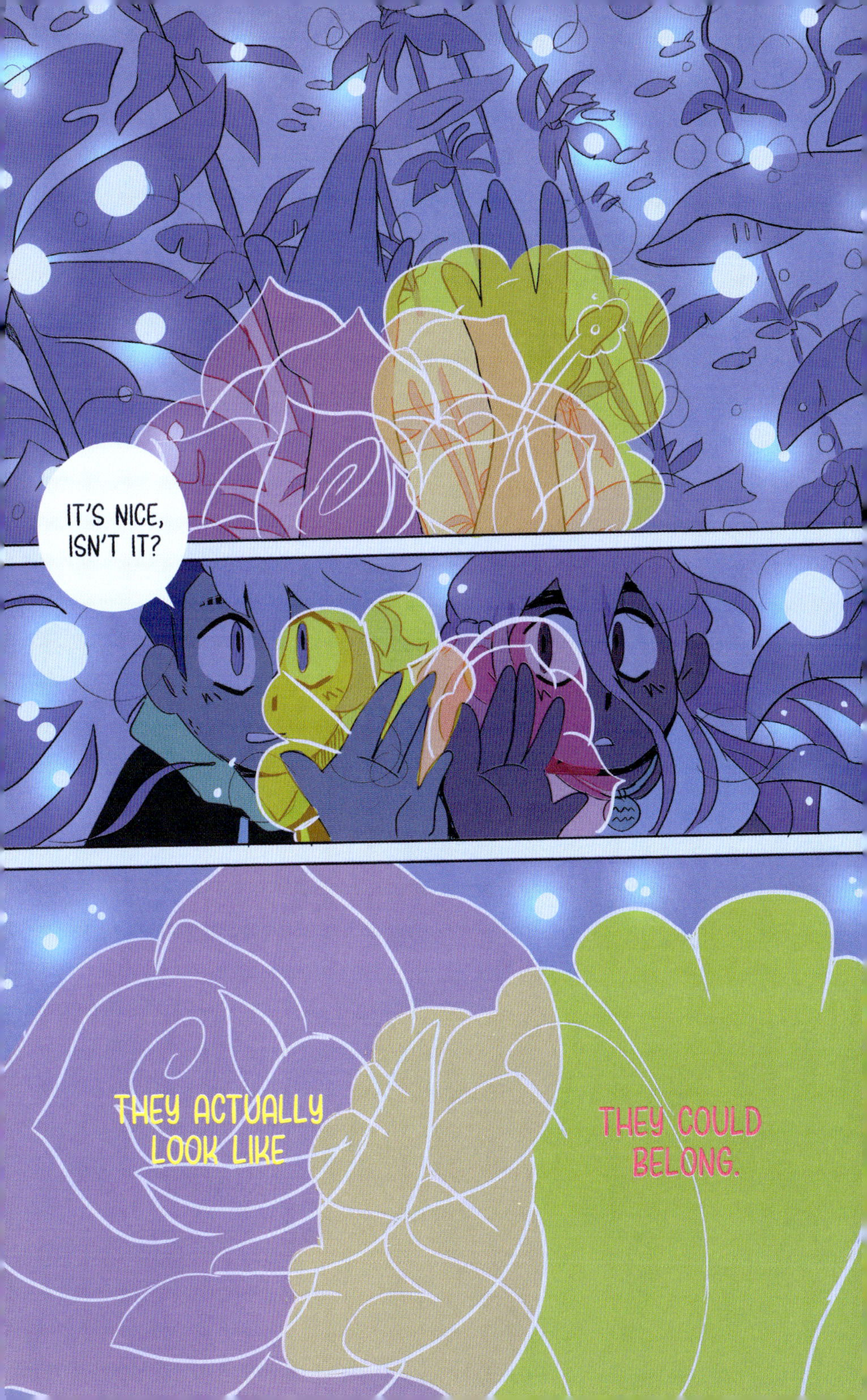
IT'S NICE, ISN'T IT?
THEY ACTUALLY LOOK LIKE
THEY COULD BELONG.

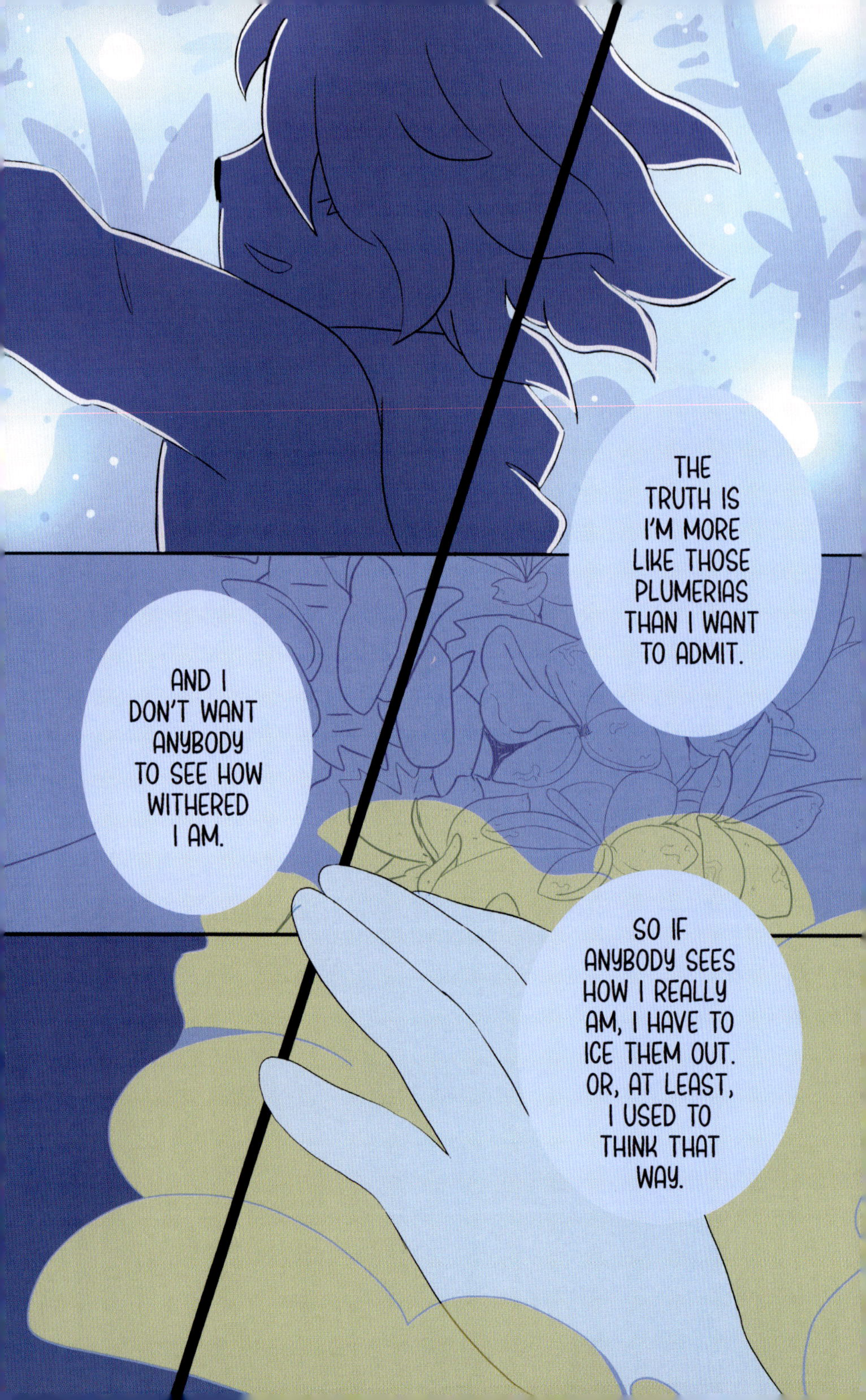
THE TRUTH IS I'M MORE LIKE THOSE PLUMERIAS THAN I WANT TO ADMIT.
AND I DON'T WANT ANYBODY TO SEE HOW WITHERED I AM.
SO IF ANYBODY SEES HOW I REALLY AM, I HAVE TO ICE THEM OUT. OR, AT LEAST, I USED TO THINK THAT WAY.

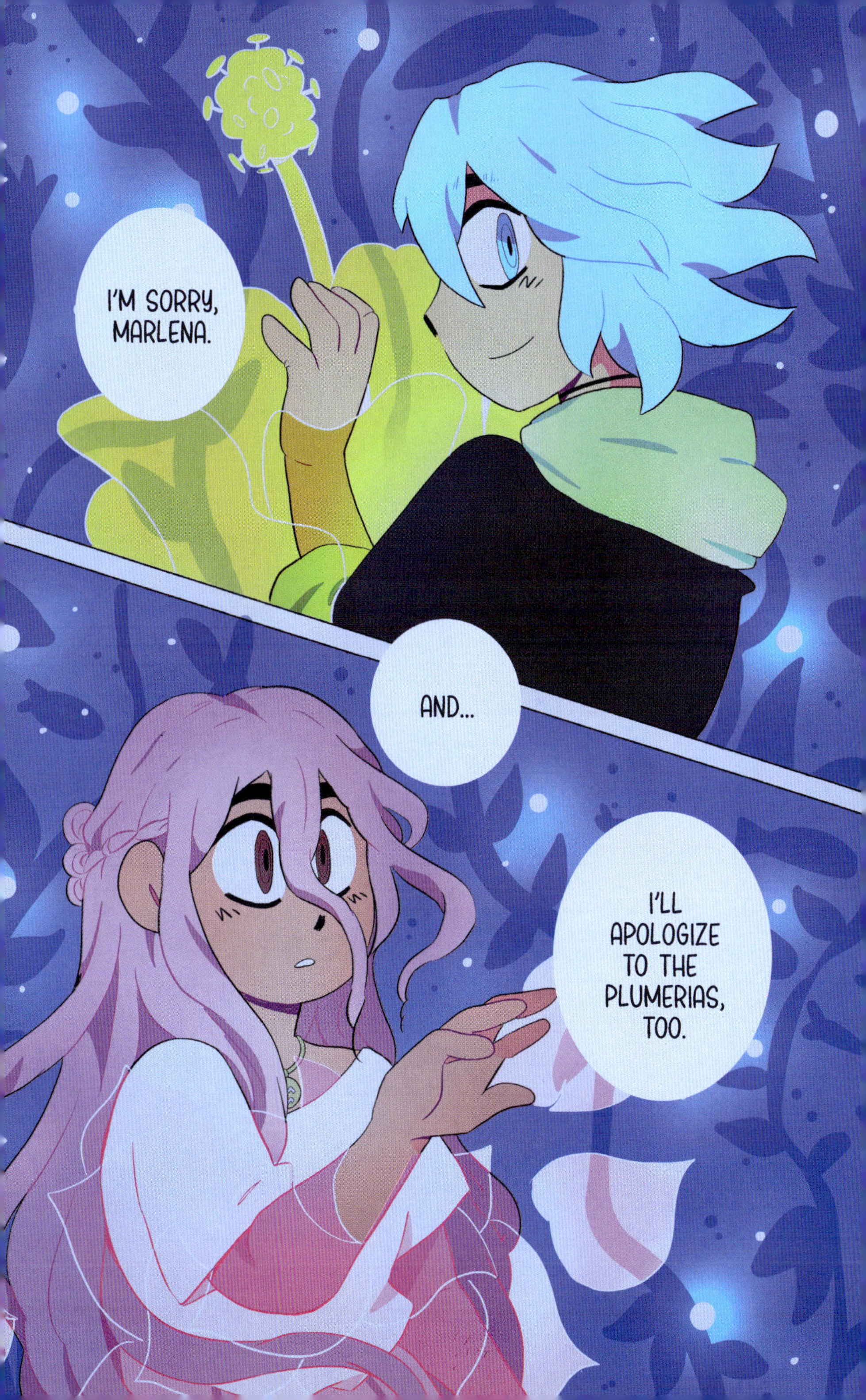
I'M SORRY, MARLENA.
AND...
I'LL APOLOGIZE TO THE PLUMERIAS, TOO.

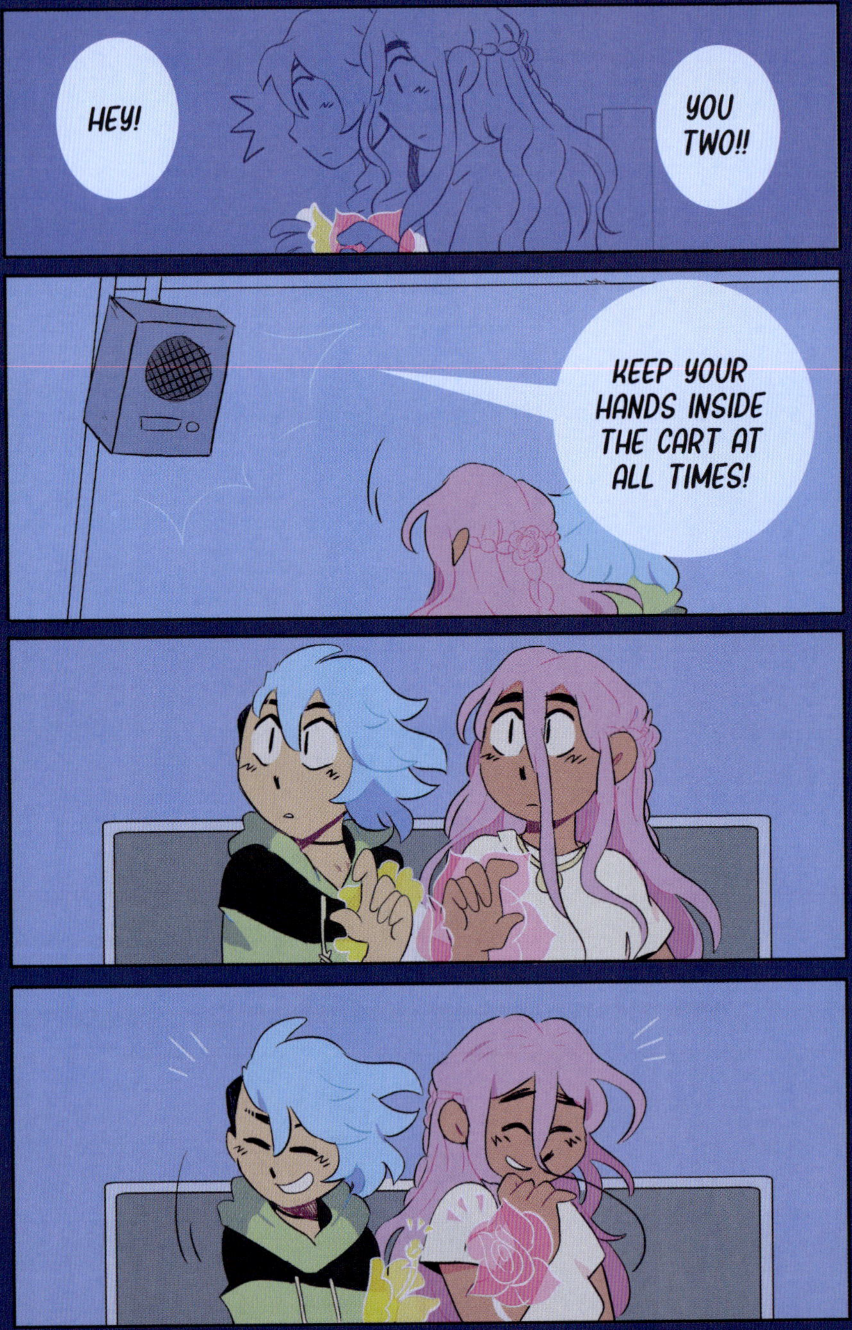
HEY!
YOU TWO!!
KEEP YOUR HANDS INSIDE THE CART AT ALL TIMES!

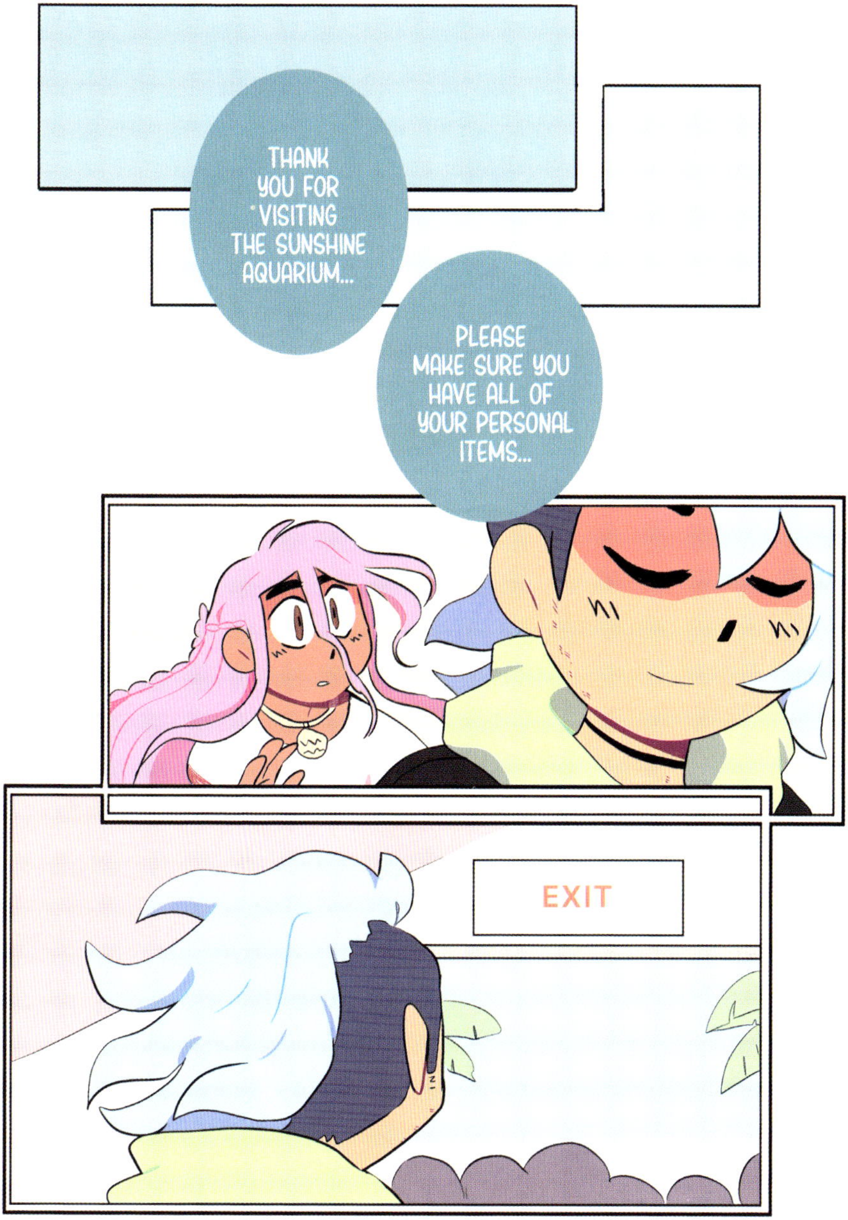
THANK YOU FOR VISITING THE SUNSHINE AQUARIUM...
PLEASE MAKE SURE YOU HAVE ALL OF YOUR PERSONAL ITEMS...
EXIT

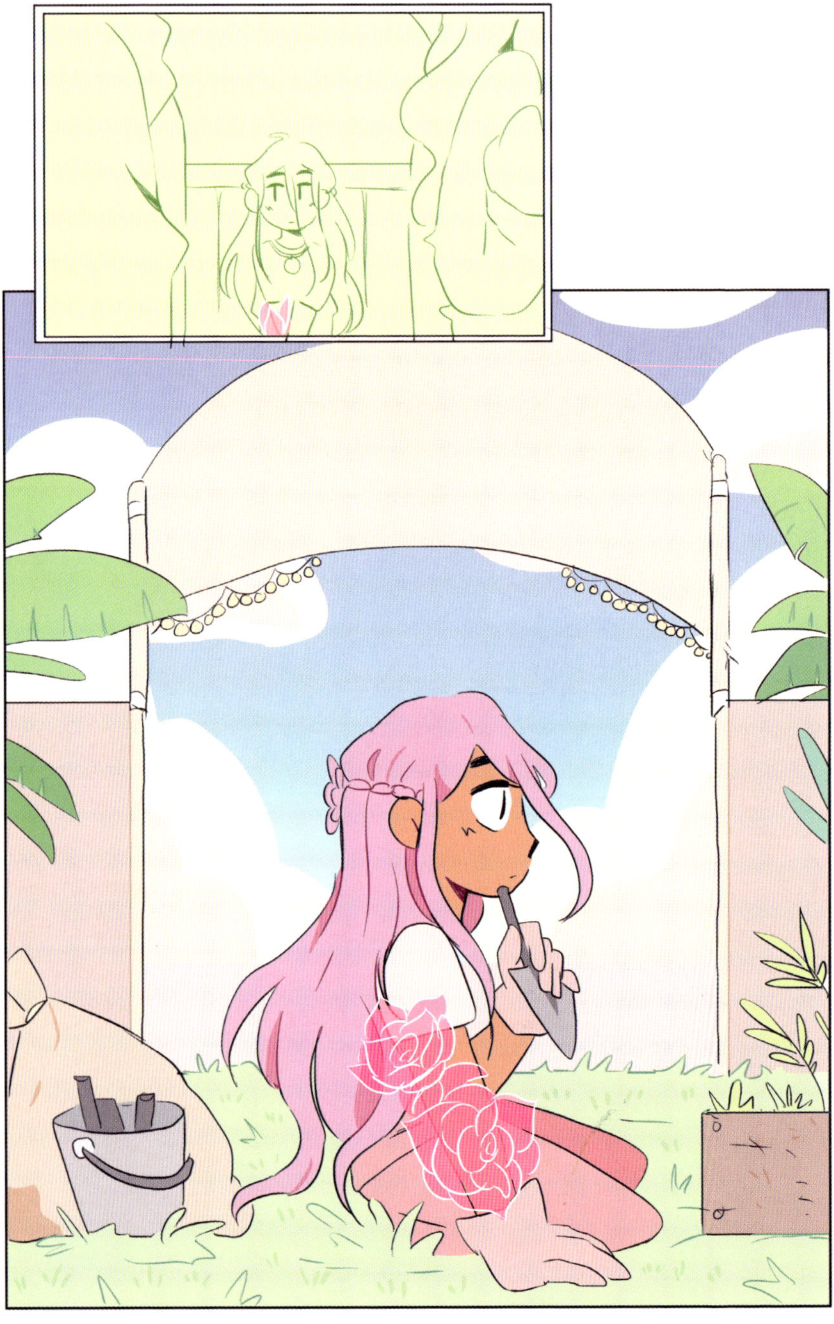

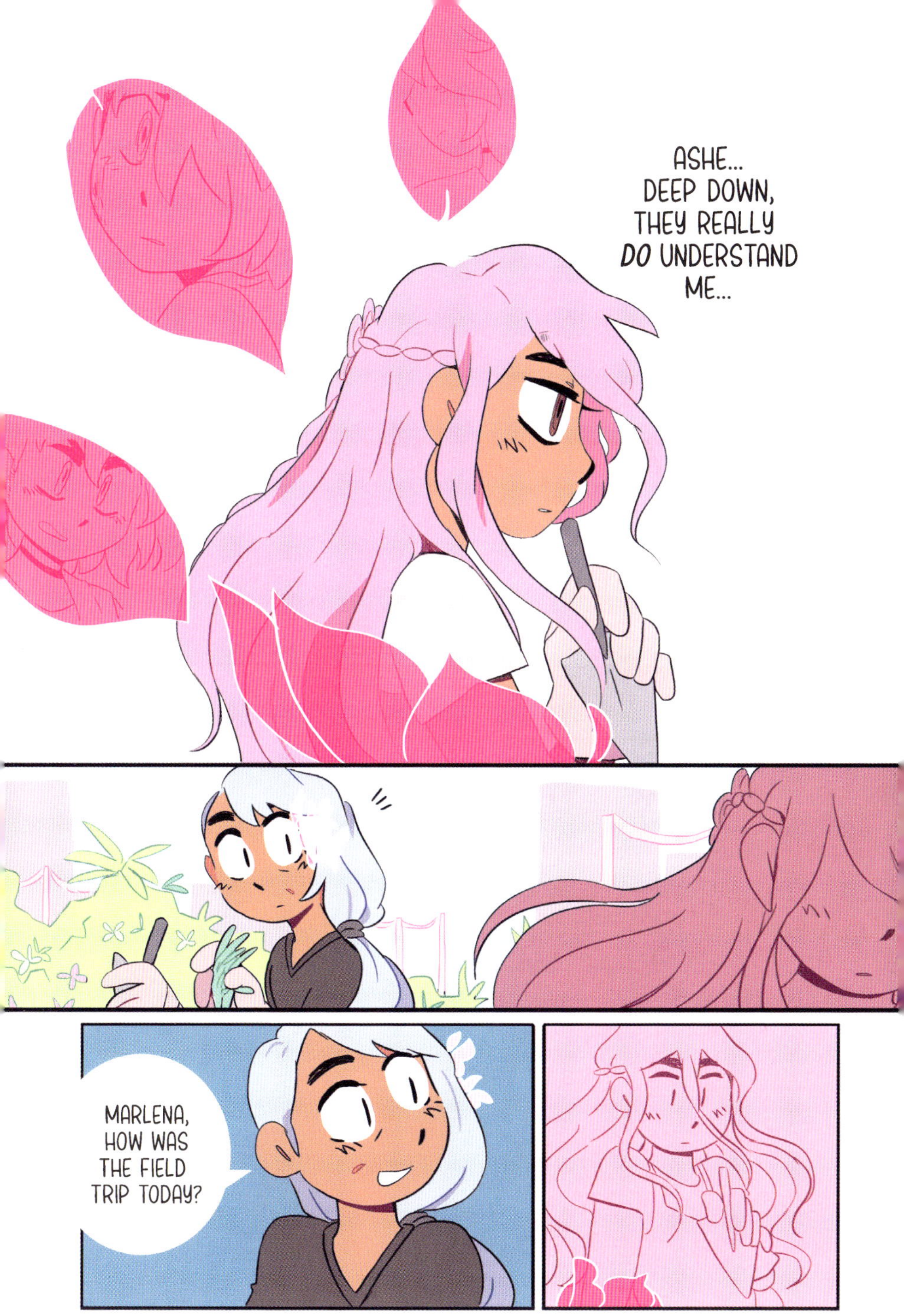
ASHE... DEEP DOWN, THEY REALLY *DO* UNDERSTAND ME...
MARLENA, HOW WAS THE FIELD TRIP TODAY?

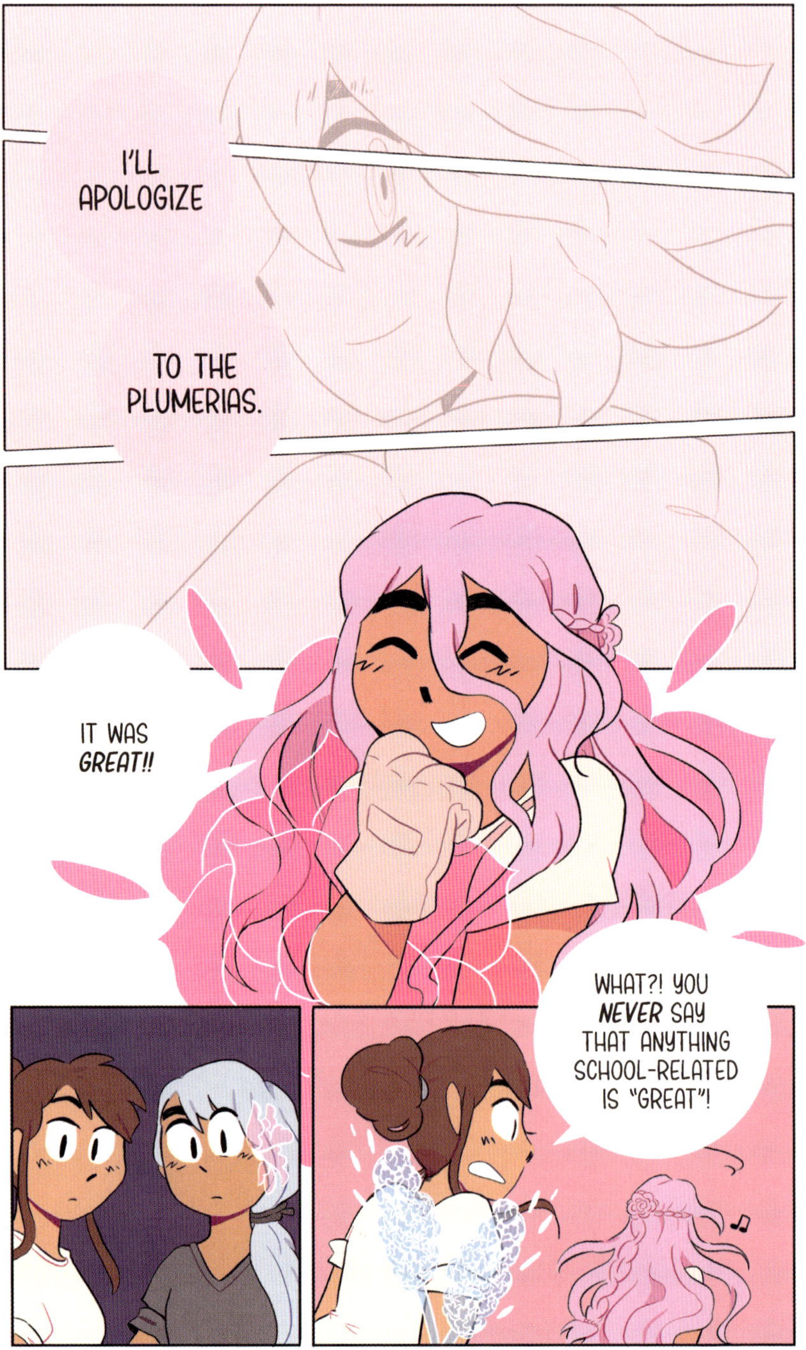
I'LL APOLOGIZE
TO THE PLUMERIAS.
IT WAS GREAT!!
WHAT?! YOU NEVER SAY THAT ANYTHING SCHOOL-RELATED IS "GREAT"!

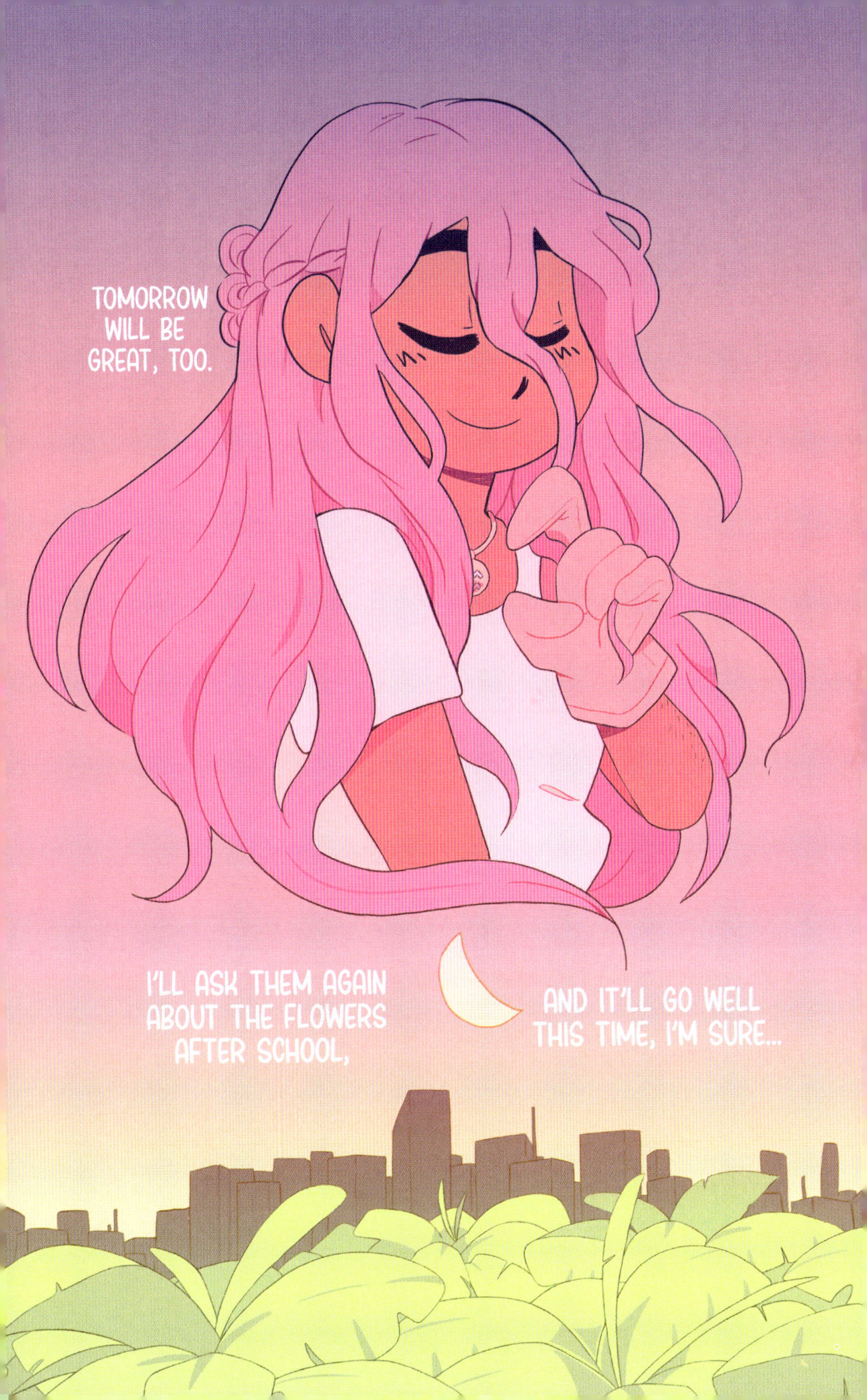

TOMORROW WILL BE GREAT, TOO.
I'LL ASK THEM AGAIN ABOUT THE FLOWERS AFTER SCHOOL,
AND IT'LL GO WELL THIS TIME, I'M SURE...

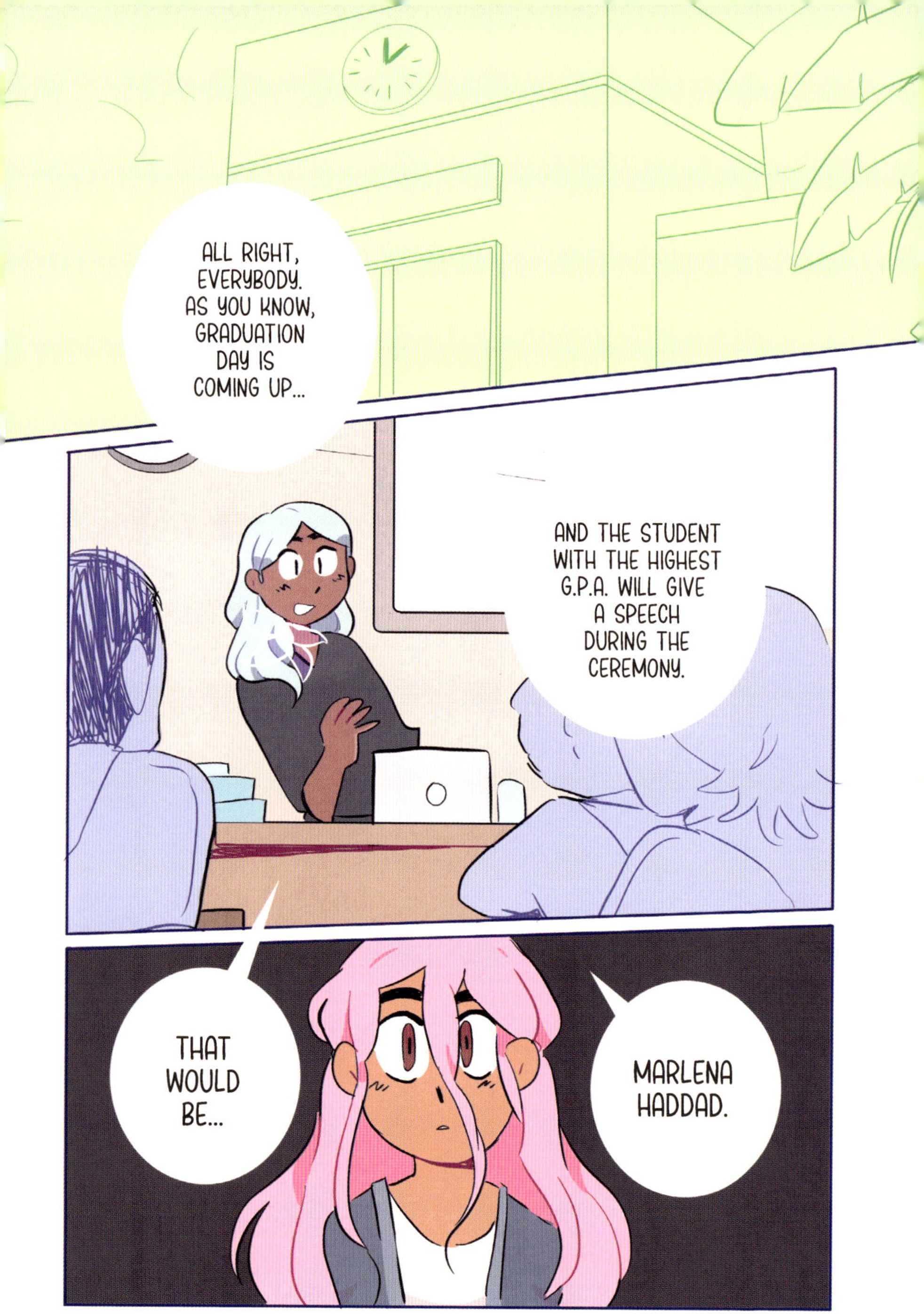
ALL RIGHT, EVERYBODY. AS YOU KNOW, GRADUATION DAY IS COMING UP...
AND THE STUDENT WITH THE HIGHEST G.P.A. WILL GIVE A SPEECH DURING THE CEREMONY.
THAT WOULD BE...
MARLENA HADDAD.

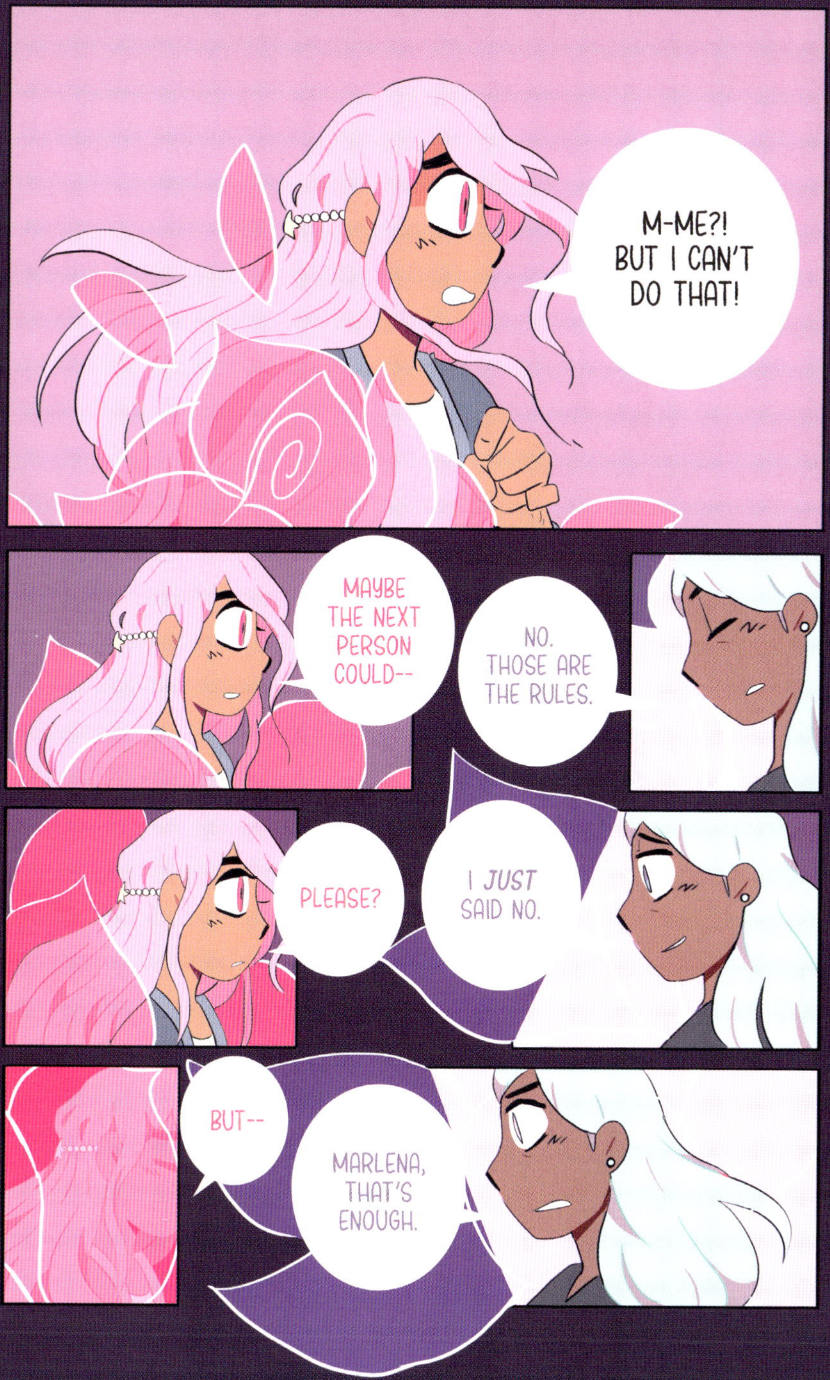
M-ME?! BUT I CAN'T DO THAT!
MAYBE THE NEXT PERSON COULD--
NO. THOSE ARE THE RULES.
PLEASE?
I *JUST* SAID NO.
BUT--
MARLENA, THAT'S ENOUGH.

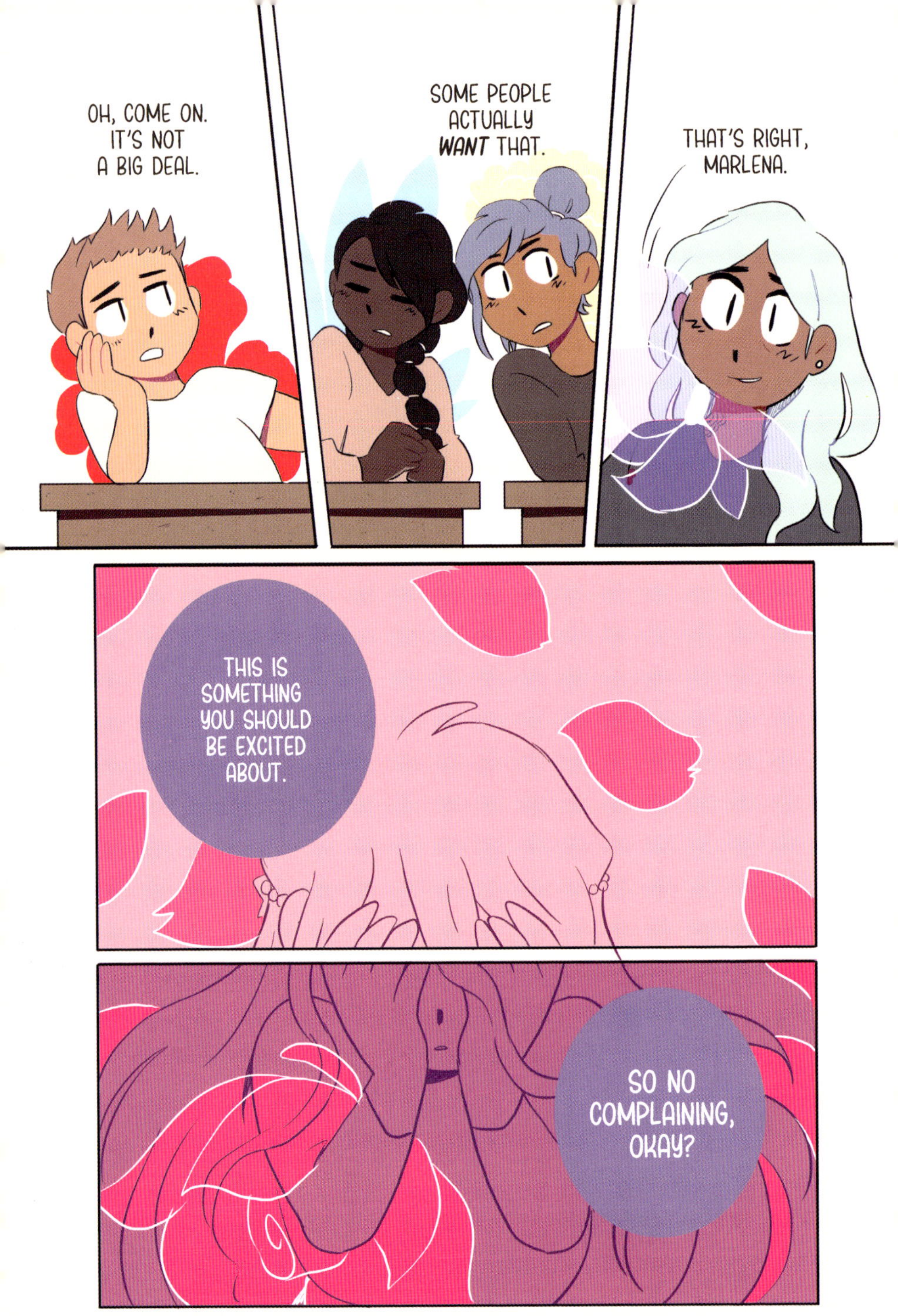
OH, COME ON. IT'S NOT A BIG DEAL.
SOME PEOPLE ACTUALLY WANT THAT.
THAT'S RIGHT, MARLENA.
THIS IS SOMETHING YOU SHOULD BE EXCITED ABOUT.
SO NO COMPLAINING, OKAY?

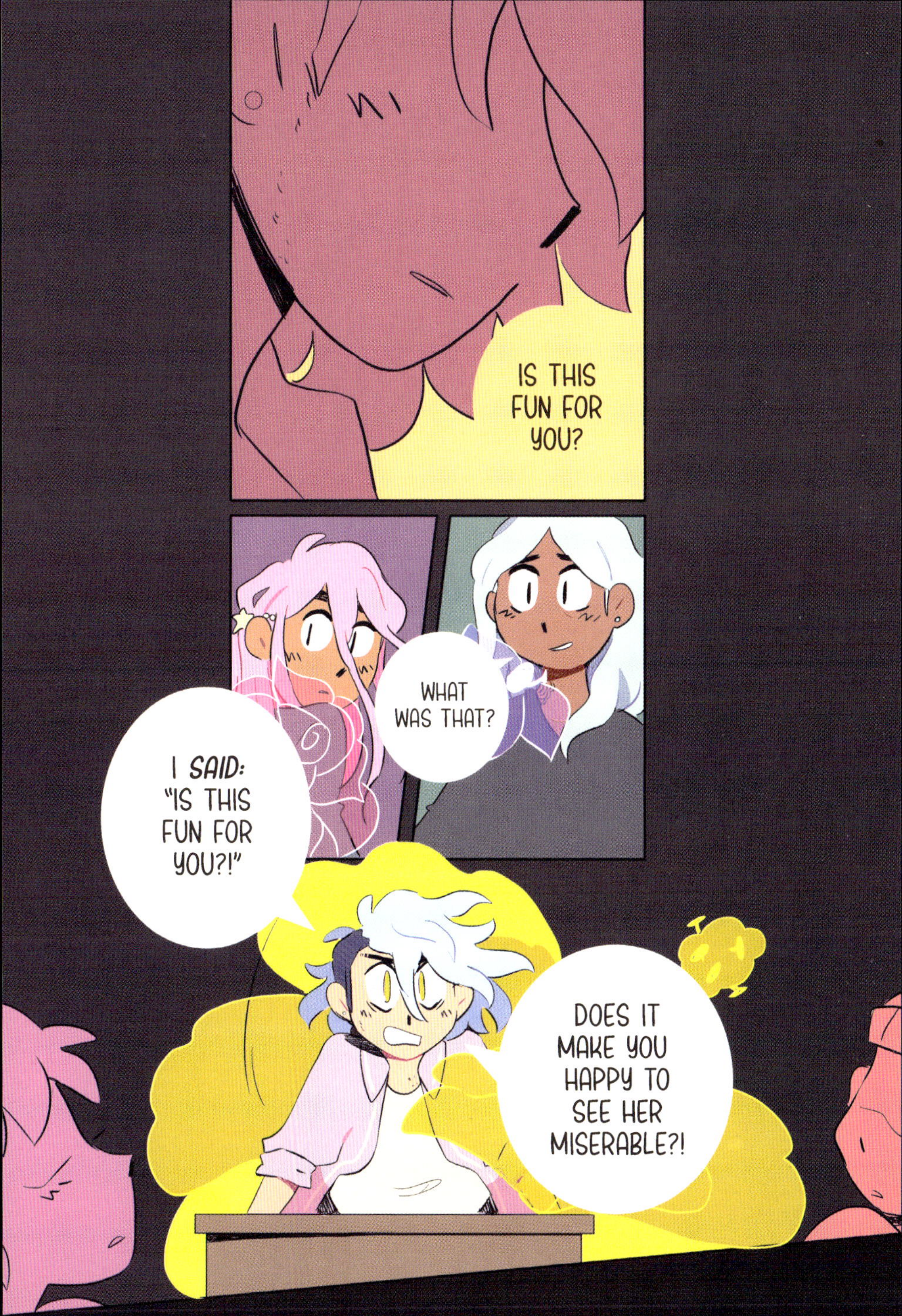
IS THIS FUN FOR YOU?
WHAT WAS THAT?
I *SAID:* "IS THIS FUN FOR YOU?!"
DOES IT MAKE YOU HAPPY TO SEE HER MISERABLE?!

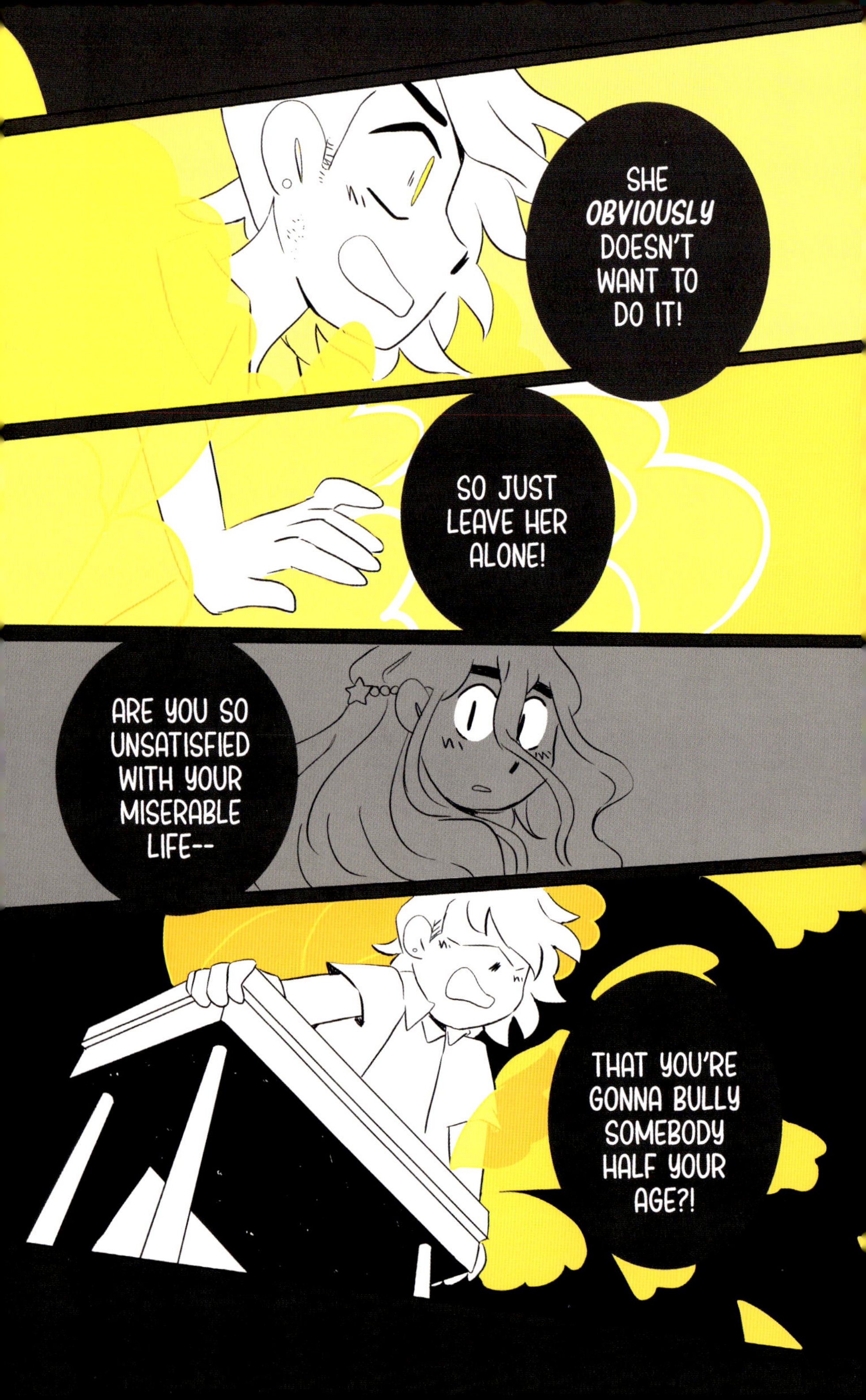
SHE *OBVIOUSLY* DOESN'T WANT TO DO IT!
SO JUST LEAVE HER ALONE!
ARE YOU SO UNSATISFIED WITH YOUR MISERABLE LIFE--
THAT YOU'RE GONNA BULLY SOMEBODY HALF YOUR AGE?!

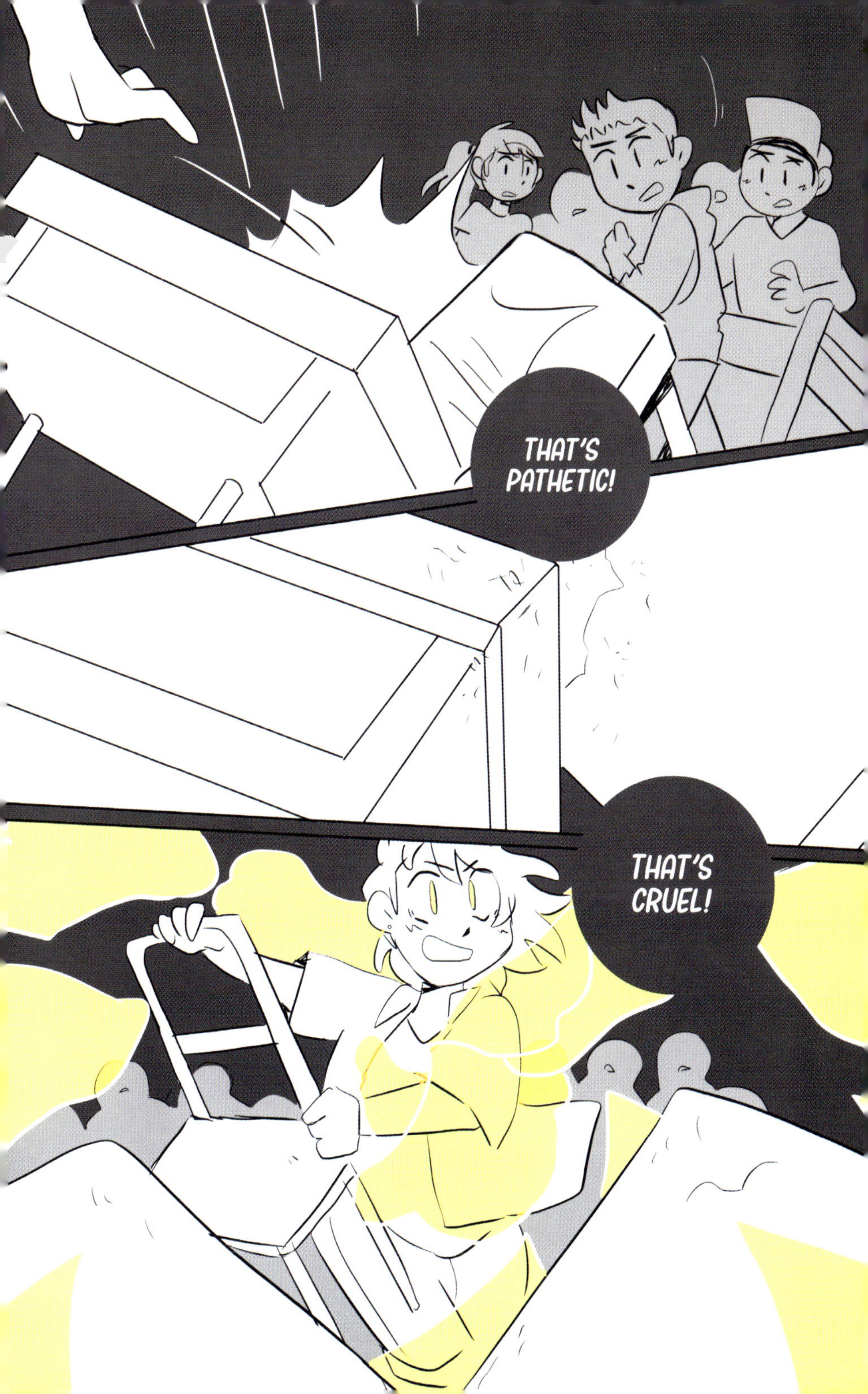
THAT'S PATHETIC!
THAT'S CRUEL!

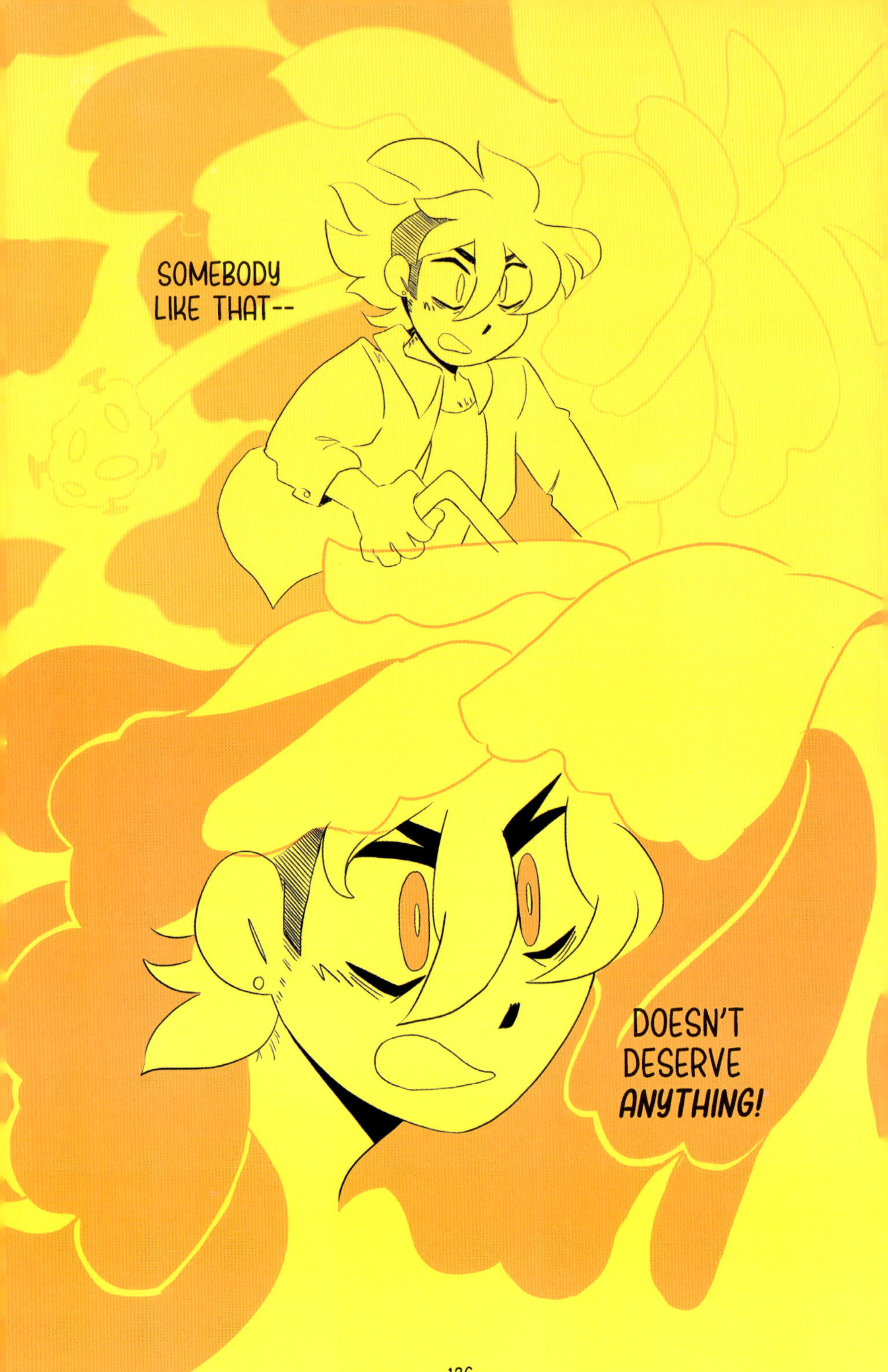
SOMEBODY LIKE THAT--
DOESN'T DESERVE ANYTHING!

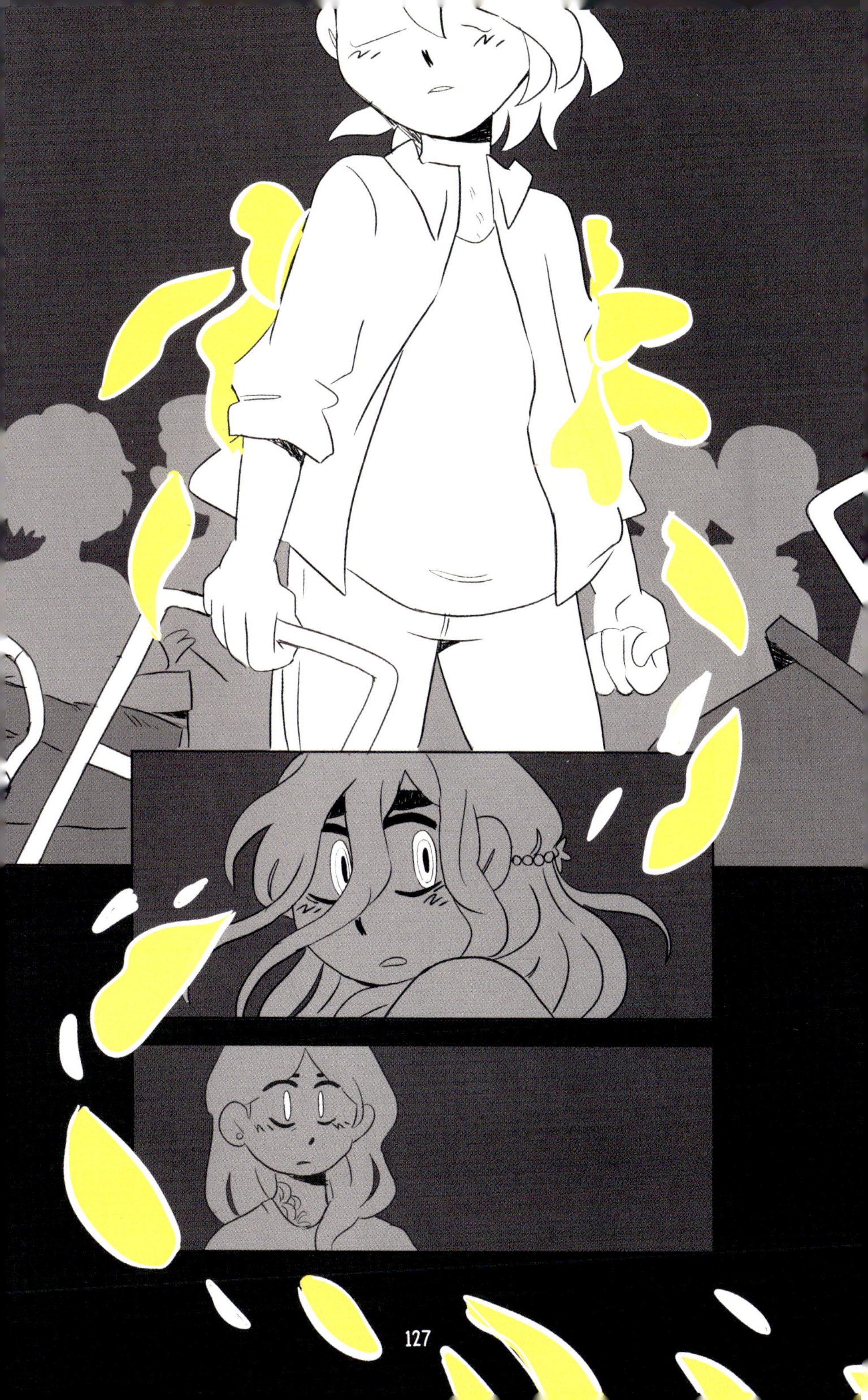

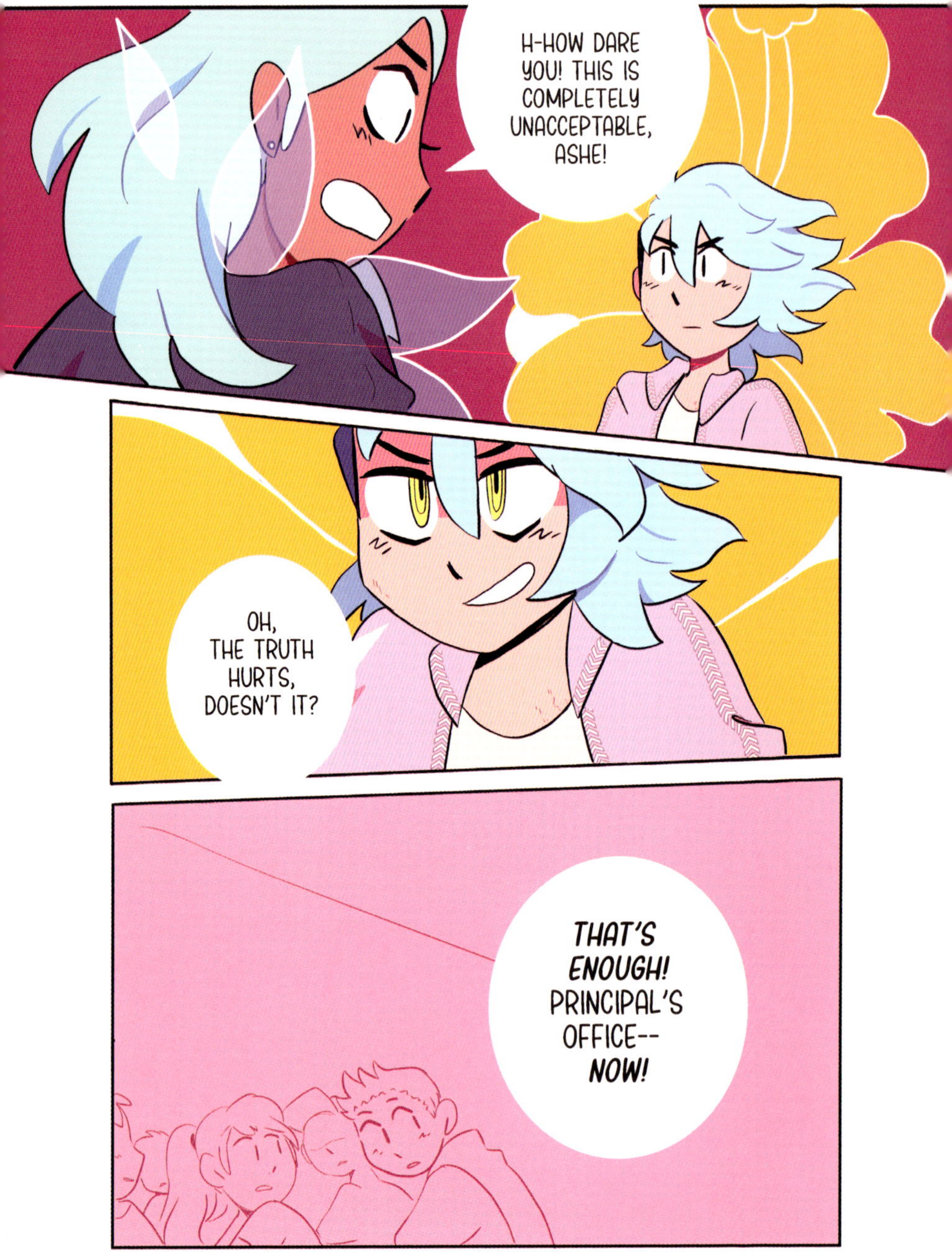
H-HOW DARE YOU! THIS IS COMPLETELY UNACCEPTABLE, ASHE!
OH, THE TRUTH HURTS, DOESN'T IT?
THAT'S ENOUGH! PRINCIPAL'S OFFICE-- *NOW!*

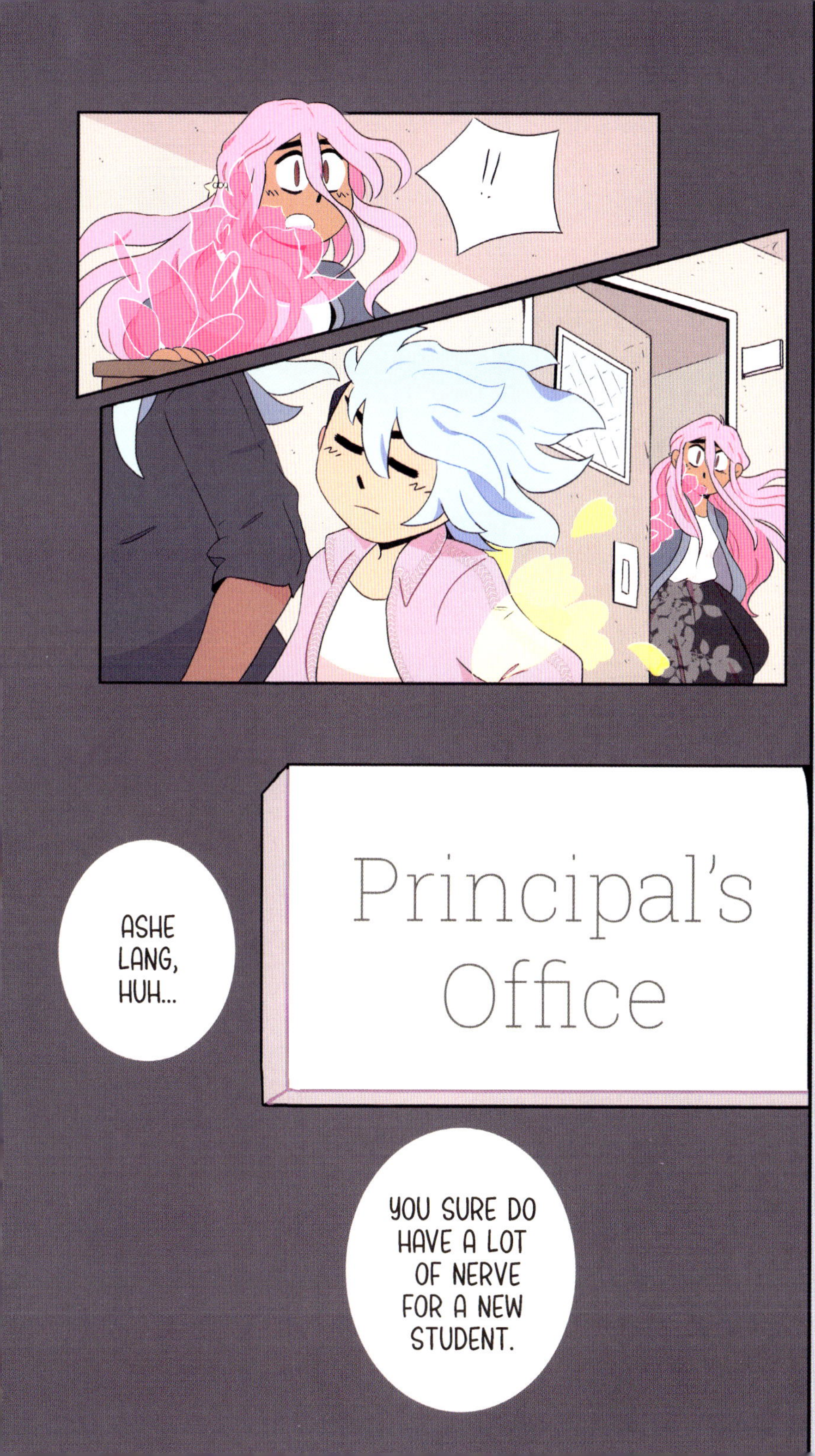
!!
Principal's Office
ASHE LANG, HUH...
YOU SURE DO HAVE A LOT OF NERVE FOR A NEW STUDENT.

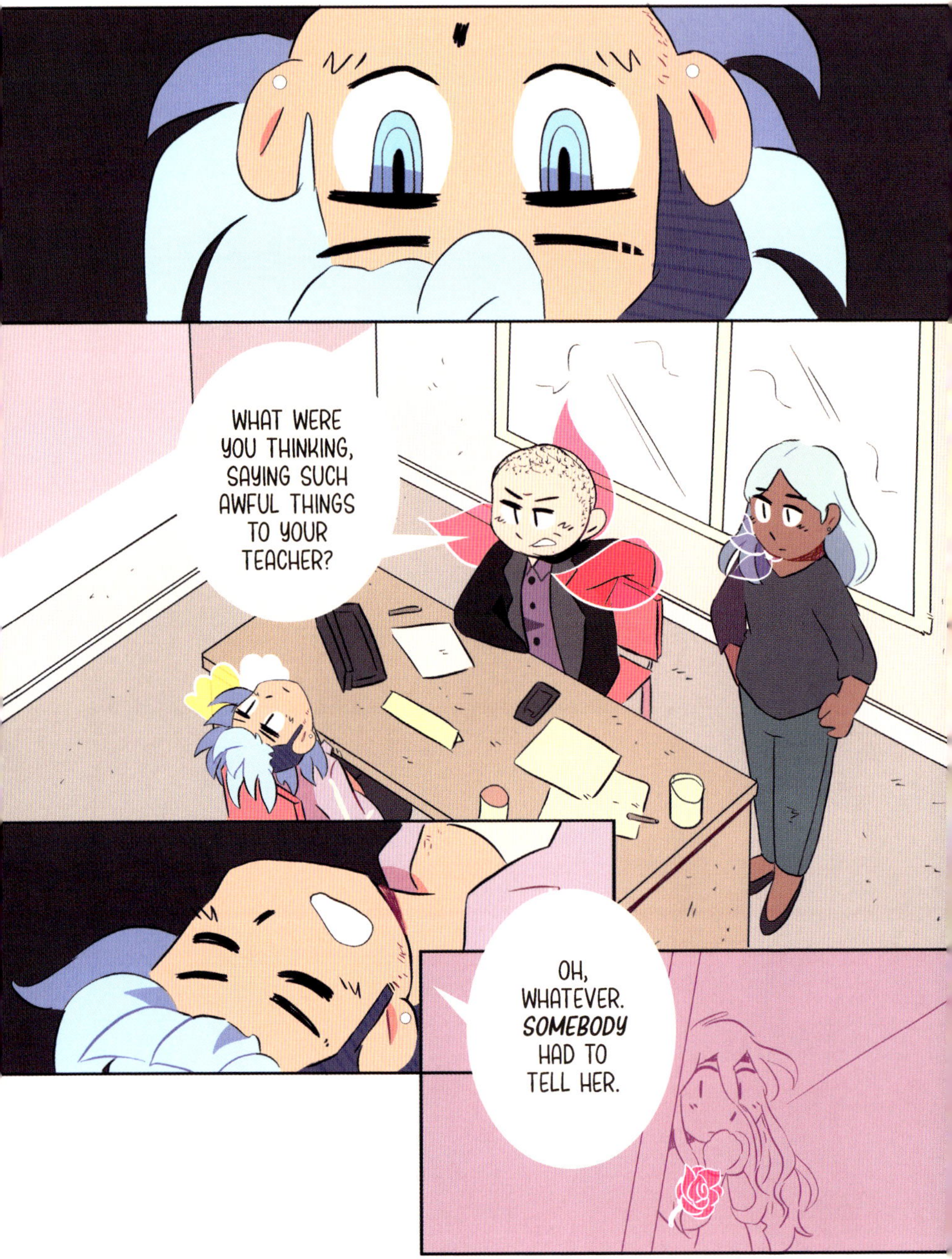
WHAT WERE YOU THINKING, SAYING SUCH AWFUL THINGS TO YOUR TEACHER?
OH, WHATEVER. *SOMEBODY* HAD TO TELL HER.

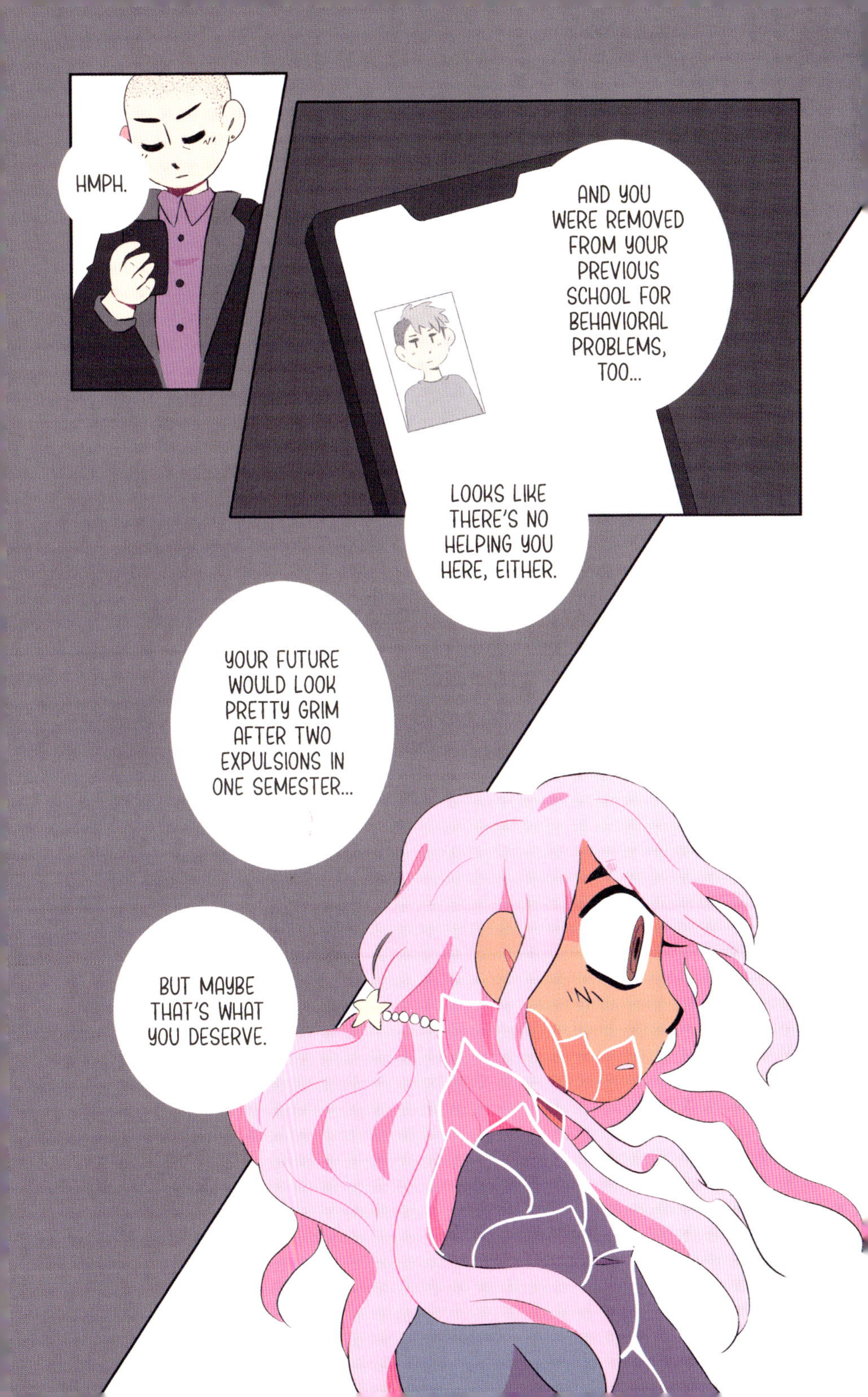
HMPH.
AND YOU WERE REMOVED FROM YOUR PREVIOUS SCHOOL FOR BEHAVIORAL PROBLEMS, TOO...
LOOKS LIKE THERE'S NO HELPING YOU HERE, EITHER.
YOUR FUTURE WOULD LOOK PRETTY GRIM AFTER TWO EXPULSIONS IN ONE SEMESTER...
BUT MAYBE THAT'S WHAT YOU DESERVE.

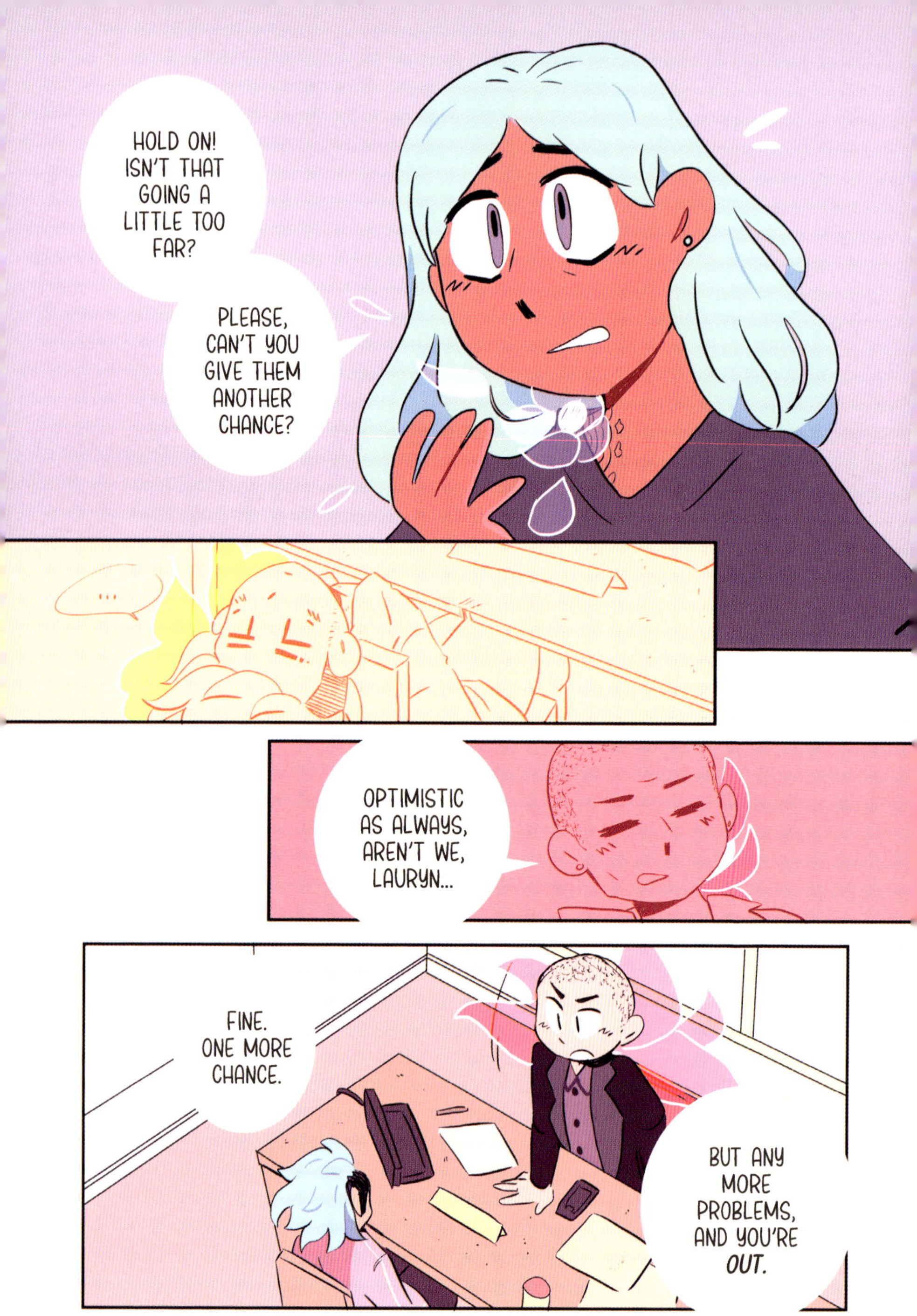
HOLD ON! ISN'T THAT GOING A LITTLE TOO FAR?
PLEASE, CAN'T YOU GIVE THEM ANOTHER CHANCE?
...
OPTIMISTIC AS ALWAYS, AREN'T WE, LAURYN...
FINE. ONE MORE CHANCE.
BUT ANY MORE PROBLEMS, AND YOU'RE *OUT*.

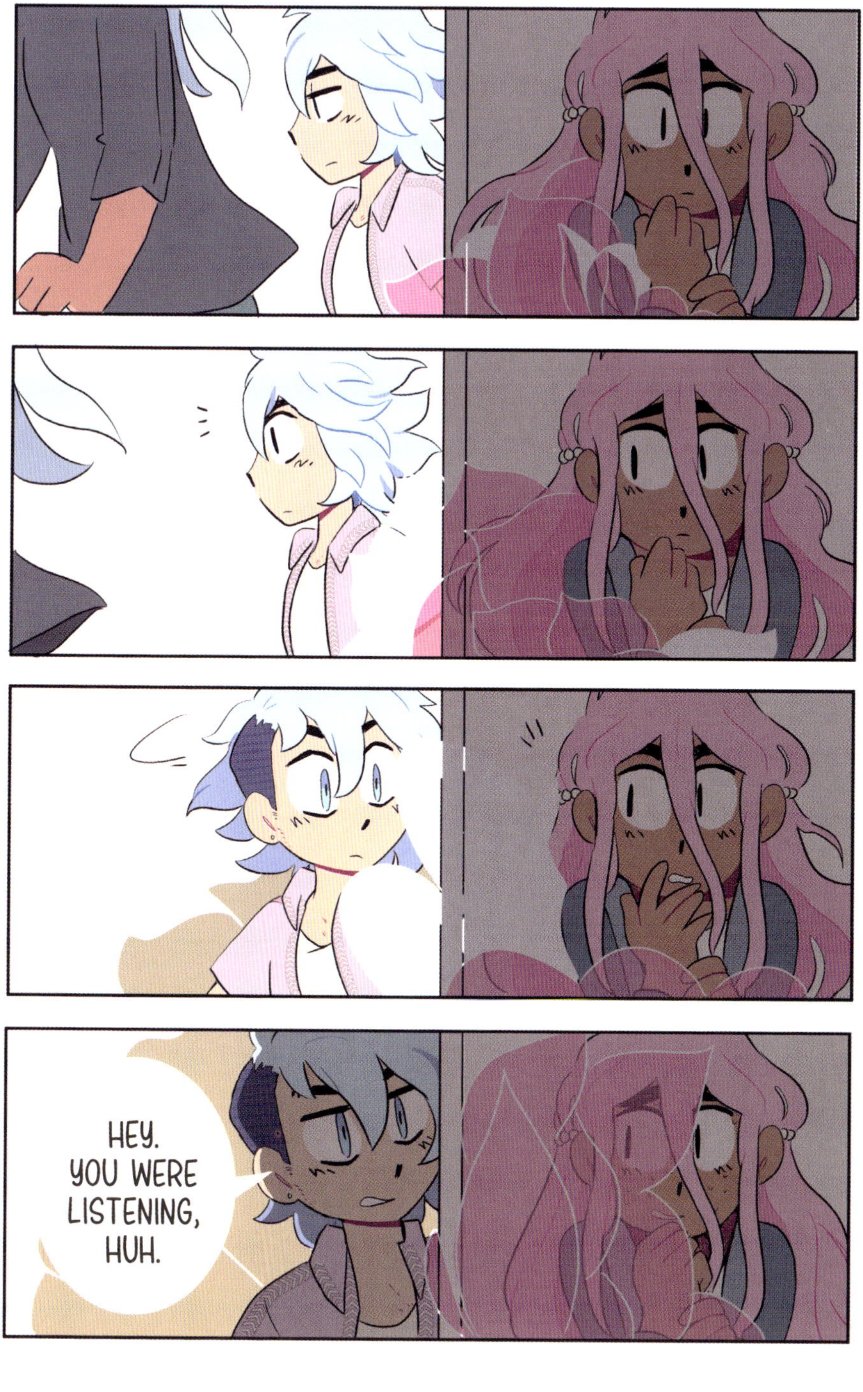
HEY.
YOU WERE
LISTENING,
HUH.

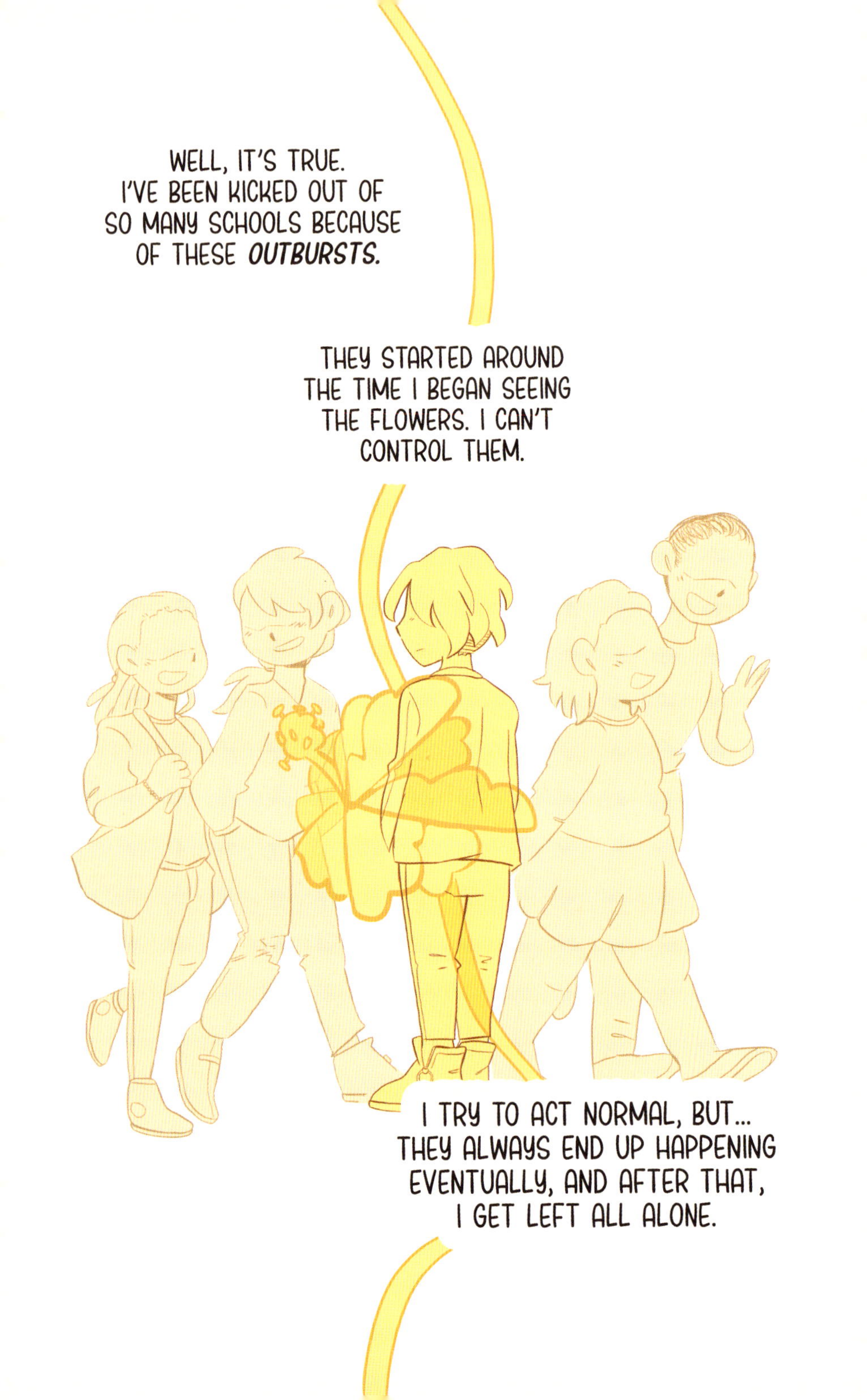
WELL, IT'S TRUE. I'VE BEEN KICKED OUT OF SO MANY SCHOOLS BECAUSE OF THESE *OUTBURSTS.*
THEY STARTED AROUND THE TIME I BEGAN SEEING THE FLOWERS. I CAN'T CONTROL THEM.
I TRY TO ACT NORMAL, BUT... THEY ALWAYS END UP HAPPENING EVENTUALLY, AND AFTER THAT, I GET LEFT ALL ALONE.

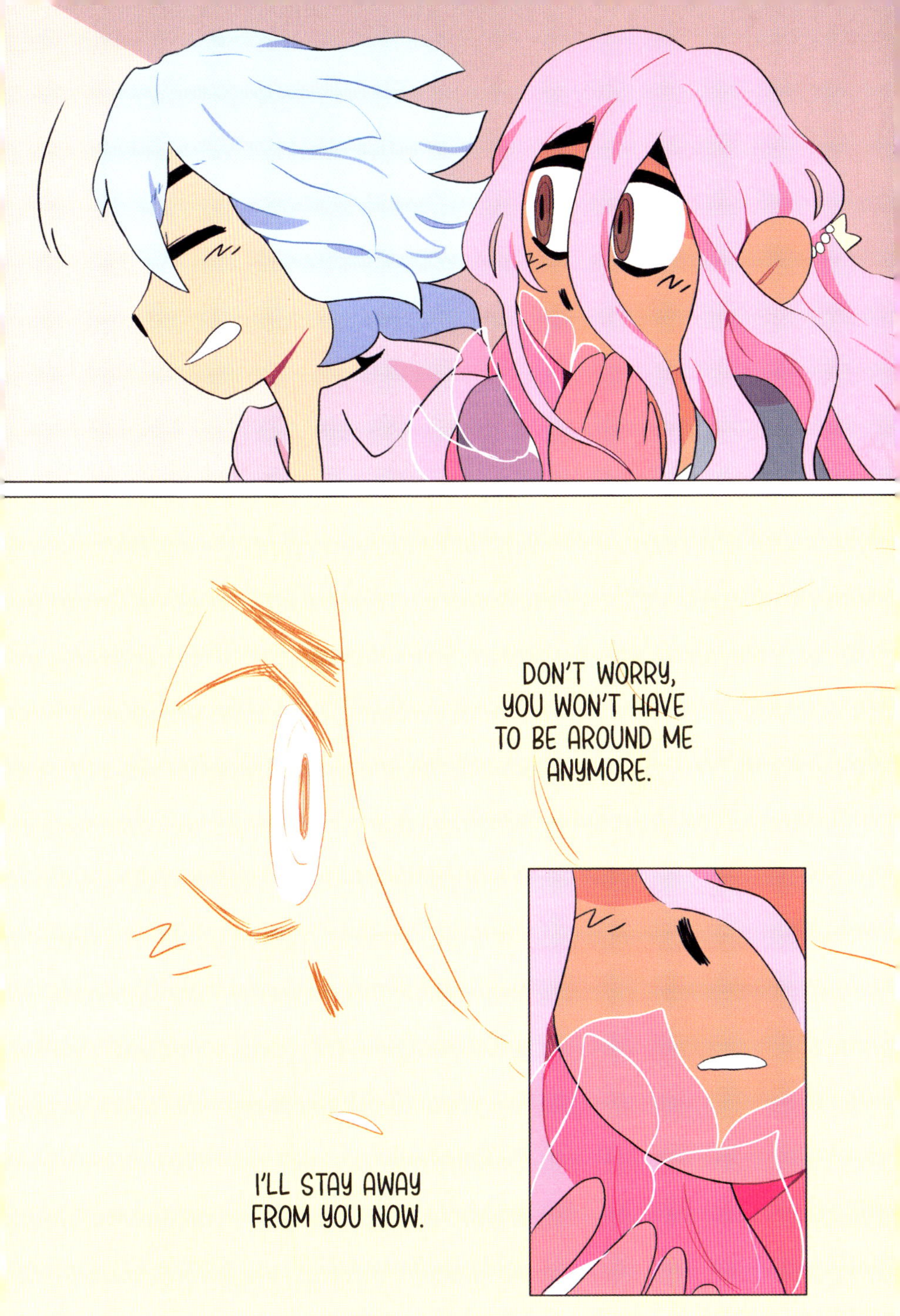
DON'T WORRY, YOU WON'T HAVE TO BE AROUND ME ANYMORE.
I'LL STAY AWAY FROM YOU NOW.

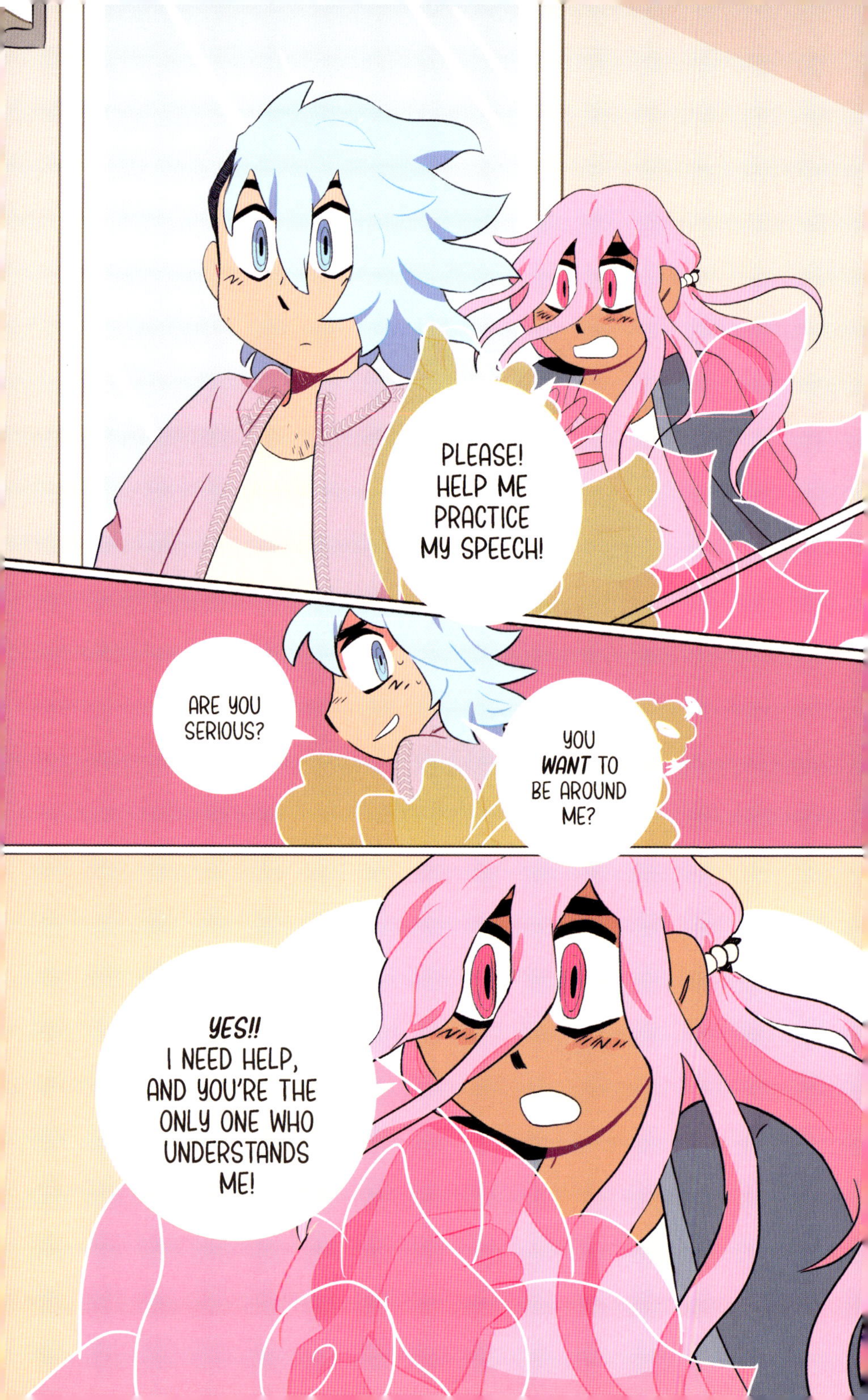
PLEASE! HELP ME PRACTICE MY SPEECH!
ARE YOU SERIOUS?
YOU **WANT** TO BE AROUND ME?
YES!! I NEED HELP, AND YOU'RE THE ONLY ONE WHO UNDERSTANDS ME!

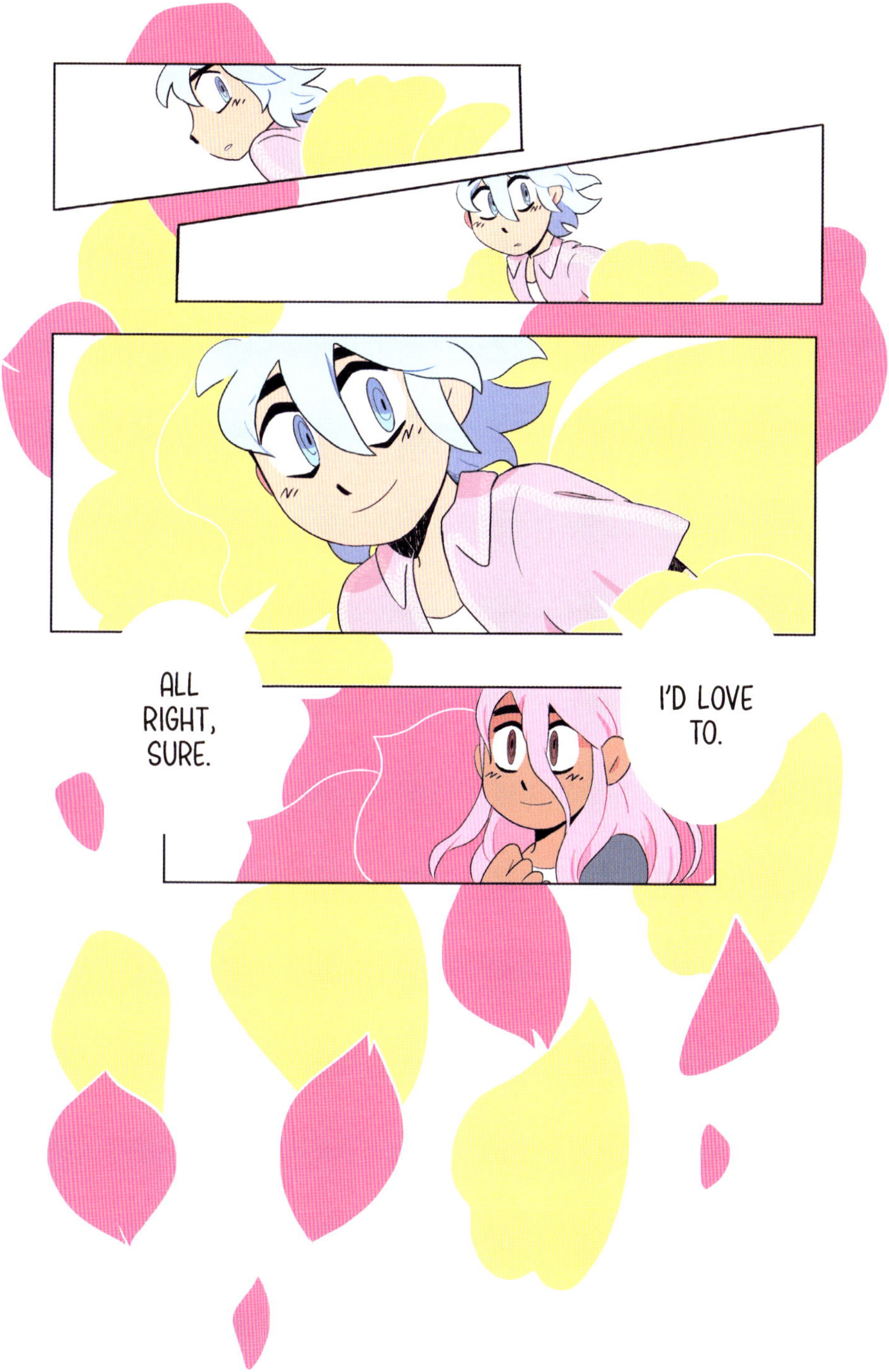
ALL RIGHT, SURE.
I'D LOVE TO.

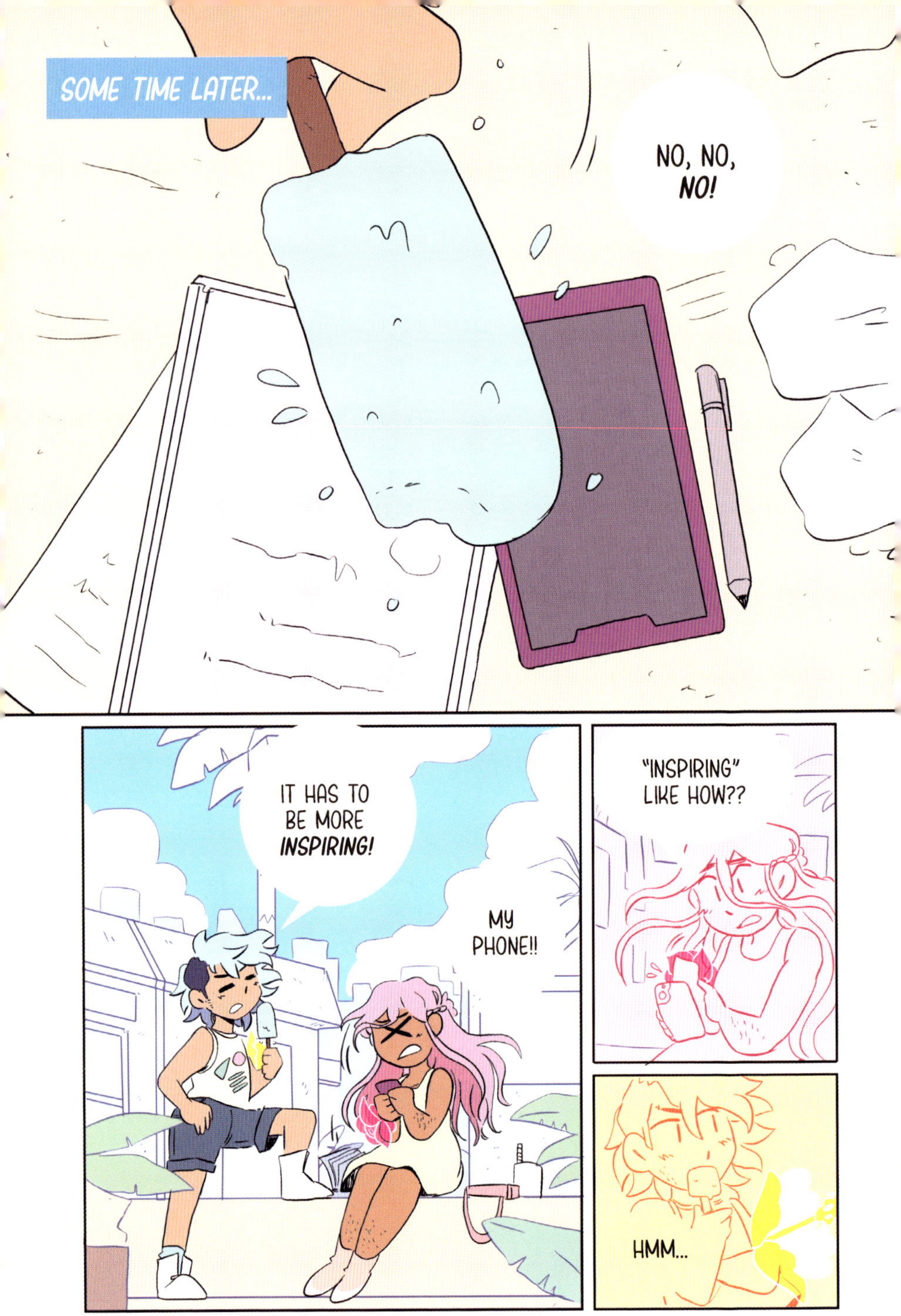
SOME TIME LATER...
NO, NO, *NO!*
IT HAS TO BE MORE *INSPIRING!*
MY PHONE!!
"INSPIRING" LIKE HOW??
HMM...

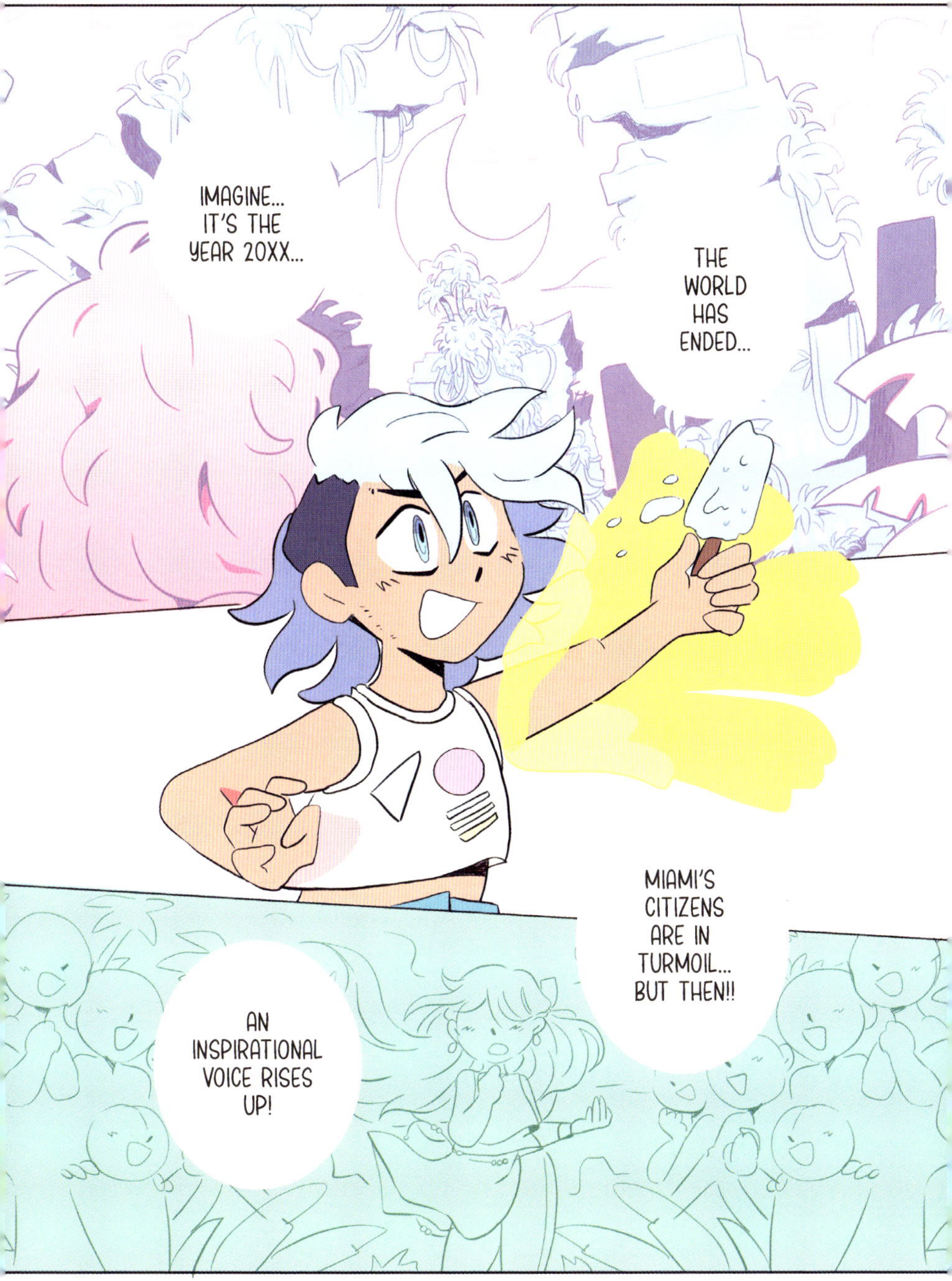
IMAGINE... IT'S THE YEAR 20XX...
THE WORLD HAS ENDED...
MIAMI'S CITIZENS ARE IN TURMOIL... BUT THEN!!
AN INSPIRATIONAL VOICE RISES UP!

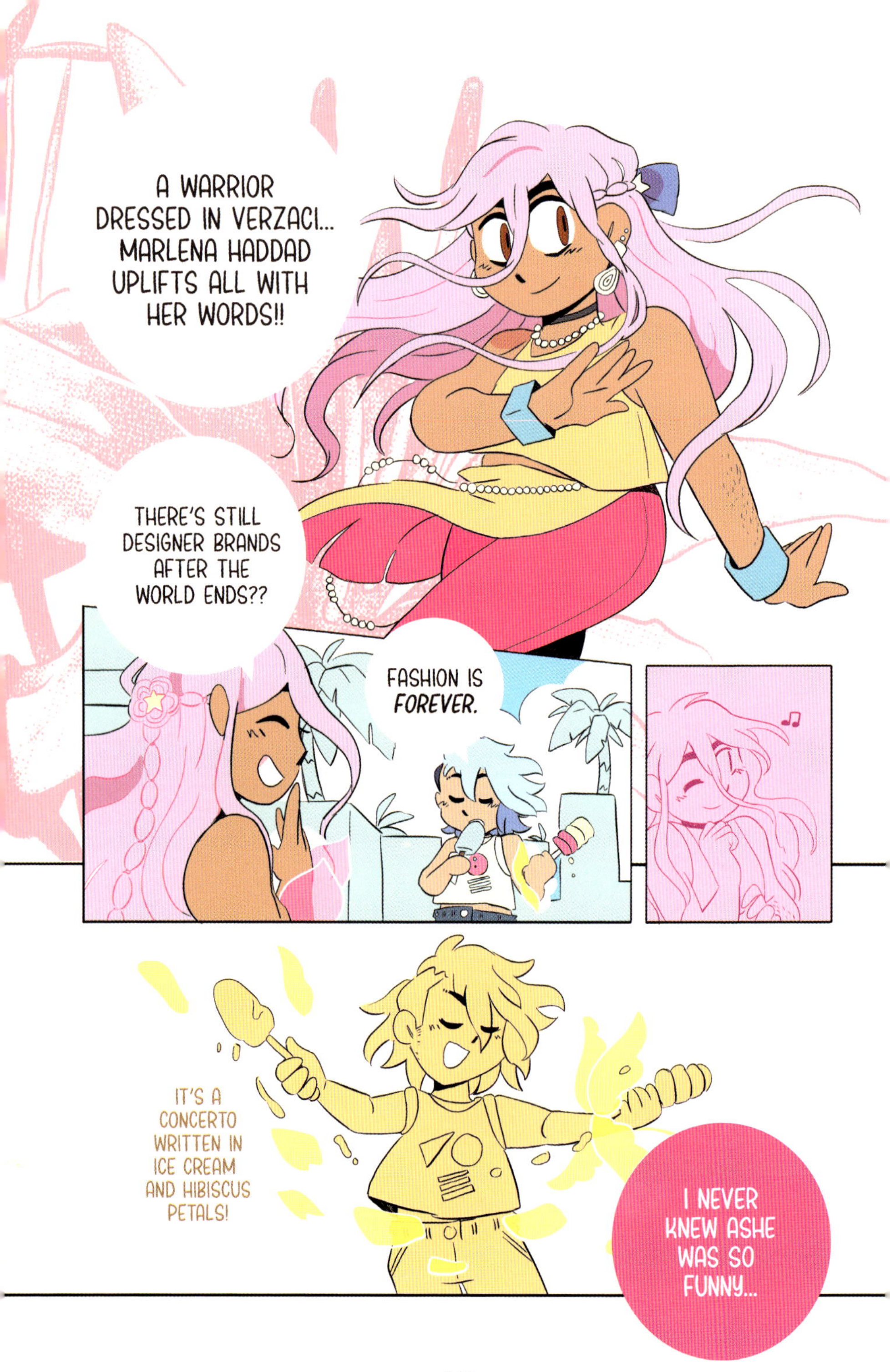
A WARRIOR DRESSED IN VERZACI... MARLENA HADDAD UPLIFTS ALL WITH HER WORDS!!
THERE'S STILL DESIGNER BRANDS AFTER THE WORLD ENDS??
FASHION IS *FOREVER.*
IT'S A CONCERTO WRITTEN IN ICE CREAM AND HIBISCUS PETALS!
I NEVER KNEW ASHE WAS SO FUNNY...

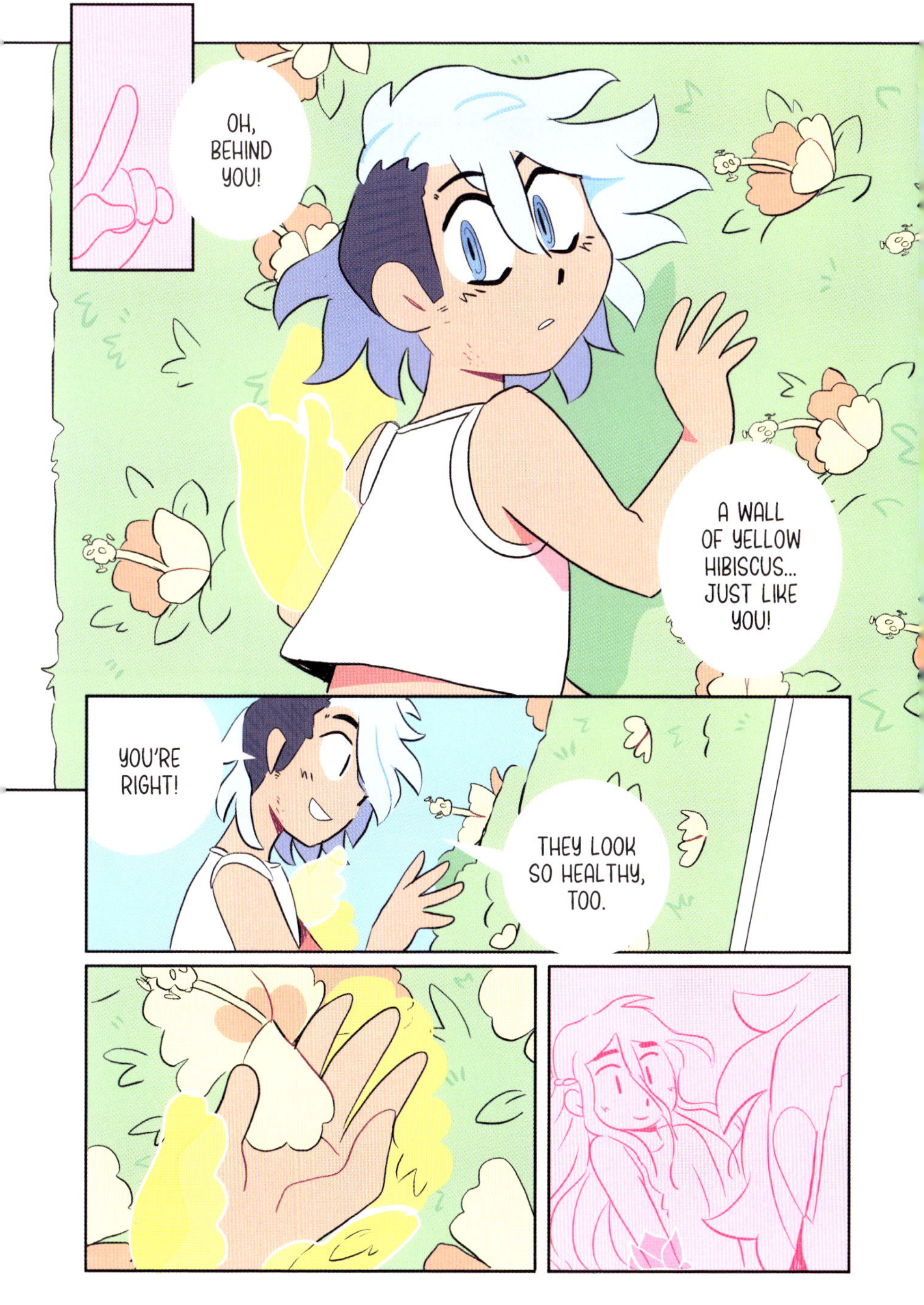
OH, BEHIND YOU!
A WALL OF YELLOW HIBISCUS... JUST LIKE YOU!
YOU'RE RIGHT!
THEY LOOK SO HEALTHY, TOO.

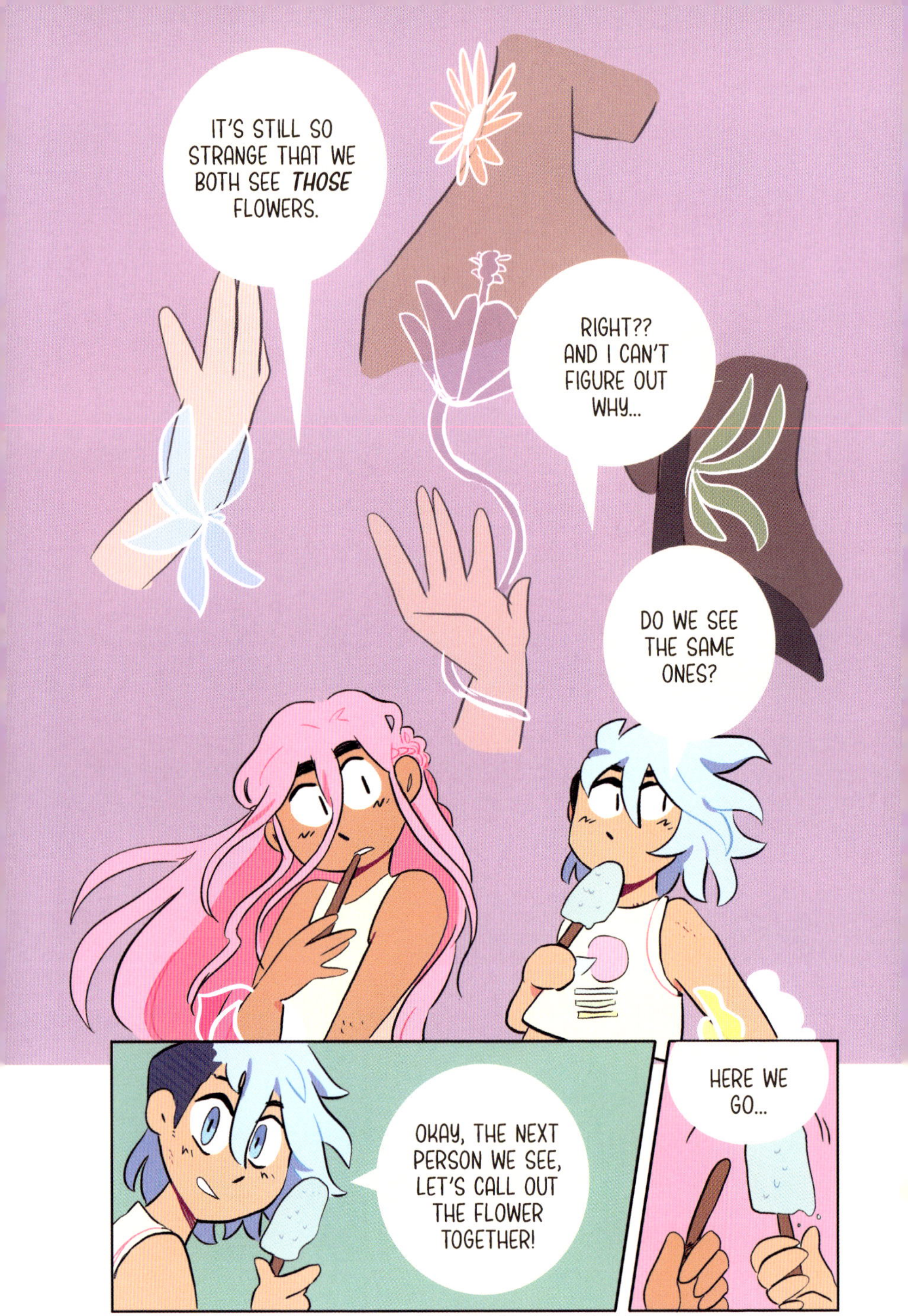
IT'S STILL SO STRANGE THAT WE BOTH SEE *THOSE* FLOWERS.
RIGHT?? AND I CAN'T FIGURE OUT WHY...
DO WE SEE THE SAME ONES?
OKAY, THE NEXT PERSON WE SEE, LET'S CALL OUT THE FLOWER TOGETHER!
HERE WE GO...

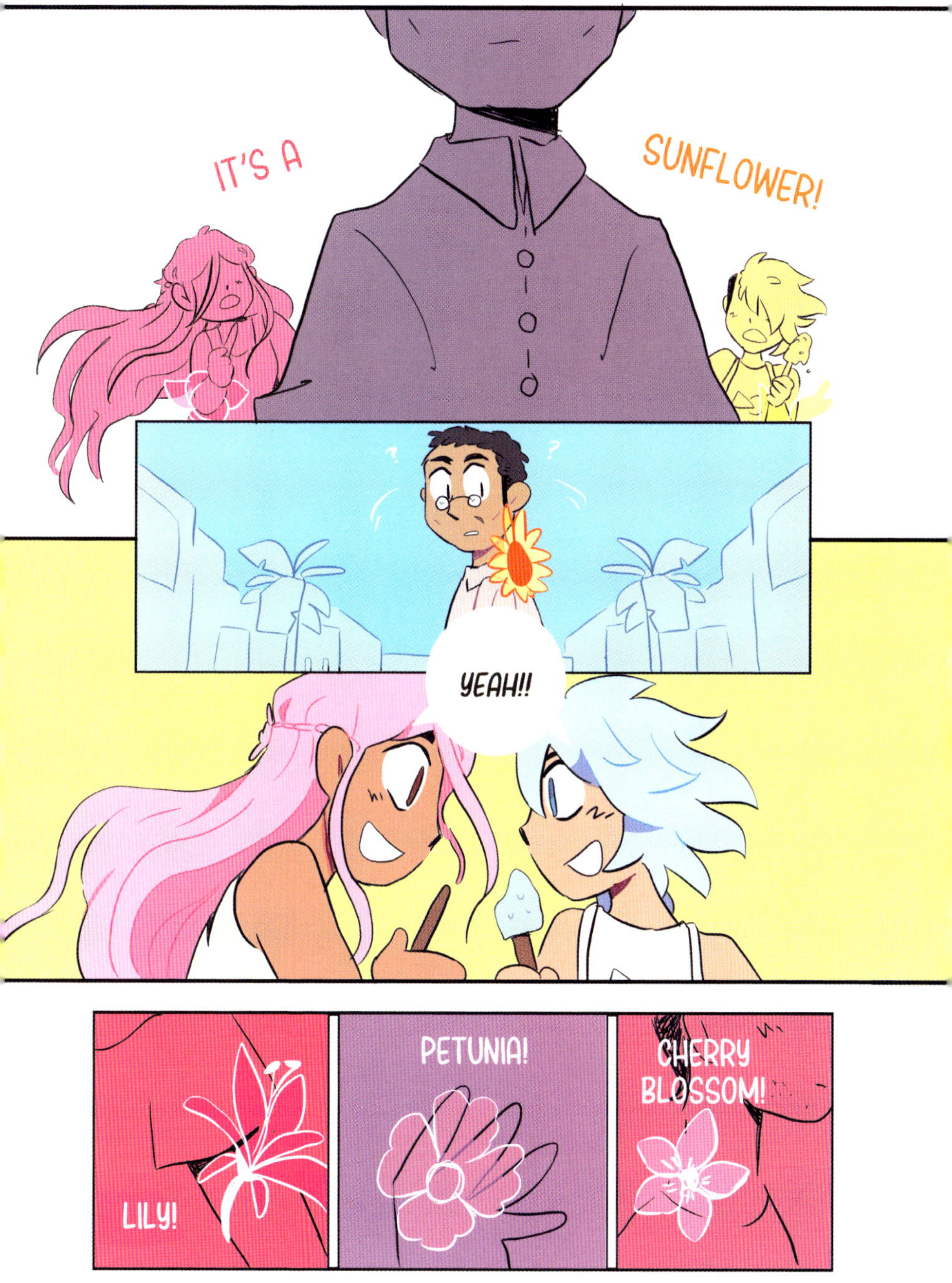
IT'S A
SUNFLOWER!
YEAH!!
LILY!
PETUNIA!
CHERRY BLOSSOM!

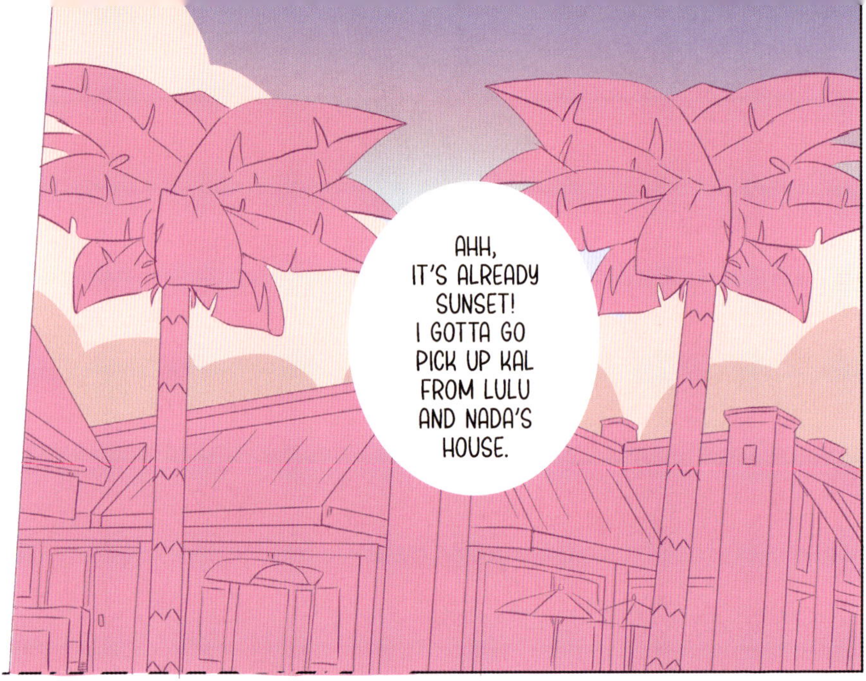
AHH,
IT'S ALREADY SUNSET!
I GOTTA GO PICK UP KAL FROM LULU AND NADA'S HOUSE.

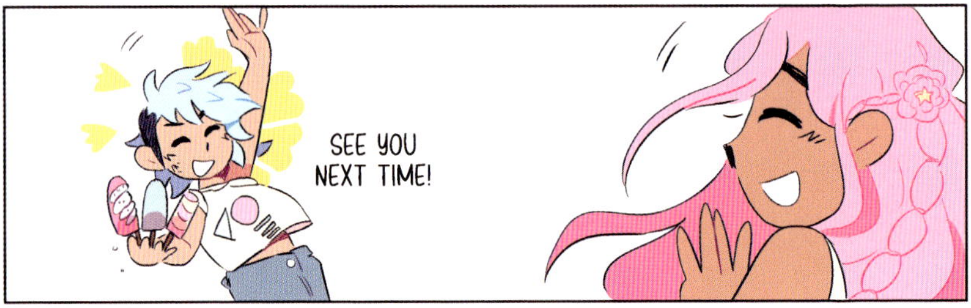
SEE YOU NEXT TIME!

THAT WAS SO MUCH FUN... ASHE IS ACTUALLY PRETTY COOL!

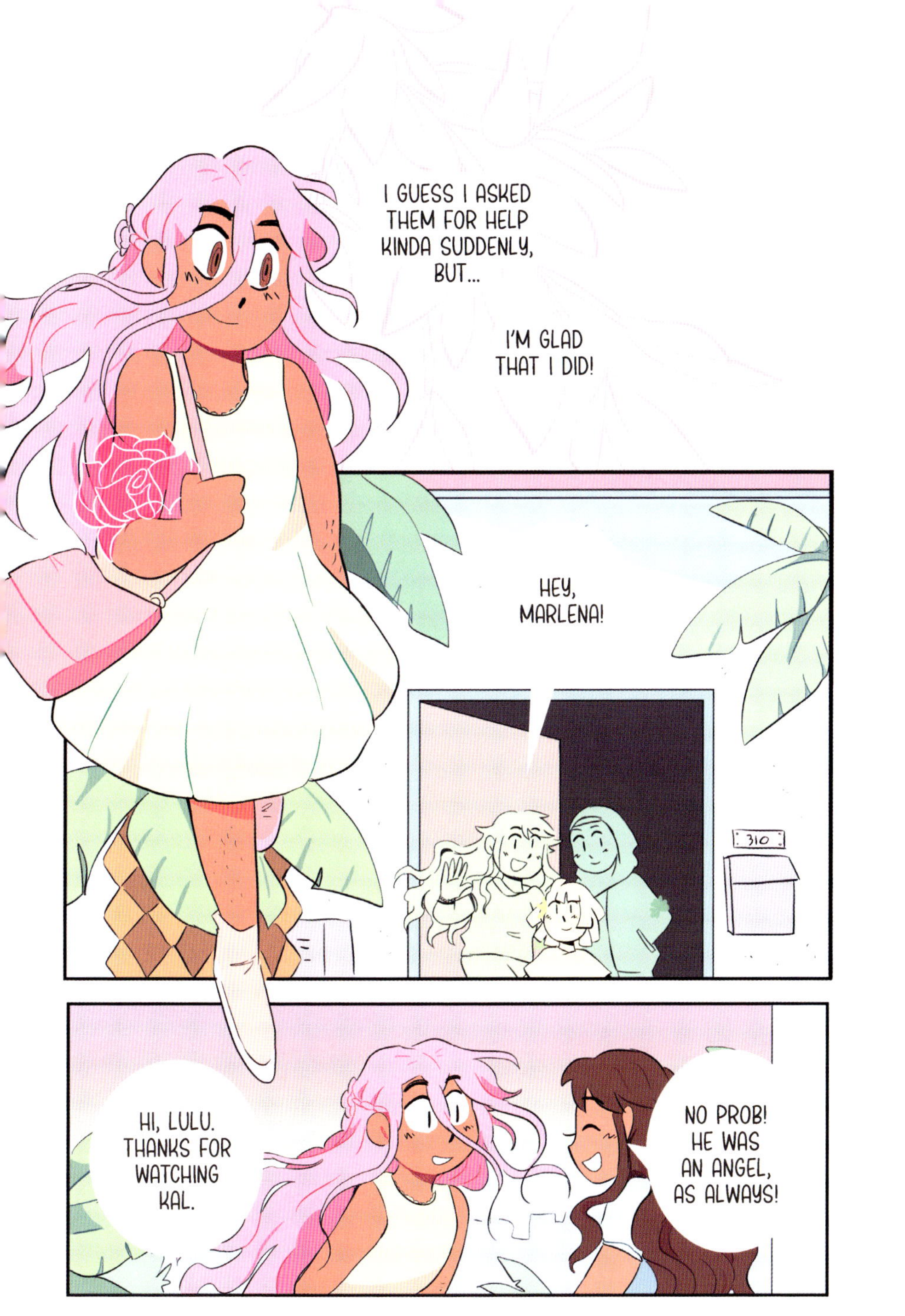
I GUESS I ASKED THEM FOR HELP KINDA SUDDENLY, BUT...
I'M GLAD THAT I DID!
HEY, MARLENA!
310
HI, LULU. THANKS FOR WATCHING KAL.
NO PROB! HE WAS AN ANGEL, AS ALWAYS!

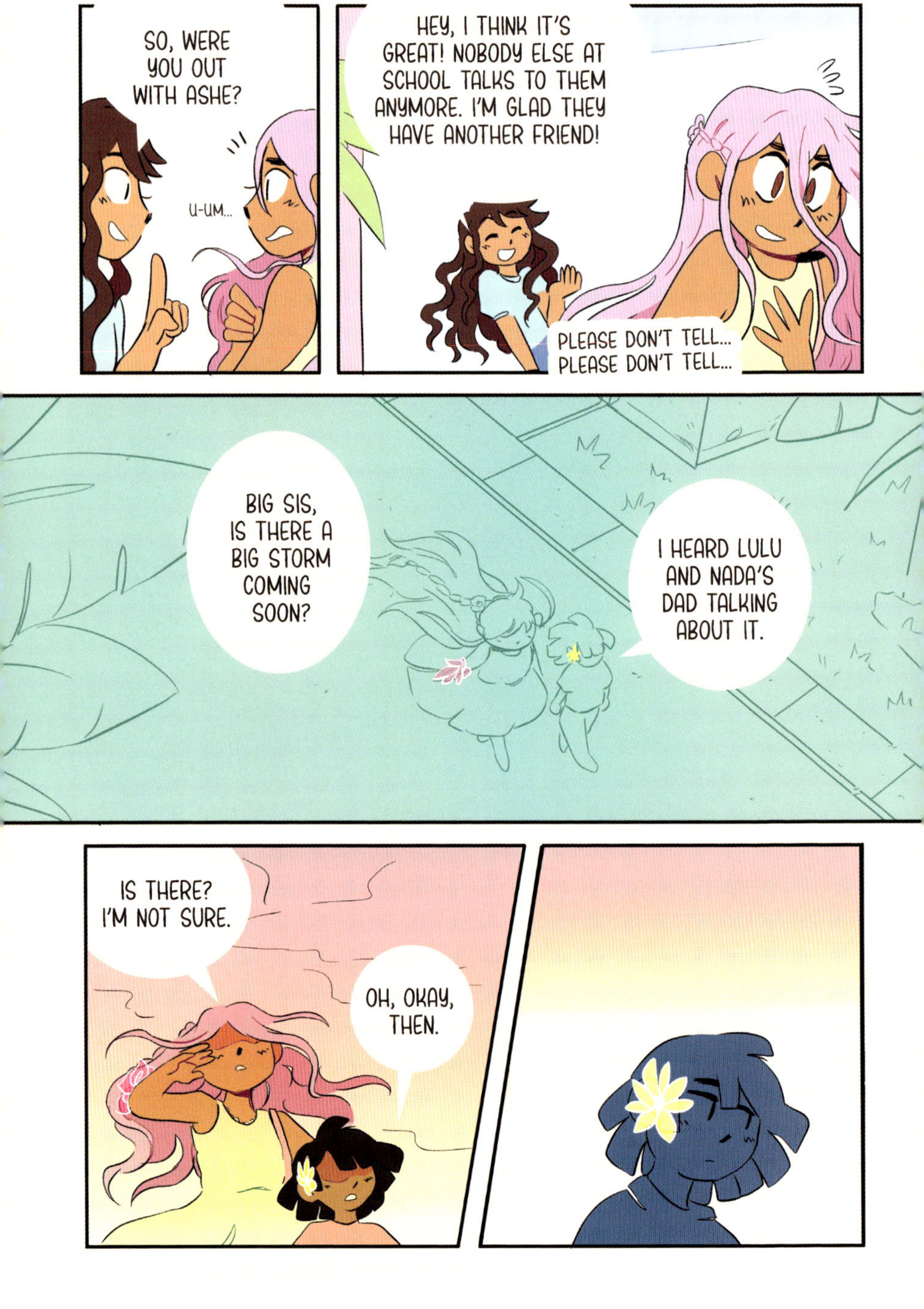
SO, WERE YOU OUT WITH ASHE?
U-UM...
HEY, I THINK IT'S GREAT! NOBODY ELSE AT SCHOOL TALKS TO THEM ANYMORE. I'M GLAD THEY HAVE ANOTHER FRIEND!
PLEASE DON'T TELL... PLEASE DON'T TELL...
BIG SIS, IS THERE A BIG STORM COMING SOON?
I HEARD LULU AND NADA'S DAD TALKING ABOUT IT.
IS THERE? I'M NOT SURE.
OH, OKAY, THEN.

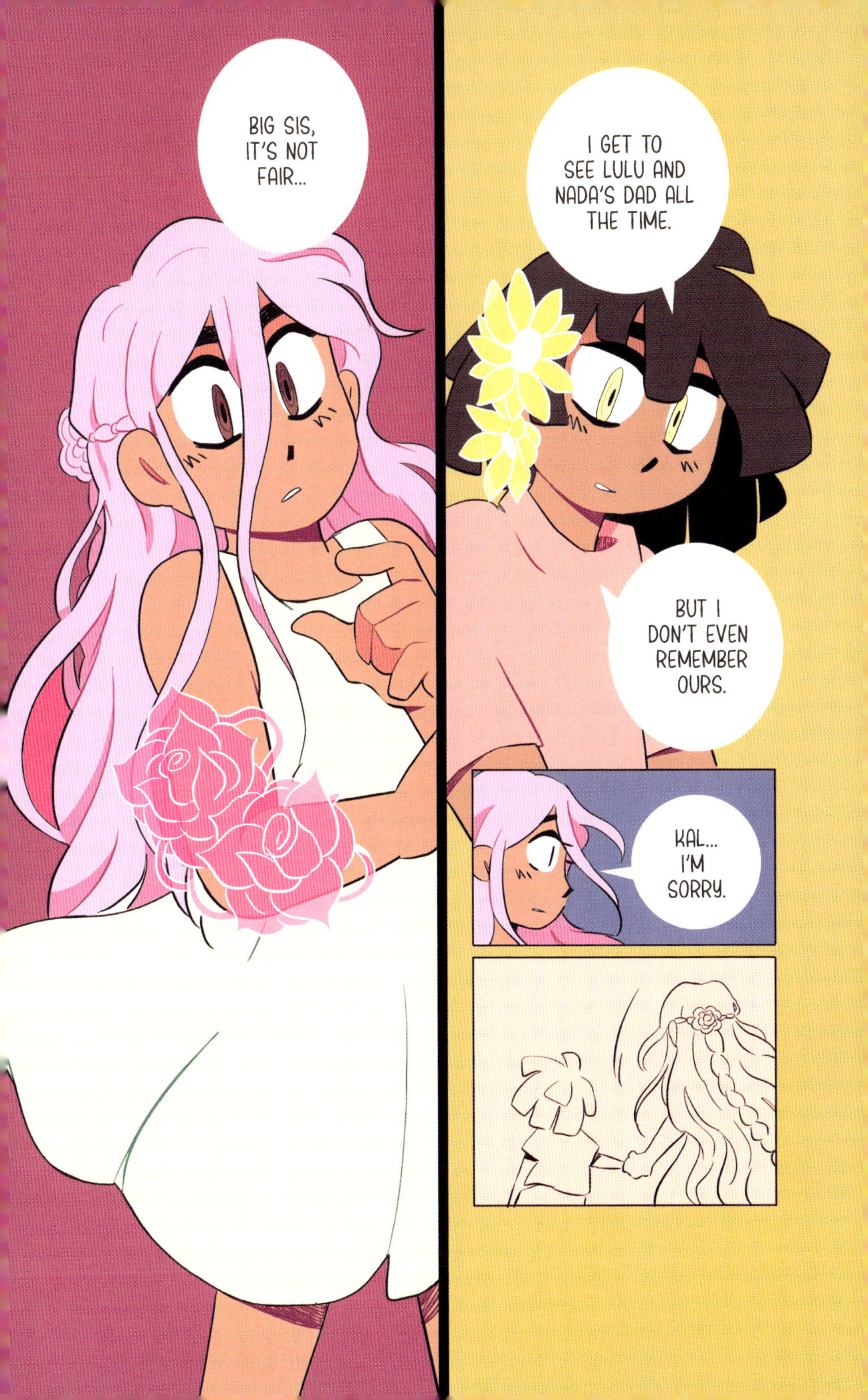
BIG SIS, IT'S NOT FAIR...
I GET TO SEE LULU AND NADA'S DAD ALL THE TIME.
BUT I DON'T EVEN REMEMBER OURS.
KAL... I'M SORRY.

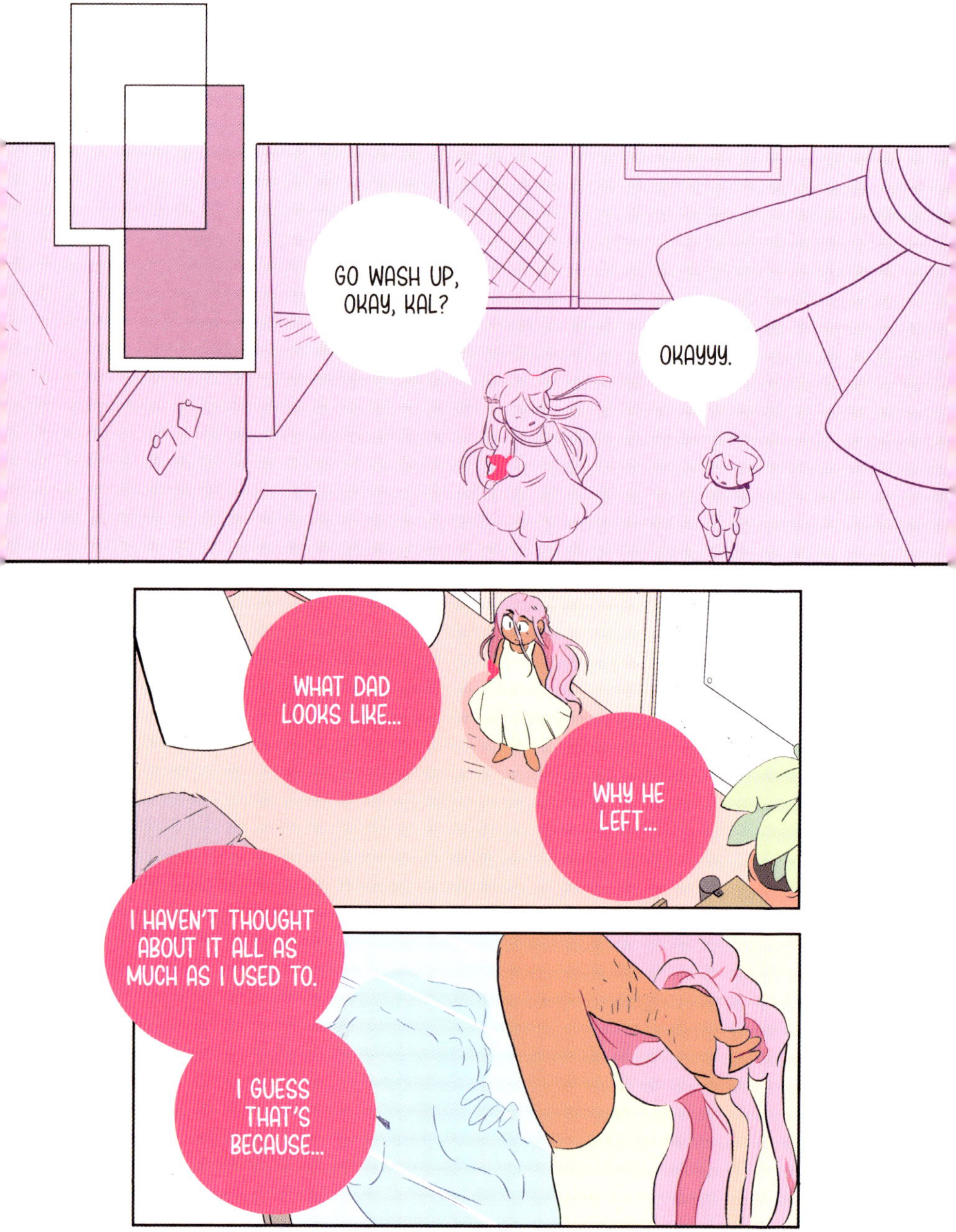
GO WASH UP, OKAY, KAL?
OKAYYY.
WHAT DAD LOOKS LIKE...
WHY HE LEFT...
I HAVEN'T THOUGHT ABOUT IT ALL AS MUCH AS I USED TO.
I GUESS THAT'S BECAUSE...

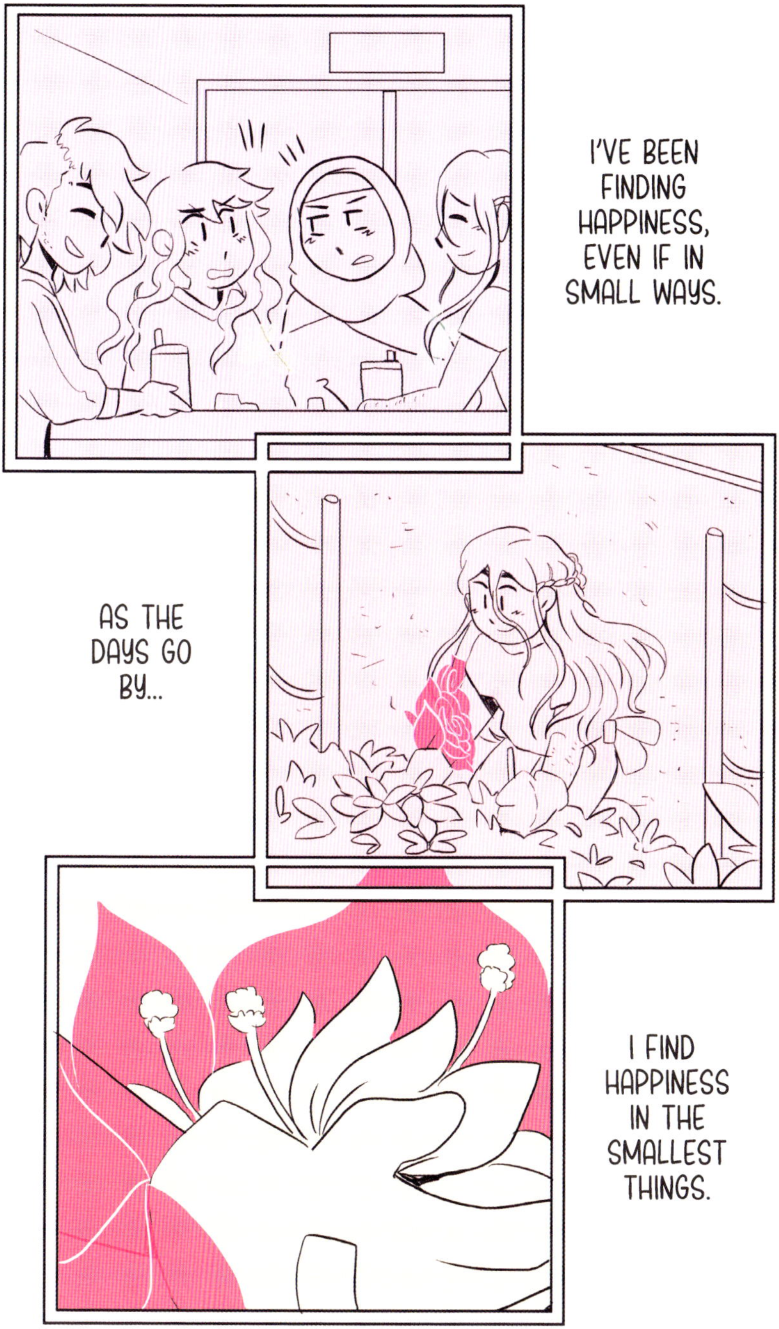

I'VE BEEN FINDING HAPPINESS, EVEN IF IN SMALL WAYS.

AS THE DAYS GO BY...

I FIND HAPPINESS IN THE SMALLEST THINGS.

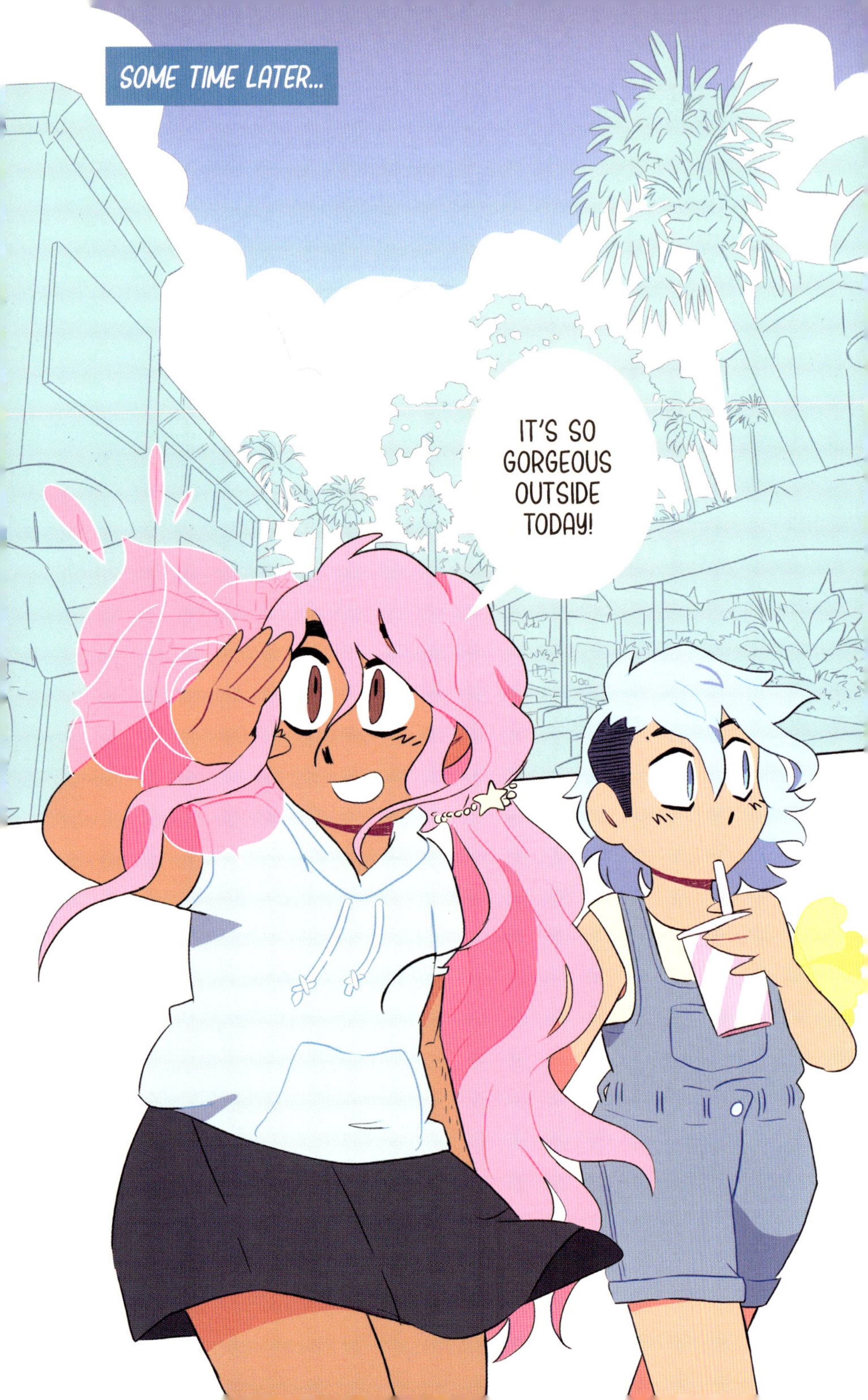
SOME TIME LATER...
IT'S SO GORGEOUS OUTSIDE TODAY!

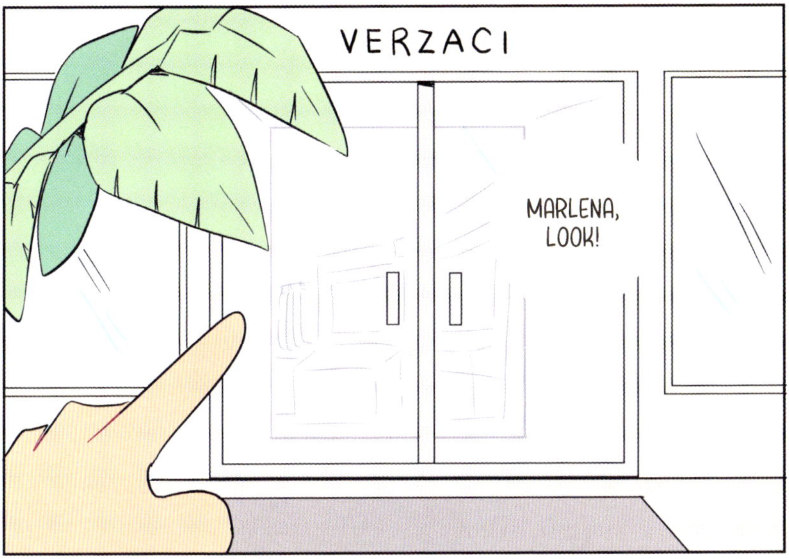
VERZACI
MARLENA, LOOK!

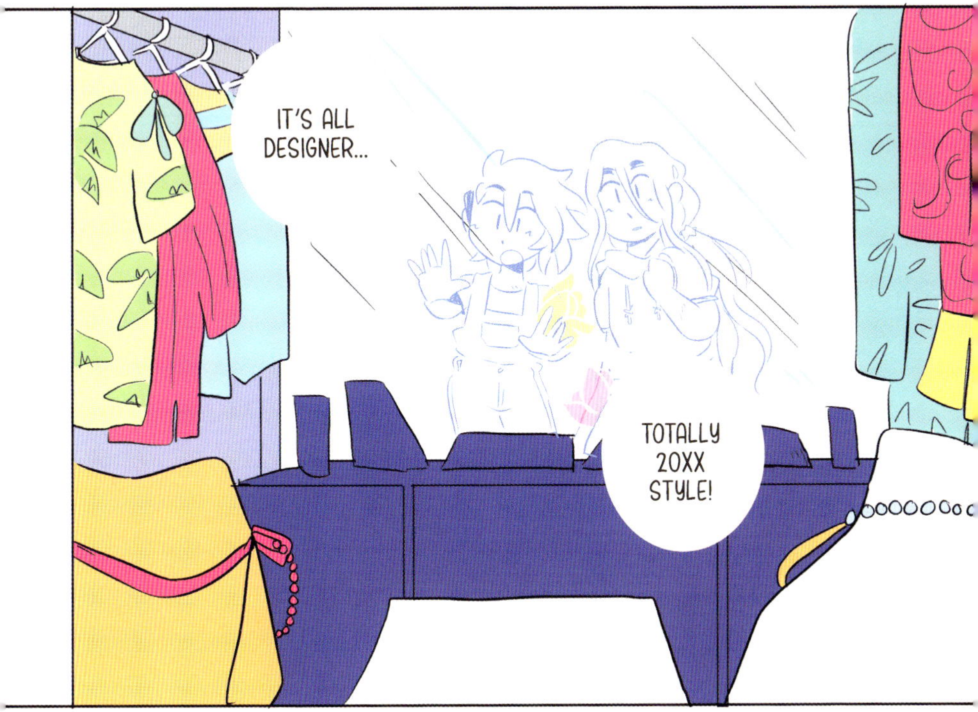
IT'S ALL DESIGNER...
TOTALLY 20XX STYLE!

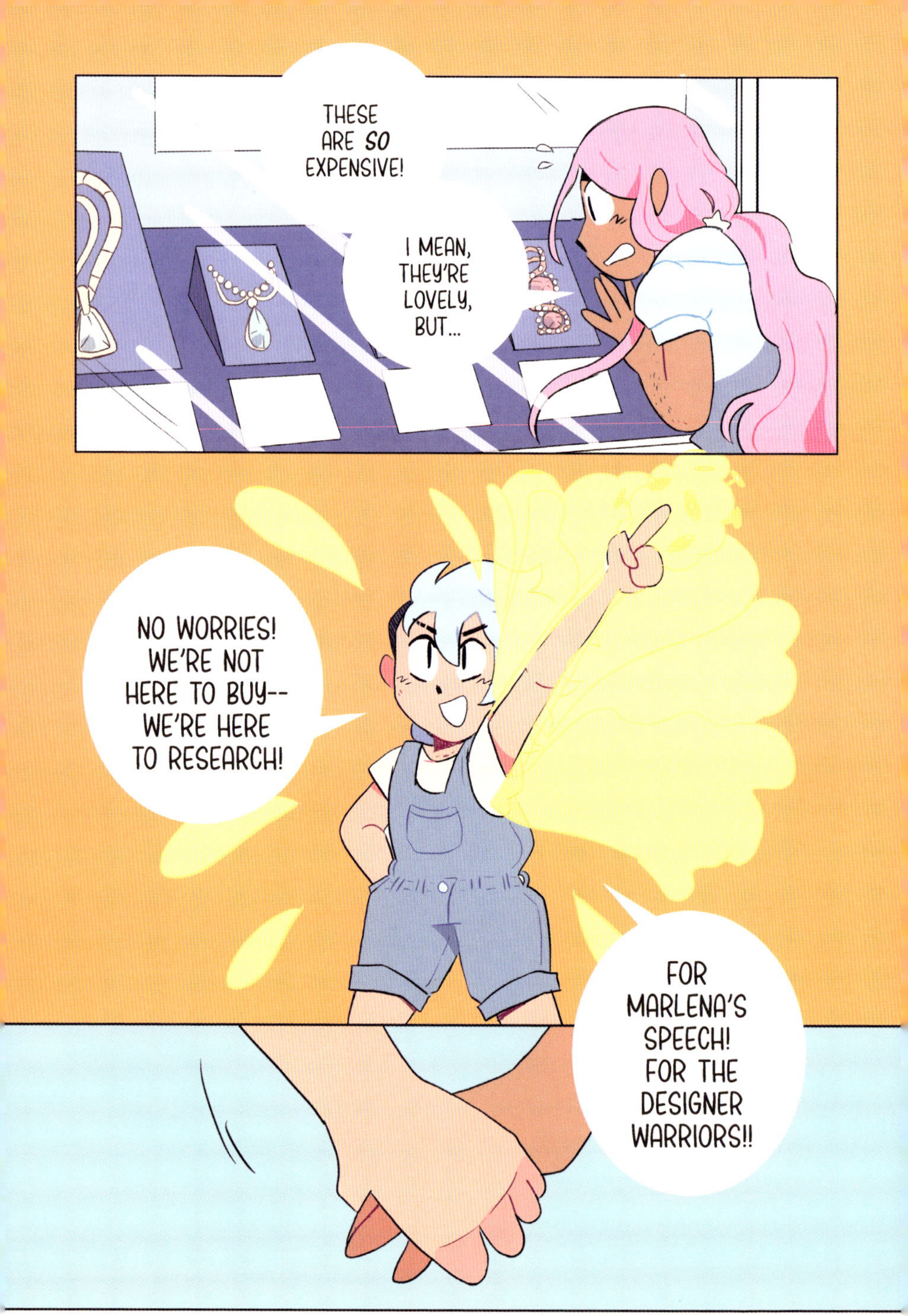
THESE ARE **SO** EXPENSIVE!
I MEAN, THEY'RE LOVELY, BUT...
NO WORRIES! WE'RE NOT HERE TO BUY-- WE'RE HERE TO RESEARCH!
FOR MARLENA'S SPEECH! FOR THE DESIGNER WARRIORS!!

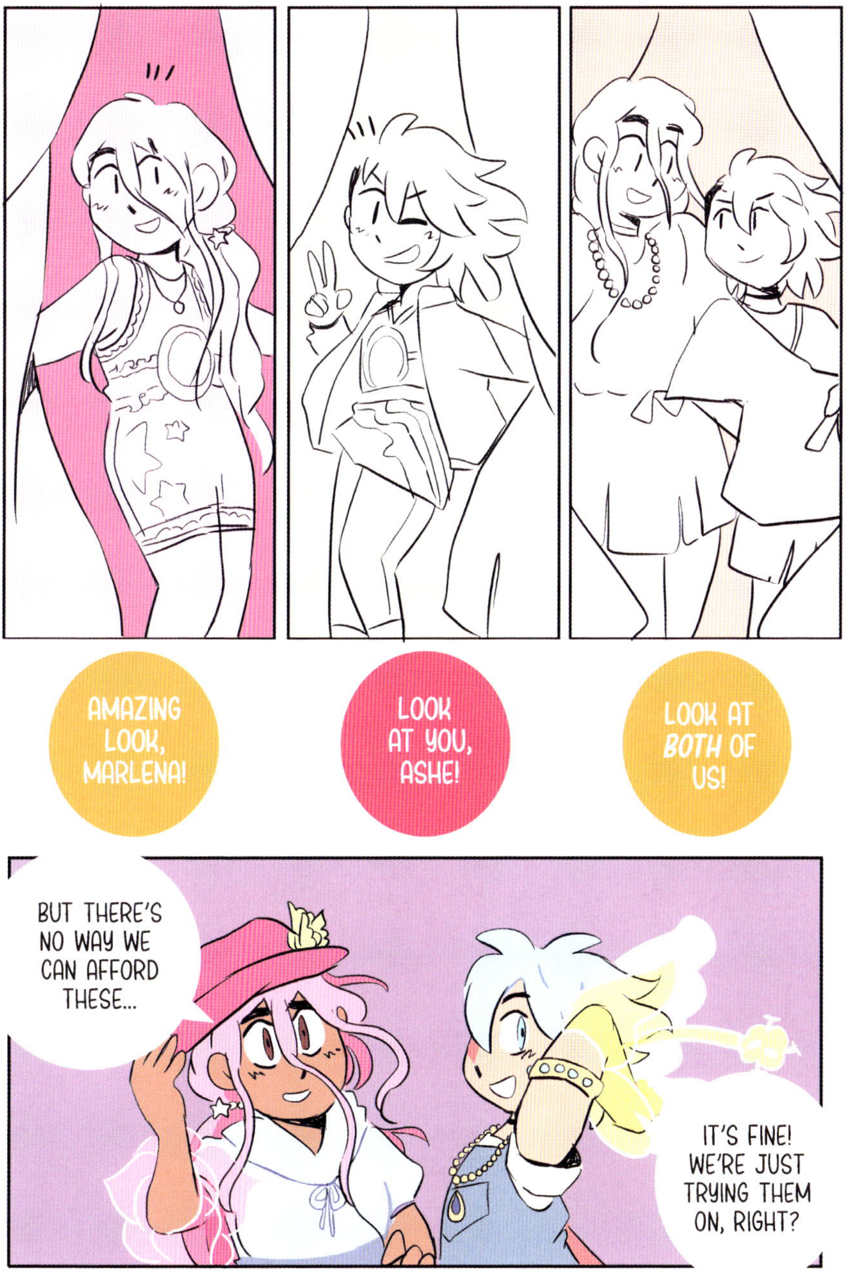
AMAZING LOOK, MARLENA!
LOOK AT YOU, ASHE!
LOOK AT *BOTH* OF US!
BUT THERE'S NO WAY WE CAN AFFORD THESE...
IT'S FINE! WE'RE JUST TRYING THEM ON, RIGHT?

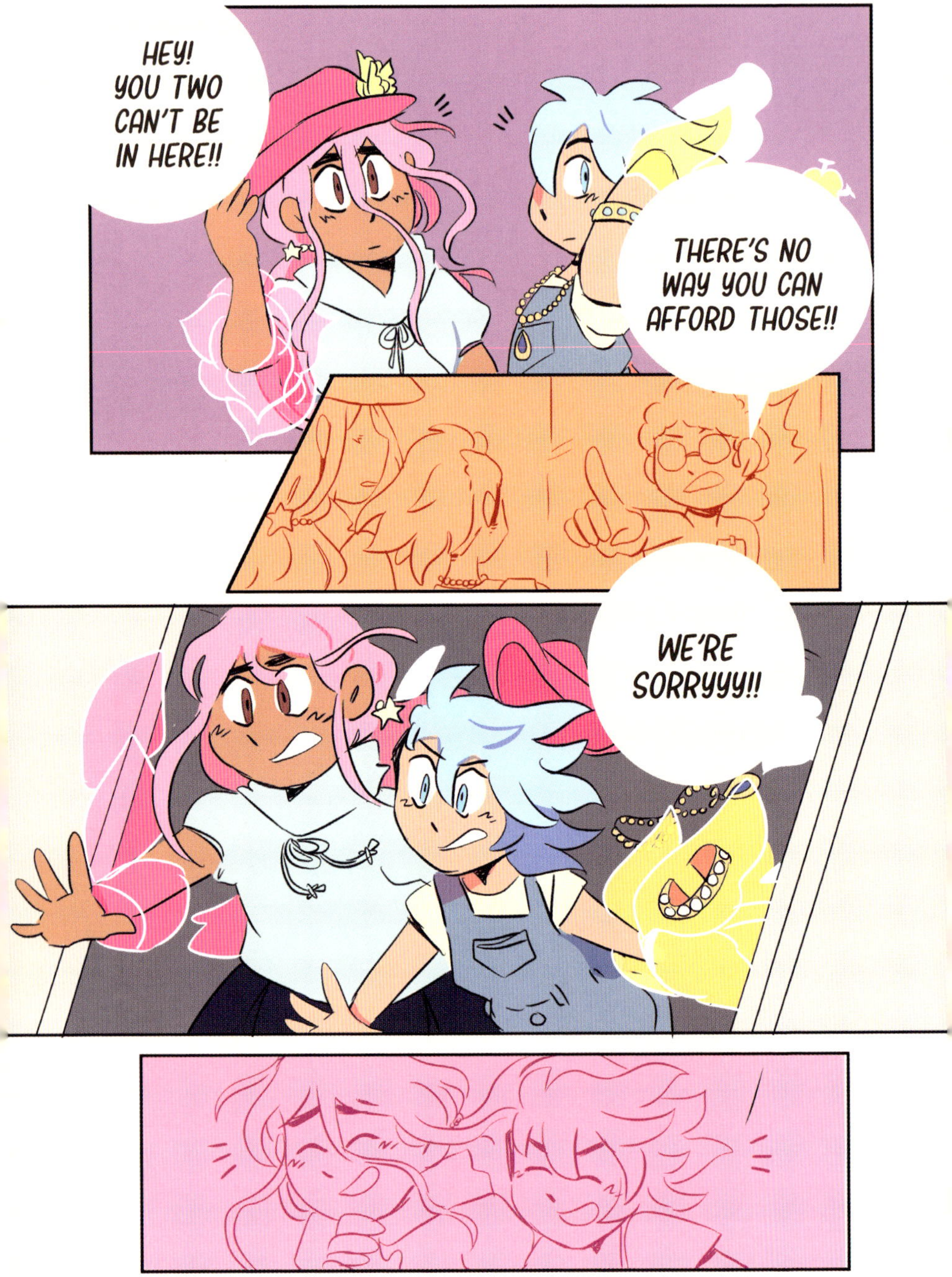
HEY! YOU TWO CAN'T BE IN HERE!!
THERE'S NO WAY YOU CAN AFFORD THOSE!!
WE'RE SORRYYY!!

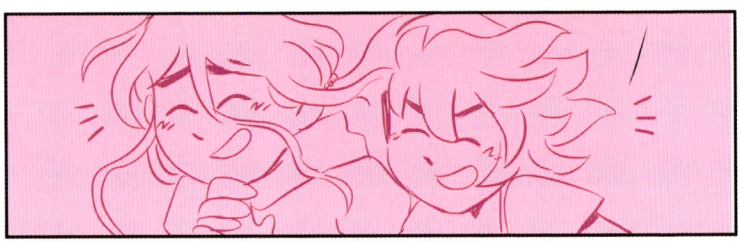

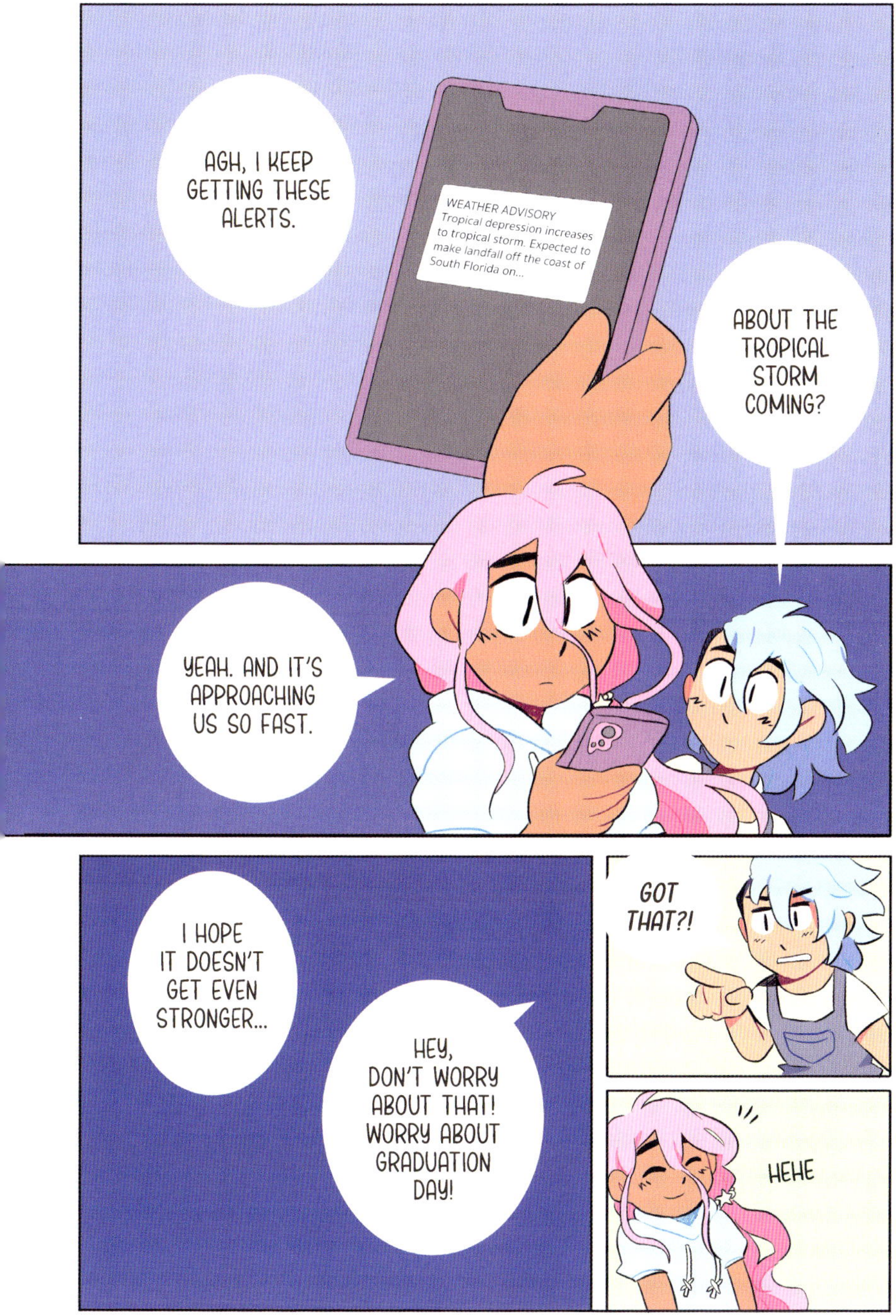
AGH, I KEEP GETTING THESE ALERTS.
WEATHER ADVISORY
Tropical depression increases to tropical storm. Expected to make landfall off the coast of South Florida on...
ABOUT THE TROPICAL STORM COMING?
YEAH. AND IT'S APPROACHING US SO FAST.
I HOPE IT DOESN'T GET EVEN STRONGER...
HEY, DON'T WORRY ABOUT THAT! WORRY ABOUT GRADUATION DAY!
GOT THAT?!
HEHE

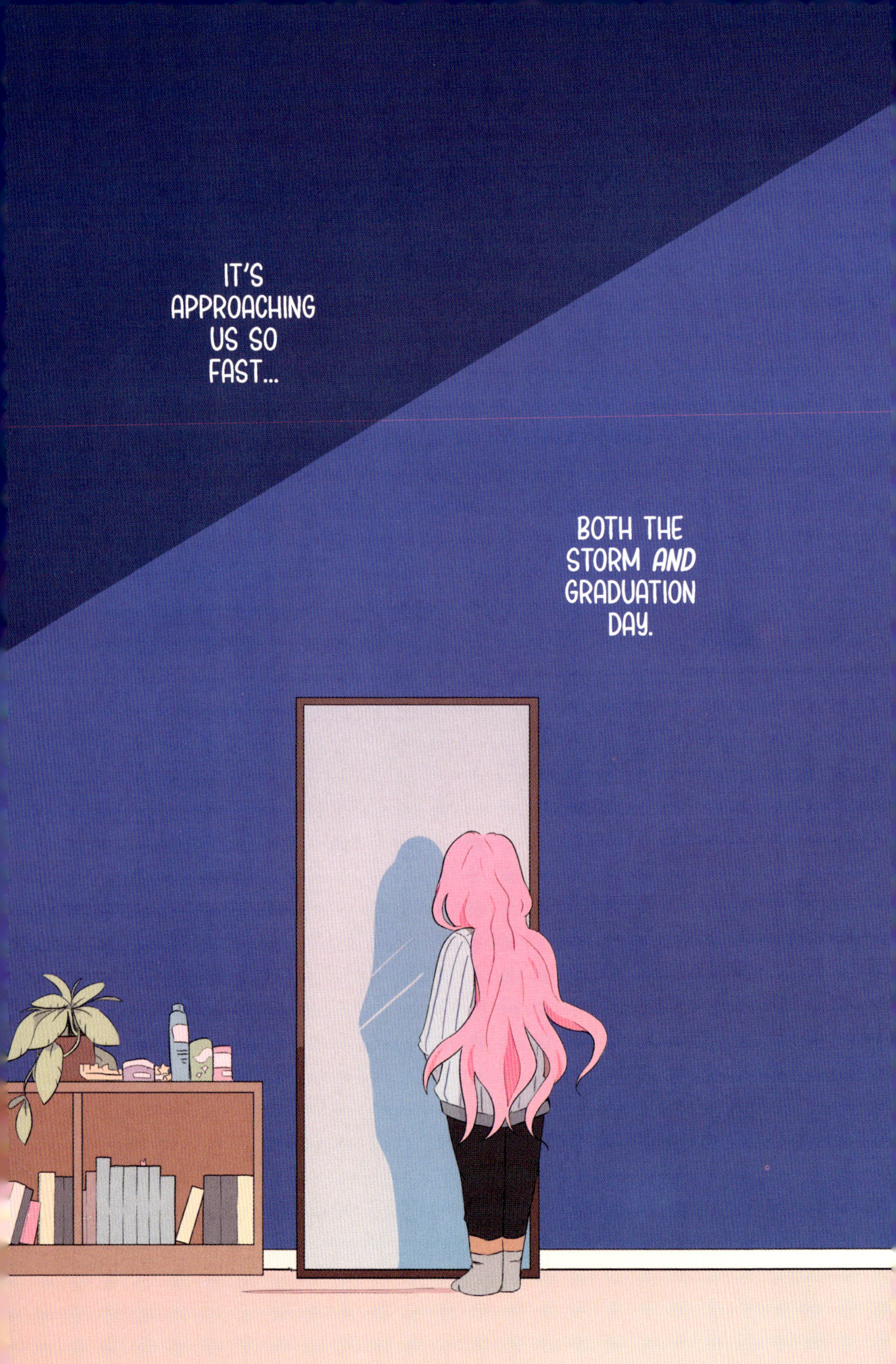
IT'S APPROACHING US SO FAST...
BOTH THE STORM *AND* GRADUATION DAY.

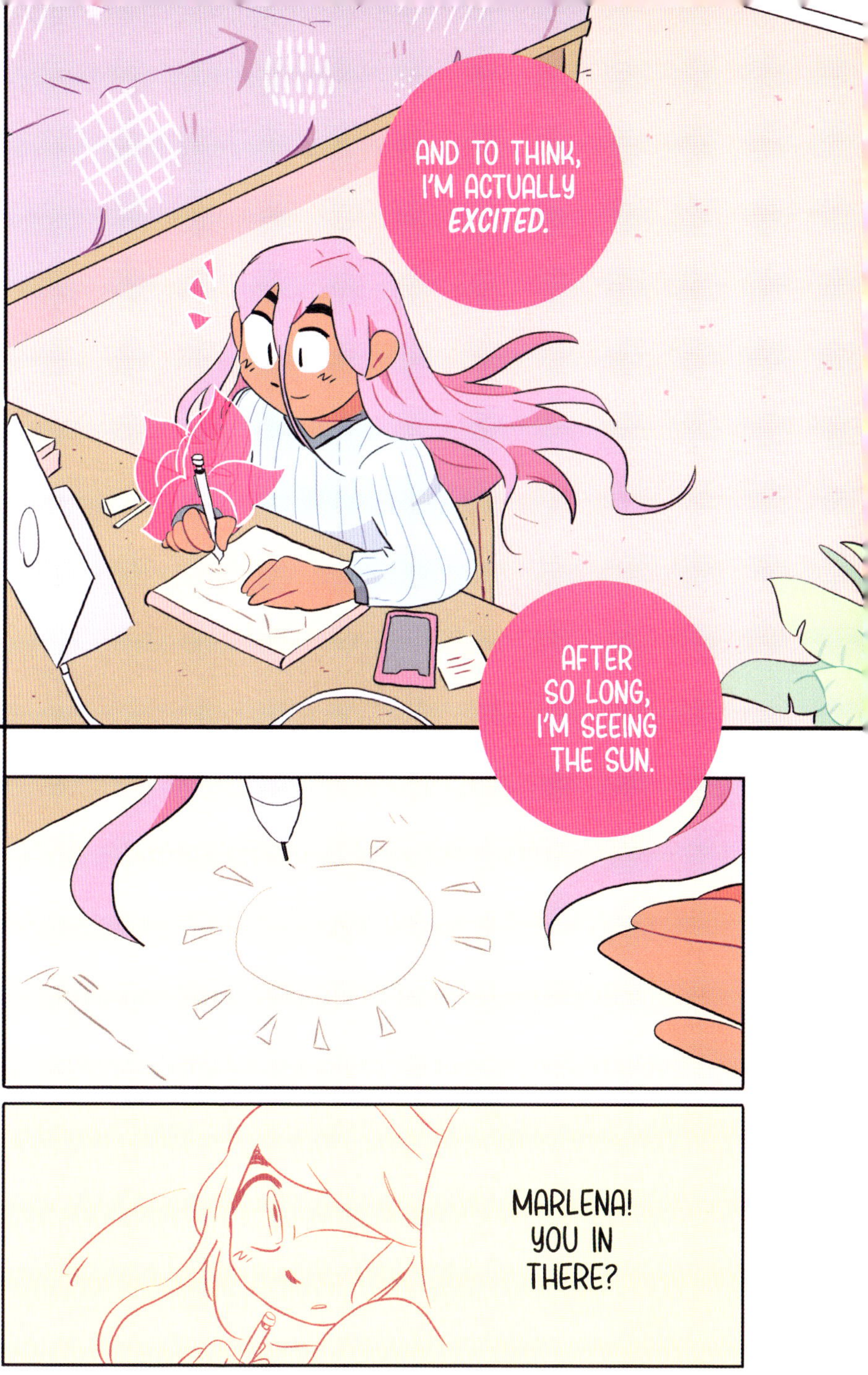

AND TO THINK, I'M ACTUALLY *EXCITED.*
AFTER SO LONG, I'M SEEING THE SUN.
MARLENA! YOU IN THERE?

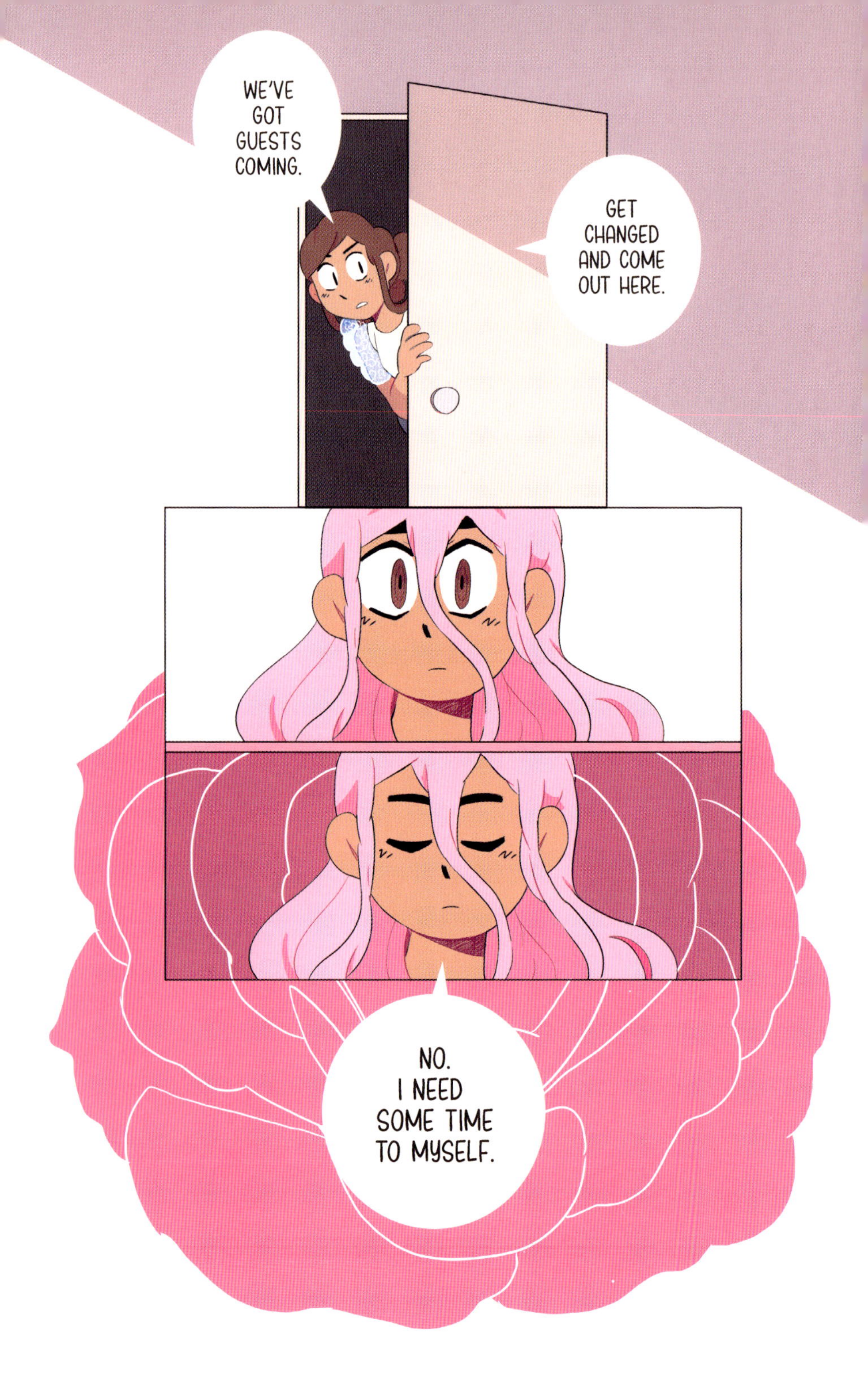
WE'VE GOT GUESTS COMING.
GET CHANGED AND COME OUT HERE.
NO. I NEED SOME TIME TO MYSELF.

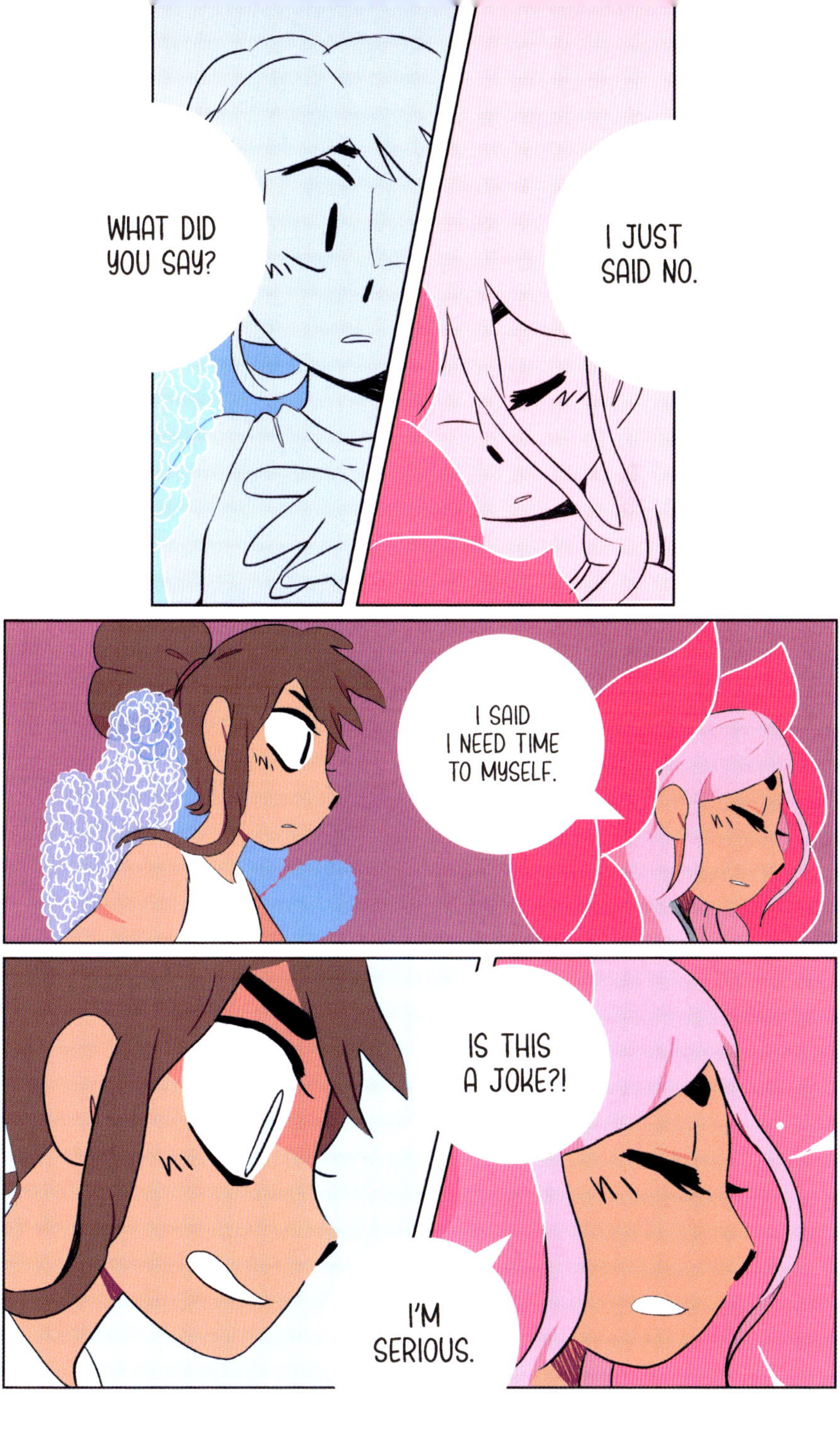
WHAT DID YOU SAY?
I JUST SAID NO.
I SAID I NEED TIME TO MYSELF.
IS THIS A JOKE?!
I'M SERIOUS.

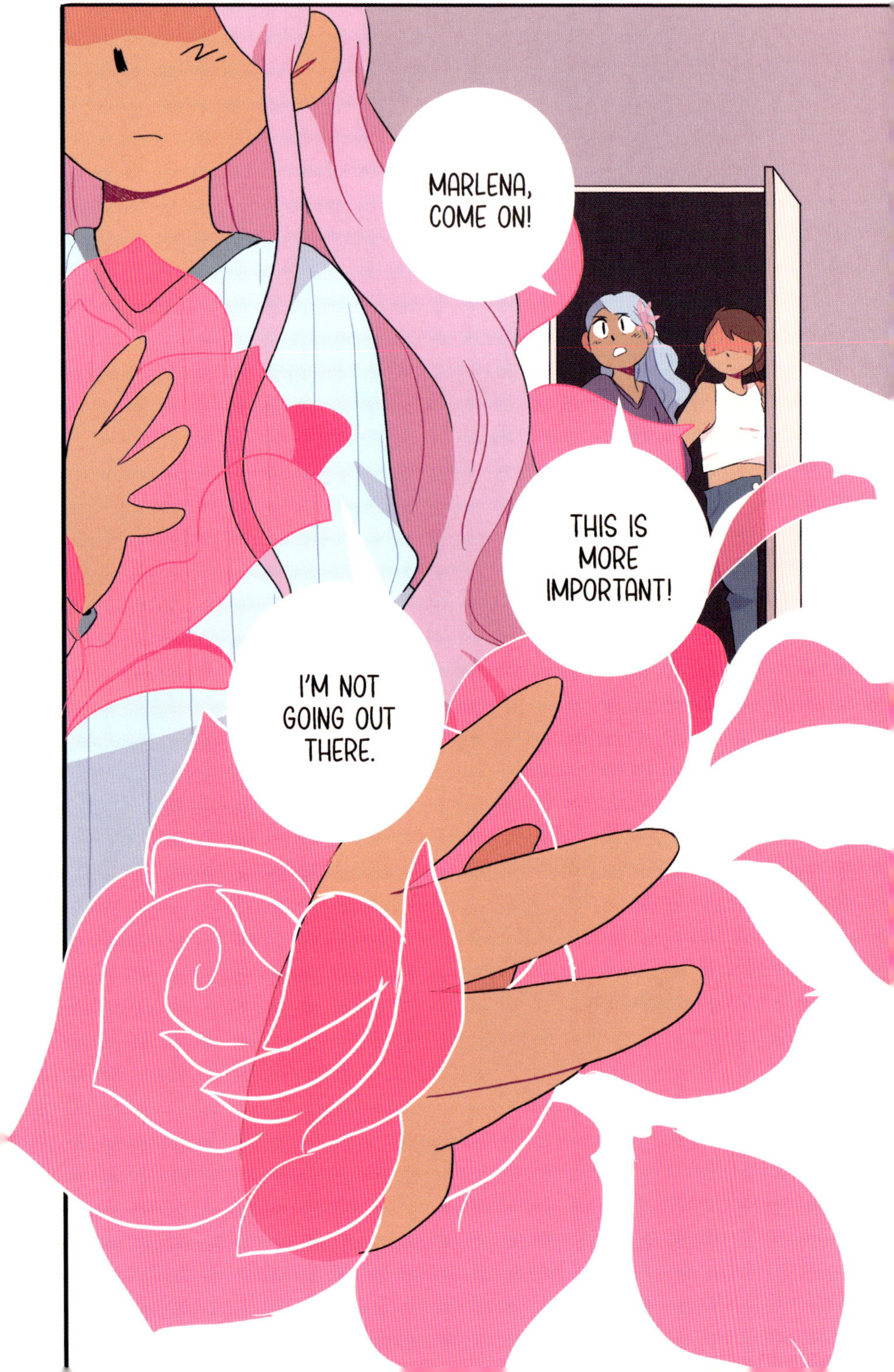
MARLENA,
COME ON!
THIS IS
MORE
IMPORTANT!
I'M NOT
GOING OUT
THERE.

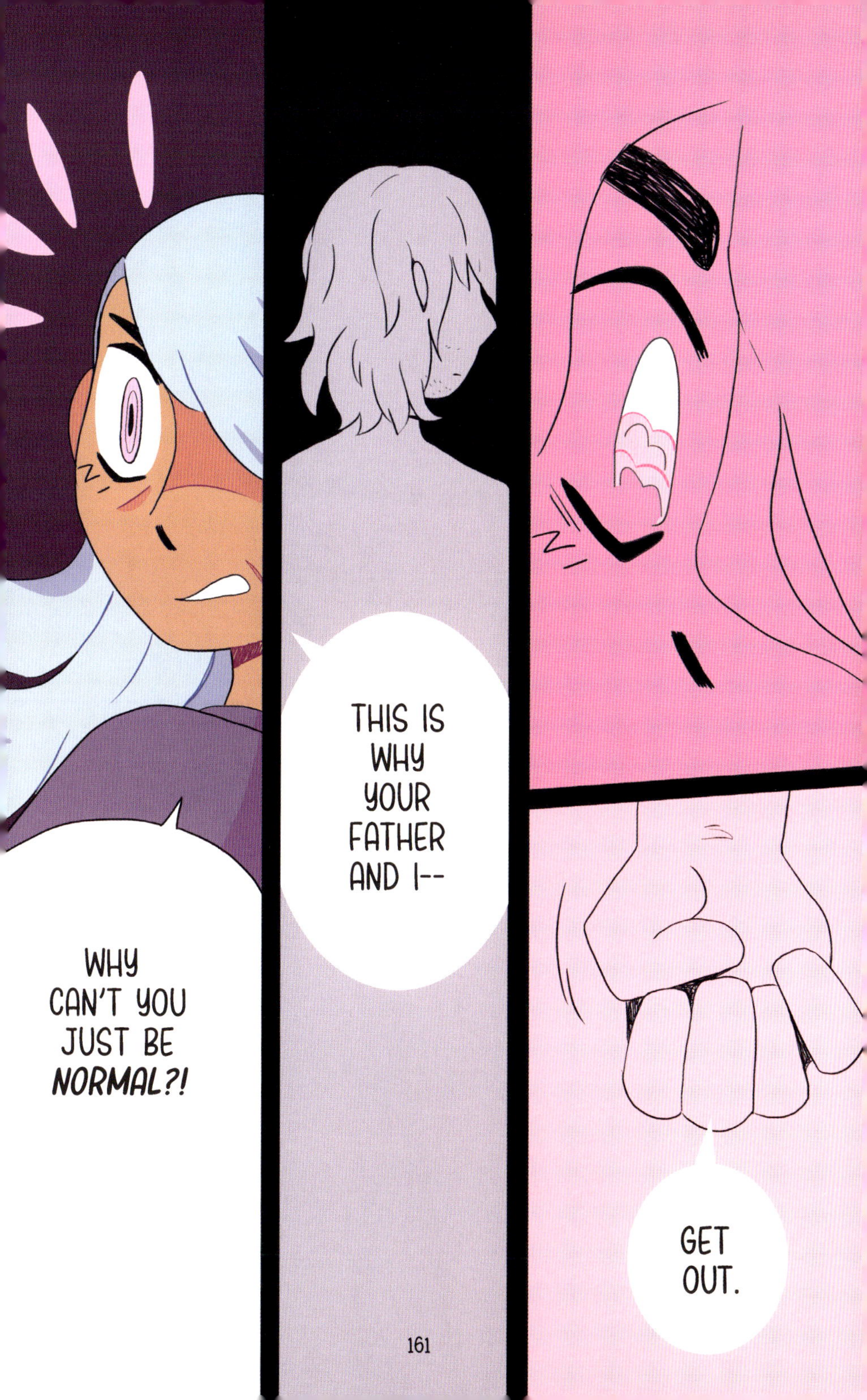
WHY CAN'T YOU JUST BE NORMAL?!
THIS IS WHY YOUR FATHER AND I--
GET OUT.

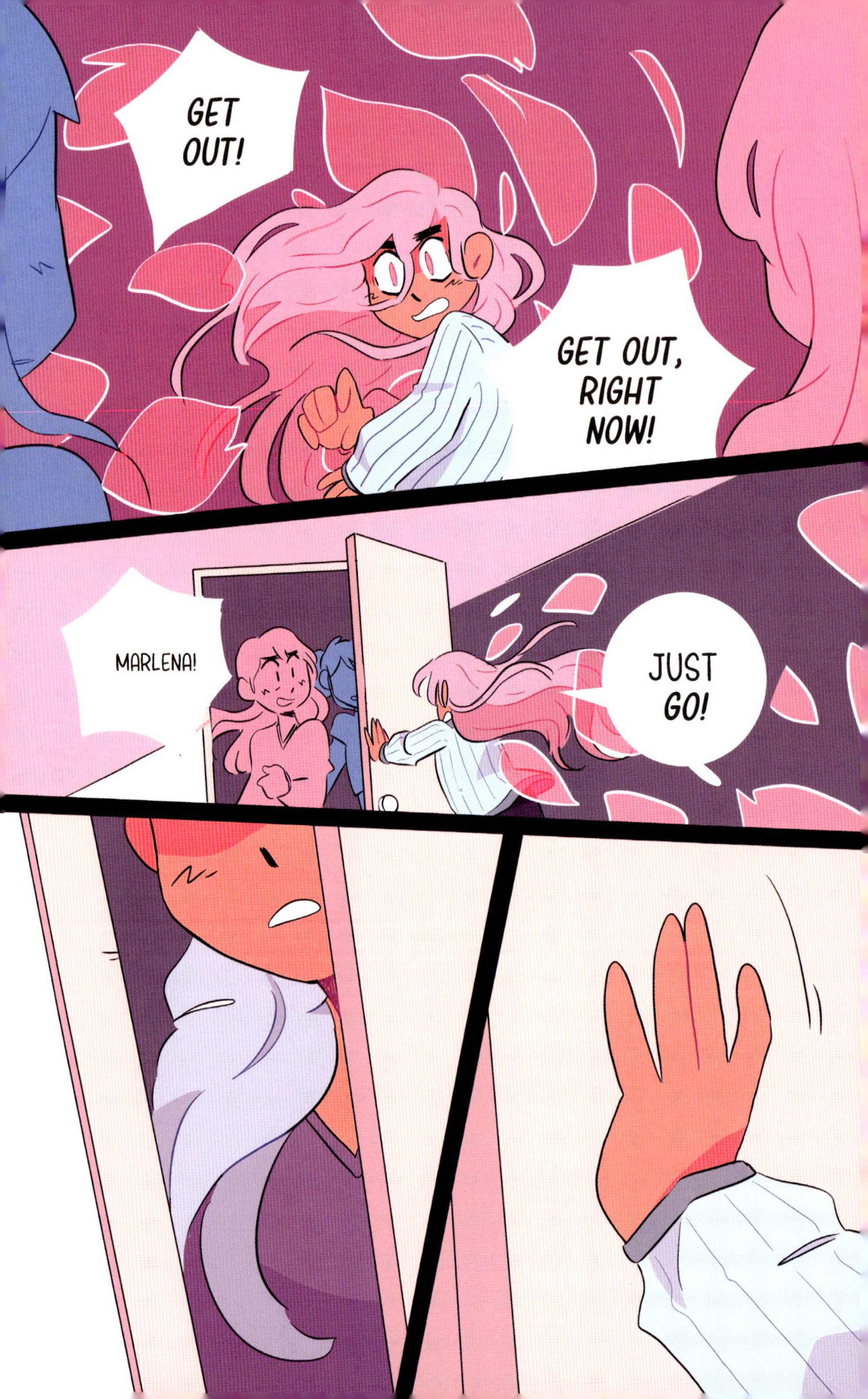
GET OUT!
GET OUT, RIGHT NOW!
MARLENA!
JUST GO!

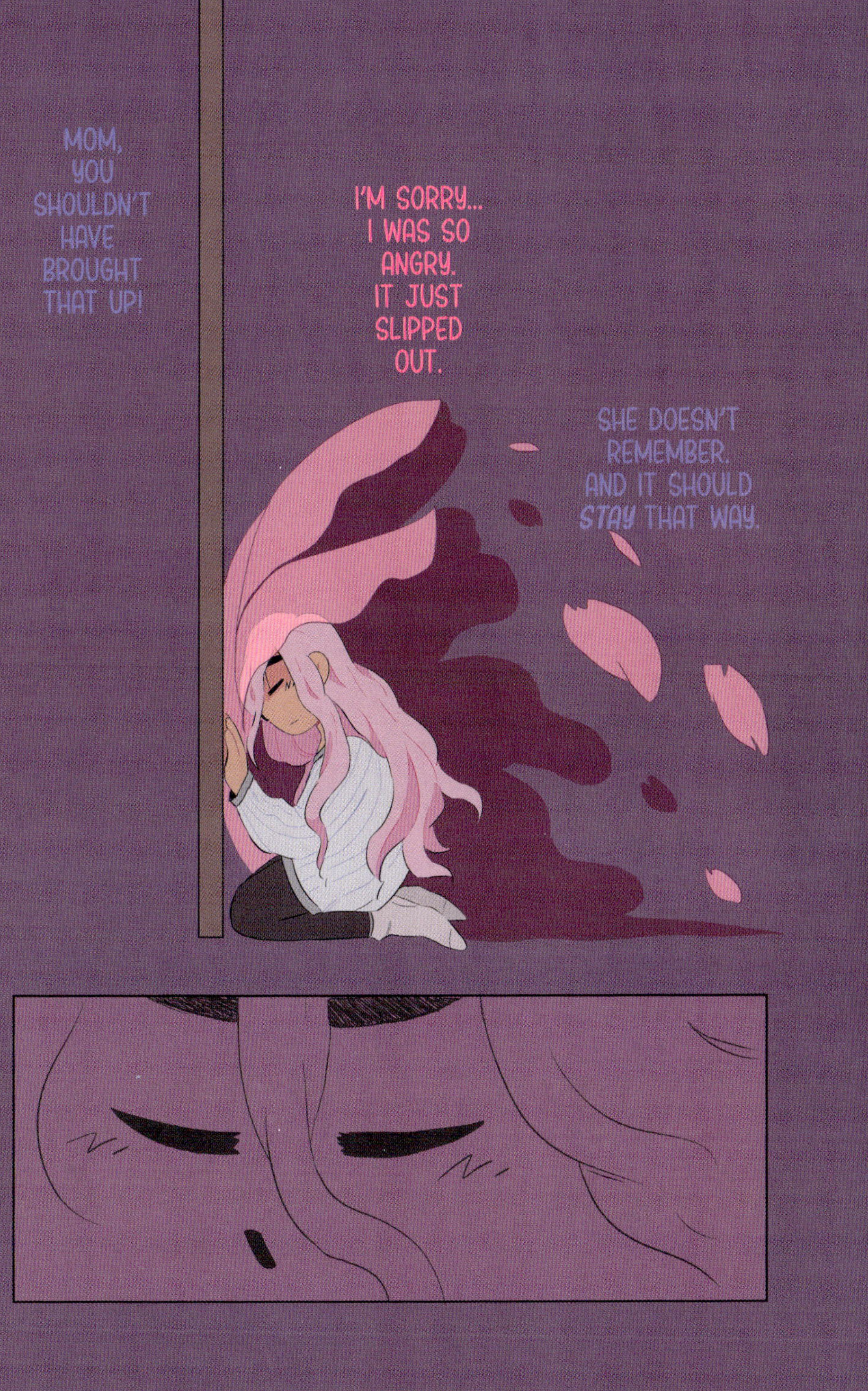
MOM, YOU SHOULDN'T HAVE BROUGHT THAT UP!
I'M SORRY... I WAS SO ANGRY. IT JUST SLIPPED OUT.
SHE DOESN'T REMEMBER. AND IT SHOULD *STAY* THAT WAY.

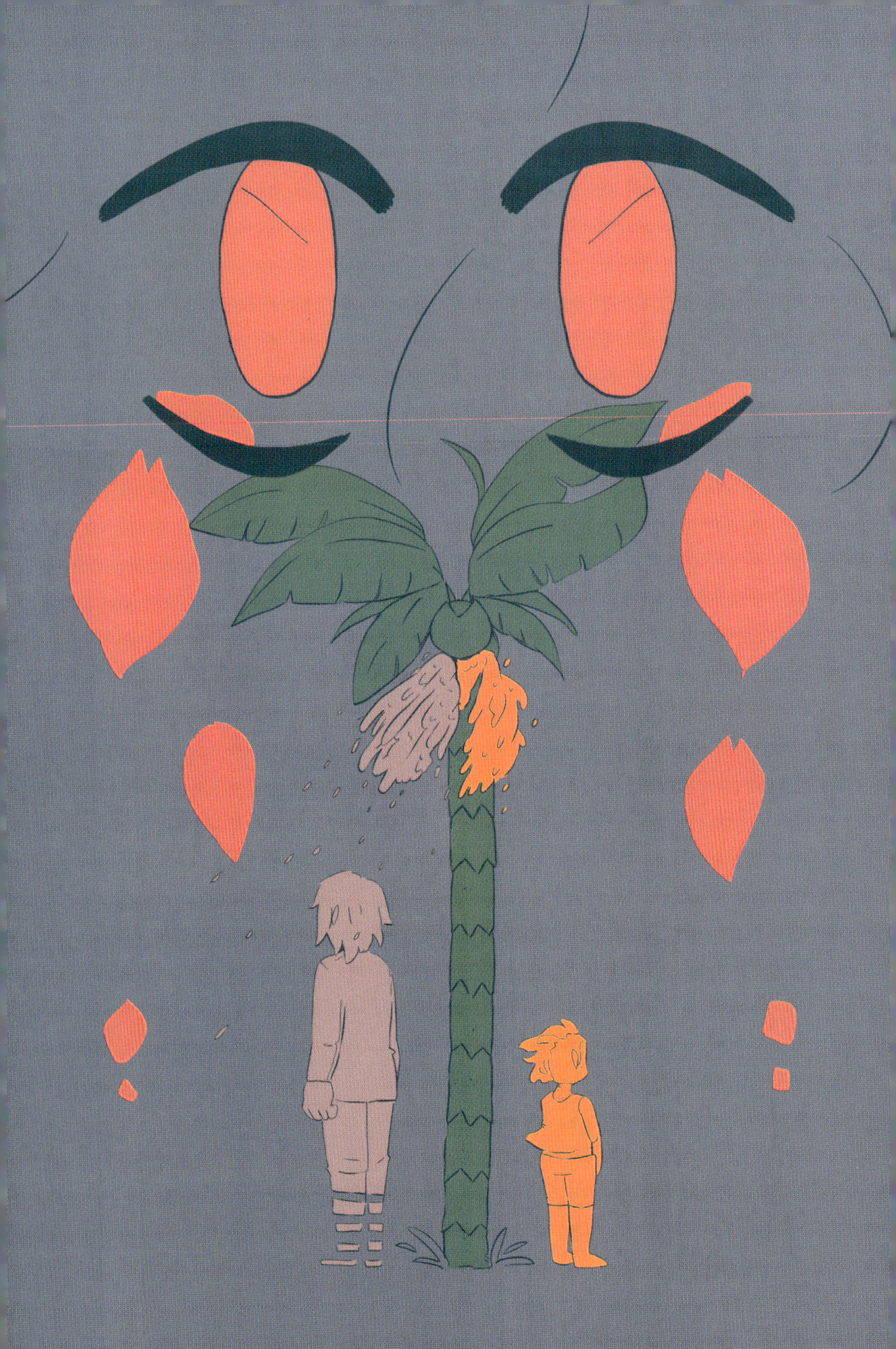

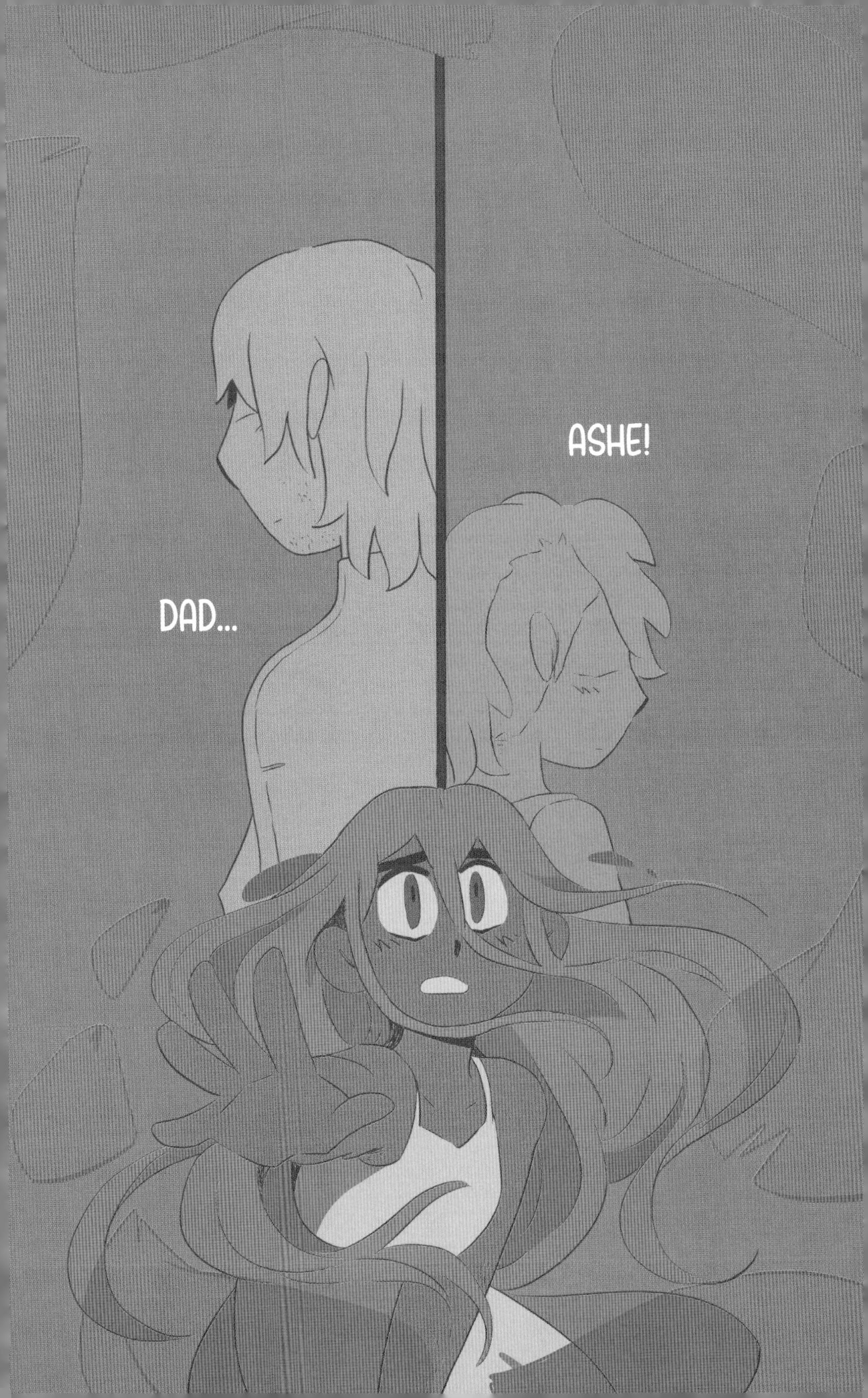
ASHE!
DAD...

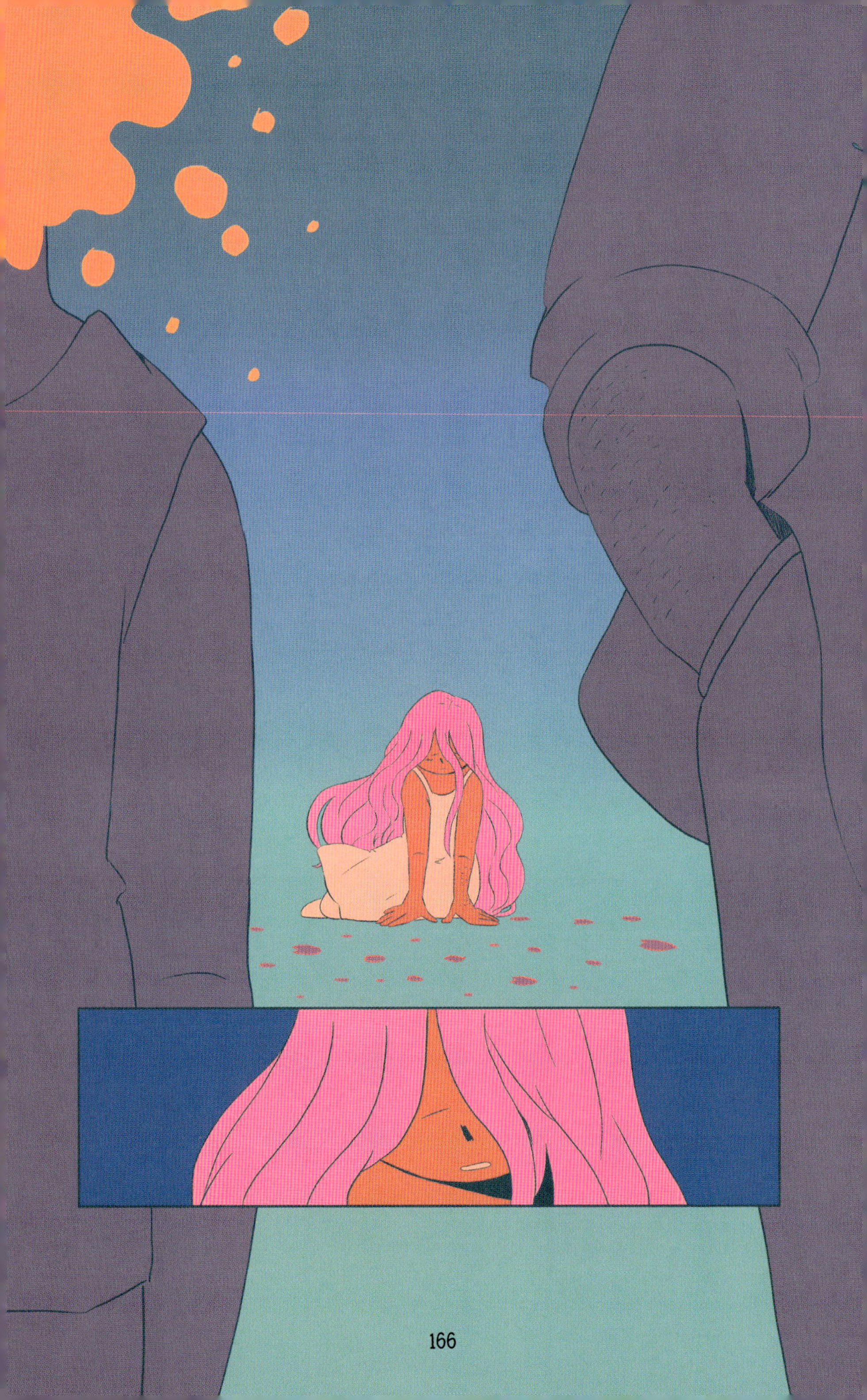

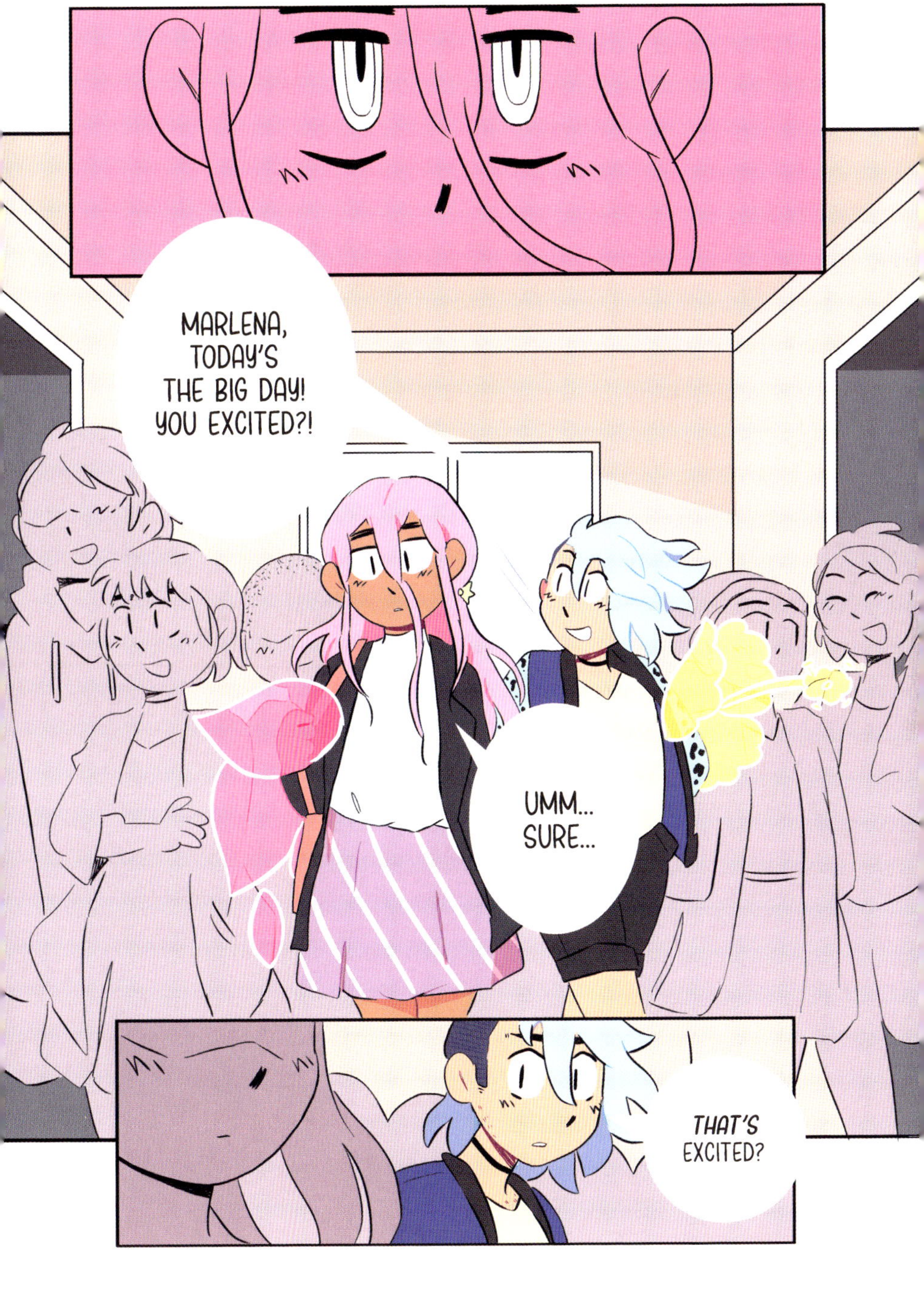
MARLENA, TODAY'S THE BIG DAY! YOU EXCITED?!
UMM... SURE...
THAT'S EXCITED?

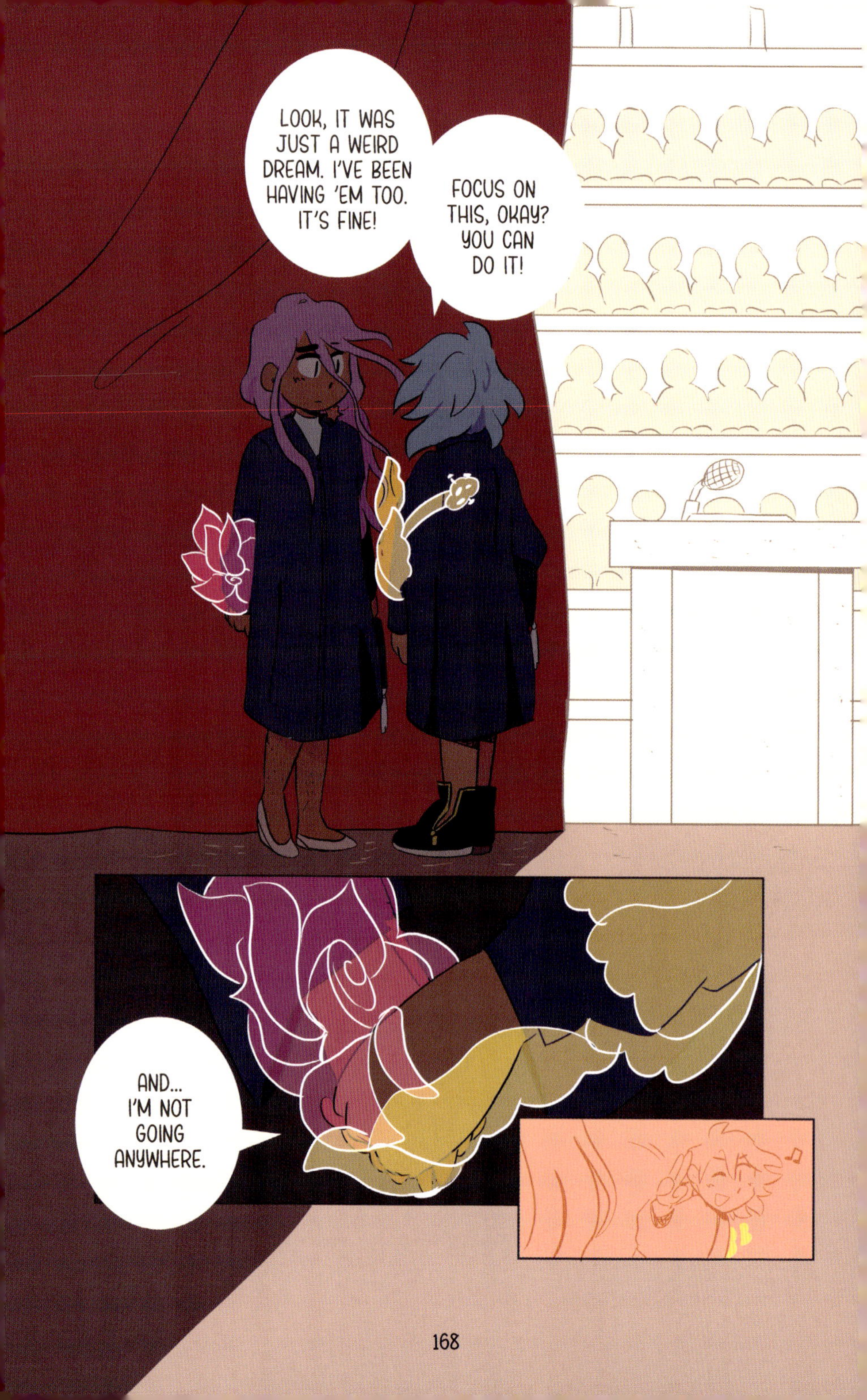
LOOK, IT WAS JUST A WEIRD DREAM. I'VE BEEN HAVING 'EM TOO. IT'S FINE!
FOCUS ON THIS, OKAY? YOU CAN DO IT!
AND... I'M NOT GOING ANYWHERE.

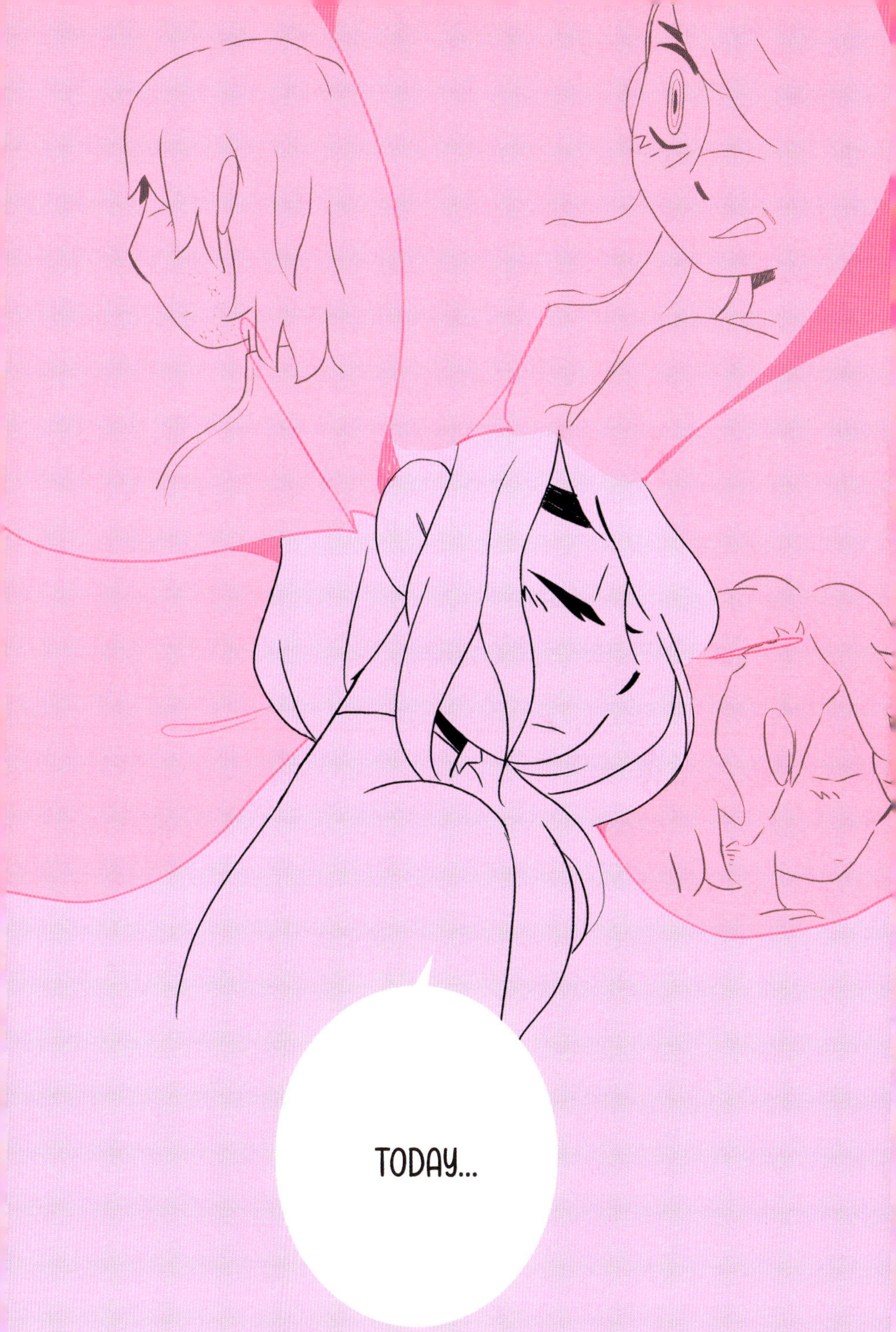
TODAY...

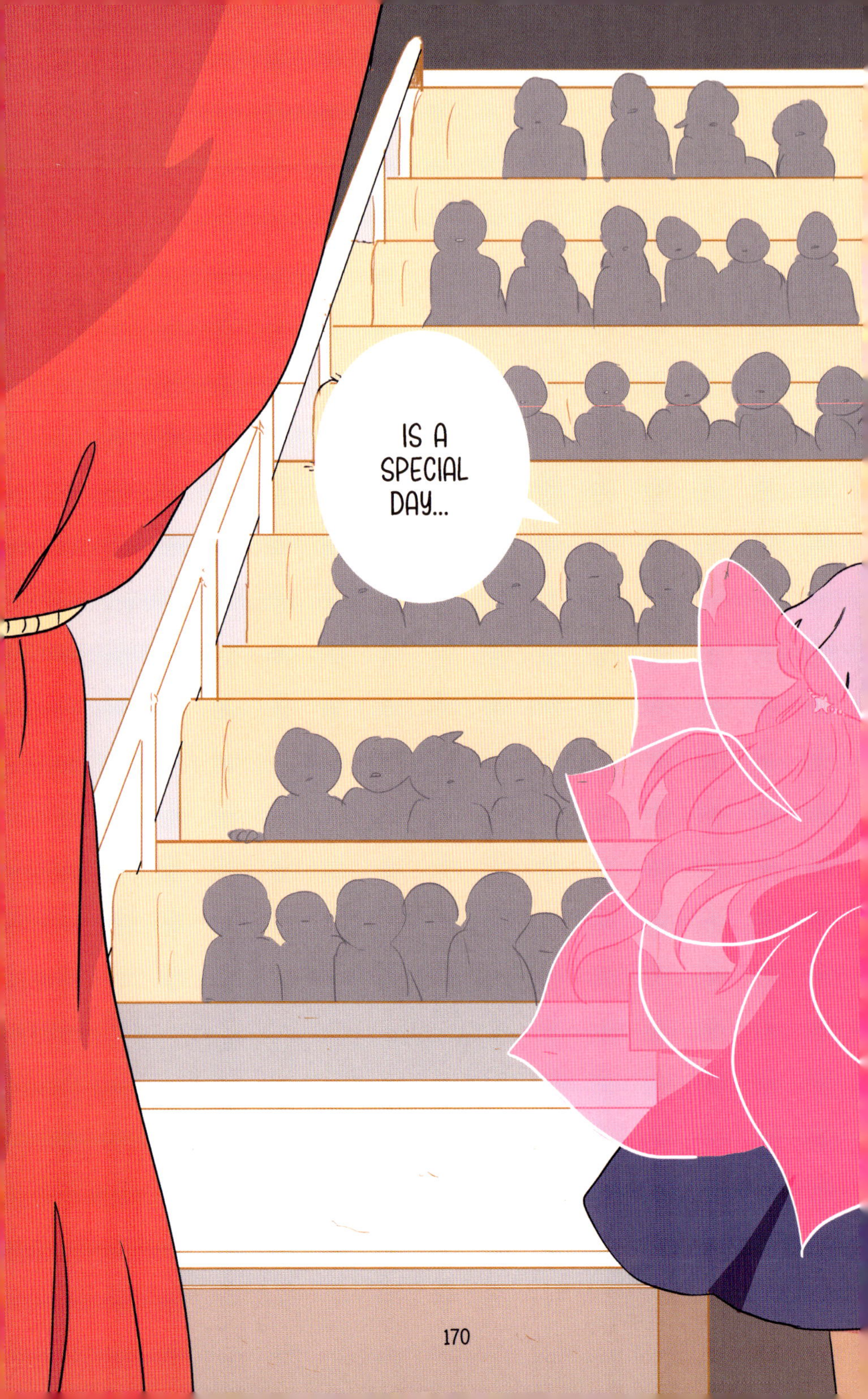
IS A SPECIAL DAY...

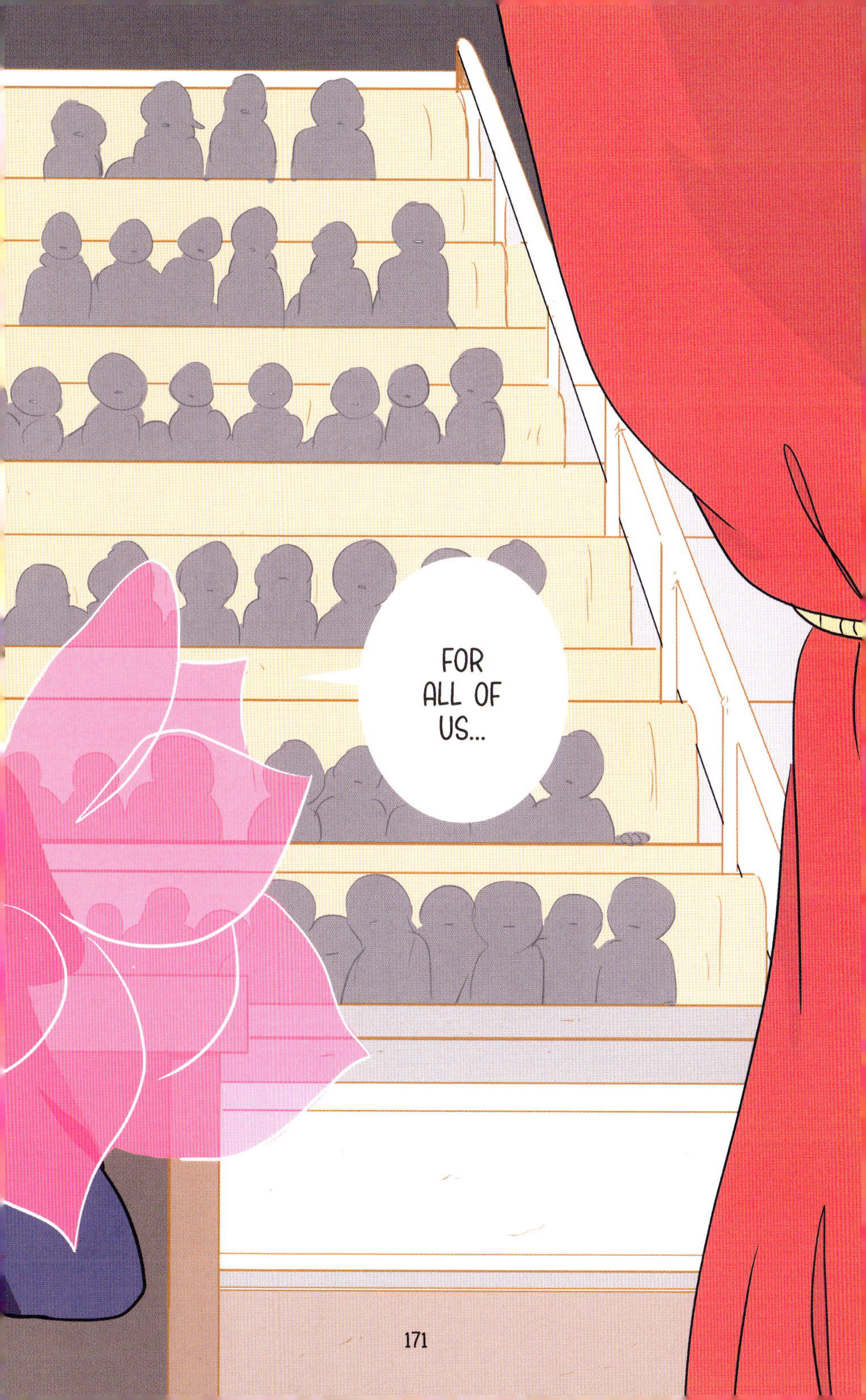
FOR ALL OF US...

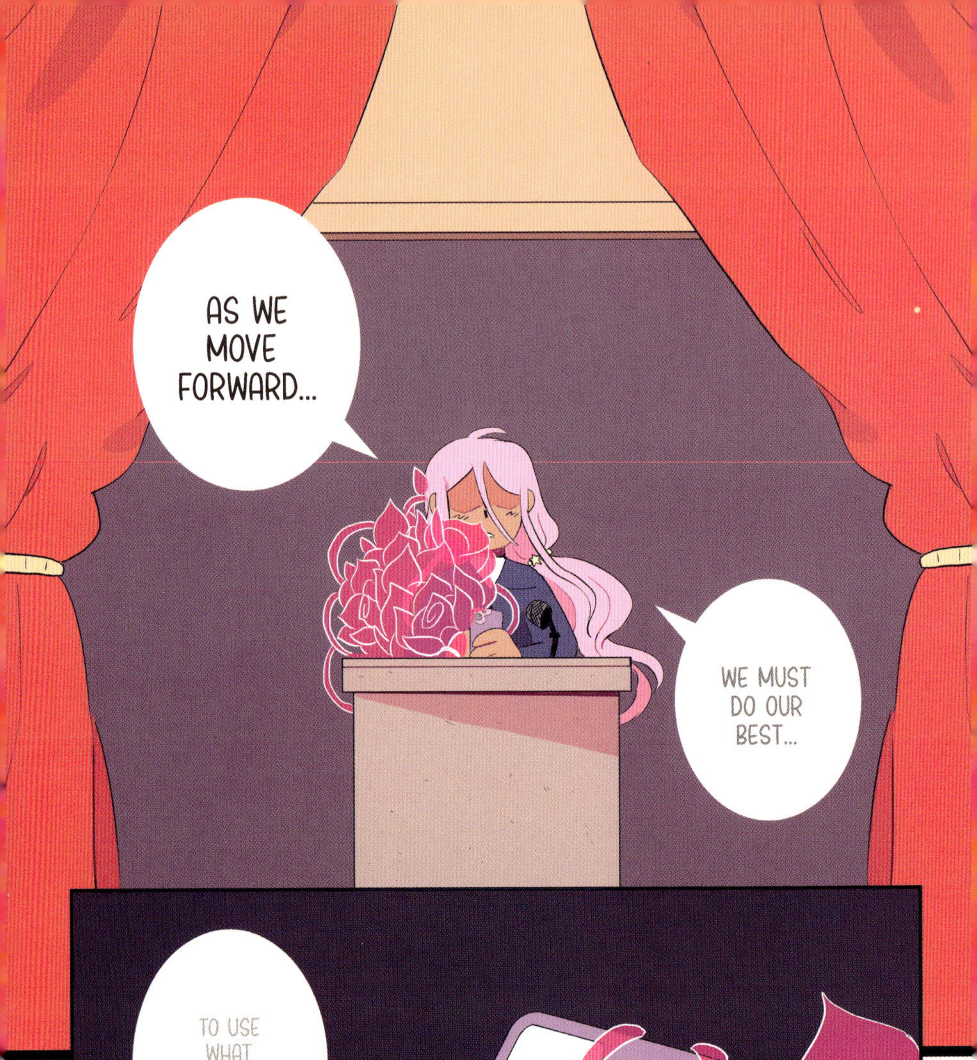
AS WE MOVE FORWARD...
WE MUST DO OUR BEST...
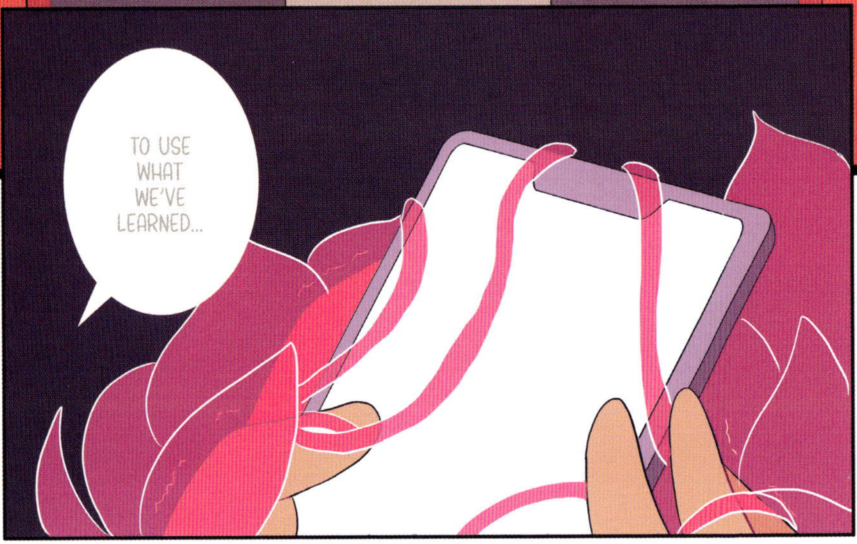
TO USE WHAT WE'VE LEARNED...

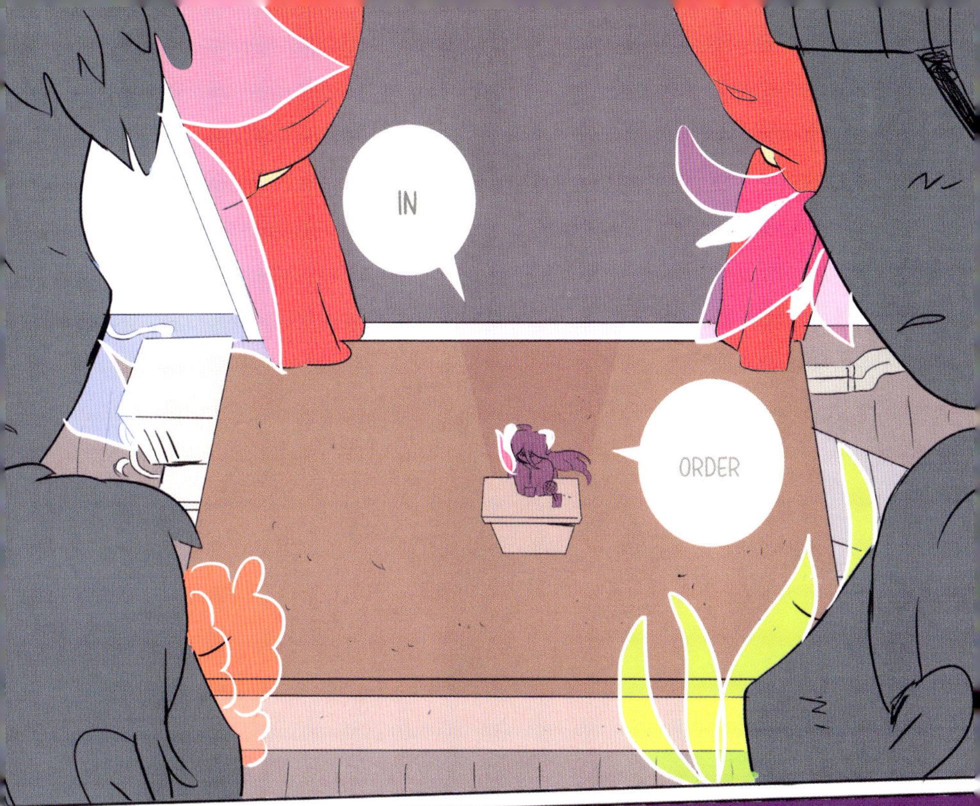
IN
ORDER

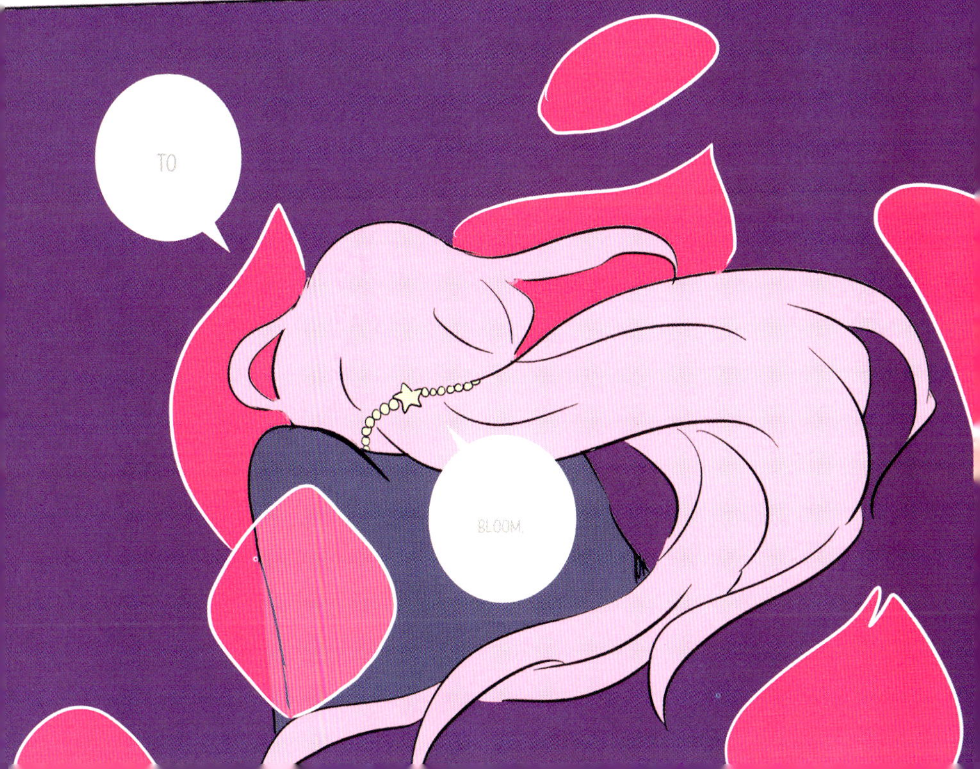
TO
BLOOM

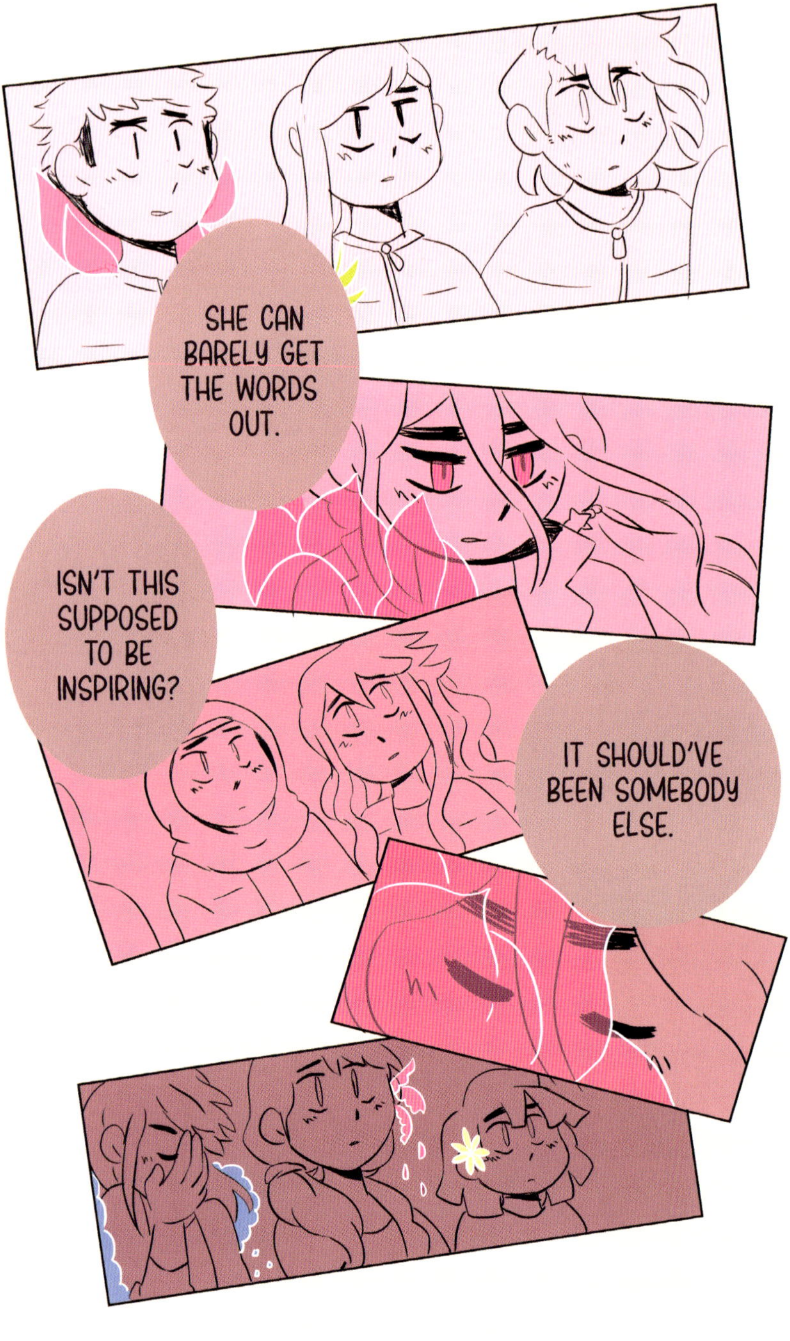
SHE CAN BARELY GET THE WORDS OUT.
ISN'T THIS SUPPOSED TO BE INSPIRING?
IT SHOULD'VE BEEN SOMEBODY ELSE.

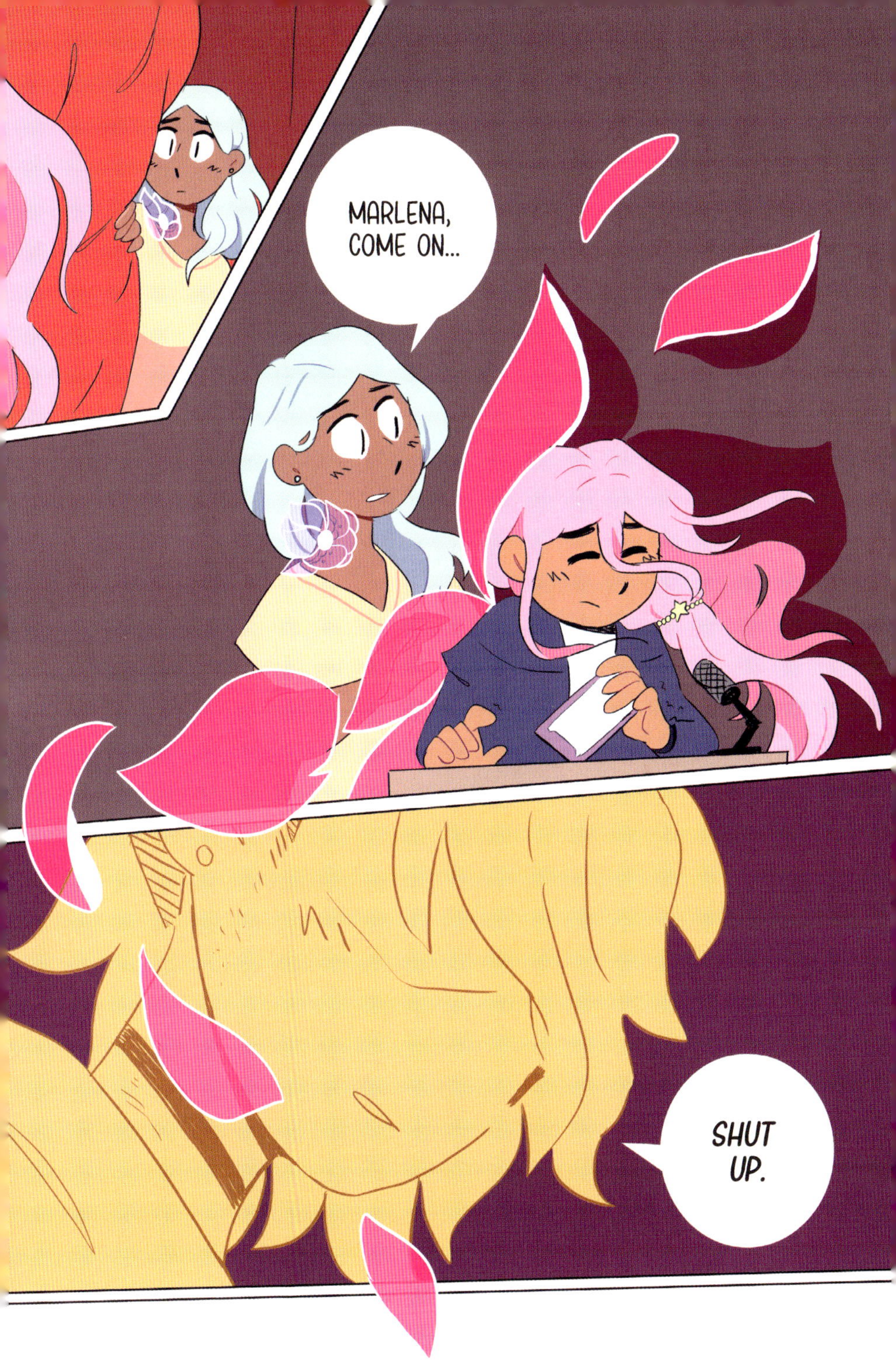
MARLENA, COME ON...
SHUT UP.

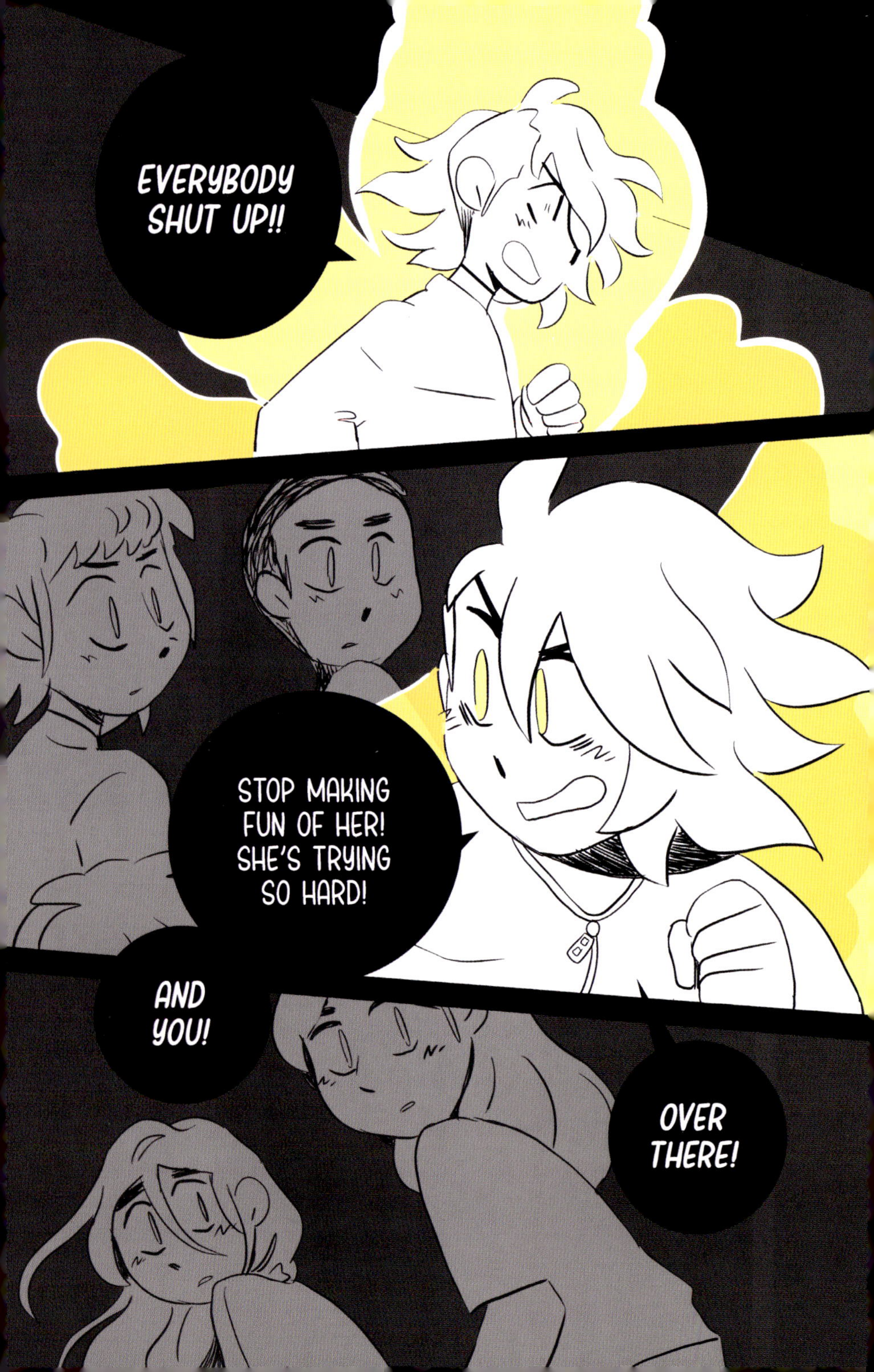
EVERYBODY SHUT UP!!
STOP MAKING FUN OF HER! SHE'S TRYING SO HARD!
AND YOU!
OVER THERE!

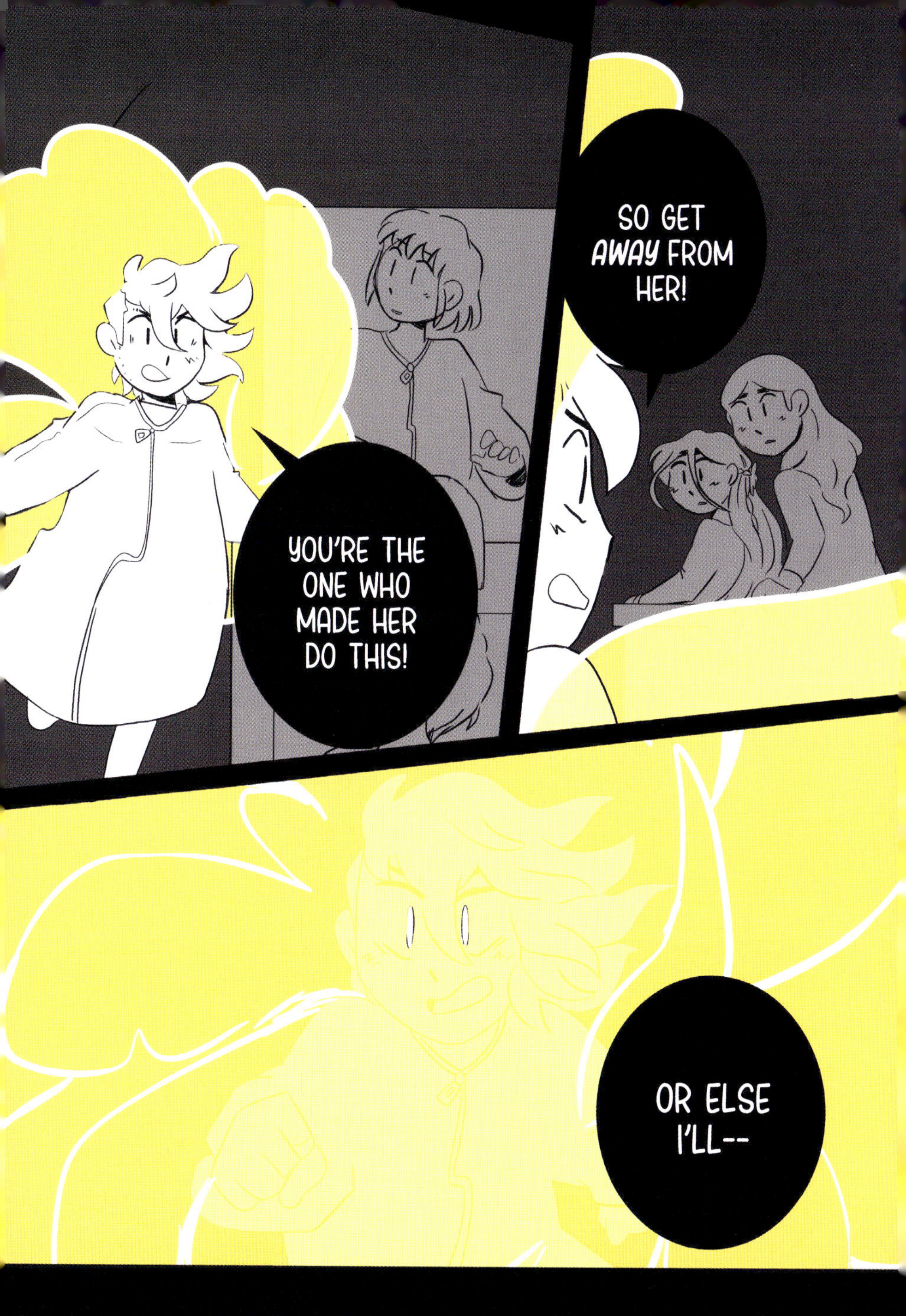
YOU'RE THE ONE WHO MADE HER DO THIS!
SO GET AWAY FROM HER!
OR ELSE I'LL--

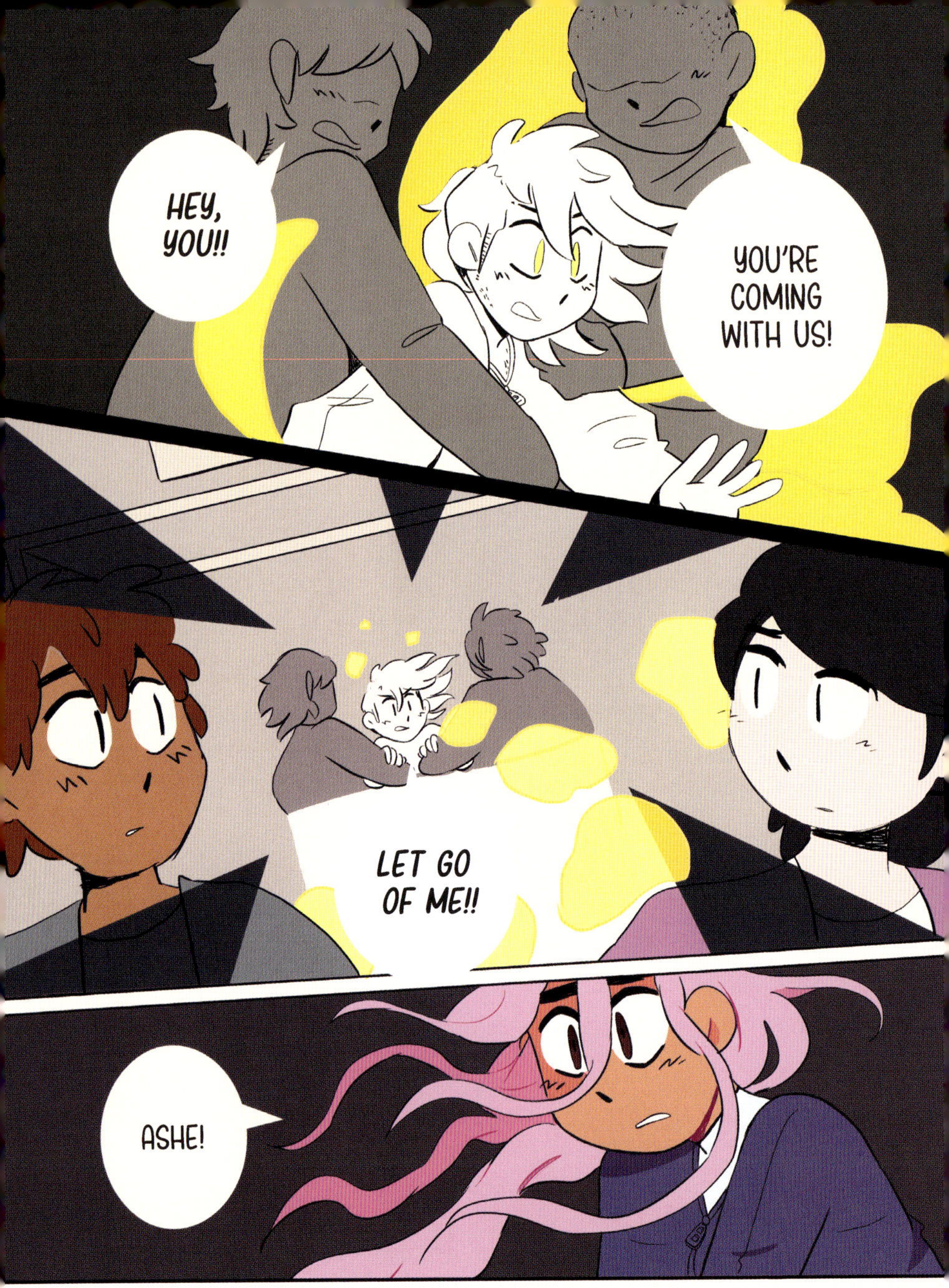
HEY, YOU!!
YOU'RE COMING WITH US!
LET GO OF ME!!
ASHE!

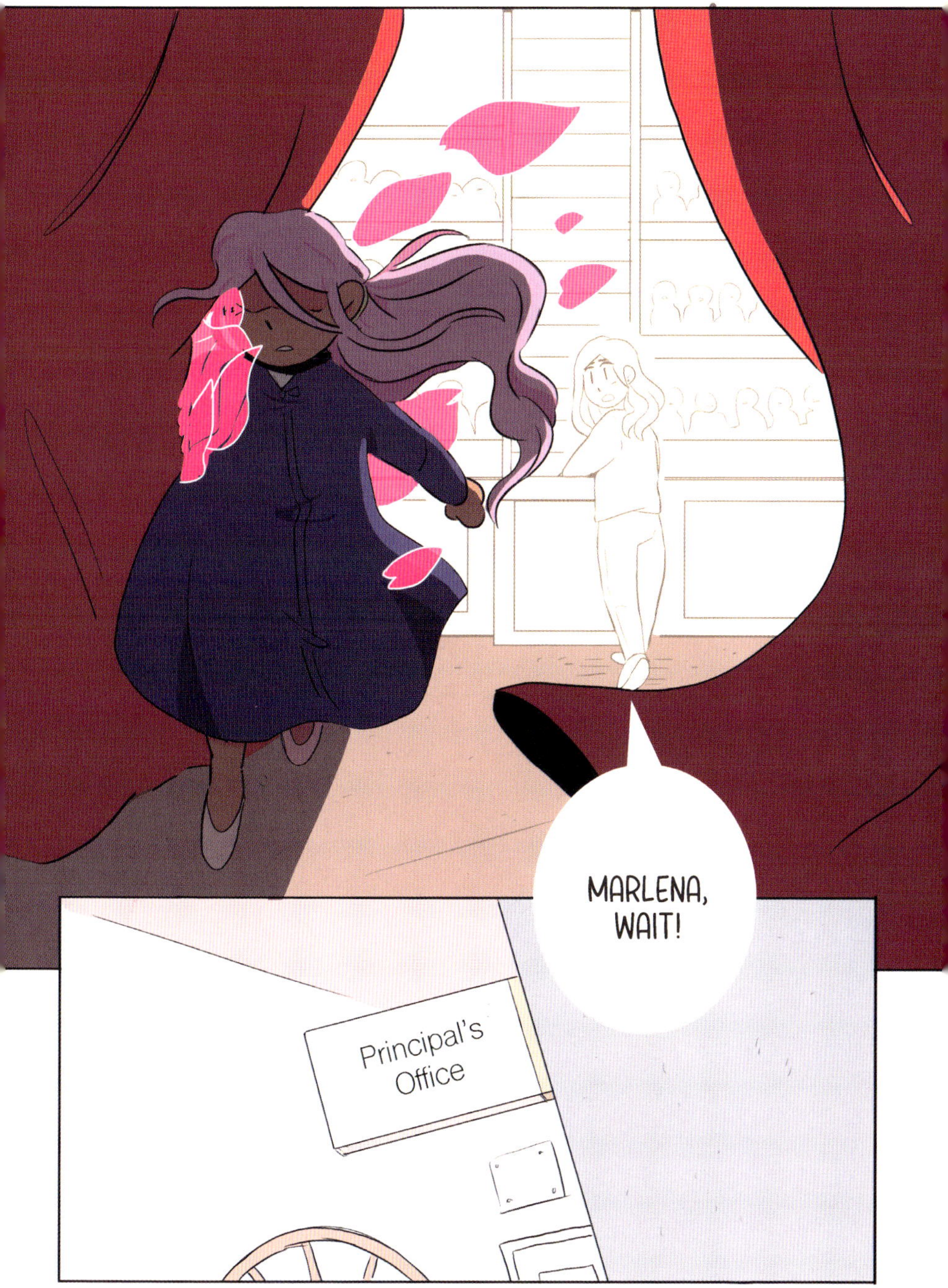
MARLENA, WAIT!
Principal's Office

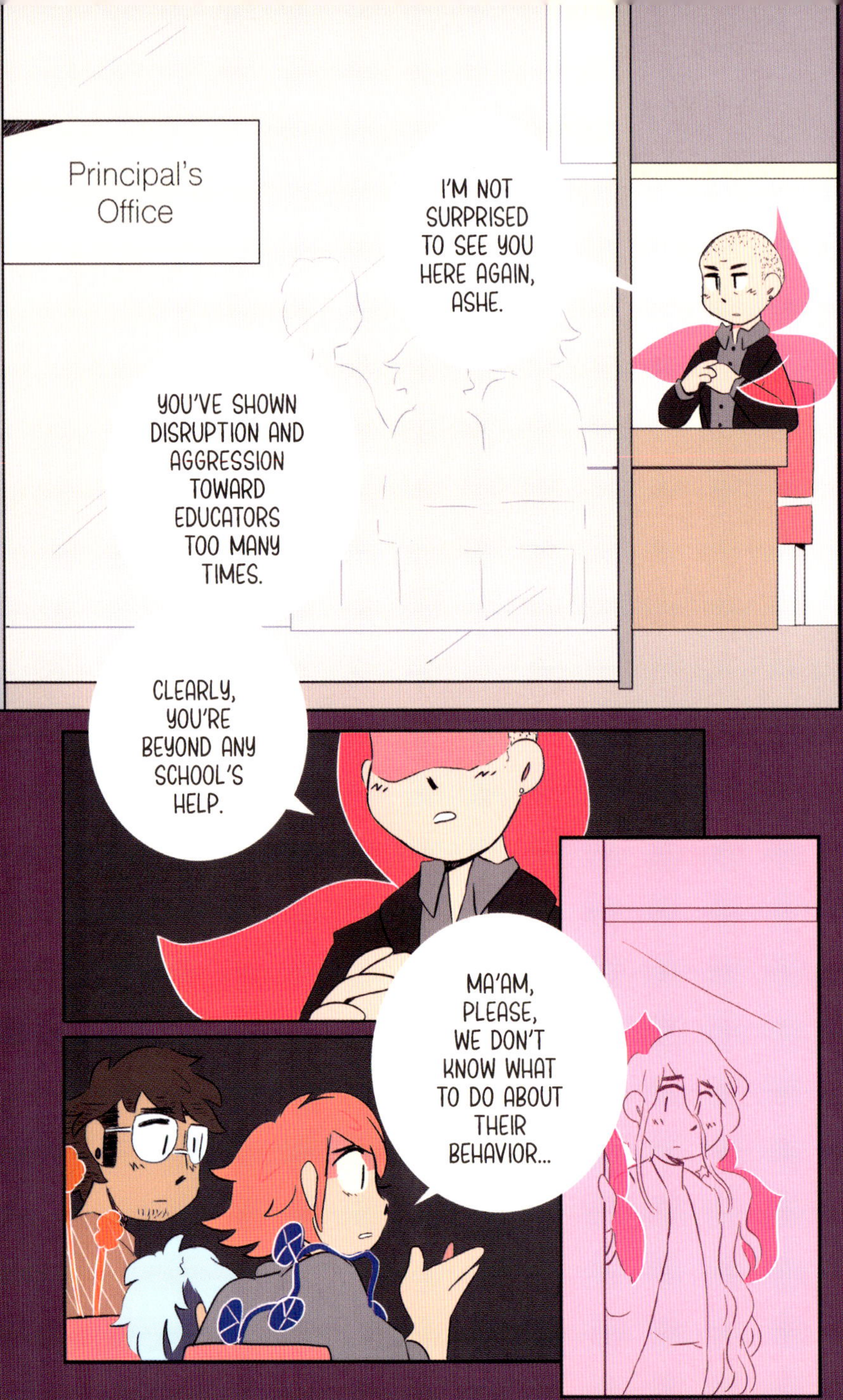
Principal's Office
I'M NOT SURPRISED TO SEE YOU HERE AGAIN, ASHE.
YOU'VE SHOWN DISRUPTION AND AGGRESSION TOWARD EDUCATORS TOO MANY TIMES.
CLEARLY, YOU'RE BEYOND ANY SCHOOL'S HELP.
MA'AM, PLEASE, WE DON'T KNOW WHAT TO DO ABOUT THEIR BEHAVIOR...

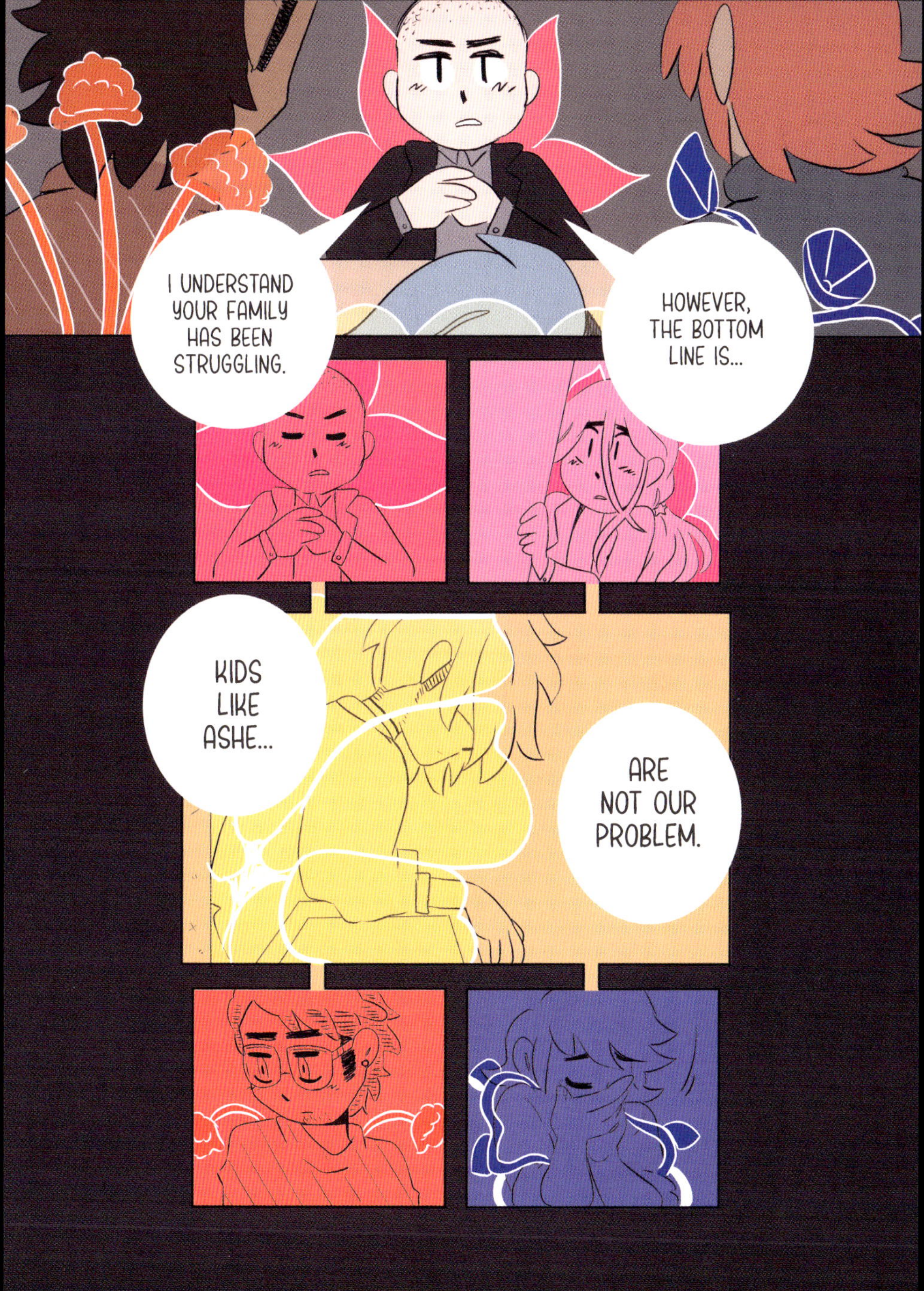
I UNDERSTAND YOUR FAMILY HAS BEEN STRUGGLING.
HOWEVER, THE BOTTOM LINE IS...
KIDS LIKE ASHE...
ARE NOT OUR PROBLEM.

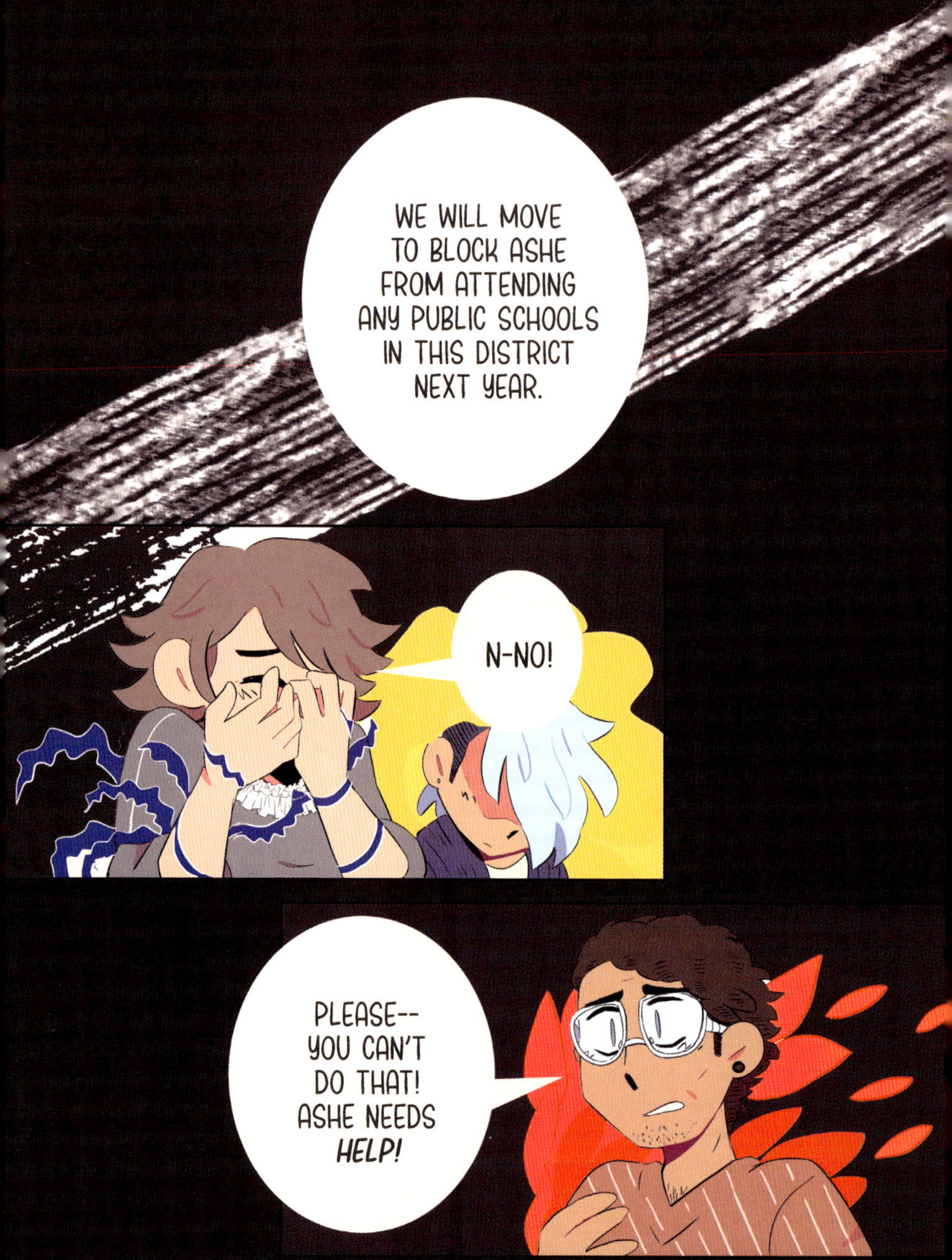
WE WILL MOVE TO BLOCK ASHE FROM ATTENDING ANY PUBLIC SCHOOLS IN THIS DISTRICT NEXT YEAR.
N-NO!
PLEASE-- YOU CAN'T DO THAT! ASHE NEEDS *HELP!*

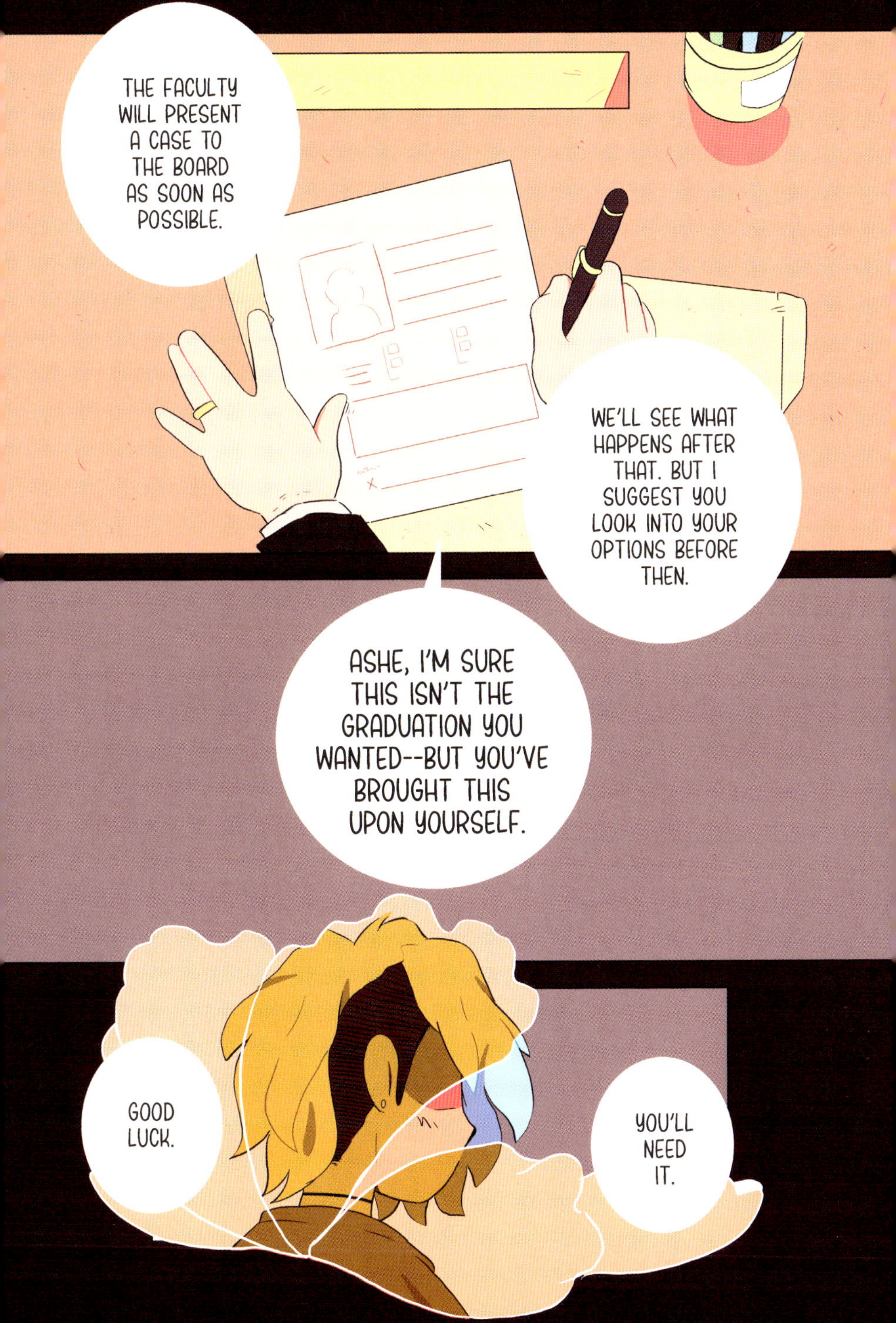

THE FACULTY WILL PRESENT A CASE TO THE BOARD AS SOON AS POSSIBLE.
WE'LL SEE WHAT HAPPENS AFTER THAT. BUT I SUGGEST YOU LOOK INTO YOUR OPTIONS BEFORE THEN.
ASHE, I'M SURE THIS ISN'T THE GRADUATION YOU WANTED--BUT YOU'VE BROUGHT THIS UPON YOURSELF.
GOOD LUCK.
YOU'LL NEED IT.

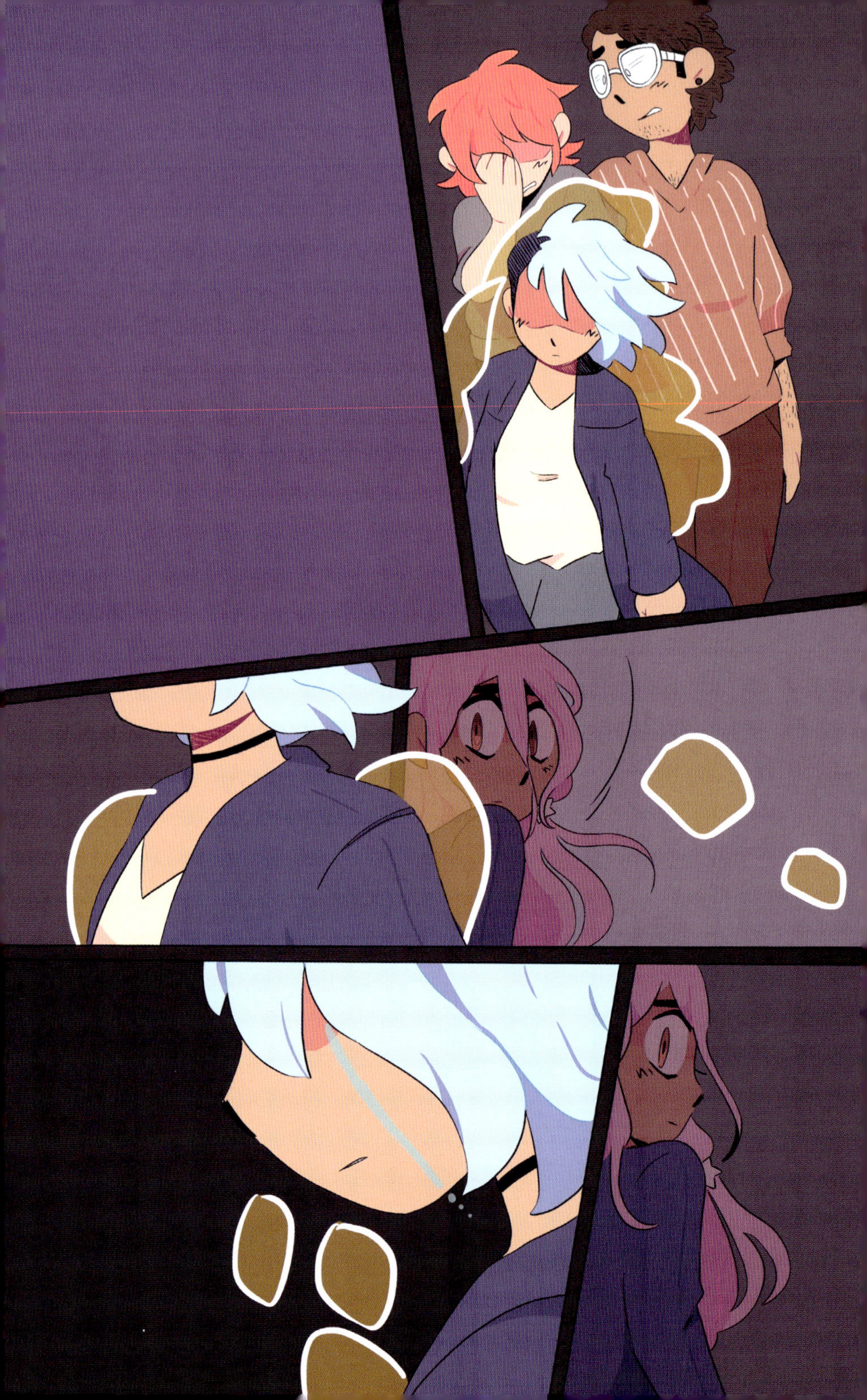

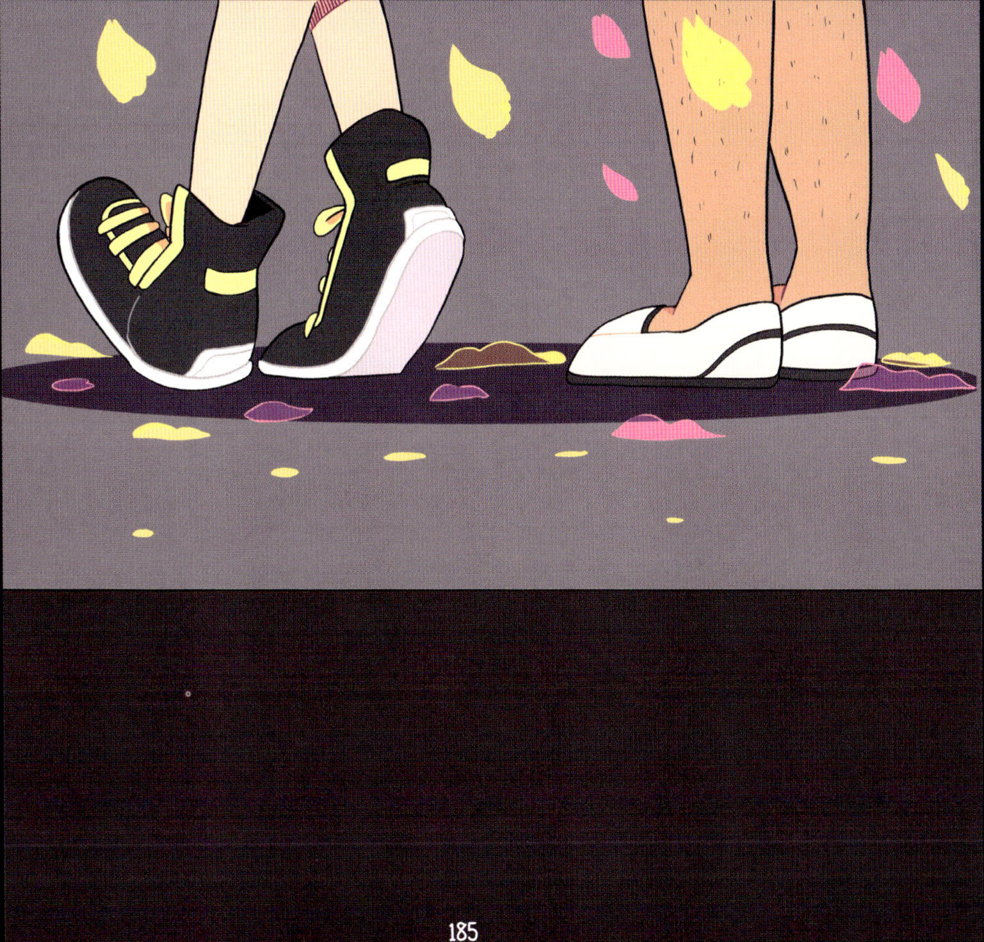

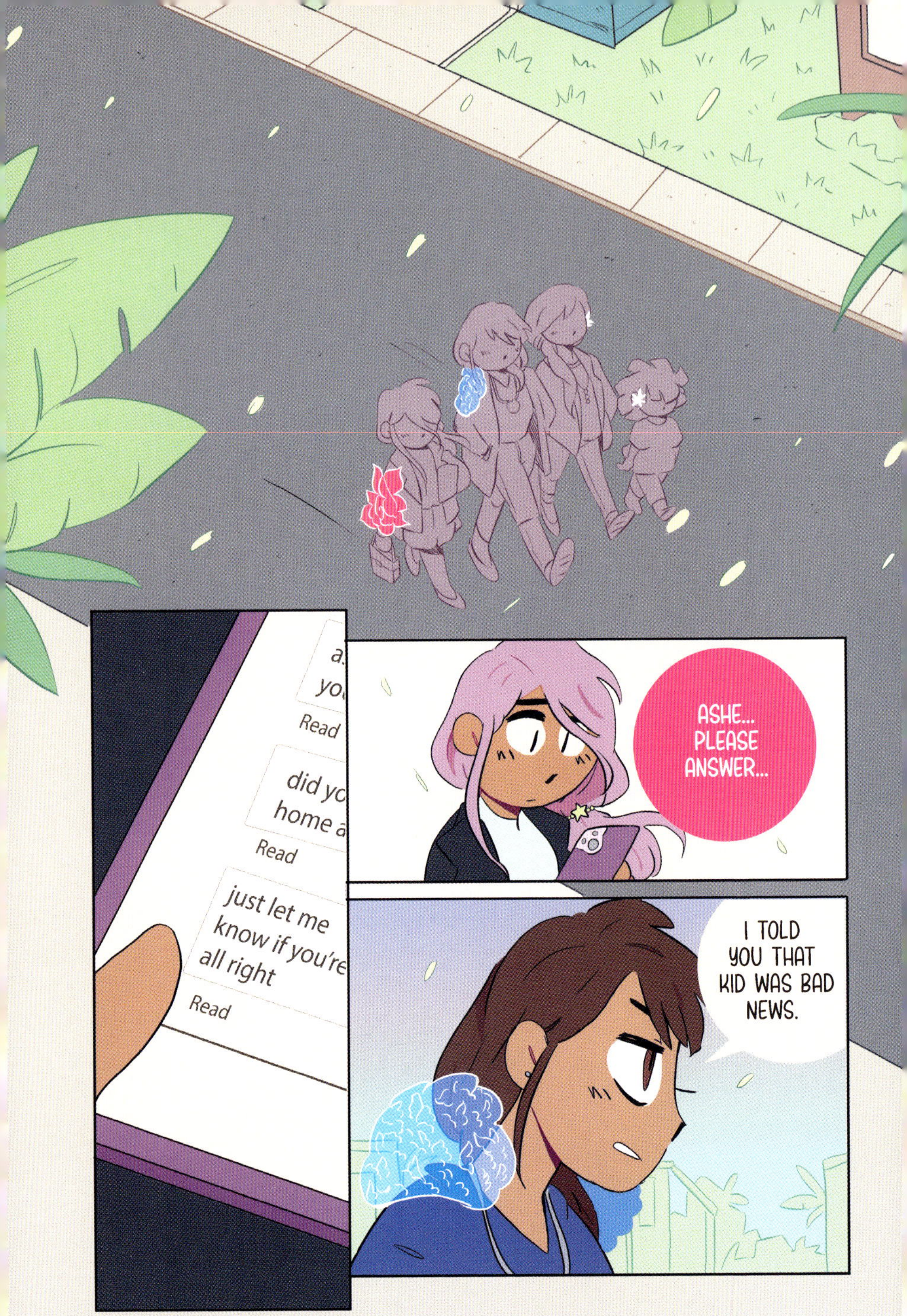

a
yo
Read
did yo
home a
Read
just let me
know if you're
all right
Read
ASHE... PLEASE ANSWER...
I TOLD YOU THAT KID WAS BAD NEWS.

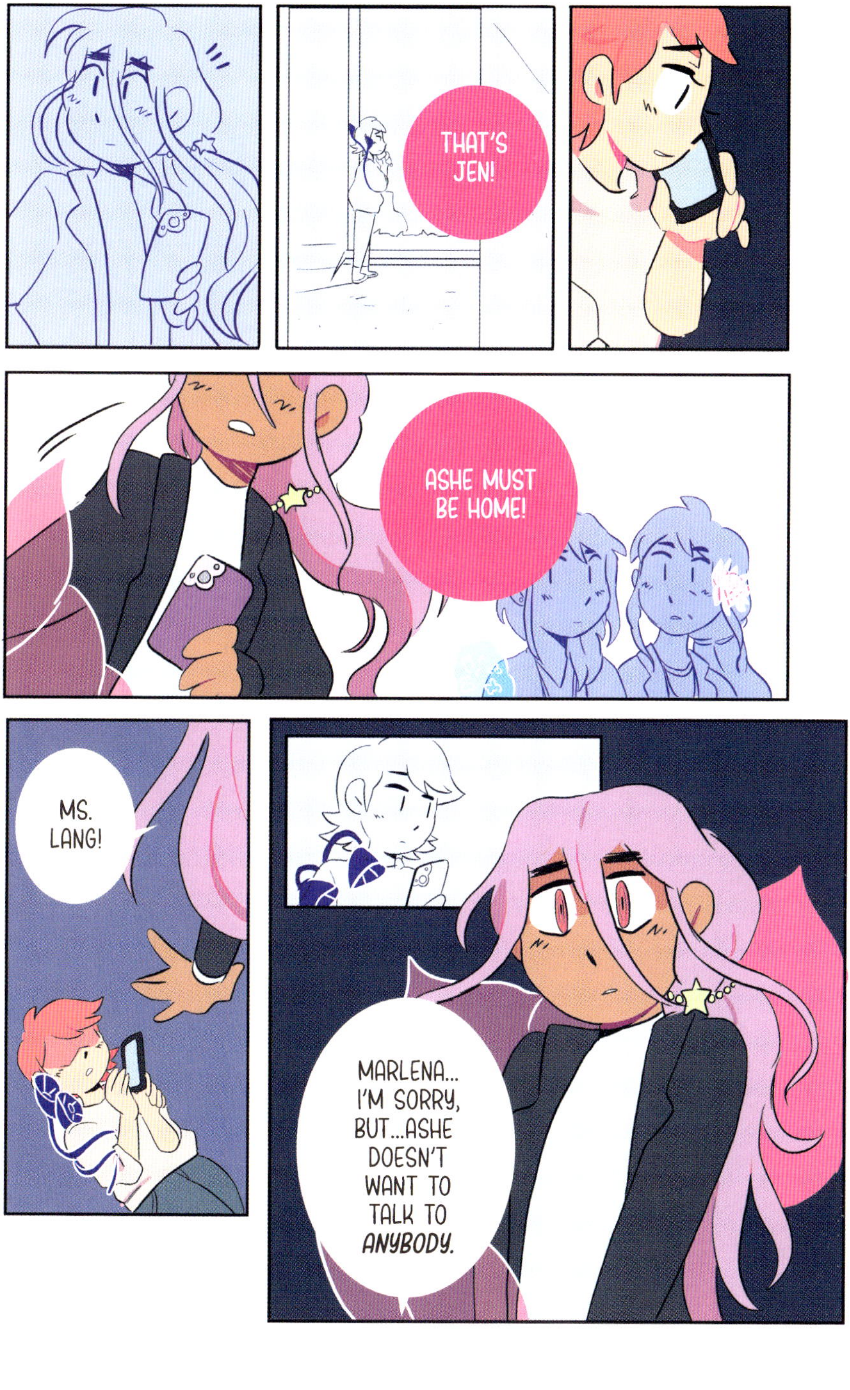
THAT'S JEN!
ASHE MUST BE HOME!
MS. LANG!
MARLENA... I'M SORRY, BUT...ASHE DOESN'T WANT TO TALK TO *ANYBODY.*

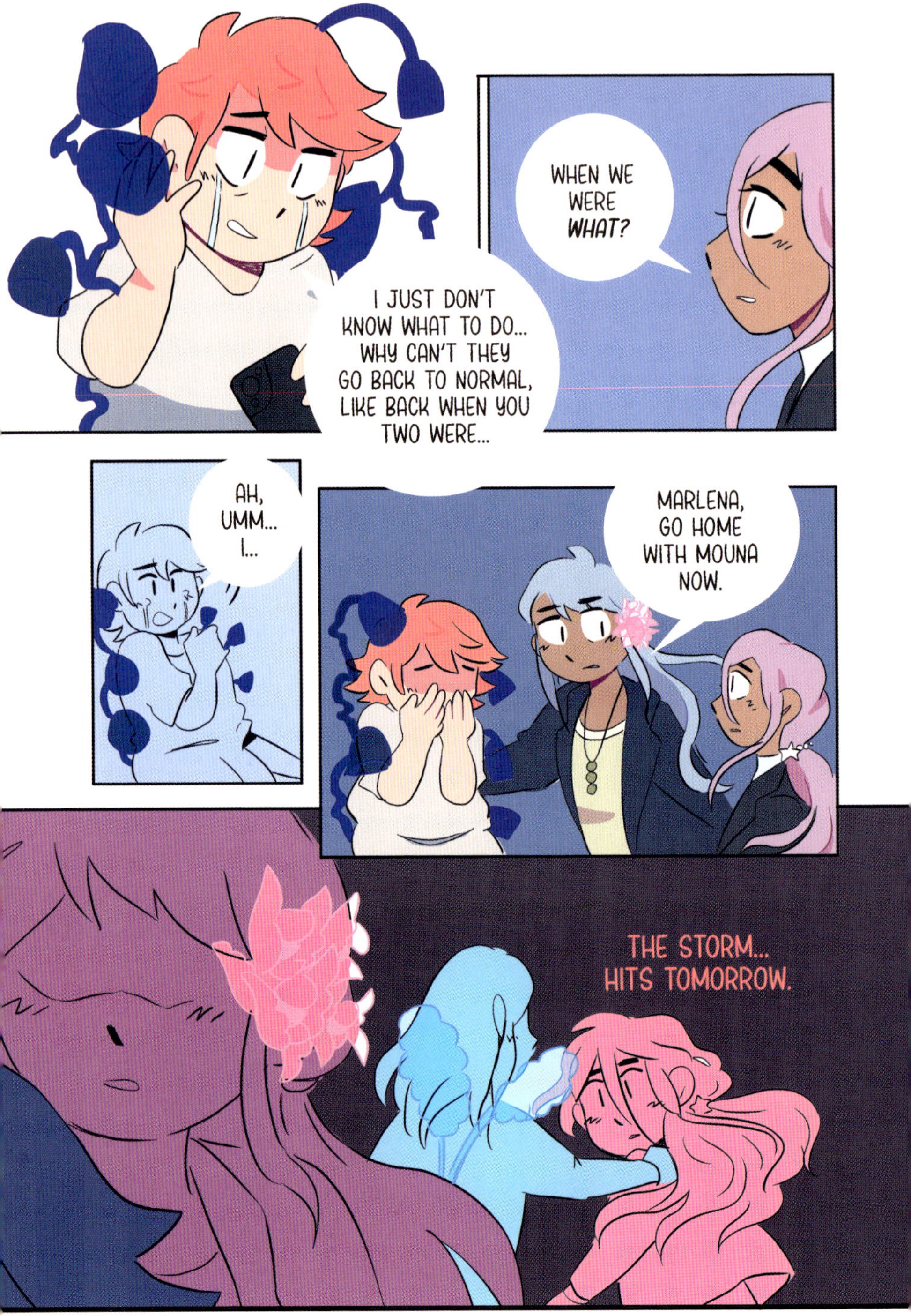
WHEN WE WERE WHAT?
I JUST DON'T KNOW WHAT TO DO... WHY CAN'T THEY GO BACK TO NORMAL, LIKE BACK WHEN YOU TWO WERE...
AH, UMM... I...
MARLENA, GO HOME WITH MOUNA NOW.
THE STORM... HITS TOMORROW.

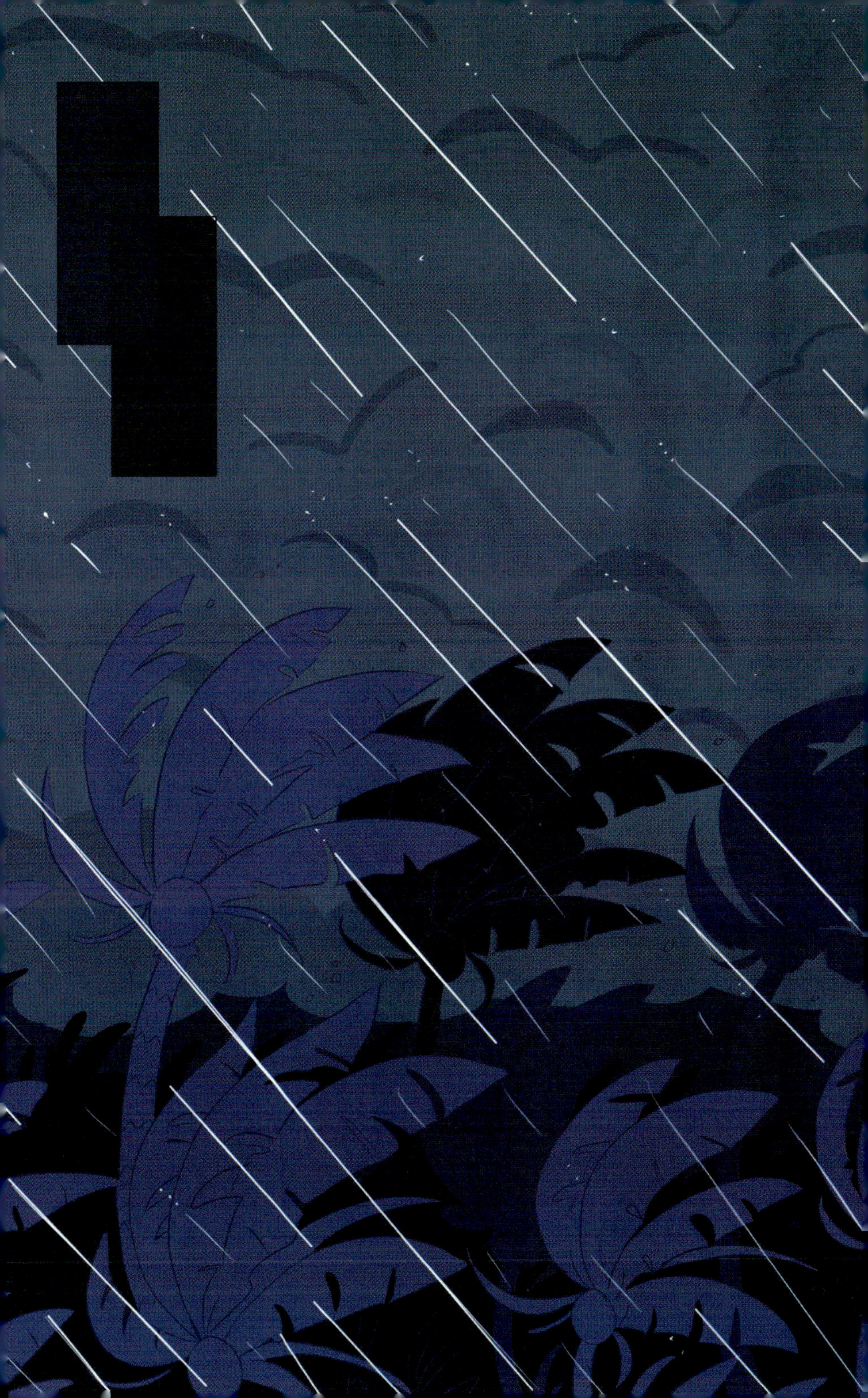
[redacted]

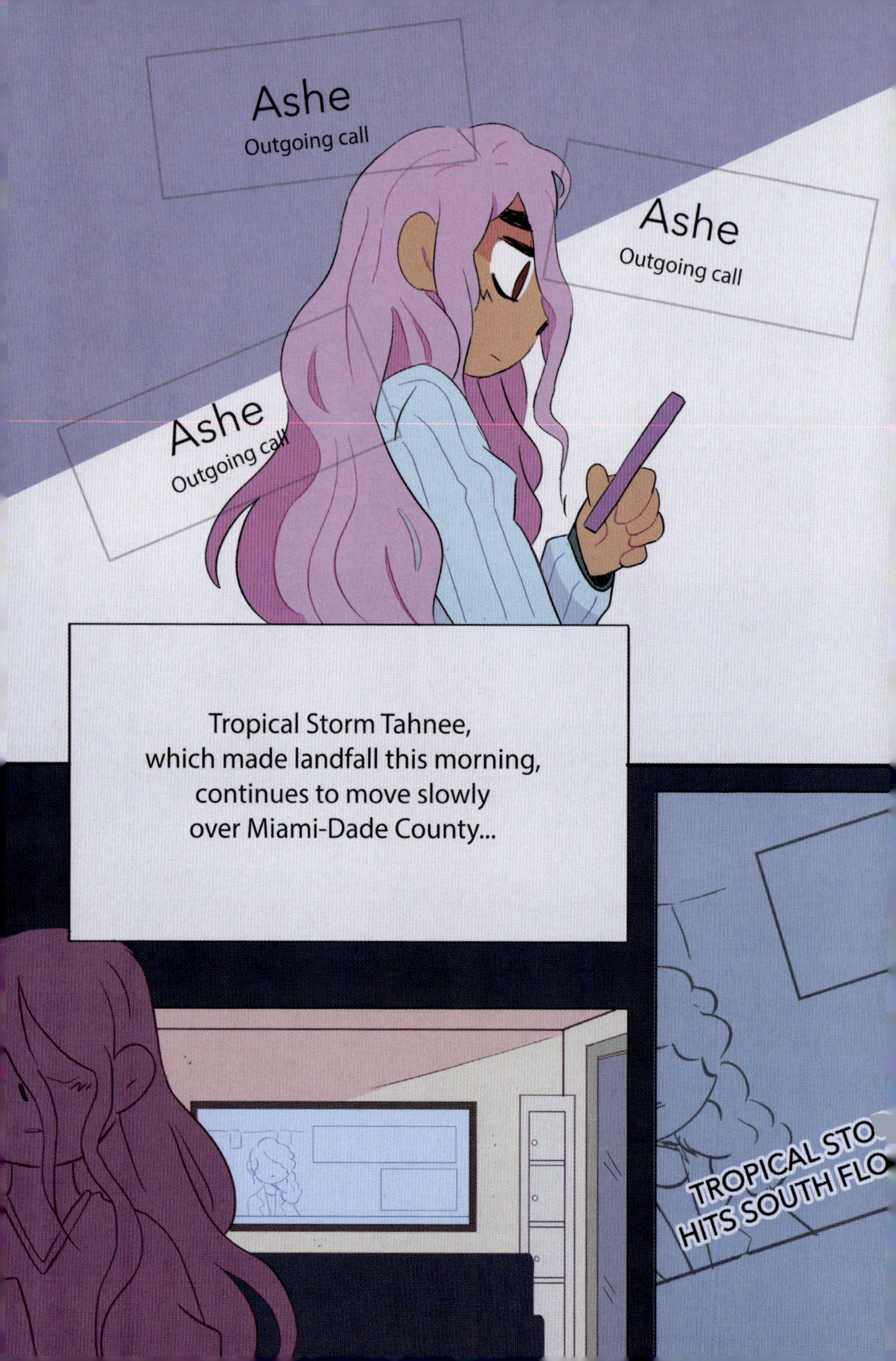
Ashe
Outgoing call
Ashe
Outgoing call
Ashe
Outgoing call
Tropical Storm Tahnee, which made landfall this morning, continues to move slowly over Miami-Dade County...
TROPICAL STO
HITS SOUTH FLO

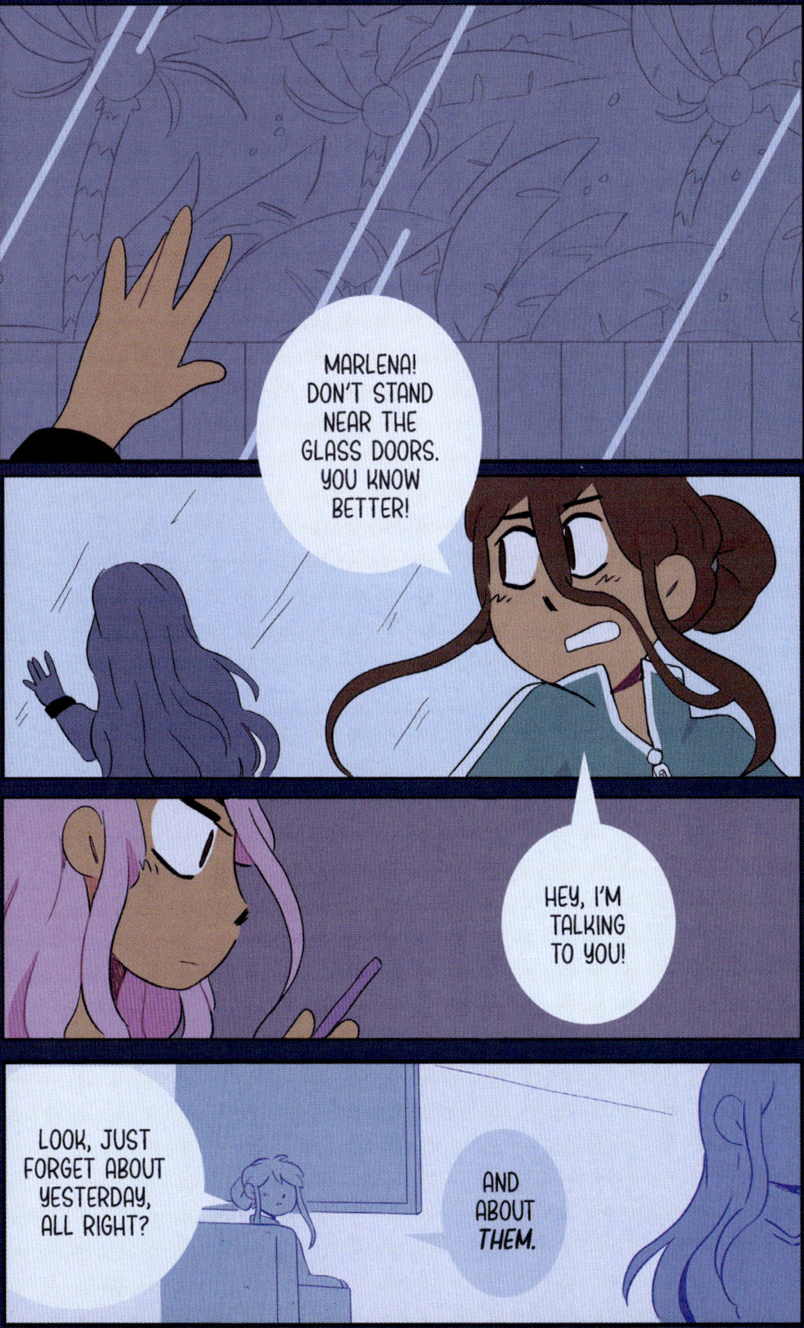
MARLENA! DON'T STAND NEAR THE GLASS DOORS. YOU KNOW BETTER!
HEY, I'M TALKING TO YOU!
LOOK, JUST FORGET ABOUT YESTERDAY, ALL RIGHT?
AND ABOUT *THEM.*

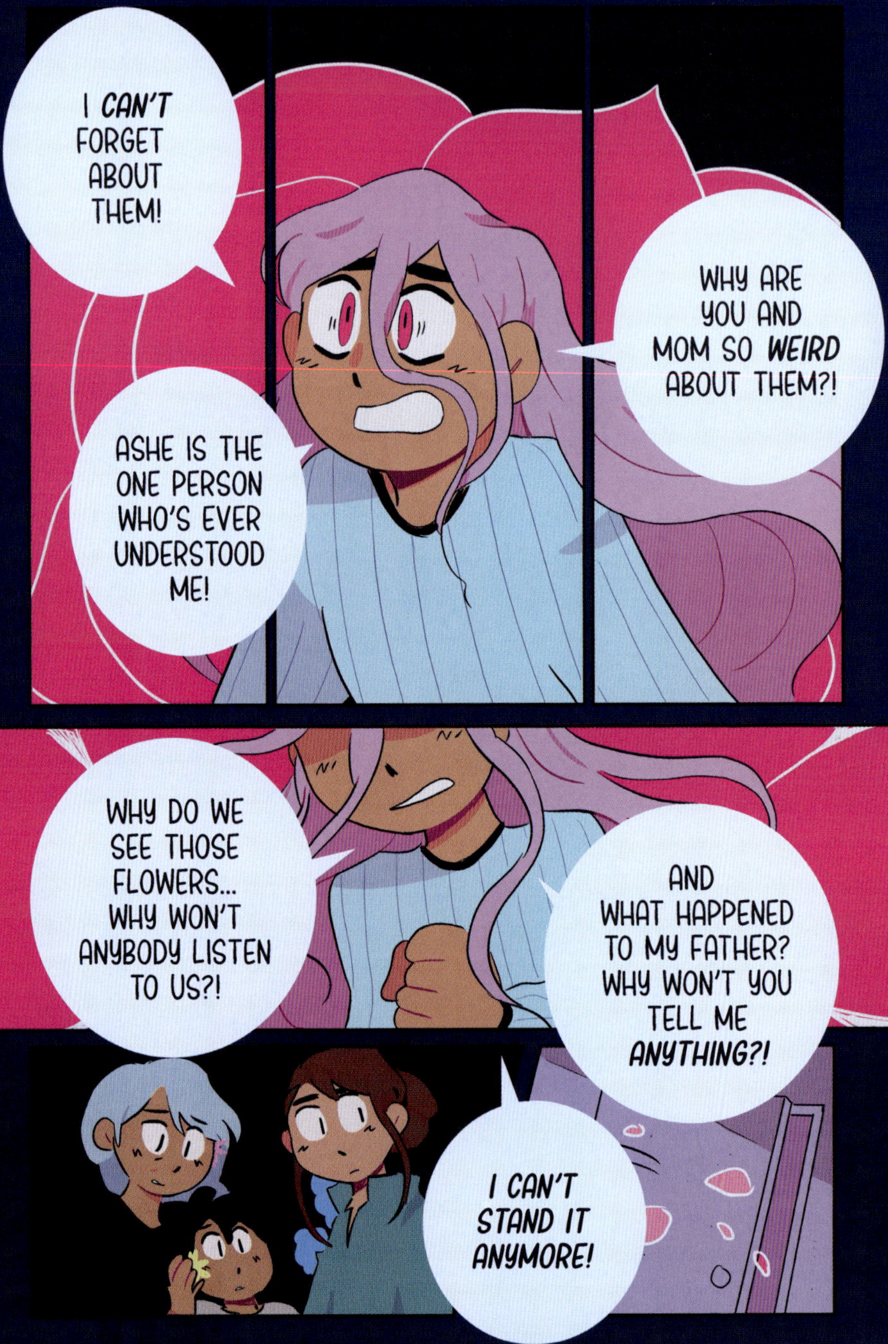
I CAN'T FORGET ABOUT THEM!
ASHE IS THE ONE PERSON WHO'S EVER UNDERSTOOD ME!
WHY ARE YOU AND MOM SO WEIRD ABOUT THEM?!
WHY DO WE SEE THOSE FLOWERS... WHY WON'T ANYBODY LISTEN TO US?!
AND WHAT HAPPENED TO MY FATHER? WHY WON'T YOU TELL ME ANYTHING?!
I CAN'T STAND IT ANYMORE!

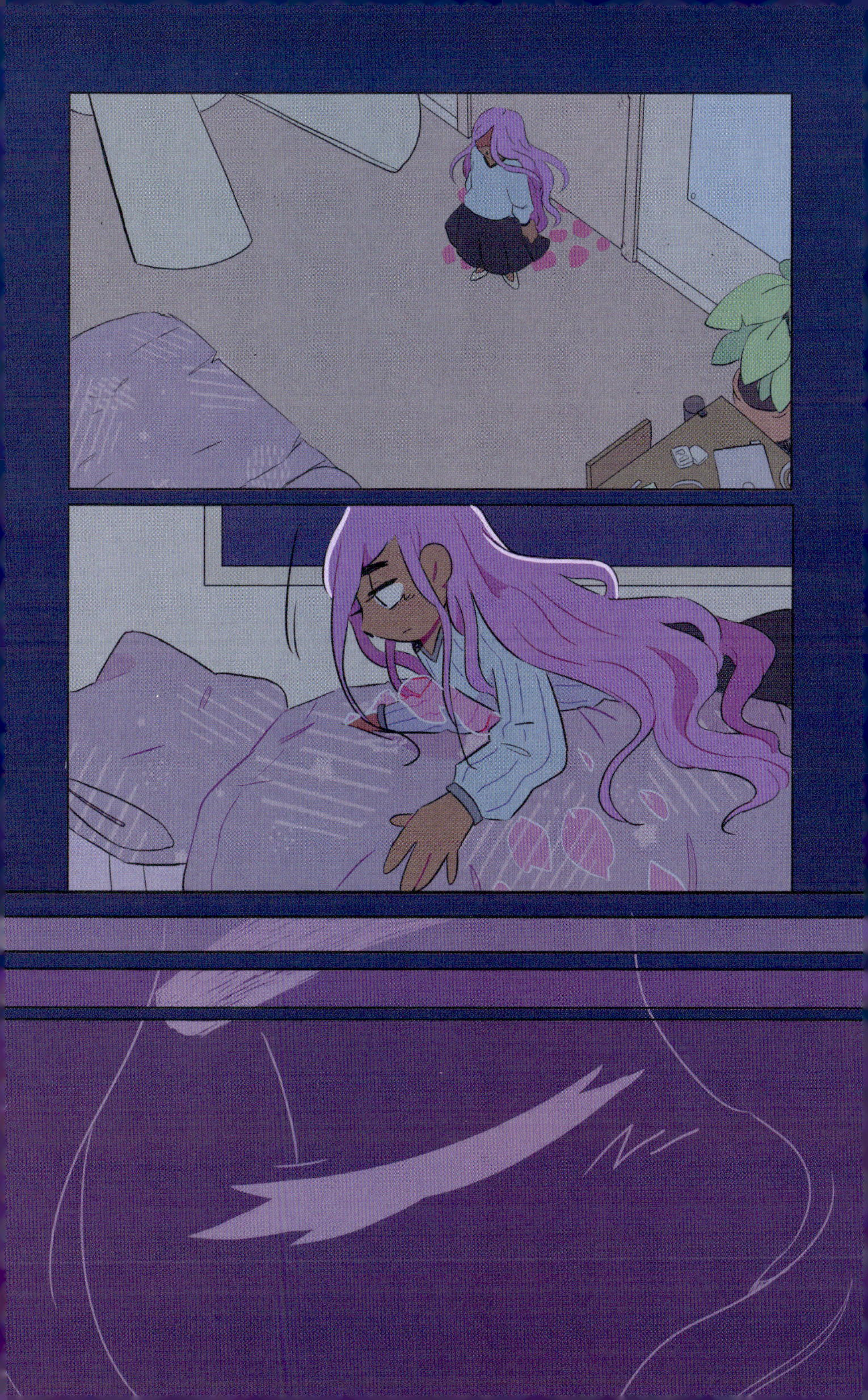

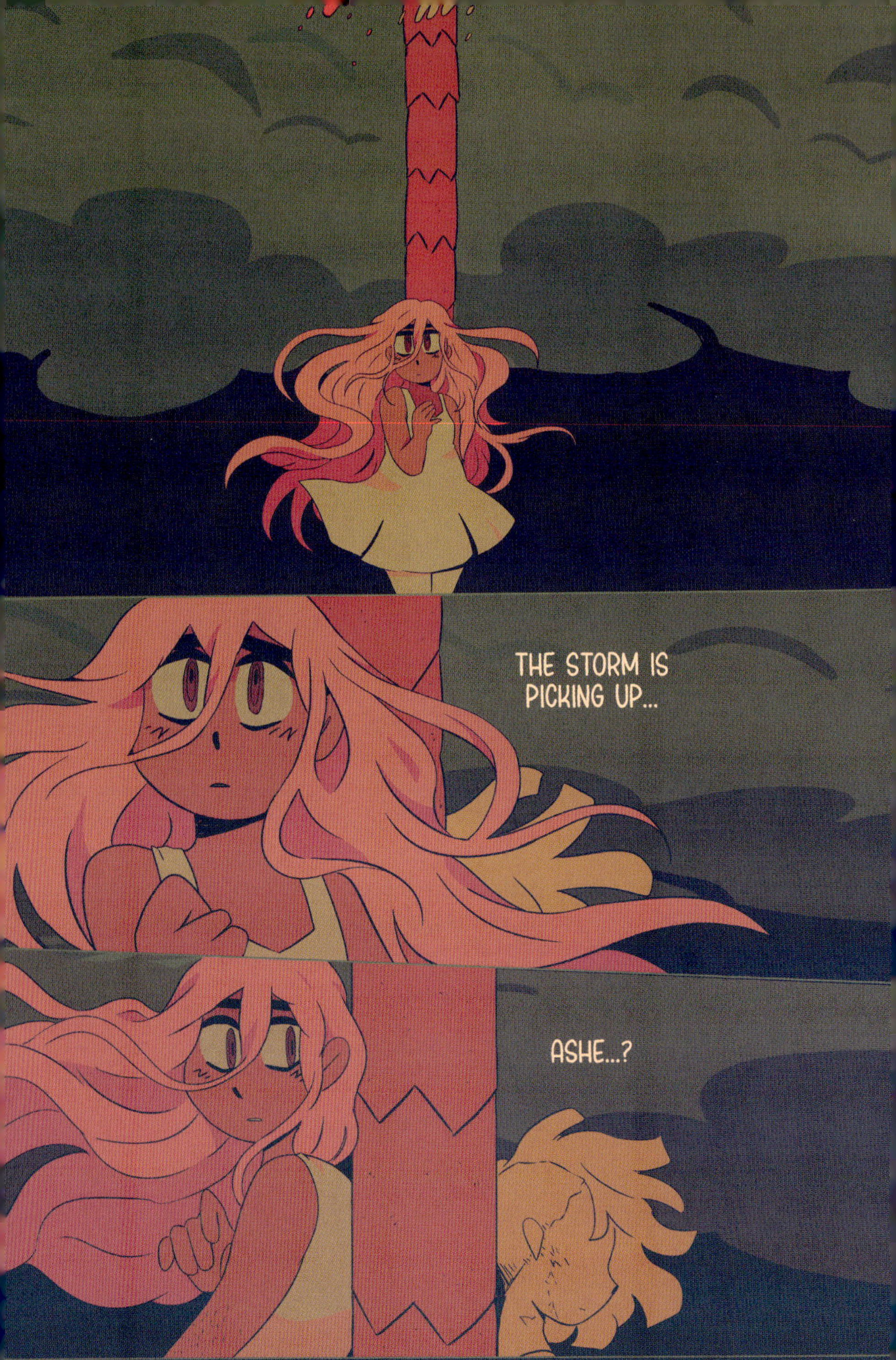
THE STORM IS PICKING UP...
ASHE...?

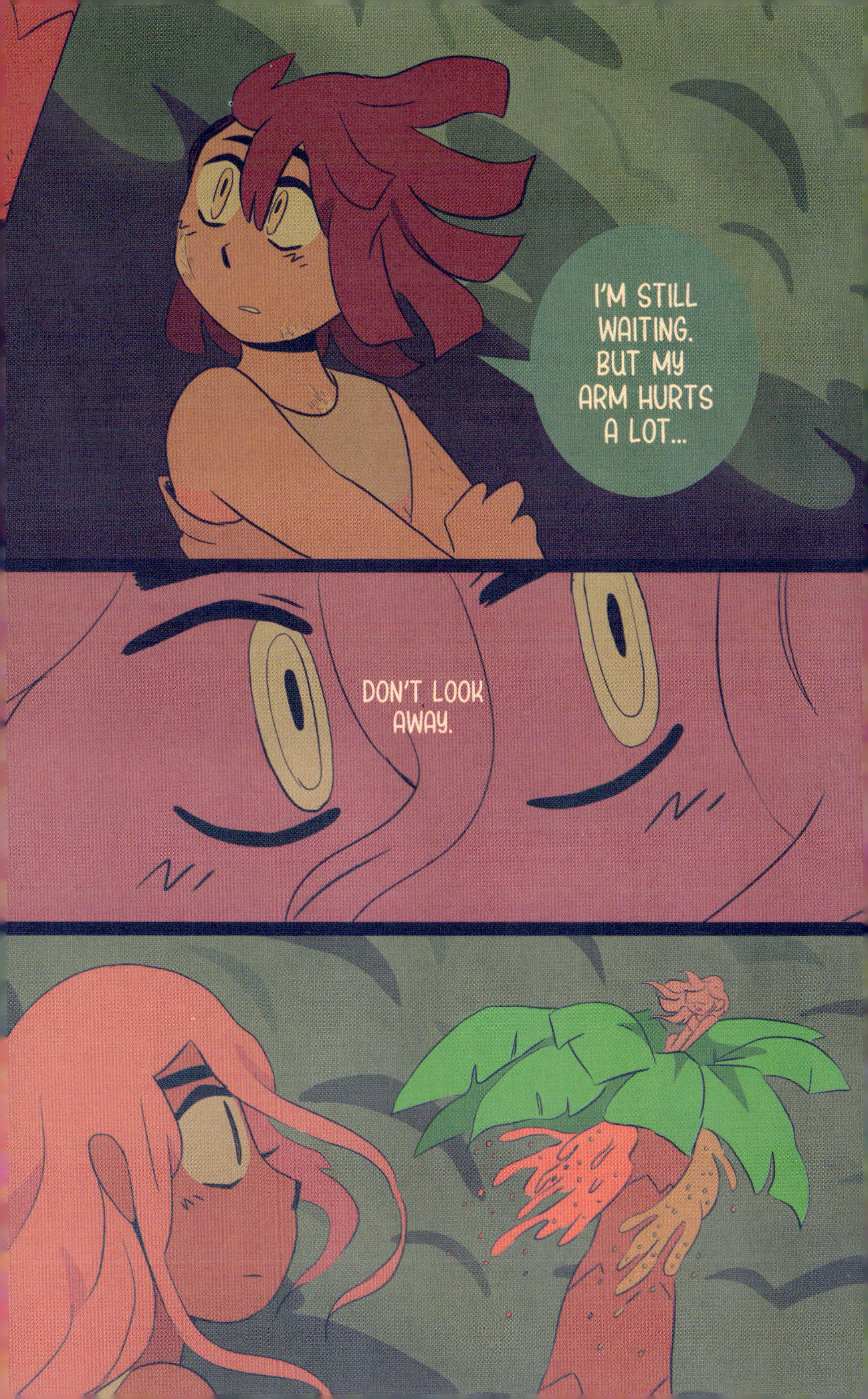
I'M STILL WAITING. BUT MY ARM HURTS A LOT...
DON'T LOOK AWAY.

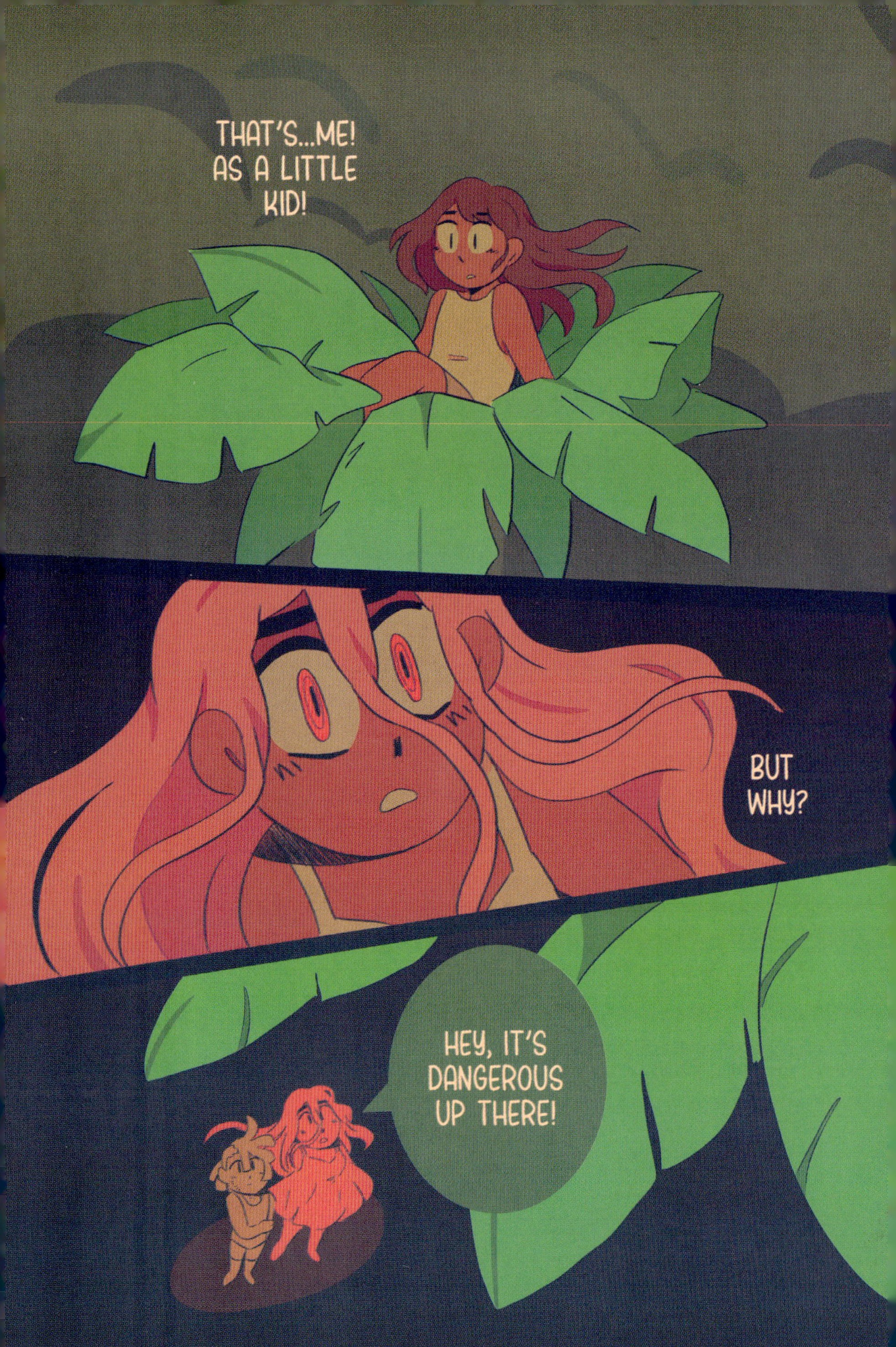
THAT'S...ME! AS A LITTLE KID!
BUT WHY?
HEY, IT'S DANGEROUS UP THERE!

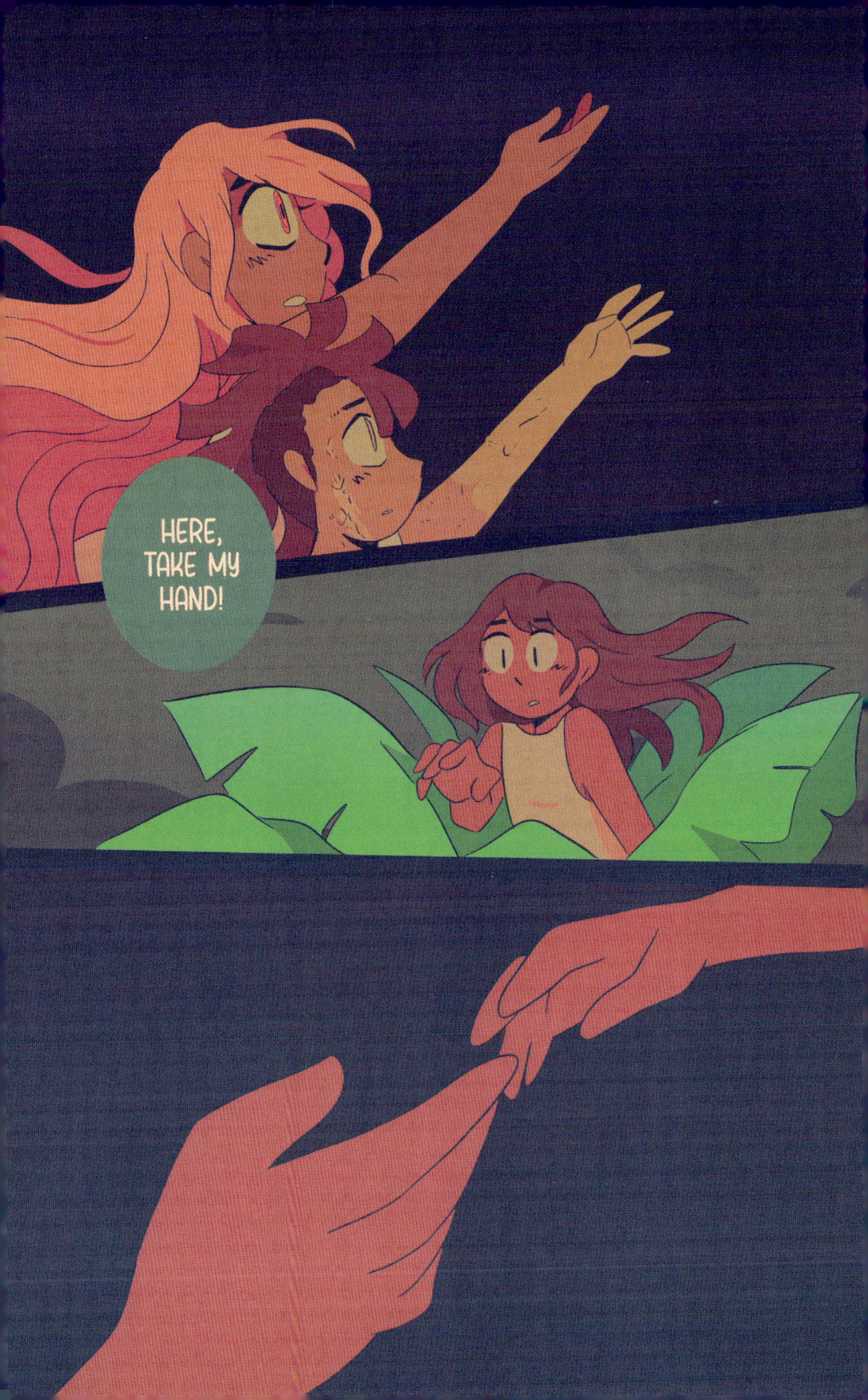
HERE, TAKE MY HAND!

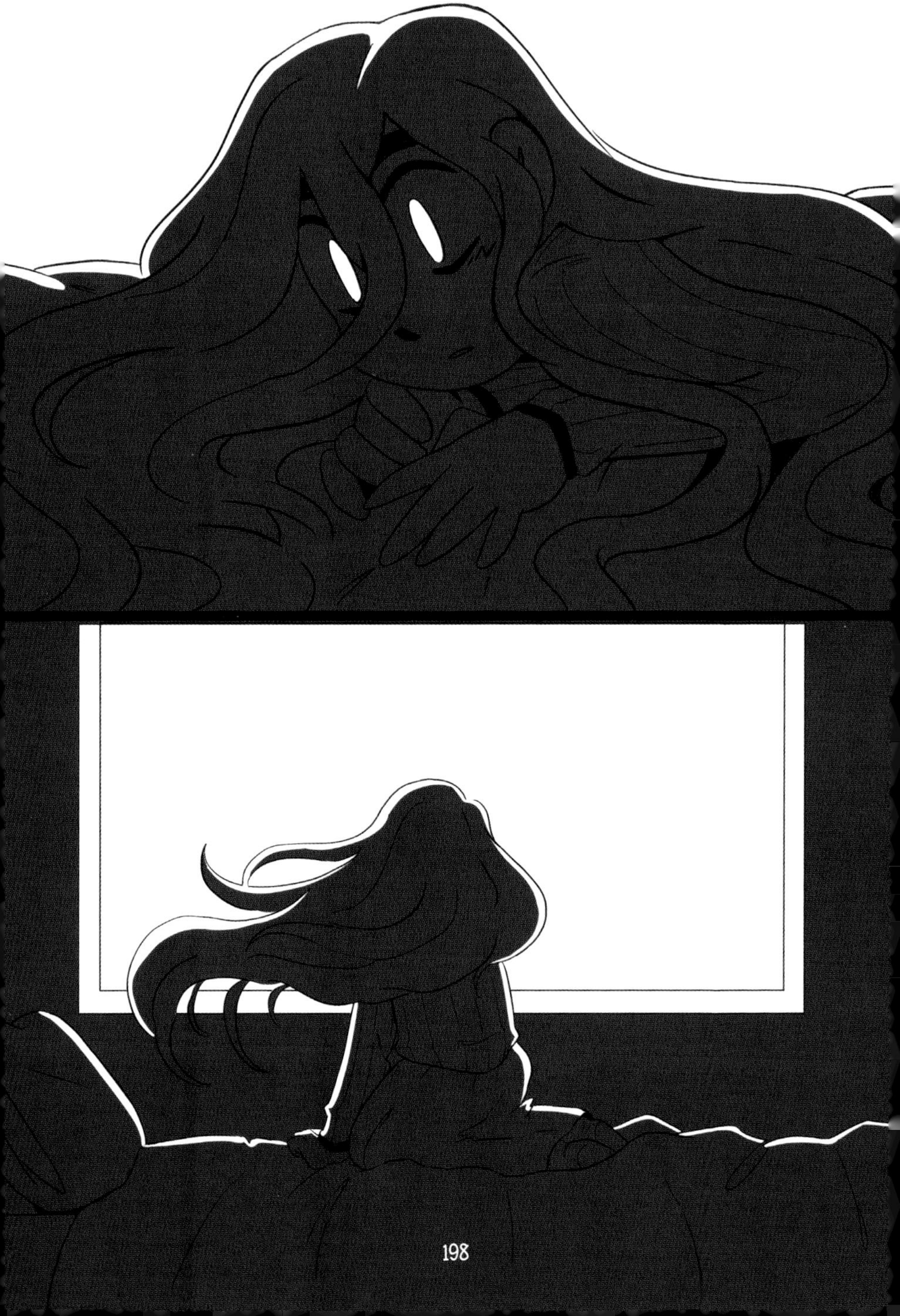

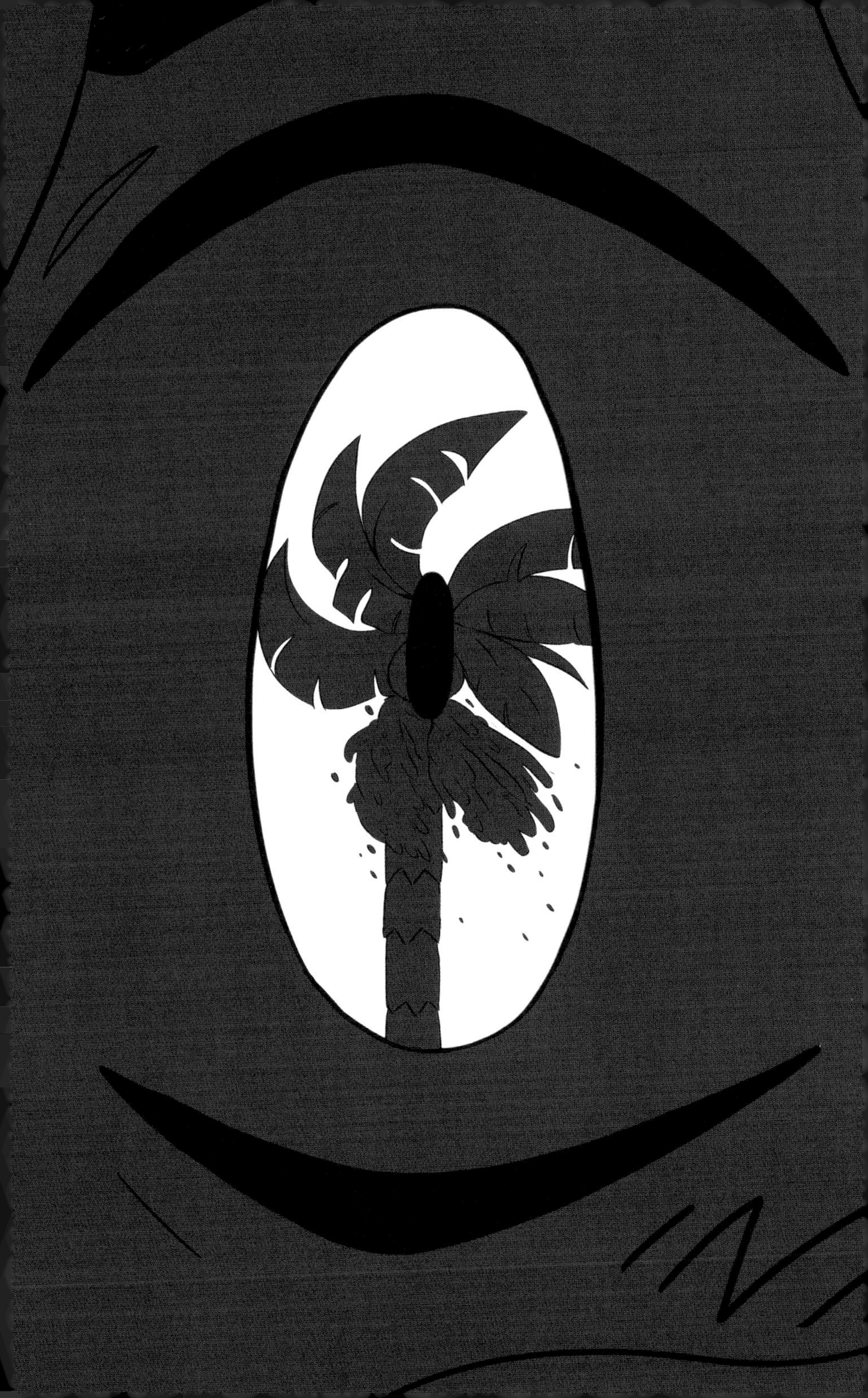

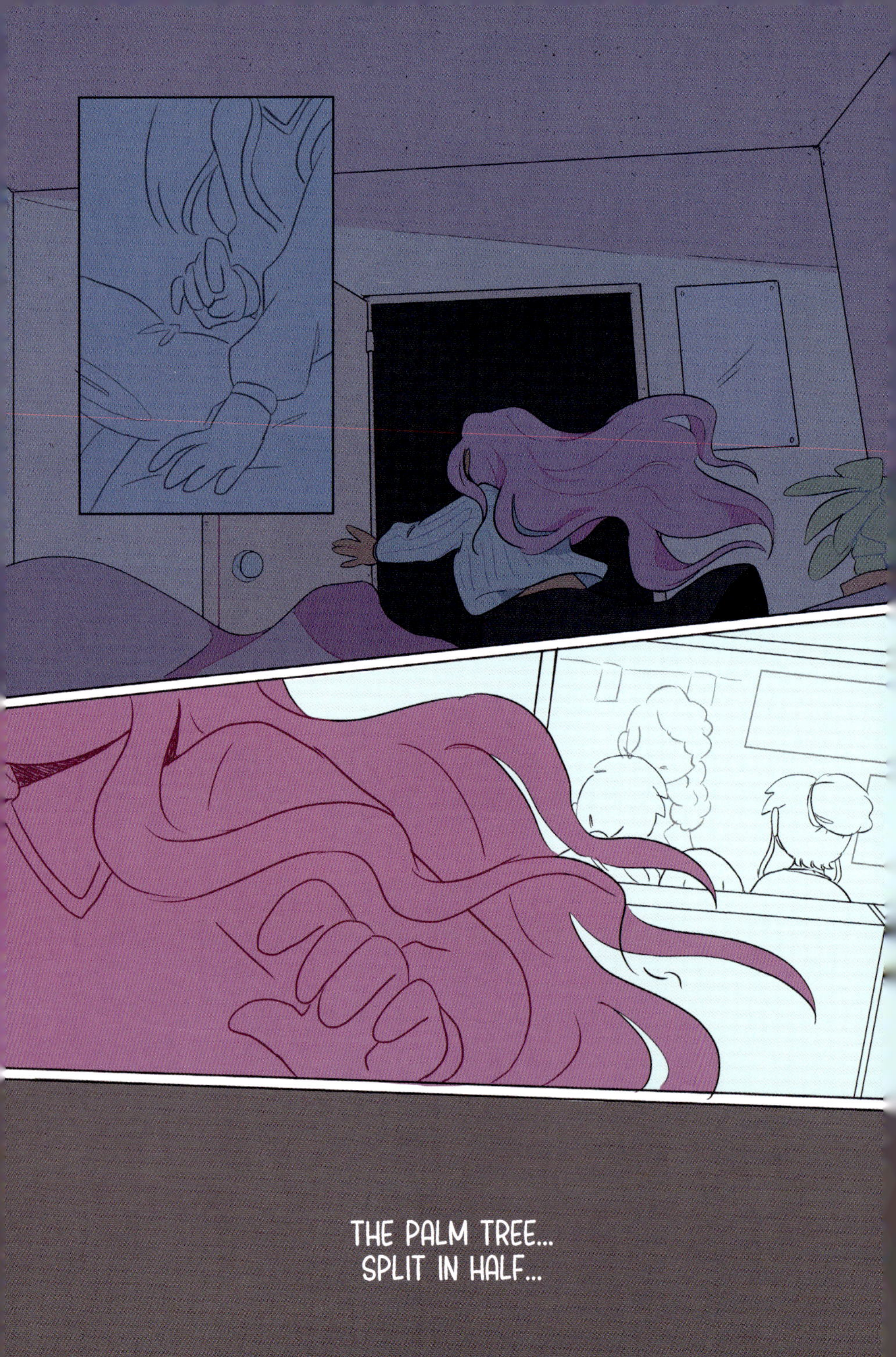
THE PALM TREE...
SPLIT IN HALF...

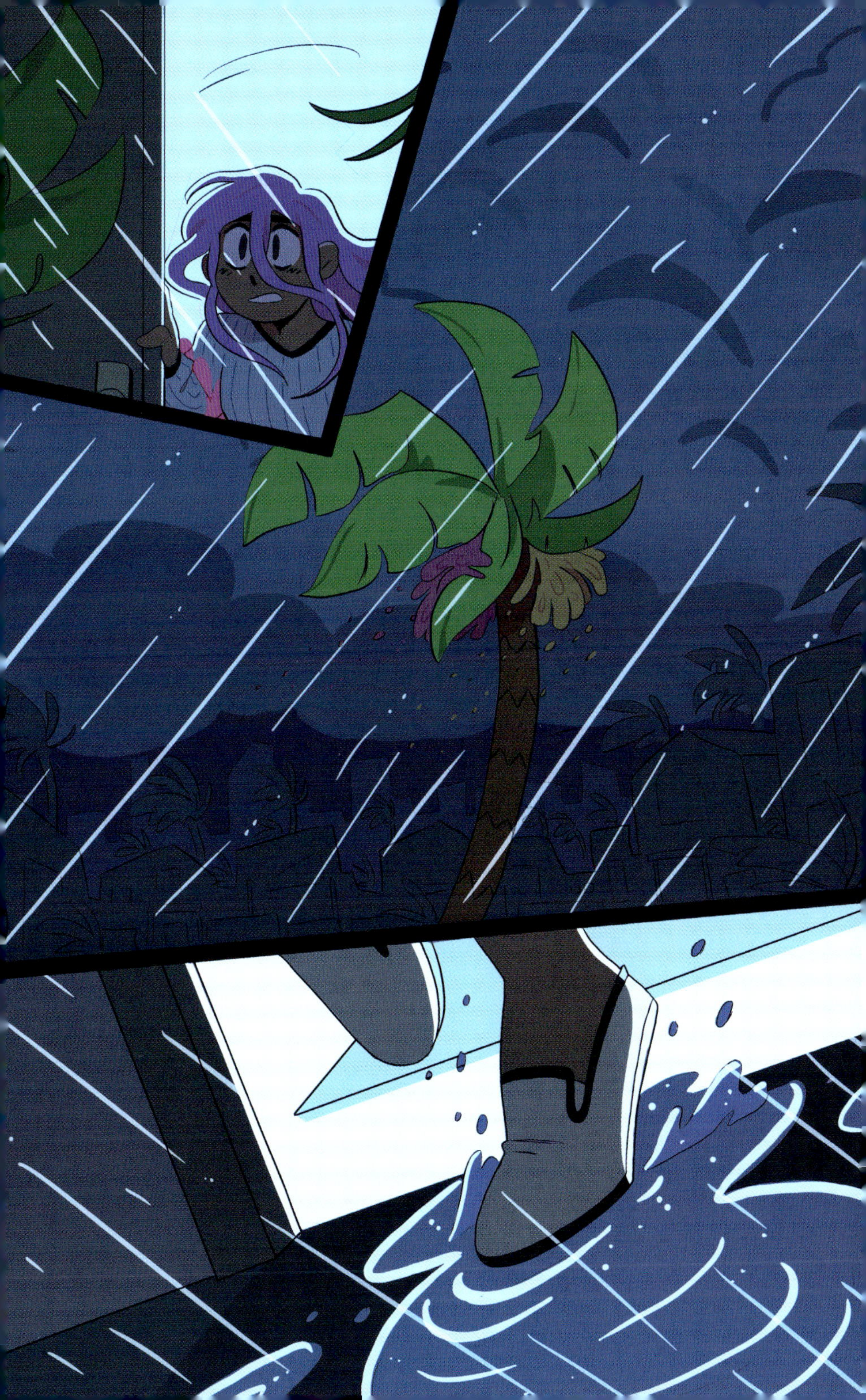

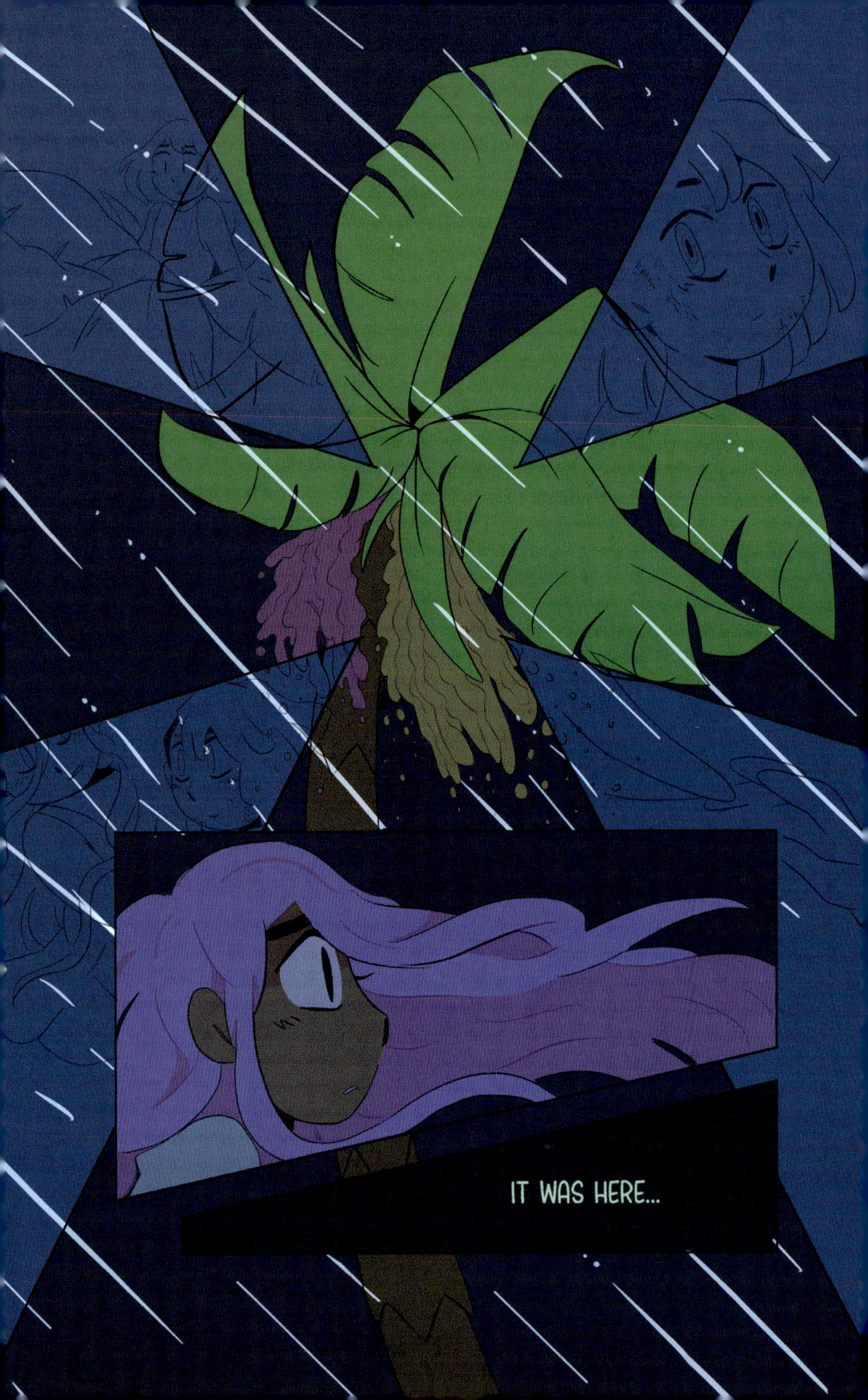
IT WAS HERE...

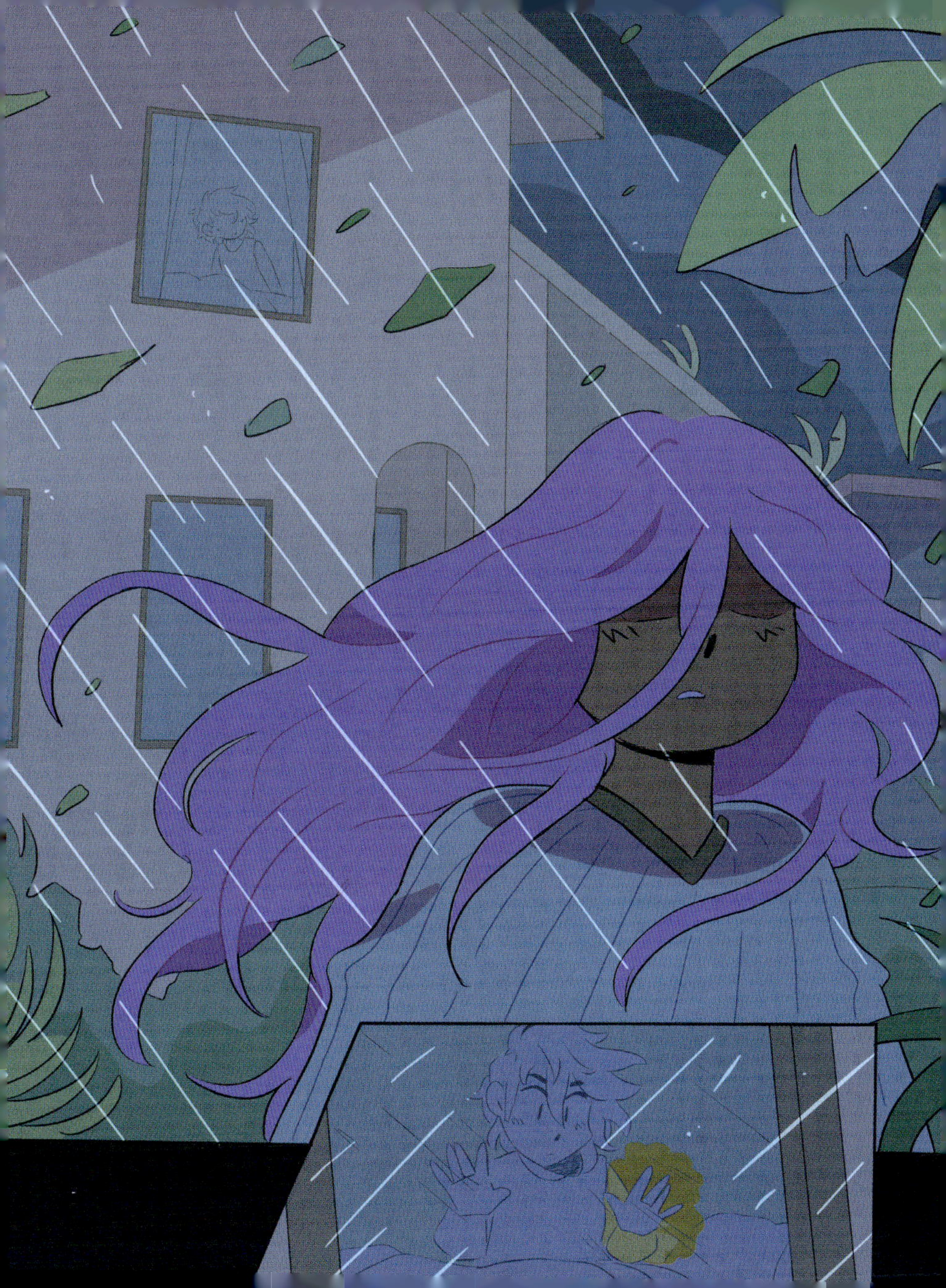

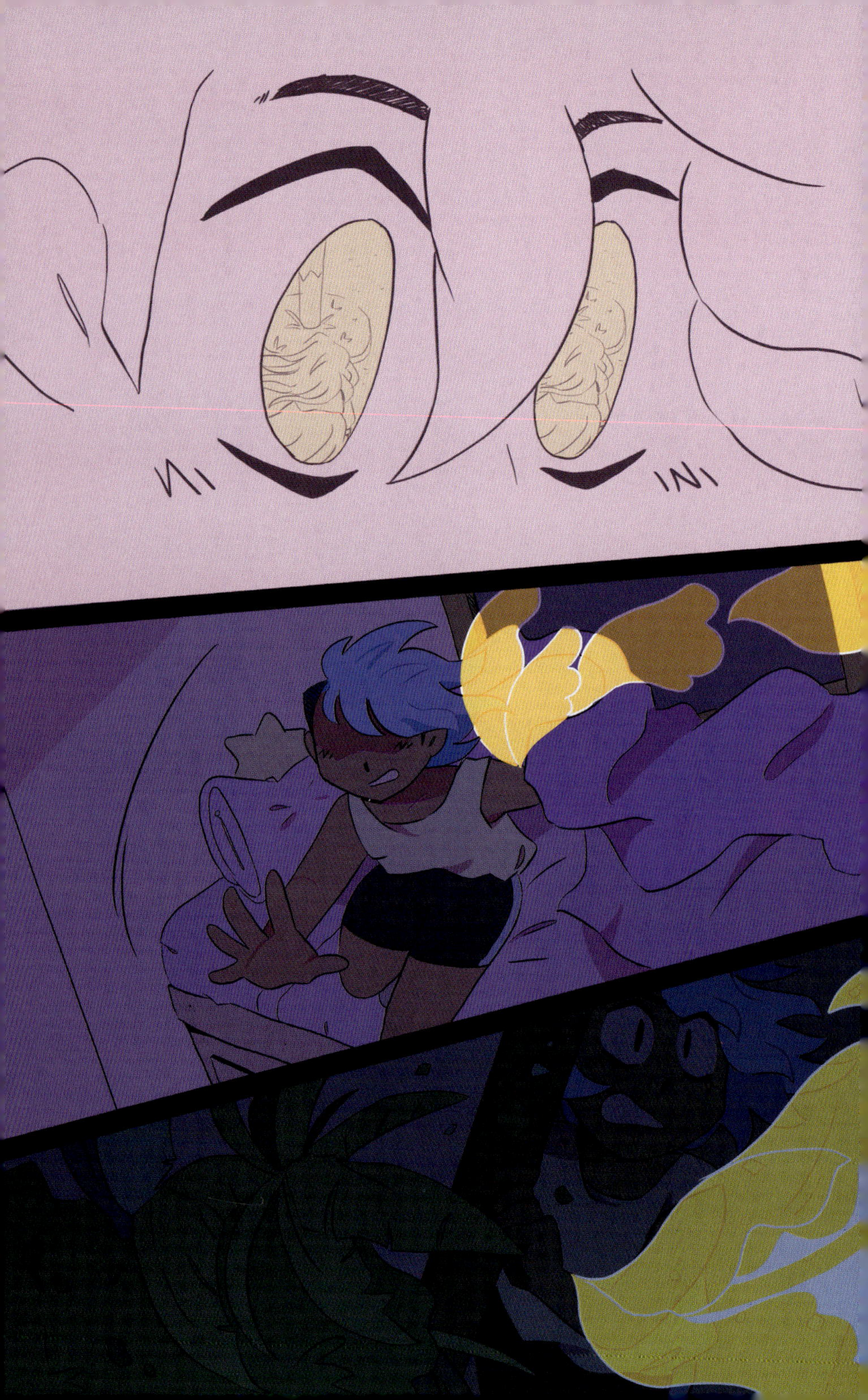

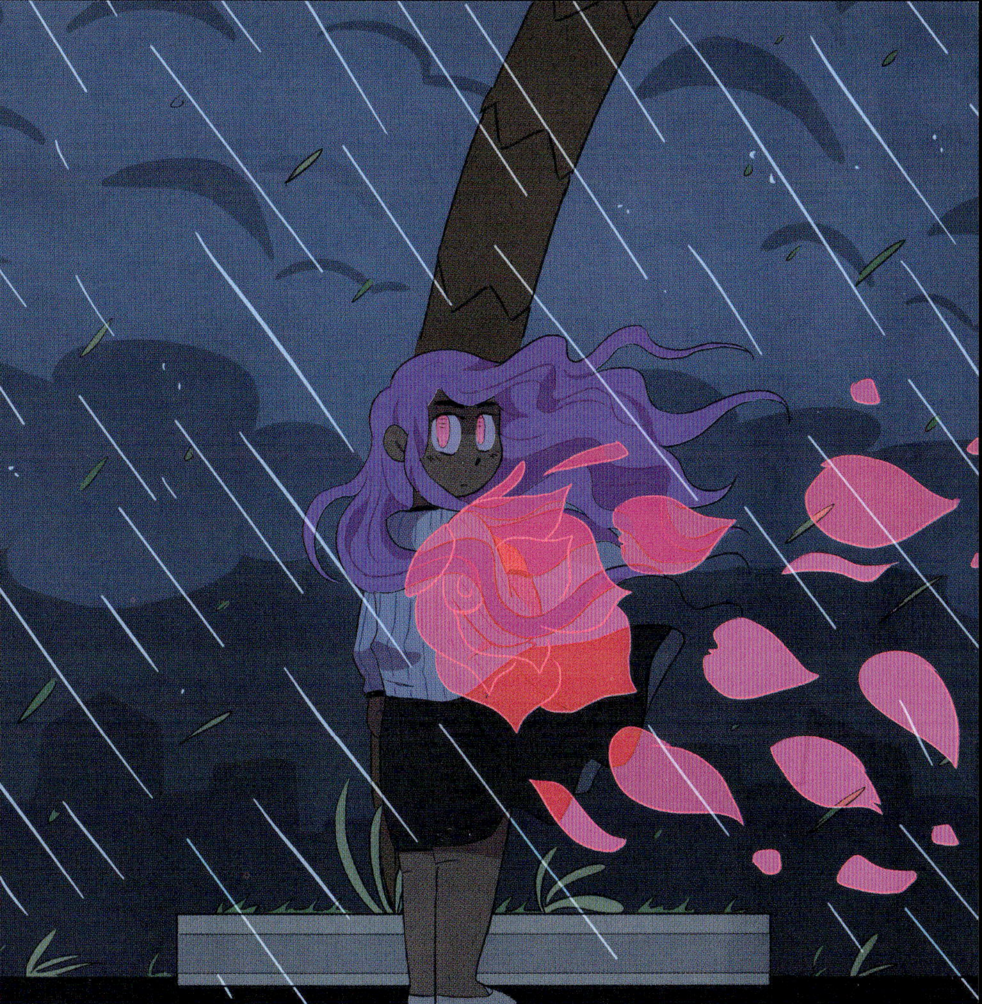

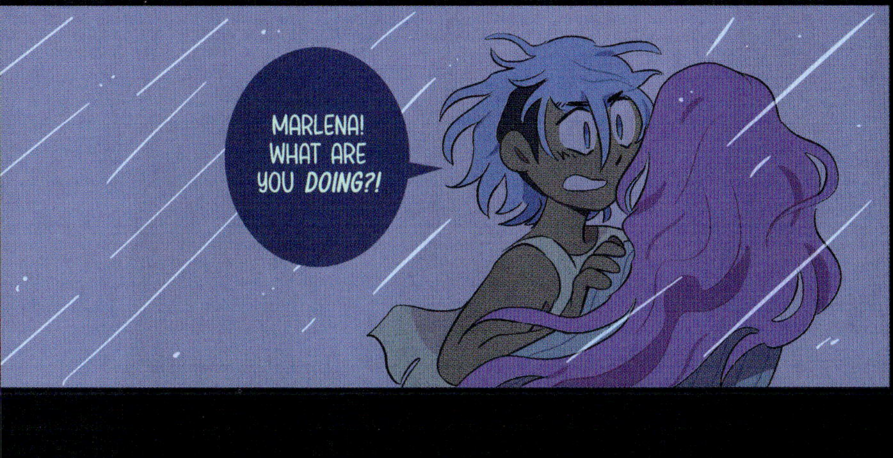
MARLENA! WHAT ARE YOU *DOING?!*

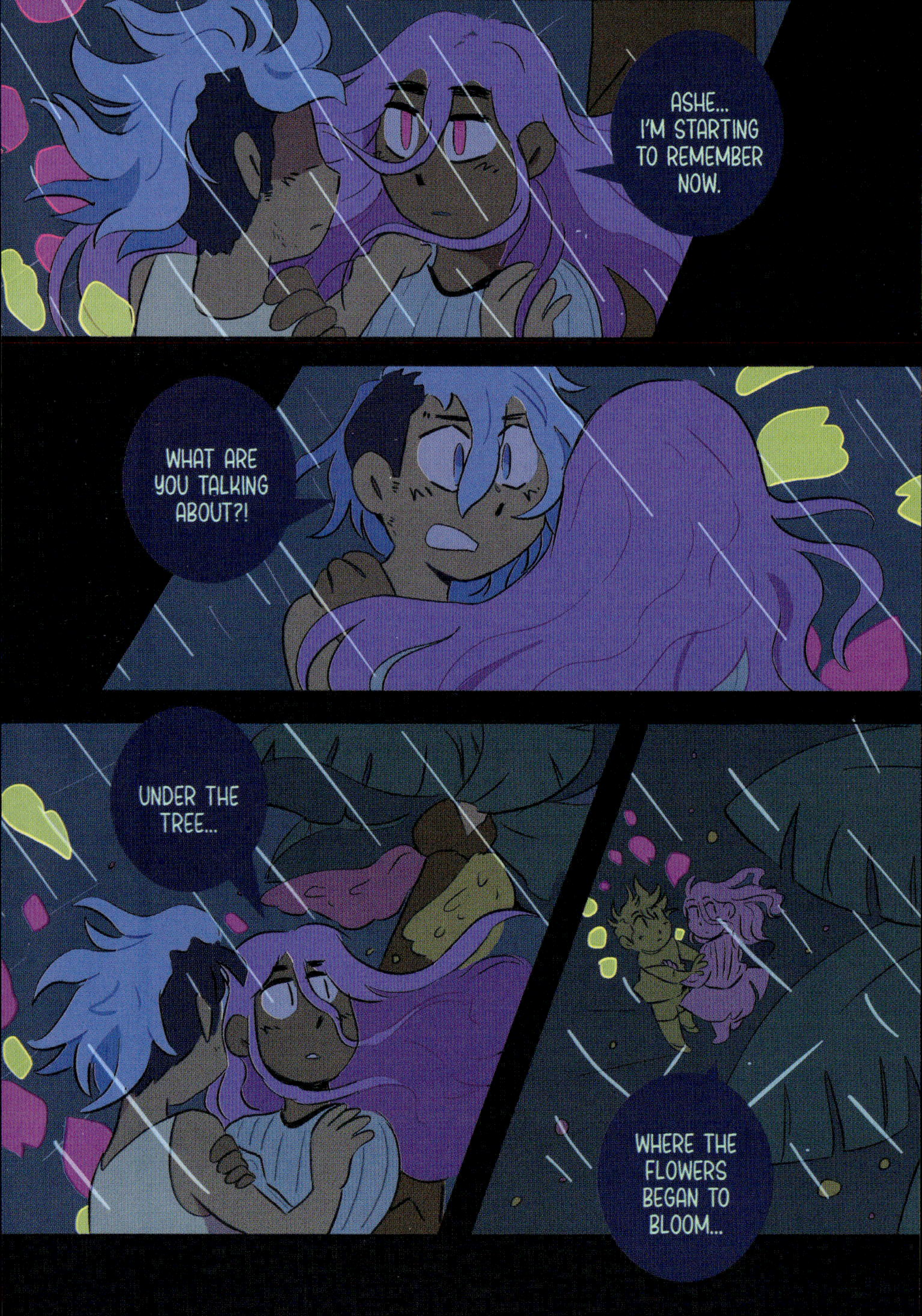
ASHE... I'M STARTING TO REMEMBER NOW.
WHAT ARE YOU TALKING ABOUT?!
UNDER THE TREE...
WHERE THE FLOWERS BEGAN TO BLOOM...

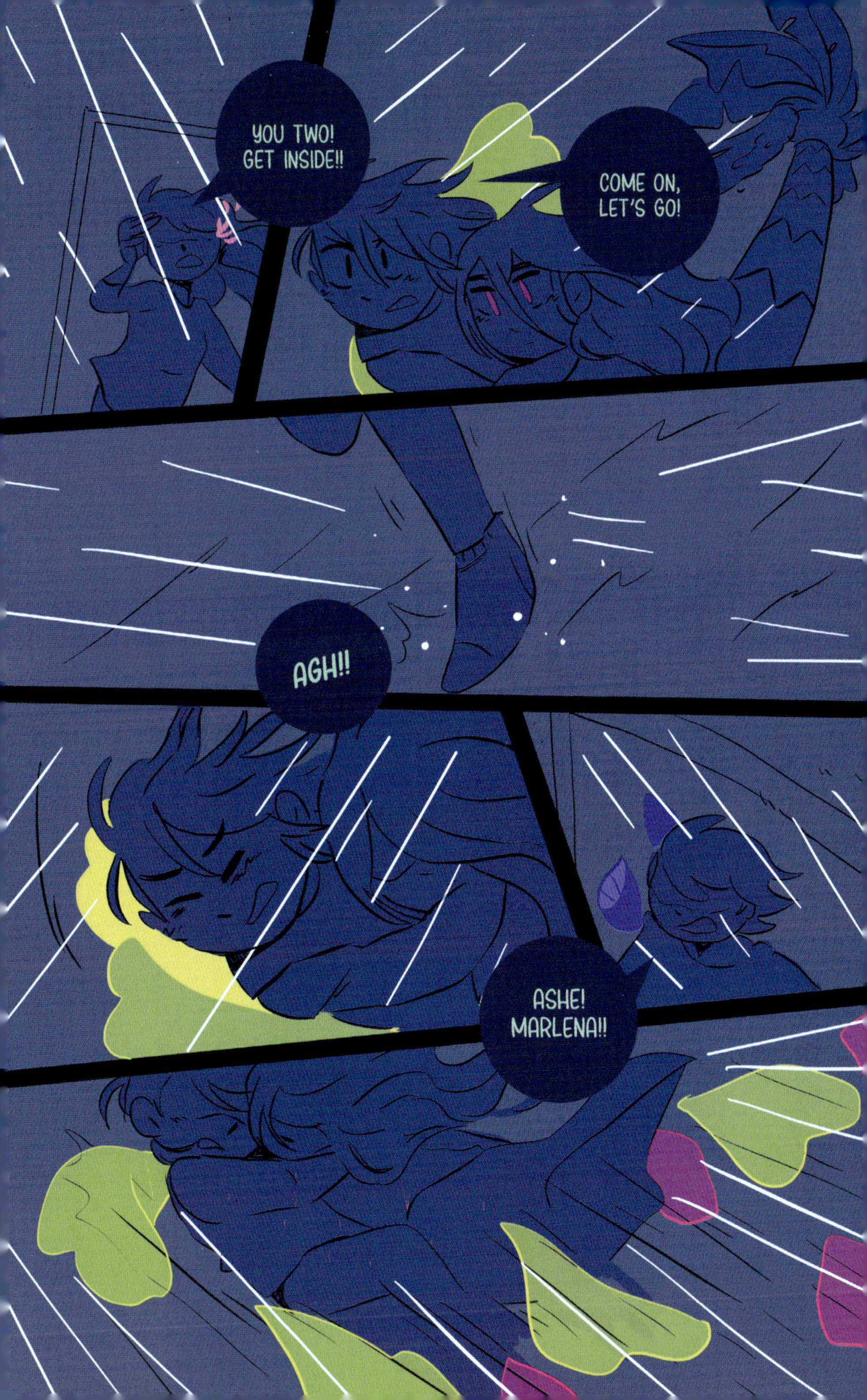
YOU TWO! GET INSIDE!!
COME ON, LET'S GO!
AGH!!
ASHE! MARLENA!!

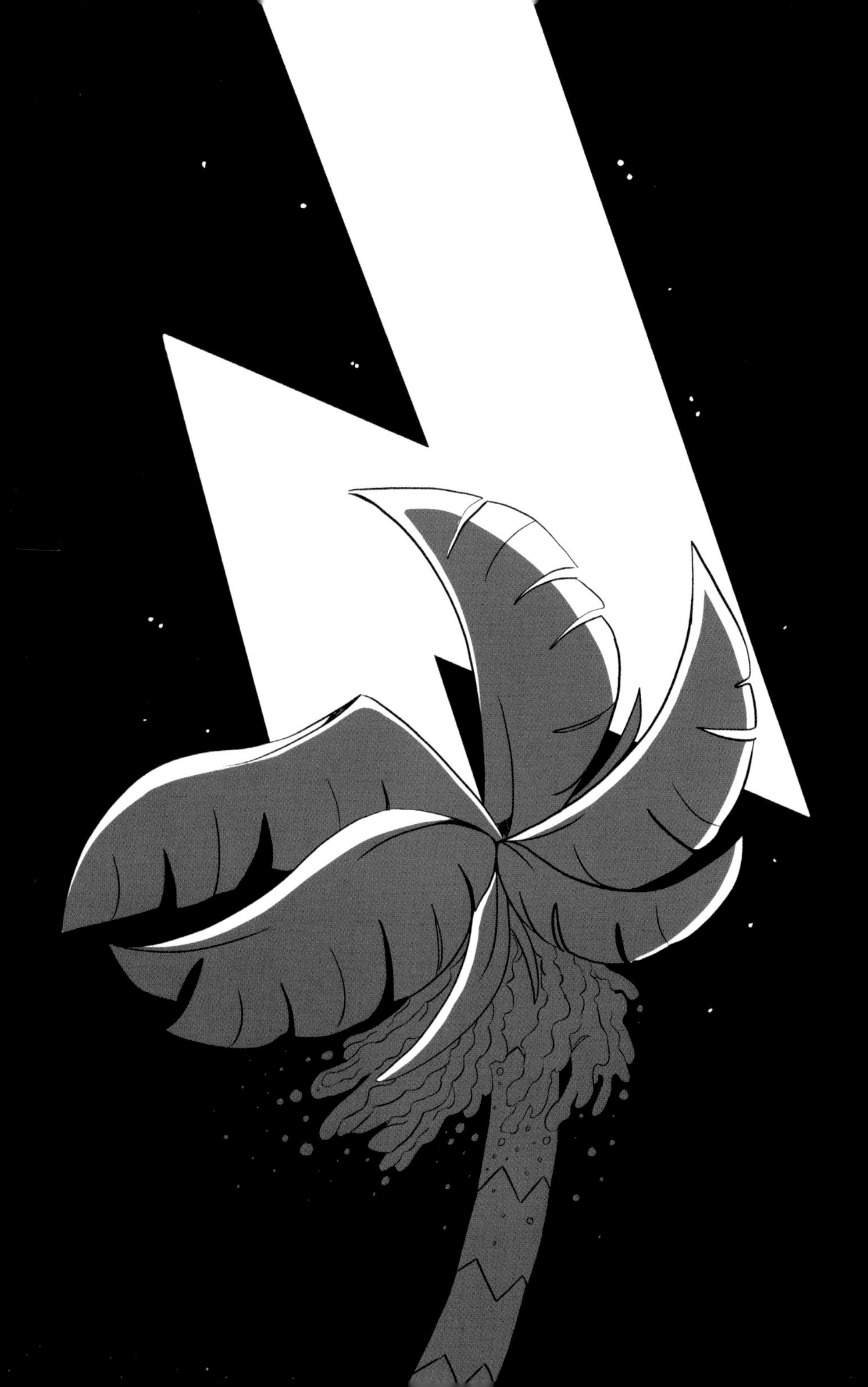

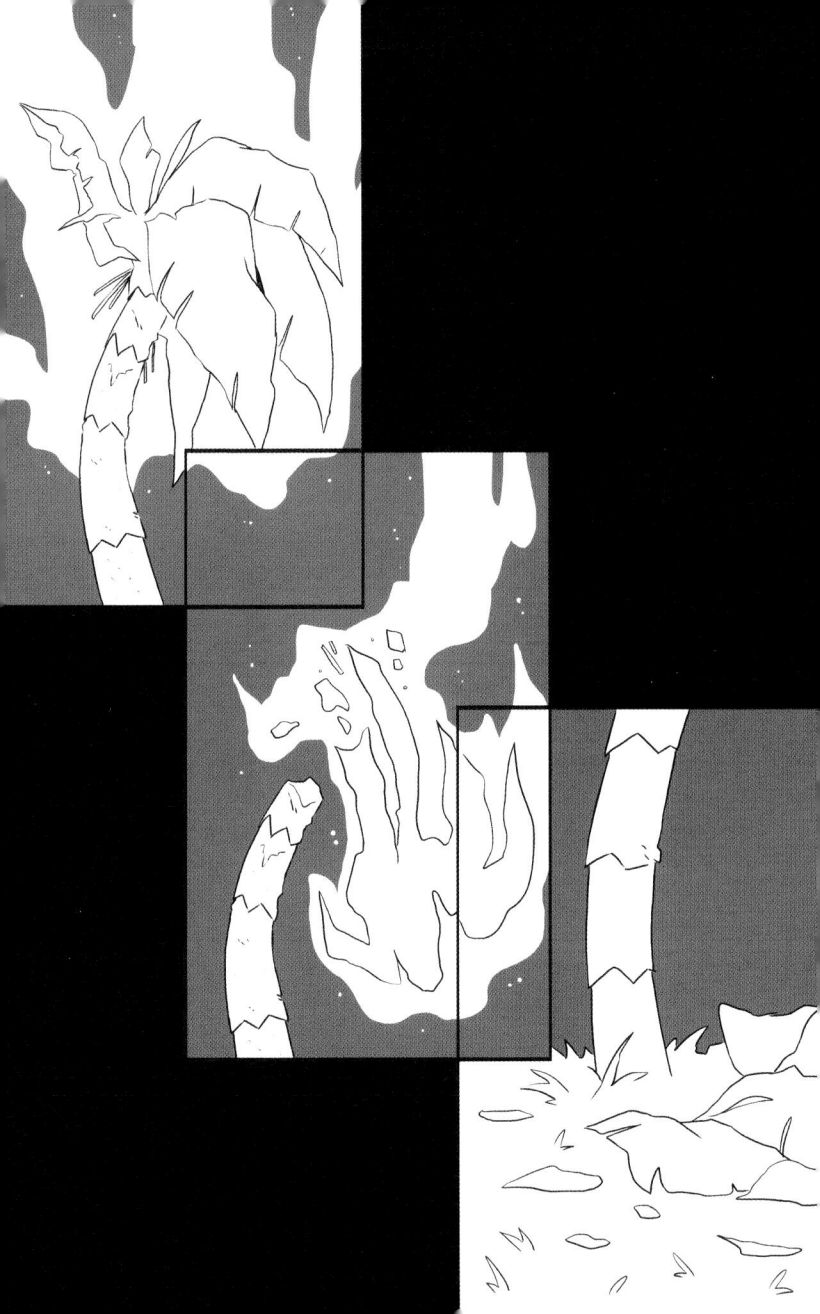

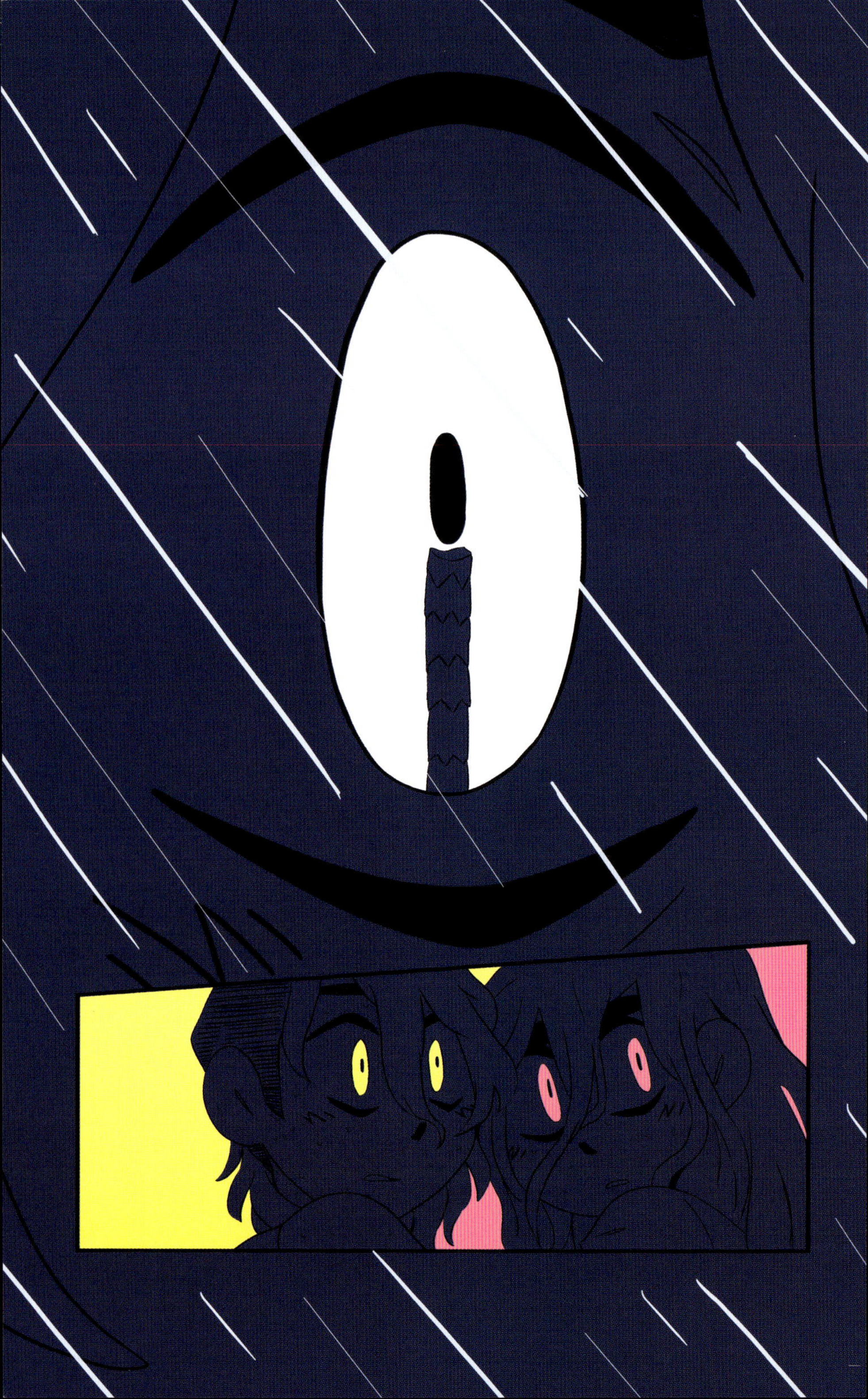

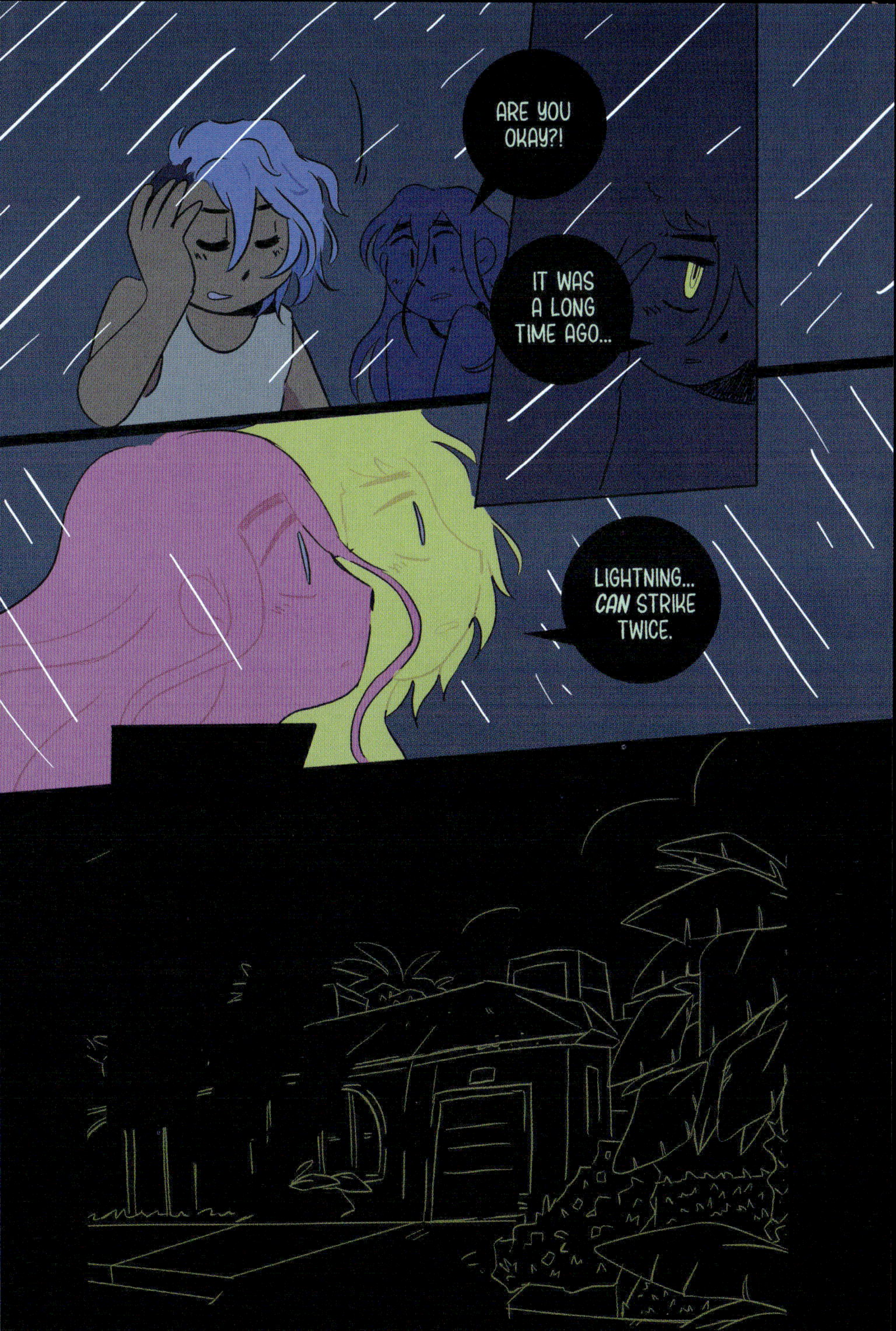
ARE YOU OKAY?!
IT WAS A LONG TIME AGO...
LIGHTNING... *CAN* STRIKE TWICE.

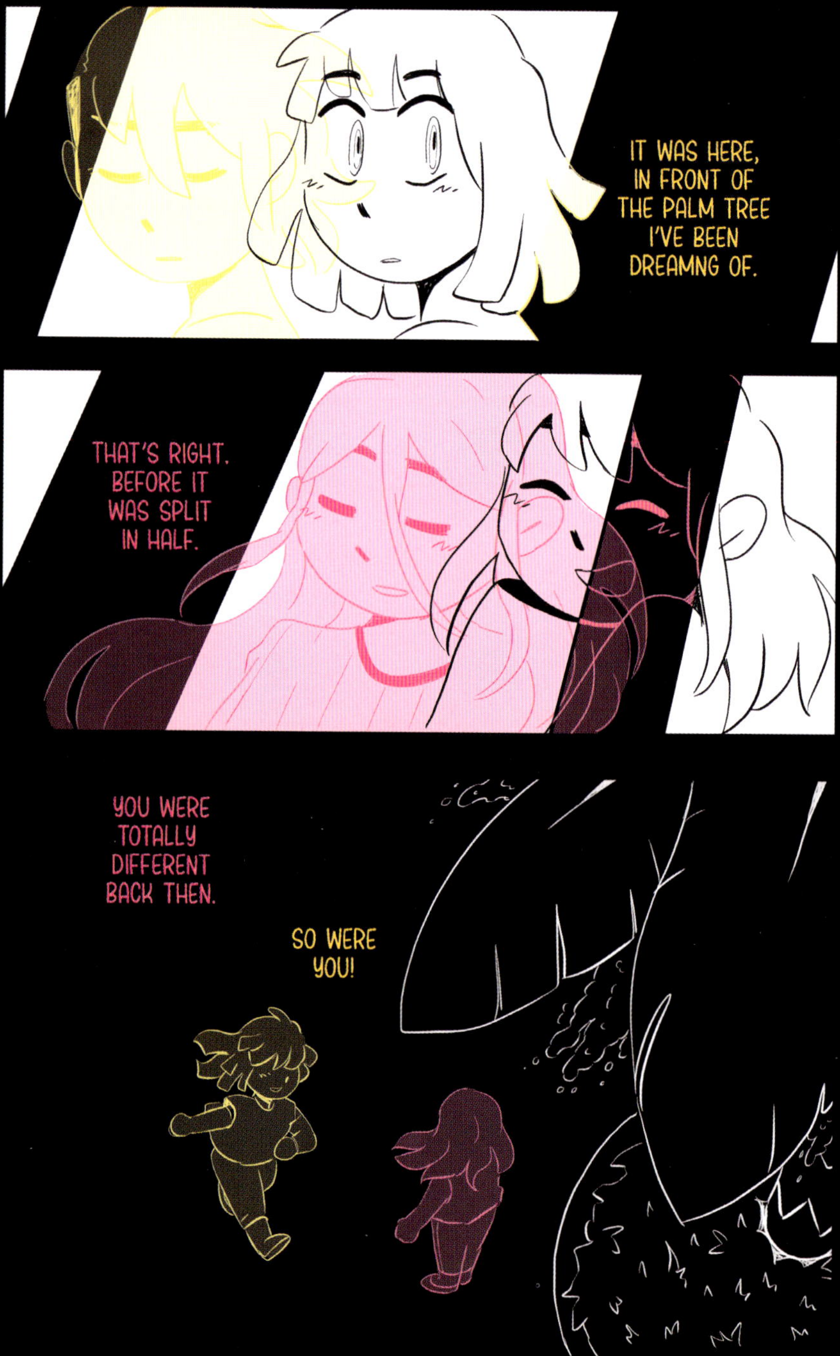
IT WAS HERE, IN FRONT OF THE PALM TREE I'VE BEEN DREAMNG OF.
THAT'S RIGHT. BEFORE IT WAS SPLIT IN HALF.
YOU WERE TOTALLY DIFFERENT BACK THEN.
SO WERE YOU!

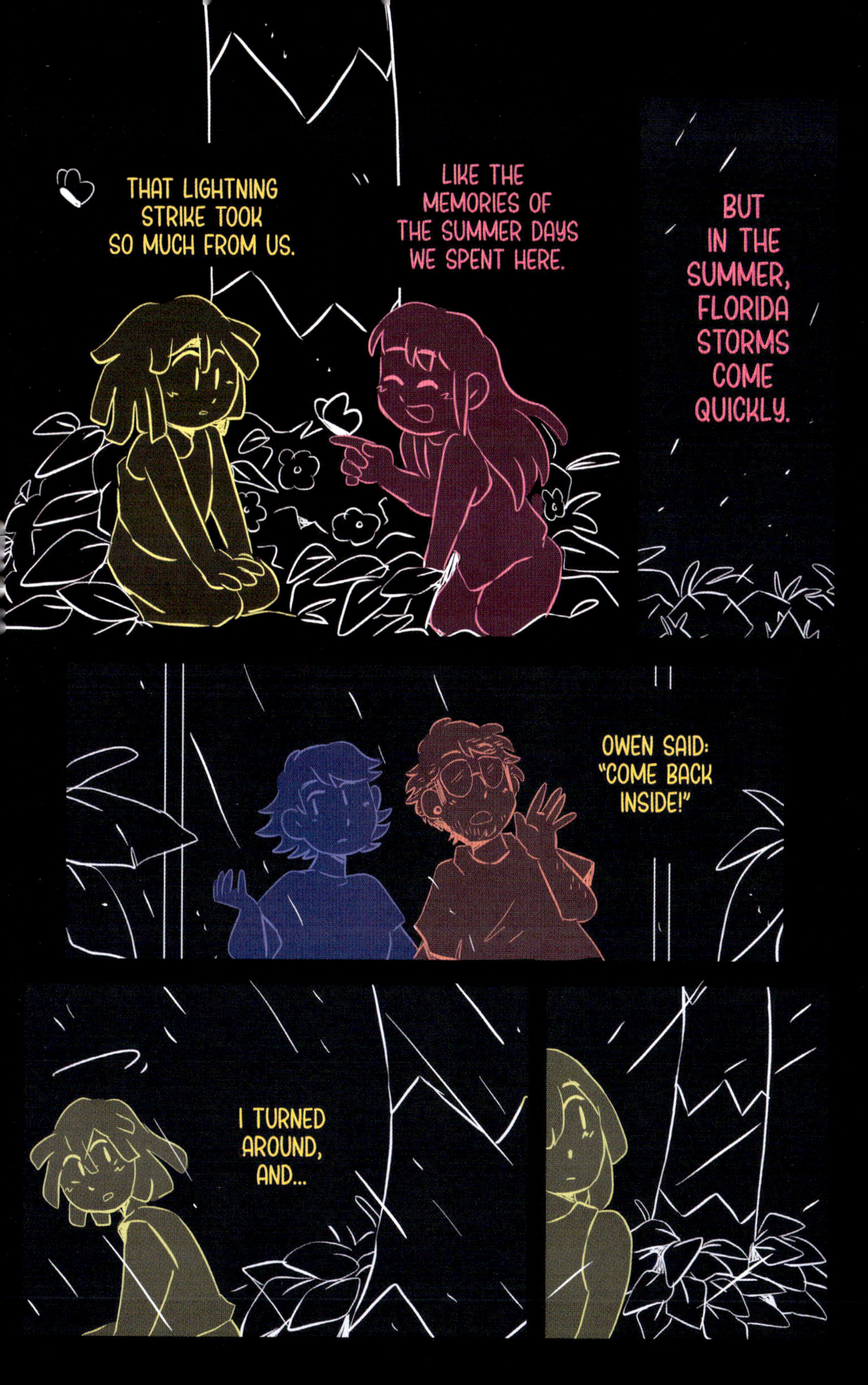
THAT LIGHTNING STRIKE TOOK SO MUCH FROM US.
LIKE THE MEMORIES OF THE SUMMER DAYS WE SPENT HERE.
BUT IN THE SUMMER, FLORIDA STORMS COME QUICKLY.
OWEN SAID: "COME BACK INSIDE!"
I TURNED AROUND, AND...

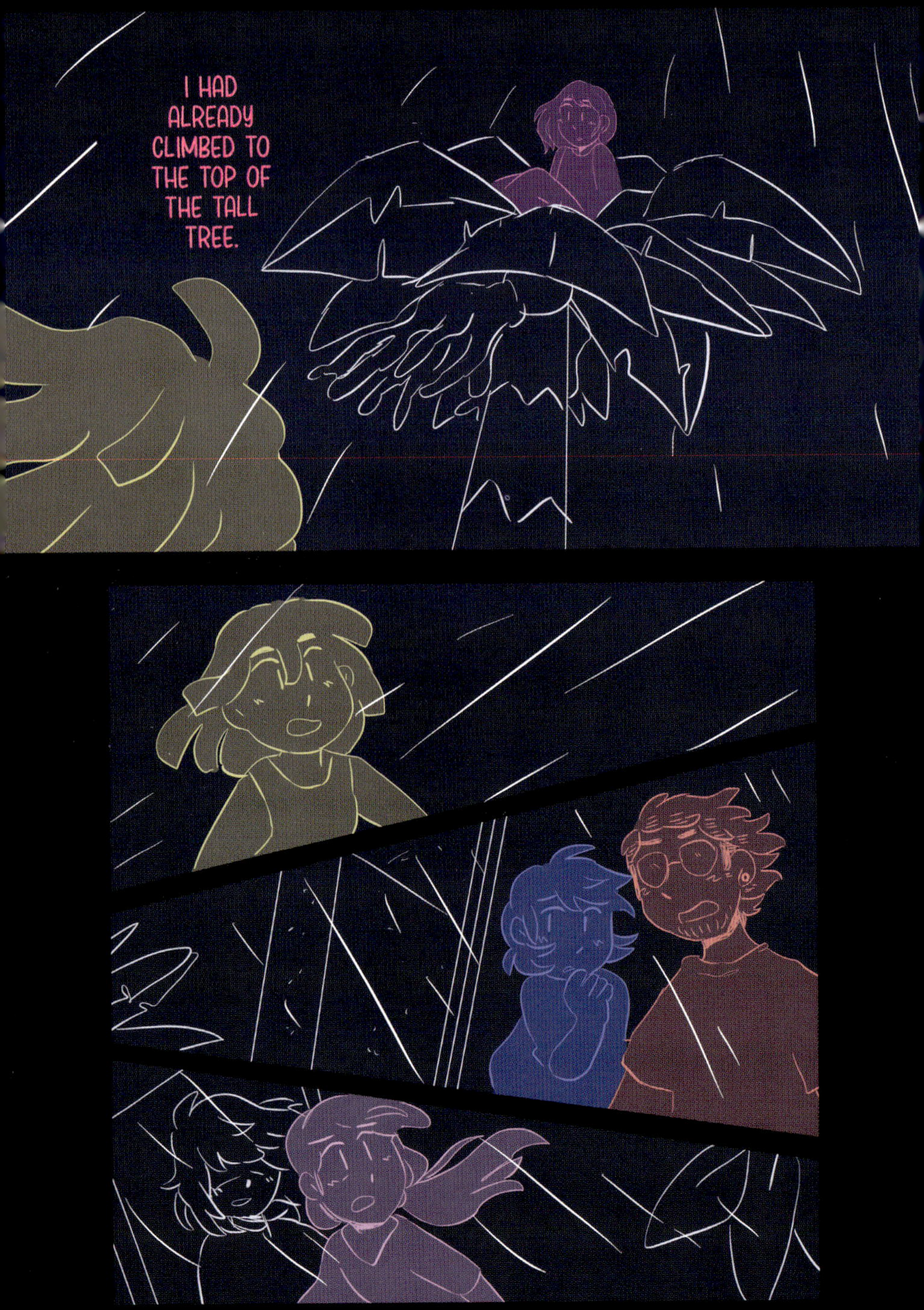
I HAD ALREADY CLIMBED TO THE TOP OF THE TALL TREE.

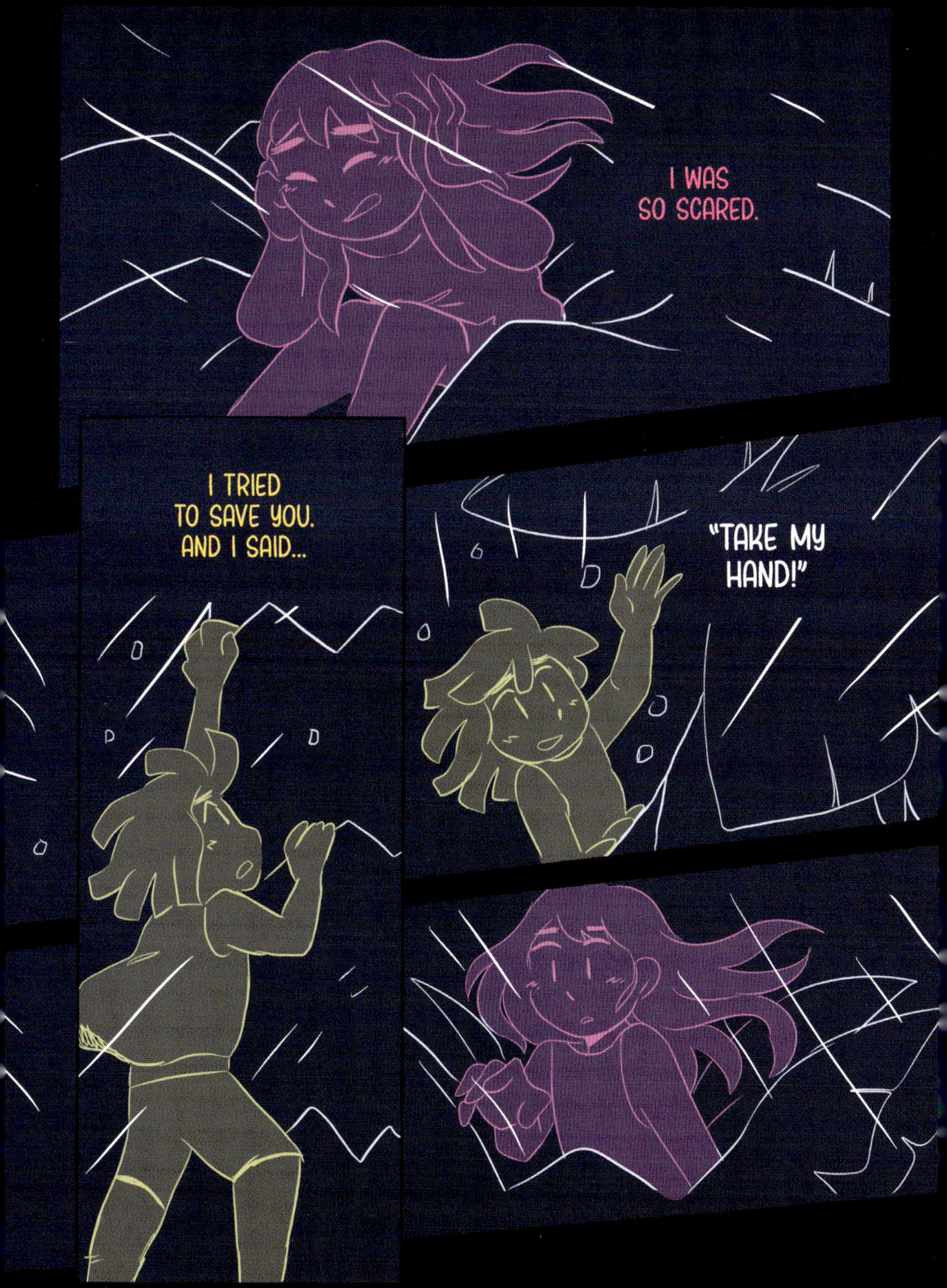
I WAS
SO SCARED.
I TRIED
TO SAVE YOU.
AND I SAID...
"TAKE MY
HAND!"

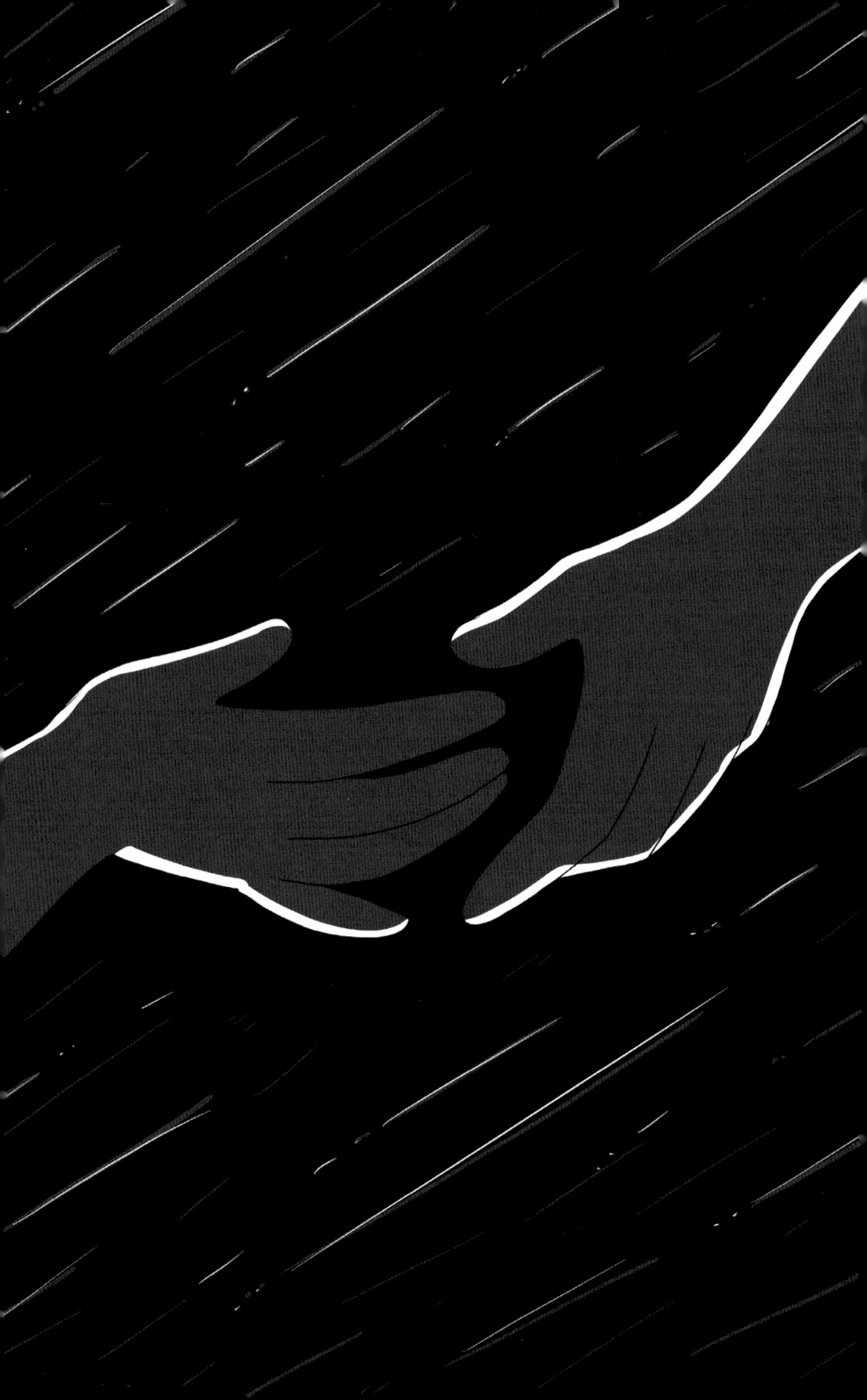

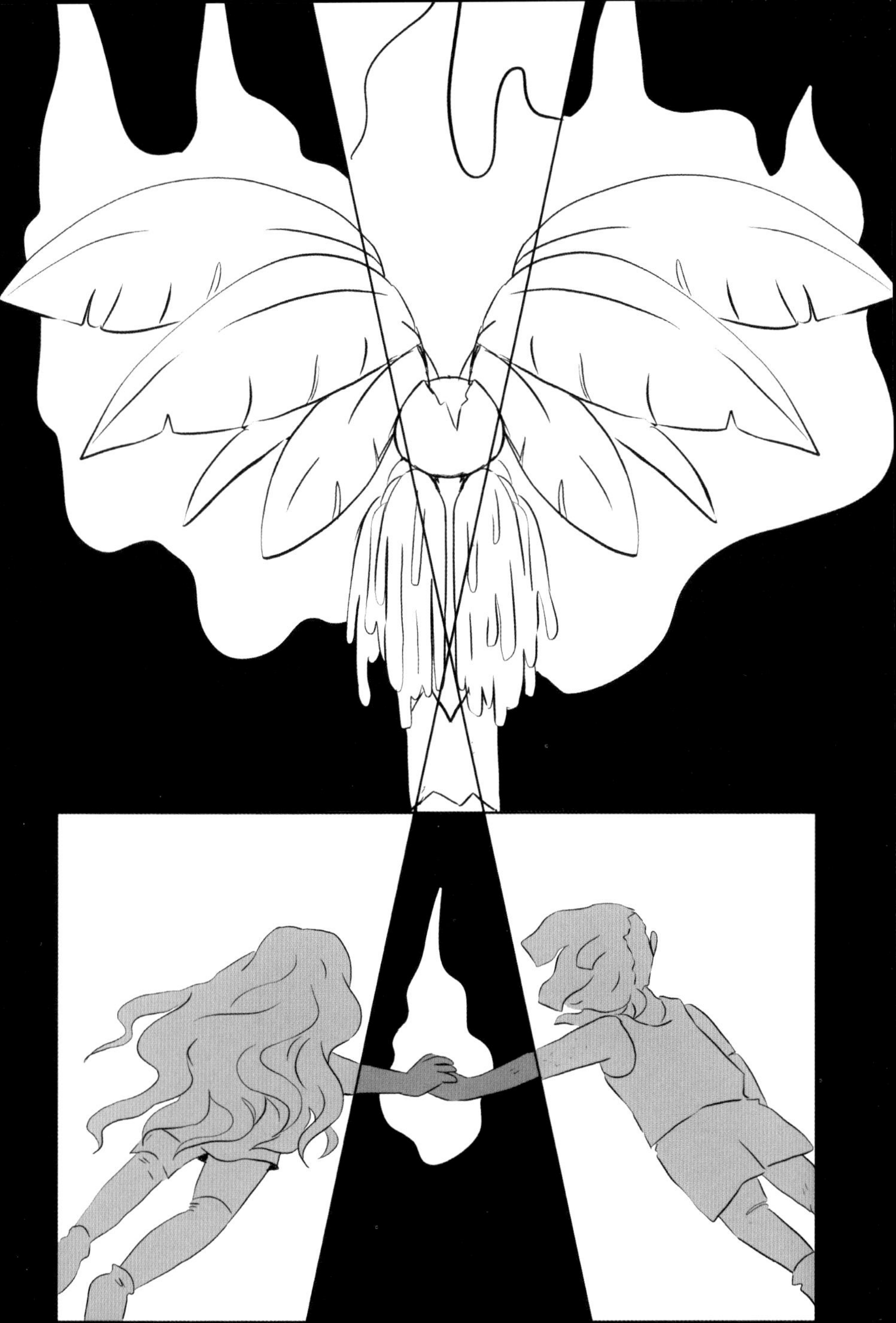

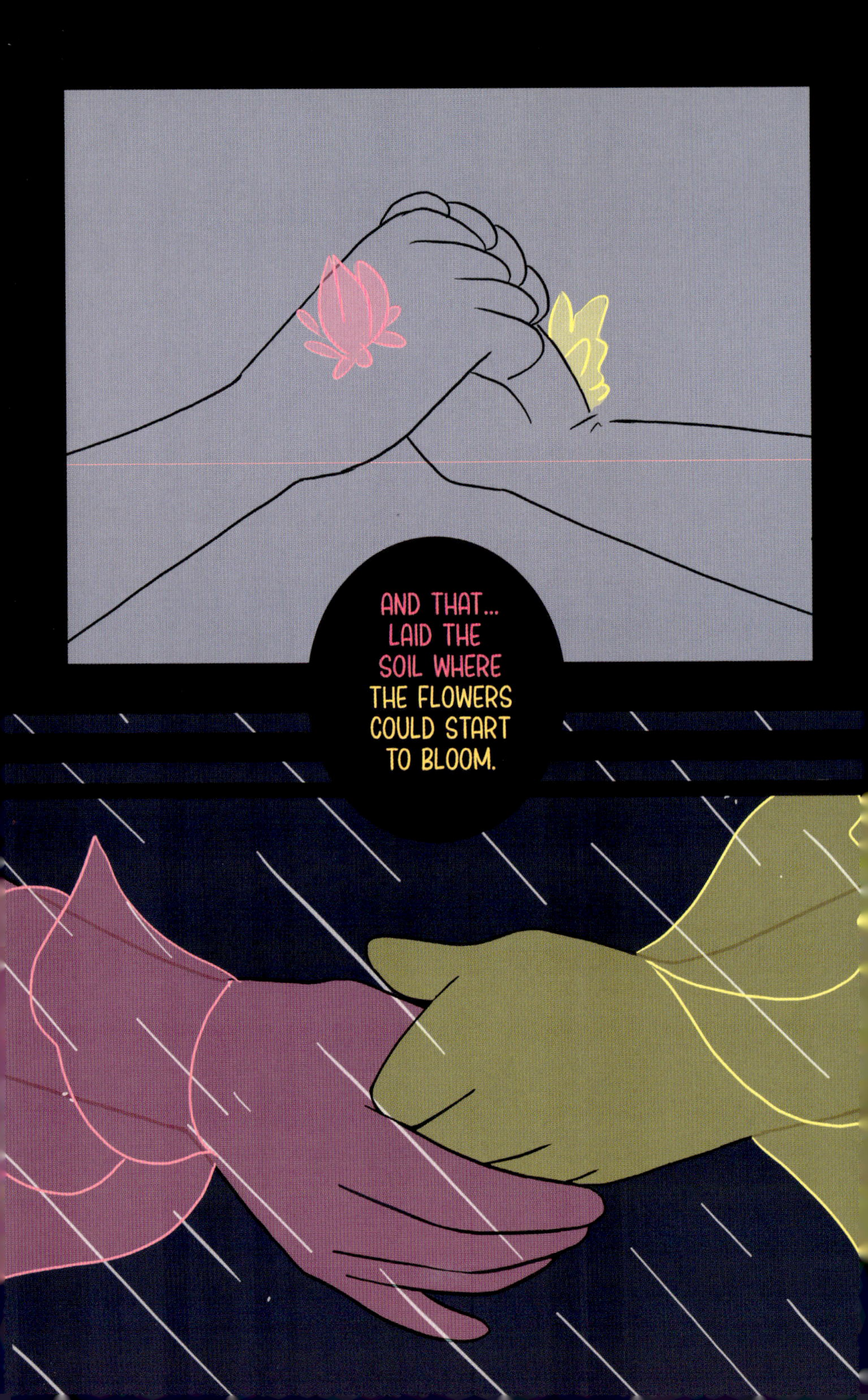
AND THAT... LAID THE SOIL WHERE THE FLOWERS COULD START TO BLOOM.

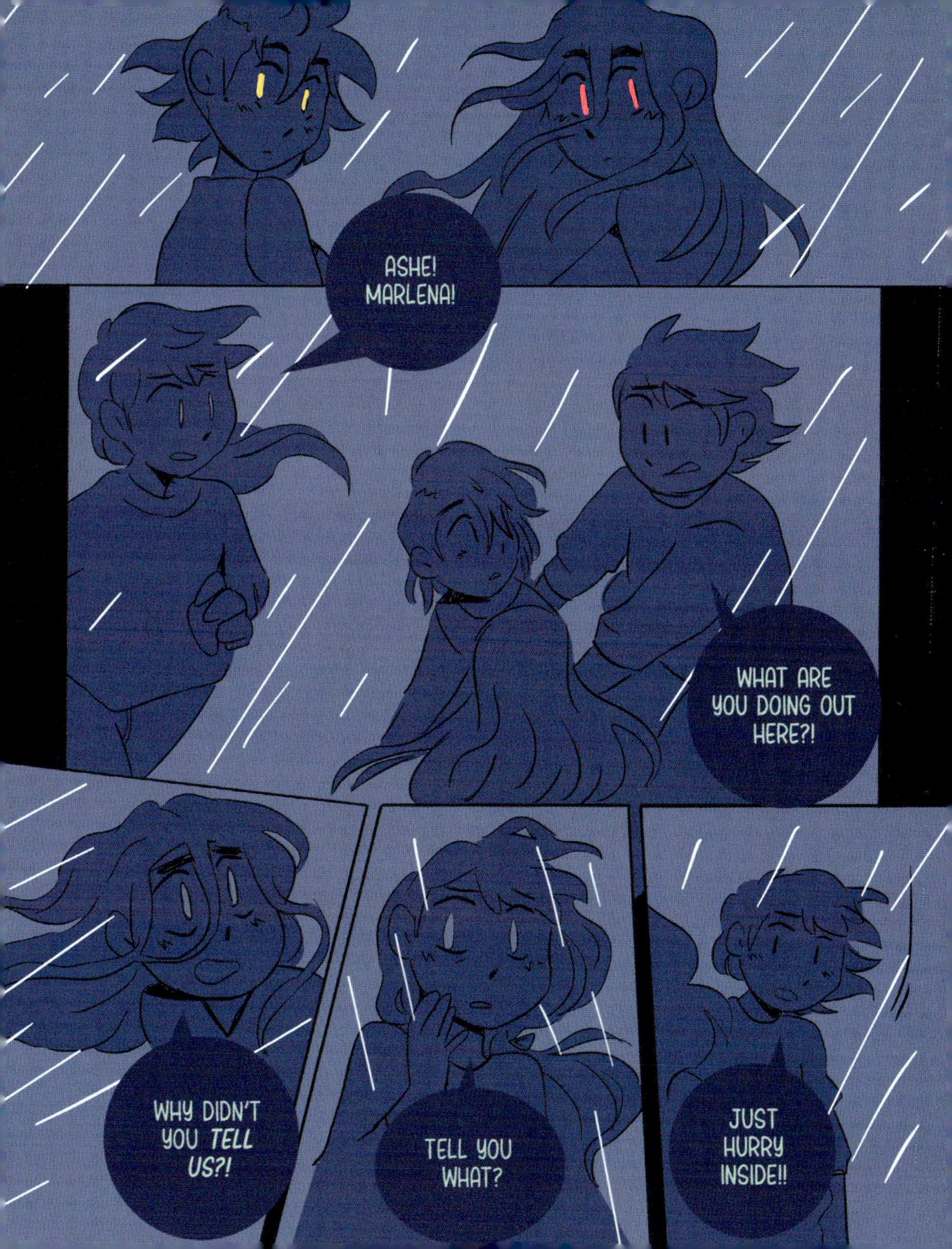
ASHE! MARLENA!
WHAT ARE YOU DOING OUT HERE?!
WHY DIDN'T YOU *TELL* US?!
TELL YOU WHAT?
JUST HURRY INSIDE!!

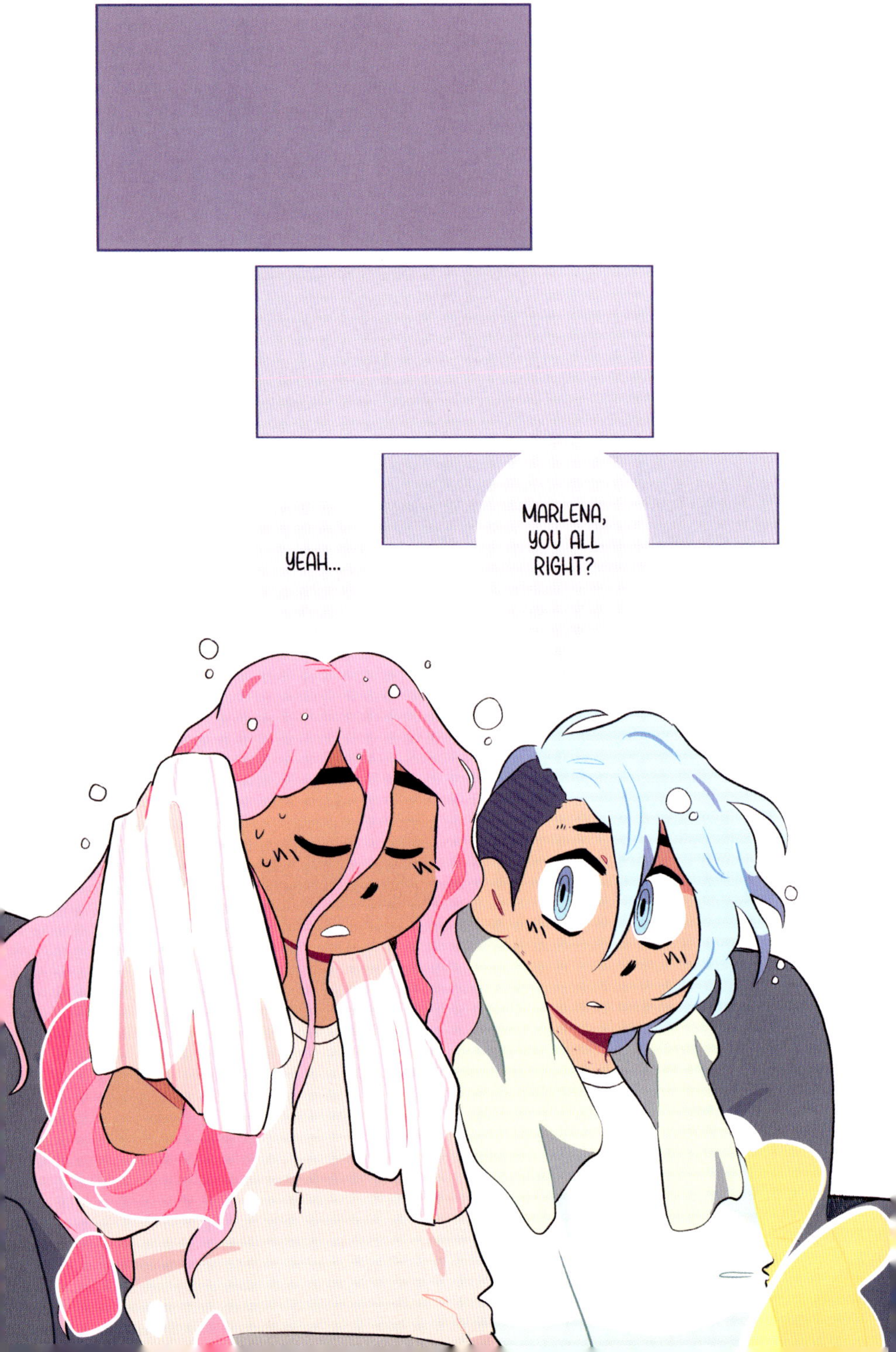
MARLENA, YOU ALL RIGHT?
YEAH...

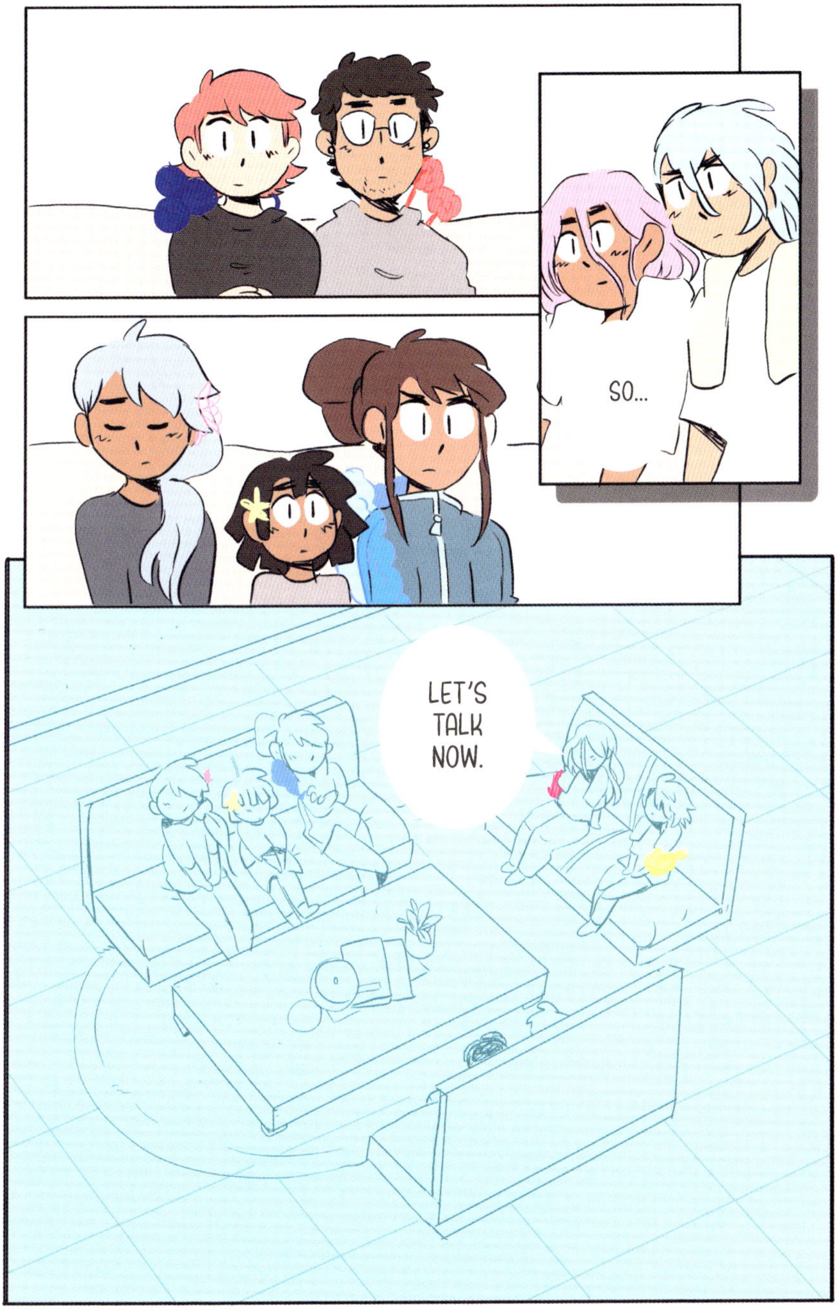
SO...
LET'S TALK NOW.

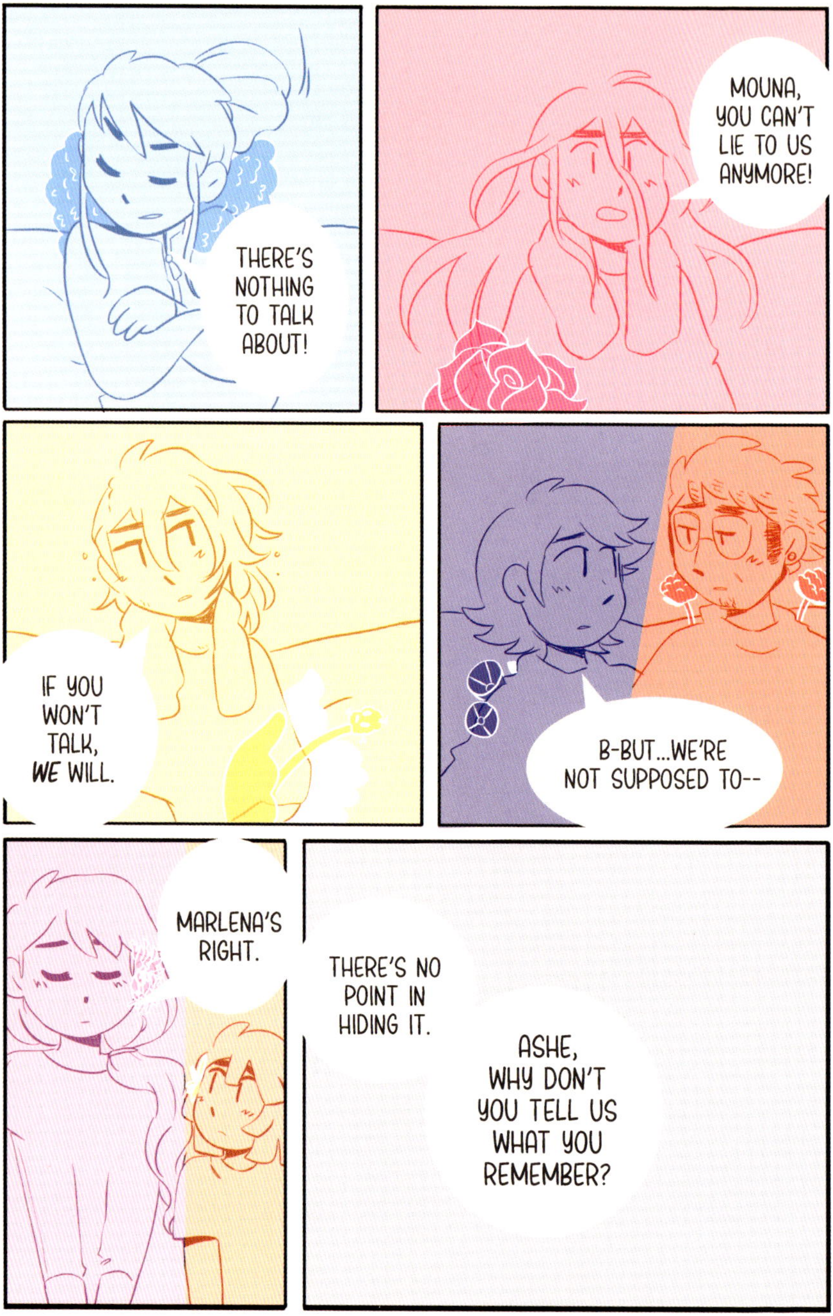
THERE'S NOTHING TO TALK ABOUT!
MOUNA, YOU CAN'T LIE TO US ANYMORE!
IF YOU WON'T TALK, WE WILL.
B-BUT...WE'RE NOT SUPPOSED TO--
MARLENA'S RIGHT.
THERE'S NO POINT IN HIDING IT.
ASHE, WHY DON'T YOU TELL US WHAT YOU REMEMBER?

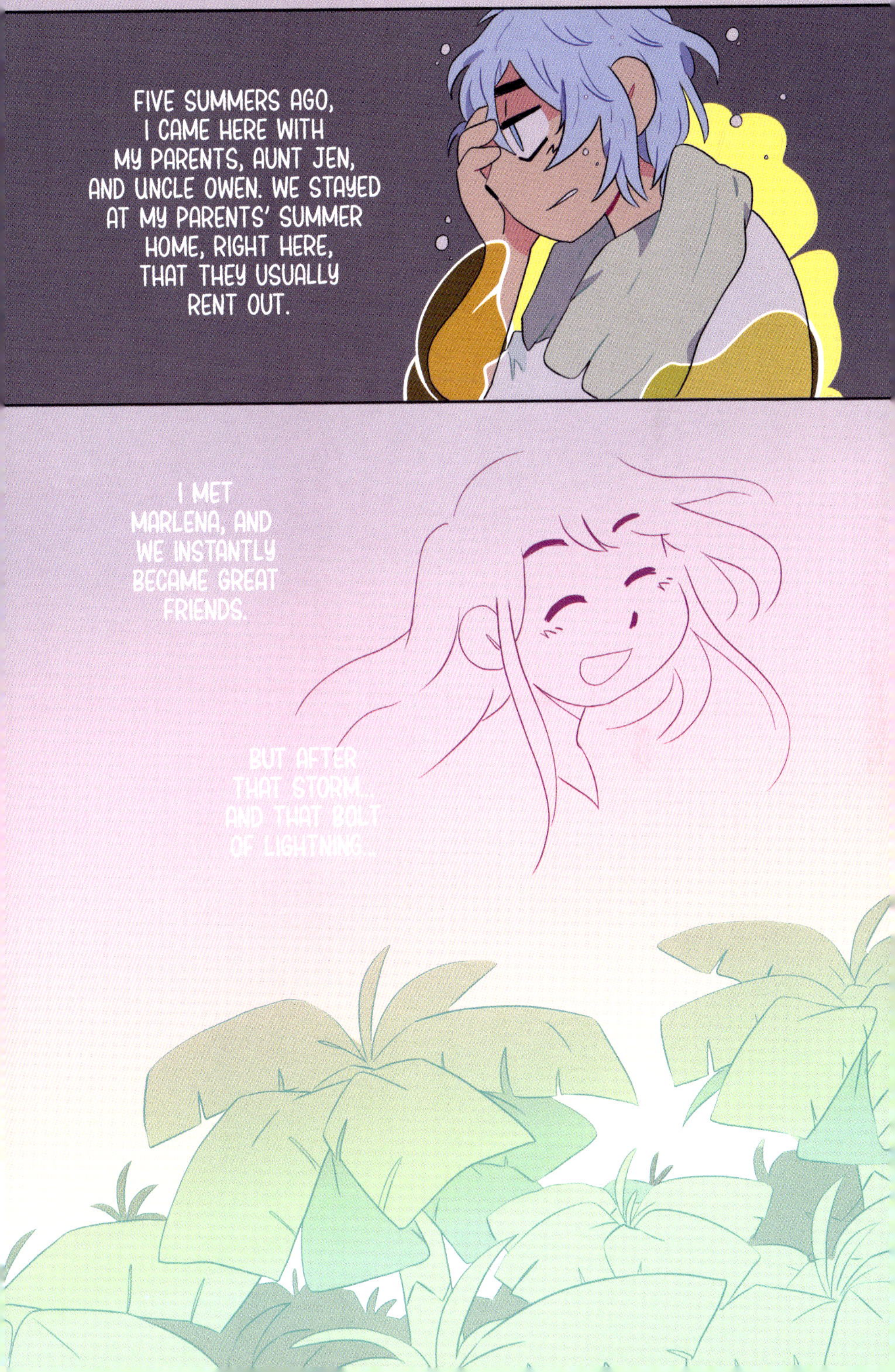
FIVE SUMMERS AGO, I CAME HERE WITH MY PARENTS, AUNT JEN, AND UNCLE OWEN. WE STAYED AT MY PARENTS' SUMMER HOME, RIGHT HERE, THAT THEY USUALLY RENT OUT.
I MET MARLENA, AND WE INSTANTLY BECAME GREAT FRIENDS.
BUT AFTER THAT STORM... AND THAT BOLT OF LIGHTNING...

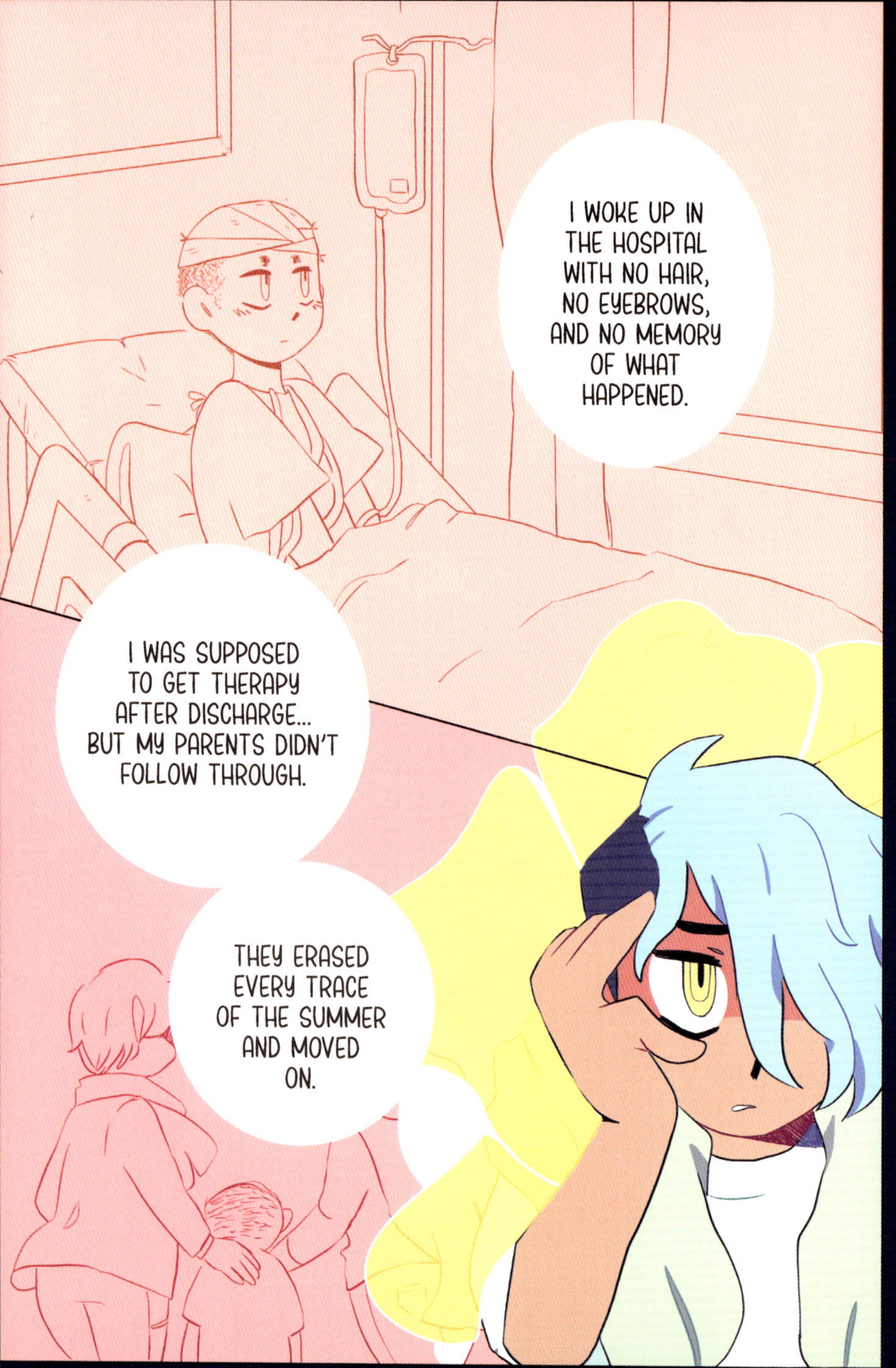
I WOKE UP IN THE HOSPITAL WITH NO HAIR, NO EYEBROWS, AND NO MEMORY OF WHAT HAPPENED.
I WAS SUPPOSED TO GET THERAPY AFTER DISCHARGE... BUT MY PARENTS DIDN'T FOLLOW THROUGH.
THEY ERASED EVERY TRACE OF THE SUMMER AND MOVED ON.

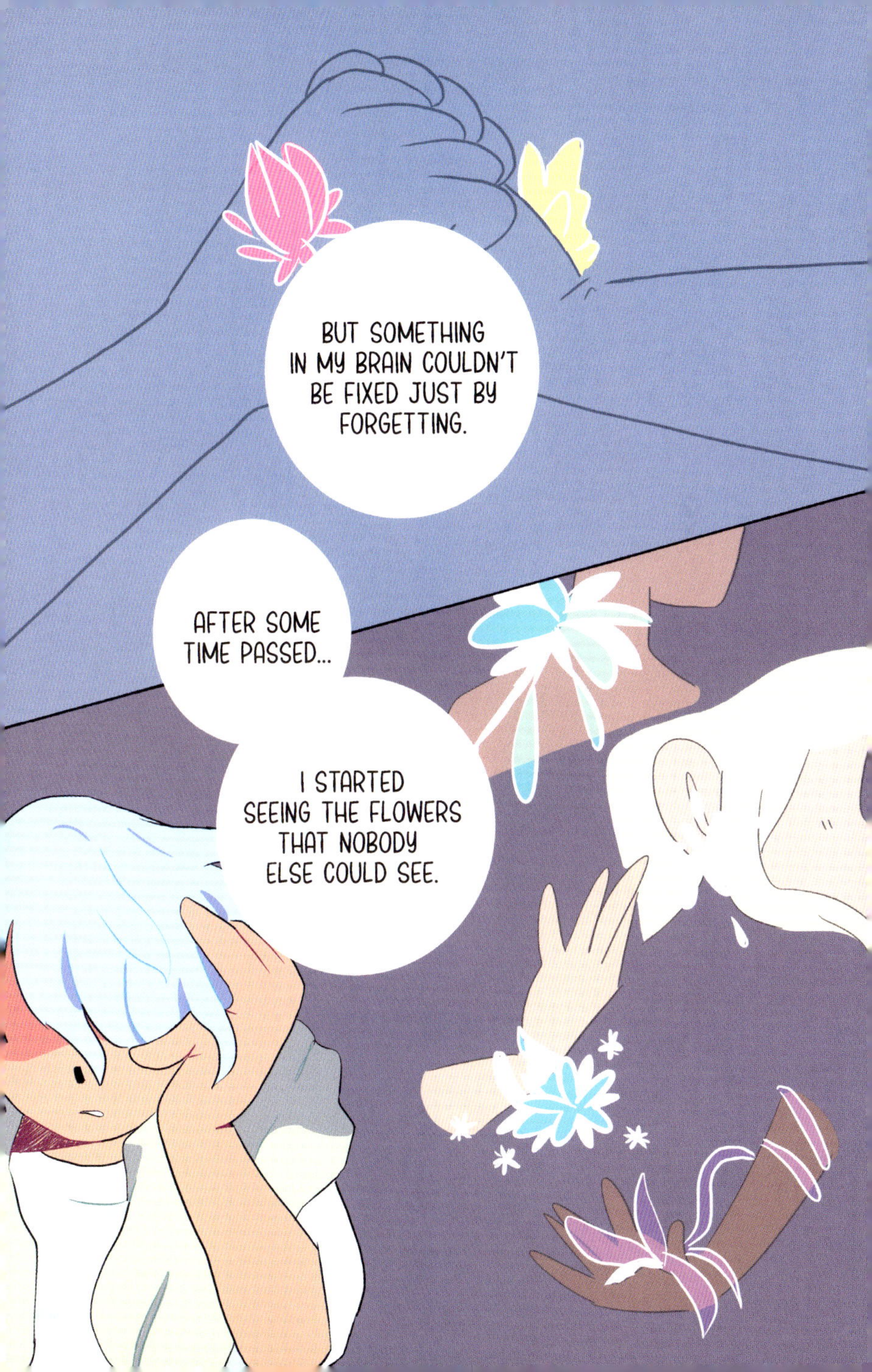
BUT SOMETHING IN MY BRAIN COULDN'T BE FIXED JUST BY FORGETTING.
AFTER SOME TIME PASSED...
I STARTED SEEING THE FLOWERS THAT NOBODY ELSE COULD SEE.

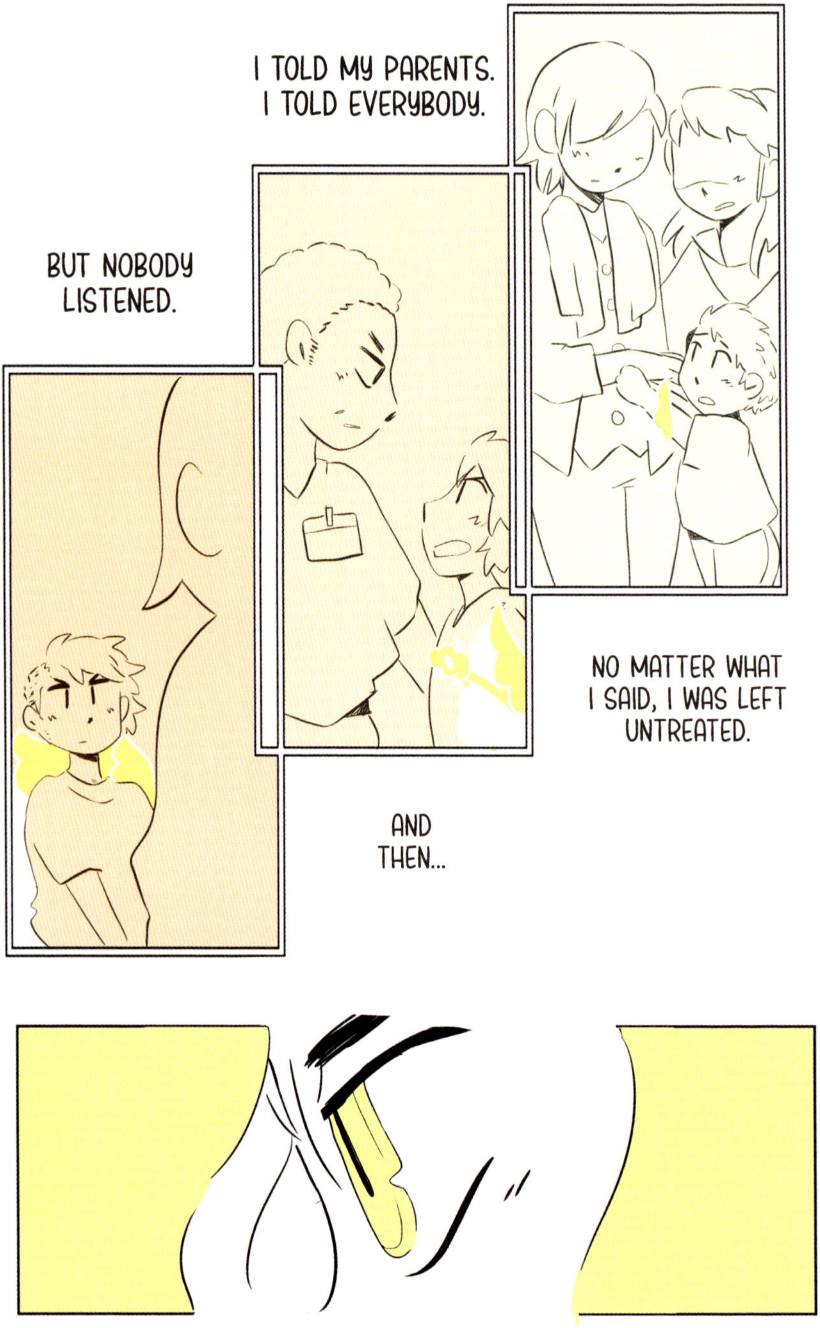
I TOLD MY PARENTS.
I TOLD EVERYBODY.
BUT NOBODY LISTENED.
NO MATTER WHAT I SAID, I WAS LEFT UNTREATED.
AND THEN...

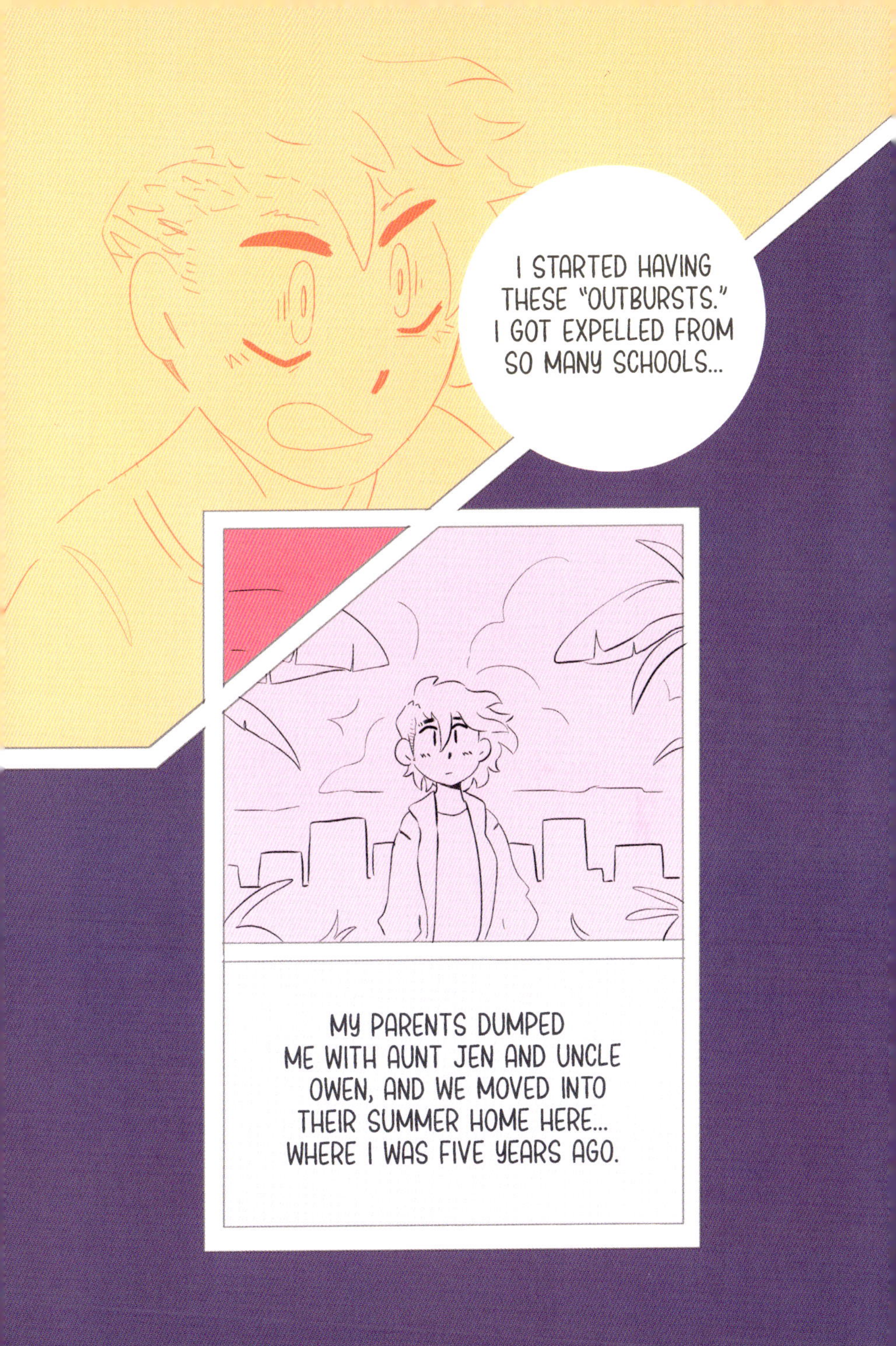
I STARTED HAVING THESE "OUTBURSTS." I GOT EXPELLED FROM SO MANY SCHOOLS...
MY PARENTS DUMPED ME WITH AUNT JEN AND UNCLE OWEN, AND WE MOVED INTO THEIR SUMMER HOME HERE... WHERE I WAS FIVE YEARS AGO.

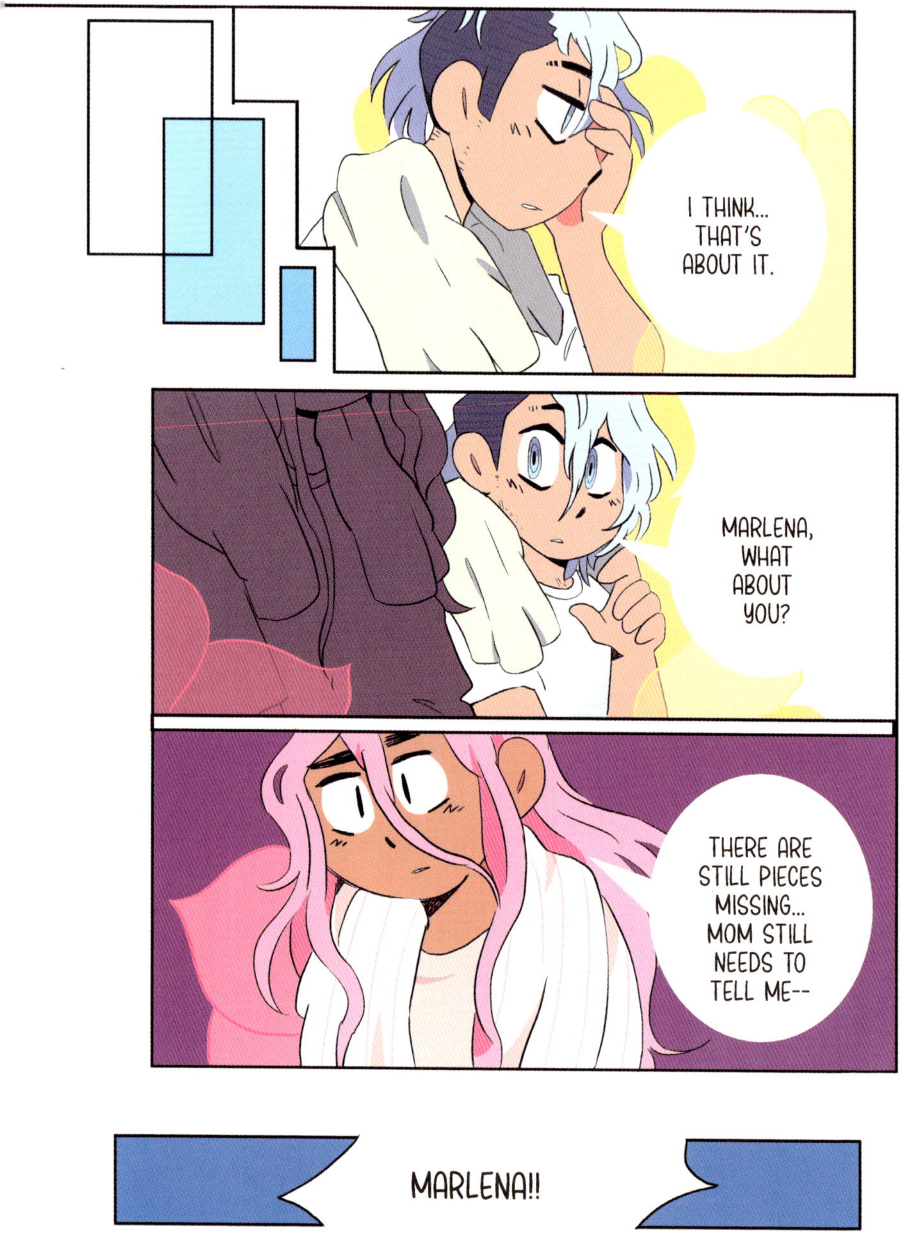
I THINK... THAT'S ABOUT IT.
MARLENA, WHAT ABOUT YOU?
THERE ARE STILL PIECES MISSING... MOM STILL NEEDS TO TELL ME--
MARLENA!!

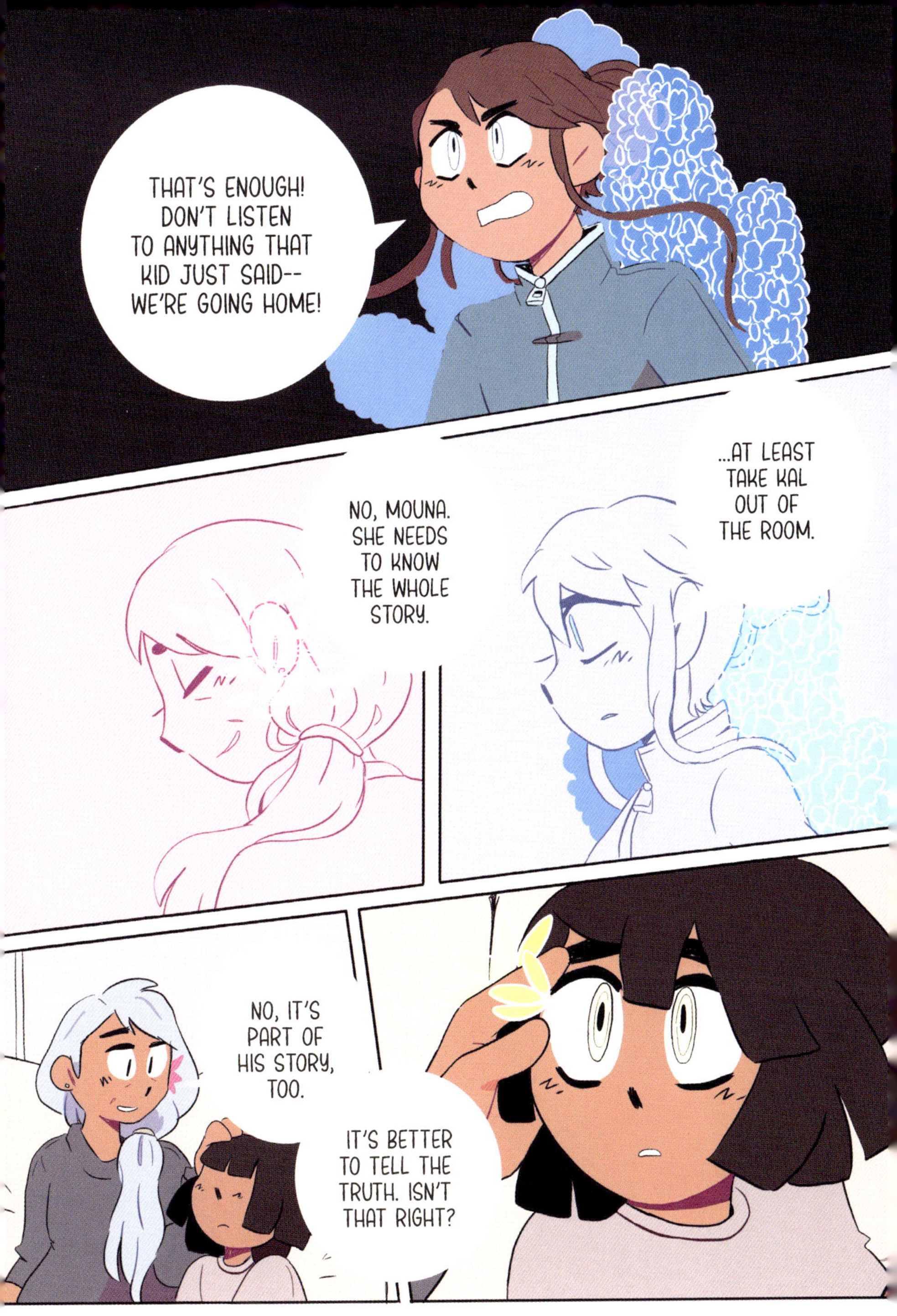
THAT'S ENOUGH! DON'T LISTEN TO ANYTHING THAT KID JUST SAID-- WE'RE GOING HOME!
NO, MOUNA. SHE NEEDS TO KNOW THE WHOLE STORY.
...AT LEAST TAKE KAL OUT OF THE ROOM.
NO, IT'S PART OF HIS STORY, TOO.
IT'S BETTER TO TELL THE TRUTH. ISN'T THAT RIGHT?

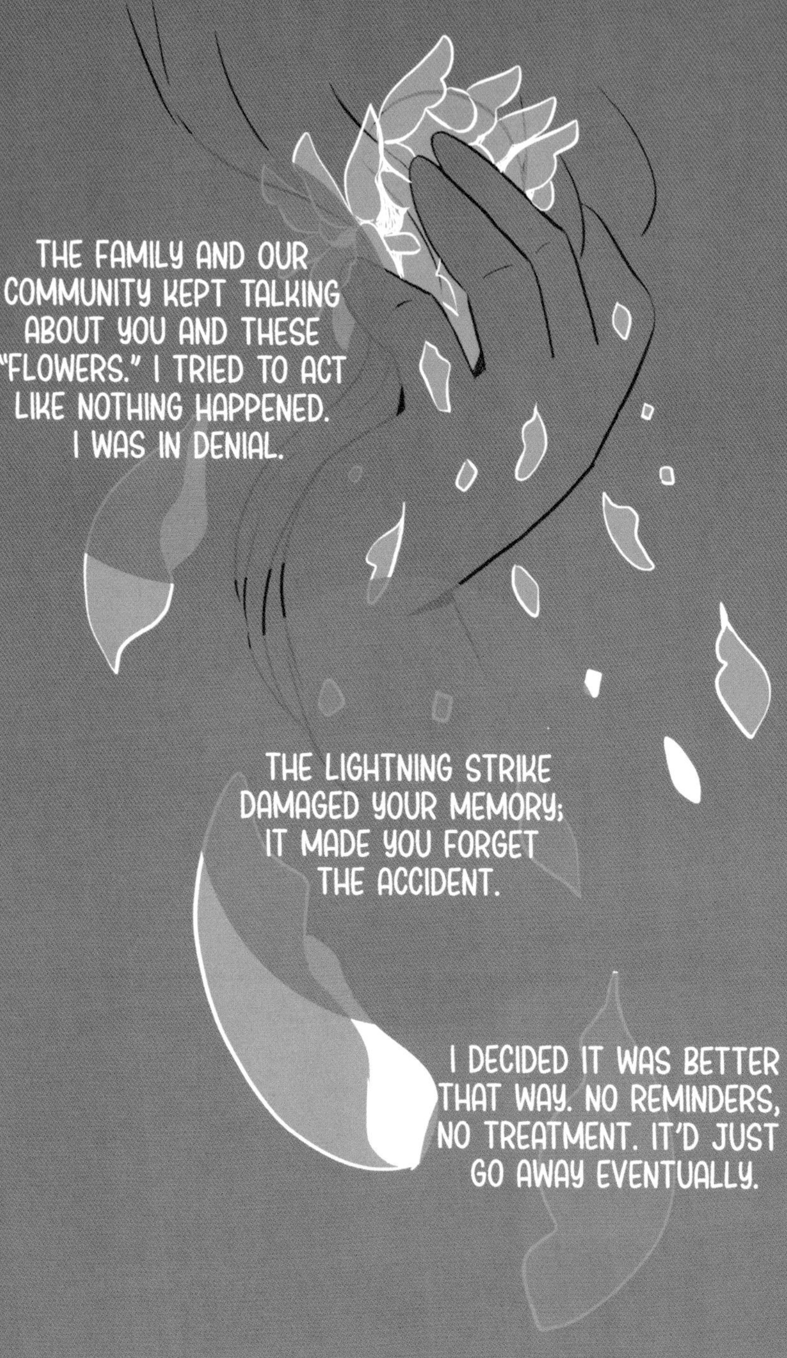
THE FAMILY AND OUR COMMUNITY KEPT TALKING ABOUT YOU AND THESE "FLOWERS." I TRIED TO ACT LIKE NOTHING HAPPENED. I WAS IN DENIAL.
THE LIGHTNING STRIKE DAMAGED YOUR MEMORY; IT MADE YOU FORGET THE ACCIDENT.
I DECIDED IT WAS BETTER THAT WAY. NO REMINDERS, NO TREATMENT. IT'D JUST GO AWAY EVENTUALLY.

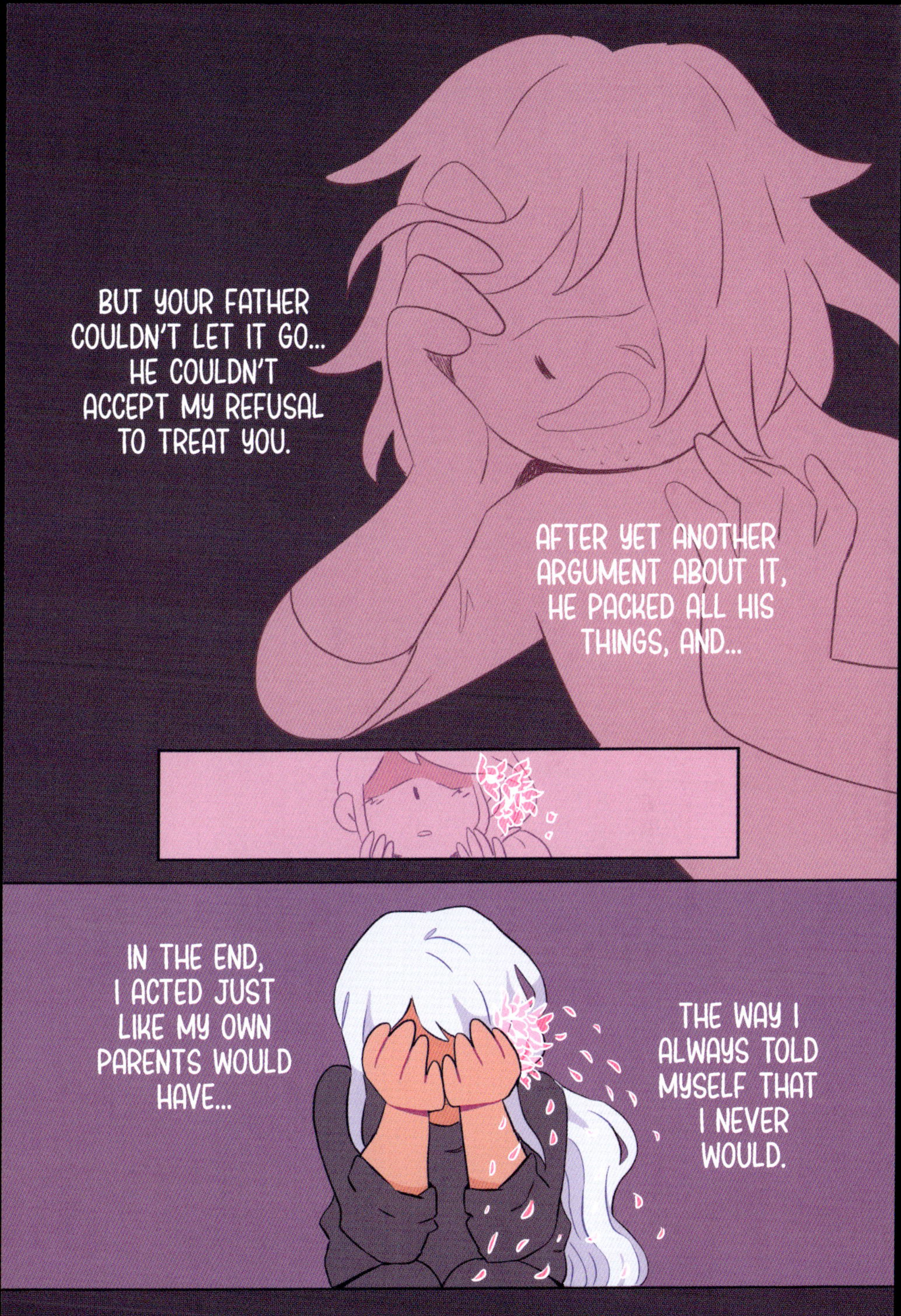
BUT YOUR FATHER COULDN'T LET IT GO... HE COULDN'T ACCEPT MY REFUSAL TO TREAT YOU.
AFTER YET ANOTHER ARGUMENT ABOUT IT, HE PACKED ALL HIS THINGS, AND...
IN THE END, I ACTED JUST LIKE MY OWN PARENTS WOULD HAVE...
THE WAY I ALWAYS TOLD MYSELF THAT I NEVER WOULD.

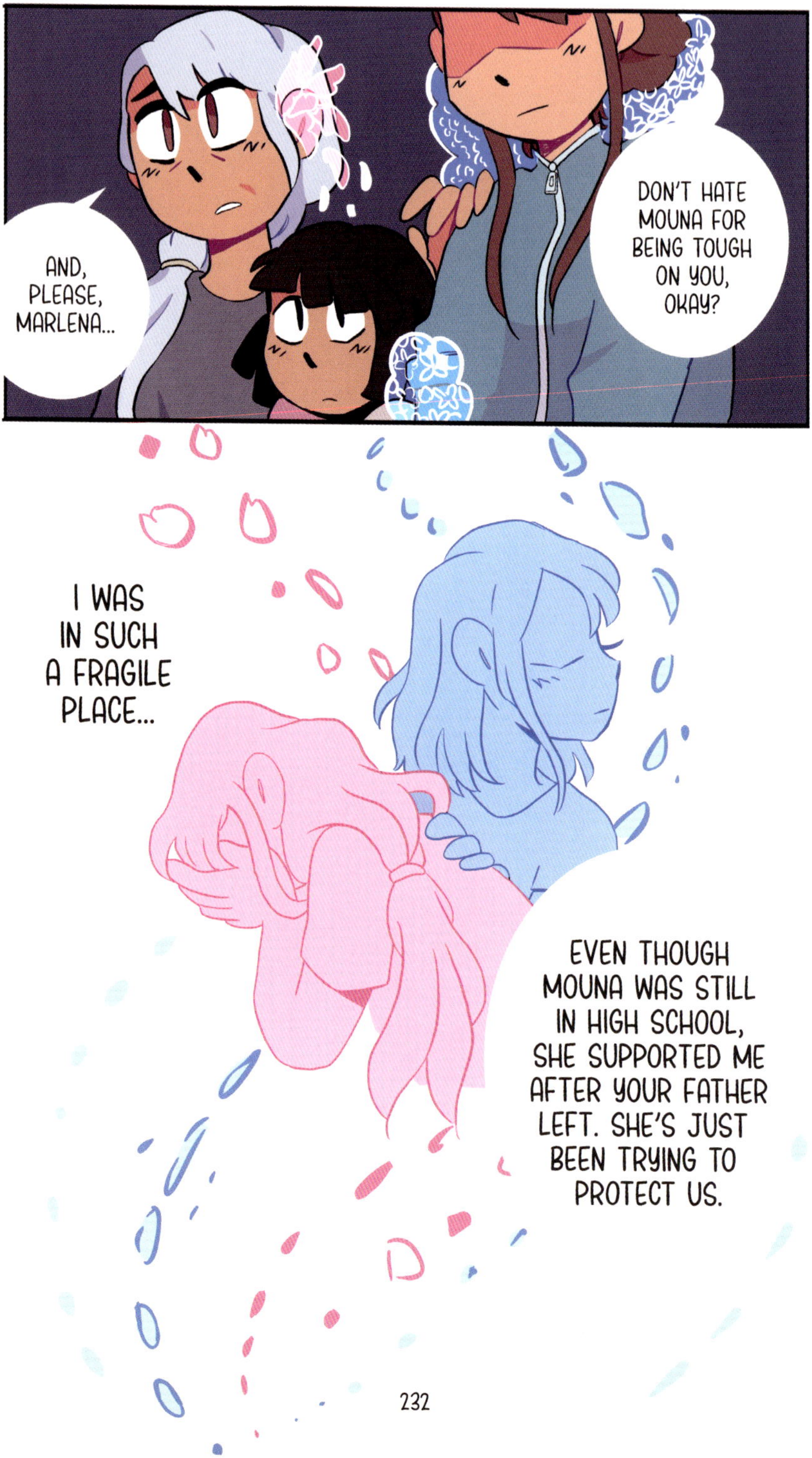
AND, PLEASE, MARLENA...
DON'T HATE MOUNA FOR BEING TOUGH ON YOU, OKAY?
I WAS IN SUCH A FRAGILE PLACE...
EVEN THOUGH MOUNA WAS STILL IN HIGH SCHOOL, SHE SUPPORTED ME AFTER YOUR FATHER LEFT. SHE'S JUST BEEN TRYING TO PROTECT US.

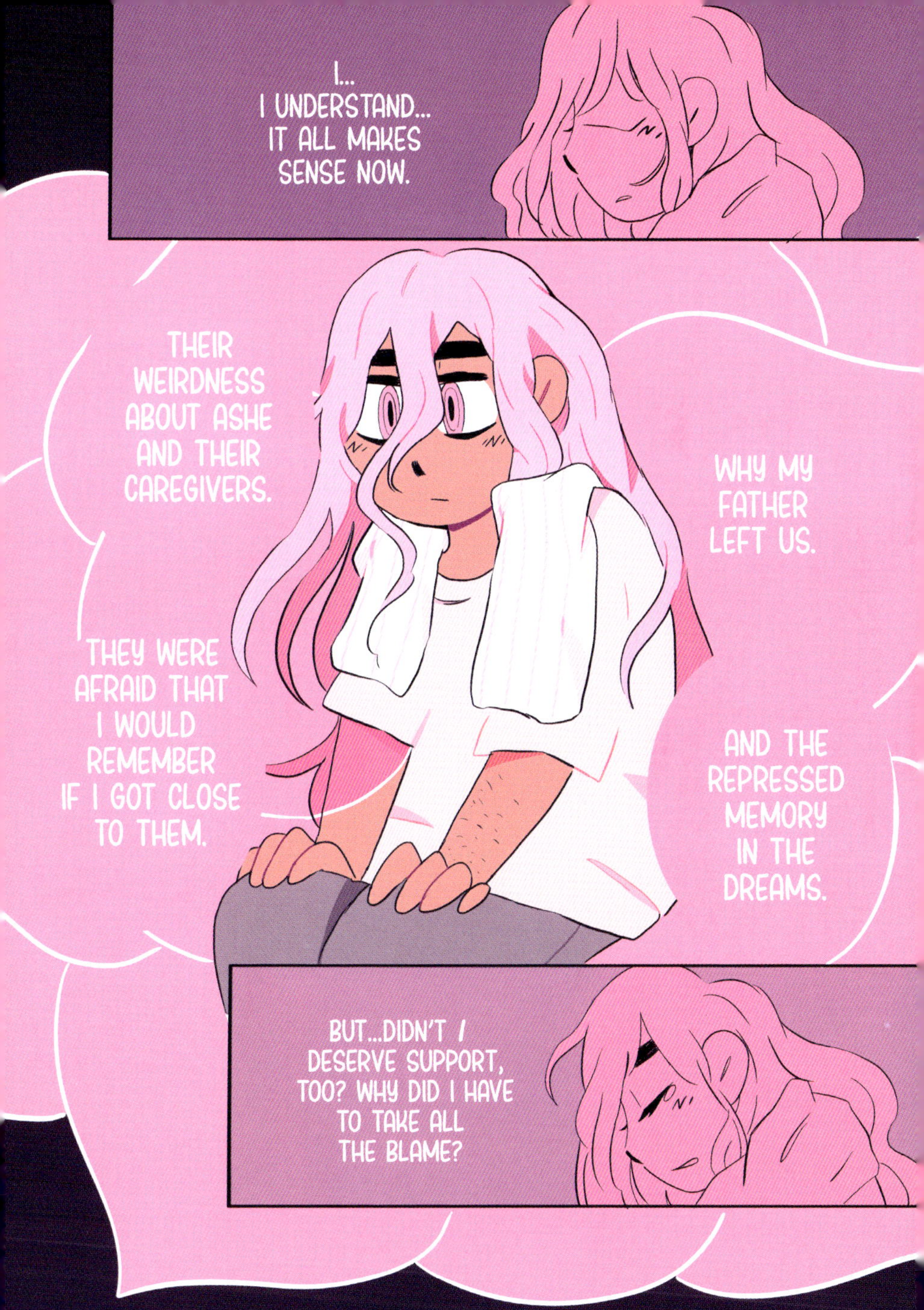
I...
I UNDERSTAND...
IT ALL MAKES
SENSE NOW.
THEIR WEIRDNESS ABOUT ASHE AND THEIR CAREGIVERS.
WHY MY FATHER LEFT US.
THEY WERE AFRAID THAT I WOULD REMEMBER IF I GOT CLOSE TO THEM.
AND THE REPRESSED MEMORY IN THE DREAMS.
BUT...DIDN'T *I* DESERVE SUPPORT, TOO? WHY DID I HAVE TO TAKE ALL THE BLAME?

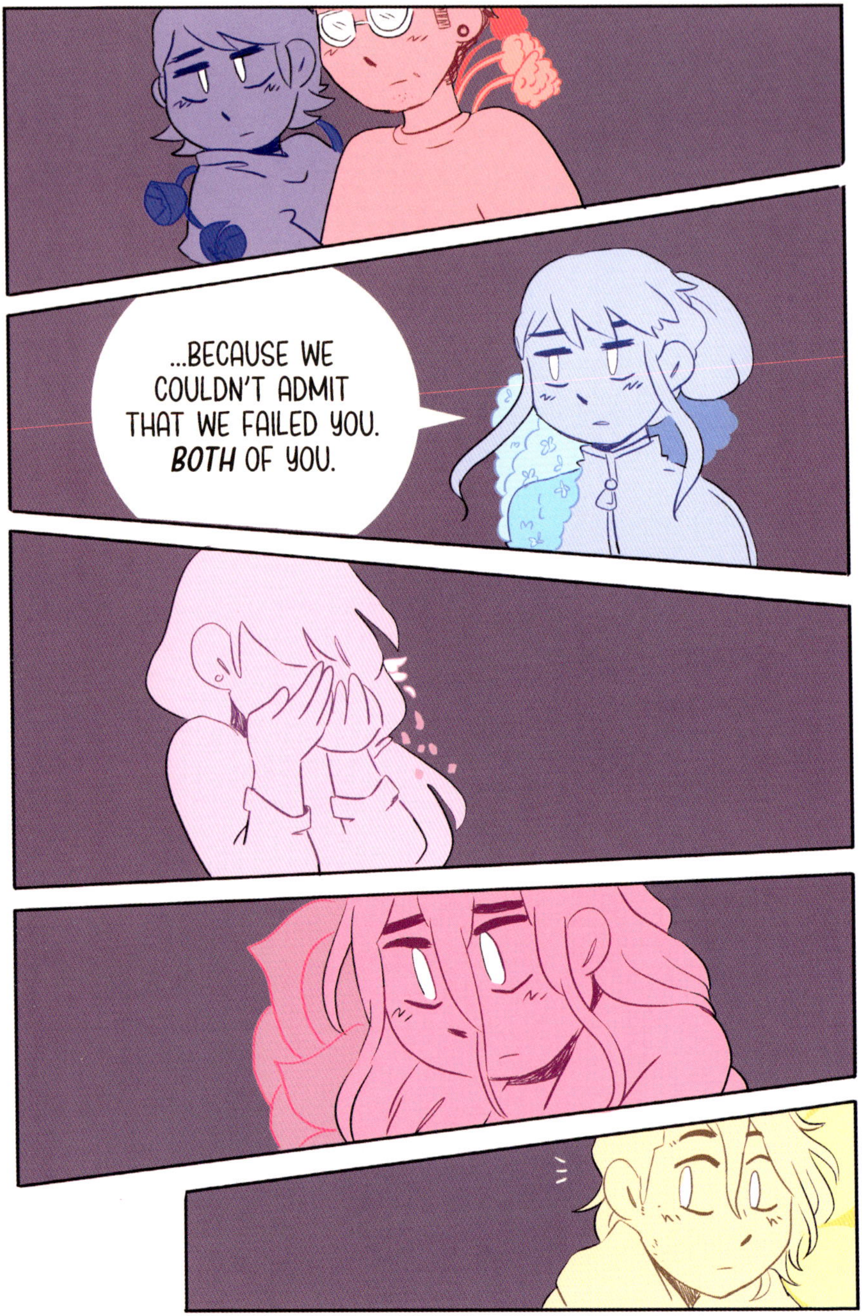
...BECAUSE WE COULDN'T ADMIT THAT WE FAILED YOU. *BOTH* OF YOU.

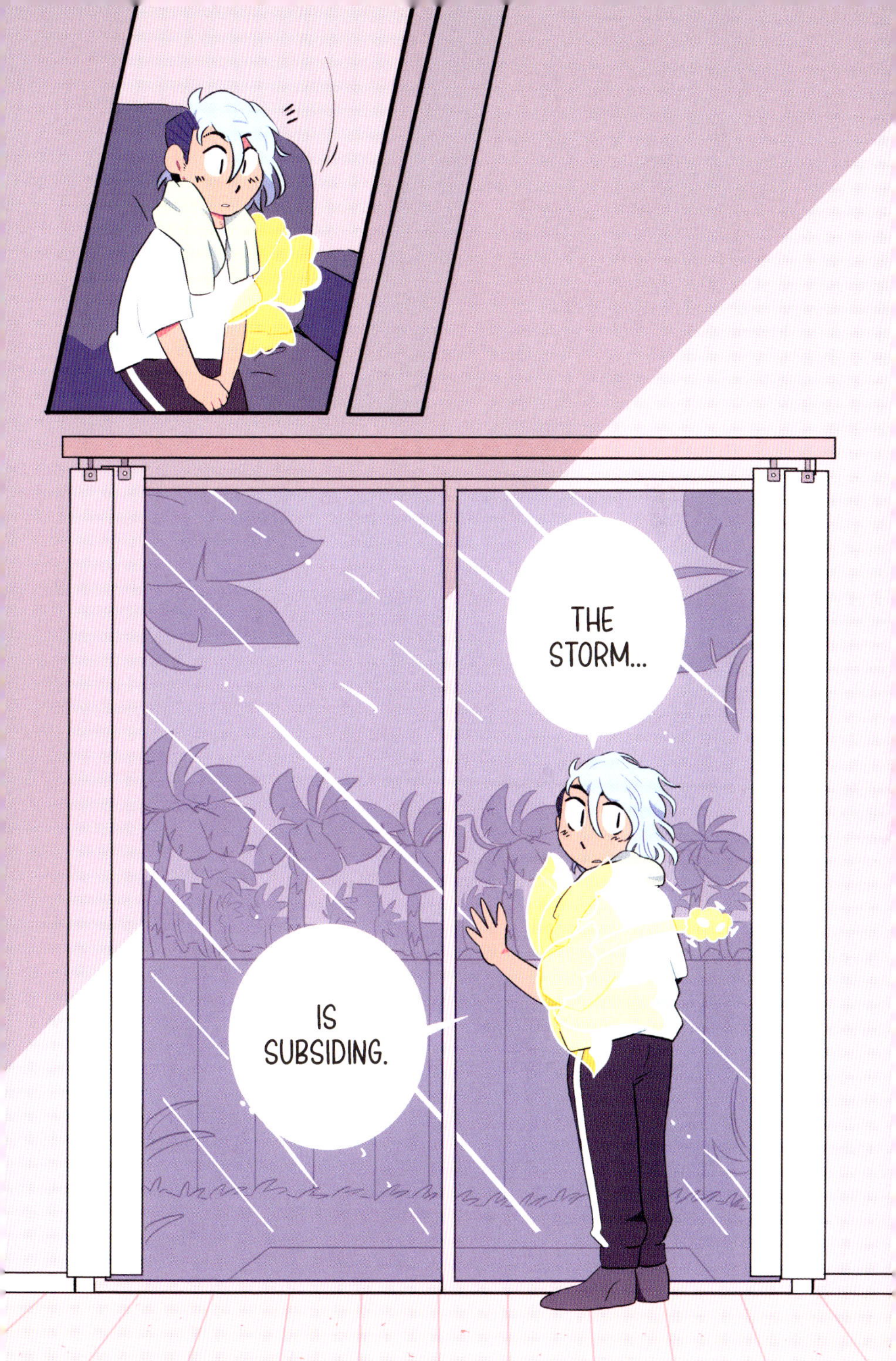
THE STORM...
IS SUBSIDING.

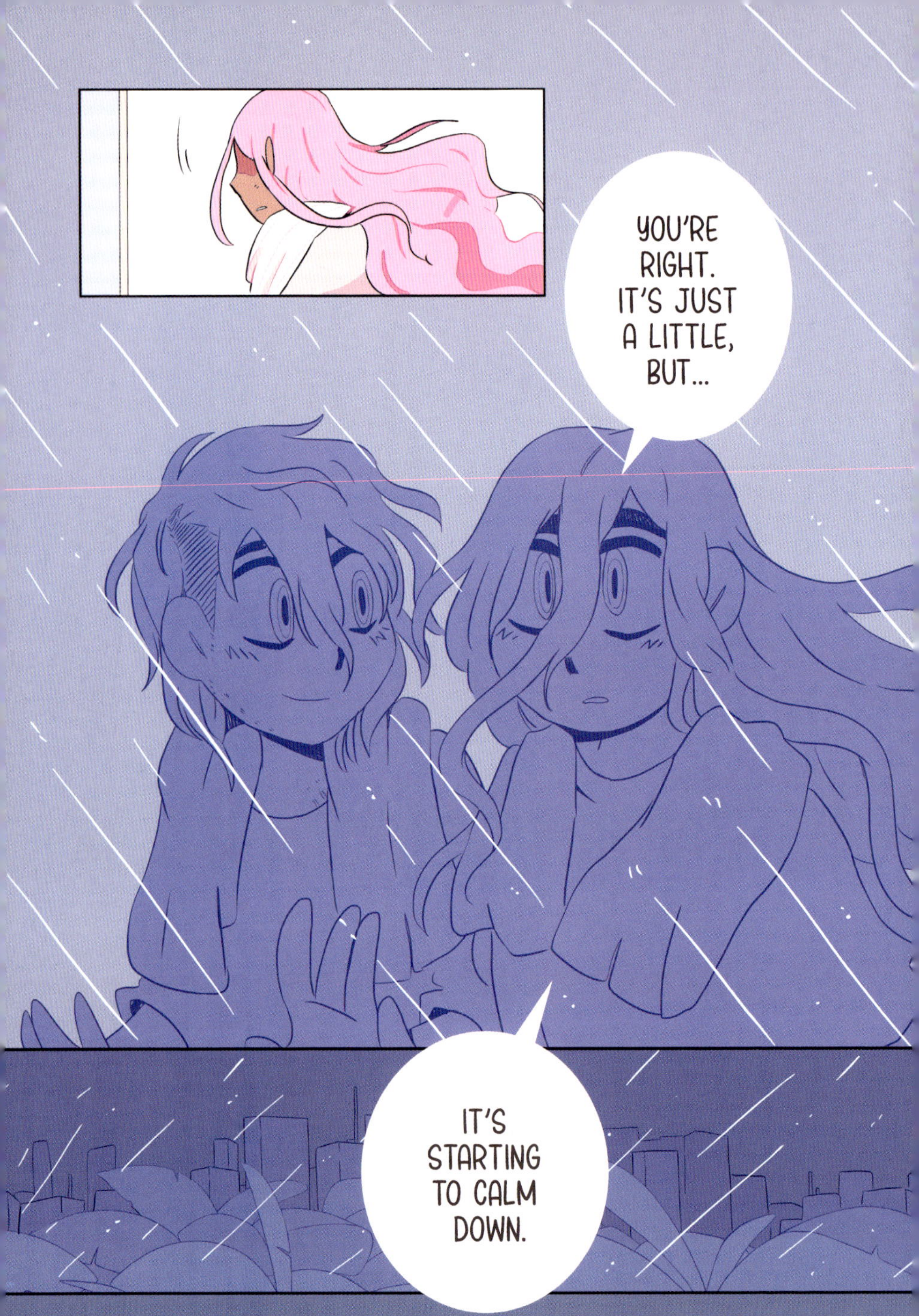
YOU'RE RIGHT. IT'S JUST A LITTLE, BUT...
IT'S STARTING TO CALM DOWN.

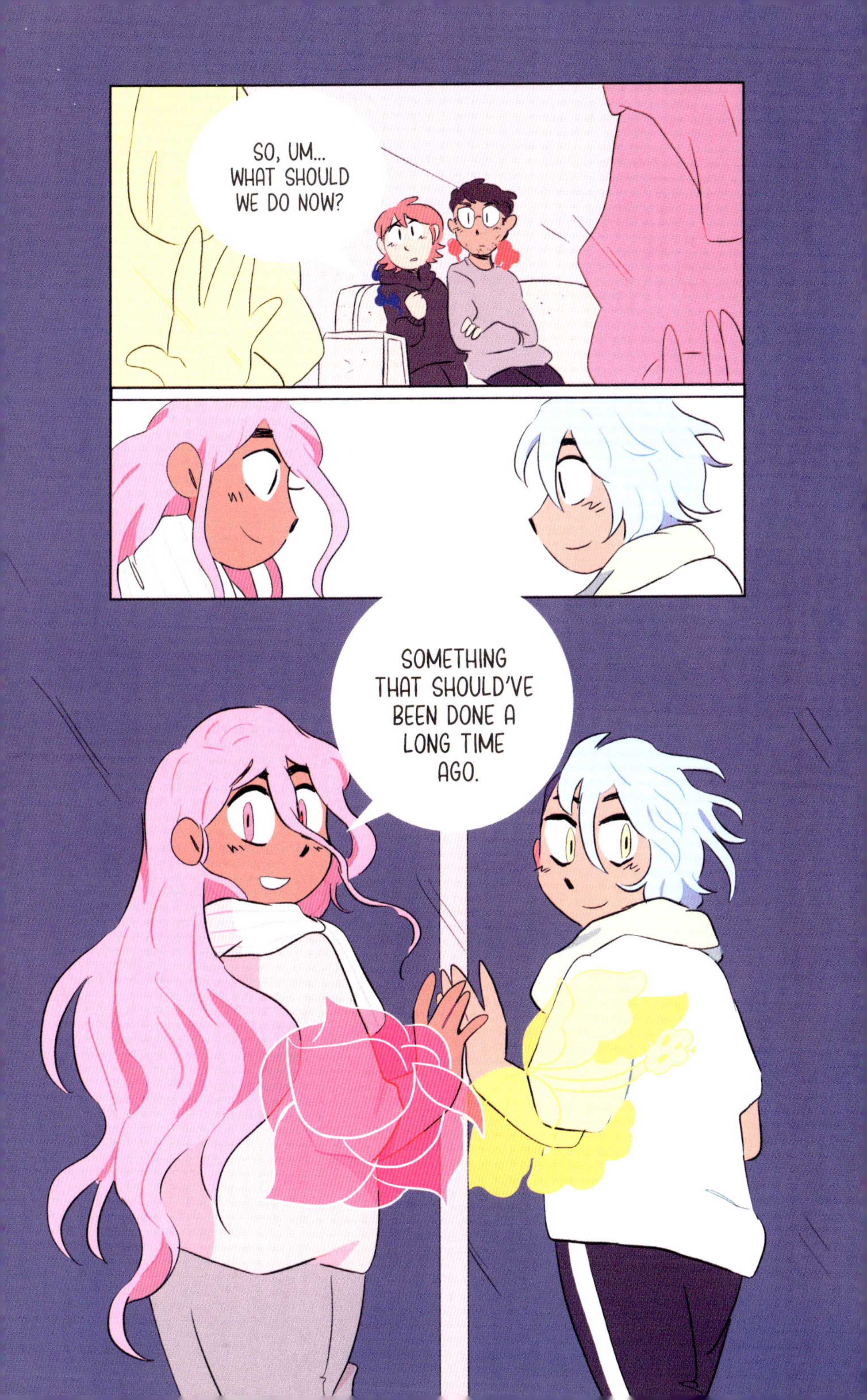
SO, UM... WHAT SHOULD WE DO NOW?
SOMETHING THAT SHOULD'VE BEEN DONE A LONG TIME AGO.

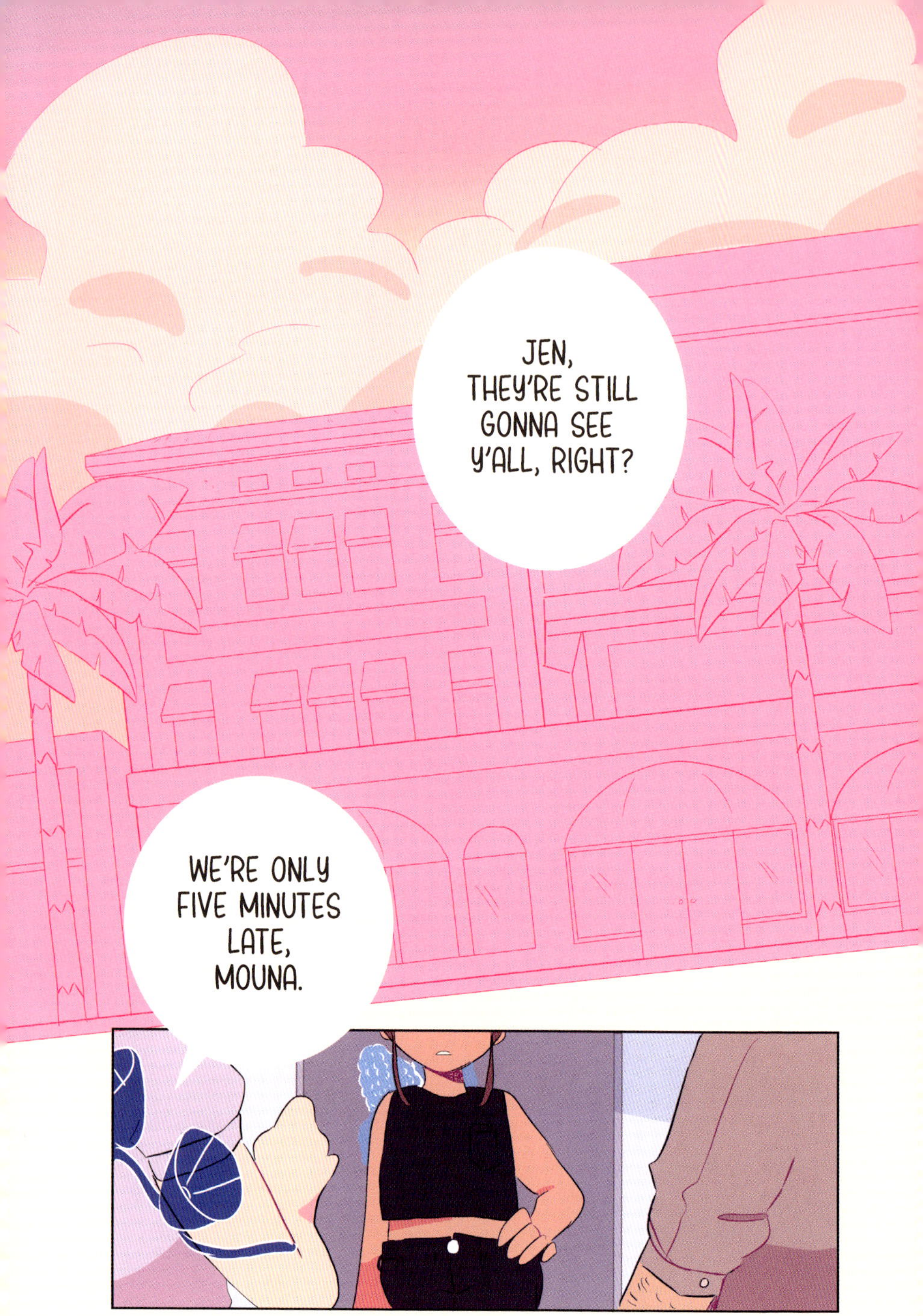
JEN, THEY'RE STILL GONNA SEE Y'ALL, RIGHT?
WE'RE ONLY FIVE MINUTES LATE, MOUNA.

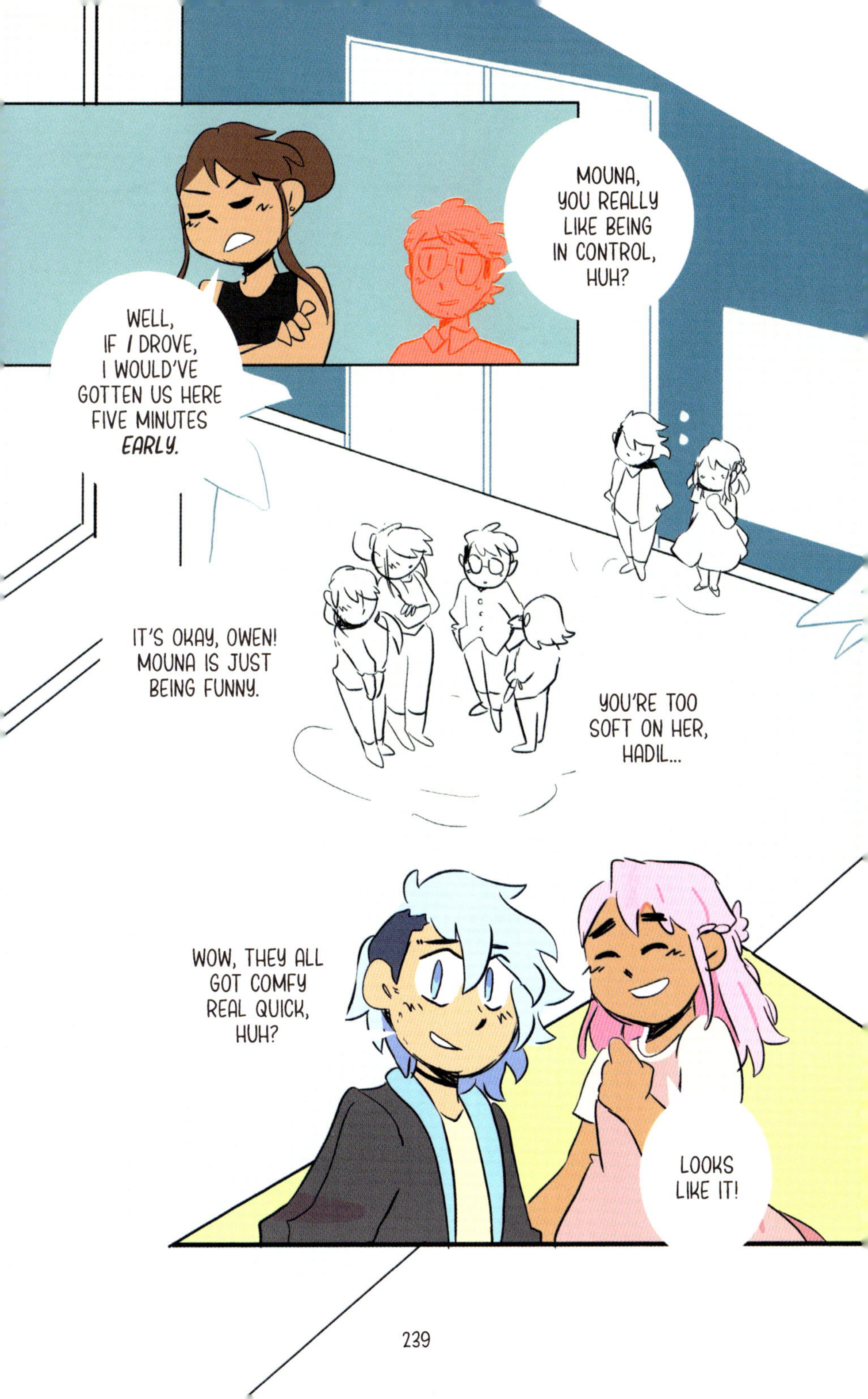
MOUNA, YOU REALLY LIKE BEING IN CONTROL, HUH?
WELL, IF I DROVE, I WOULD'VE GOTTEN US HERE FIVE MINUTES EARLY.
IT'S OKAY, OWEN! MOUNA IS JUST BEING FUNNY.
YOU'RE TOO SOFT ON HER, HADIL...
WOW, THEY ALL GOT COMFY REAL QUICK, HUH?
LOOKS LIKE IT!

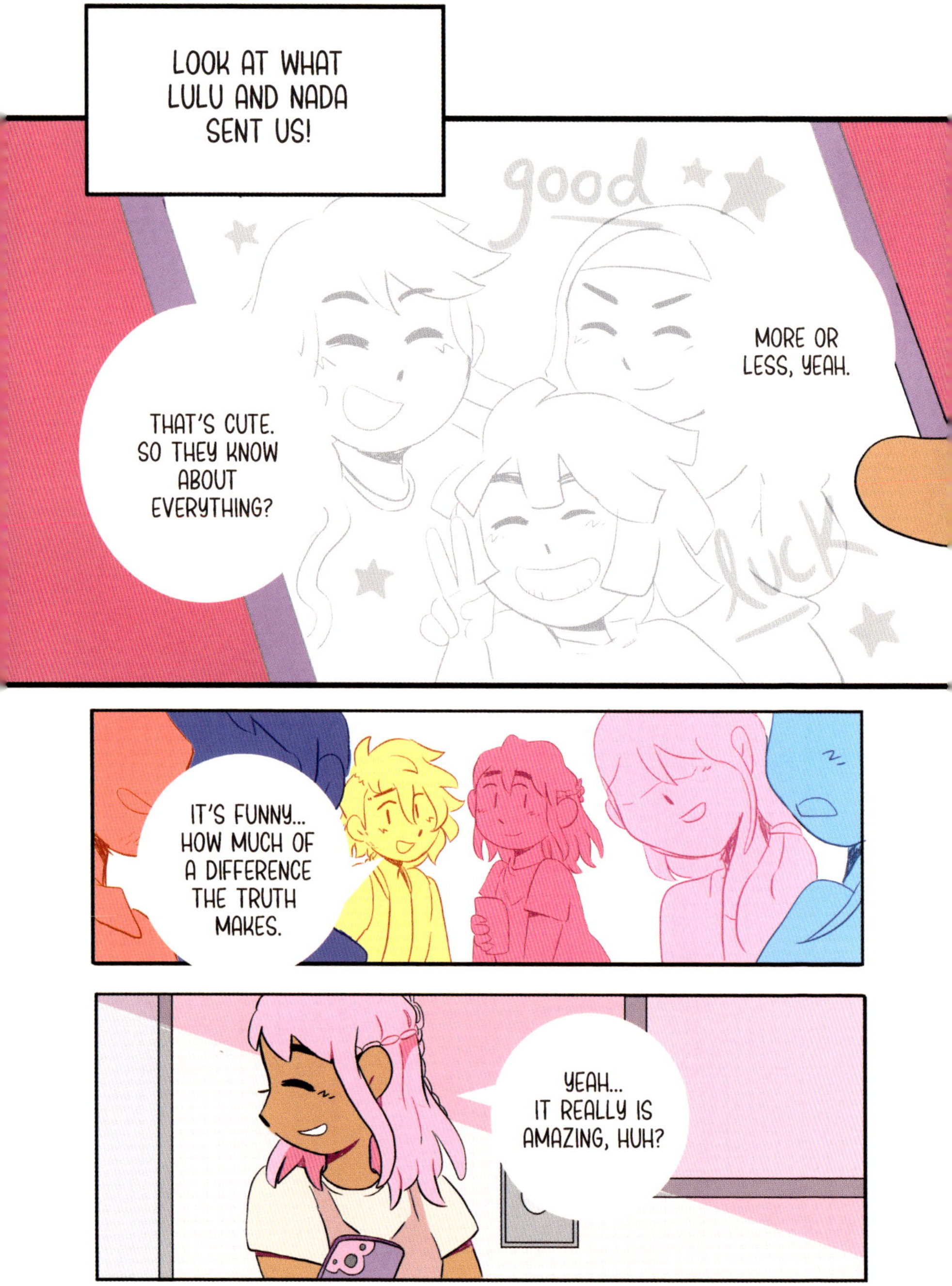
LOOK AT WHAT LULU AND NADA SENT US!
good luck
THAT'S CUTE. SO THEY KNOW ABOUT EVERYTHING?
MORE OR LESS, YEAH.
IT'S FUNNY... HOW MUCH OF A DIFFERENCE THE TRUTH MAKES.
YEAH... IT REALLY IS AMAZING, HUH?

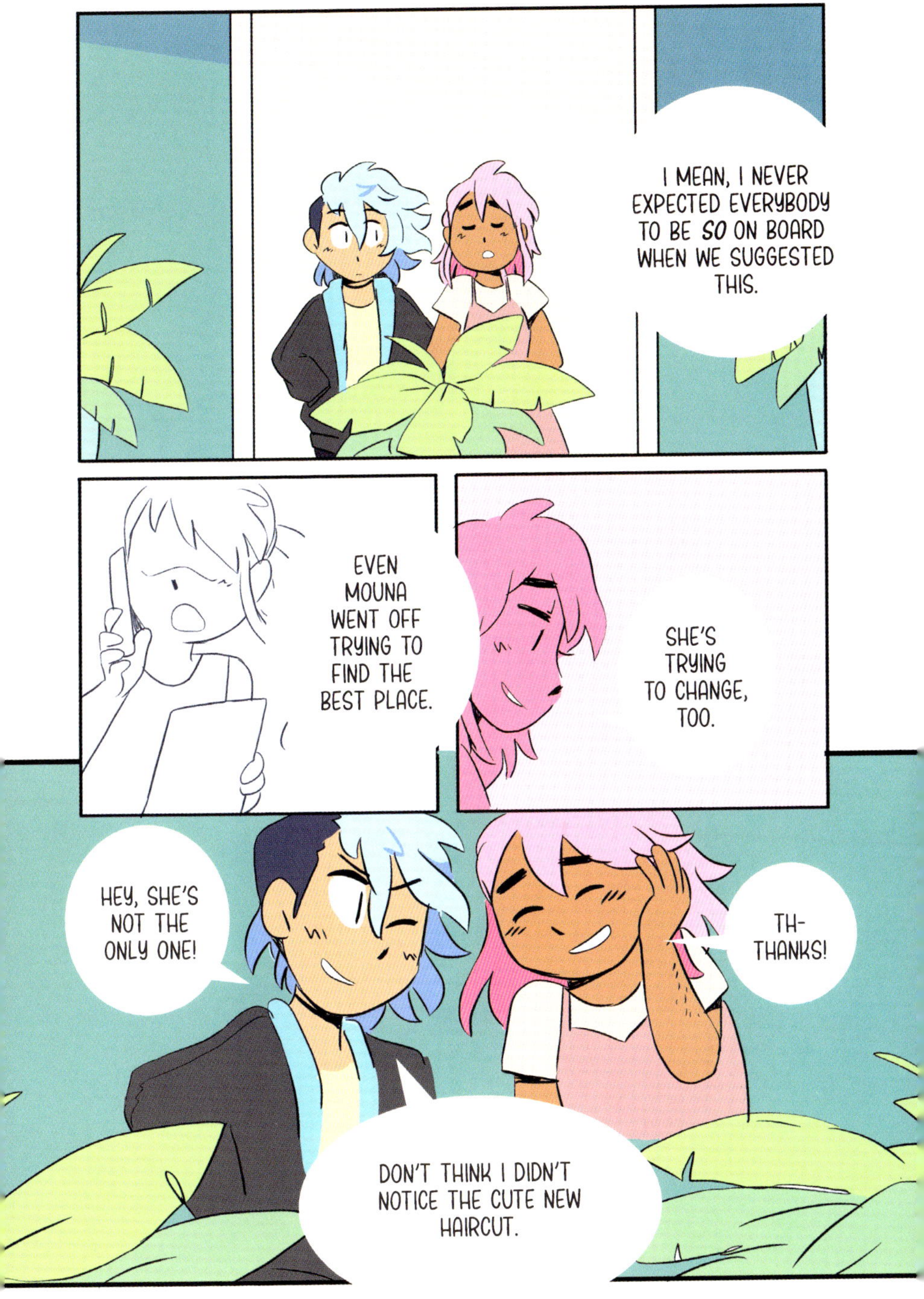
I MEAN, I NEVER EXPECTED EVERYBODY TO BE *SO* ON BOARD WHEN WE SUGGESTED THIS.
EVEN MOUNA WENT OFF TRYING TO FIND THE BEST PLACE.
SHE'S TRYING TO CHANGE, TOO.
HEY, SHE'S NOT THE ONLY ONE!
TH- THANKS!
DON'T THINK I DIDN'T NOTICE THE CUTE NEW HAIRCUT.

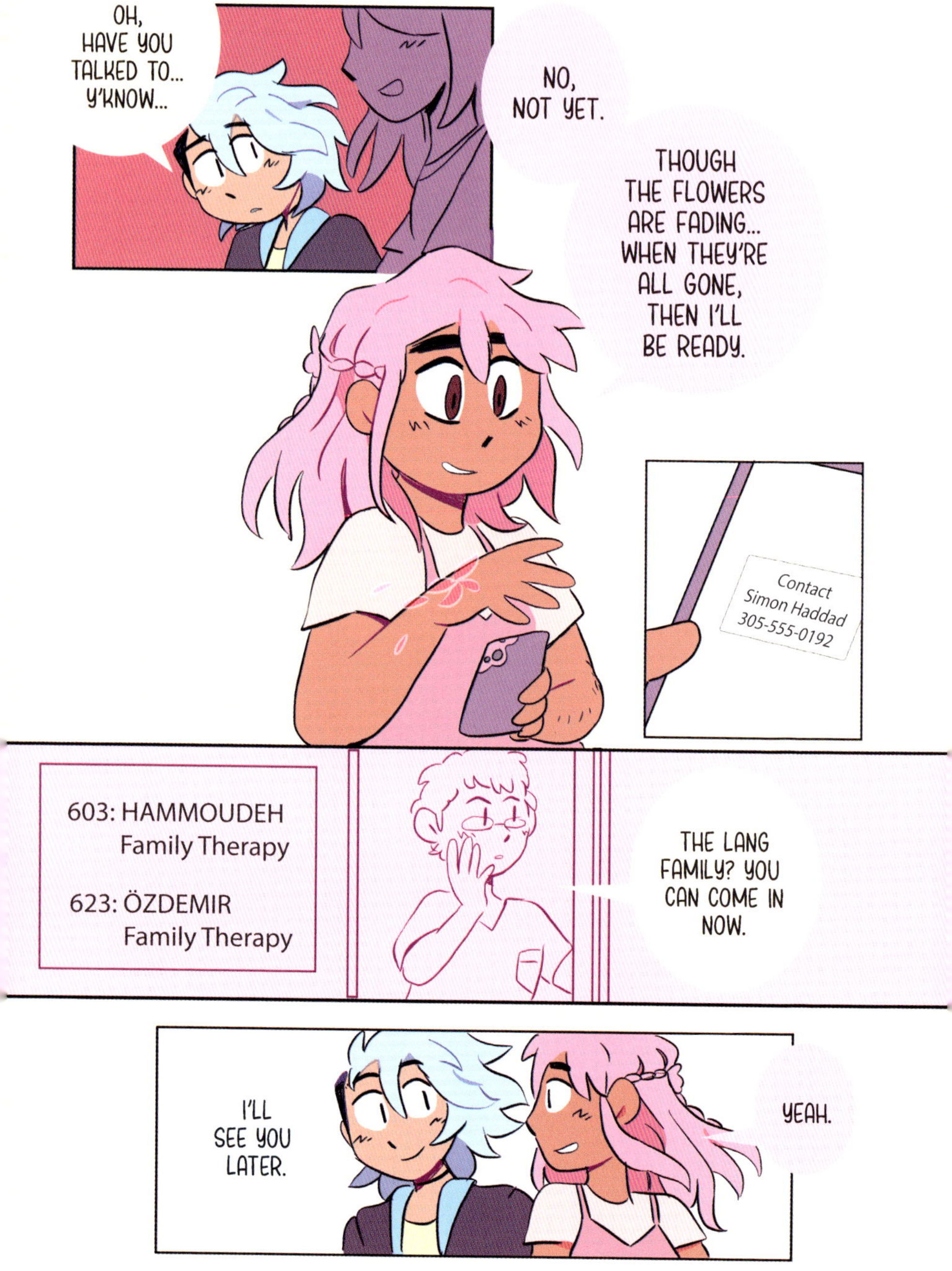
OH, HAVE YOU TALKED TO... Y'KNOW...
NO, NOT YET.
THOUGH THE FLOWERS ARE FADING... WHEN THEY'RE ALL GONE, THEN I'LL BE READY.
Contact
Simon Haddad
305-555-0192
603: HAMMOUDEH
Family Therapy
623: ÖZDEMIR
Family Therapy
THE LANG FAMILY? YOU CAN COME IN NOW.
I'LL SEE YOU LATER.
YEAH.

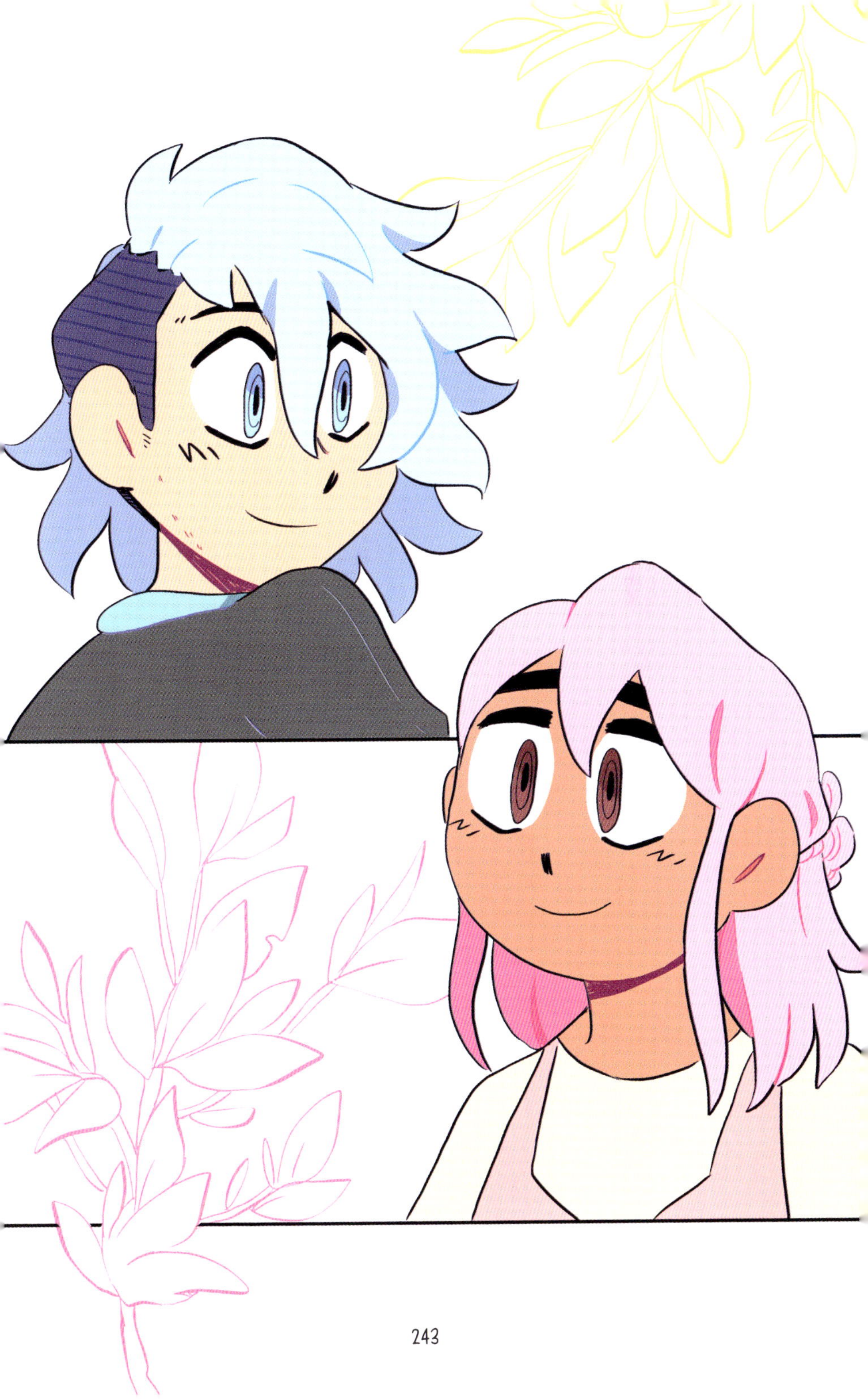

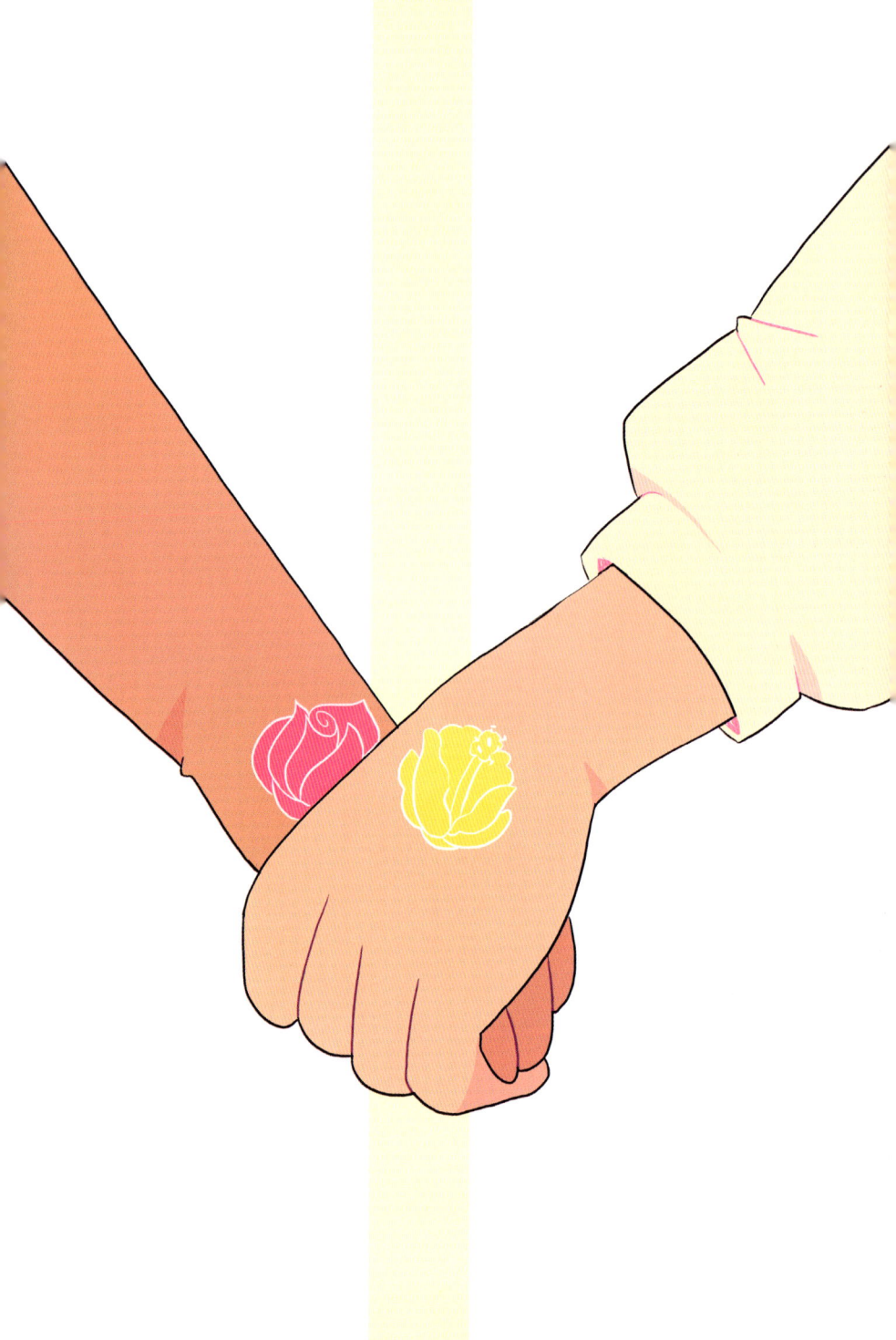

Turn the page for a teaser of

NAYRA AND THE DJINN

by Iasmin Omar Ata

NAYRA
and the DJINN
Iasmin Omar Ata

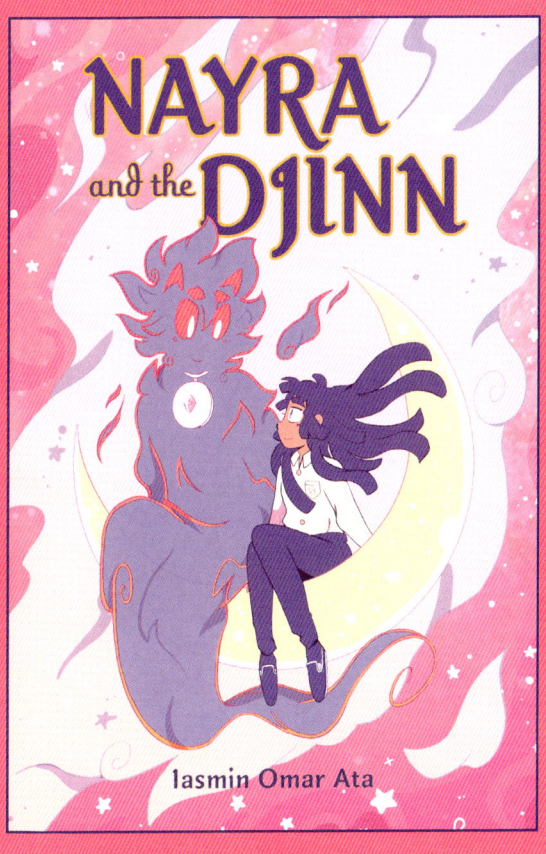

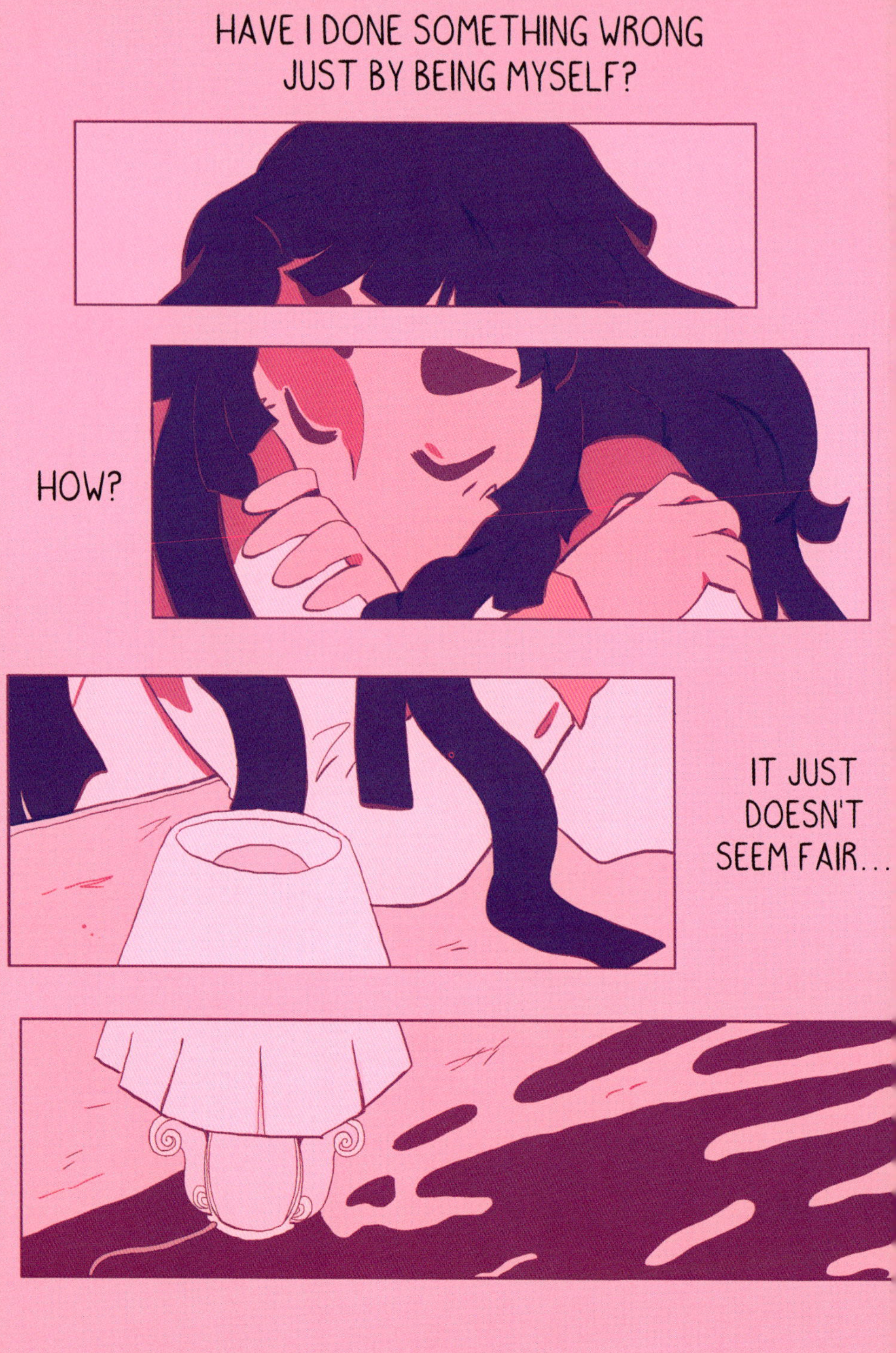
HAVE I DONE SOMETHING WRONG JUST BY BEING MYSELF?
HOW?
IT JUST DOESN'T SEEM FAIR...

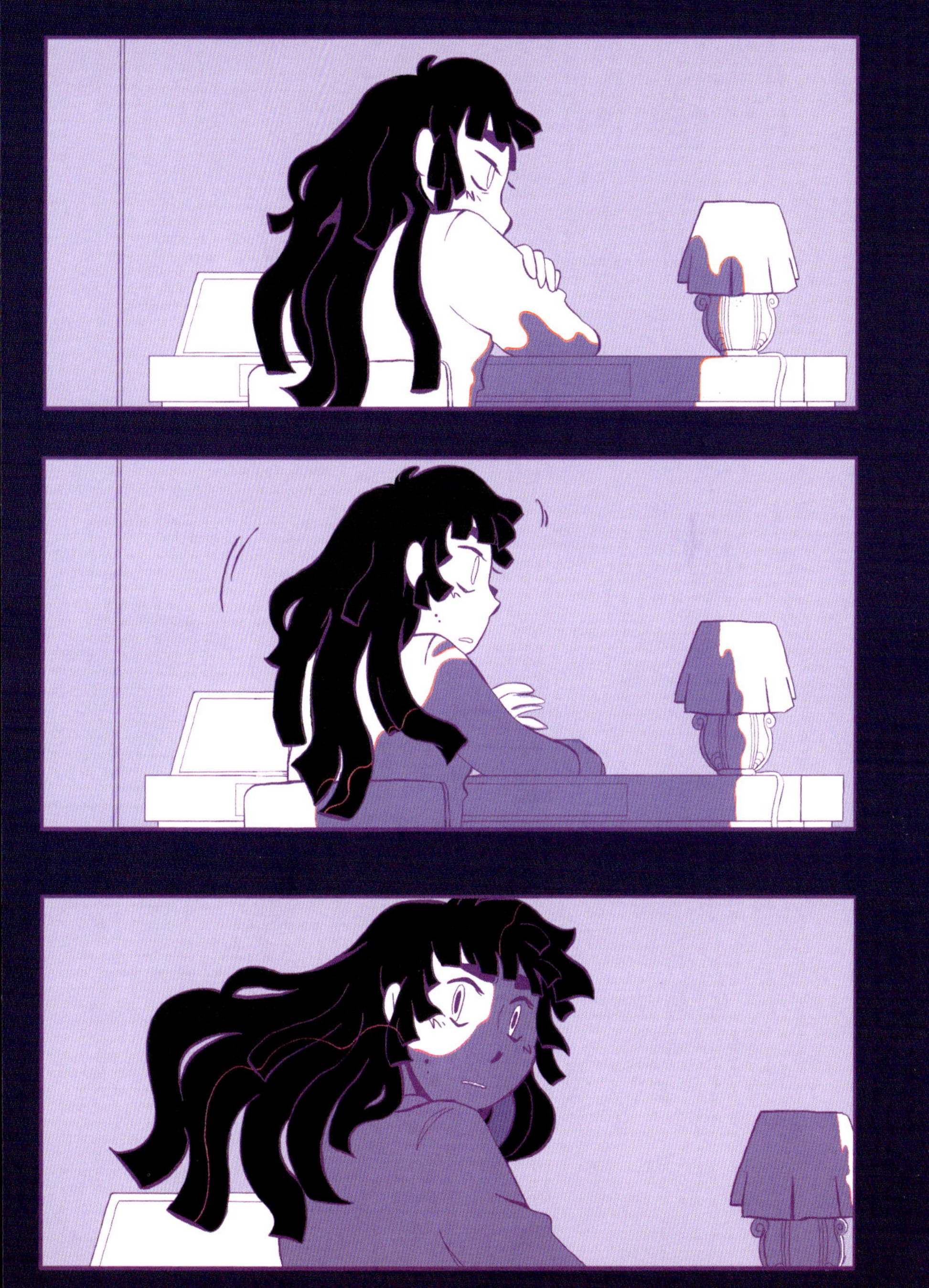

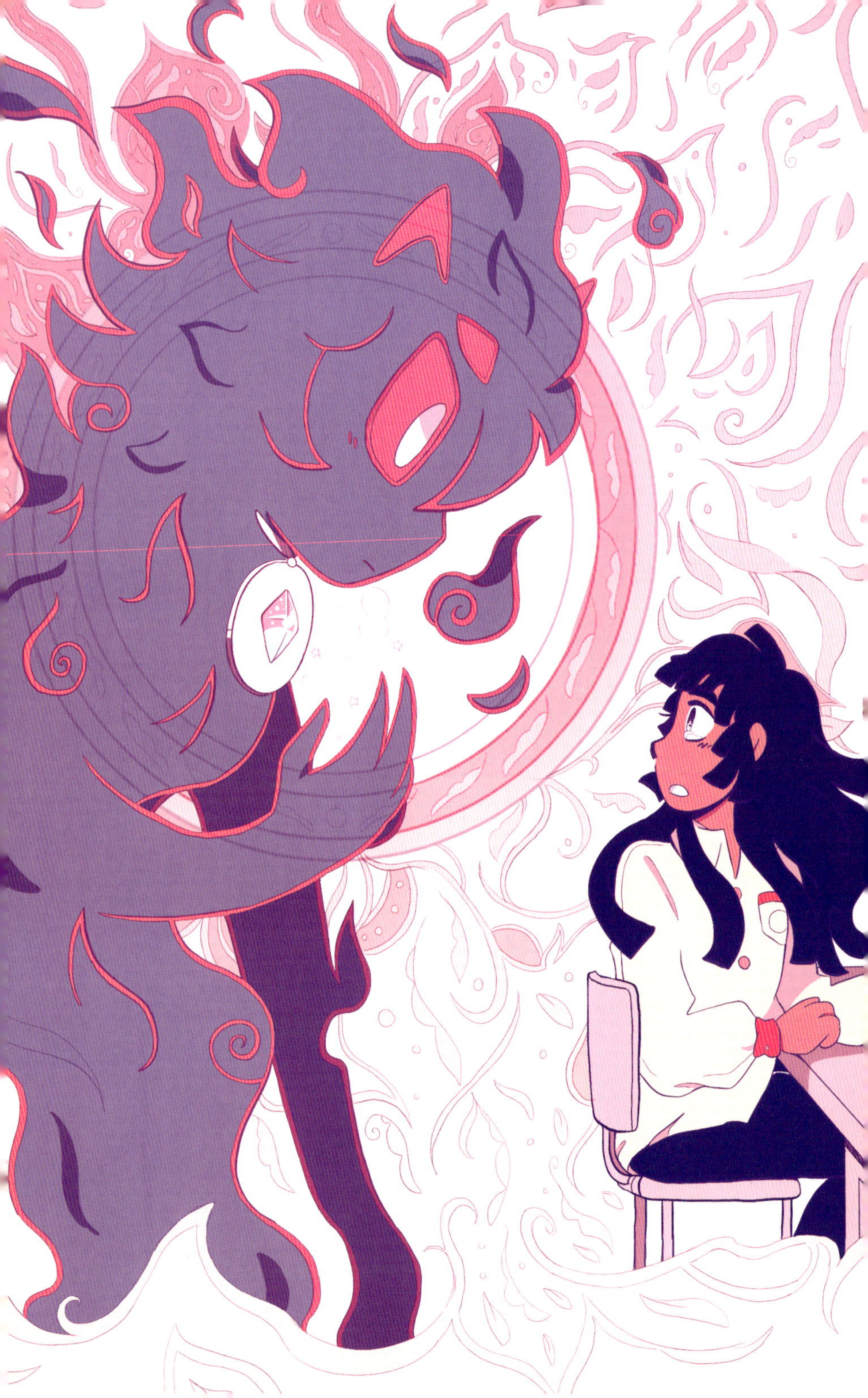

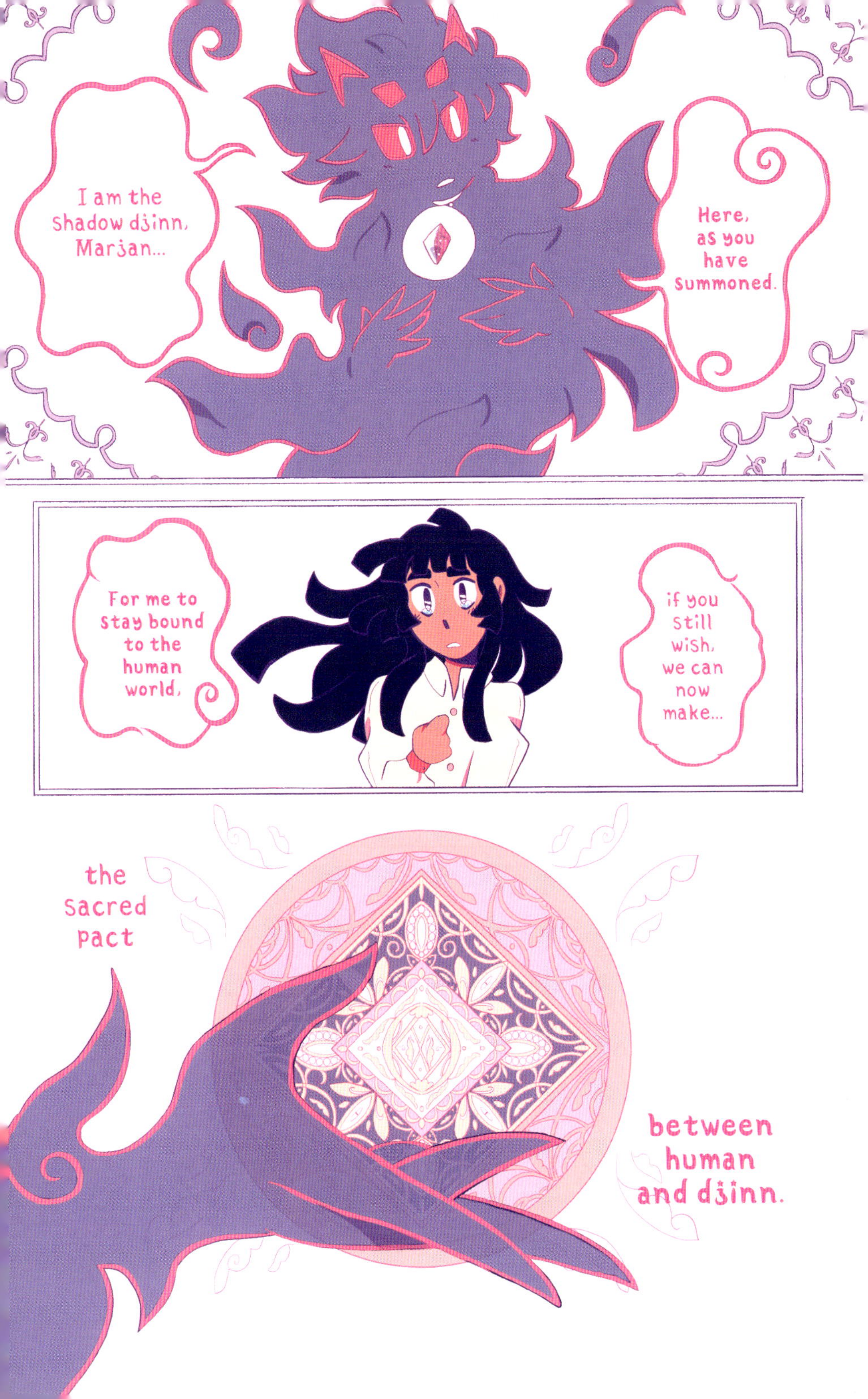

I am the shadow djinn, Marjan...
Here, as you have summoned.
For me to stay bound to the human world,
if you still wish, we can now make...
the sacred pact
between human and djinn.

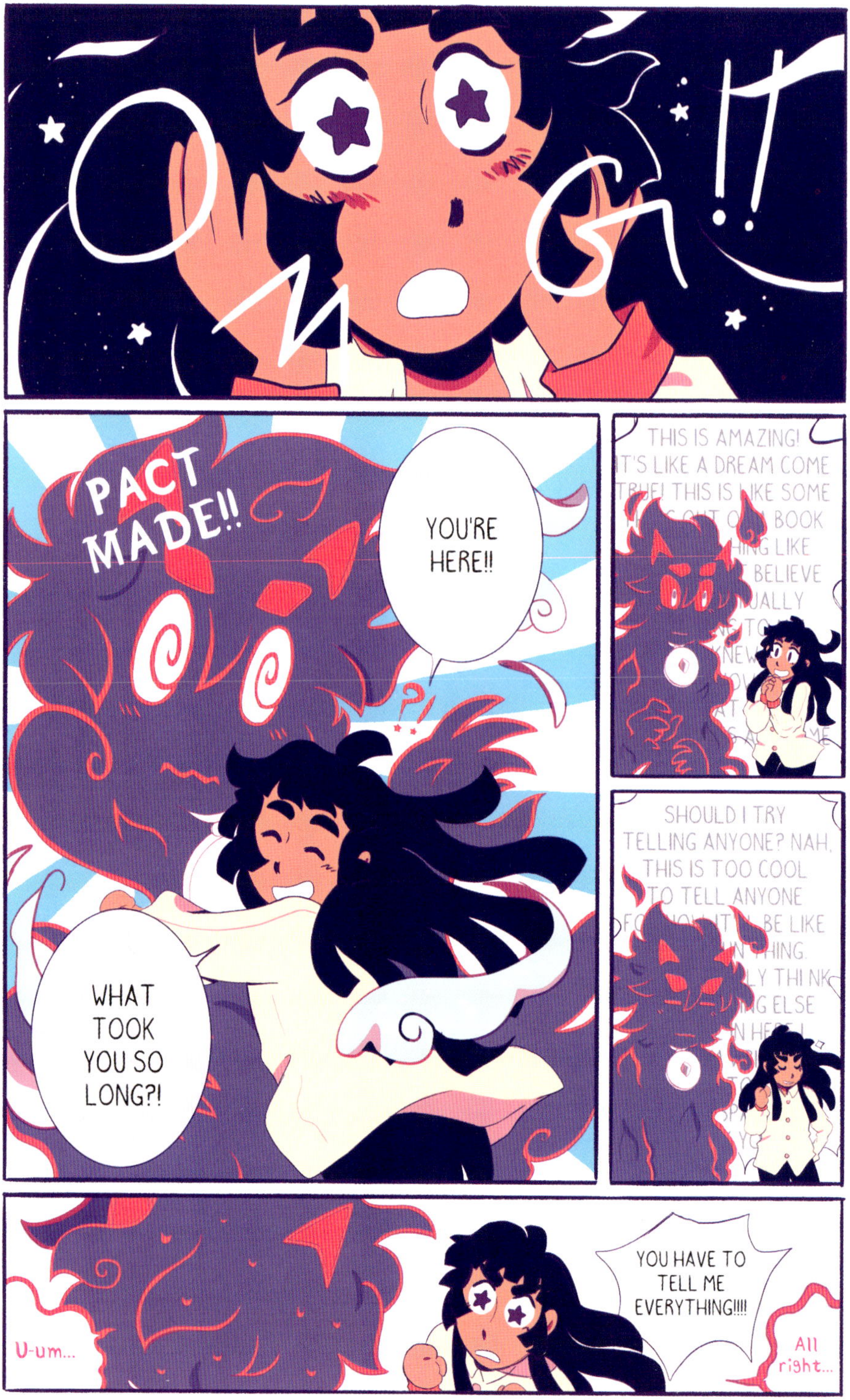
OMG!!
PACT MADE!!
YOU'RE HERE!!
WHAT TOOK YOU SO LONG?!
THIS IS AMAZING!
IT'S LIKE A DREAM COME
SHOULD I TRY TELLING ANYONE? NAH, THIS IS TOO COOL TO TELL ANYONE
U-um...
YOU HAVE TO TELL ME EVERYTHING!!!!
All right...

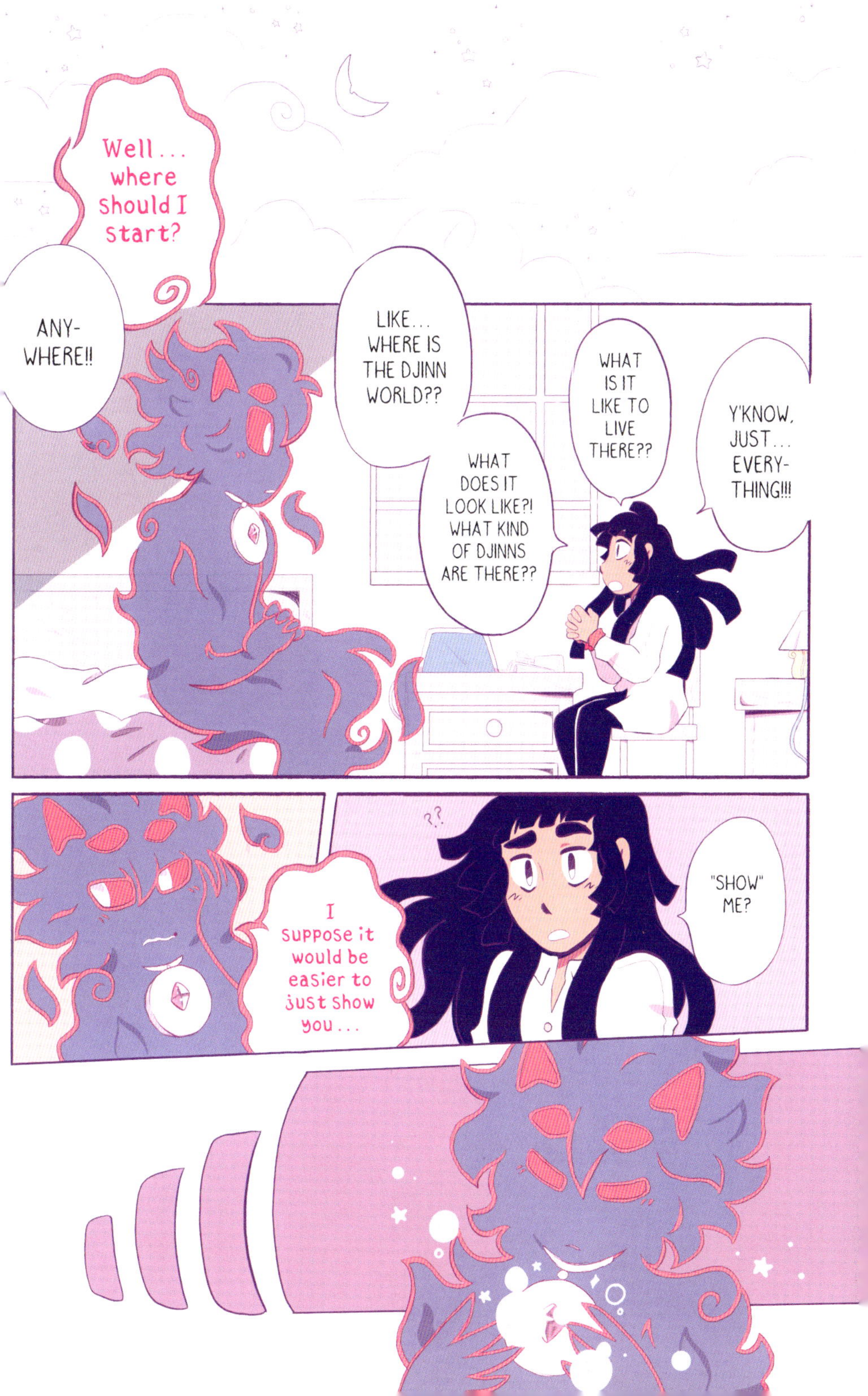
Well... where should I start?
ANY-WHERE!!
LIKE... WHERE IS THE DJINN WORLD??
WHAT DOES IT LOOK LIKE?! WHAT KIND OF DJINNS ARE THERE??
WHAT IS IT LIKE TO LIVE THERE??
Y'KNOW, JUST... EVERY-THING!!!
I suppose it would be easier to just show you...
??
"SHOW" ME?

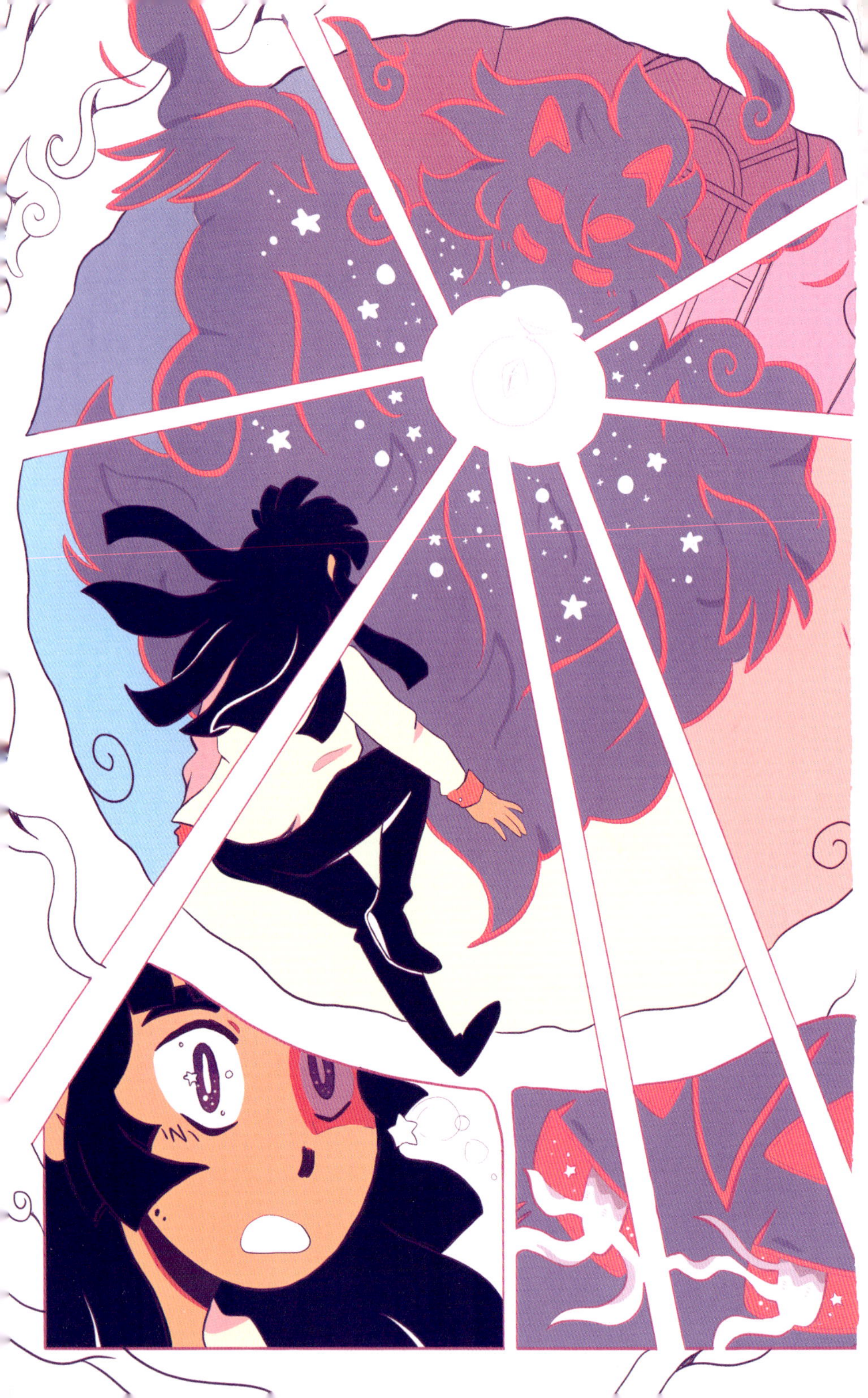